The Diviners

The Diviners

A Novel

Rick Moody

LITTLE, BROWN AND COMPANY | New York | Boston

Little, Brown and Company
Time Warner Book Group
1271 Avenue of the Americas, New York, NY 10020

ISBN 0-7394-6601-1
ISBN 978-0-7394-6601-8

Book designed by Paula Szafranski

Printed in the United States of America

For Melanie Jackson

The Diviners

Opening Credits and Theme Music

The light that illuminates the world begins in Los Angeles. Begins in darkness, begins in the mountains, begins in empty landscapes, in doubt and remorse. San Antonio Peak throws shadows upon a city of shadows. There are hints of human insignificance; there are nightmares. But just at the moment of intolerability there's an eruption of spectra. It's morning! Morning is hopeful, uncomplicated, and it scales mountaintops, as it scales all things. The light comes from nowhere fathomable, from an apparently eternal reservoir of emanations, radioactivities. Light edging over the mountaintop and across the lakes of the highlands, light across the Angeles National Forest, light rushing across skeins of smog in the California skies. Light on Redlands, light on the planned communities, light on the guy tossing the morning newspaper from a Toyota with a hundred and ninety-three thousand miles on it. Light on the Santa Ana River, on a drunk sleeping tenderly beside its dregs, light on the Santa Ana Mountains, the San Bernardino Mountains, light on the Prado Basin, where a stabbing victim welters in her wounds. Light on East Los Angeles, on gangsters who haven't slept yet. Light upon the unvisited downtown expanses of Los Angeles. An empty city bus idles at a red light. Light on the La Brea Tar Pits, on the Pleistocene and Holocene residents of the city, light on the system of viaducts coming down from the mountains, from the trickle of the Colorado River, light on the faint traces of the San Andreas fault, light on the cracked and empty sidewalks, light moving faster now, or apparently faster, the Magic Hour of dawn on the tanning-salon faces coming out of endless parties from the night before. Light upon the freeways, light upon tinted windows, light upon limousines. Even the back lots are perfect with it. Cinematographers everywhere are awakened, as if light calls upon them to arise. Light upon the stray dogs and jackrabbits and condors and Mediterranean fruit flies, nestling in the valleys. Light surging toward the beaches now, toward the great and somnolent ocean, light upon lovers, light upon Manhattan Beach, light upon Hermosa Beach, light upon a pair of punk rock kids in leather pants smoking weed beneath the pier at Redondo Beach, light upon sleeping lovers on a beach, light upon all Los Angeles, and then the light *beyond* Los Angeles, until the city is a memory receding in the progress of morning, just a layer of auburn air and music pulsing from a dream, light upon the waves, faster now, or so it seems, light over surfers, bobbing on the waves, light over the channel islands, and then light in the immensity of the sea, giving up the comfort of the coast.

Light upon the great Pacific, upon the North Central Gyre, circulating clockwise through this immensity, illuminating the strata of the deep from the Aleutian Islands to the West Wind Drift. What was oppressively dark now has a greenish cast with hints of blues and grays: indigo, slate, milori, zinc, Sevres. Light upon the seawater, therefore, and its potassium, manganese, calcium, and chloride, the particulate of eroded rock. Light upon the invisible phytoplankton and all organic material. Light upon sea vegetable, light upon coral reefs, light upon the Pacific gray whale, wending its way south to warmer climes, and light upon other cetaceans, light upon the continental shelf, all the way down to the continental shelf, light upon the Pacific anomaly known as La Niña, for it is the new year of La Niña, with her particular weather madness. Light upon schools of Pacific marine life, light upon sharks, light upon tuna and other harvestibles. Fish are surging toward the surface of the Pacific with the enthusiasm that they have for feeding when it is light. What a beachhead the light makes here across the northwestern edge of the Hawaiian Islands, Kauai, Nihau, then up toward the atoll of Midway, known for its naval battle. Light upon guano deposits and seabirds perched about the buildings housing the permanent naval staff of Midway, a staff numbered year-round at twenty-three. Light is no respecter of the international date line, though any complete account of the instant of morning must include it, light hastening over the international date line. Were an ensign from Midway to travel out a few nautical miles, he would expunge an entire day, he would have one day less in his tour in the Pacific. Somewhere in the helter-skelter of this morning is tomorrow.

Light upon the western Pacific, where the trenches are, where the fish themselves are the light source. Eyes attached to long stalks that glow with some interior phosphorus or radium. Drifting, miles down, in a blissful state, free of man, in the heterogeneity of marine creation. Light upon all these trenches and all these scars and striations of the ocean floor marking the subduction of tectonic plates, where the molten earth bubbles up and makes its presence known in the indigo surface of the ocean. In the trenches, light is hope or fantasy. Light as possibility and as revelation.

Light upon the Volcano Islands of Japan, western Pacific. No more than five miles long, the archipelago, but large enough to entertain the most brutal of battles in the last global war. Twenty-six thousand lost, in aggregate. Light upon the Japanese soldiers still in the caves there, whispering their sutras, drinking condensation from the cave walls, awaiting word from the emperor, unaware of Japanese deflation and the three recessions in the past ten years. Light upon Mount Suribachi and the tattered American flag that once flew there before Iwo Jima was returned to the prefectural government of Tokyo; light upon the dark history and the porous volcanic rock of Iwo Jima, on its sulfur mining and its sugar refineries. There is also the briefest commencement of dawn on the Bonin Islands, another group of volcanic extrusions near the Tropic of Cancer, where, on this day, rosewood is to be harvested, with its streaky purple timber, for fine cabinets. Light upon the monsters of this island retreat, Godzilla, Baragon, et al., whose creation is owing to the nuclear history of the region, light upon the bright flash of the nuclear explosion, for now the rising sun of morning, streaming in the east, is upon the island of Kyushu, southerly in the Japanese archipelago, light upon the great expanses of green of Kyushu, and now dawn upon Nagasaki, where the second of the explosions was detonated, light of dawn reflective of that other light. Light on the island of Kyushu as source for the growth there of tobacco crops and tea leaves, light upon the tip of South Korea, light upon the Yellow Sea, light beginning to make itself felt up and down the peninsula of Korea, upon Inchon and Nampo, the comparatively shallow Yellow Sea, illuminated in viridians, light at the speed of light on an axis of rotation, toward the Chinese coast, toward Shanghai, where there was the tail end of a typhoon just last week.

Light upon the Nanjing Road, traveling westerly, on buildings of British design, light on the four-story French additions to the neighborhood, light on the high-rises that date back just ten years or so, light upon the glass boxes of Chinese capitalism, light upon the suburban areas that have filled in the farmland outside of Shanghai, light upon the factories, where the citizenry is busy this day making fax machines and semiconductors, light upon the railroads heading west, light upon political informers, light upon underground poets of Shanghai, light upon the faithful of China, and light upon the Yangtze, backward up its course, backward through Huize, Yunnan, Sichuan provinces, through the most populated parts of the most populated country, through industrial parks and endless agriculture, through poverty, through thousands of miles along the tributaries of the Yangtze, upward, for the Yangtze flows down from the roof of the world.

Now the light, bittersweet, amber, between the foothills of the Himalayas. Today the clouds have parted long enough that the tips of the Chinese peaks can be seen within the luxury of clouds. From a great distance, from jetliners traveling from Calcutta to Japan, light upon the peaks, first the lesser peaks of the east, on the Chinese border, and then light upon Namcha Barwa and Gurla Mandhata and Everest, light upon the valleys, light nosing into the valleys, light upon the mouths of the Mekong and Ganges, and light upon the monasteries that have yet to be sacked by the Chinese government, monasteries untouched by the secret police, light upon a certain constellation of monks chanting in overtones, blowing on their summoning horns. Light upon the Himalayas, serene, unpredictable, where climbers are embarked with gear and sherpas, light moving westward, over the Karakorum Range, light upon the two pounds of plutonium that someone lost in the mountains here, as yet unlocated, light upon the terrain annexed by the Chinese, and light upon warring factions, light upon Jammu and Kashmir, where Hindus and Muslims have weapons trained on one another, light upon the Ladakh region of Jammu and Kashmir, above the tree line, light upon the Kargil region, light upon the Shia Muslims, light upon the Hindus of the Kargil region, light upon Srinagar, Badgam, Puilwama, Muzaffarabad, light upon Poonch, Rajouri, light upon the many tongues, light upon the many ethnicities, light upon the kids roaming in the streets of the cities, throwing rocks at occupying armies, light upon the conscripted young men from Bombay and Calcutta serving in the army in Jammu and Kashmir. Light upon the inductees who just want to get home in one piece, light upon the Kashmiris in the street, the members of Al Mujahid Force, Muslim Mujahideen, Al Barq, Al Jehad Force,

Harkat ul Mujahideen, Hizbul Mujahideen. Light upon the Pir Panjal range, where freedom fighters are encamped and well stocked with rocket launchers and submachine guns.

Light upon the Madrassas, in Peshawar, the Madrassas as numberless as the petals on the lotus blossoms of the world. The Madrassas have taken in all the boys, light upon their affection for the game known as football, light upon the game they play this morning in a dirt lot near the Khyber Pass. Light upon the sheer cliff walls of the Khyber Pass, light upon the troops belonging to a military dictator bent upon keeping as many Afghan refugees on the other side of the pass as is possible, light upon fleeing Afghan refugees, light upon men whose beards are of insufficient length. Light upon fugitive barbers. Light upon the Silk Road, where Nestorianism took refuge when driven out of Constantinople. Light upon the afflicted rapists of Afghanistan who are busy, allegedly, defiling the boys of Dehi-i-Haji and Juwain. There are men who follow every wayward devil. Light upon men fleeing into the hills, light upon Tajiks and Uzbeks, and Kurds, and Arabs, light illuminating the plateau of Iran, over the mountains and into the Dasht-e-Lut, where the hills heave up abruptly, sheer, blue, gray. Not a soul to be seen, except these horses and their riders, fleeing. Though the smokestacks of a natural-gas facility are apparent upon the horizon as the light breaks over the desert, even here the conflagration in the east is hallucinatory. There is the sound of Kurdish epic poetry on the breeze; there are imaginary pistachio trees, with their delights. Up ahead on the rocks, an oasis, at least until the advent of further light, when all the riches of Persia appear instead to be part of memory. The sleepers in the desert are weary but cannot wake, and the dawn sweeps westerly over them, further into Mohammed's country. As far as the eye can see, the prophet and his vision, the dawn is his metaphor. He seeks refuge in the Lord of the rising day. The Lord has no qualities and there are no words with which to name his qualities. Dawn is for all the peoples of Mohammed's country:

Persians, Kurds, Arabs, Palestinians; dawn is for Baghdad, dawn
is for Mecca or Medina, or it is for Damascus or for Jerusalem.
Here is the dawn, see the sky bespangled with the signs of the zo-
diac. Here's the muezzin. Light upon the first cup of tea, light
upon the faithful inclining toward prayer, light upon refugees in
camps getting up to pray, how long until their knees give out
from it, light upon believers, light upon the settlers of the West
Bank, light upon them and their weapons and their certainty,
light upon all the armed forces who refuse to serve, light upon Jerusalem and Beirut and Cairo, light upon the authors of Torah,
light upon Talmudic scholars, all weepers at the Wailing Wall,
light upon the remains of the temple at Jerusalem, light upon the
Egyptian ruins, light upon the remnants of Mesopotamia, light
upon the thousand and one nights, story without end. Dawn is
more reliable than conceptions of dawn, so all of this splendor
diffuses into the fog at the very shore of the Mediterranean.
Weary is the morning, having come so far, weary of toil. Morning is eager to bathe in the sea. All the bathers on the scorched
sands see it now, dawn, coming over the buildings, its fingertips
brushing across the promontory at Jaffa; four thousand years this
promontory of bathers, a million and a half dawns witnessed
here, every dawn with a naked body to enumerate its colors.

   As if to indicate metamorphosis. Light upon the twin halves of
Cyprus, the Turkish half and the Greek half, the middle of the
middlemost body of water in the middle of the world, center of
the things. Omphalos. Ruins everywhere, ruins of Cyprus, Turkish and Greek. And then ruins in Turkey and ruins in Greece.
Light upon the ruins, light upon the ferment of Turkey, and then
light upon the islands of the Aegean, light upon Patmos, where
Saint John hallucinated his revelation, light upon these allegories
and riddles; light upon Rhodes, light upon Lesbos, light upon
the islands through which Ulysses circulated, in loneliness and
exile, to the very brink of Purgatorio. Light upon Crete, light
upon Knossos, the knowledge of the light, the knowledge of the

dawn, light upon the Neolithic past there, upon archaeologists with their tiny paintbrushes, creeping down ladders into the sites of their digging, light upon the dynasty of Minos, light upon the Minotaur and the labyrinth, the solution to which is simply to follow the light as it moves through the labyrinth. Light upon the westernmost edge of Crete, the city of Falassarna, light upon the occasional Albanian still trying to make it across the Adriatic on a rubber raft, light upon the Albanians ditching rafts on the coast of Puglia, light upon the beaches at Brindisi and near Bari, light upon the beached rafts of Brindisi, Albanians fleeing inland like the stray cats of Lecce wandering the Roman ruins, light upon the oft-conquered Puglia, and light upon Sicily now, with its light and darkness, its history of blood feud, light upon its hills, and light upon the Tyrrhenian Sea, and thus light upon Rome, all of the light beginning to peek through the streets of Rome, so that light is now visible, beginning to shine upon the Pantheon, that massive structure of such permanence that even a McDonald's just across the square from it cannot spoil its perfection, light upon St. Peter's, where the pope is trembling, light upon the Coliseum, light upon the piazzas and their Berninis, light opening its lens wider now, light hurtling up the longitudes, light upon Western Europe and a history founded on light as a mythological tool, light as a separation from night, light upon Milano, Firenze, Venezia, Nice, Monaco, Barcelona, light upon the church in all its incarnations, light upon all the cities of Western Europe and upon those up early to get to work in these cities, light upon those who wake to read the paper, a Parisian at a café, light upon a Spaniard in Pamplona, drinking a Turkish espresso, light upon Madrid, city encircled by fire, light upon Lisbon, and light farther north, in London, light upon the pigeons of Trafalgar, and light upon the pickpockets of Piccadilly Circus, light upon the orderly shops of the Fulham Road, light upon the bobbies and light upon the lorries and the black taxis, light upon the disenchanted royal family. Light upon Belfast, light upon the coils of barbed wire in

Belfast, light upon lads scraping themselves up from the paving stones in front of a pub, a bit worried about an ominous van parked in front of that nearby bank, dawn breaking over the opera house, where there is considerable hope for improvement.

Cold and severe dawn falls upon the ocean once again, ricocheting in the play of waves; another ocean, stretching down toward the Falklands, down toward the Cape of Good Hope, this ocean of nuclear submarines whispering along ocean floors, this ocean of imperial vessels, of Erik the Red, of Christopher Columbus, of Leif Eriksson. Light upon the arctic frigidness of the North Atlantic, too, light upon the perpetual north of the North Atlantic, and light upon Iceland, therefore, light upon Mount Hekla, the volcanic peak of Iceland, held for many years to contain the mouth of hell. This time of year, dawn is late; the fishermen of Iceland are well into their tasks. In Reykjavík the prodigious revelers of the city square are just getting up from another binge, heading for thermal baths to try to blunt that sickness; light upon the expanses of volcanic rock between here and Keflavik, light upon the hot springs, the geysers, the black beaches of the south coast, light upon the mouth of hell.

Light upon the open sea, the Winslow Homer green of the North Atlantic, upon the blue whale, the right whale, the songs of North Atlantic whales, light upon the fish coming to the surface, light upon the currents of this well-traveled sea, light upon the circulations of the Gulf Stream, the North Equatorial Current, clockwise, into the light now, these currents, light upon Greenland, the light of the Inuits, the light of the many names for light, light upon the Nunavut territory, upon Baffin Island and Baffin Bay, light upon the coming of winter in the arctic, light upon the very end of the hurricane season, light upon the fishing boats coming back empty-handed from the Grand Banks, light coming down the coast now, where Leif Eriksson landed and turned back, light upon Newfoundland, light upon moose frozen in headlights on the highways of Newfoundland, light upon

Cape Breton, light upon Nova Scotia, where the tides are so violent that the coast can come and go seventy feet in an afternoon, light upon Campobello, and light upon Eastport, state of Maine, United States of America.

It's possible that the sleepers just beginning to wake know nothing beyond Eastport; they have stuff on their mind, there are car payments, there are mortgage payments, there are utilities, there is heat to worry about. It has gotten cold down east already. International concerns are not pressing. On the pier in Eastport, next to that deep water, a pair of teenagers in a pickup, having made out all night, having slept in the truck, hand in hand, are now watching the dawn fretfully. They are going to get yelled at. What a sunrise. The crimson sun beginning to dash itself on the islands. Autumn on the coast of the state of Maine, in New England. The light only tarries here for a brief spell. There have been snow flurries. The best autumn colors are in the past. People are getting their boats out of the harbors, up on stilts, in the Casco and Penobscot bays. Light upon the mariners of the eastern seaboard, light upon the mariners from here down the coast, light upon the fishermen of Kittery and Portsmouth and Newburyport, light upon Provincetown. Light upon the scrub pines. Light upon the towns of the Cape, from which the mariners of yore set out to hunt the whale, light upon the mansions of Newport and the designers of sailboats, and light on the lighthouse, for example, of Narragansett Bay, at Point Judith, the lonely lighthouses whose job was once to augur the dawn, light upon surfers of Point Judith, light upon Watch Hill, and then light upon the casinos of Connecticut, and light upon the nuclear submarine base at Groton, and from here dawn has a straight shot down the coast, a straight shot on the interstate clogged with truckers on amphetamines, infernal all the way through New Haven and Bridgeport. These towns are dead, and the light does nothing but show up the rubble. The light shows up their corrupt politicians, their pedophile mayors, their distracted suburbanites; everybody's just trying to get past the cities of the dead, bent upon the gates of New York City.

How fast does it happen on this particular day? How fast does the sunlight rush westerly, dappling the world? The figure is 1,670 kilometers an hour, or about .23 miles per second, which is the speed of the rotation of the third rock from the sun. Day leaves no latitude behind. Therefore, twenty-four hours have elapsed, or twenty-three hours and fifty-six minutes, all of this according to the quantum theory of light, as described by Feynman. Suddenly there is the behavior of sunrise on waves, like the light over the Whitestone Bridge, where commuters are trying to get a jump on rush-hour traffic heading in on the Van Wyck, past the airports, the dawn on their left. You can see morning from the bridge. Light upon the Empire State Building, light upon the Chrysler Building, light upon the World Trade Center. Light upon those gruff, show-offy digits. Light upon Shea Stadium, site of the recent Subway Series. Light upon LaGuardia Airport, the most congested airport in the country, light upon the Brooklyn-Queens Expressway, light upon Floral Park, light upon Maspeth, light upon Inwood, light upon the Bronx Zoo, light upon Riverdale, light upon Yankee Stadium, light moving apparently instantaneously from here to the isle of Manhattan, its office buildings still illuminated with emergency fluorescence. Manhattan, New York City, beginning of another day.

New York City, noteworthy for its insomniacs. Light upon all the insomniacs, across this city, metropolis of insomniacs. They are there, in the despair of another night, out on the couch in the living room to avoid waking their husbands or wives, or insomniacs are in the tub, and they are reading, or they are thinking, or the insomniacs are regretting at the instant of the dawn. No one asks how they spend the middle of the night, no one who doesn't suffer with insomnia wants to know. The insomniacs are the witnesses to the dawn, they are in the tub and looking out on the air shaft, through the one tiny window, where a tiny patch of sky is visible, or they are at the breakfast table, trying to read something so boring that it will put them back to sleep. Every block has insomniacs, and here's the first light of a day in November breaking over them. A woman whose car is going to be repossessed, a guy who falsified his résumé to get an adjunct teaching position, an artist who cannot make her rent, a dot-com programmer whose company is about to exhaust its financing. The insomniacs! They welcome the day! One of them is about to take the dog out for a walk. One of these insomniacs is listening to the international news to see if the Japanese markets are up. A long, low moan escapes him when the intensity of the decline becomes clear. Whoever it is who made the dawn made it as a gift to these insomniacs, that they wouldn't feel so alone, that they would have something to do in their apartness, namely watch the celestial display of first light. Some of them do it, some of them go up to the roof just to see the light caroming off the buildings in Jersey City. Even the insomniac will feel some hope at dawn, even the homeless man on the grates in front of the Eye and Ear Hospital may feel a bit of relief, even the guy who hasn't been out of his apartment in years, even the racially oppressed, even the poor, even the unemployed, even they feel a transitory joy. Even the woman on the ground floor of the brownstone in Park Slope, who yanks back her blindfold, recognizing that she can put off rising no longer, rushes unsteadily from her full-size mattress, and makes a run for it, for the bathroom. A day of dawns. A jubilee. Morning, just after the election, year two thousand.

I

Rosa Elisabetta Meandro, in insubstantial light, entrails in flames. Rosa Elisabetta of the hammertoe, Rosa Elisabetta of the corns. Rosa Elisabetta of the afflictions. She has hinted about the nature of her sufferings to certain persons up the block, certain persons on Eleventh Street, Brooklyn. Emilia, whose son sells the raviolis, for example. She has whispered to Emilia about the colitis. She has indicated problems relating to her gallbladder. Stones. Also headaches. These headaches begin with visitations, with rainbows, celestial light, an inability to remember numbers. Rosa Elisabetta might smell the overpowering perfume of cocktail onions, after which there is Technicolor. Two or three days sick in bed, lower than a dog is low. If she's enumerating the complaints for Emilia, there is the colitis, there are the corns, there is the pancreas, there are the headaches. At least four things. Gas, though it's not proper to talk about it. On nights when the garlic has not been properly sautéed according to the cuisine of her ancestral homeland, Tuscany, then there is also the gas. Perhaps it is correct to include this in the list of complaints, assembled at 6:13 AM, as she burrows down further into bedcovers, into the folds of her four-poster. She doesn't know how much longer she can resist the cramps, the pressurized evacuation of her last meal and everything else eaten in the past twenty-four hours, everything, at least, that has not already been evacuated. *Best to be pleasant about it;* this is what Emilia said when Rosa Elisabetta Meandro was telling her about the scabs. There are these scabs that don't heal; when she gets a cut, saws into herself accidentally in the kitchen, dicing vegetables, there is the mineralization of the cut. The cut doesn't heal, not as it should. What's that all about? She was also going to tell Emilia about the halitosis, that day, which she can smell by cupping her hands and attempting to exhale and inhale quickly, while lying in the four-poster. It is no longer the smell of the garlic sautéed, nor is it the smell of the cocktail onions, nor is it the smell of port wine, nor is it stewed peppers. It's some new smell, and this is what Rosa was trying to tell Emilia the other day, no doubt about it. The look in the eyes of Emilia was a look of pity, which is a look that makes Rosa Elisabetta Meandro irritable, though she tries to be pleasant, and this righteous anger, even in the dawn light ebbing into the garden apartment through the windows facing the street, is a refreshing sentiment, a motivator, as she breathes out cupping her hands.

Consider the formidable Rosa Elisabetta of the past. Consider the archaeology of her phases. Kingmaker in the civic politics of the Fourth Ward, parader with infant ghouls and vampires on Halloween, soup kitchen volunteer; Rosa Elisabetta, institution. Dignified mother of the block, guardian of the parking spaces of longtime residents of the neighborhood, protector of the community, of local parishes, registrar of voters. Once she was all these things. A lover of families. As she enumerates them, however, Rosa Elisabetta can feel the sweat pooling in the folds of her abdomen; she can feel cramps beckoning from south of her equator. What was it that Emilia surely wanted to say about her bad breath? Maybe nothing. Her father had bad breath. Foul breath. It was his guts. She was there with the priest, such a nice priest, and the breath of her father smelled like a gizzard. She won't talk to Emilia anymore. How can anyone think such a thing? The cupping-hands experiment does not bear out results. Nothing at all like the smell of death.

She held the little children in the day care center while their mothers worked in Manhattan. She sang songs to these children, songs by important American singers from the age of big bands. Not one of these little children said to her: *Your breath smells like something died in your mouth.* She liked to present the boys with chocolates; she liked to warn them about the dangers of amorous contact. She told the little boys and girls: Avoid becoming inflamed. Never be alone in a room with a man who is too thin. Never walk near an idling automobile if it has tinted windows. Next she would speak of the constellations, how the constellations were catalogued during the Roman Empire. She knows about the Roman Empire from her father and his father, and she knows about it from the priests in the schoolyard of Dyker Heights, where she lived as a girl. She also once watched a miniseries on the subject of the Roman Empire. The emperors poisoned one another. The emperors knew a lot about poisons. She lifted and carried children, kissed them on their dirty necks. It is not right that Emilia from the ravioli store should even consider saying anything about the colitis, the gas, the headaches, the corns, the scabs, the breath, or the hair that is falling out. Or the blindness, or the incipient deafness, or the fact that Rosa is too skinny. Her dresses hang off her, like sheets draped over furniture in shuttered houses.

The cat is disturbed by a migrating foot from his spot in a spiral of bedclothes at the end of the bed. The cat resembles the black-and-whites of civic policing, but she does not like the name her daughter has given him and will not utter it. The animal hops gamely to the floor, waits. Will Rosa feed him? Now Rosa Elisabetta smooths her threadbare nightgown over her legs, pulls an old pink sweater from a squeaky dresser drawer just opposing, and wraps it around herself. Winches herself up on swollen knees and hips. This is her submission to the order of aging and infirmity. She knows what is to come now, how long it will take. She passes across the hardwood floor with its inlays of cherry and mahogany, into the sitting room, careful to avoid stacks of reading material beside the chair, some large stacks, in front of the French doors leading out to the garden. She flips on the television on the way past, 6:21 AM. A twenty-four-inch monitor that she bought used from a newspaper advertisement. The static of the picture assembling. She doesn't have time to look because all at once she is doubled over, indelicately emitting pollutants, she's awake and will be awake, clutching at her insides. She can hear the device, the old television set, from the bathroom. The volume is calibrated to allow this pleasure. Its music is generous from the agony of the bathroom. She bolts the door, leaving the cat on the other side. She begins to weep as the tremors begin. She weeps for the indignity. She hopes she will not bleed. She worries that it will not stop. She could live with it for a while, the colitis, if only she didn't bleed. She reaches for a magazine on the tank. The wallpaper in the bathroom, floral print, is peeling, and there is paint flaking from the ceiling. She tries to pretend that the concerns of the magazine are her concerns. Allegations about the outgoing president and his wife. His wife's lesbian secret. A powerful weight-loss program has enabled certain celebrities to shed up to seventy pounds. One chubby actress had her stomach stapled, live on the Internet. Will Rosa Elisabetta faint? Perspiration courses down her brow. She has fainted in the past. An awful embarrassment, the fainting, because then her daughter or the Polish woman who comes to clean will find her on the floor. Another actress, this one too thin, needs to put some weight back on, drinks milk shakes that weight lifters drink. Just the ticket. She thinks she can hear them talking about it on the television. Weight loss. Rosa throws the magazine into the claw-footed bathtub. Her face is slick. The cat is mewling outside the door, beckoning. There is a moment of pain, but then she attends instead to the soothing television voices. In the morning she likes to have on the perky one, the perky one, because the perky one keeps at bay the fear of death, but it doesn't sound as though she remembered to turn on the perky one, it sounds as though she got the one with the speech impediment. She likes the one with the speech impediment because he might explain things properly. But she prefers the perky one. She is comforted by all overheard voices, especially on mornings like this. And these voices are mixed with discussions from the past, in her head, enmity between her grandfather and her father, for example; she has been known to have a conversation with her estranged husband while shitting her brains out.

She will need someone from the neighborhood to keep an eye on her parking space. She has no car, but still. People are moving in, young people, they don't even know. Your car is secure for a total of six days through the kindness of neighbors. The young people don't understand until they have lived here as long as she has lived here, forty-six years. If she catches one of these young people trying to take her parking space, no matter about the colitis, she will give him or her a talking-to. From time to time, she has put on her robe and pulled open the door and called up the steps in the darkness. "Take your car back to Omaha! Don't you come around here again!" Imagine taking people's spaces when these people have lived here since before your parents were born. They move into the neighborhood, these young people, and the girl doesn't even have a ring on her finger. Honestly. That first September her daughter was in college, she put an advertisement in the paper, apartment to let, like in the old days, when the floozy from the bar performed an incantation on Rosa's husband. Just like then, renting the room. Except this couple calls to see the apartment. No wedding rings. They are different colors; one is a black man and one is an Italian girl. She shows them around, the original balustrade, cast iron, painted black, finials. She makes remarks about southerly light; she makes remarks about original moldings and plastering; she speaks of the Romanesque and Italianate uses of brownstone, things she has been told to say by a Realtor on Seventh Avenue whose services Rosa did not retain. She doesn't say anything to this couple that she wouldn't say to anyone at all, treats them as she would treat anyone, makes pleasantries, even when the black man is offering his know-it-all comments about wiring in the building, asking if the wiring has been rewired since the building went up. When exactly. She says, "You ought to see the garden, honey," ushers the girl back onto the patio, through her own apartment. She has the tomato vines, some basil and parsley, painted daisies, coneflower. Warm, everything flowers later into the season. Rosa takes the girl by the shoulder, in the dappled sunlight of the patio, where she used to hang the laundry, and she says to her, "I figure out who your mama is, I'll call her, and I'll tell her you were here with that man, and I will help her give her a talking-to. So now you get your black boyfriend and you get out of here same way you came in; don't let me see you on this street again, do you hear me? And you better hope none of the boys on this block saw you with that boyfriend, not if you want to make it to the subway in one piece."

There are couples like this on the block now, all sorts of couples, and the boys on the block, who used to have a sense of honor, they don't do a thing about it. Maybe the neighbors all treat these couples to a look of chastisement on the way past, but that's the end of it. A disgrace. Rosa Elisabetta herself is no longer the kind of person who lives on this block. Rosa is a specter, a revenant of a Brooklyn past, someone buried under layers of sediment, which is why she has the smell of death on her.

The pancreas, the problem with the pancreas, and the corns, and other complaints. She thinks, I will no longer drink the *vin ordinaire,* I will only drink the white wine and the Communion wine. Voices in the next room, gathering to speak of such terminologies as *grave uncertainty, political instability, intervention of the courts,* none of it particularly clear to Rosa. She pays the most attention to the school board and the city council, the social clubs, and she only pays attention to these because in the old days she paid attention to them when her father and her father's friends had an interest in politics. They knew how to look after what was theirs. She would give out leaflets over by the subway. Now she's not even sure who is running for the school board, if there is even a school board candidate.

Like trying to evacuate pieces of glass, like glass or maybe pieces of your brain coming out of your posterior, bits of your insides, bits of your organs, like your pancreas, for example, or the gallbladder. Black bile, green bile, stones. All the humors. Such a stink. She moans, while the voices debate about concession and recount, and so Rosa resolves not to give in herself and reaches into the cabinet underneath the sink, if she can just reach from where she is, where she keeps a special something. At the exertion, another molten river floods from her. Usually after an hour or so she feels better. When it is clearing itself up, she doesn't really need the bottle, the quart bottle purchased from the criminals at the bodega. Doesn't like to patronize them, because they do not ask after her family. She's sure that they are selling illegal drugs to schoolchildren, but nonetheless, there's the fact of convenience. The mildew smell is nauseating, too. When the Polish lady comes, she will have to tell her about the smell. Rosa Elisabetta doesn't know if she'll be able to keep down the malt liquor. Sometimes she spits it up. Sometimes she has to spit up some of the malt liquor in order to calm her stomach. Into the sink, sometimes into the tub. It's like in the miniseries about the Roman emperors. One fellow, he had the sour stomach, and then his grandmother fed him. Rosa unscrews the cap on the malt liquor, a feverish chill overtaking her; she can hear the chatter from the next room, beautiful and serene now that she's unscrewing the cap of the malt liquor. The voices sound like birds. The flocks of Prospect Park in spring, like that rooster that was crowing in the park last summer, someone left a rooster in the park, and it was doing its job in the mornings. She decides to risk the malt liquor. Everything is nauseating on a morning like this, the old tile floor in the bathroom of the brownstone, the mildew, the stink, the interracial couples of the neighborhood, the diaspora of her contemporaries to Long Island and to Westchester, to the state of Florida. She drinks deep, gags, drinks more, gags. Drinks more. Rosa Elisabetta, the last person in this neighborhood to have officiated in stickball and to have carried lasagna next door when people moved in, the last person to have drunk red wine out of jugs at the block party, where the priest came by and made jokes about baseball. They all drank wine, her family drank wine, even as a girl she drank wine, her friends had wine on Sundays at church, and no one worried about whether the priest was molesting anyone.

Rosa Elisabetta won't allow herself to be pushed out of her own neighborhood, where she raised up a daughter by herself and grew old. The neighborhood where she learned the one thing she learned, that a daughter was what God had promised. The perfection of daughters, daughters running in the park, daughters playing on the swings, daughters at the zoo, daughters smelling hyacinth in the botanical garden, smelling lilies. She made a dress for her daughter out of gingham, put up her daughter's hair in pigtails, took her over to the neighbors to ask if her daughter was not the prettiest girl on the block. She raised a daughter and worked in the principal's office of the elementary school, and no one can take her parking space away from her.

Replenishment of fluids. Vital to her condition. She knows what a flat cola will do for an elementary school child in the throes of a stomach complaint. She knows how to stop a nosebleed and how to apply a tourniquet. She will stay here until she has replenished. The malt liquor is half empty, and she is feeling as though she might be up and around before noontime after all. She is starting to feel like a matriarch, like a God-fearing Catholic. So she reaches back and toggles the lever, to flush away the bits of her that she has ripped loose, and the toilet gurgles darkly after clearing only a portion of the evidence. "Oh, don't tell me. Don't you dare tell me." Yet while this anxiety about plumbing — like anxiety about all home maintenance issues, and anxiety about medical issues, and anxiety about automotive issues, and anxiety about political issues — weighs heavily on Rosa Elisabetta, a fresh bout of muscular contractions overtakes her, and she can do nothing until its temblors have coursed through her. Then, coated with sweat and smelling like malt liquor, she reaches over, runs the tap, as if the sound of the tap will help, maybe the sound of the tap, instead of voices talking about the state of Florida, and she gets a handful of water, spills it across her face. It splatters the neckline of her nightgown and her sweater. She hates the color of her towels. She avails herself further of the malt liquor. She will finish the bottle.

Rosa is going to have to get herself well enough to search out the plunger in the kitchen, and then she is going to have to plunge the john, because she doesn't want to make it anyone's business, though she can barely make it up the block to the bodega on a good day. She only does it to purchase supplies when her daughter is at work, so no one will see. Otherwise, she has everything delivered. She won't have the plumber in here because of the blood, because she knows there's blood. She won't have it. She heaves, nothing comes up, and then the last of the malt liquor goes down. The first sip tastes like ambrosia, the last like formaldehyde.

She drops the empty into the claw-footed bathtub. It rolls back and forth without shattering. The trash can that she purchased at the discount store on Atlantic is over by the door. She doesn't like going there, Atlantic Center. It's full of the wrong kind of people. She went that one time because there were bargains. She reaches for a second bottle under the sink, just to be sure of the existence of the second bottle, and she gets a finger around the top of it, but then the quart bottle topples and rolls back into the sink cabinet, upending a toilet brush and a can of cleanser. She takes the name of her Heavenly Father in vain. She must have lost five pounds now, maybe more, and the room stinks, and the toilet is all clogged, and all she asks for is a little bit of relief.

The voices clamoring about Palm Beach County are like the souls clamoring to get into purgatory, or like the bees making a nest in their honeycomb. In the countryside. In an Italian village. In Siena. *Il mio caro paese.* She can see it now, her father and her father's father. Amateur magicians. In the old country. She knows all the stories. She can see the cypresses, farmers bent along rows of grapevines. Olive groves. She pushes up the lid of the toilet tank and plunges her hand into the tank, its rusty H_2O, and the lid, which is so heavy, slips sideways, hits the lip of the claw-footed bathtub, crashes to the floor, where it actually breaks clean in two. Rosa Elisabetta castigates the toilet lid with a string of ornamental curses. Outside the door, the cat gets traction and skitters off to the farthest closet he can find. Upstairs, too, from the racket she's causing she can hear that her daughter has waked, the planks of the hardwood giving with her daughter's ungraceful footfalls. Where is that pint bottle? She knows she put the pint bottle in the toilet tank, because her daughter was haranguing her. Her daughter was in the closet, throwing things out, mementos, items that Rosa needed, and that was when someone must have taken away those other items in the closet and perhaps also the one in the toilet tank. Someone has thrown them out. Her daughter is always straightening. She comes and she straightens up. And her daughter hired the Polish woman who also comes, and they straighten up together, but Rosa Elisabetta knew what that was all about, she knew what was getting straightened up.

Voices call out about the weather. Chance of showers. Drizzle approaching.

The worst of all possible things, which is that she hears her daughter's front door closing, hears steps in the stairwell. The lumbering tread. She's in her pajamas and coming downstairs to look in on Rosa. How could the great-granddaughter of magicians be such a dinosaur! Her grandfather, her great-grandfather, they were revered men of the village. They turned the lands of the poor and the afflicted to good. Gypsies followed them wherever they went.

The Viscusis came to the barren parts of the land with special tools, divining rods. These tools had been blessed by a sympathetic priest. The Viscusis said some powerful magical phrases, and then when they dug in that spot, they found water. Clean water, pure water. All the wells in their town, those wells had been selected and dug by Viscusis, so the Viscusis stood for water, for things growing, for cultivation, for husbandry. The wine that you drank from that town, the town where she was from, where her father and her grandfather were from, that wine came from grapes that were nourished by the wells dug by Viscusis.

Rosa's mistake was marrying Claudio Meandro, who was only good for one thing, and that was drinking up the product. Well, he was good for other things, too, for whoring and never bringing home a wage and abandoning his wife and daughter. She can hear her daughter wheezing, even with the television on. The rudeness of her daughter's breathing, which is the husky breathing of a chubby woman, the breathing of someone who is undersea diving. And that was just her coming *downstairs*.

"Did you feed the cat?" her daughter yells from the stairwell.

"Don't come in here!" Rosa calls from the bathroom.

"Why do you have to chain the door?"

Her chubby hand now on the other side of the doorknob.

"Why is this chained?"

"I'm in the bathroom!" Rosa calls, and the exertion prompts a fresh stream of her insides. "Don't come in."

"Are you okay?"

"If I needed you in here with me I'd call you."

"I heard a crash."

"You did not."

The neighbors in the next building will be able to hear the shouting through the cement, through the brownstone, through the Sheetrock, through the plastering. She gets up off the john now and crouches; her legs and her bottom are covered with the mess of her condition, she's a mess, and she tries to flush it away, again; she wants all of this gone, this indignity of the present, feminine-itch commercials, television programs about people on some island eating rats to stay alive so that their pictures might appear in magazines devoted to the subject of weight loss. She will brain that daughter if she comes in here. How did she give birth to a fat woman?

Her grandfather was summoned by the mayor of the village, a man with guns and power. The mayor said, I'm not getting a crop to grow here on my lands while you have many crops growing on the lands you oversee. You are harvesting all the crops, and I can't bring my grapes to market, and what I want is for you to bring your magical spells to my land here. I want you to make my lands fertile. Or else I'm going to run you out of town, and that will be the end of your vineyard. And your kids and your kids' kids, they'll be forgotten here, they will be outlaws, and the name of Viscusi will be forgotten here for all the rest of time. This was after the war, understand, and there was a lot of ill humor around. And there was also the matter of the well at Pienza, which owed its fame to Pius II. The mayor was outraged, *completamente oltraggiato,* that none could design a better well than the one at Pienza.

"I can't stay here and be after you all morning, Mom."

"Give someone some peace and quiet if they need it."

Rosa tries to flush away the evidence one more time. A serious tactical error. Now the worst possible thing happens, which is that the *merda* begins to come up, the water swirls ominously, and soon what will not go down through the drains, out to the sewage treatment plant, it comes up, backs up, and she can hear herself crying out in dismay, but she hears it almost as if it is happening to someone else. She doesn't know what's in her, what worm or parasite causes her to suppurate like this, part of her pancreas, part of her bowel; there's that moment of hesitation, that meniscoid pause in the process of boiling up, before it swells over the lip of the toilet —

"Are you listening about the election?"

— and begins to flood the floor. The insides of her twisting and burning. And that's when the headache starts, she can feel it beginning to start, the headache is upon her now, too, the Technicolor. She is beginning to have the vision, the phantasms that precede the next onslaught of pain, and the vision is of her grandfather and her grandfather's father, and they are desperate men, because they cannot find the water in the fields belonging to the mayor. They cannot find the water. After dusk, after church, they are wearing the clothes they wore to church, and there is the light of the old country, the light that inspired those old masters, the perfect light of the Tuscan country, and they go out into the fields, past a matrimonial procession winding up the streets toward the town square, and the wedding is making its tortuous way toward the well in town, a beautiful old well where the men and their wives will pour out long drafts of water, and they will drink wine and they will drink water, and they will revel and dance. Her father's father and grandfather are not in the wedding party, they are working, and they have the polished sticks of their profession, diviner's wood, this wood that for generations has made for good crops for the villagers of their town, and all they have to do is find one single well on this property. They have done it many times.

Rosa Elisabetta takes off her sweater and pulls the nightgown over her head. There are only glimpses of her in the mirror above the sink, a mirror veined with flaws, a translucent elbow, a swollen knob at the bottom of it, here are the gray tendrils of her curls around the severe lines of her chin and cheeks; the light moves

over her and through her in her nakedness, the light is an afflic-
tion, she bears up under it, because she is a beauty even as an old
woman, the men will clamor to lie with her, and she climbs into
the bathtub and leans her striated face against the porcelain of
the side of the tub; she knows the feel of the polished wood of the
divining rod, it is the wood of the umbrella pine and it has been
polished and tanned until it is like the hide of a cow; she knows
that creation of this divining rod is controlled by emissaries from
the heavens. A vision is upon her and this is its material.

Her grandfather had the women chasing after him all the way
to his death. The women followed after him and his father, even
that night, *le amiche* abandoning a wedding party and its black
sedans, jumping out of moving cars, and they were following her
grandfather and his father as they worked their way across the
farm belonging to the mayor. A procession of diviners. The men
were working their way across the fields, with the sticks of their
trade, but they were finding nothing. They had begun to sweat.
They had begun to worry. The *ragazzi* trailed the grandfather
and the great-grandfather, across the fields, the *ragazzi* already
drinking wine. No one knew where this drinking wine would
lead, except that at the end of drinking wine, the men would find
the water, because it was always so. And there would be a bonfire, and the hermit who lived in a shack by the railroad tracks
would bring out his concertina and his pet rat. This was the one
field between here and the city where there was no water. They'd
never before faced the possibility of failure, the Viscusis, because
they knew Gypsies. That's how the story went, thought Rosa
Elisabetta, in the bathtub, her soiled clothes on the floor.

The mayor would not take no for an answer.

There was nothing to do but fabricate a response from the
divining rods. Nothing to do but fake it. It was her great-
grandfather who suggested this. Her grandfather didn't want to do
it. Because he was a moral man and he felt that it would do no good
for their reputation. *Tuttavia, ha detto troppo una bugia assurda.*

Here is what the divining rod felt like in the hands of the men. Smooth but burdensome. You carried it as if it might break apart at any moment, as if it were a ceramic relic from the sixteenth century, and then you carried the divining stick into the field, and when the water was there under the ground, the stick trembled, as if it were in the midst of a Bernini ecstasy. The way her grandmother trembled, her grandmother who almost became a nun, or the way her mother trembled, who was among those who followed the men around in the field that very night with the wine. They watched the wedding, they jumped out of the car, they followed the men into a field, waiting for the men to find the water so that they could have the bonfire. Soon they would dance to the music of the concertina. That night, the Viscusis had to work fast, because that night they added a new skill to their repertoire: lying.

The mayor and his lackeys, armed, emerged from a copse, and now they watched as the Viscusis came to the most distant hectare of the mayor's lands. They stood off to one side, and Marco Viscusi, her grandfather, held the divining rod, and it trembled in his hands, a steady, unearthly trembling, if a playacted one, and Claudio said, "Father in heaven," or muttered another oath that would make it seem as though this were the work of the angels who sat right at the lip of the proscenium of all the hosts.

"Dig here, dig here," Marco told them. But the mayor threw down the shovels and said, "No, you dig. We'll be back in an hour."

"Okay, I'm coming in now, Mom. Okay? I'm going to go ahead and remove the chain."

She smelled them, Rosa Elisabetta, flush against the past, the cocktail onions, the breath of her husband, Meandro, the foul collars of his work shirts. And then her daughter pounding on the door outside, shouting to be let in. She could hear the voices yammering in the other room: bladder-control problems, the recount. She could hear the unfed cat whining. But she was a century back, when the Viscusis were sprinting across the fields, gunfire crackling over their heads, gathering up their things, making for the coast, leaving even their umbrella pines behind, that the mayor might burn them that night in his fireplace, cursing the name of Viscusi. Let this be a lesson to others! Off to America, in the company of the easy women from the fields, one of them already with child. That would be her own mother, the tyrant of Dyker Heights.

2

Statuesque, plus-size, smoggy sunlight in her dirty-blond hair, in front of the hospital, concealed in dark glasses, as if she might want to spray bullets into the crowd. She flags down the car, though it needs no flagging down. The woman in the gray raincoat and black designer suit climbs in. Slams the door. It rattles on its hinges. Arranges herself on the plush seat of the Lincoln Town Car. The car service driver, of subcontinental extraction, is perplexed in the rearview, *would she slam her own doors?* But she pays no attention, since she is already embarked on instructions: "Rockefeller Center. Here's how we're doing it: We're making a U-turn here and we're going back to Ninth, where we're going west until we get to Smith. At Smith, first available left, then we're going all the way over to Hicks, and then across Atlantic, *not* onto the BQE, along Hicks, using the back entrance to the bridge." As if he mustn't understand because he's an immigrant. He has a child at home, you know, a boy, an American boy, a boy raised in America. He, too, has shouted the words *Away from that socket!* He has an education, which is better than an American education, which is shit. He does not eat every day at a restaurant with a plastic exterior. The woman knows nothing of these things. He nods, imperceptibly, and they are off, into the part of rush hour that is composed of employees who are late.

The large woman affixes herself immediately to the cellular telephone, or rather to its tiny pendulous headset. As if she's talking to herself, as if she has just alighted in the car after a stay in the psychiatric wing of the Methodist Hospital. The boundary between telephone call and additional shouted instructions is difficult to pinpoint. "*Off* of Smith Street! You think I'm paying you to park?" As if she wants to ensure that he should listen to the entirety of her conversation.

He learns many things. He learns about her place of business: "I'm not going to be in time for the meeting. Right. Drilling out in front of the house. They struck a water main. Six feet of water in the street. A union guy got hurt. There's a liability angle, according to my lawyer. Electricity's out, too. I don't care what you tell them. We are in extended discussions with what's-his-name, right, from the television show. He wants to be attached. Broad audience appeal. Just remind them. Use these words. Broad appeal. Can you remember? I'll reschedule."

The intersection at Atlantic Avenue has been under construction since the Persian Gulf War, which is when he arrived. At night it's an archaeological dig. The city is in layers below the surface. They are burying a military bunker here, under the subway station, and under the bunker they are burying antiquities stolen from the nations of the Tigris-Euphrates river valley. The men are wearing hazmat coveralls, and sparks are raining from their welding equipment. It's all a tangle when he tries to get across Atlantic Avenue, even down by the other hospital. This passenger is like one of the cats in the zoo. Big cats before feeding hour. Pacing the cages as if they are going to devour the very walls. His boy loves them. His boy is full of joy, and the displeasure of the cats is a revelation to him. His boy has very little memory, and so every day is full of novelty. A leaf of the newspaper skittering above a sidewalk is a revelation. All smells are beloved of his boy. The smell of refuse delights him.

"Dr. Weiss?" she's saying. "Is it a bad time?"

Saturated with artifice.

"No, no, no. Of course. Well, something's going to be done. To ensure stability in the markets. Something has to be done. That's not what I called about. I had to phone the paramedics to come pick her up. They know her by name now, they've been over so many times. They actually call her Rosa. Rosa this, Rosa that. Snickering behind her back. I heard some crashing around. Like a demolition crew had moved into the basement. Which is basically true, because it looks demolished. She'd locked herself into the apartment, had the chain up. She shut herself in the bathroom. God knows how long. The cat was starving. I don't know when she feeds the cat. The cat looks like it has anorexia. No, I couldn't get in, and she wouldn't come out of the bathroom, so what was I supposed to do? The television was turned up so that I could hear the news anchor in my own bathroom. I asked her repeatedly to let me in, I was firm but I didn't *engage,* and I could tell she'd been at it, you know? A certain way she sounds. Too flexible. You know pretty much as soon as you hear her."

When he is not driving, he loves to be driven. He loves to see the lights, the skyline, the traffic shimmering above the water. In his own country, you get to know people in traffic jams. You learn their children's names, their grandchildren's names. You talk politics. You are with these people for a long time. You have a fistfight, and then later you invite your combatant to dine with you, should you ever emerge from the traffic. Once, he started a poetry circle with young people he met in a traffic jam. Like many drivers of car service vehicles, he has an advanced degree. In European literature, from the University of Delhi. He is most interested in televised narratives. They had American programming, dubbed, on the satellite stations of the Punjab. The program he most admired concerned oil barons of Texas. This program was, of course, deeply indebted to the nineteenth-century novel, to the three-volume sagas. He believes Horatio Alger is shit, actually, though his work is to be studied as a foundation for the American television serial, which is a thing of beauty.

The dispatcher sounds like the muezzin calling to the Muslims. Certain words are repeated. *Thirty-one, thirty-one, JFK, thirty-one, two twenty-eight, pickup, Seventh Avenue, two twenty-eight.* He fiddles with the volume on the radio so that it appears that he's not listening to the telephone conversations in the backseat.

"I had to break the chain on the door. Just give it a good shove. I just leaned into the door some, gave it a good shove, and the chain came right out of the wall. I'll spackle it. Anyway, then I walked right up to the bathroom door and I said, 'I know you haven't fed the cat. I know you're lying to me. I can tell when you're lying to me. What do you think it's like to be lied to constantly? Do you think that's pleasant?' That's what I said. She gets outraged, like it's an invasion. She's yelling that she needs some time to herself and will I please go away. The thing is, it *smells* pretty awful. I can tell even from out in the hall that there's some kind of emergency going on in there. I just say, 'Fuck it, Ma, I'm coming in,' and the guy on the television is yammering about concession speeches, and the cat is yowling about wanting to get fed, and I force the bathroom door, and that's when I saw the *blood*."

One drive he particularly likes: to Coney Island. He has a story about the roller coaster named the Cyclone. His wife, to whom he was engaged to be married when aged sixteen, according to the wishes of their parents, is always worried about their son. She is unnecessarily worried; she follows him about, keeping his hands out of things, because he has to put his hands on everything to feel what it is like. If there is rice pudding dessert on the countertop, as there sometimes is, his son must put his hands in the rice pudding dessert. He likes the texture of rice pudding. If there is curry or a korma or a biryani on the table, his son will attempt to put his hands *in* or *on* the dinner, before eating it, even if it should burn him. When there is rain, his son proceeds first through the door and into the street with his hands aloft, as if he wishes to catch rain. His wife takes their son to the school for other children who attempt to catch rain, and this school, because it is operated by the City of New York, is worthless, and though his son at one time had the possession of a few words, he is no longer using very many words, and his wife prefers that he stay in the house except when he is at the worthless school operated by the City of New York. His own beliefs are different. He believes that his son needs to be exposed to many things. His son needs to see the Statue of Liberty; his son needs to smell the herbs of the botanical garden and the animals of the zoo. When he is able, he sneaks his son to the cinema, where they see action films and sometimes Bollywood.

Then there is the amusement park called Coney Island. There is the boardwalk of Coney Island, there are the shouts of barkers at the playground, which are also like the calls of the muezzin, and there are the tastes and smells of the playground. He has journeyed to the playground of America. He has returned home to his wife, who is watching a television program about someone wishing to be a millionaire. To his wife, he says, "I want to take my son to Coney Island." His wife objects, of course, to the trip to Coney Island. She says that their son is a learning-disabled boy, which is not a term that he cares to use. He prefers to think that his son is a sorcerer's apprentice, so advanced in the studies of his craft that he has no time for the things of this world. His wife protests anew and then she breaks away from the conversation while attempting to guess the correct answer of the contestant who wishes to be a millionaire. She ridicules this contestant. Then she protests again.

Nevertheless, it's his decision because he is the one spending twelve hours a day driving this car. And so it is decided. They will go to Coney Island, though his wife says that there are rules about who can ride. Here's how they go: via the Brooklyn-Queens Expressway, to the Gowanus, to the Belt Parkway, to Ocean Parkway, and they park their Chevrolet sedan to unload the women in their *salwar kameez,* his wife and her cousins, so that they might walk along the boardwalk. What a day. Sparkling. It is glorious for every person who lives there, no matter where he comes from, whether he comes from the steppes of Central Asia, or the desert of the Middle East, or the jungles of Africa, or the rain forests of South America. The bridges, the Statue of Liberty, the view of New Jersey, where his cousins live, this is glorious. The sea is glorious. The open water is glorious. They shoot plastic rifles at plastic ducks, and he gives his son a key chain with a Bengali tiger on it. They eat the snack called french fries. His son has an abiding need to put french fries into the mouths of everyone present. Even some strangers are willing to have these french fries put into their mouths.

And then when the moment is right, and the sun at its zenith, they begin to make their way toward the Cyclone. His wife says, "No, no! Not on that thing!" But he does not pay attention to her imprecations. The ticket booth is before them, and he hears the cries of riders of the Cyclone hurtling through space. The man in the ticket booth is weathered from his many years at the Cyclone, such that he looks like one of the seagulls of the Coney Island boardwalk, which are so gray and so fat and so nasty that you cannot pause from putting a morsel of food into your mouth, unless a seagull should take it from you. His son has recently learned this painful lesson.

"Excuse me, sir, is it possible that I may bring with me my boy here, onto the ride?" Pointing to his son, whose beatific expression is marred only by the strands of drool and by his squashed features. The man in the booth of the roller coaster called the Cyclone cannot be bothered with the semantic categories of intelligence. He has seen it all before. He has seen the riders with no arms; he has seen the riders with withered legs. He has seen blind persons, who fold up their canes and remove their sunglasses. He has seen it all, an ebbing and flowing of physiques. Into this door, America goes, and pays for its ticket, and from this one America emerges, wobbly in the knees — if it still has knees. The man in the booth waves his hand in a dismissive way, as if to say that the roller coaster is no discriminator of intelligence. Only size matters, just size, and his son is now fifteen years old, and he is interested in many kinds of mischief with regard to his bodily secretions, but there is no disputing he is large enough for the ride. "Excuse me, sir, but now I thank you. It's a momentous day, sir, on which you should treat my son with respect, because he represents the renewal of blessings upon this country. Thank you for your consideration." The man in the booth spits into a paper cup.

He could go further, of course. He could speak of the Indus River civilization; he could speak of the millennia of accomplishment on the part of the Vedic Aryan civilizations, of Graeco-Bactrian art, a thousand years before that Jewish woodworker ever got his failed business going in the city of Jerusalem. He could speak of Mongol invasions, British occupations, of the Civil War, of Jinnah and Nehru and Gandhi, of his own father, a shopkeeper, in the rioting, of his father's uprooting of the family from what is now Pakistan, where it was said that a Sikh family could no longer be safe. He could speak of the Sikh emigration, of its scattering, of the Punjab and its ferment, of the Sikh tendency, at least in his family, toward restlessness. He could speak of coming here, of always knowing he was going to come here one day, for the boy, so that the boy could ride this roller coaster, so that the boy could know these things that his father did not know when he was getting concussed on the streets of Delhi. Yet he says nothing. He smiles, and he leads the boy and the women up through the maze to the tracks of the Cyclone. Here is the car of the roller coaster disgorging itself of a dozen teenagers. He and his son take up position in the frontmost car, and the jaded operators of the roller coaster pull fast the restraining bar, and his son is speaking the strange clicking language that he favors, which sounds like an exotic African tongue, and then there is the sound of the chains dragging the car of the roller coaster toward that first summit, and all the women in the back are screaming, and his son is seeing Shiva the destroyer.

There is an interval of dramatic silence in the monologue of the large woman in his car, because she has arrived at an inexplicability in her recitation of events. Her eyes are filled with moisture, which Ranjeet can see in the rearview, but this woman will not be made a mockery of, not in a car service vehicle, which is at the present moment stuck in a sequence of lights before the Brooklyn Bridge, at the edge of an empty section of warehouses near the neighborhood called Dumbo, a neighborhood of strangely dressed young people. After the interval of silence, she rises toward the summit of her own narrative.

"Well, of course the first thing I had to do was clean all of that up, because I wasn't going to leave that all over the floor, the john all backed up for when the paramedic guys arrived. I mean, I'm not going to go back to the house after that and clean it up, and I'm not going to leave it for the cleaning woman. So the first thing is I'm down on my hands and knees, and I'm cleaning this up while she's in the tub berating me, saying all the usual stuff. I was a disgrace, blah blah blah, why can't I get married, like, why do I have to be like I am, which is a disgrace, why is her only daughter one of *those* sorts of women, and does this reflect badly on her in some way? I mean, it's not like she had a lot of boyfriends after Dad left. Same old list of grievances, I don't have to tell you. She gave me curlers once, did I tell you that, and she'd invite guys from off the street — no, okay, sure, I understand. Yeah, I'll finish up . . ."

Did they envision in the last century that one day this bridge would welcome men and women from India and Pakistan and

Bangladesh, men and women from Ivory Coast, or Ghana, or Malaysia, or Sri Lanka, welcome them into the conspiratorial enterprise of Manhattan, promising, for example, that a man like Ranjeet could enroll his son in the schools here, so that his son would not be lying in an empty room with a cement floor at the back of a tiny apartment in Delhi because no academy would take him in or teach him anything, such that he would have to take up begging, and no one would have him, except perhaps Christian churches, no one would massage his strange toes, no one would kiss his strange Mongolian eyes? The bridge, with its stone towers, east and west, seems to answer resoundingly *yes* to such a question as this, when imagined by a car service driver during dull stretches of traffic, and he finesses the merge onto the FDR before she has even finished explaining again to the psychiatrist about her mother's sickness, which Ranjeet can't yet diagnose, though he does hear something about a pancreas. This is a thing he does not know well. The women do not drink alcoholic beverages in his family; the men do not drink alcoholic beverages, except that occasionally they do, occasionally they go out into the parks and they drink and take off their turbans, at least in his family they do this, though they do not let it affect their many responsibilities.

"I'm supposed to have this meeting this morning. About the new project, and it's ruined, it's ruined. How the fuck am I supposed to get one of these movies made if I'm always back at the house trying to keep her from ordering me zircon-encrusted jewelry from some newspaper circular so I'll be able to attract the right kind of man? Or calling the call-in programs, saying that the immigrants don't respect the nation, even though she's practically an immigrant herself, and she's leaving me notes about how I'm supposed to produce an heir or else."

A spell begins to overcome Ranjeet. The spell of that perfect word, that pair of syllables that changes everything. *Movies.* It is a word as perfect as the two perfect etymological American exports: *okay* and *Coca-Cola*. The word *movies* may have its origin in Sanskrit, *movati*, in which one *pushes* or *shoves;* movies, culturally speaking, involve a fair amount of pushing and shoving. It is a global romance, a word of American promise as is no other, a word that summons the glittering prizes offered by this land of opportunity, the word *movies*. He knows about movies; he knows about films of bodybuilders, about teen sex comedies. He knows about sequels. His son also likes animated cartoons with violent passages. The word *movies* transports Ranjeet Singh, leading him to power up his own cell phone in order to call his cousin Hardeep in Jersey City. He must shout because his cell phone is not effective. They are now a two–cell phone Lincoln Town Car, hurtling under the Williamsburg Bridge, alongside the East River, in Manhattan. There is a Coca-Cola sign, look there. To the wife of Hardeep, he says that he cannot talk to her now, "Please don't start about purchases you have just made, just please hand the telephone to Hardeep," and then, in Punjabi, a dialect known for its colorful curses, he tells his cousin Hardeep the situation. There is this rather large blond woman in the car, and he does not know for certain, but he believes that the woman in question is employed in the business of the movies. Could it possibly be that she is in the movies? Could it possibly be that he has a famous person in his car? Once he had a politician in his car, the president of the borough of Brooklyn in his car, but this did not impress him. Not like the present instance. Because of the nature of his studies at university, he tells Hardeep, he knows movies. Wait, let him listen a little more. And Ranjeet strikes a pensive pose.

"Yeah, of course, these things really make me want to engage in acting-out behavior. I mean, the terminology makes me want to vomit, but I don't know what else to call it, so for today, I'll just say I'm having thoughts. Okay? Does that make you happy? Does that mean that I'm no longer exhibiting resistance? I missed a really important meeting this morning. I used to have a career, you know? I actually made the occasional movie once upon a time. Now I'm cleaning the shit out of the bathroom of my alcoholic mother, who has soiled herself and is sitting in the dry bathtub, drinking, with the television blaring, and I'm thinking about acting-out behavior."

In their country Hardeep was instrumental in the beginning of the hacker phenomenon. He claimed to have authored a virus. A message would pop up on pornographic Web sites telling the user that a woman's body is a holy temple of God. Now Hardeep is writing code for large corporations, Web-based products, business applications. It pays handsomely. Hardeep and his wife and children live in a condominium in Jersey City, near the Newport Center. Ranjeet tells his cousin that he must urgently search online databases for the identity of this woman from the movies, and Hardeep asks, in his husky voice that sounds brusque even when he is being sentimental, if Ranjeet happens to know the name of the woman from the movies, and Ranjeet is forced to concede that he does not know her name, for she has not given it. She does not need to give her name to secure a car.

"Don't do the detachment thing, please," the large passenger is now saying into her pendulous transmitter. "I don't need a bunch of questions about how I *feel* about it. I'll tell you how I feel about it. I feel like I have nowhere else to turn. I feel like I'm stuck with a madwoman. And she's not even in the attic; she has the better apartment. It's more like I'm in the attic, and the whole thing is reversed, and I'm the one who's going out of my mind, and I'll die first, of boredom, because I can't take her complaining and her incoherence, her demands and her spontaneous hemorrhaging —"

Ranjeet makes for the Forty-second Street exit. Which means that he will be going past the United Nations. He tells Hardeep that there is absolutely no chance that the woman is a movie actress, because she is very plump, and in this country she would not be a film star, by reason of plumpness. There are character actors who are noted for their plumpness, but they are considered fit only for ridicule. Perhaps in India, where a large wife is to be adored, Hardeep's wife being an example, she could be an actress. There she would make the sky feel badly about its imperfections. "Perhaps she is a film editor," Hardeep offers. So Ranjeet is considering just saying something to her, shouting across the seat, over the rhythmical chants of the dispatcher, *Forty-eight, pickup, forty-eight,* "Excuse me, plump young lady, because I'm a film scholar in my homeland and I cannot help overhearing that you are involved in the movie business. I would like to inquire about your employment. In what area particularly are you involved in this film business? You are perhaps an agent? Or a casting director?" But before he can say anything, she shouts in such a way that there is no mistaking that it is he with whom she is attempting to communicate, "Excuse me, uh, I've had a little change in plans, and now we're going to have to go back down to Fourteenth Street; I'm really sorry —"

A turn on Forty-second! No! The whole of this Western civilization rises up against a turn on Forty-second Street! Once you are on Forty-second Street, you must stay on it, this artery. Yet if this is so, then how do people get on and off of Forty-second Street? They get on at one river and then they go all the way to the other river, passing the Grand Central Station, the New York Public Library, the Disney Store. Bisection, boundary, limit, emblem: Forty-second Street. There must be persons, visiting from other countries, who have been stuck going back and forth on Forty-second Street for tens of decades!

On the phone, Hardeep protests that the description is inadequate. There are many upon many upon many film producers with blond hair, much of it artificial in color. And there are many plump celebrities. It could be that Ranjeet has in his car a certain very plump talk show host. Actually, there are several plump talk show hosts. It seems that being very plump is an indicator of potential for talk show hosts. Here, Ranjeet demurs. It is definitely not the plump talk show host in question, and he knows this for

the reason that his son has a violent hatred of the one plump talk
show host. Any time the very plump talk show host appears on
the television, his son must be restrained. "Well then," his cousin
offers, "if it is not the talk show host, it could be that woman
from the situation comedy, the one who had her stomach made
smaller." The conversation goes on this way, and Ranjeet becomes exasperated, says that his cousin is shooting at the fishes,
and he looks back in the rearview mirror and sees that the plump
woman is now yanking possessions out of her bag in an animated
manner. He sees that there is a baseball cap in there, she pulls the
baseball cap out of the bag for a moment, and he nearly rear-
ends an expensive vehicle, perhaps a Jaguar, by the Flatiron Building, because he is attempting to read the words on this cap that
he sees in the backseat, the cap that says *A Low Life in High Heels.*
Hardeep is yelling that he cannot stay on the line all day, but
Ranjeet pleads with him, please please, just to punch the words
into his computer to see if anything will come out of the computer, *A Low Life in High Heels,* and Hardeep employs the search
engine because everything is available on a search engine, for this
is indeed the age of information, and soon there will be search
engines right here in the Lincoln Town Cars, or so the dispatcher
has said.

In fact, there is a movie with this very title, *A good-natured but
somewhat pretentious biographical picture about a minor character in
Andy Warhol's Factory, featuring new music by Lou Reed.* This is
what Hardeep reads to his cousin. And who are the principals of
this movie, the director, the writer? For these are things that can
be discovered with the search engine, as Hardeep has described
it, and soon Hardeep lists these people and adds his own interpretation of the commentary, "A man from Miami prefers to
dress in the clothes of a woman, as you would often see on American television. Yes, of course there was a producer involved in
the film," Hardeep says, "and I am looking at a photo of her right
now, and she has very large cheeks, like she is carrying nuts in

them, and she has blond hair. It looks as though it is not real hair but rather hair that is dyed. Is this enough information?"

Ranjeet replies, "You are the best cousin I could ever have."

Now they have arrived at Fourteenth Street, where endless construction is also being practiced by extortionists in unions. Passengers have told him so. There is a construction site that has a large rubber rat out in front of it. It has contented features, this rat, and near to it there are men speaking angrily through bullhorns. They stand flush against the enormous, distended belly of the rat. Ranjeet plunges ahead in the Lincoln Town Car, makes it across Broadway, and soon he is at the stop designated by the plump woman, who is again organizing her personal effects. The adventure is coming to a close. She asks the price. He asks the same question of the dispatcher, whose plosives thunder through the two-way radio. Bills are exchanged. Ranjeet can see that this moment is poised to escape and he realizes that he cannot avoid bringing up the issue; he must bring it up, for to do so is to wrest the promise of a lifetime from the jaws of defeat.

"Excuse me, I am sorry to —"

"No time," the woman says.

"But I —"

She fumbles with her purse; she closes its latch. She lurches across the backseat in order to avoid opening the door on the traffic side.

"I believe that I overheard that you are in the business of cinema. I was once a student of cinema. Before I came —"

"My assistant will be glad to read your script."

"I have no script," he says quickly, as she plants one foot on the curb, exactly as in fifty thousand movies past. "I have only advice. About television."

3

There are no rules in the self-help universe. Your average addict hates rules. The Second Avenue Clubhouse, on Fourteenth Street between First and Second avenues, therefore observes few rules. Those twelve traditions everyone talks about? The Clubhouse doesn't observe them. The Clubhouse puts the group ahead of the sick-and-suffering individual, denies addicts entrance if unwashed, passes the basket twice, collects a yearly membership fee. The addicts who run the Clubhouse are unelected. They refuse to step down. They rule completely. For these reasons, new and untested flavors of twelve-step meetings have found favor here. Down the hall there is Self-Mutilators Anonymous, Shoplifters Anonymous, Nightmares Anonymous, a smattering of sex-addict meetings, including the very anonymous Pedophiles Anonymous. Candlelight meditation meetings for Adult Survivors of Incest.

Vanessa Meandro climbs the stairs, out of breath, sweating. Vanessa imagines that she has compassion for all sufferers of obsession, or she says she does; the pedophile walking down the block alone and passing by a blond nine-year-old girl on a bicycle, guys who spend the day fucking other guys in the woods in the

Vale of Cashmere. And yet she has no compassion for sufferers of her own particular difficulty. She strides, in her despond, through the entrance and into the Clubhouse, which is a three-bedroom apartment in the kind of postwar building that used to be considered shabby and uncomfortable but that now rents exorbitantly. The carpeting has stripes of grime. Vanessa passes the Clubhouse bulletin board, which advertises triple-winner meetings for alcoholics who are post-traumatic-stress-disordered, self-employed, compulsive gamblers. Where else would they go? Especially if they are also interested in vegan dietetics, clutter clearing, lucid dreaming, rebirthing, and courses in miracles?

The meeting has already started. Vanessa dreads the door that opens into any self-help group. In her instant of hesitation, she believes that people in the meeting sometimes know who she is. There have been articles written about her, articles that have appeared in large glossy magazines. She once wrote a piece herself, too, for an anthology entitled *Creative Control,* published by a small independent press. Film students read and debated this book. She imagines that the fellow sufferers know who she is, if only because this would make her feel worse. There is nothing to do but cross the threshold into the meeting. There is nothing to do but accept the gazes of her fellow addicts. They're reading the twelve steps, steps she has entirely ignored. There are a lot of very large people in the meeting, large women, large men. Often there are complaints about the size of the seats. She stumbled into a business meeting once, and rancor about the folding chairs was its sole topic. If the meeting were catering to the needs of this constituency, they should make the chairs larger!

She'll have to crawl over a half dozen of the beleaguered to get to the vacant seat in the corner. She doesn't know if she can. An anemic sunshine illuminates dust in the window facing south. Faces of the sufferers are lit up with it, with anemic sun. They are trying hard to make this a better day. Maybe they have acted out already this morning, they have given in to their urges, and they are trying to appear as though they will not do it again. If only there will be evidence of remission. Just for today. They are fervent, for this hour. A coffee pot in the corner cooks down the astringent tar. No cookies, anywhere. In the front, a girl so badly anorexic that she resembles a famine appeal introduces herself again. Paisley, compulsive overeater. Paisley asks, cheerfully, "Anyone new here today or attending their first few meetings?"

The woman sitting next to Vanessa smiles in her direction, inviting her to make herself known. Vanessa fluffs her hair nervously. She does some nervous stretching. "Is that a hand back there?"

"I'm Vanessa."

Everyone cries out a greeting to the newcomer. Paisley reiterates that it's not to single out the newcomers that they're so identified, it's so they might feel welcome! This *is* a safe place, Paisley reassures them. Then there's some more nonsense about the steps, during which Vanessa takes out her personal digital assistant and begins scrolling through the appointments she's missing. Meetings here at the Clubhouse are an hour and fifteen minutes, with a fellowship portion in the middle, where you can't eat anything. The sufferers stand around nervously, knotting and unknotting their fingers. Last week, Vanessa heard a woman blustering during the fellowship break, enlisting friends in her plan to keep more movie theaters from opening downtown. Just too many movie theaters downtown! Vanessa wanted to invite her to go back to her cave and rot. No one was listening to the woman, but no one was brushing her off, either. She was just there, anxiously murmuring during the five minutes of fellowship.

Since no addict can abbreviate her remarks, since everyone has to blather on until he or she has enumerated everything that has happened in the last twenty-four hours, including specifics about irregularity and skin rashes, one volunteer holds a stopwatch during the meeting to make sure that people don't go on beyond their allotted four minutes. Vanessa wishes for an even shorter duration. These are the dullest storytellers on earth. They would bore rock formations. They are worse than habitual dream recounters or film agents with their plot summaries. She would like to create some special quarantine for film agents and dream recounters. The next ward over would have the compulsive overeaters.

Now Paisley welcomes her close personal friend, a real power of example, Dean, and Vanessa realizes that she actually recognizes Dean. Dean is not just a regular obese woman with knee trouble, acid reflux, and diabetes. Dean is a former supermodel. Dean is a *Vogue* cover girl, a former lingerie model, and, if the reports are right, an unrepentant heroin addict.

"Hi, I'm Dean, and I'm a food addict. I have to talk first about my esophageal ulcers, because they are very real for me right now." After which Dean proceeds to the recital, first time as a girl, when, lanky and unloved, teased for her horsey legs, her bulbous nose that she didn't get fixed until later, she put her fingers down her throat after some uninvited attention from a drunk friend of her father's. Gulping down drinks with Kahlua in them while the friend, a local minister, tells her about the glory of the Divine, the look in his eyes a mixture of famishment and terror; she goes upstairs to the bathroom, thirteen years old, puts her hand down her throat, bathroom interior like one of those anti-gravitational swimming pools that astronauts train in. A pleasant thing, ridding herself of the Kahlua, the stolen drinks, ridding herself of the ambiguous glory of the Divine, ridding herself of some middle-aged man with salt-and-pepper beard, so she keeps putting her fingers down her throat, and it is good. It is good to observe purity doctrines because these are doctrines about the glory of the Divine. It is good to refuse food or to feast only on feast days, the saints did it, but some days she would eat a half gallon of ice cream, put her fingers down her throat, try to get her hand out of the way before it all came up; she began to like the look of it on her face, a little bit of vomit, because everyone liked her face so much, which was a face perfected by surgery, its pathos amplified by some rape; every woman gets raped, guys are rapists, that's the truth of the story, Dean says. Some nights she liked the look of last night's ice cream on her chin, the chin that was so prominent on the cover of some magazine or another, it looked good to her, vomit on her chin, reminded her somehow of the guys who blacked out the teeth of actresses on subway posters. It all worked fine for a while; she smoked, she had her teeth brightened and then capped, didn't have a living tooth in the back of her mouth, couldn't eat more than a cup of soup most days because of how much damage she'd done; in the morning she was empty. She liked mornings when there was both mist and sunshine over the park that her house overlooked, and she was empty, and there was baroque music playing, it was all good, and then the bleeding started. Who cared? Her father had an ulcer, her brother, everyone ulcerated, that was just part of being an American, you bled internally, you oppressed other countries, outside you looked great. But when her esophagus started bleeding, it got her attention, the bleeding got her attention, like the night she ate three hundred and sixty-five caramels, it just seemed like a good number, she was on the phone talking to some guy who'd just had an IPO for a company he started, sold surgical tools and medical materials over the Web, he was twenty-eight, and the stock had appreciated 113 percent on the first day, and he had given her chlamydia, this guy, though she hadn't told him, and she talked to him and let him tell his stories about his IPO, she let him suggest that she buy some shares, and that was really funny, in a depressing sort of way, and then she went into the bathroom, and there was all this blood, the color of it was shocking, it was Technicolor blood, some of the caramels coming up whole, that's how horrible it was, they were like the cubist blocks of some painting, the caramels when they came up, but the blood was more red than red, it was like cadmium, fresh from the earth, filings of cadmium from a mine somewhere exotic, the disintegration of her. There was only ice cream and Kahlua, or she was on a diet that consisted entirely of the licorice called the Twizzler because that was what the doctor told her, the doctor of her interior monologues told her to eat only Twizzlers, fuck what anyone thought, she went out to lunch with her agent, who was always trying to keep everyone away from her, except socially acceptable guys like the IPO guy who gave her chlamydia, then she ordered salad and pushed the salad around on the plate in the most brazen way, like when she was a kid and her mother tried to give her laxatives; it was good for a girl to have laxatives. Meals were more like plowing than eating. The day comes when she can no longer eat a meal at all. She tries the occasional Twizzler, just because there is an obscene beauty to the Twizzler. It's American; it reminds her of times past when candy was still a surprise. These guys are still calling, leveraged-buyout specialists are calling, and movie executives are calling, not the kinds you want to call. She's embarrassed by it but doesn't know how not to talk about it, these guys are calling, and basically she thinks they're probably porn business people, that's what they look like, always with the gold chains, and then she can't go a day without putting her fingers down her throat, it's every day, and sometimes the night, sometimes it's the last thing that happens after she looks at the meteor showers over her bungalow on Long Island, she goes into the bathroom, insults herself with her right hand, gets her hand out of the way as the food comes up, looks at herself in the mirror, her pride, the sweat on her brow, she uses some deluxe mouthwash, doesn't smile now, because smiling gives away the lie, avoids men, except when they force themselves on her, never kisses them, just sleeps with them, until she goes to the ear, nose, throat specialist to the stars, and the specialist takes one look at her throat and explains in graphic detail what is going to happen soon: intravenous drip, psychiatric hospital, halfway house, or all three. Later, she goes to a Christmas party with her father — her mother is dead, having left a slim corpse — and who should happen by but the minister. Her father's friend. Since she last saw him she has become the exemplar of heroin chic photographs. Even though she has never been a heroin addict, she looks dead, and a medieval glow hovers around her. She can't do her own shopping, she doesn't know how to balance her checkbook, but she has read and memorized portions of the *Imitatio Christi*. So she comforts her father's friend late into the night, and she explains that he has fallen far from his path, and she goes upstairs and coughs up a couple of cups of blood.

Vanessa whispers to the obese woman beside her. She's just remembered an important business obligation, sorry, really sorry, but she's already squeezing herself over the cramped legs of the woman, whose eyes are so filled with sorrow that it's impossible to meet them, really sorry, and there's a horrible scraping of chairs in the back row as Vanessa tries to get to the aisle as quickly as possible. Dean never once raises her eyes to this commotion. Her voice is a benediction. And now, impassioned, she describes the instant of her epiphany, when she gives up and comes to her first meeting, when she sees that there is another way, another life.

But Vanessa is out the door. She makes for the stairs. There's no good in the world at all until she hits the street. Oh no, the car service guy is still there, the Sikh. Oh no. He has parked, lying in wait for her. All these people, these thousands of lives and stories careening past on Fourteenth Street, and this guy has to be waiting for *her*. He's mouthing something from the front seat. He's shifting around in the front seat as if he's going to get out. She can hear the door opening. And then a cab, one of those new sport utility taxis, its beacon illuminated, disgorges another obese woman. This woman has a cane and she's headed for the meeting, no doubt, and Vanessa shoves past her and into the taxi.

"World Trade Center, please. And see that guy right there? The guy in the Lincoln Town Car? That guy. If he starts following you, perform evasive maneuvering. I don't know. Steer clear. Get the hell away from him. Whatever you do."

The driver, a Hispanic guy in his late forties, looks skeptically in the rearview.

"Take the FDR."

Across Fourteenth Street, toward the power plant. He makes the turn and they are on the Drive. She's just caught her breath when he careens around the southern tip of the island and then up the West Side Highway, under the skyway at World Financial Center. Jersey City looms like a bitter twin across the Hudson. The wet-hemp smell of the river. The cab pulls up at Vesey and Church. She says, "Leave the meter running."

Who actually looks at the towers? Everyone ignores them. They are eyesores. Like the telephone poles of rural electrification that bisected the pristine countryside, they rise up out of nowhere and inflict themselves on you. Who gives a shit? The Port Authority took ten years to build them, who gives a shit? Who gives a shit that they're so tall? Who gives a shit that they dwarf the Empire State Building? Who gives a shit? The only feature worthy of comment, as she heads across the plaza, is the gravity of their relationship. They lean in against each other, like lonely people, across the plaza, desperate for company. They lean so far in that you can't look away. Somebody's terrier, off the leash, bobs along at plaza level, in the penumbra of the towers, looking almost subatomic. The towers don't make you want to write a sonnet. They don't make you want to dance. They make you want to write a cost-benefit analysis.

Or they make you want to eat. They make Vanessa want to eat, and so she's down in the concourse underneath, a shadow city made possible by the scale of the aboveground development. There are any number of possibilities for foods that she shouldn't eat. These foods call to her. There's a Nathan's Hot Dogs, there are the burger joints. She could easily eat several of those hot apple pies. But she doesn't want McDonald's. She has come for one thing, for one cure. The word for her cure is *doughnuts*.

Toward you, Krispy Kreme, we swim, as in the waters of the Ganges. Krispy Kreme, beacon for the forgotten and disenfranchised. Krispy Kreme, with your bounteous offerings. Who else loves so unconditionally and gives so unstintingly? Who else puts others first so graciously and humbly? You, Krispy Kreme, mother for the motherless. You stand for all embraces. You are like candle-light or overheard surf. You are like a waterfall in a sylvan interior. Krispy Kreme. From your humble origins in Winston-Salem, where Vernon Rudolph's secret yeast-raised-doughnut recipe first caught on with consumers, through your brand-spanking-new mix plant and distribution plans in the nineteen-forties and -fifties, your expansion throughout the Southeast during the civil rights era, not to overlook the tragic passing of your founder. From your sale to the Beatrice Foods Group unto your initial public offer-ing, a scant seven months ago. Holy syllables, holy Krispy Kreme, holy hot doughnut–machine technology, holy franchising empire.

Just a little stand, here, beside the Rite Aid pharmacy, to which Vanessa trots with such purpose that the commuters coming up the PATH train escalators veer out of her way. Doesn't matter that the Krispy Kreme at concourse level is neither flashy nor fashionable. She will not be diverted from the mission, which is the mission of doughnuts. Is the sign illuminated? Do you need to ask? The sign that indicates that the doughnuts are fresh. Yes, there is a *light* at Krispy Kreme, which indicates that the original glazed doughnuts of Krispy Kreme are just off the assembly line. She looks for the indicator lamp; she looks for a sympathetic light in the eyes in her fellow men and women. Yes, the light is still illuminated! How is it possible? How could they still have the doughnuts so late in the morning? Is it some kind of synchronic-ity? Is it a further proof of the parking-spot god, the subway-seat god, the Overeaters Anonymous god who apparently smiles on the needs of Vanessa Meandro? She is destined to have a dough-nut that melts in her mouth, a doughnut that tastes like the happy ending of a romantic comedy as purveyed by a vertically integrated multinational entertainment provider under German ownership.

The line is not long. Her cheeks are flushed. She knows that the girls at the register at Krispy Kreme will not be supermodels.

She knows that they are not going to look at her with the pitiful look that she gets when she buys the five or six boxes of Entenmann's chocolate-chip cookies at D'Agostino's. She's not going to get that look. It's good to be back. She hasn't been here since she had that meeting at Windows on the World with the guys from the digital video company.

"Four original glazed."

Impatient, shoving the Jackson into the hands of the Krispy Kreme employee, Rosie. She doesn't even wait to be in the open space of the concourse before she has one in her mouth. And here's the lesson. The great spiritual benefit of the Krispy Kreme original glazed doughnut is the sensation of nothingness. The satori that is Krispy Kreme is the obliteration of self, the silencing of the voices that are attached to the oppressions of life. As soon as she has the original glazed doughnut in her mouth, relief floods in. If only the delights of the Krispy Kreme original glazed could be evenly distributed across the expanse of an entire hour, instead of lasting just the one or two minutes it takes to get the delicious yeast-raised dough into her mouth. Why is the delight of an original glazed doughnut so brief? Why is her dissatisfaction so quick? She hasn't even finished wiping the glaze from her fingers with a Krispy Kreme napkin before she's ready to have the next. Back in the cab, Vanessa provides a new destination: corner of Eighth Avenue and Twenty-third. The driver can't understand her at first, because her mouth is full. She repeats it, and then she offers, "My dad left when I was a kid."

It's the *cane* that does it, understand. The refined sugar. The obsidian gum of that divine cane. A black juice boiled in a vat, sticky, hard to handle. Black gum, better than the fruit of poppies when first it made its way around the globe. The cane. The cane tells us about the slave at the end of the lash, the cane tells us about the colonial adventure among the Carib, it tells us about the trusts and the trust busters, it tells us about monopoly, it tells us about profit, it tells us about novelty, it tells us about intoxication, it tells us about the dulled wits of the populace, it tells us about candy shops, and the moms and pops thereof, it tells us about Hershey, Pennsylvania, it tells us about the folks at Cadbury, it tells us not to listen to any voice but the bloodstream and its cry of plenty when the cane hits it, it tells us always to hew near to that cry, and when we are contented, always to yield again. And therefore Vanessa will say anything now. The cane has loosened the screws; the cane has made all men her friends. Doesn't the driver speak English? Does he speak some abridged version of English? Doesn't he realize that this is a story that has not been told to the trade magazines? She swallows down the end of the second original glazed doughnut with difficulty. The cane wants her to speak. The cane wants her to praise its reign. And she can't stop herself, even when she happens to look out the window and see the car service guy from Brooklyn. Pulling alongside. Smiling and waving at her.

"My mother was a shrew. My mother didn't listen to anyone and was constantly pestering everyone around her with her demands. Maybe that's why he left. My dad. My mother drives people off. I don't know. It was his birthday, and it was this time of year, by coincidence. Mom had just taught me, you know, that I was supposed to get people presents, for their birthdays, for the holidays. So I bought my father a clip-on bow tie. I was so excited. A bow tie. I think I got it on Orchard Street. Wrapped it up in some purple tissue paper. We already had an artificial tree up for the holidays, even though it was kind of early. My mother insisted on the flame-retardant tree. I knocked on the door and I said, 'Daddy, I got you a present.'"

She's begun the third doughnut. Autonomous reflexes have come into play, the grasping motion has taken place, and she has reached into the bag, and the doughnut has been placed in her mouth, and it has gummed up the fine muscle coordination required for the pronunciation of certain words. A gap in the narrative of some duration. They pass the club called Westworld, on the West Side Highway, where she once went with a gay friend. Across Fourteenth, a run of synchronous green traffic lights, toward Twenty-third.

"I'm pounding on the door and I don't hear anything at first. I know he's in there, but I don't hear anything, and I try the doorknob and peek my head in, and he says, 'Vanessa, I'm still sleeping; I'll be out in a little bit.' So I wait outside in the living room, and an hour passes, or at least it seems like an hour. He still hasn't come out to the living room. That's when I get this irrational fear, you know, that Dad is dead or something. I don't know why I get this thought, but I do. Even though he's in there, even though I hear his voice, I get this idea that maybe Dad is dead, you know what I mean? I was thinking about death before any kid should be thinking about death, and I'd start eating stuff. So I started eating some of that cereal, uh. You remember that cereal? There was Quake and there was Quisp. You had to vote for one or the other. I was eating Quisp. Maybe a whole morning passed that way, with me just eating Quisp and thinking about television or something, but I decided, and this was a mistake, you know, I decided that the thing to do was to put on the clip-on bow tie, myself. Just wear it in there, I said to myself, where my dad will see it on me, and he will be impressed with this bow tie. Kids throw good love after bad love. So I open up the tissue paper, I take out the bow tie. I was wearing some kind of blouse that my mother had made for me, a blouse that I hated because I liked to wear boys' clothes, and I put on the bow tie, which was gold or silver, something synthetic, and I knocked on the door again, and then I turned the knob, and I go in there, and, of course, well, you know what my parents were up to, right? I just remember the general posture."

The car pulls up at the franchise on Twenty-third Street. Vanessa leaves her raincoat in the car and, just before slamming the door, she asks the driver if he wants anything. Maple glazed? He doesn't respond. The meter is still running. She goes in.

Krispy Kreme is empty except for the two actresses in the back, talking on their cell phones. They're drinking in the Krispy Kreme ambience, but they aren't actually eating any of the product. They're calling their agents. Vanessa goes straight to the front of the store and demands hot doughnuts. But a young woman behind the counter, wearing a barrette that matches her uniform, tells Vanessa that the supply has been consumed.

"What do you mean you don't have any hot doughnuts? I just had some hot doughnuts down at your, at the, I just had some. You must have —"

"I'm afraid not." Her accent has a Caribbean lilt. Maybe her ancestors worked on the cane, in the fields. It doesn't change the situation. "I just have what you see here."

"Here's what I want. You still have some of those pumpkin spice ones? I'll have two of those, and then I'll take two of the glazed sour cream. And two cinnamon twists. I have to get these back for a birthday party for my assistant. Right away. I promised her hot doughnuts. She's going to be really disappointed."

The sales technician has heard it all before. She has heard the fabrications of the beat cops, back for their fourth bag, worn down by the scofflaws of the city. She has heard the lies of the balding guys from the car dealership over on Tenth Avenue. The doughnuts are for the service department! Vanessa knows well that the employees of Krispy Kreme have many stories to tell, stories of doughnut abusers. In an effort to avoid regret herself, she stops on the way out by the table of actresses on cell phones.

"You guys look so great," Vanessa says. "You're really beautiful. I'm getting doughnuts today for a casting call. This movie's going to be fabulous, a costume drama, you know, epic scope. You should definitely come read for us."

One of the blondes freezes at the table. Her face a jumble of skepticism and that intoxicant, hope. Who is this film world angel who has graced them at the Krispy Kreme?

"Really," Vanessa says. "The movie is called, uh, it's called *The*

Tempest of Sahara, right, and you should call Stan Gneiss, the casting director. Do you know him? Tell him Naomi sent you. Naomi Power."

She puts a hip into the door of Krispy Kreme and hits the street, with a pumpkin spice doughnut in her mouth, the old-fashioned cake-style doughnut. Now another interval of nothingness. It's seconds before a thought occurs to her again. And that thought is: shortage. Which is when the Sikh guy in the turban, who has double-parked his car directly behind the taxi, calls out, "Ms. Meandro, please, just a moment of your time!"

She bolts for her taxi, almost drops the bag of doughnuts on the way. She tells the Hispanic driver that they absolutely have to stay ahead of the Sikh guy, they have to lose him. She tells the driver to take some impossible route, with lots of doubling back, to Pennsylvania Station. Lose him by Macy's at that big Broadway merge.

"My parents were making love, and I was interrupting them in my silver bow tie. You get the picture. My mother had figured out a way to put herself between me and my father. You know? That's what the therapist is always saying. I don't experience any kind of intimacy because it has to be in a triangular shape. I'm always thinking about triangular constructs. Anyway, my mother rolls off my dad and tells me to get the hell out, go make myself breakfast. So I do. I go out, I make myself *another* breakfast, I take it out on the patio, more Quisp. On the patio I hear shouting. Not that shouting is anything new. But when I come back in, my dad is not there. That's not new, either, except that this was the last time I saw him. A moment like this, most of it is submerged, you know. Only a tiny little bit of it protrudes above the surface. Just the tip, really."

Glazed sour cream is preposterously good. But by the time she gets to the second one, she's already had enough doughnuts for the day. And yet how long does a feeling like that last? It doesn't last very long. She wants another, though the thought nauseates her. If the taxi driver could just swerve right, here in the flower district, drive through a storefront, glass and exotic tropical plants scattered everywhere. Then she'd stop eating doughnuts.

"I don't even remember that much about it. I know he was there and then he wasn't there, and my mother has her version. In her version, I drove him off. But I didn't drive anyone off, because I was, what? I was seven."

She leans close to the perforated spot in the bulletproof divider.

"What do you think? My mother claims it was the bow tie. That's her opinion. I get him a bow tie for his birthday, and my mother says it's that I wasn't ladylike. Why couldn't I wear clothes like a girl? Why didn't I want to wear designer jeans in the late seventies? She has a lot of opinions on this stuff. Never wear black tights. Always wear nylons. Use curlers. Always have on a dark shade of fingernail polish. I remember her coming to a field hockey game once. I was playing in the park, and she's sitting on the sidelines, knitting some really fem sweater and starting all these conversations so she can tell people that she's knitting the sweater for me. I could hear everything she was saying."

As soon as the taxi halts at the back entrance to Penn Station, Vanessa is out. And it's the same at Seventy-second Street on the West Side and the Upper East Side location, the glazed devil's food doughnut; the lemon-filled doughnut; the raspberry jelly–filled, with its excess of confectioner's sugar, the powder somehow like the wigs of French aristocrats just before the Revolution; custard-filled doughnuts, dessert of libertines, fifteen grams of fat per. She wants to see a line of morbidly obese people at the register, noshing, in the line at Krispy Kreme, ordering four or five doughnuts apiece. She knows the location of all the distributors, and she labors back and forth across Central Park, with the tab on the taxi closing in on fifty dollars. And then, at last, she heads for 125th Street. When she was at film school at Columbia, she used to go to the Twin Donut on Broadway, right under the elevated subway, but Twin Donut seems a lifetime away. Her romance is with Krispy Kreme now. It's not only the remoteness of 125th Street, as a locale for a doughnut adventure, it's not only that she's going to be the only white face in the Krispy Kreme of 125th Street, it's that she has the most decadent doughnut possible on her mind. It will be her fourteenth doughnut of the morning, and the contemplation of this sweetmeat is such that she hasn't even explained it to her taxi driver. Yes, the most perfect representation of her isolation and restlessness is the *triple-chocolate variety*, with Bavarian chocolate custard, chocolate icing, and chocolate chips. You really have to put off the triple-chocolate doughnut until last, because if you start with it, it's possible that you could go into a coma before you get to 125th, and then you will not have visited every single freestanding Krispy Kreme in the city of New York, then you will not have skipped out on a morning's work, then you will not have driven yourself even further from the possibility of human affection. The light is elegiac. You'd need a blue filter to correct for its sentimentality. Empty polyethylene bags with the names of local pharmacies emblazoned on them lift off in the open intersection. Inside, Vanessa takes her place in line.

The clerk, who's making do with hourly wages, picks at an incredibly long fingernail for a moment before moving to fill Vanessa's order. She stares vacantly at a ring on the countertop left by somebody's extra-large coffee. The patrons of Krispy Kreme are still for a moment, in the compulsion of ordering and devouring. Just then, someone taps Vanessa on the shoulder.

The Indian guy.

4

Annabel Duffy calls her boss *Minivan* because her boss is that large. The size of a minivan. In the interiors of her consciousness, Annabel begins or ends all business-related exchanges thus: "Minivan, can I get you some coffee?" She thinks, "Gosh, that designer suit looks fetching on you, Minivan." She thinks, *Minivan, Minivan, Minivan.* Because it's the one effective rejoinder to the oppressions that Vanessa Meandro visits upon her. Like the day Annabel came to interview at 610 Fifth Avenue. Minivan had apparently decided to break down Annabel until she was a quivering protoplasmic blob. Minivan indicated, in this preliminary interview, that she'd interviewed nothing but "anal-compulsive gay men" for three days, and Minivan made it clear that she could not work with these men because they were "prima donnas." What Minivan needed — and as she made her need clear, she rose up, swelling and posturing — was someone who would submit, someone who could sleep on a bed of nails, someone who could take an hour on the rack and demand more, someone who would be an untouchable, in the Hindu sense, without complaint, who would even be grateful for it. Did Annabel think she was this person? Bullshit. Annabel had no idea what submission meant! Annabel did not yet know what was required because she had not yet been forged in the underworld furnace of Minivan. It was clear to Annabel that Minivan was appraising Annabel's presentability as she made this observation, that she was checking out Annabel's skin tone, which was a much darker skin tone than that of any other employee in the office. But there was something carnivorous about the gaze, too; she was checking out Annabel's breasts and ass, and because of this, Annabel made her first subversive assumption about Minivan: *big dyke.*

Still, no informed hypothesis about Minivan's personal life has ever been borne out by cold, hard facts. Minivan has never appeared to have a personal life. No men, no women. And Annabel, as the ass't, has dealt with every aspect of Minivan's character. Annabel makes Minivan's appointments at that spa in Arizona that specializes in overeaters. Annabel fires Minivan's therapists every few months and gets new referrals. Annabel has learned about Klonopin, Ambien, Paxil, Wellbutrin, and Halcion; she has learned about cocktails of mood stabilizers, antidepressants, and antianxiety medications; she has substituted lithium for Depakote, Serzone for Lamictal or Lexapro or Zoloft, which she substituted for Prozac, has held out antianxiety medication in her palm because Minivan, with remarkable insight into her own character, has noted that she isn't to be trusted to keep the prescription in her own desk. Since Annabel has been doing all of these things for Minivan, Annabel believes she would have known about a girlfriend if a girlfriend in fact existed.

Annabel knows, furthermore, that Minivan technically still lives at home, though this is a fact shrouded in secrecy, especially this day, because Annabel has been on the phone with the detox ward of the hospital in Brooklyn where Minivan's mother was incarcerated as of one or two hours ago. Normally, her mother would have called by this time in the AM, in order to launch into some strange, ominous subject, like yesterday's car crash involving a guy driving up onto a sidewalk in midtown and taking out two or three pedestrians. After which Minivan's mother, referred to around the office by the name of Rosa, even by Minivan herself, is likely to go on to a torrid sociopolitical subtopic that will include Rosa herself, the mayor of New York City, the Federal Bureau of Investigation, pollution in the Gowanus Canal, gentrification in Red Hook, the new crosswalk at Radio City Music Hall, campaign finance reform, and shadowy state and federal agencies as yet unknown to the general public. As Annabel listens to these monologues, inevitably there is an urgent cry from the corner office: "Are you doing your nails or something? Do I pay you to do your nails?"

The name of the company shall be Means of Production, referring here to a meanness of character, a paucity of compassion. Minivan will not commit to this interpretation because she will not commit to any interpretation. Minivan is about pragmatism, realpolitik. Every complaint about Annabel Duffy's on-the-job performance also contains discussion of Annabel's weight, as Annabel is willowy, svelte, twiggy. "You know you're not supposed to be able to see all the bones in your elbow. If you can see them, there is a problem. Think about it." Or: "Is this a political thing with you? Not eating? You're expressing solidarity with subsistence farmers of developing nations?" Or: "You're making me look bad, Duffy. I didn't hire you to look like a model. You're here in a miniskirt in order to make me look like a whale. Am I right? Wear a garbage bag or something. Wear a warm-up suit. Go down to Old Navy and buy a fucking warm-up suit that's four sizes too big and wrap yourself in Ace bandages or something. This is not an environment that I can work in. Go eat a sundae. Get two sundaes, in fact. Bring one back for me."

Whereupon Minivan will insist that Annabel really do it, really get the sundae as described. Likewise, Annabel has taken entire gross boxes of chocolate bars out of Minivan's office, per her direction, replacing them with a more dainty jelly bean display. She's ordered pizzas at ten o'clock at night, multiple pizzas. Back-to-back lunches for Minivan. Followed by drinks, followed by dinner, followed by a separate dessert engagement with some other agent. Annabel has ordered four sides of bacon for Minivan from a room service menu, in the Gallic tongue, because Minivan, lounging at poolside in the south of France, claims her French isn't up to the task.

Traditional Hollywood fare. Like all those mailroom stories, some of which Minivan is fond of telling herself. The producer, for example, who used to walk around in the parking lot first thing in the morning, checking the hoods of the cars of his employees to see how warm they were. The guy with the warmest hood was insufficiently ambitious. Gluttony, selfishness, megalomania, chocolate addiction, pathological lying, promiscuity, obsessive-compulsive disorder. The world of cinema. And yet there are two reasons why Annabel continues to work for Vanessa Meandro. The first reason is a steadfast if misguided belief in the possibility of tenderness. As Annabel conceives of it, the moment of tenderness is not a theory, but a genuine probability, like democracy in China or a Middle East peace accord. The moment of tenderness is a possibility in all interactions. It is the neutrino of human events. The moment of tenderness becomes ever more predictable, statistically, the worse things get. Bad luck is the catalytic agent for tenderness. The moment of tenderness cannot be resisted forever. Minivan, one day, will have to express kindness, if only by accident. There is no other way to think about the world. The longer Annabel works, the more likely is the moment of tenderness, the more Annabel wants to be present when the inconceivable happens, when the world of light opens in Minivan like a flower. Greatness in the film world happens in inconceivable moments. When the predictable torrents of horror films for teenagers have overspilled the drains and sewers and engulfed the corners of all the sidewalks, then the rain will stop, and the sun will rise, and only Annabel will continue to believe in it, a moment of tenderness.

The existence of the moment of tenderness, however, is in dispute according to all others employed at Means of Production. These hard-core empiricists number exactly four. Another personal assistant, Jeanine, who is responsible for travel arrangements and most of the call logs for Minivan. A development girl, Madison, who once had Annabel's job and whose hazel eyes are bottomless. A celebrated action film star, Thaddeus Griffin, who is sharing the cost of the office suite with Minivan while he tries to parlay his action film credits into independent film respectability. And the bookkeeper, a middle-aged woman called Lois DiNunzio, who has successfully eradicated all signs of human emotion. These four employees (and the occasional heroin-addicted intern from Tisch School of the Arts) coexist badly within the domain of Minivan and yet they agree on one thing: the complete implausibility of any moment of tenderness. They give Annabel endless amounts of shit for believing in this moment of tenderness. They have each recounted, in whispers, the Christmas-evening harangue from Minivan, when they were called selfish, witless, moronic, and weak. Or, moving from adjectives to nouns, they were called such epithets as coke slut, mannequin, industry whore. For these reasons and others, Annabel's fellow employees have asserted that the moment of tenderness does not and cannot and will never exist.

Maybe if it were *only* the moment of tenderness, Annabel would not have stuck it out for five years, having taken the position fresh from the college in western Massachusetts with the experimental curriculum. The other reason to stay is her screenplay. During the workday, Annabel acts out the ingenue roles of Juliette or Justine, while at night she has begun working on a screenplay about the wife of the Marquis de Sade, called *Fire Eater*. Despite the lack of easy financing inherent in the kinds of projects Minivan favors, she has continued to make great movies.

And Annabel knows, eventually, that even if she must be subjected to the very kind of torture that the Marquis visited upon his wife, which includes, in Annabel's screenplay, experimenting with erotic asphyxiation, penetrating his wife with devices, encouraging others to do so, fucking teenage boys in front of his wife, demanding that teenage boys fuck *him* in front of his wife, sexually abusing the children of his parish, and forcing his wife to sodomize him, Annabel knows eventually that Minivan will see the light about *Fire Eater,* and Annabel's project will fit right into a Means of Production release schedule that in the past has included an entire film made about Charles Manson's final remarks before sentencing; a film about the last years of the life of Mark Rothko; a film about the arrest of the Weather Underground; a George Jones biopic; and the celebrated Means of Production love story, *Offenders,* about the schoolteacher, Mary Kay Letourneau, who romanced her middle school student. *Offenders* had that incredibly moving passage where the teacher and her thirteen-year-old lover go skydiving together, just before neighbors inform on them. Here's the moment that critics, at least at the alternative weeklies, liked so much, that moment in the trailers when Mary Kay's thirteen-year-old lover gets ready to leap out of the plane at the behest of their instructor. He has no fear, and the blue sky outside the plane looks almost colorized, a tissue paper cloud here and there. He's attached to the cable that ensures that the parachute opens properly, and he looks back at Mary Kay, a goofy grin on his face because he's afraid of nothing. He thinks that the whole world is a professional-wrestling episode. Mary Kay, however, knows what this dive means. Suddenly she's reaching out to him, but he's gone, their hands failing to meet, causing her to jump, too, and the plane banks left, and their chutes open, and the sere flatlands of the Northwest are below them, and a married woman has just thrown away her life for a profane love. Never has the wailing of the wind sounded so desolate. The absence of music makes the film more persuasive. Lili Taylor's finest moment, really.

Annabel knows that a certain rarefied segment of the filmgoing public has exited at the conclusion of every film produced by Minivan determined to overthrow a despot or to work for the legal-aid society or maybe just to make a film. Everyone at her school in western Massachusetts, the one with the free-form curriculum, felt this way. Half of them have trooped through the Means of Production office, it seems, trying to get Minivan to back their documentary on the making of Miles Davis's *Bitches Brew*. No? How about a film about the new East Village orgy scene?

The combination of the possibility of tenderness and a series of movies, not one of which cost more then ten million dollars to make, films that saved the lives of fifty thousand college students in the Northeast, this is enough for Annabel. She willingly shows up for work today, to be told by her boss that she looks like an Eritrean refugee. And here is her boss now, moving past Annabel's desk, and then Jeanine's, followed, inscrutably, by a Sikh guy in a turban. She drops a bag of Krispy Kreme doughnuts on Annabel's desk.

"Want me to save these?" asks Annabel, holding the abject bag in her hands.

"Send in DiNunzio. Clean out the empty office. Squeegee the windows."

To herself, Annabel pronounces the word *squeegee* as though it is a completely new word. The inexplicable Sikh guy, meanwhile, is smiling the most generous smile she's ever seen, as though his smile could repair entrenched diplomatic problems. He's standing in the hall by the sequence of portraits of great contemporary feminists by photographer Miranda Grossinger that Minivan has been collecting. Miranda wants to make a movie, too, and she has therefore been more than happy to improve the decor at Means of Production. The Sikh is leaning dangerously close to the photograph of Avital Ronell. He's in danger of knocking the photograph off the wall because he's so full of surprise and delight.

"Duffy, did you read the treatment? Do you have the coverage?"

Which treatment? Which coverage? Minivan's head appears, disembodied, leaning out through the door frame. Annabel nods blankly. She knows better than to deny having read anything. On her day off, Election Day, which was not really a day off, she chased down a new wristwatch for Minivan and fired another intern, she worked on her script at the office, and only then did she go to stand in the line to vote on Seventh Street, where the elderly Hispanic ladies manning the booths were showering the voters with abuse. When she finished voting, it was after nine. Which was when Thaddeus came over. His wife, the commercial actress, had gone to San Diego to work on something, so Thaddeus was waiting on Annabel's stoop when she got home. He complained the whole way up the four flights, as usual, "Haven't you ever heard of elevators? Everywhere else they have elevators. They comply with the Americans with Disabilities Act. I have a tobacco-related disability. I'd prefer to have a ground-floor romantic liaison, if you please."

Thaddeus Griffin. She's seen him holding a gun so many times that it seems as if he should always be carrying one, an ArmaLite or a Kalashnikov. Thaddeus Griffin, in *Single Bullet Theory;* Thaddeus Griffin, starring with a token African American pal, in *Single Bullet Theory II.* Thaddeus Griffin, starring in *Full Magazine,* about a heartbroken editor for a mercenary periodical who gets involved in a conspiracy to shoot the president, here starring alongside another token African American pal. Thaddeus, in fact, has never made a good film, despite having been brought up in New York City and despite having attended Union College in Schenectady, where he nearly graduated with a degree in marine biology. Thaddeus Griffin, the guy who comes to her house and weeps about his marriage and then with almost bloodless suddenness simulates a forced jocularity that would pass for charm on the networks. Everything is a joke! He can imitate any-one! He imitates his agent! He imitates studio heads and televi-sion personalities! He does his ongoing impression of Minivan! He'll get an entire sushi roll in each side of his mouth, like when they were at that place on Ninth Street, and he'll start talking about Michel Foucault and how knowledge *is* power, with sushi rolls in his mouth. Despite renting an office with Minivan for a year and a half, he has yet to be cast in anything, even though he has given Minivan free script advice and taken her out to Bal-thazar for dinner with one of the principals of DreamWorks, even pitched a script about the death of Trotsky to the studios for her. The favor bank has worked in one direction only.

Thaddeus's campaign to know Annabel more perfectly is co-incident with his fading prospects around the office of Means of Production. The campaign went like this. First, of course, he proposed to read the draft of *Fire Eater,* which he claimed to like. Then he invited Annabel out for drinks to discuss the script, at the history-laden Cedar Tavern. Three times people stopped him to say, "Hey, you're the guy who killed that terrorist with a cross-bow," which was, of course, the climax of the original *Single Bul-let Theory.* It was during this sequence that Thaddeus, with great concentration, uttered the words, "Jesus wept, motherfucker," displaying a conviction rarely seen in modern cinema. You had to see it in context, really. And this was how he signed a cocktail napkin, for a fan, in the middle of the ring left by his neat scotch: *Single Malt Theory, Thad Griffin 2000.*

"The script is really good," Thad offered, when they were alone. "Really out there. I like it. I admire what you know." Say-ing it in such a way that it was clear the opposite was the case. This seemed like the problem of celebrity, that the celeb could not uncouple him- or herself from the burdens and privileges of fame. The safe, uncontroversial remark that the celebrity was trained to deliver became his only refuge. With Thaddeus, she could not walk the street unperturbed. He would say, "We have to keep moving." Maybe Thaddeus selected his profession for this reason, so that he would always have an excuse to move. At the same time, maybe he was not as famous as he thought; maybe nobody gave a shit about his films, which were generally acknowledged as all but worthless. Annabel believed that action films were inherently conservative anyhow, that they existed solely to offer support to libertarian positions on the Second Amendment. When you thought about it that way, you found pity for Thaddeus and his occasional attempts to be one of the people. You could see that Thaddeus had long since lost something, some set of skills that other people had: the ability to sit in a room without attempting to command its attention, the ability to look up at the smoggy night sky and know that it existed without any input from him at all and without the cooperation of tabloids.

"The thing about reading the Marquis," he said, "the thing is that the Marquis really changes the way you think. I mean, you could just be going about your business and then you open up, uh, what's that one called? You open up *Philosophy in the Bedroom,* and you hear what's his name, the philosopher character, you hear him say, 'Thrice Fuck of God, I discharge' or whatever, and you know you are really being taken to a place where you don't ordinarily go, a place in your body, a place in your emotional life. All the women with the strap-ons, the innocent girls. You're in a lower part of nature, you know? You're in one of those videotapes that record lions out on the Serengeti taking down the gazelles and ripping into them. You're there, and now you know about bloodlust and power and the inner lives of men."

Low lighting and bar noise. He was trying hard.

"So tell me why you want to work with this material, anyhow? I mean, why not write a screenplay about a blond girl who wants to give etiquette lessons to disadvantaged classmates and who in the process becomes president of the United States?"

The waitress, who had passed through a sullen period, was

now happy and attentive. She had just realized she was serving a *movie star.* She hovered near the table.

"The Marquise's life was like the lives of black women."

"How do you figure? Ten words or less."

"Her life was about intellectual and sexual slavery."

"Why not write about slavery, then?"

"I might."

Thaddeus polished off the last of a second scotch, attacked a third. A cop show, sound off, performed its rote dance on the monitor above the bar. He stared at it, absently, while formulating his comeback.

"Thing is, while I was reading the script, I did have that sensation that I could start eating steak tartare out of a dog bowl and it would be liberating somehow. I had to think. I mean, I couldn't help myself from thinking one thing the entire time. I was thinking, This woman is really articulate, this woman has had a great education, this woman knows things other people just do not know. But I was also thinking this other thing —"

"Let me guess," she said.

Thaddeus manufactured a facsimile of surprise. "Okay, go ahead. Guess."

"You were thinking you'd never fucked a black girl before."

"I can't believe you talk like that, Annabel," he said with mock horror. "It's making me perspire. Wait. Let me collect my thoughts. Actually, believe it or not, I *have* had relations with a black woman before, because I wasn't born yesterday. And I did have that black secretary character working with me in *Oath of Citizens.* On the novelty scale, the skin color thing just isn't that high up. The novelty scale, in fact, is not that big a deal. Although it is true that I've never fucked a black girl *in the ass* before."

Which indicated that it was now time for Annabel to leave. With a pig there was always a time to leave. A decisive moment. Many had walked out of the Cedar Tavern. Over the century of

its existence as a local tavern, many had walked out on provoca-
teurs, drunkards, decadents, on hidden drug problems, on voluminous anxieties, on unquenchable insecurities, unnamed wives.
What did these men offer? They offered to take you to your room
and then they offered to leave you in a bad, abrupt way. They
were there, they were not there, hard to tell which was which,
and then they came crawling back.

"Wait, I'm *trying* to talk about the script, I swear."

"You're twelve years older than I am. I've met your wife. She
gave us those . . . those maple thingies at Christmas last year."

"Annabel! Sit!"

So he settled down. He told her that the Marquise needed to
show her devotion and her desire to leave by page sixteen, that
the church needed to be hunting down de Sade, with intent to
kill, by the beginning of act two, that the Marquise needed to be
helplessly in love with a priest, that Annabel needed to see that
film with Glenda Jackson about Marat, and that Annabel needed
to get rid of the voice-over sections because development people
don't understand large blocks of voice-over. He had two more
drinks while he was doing this, and next thing she knew they
were in Tompkins Square Park, and Thaddeus Griffin, action film
hero, dyed-blond hair swept back perfectly as though it had been
spray-painted on, was sitting on a bench sobbing, saying his work
was worthless and he was a joke, he was a fucking joke. He said
it was the worst thing imaginable, being a joke, and then he was
saying, "Take me home with you. Just take me home with you;
I'm too drunk to do anything, and anyway, that's the stupidest
thing in the world to do about loneliness, a drunken fuck. Just
take me home with you, let me see your hair-care products, let
me know if your bathrobe is tartan, or white, or one of those
Japanese kimonos. I can't think about our stories going off in
separate directions, like if I go back to my house, it's just going to
be a split-screen thing, and I can't take that."

She asked about his wife. His wife was in San Diego shooting a commercial, as she always was. She was always shooting a commercial. She had some kind of repeating character. Her residuals were excellent. The product had to do with feminine itch or bloating or medicated pads. "Did I say that my wife has an artificial eye, Annabel? My wife has an artificial eye. When you look into her eyes, you can see that the left one is artificial, because the light is reflected from it in some weird way. Did I say that my wife only buys clothes online or clothes given to her by designers, because she has a phobia about being seen shopping? Did I say that my wife and I had a photographer take a series of pictures of us strolling that we periodically release to the tabloids, just to make sure we control our public image? Take me home with you, Duffy. Recite to me the cantos of your life."

She did. And he passed out immediately.

After that, even though she was dating a couple other guys, an assistant at the Michael Cohen Agency and a dean from the experimental college in western Mass., Thaddeus would turn up without notice, because things had to be flexible, and he would call from his car, coming down the West Side, and he would ask if now was a good time, never asking if someone was there but asking nonetheless, because he never expected that they were involved in anything but some amusing film-world dalliance. As it wore on, and *wore* was a good word for what it did, it became all about Thaddeus's cock, which, despite her education and intellectual training, she somehow came to love. Why could women be smart, decisive, and brilliant and then somehow irresolute at the sight of a cock? It was one of the depressing secrets of adult life. She loved his cock because she was the Marquise, because she became the Marquise, because that was how it had to go, because by being the Marquise she overcame her, knew her, could write about her, because the Marquise had the skin of an Algerian, the Marquise was a Moor, and she was the Marquise, and she put the cock of film star Thaddeus Griffin in her mouth, and she put the cock of film star Thaddeus Griffin in her vagina, and she let the cock of Thaddeus Griffin erupt onto her dark skin because he was film star Thaddeus Griffin and he wanted to do it that way. And he bought her a nose ring, and he paid for the tattoo on her lower back, just above her behind, and he had the best guy in the East Village do it, and he attended this assignation, and he begged her to pierce her nipples, and when he said, "I want more," she felt stronger, and so in turn she gave more. She was the assistant who gave more, because she was the black assistant, and she felt stronger when she shouldered burdens ever more impossible. They wanted her to give more just to stay in the game, and she laid up dreams in the attic of her consciousness, hoping, like a remedial hoper, for the moment of tenderness. But she never did that one thing he wanted, she never let him be the guy who fucked a black girl in the ass, because he had to be desperate for something.

One day, Rosa, the mother of Minivan, called the office line, and in the middle of it, she started babbling incoherently about her grandfather or great-grandfather who possessed the fraudulently magic skill of *dowsing*. This was mixed in with her obsession with a certain talk show host. She couldn't stop talking about this talk show host. Somehow, in the recounting, Annabel and Thaddeus appropriated the word, and it became the code for all things romantic: *dowsing*. Thaddeus let it trip off his tongue, "Is there dowsing in the forecast?" This is how it happens, see. This is how the whole lie gets started and begins to get up its head of steam. Annabel Duffy, the black intellectual, is locked in an affair she doesn't really want to be having with a white action film star, who is riffling papers on her desk while an Indian guy in a turban is staring at her, smiling, and her boss is yelling at her from the next room about the call sheets and she's asking about the treatment.

"I asked if you read the —"

Thaddeus Griffin has slyly stolen up on the action. He too notices that there is a Sikh in the office, and imagines, probably, that the Sikh is delivering something.

The Sikh says, "Mr. Griffin. You are a great and underutilized actor. My honor to meet you."

"Why, thank you," says Thaddeus. "You're a new employee?"

"Yes, sir, I am the new employee in matters of television."

And the Minivan shouts out again. "There's buzz. There's a volume of background noise about this treatment. I have heard things. And I want to know what it's about and I want to know if it's any good. Jeanine, where are the call sheets? And Annabel, I want to move the office out of this neighborhood. I don't want to be in this neighborhood anymore. I don't want to see another fucking Christmas tree out the window. I don't want to have to listen to that music that the skaters skate to. I want to move downtown. And I want to know what that treatment is about."

Which treatment? Annabel shuffles the papers around. She can't find anything, can't find coverage, can't find any treatment. She looks up at Thaddeus. Lying is about to become the only way to survive, yet again. The Sikh smiles. Not even knowing what treatment it is now, what script, what book, what play, what was it that she was supposed to have seen last night, which younger playwright? How can she get the jump on Madison, to whose domain all of this material also belongs? Madison, who is hovering at the edge of the action, peeking out of her cubicle. The Sikh is smiling and Thaddeus is doing his agitated dance, his restless legs syndrome, and Madison is scowling, and Lois DiNunzio is calling to the Sikh that he should come over to her desk to sign some tax forms —

"I think I might have sent it back, the, uh, I think the script you're asking about might have been sent back."

"Are you kidding me?"

A torrent of abuse ensues. Minivan, like, well, a minivan plowing up onto a sidewalk and taking out a few pedestrians, begins a tirade. It's so predictable that it's as if she's reading it off a cue card. Your stupidity *cannot* mean the end of my business, et cetera. Like it's a monologue. There's a moment of suspense at the end, though, because sometimes someone gets fired over these kinds of things. So will Annabel get fired? And does the treatment in question even exist? Or is this another test of stamina for the black assistant?

Until Thaddeus, smirking, says, "Vanessa, give it a rest. Don't be a jerk. It's on *my* desk. I read it. It's hilarious. It's the one about *dowsing*."

5

Michael David Griffin, also known as Thaddeus, during his first Ashtanga series. At the Ashram of the False Guru. In this the seventh round of sun salutations, resistance in Michael David Griffin begins to fade blissfully away. He is perched in a corner of the ceiling, in some evolved yogi incarnation of himself, and he can see himself below. Thaddeus Griffin, in a silence of exertion, Thaddeus Griffin and the tidal movement of the breath.

He's a beginner, understand, but the time has come for the Ashtanga series. The False Guru took aside Thaddeus Griffin on the way in to tell him of the excellent programs they have under way, like installing this indoor fountain and making available some synthetic yoga wear for the women who will want to sign up with Ford and Elite. Also there are harmoniums they have purchased for instructors. Wouldn't Thaddeus like to be involved with the ashram in a more complete way? Wouldn't Thaddeus like to be a part of the brochure of the False Guru, which elucidates the one true path to serenity and worldly abundance? His response was something bland and noncommittal regarding new program initiatives. He said, "Keep reminding me," which he says when he is doing his best to forget everything just said.

Thaddeus is unshaven, and his hair is standing on end, and he is in forearm stand, and his wife is in San Diego, most likely fucking that commercial director. Thaddeus works three months a year and then does a lot of interviews on prime-time newsmagazines. His movies give teenagers something to do.

The models around him, here at the ashram, move from their elaborate series of advanced bridge poses up onto their feet, then back over their heads into a handstand, as though they are made of pipe cleaners. He would like to fuck these models. He would like to fuck each and every one. He would like them, in bridge pose, to serve as coffee tables in his apartment. He is the minister of false consciousness. Why is it that he is always thinking about these things? Why is it that he experiences spiritual advancement only when next to the perfect ass? He is in bridge pose and he is arching toward the ceiling, and then he is down, and then he is up, and then he is down and then he is up. Just three more, the instructor says. Something in Thaddeus Griffin is shattering. Not literally, like when his friend Jorie popped her hip out of its socket during the Ashtanga series here at the Ashram of the False Guru. Sounded like a champagne cork ejecting. (She was taken out screaming.) No, it's as if Griffin finds himself in the spin cycle of human souls. His mediocre career as a movie actor is colliding with the reality of the wife who is fucking a commercial director and this is colliding with the fact that he isn't working and this is colliding with the fact that he isn't producing films, either, which was his plan for escaping from the hustle of being a chump actor, which is colliding with the fact that even his young mistress will no longer put up with him. The twenty-eight-year-old mulatto genius won't sleep with him, and now plank pose, and he can feel the extrusion of toxins from muscle tissue, dioxins, PCBs, the poisonous things in him, which are many. The instructor is quoting from the Sanskrit. The rich and the privileged come to perform the Ashtanga series so that they can learn justice, the instructor seems to be saying; this is

where rich New York, which is primarily white New York, comes
to learn compassion for that part which is brown, black, red, and
yellow. This grotto, this ashram where the False Guru puts in his
indoor fountain and names it serenity. Is the instructor saying
this? Or is Thaddeus Griffin shearing apart? And is this shearing
apart not a two- or three-times-a-week occurrence? Now the instructor is leading them in the chant of the guilty white liberal.
The long low drones of the harmonium, with its bellows like the
gritted exhalations of a chump movie actor. Michael David Griffin is beginning to sob again. It is good for actors to sob; it indicates serious craft. *We would all do better / We would all do better / But
we are on deadline / We are on deadline / We would all do better / We
would all do better / We will do something for the poor and unfortunate
when we get back / But we have compassion, we really do.* The harmonium, and the Sanskrit, and another round of the full wheel,
and the head of a model goes between her legs and her ankles
drape over her shoulders.

His failures are so numerous, pouring from him during the
Ashtanga series. Like when he seduced that development girl,
Madison McDowell. He seduced her and then took her for a
weekend to the track in Saratoga Springs, and he bet twenty
thousand dollars on a filly and boy was that money gone fast.
They had breakfast at the track, and he put Tabasco on the eggs,
he ate the sprig of parsley, and he told Madison that her eyes
were the bluest eyes he had ever seen, and then he bet twenty
thousand dollars on a filly and lost. But her eyes were really
closer to hazel. Then Madison took a call from that harpy Vanessa
Meandro, and Madison cooked up an excuse to take the train
back down the Hudson to the city. He'd rented the house on
Union Avenue for a whole week. Then there was Jeanine Stampfel,
Vanessa's personal assistant. Few office assistants have been as
miserable as Jeanine. Jeanine the self-immolator. Somewhere in
the recesses of her apartment, which was actually her parents'
apartment when they were in town from Scottsdale, she was tak-

ing a common household lighter and she was applying it to her ivory skin. Here was Jeanine, in a pinafore, in her white bobby socks. Jeanine was on a fainting couch beside a leather globe that still listed Ceylon; she was taking an antique Zippo lighter out of a desk drawer and setting fire to herself. Her sharp intake of breath was like a chump-movie-actor attempt to do a standing split. Her forearm liquefied. He saw the scars.

"Excuse me," a voice whispers next to him. A young woman in black leotard and leg warmers. Always the ones in leg warmers. "Excuse me." He looks up to see where the spotter is. Across the room, by the bank of windows facing the theater across the street. The spotter is attending to someone's hunched shoulders.

"Excuse me."

Michael David Griffin says, "I'm trying to do my Ashtanga series, here. Can we talk later?"

She holds out a handkerchief. Folded perfectly, as if a secret message were contained within. Her ass is a temple. Greek city-states were founded on less. Michael David Griffin says nothing and wipes his eyes, and now his bodily fluids are on her handkerchief. She could have biological materials cloned from the weave of her handkerchief. Nervously, he hands back the handkerchief, smiles, tells her his name is Thaddeus.

"I know your name," she says.

"Then I'm at a disadvantage." In his inattentiveness he collapses onto his sticky mat. The smells coming off him are not covered in the Kyoto protocols.

"Nora." She goes into a perfect split. "Don't you want my number?"

Later, when he comes out of the changing room, hobbling, Nora is there. She extends her hand. Says she admires his work, which cannot be true. Does she like *Single Bullet Theory*? With its triple-digit body count? She's wearing one of those Greek fisherman's caps. She has elegant cheekbones. The babbling of the indoor fountain says: *Your superficial goals are good, and you may pursue them at your leisure.* Here comes the human moment. It's always here. It's the Ashtanga series that brings it out in him. Don't think of her as an expanse of skin that could rub against your skin, don't think of her as a bonbon. Think of her as a complexity to be respected, a person tortured during field hockey practice, the only Jewish kid at Christian summer camp, the girl who vomited in college every morning.

With all this in mind, Griffin allows himself to be pulled away by the mulatto genius. He pulls away from the gravitational field of Nora. The mulatto genius is waiting. He is late. When he pulls open the door of the bar across the street, he feels an uncoiling of gratitude, yards and yards of gratitude in him. He has extruded poisons; he has had a reasonable human interaction. In the bar, on a stool, the mulatto genius balances, one lanky leg stretched all the way to the floor, stabilizing. She's like a switchblade. There are many unknown things about the mulatto genius, and he has to stop calling her that. She is dressed in black leather pants and a black V-neck sweater from Agnès B., neither smiling nor frowning. If it were in a script, it would say *They kiss quickly,* and he would have a hundred questions: What does her mouth taste like, and does she close her eyes, is she wearing perfume, and is it a car-crash kiss or is it like the soft rolling of tides over a salt marsh?

On the small stage on the far wall, a soundman, wearing baggy pants and a hooded sweatshirt, plugs a cable into an amplifier.

Griffin says to Annabel, "It came to me during the Ashtanga series. I went out to the men's room, I blew chow, went back in, fought off a couple rabid fans, wept over the condition of my life, apologized to the instructor, and then I got it."

"What did you get?"

"The idea."

"Which idea?"

"About the missing treatment."

The sweatshirt yells *Check* into the microphone. The barkeep pauses in front of them.

"Make the coverage up."

"Make it up?"

"Right here and now." He warms to the idea. "I already told her it was about dowsing, diviners. Make it up tonight, like you'd spin out a story of love. Make it up like storytellers around a campfire." Did she have a pen? Did she have paper? Did they have a napkin? Could a treatment be written on a napkin in one of the bars of the city? It happened every night. Could coverage be spray-painted on the city itself, New York City, as if *of* the city itself?

"You think Vanessa will ever know? She'll never know. She only gives a shit about this script because it's leverage. *You* lose a script, *you* fucked up. She loses a script, who gives a shit, find another copy."

Then he improvises his monologue, again, about how to write, which is really a monologue about the nature of self-improvement. It's the monologue that got him the space with Vanessa, the monologue that launched a thousand temporary production gigs. The monologue about being outside of the empire, outside the establishment, the monologue about how creativity comes at the expense of conventional thinking, at the expense of formula, at the expense of abstract values like tradition and love. The monologue about creativity as revolt, as bloody insurrection.

"The problem is that all film needs to be written automatically. It needs to be written by your *pussy.* Modern movies, this is what I'm saying, need to be written by cocks and pussies. The problem with these action films, for example, is not enough cock and pussy. People need to get words like *cock* and *pussy* out into the atmosphere, they need to say *cock* a lot, the way they say *sunrise,* the way they say *pang of regret,* they need to see that *pussy* is the most beautiful word in the world and that every script in the world needs to be written with a pussy and a cock in it, needs to be written *by* a pussy and a cock. No other reason to write. We think that it's about art or commerce, we think it's about the art people over here, wearing black and smoking, or the commerce people over here, with their tit jobs and their spray-on tans, but that's not what it's about, it's about pussies and cocks, and if your pussy was *not* wet, sweetheart, when you were writing about the wife of the Marquis de Sade, then you might as well just give up the job. You should be dripping when you write a story, and your stomach should be churning with the head-splitting climax at your end of the story, the one that *gets you off.* The one where all the differences in the world, like the difference between a pussy and a cock, are obliterated in the reprise of the come shot of creation, the big grand unified come shot that made the conditions that made you and me and art and commerce and religion. Fuck art and fuck commerce. Abandon the Marquis and his marquise. Come away with me, and I'll take you places you've never seen before, because that's where we're going to write this coverage, tonight, and I'll show you how to write a story, and then tomorrow, when the sun comes up, you can put it on Vanessa's desk, and when she loves it, which she will, you can say you wrote it yourself and you can know that you wrote it with your *pussy.* You can know that your pussy made this masterpiece."

The barkeep keeps the shot glasses full. Glasses from a rack tintinnabulate as the dishwasher brings them back.

"You've never written anything. What do you know about it?"

"I know enough to have the title."

"How can you have a title?"

"The Diviners."

She says, "I don't know. Maybe."

"What do you mean? It's fabulous. What could be better? It'll look great. It's got the accent on the second syllable. Just the idea got me hard in the changing room at the ashram. I was straining against my warm-up pants. That's all we need to know. Just try saying it!"

At which point the scene changes, because he has exercised his seduction skills, naturally, skills given to him by God, and the bar vanishes away. These are the gray tones of a limousine interior. There's no connective tissue to attach the one scene to another scene, there's just the mystery of the raconteur. The location scouts have already been working, advance men and women, and suddenly Thaddeus Griffin and Annabel Duffy are in Washington Mews, that stretch of housing for professors from the university nearby, each carriage house as small as a one-bedroom but as charming as a villa. They walk halfway across the block, toward Fifth Avenue, on the cobblestones, and he finds the door he's looking for. As they close in, his arm around her waist, he raises a single gloved hand to knock, and then pauses:

"You're wondering *why.* You're wondering why a guy who didn't finish his degree has you here, on a block of professors. Well, I'll tell you why. Because a guy I used to play chess with in high school, Charles Ng, is working toward tenure here. In the Asian Studies Department. He's an incredibly promising scholar, one who has been contacted occasionally by the State Department to be of service in espionage cases and so forth. And why we are here is because Charles is about to corroborate my story, the story I'm about to tell you, which begins, of course, with the Mongol hordes."

"The Mongol hordes."

Up the block, the wife of an absentminded professor closes her front door behind herself. A corgi leads her out. They head toward Washington Square Park.

"Driven off of the grassy plains for what reason? Driven out of their homeland of millennia for what reason? If it was so perfect there; if they could found a religion there, in a land of plenty, a culture of enlightenment that persists to the present day, why leave? Charles Ng will tell you. Drought. In those days there was a great drought in the East. The rivers dried up. Primitive efforts to irrigate had created salt deposits, rinds of salt, on the vast steppe. There was no snow in the mountains, and so the runoff of the snowcapped peaks that in spring and summer slaked the grasslands never came. The lakes were mud puddles, and Asian tigers lay in the tall grass waiting for any living thing. The way of life for the Mongolian nomads involved grave danger. These grasslands had sustained the yak, the lamb, the goat, the Asian antelope, and the brave clans who had dominion over them. These grasslands were home to great flocks of fowl and herds of game. And now these grasslands were burning in the massive fires of Mongol legend. There was no cheese, nor curds, nor yogurt, the provisions that had sustained those Mongol families around the campfire. There were no meats from domesticated animals that once had made the children strong. And the pelts that kept them warm during the bitter Mongolian winter? Charlie Ng has written a bunch of books about the decades of Mongol drought and he has written about the Mongolian rainmaker, Zoltan —"

"Are you joking? Zoltan?"

"We can work on the names later. You'll see. Anyway, on the one side, the drought of the Mongolian plains. On the other side, the Roman Empire. The cradle of civilization, expanding northward with taxes, tributes, foreign tongues. It was a tinderbox, this historical moment, and Zoltan, peace lover, a man of shamanistic gods, it was he who renounced the plans of his second cousin Attila. Attila, who slaughtered Zoltan's father in order to seize control of the nomadic clans, the very clans who now rally the Mongolian archers on their stallions, set the valleys of Mongolia aflame. It was a fire of such enormity that it made our southwestern wildfires look like a backyard barbecue. The riders, galloping down across the mountains and into the empire, were safe only because they were under Atilla's control. Those who refused? They would be consumed by the fire. Get it? A valley of flames, two thousand years ago, and Attila is raping Roman women, burning villages. All the world is in flames, but Zoltan appears with the wall of flames behind him, and he's walking through a valley in flames, in, in, I don't know, in Uzbekistan, and he plucks up this forked stick, for this forked stick will be his crutch — I forgot this part — because he has a withered leg, and he says to his sidekick, the Moorish slave named Kiko, 'This forked stick is the indication of the two paths down which we can journey, the path of good and the path of ill, and I, Zoltan, my family torn asunder by the Hun, resolve to use these two as one, the two — good and ill — make one, to forge our history, the result of which will be as water, from which all living things come. My name will be written in water, and down through all the ages there will be water for the descendants of Zoltan, until history rests from its labors, and my heirs will always know that the way of peace and magnanimity is the way of water.' And from there Zoltan marches, alone, with forked stick and sidekick, into the ruins of what is now Europe."

Thaddeus has long since plunged his gloved hand into the pocket of his black leather overcoat, though it looked splendid hovering at the door knocker on Washington Mews. He pauses for effect. And now he begins to walk up the street.

"So there's no Charles Ng?" Annabel says. "No such person?"

"It's a good name, though, right?"

The generations between Zoltan and his next important heir, Babu, are thirty generations, and the names are impossible to pronounce, and yet Thaddeus lists them while the two of them are walking down University. Here now is the multigenerational saga, with its epic sweep. Every twenty years, if not sooner, some cock finds a home in some pussy, and another infamous generation is spawned, and the peoples of Zoltan move back and forth across the borders, they're ejected here, they turn up somewhere else, and in their sorrow and impermanence, they set their tents rocking, for no class of men and women has ever been more fertile than a refugee population. Thaddeus produces the flask from his coat, takes a long pull on it, hands it to Annabel, rhapsodizing. Here they are, before CBGB's, where once hordes of rock-and-roll musicians gathered in leather jackets and torn jeans, feather boas and fishnets, where once there were Mohawks, body piercings, tattoos. They stand before it, Bowery and Bleecker, while kids spill in and out of the doorway. One youngster with bright blue hair remarks, "Hey, you're, you're, you're . . ."

Thaddeus raises high his hands to put a stop to the interruption.

"Listen close." He pauses for effect. "The two most hated groups of people in all Europe were the Gypsies and the Jews. Everywhere you went, the persecution of the Gypsies and the Jews. The Gypsies walked all the way from India, across a continent, with their inscrutable language, and when they met up with the Magyars, well, they were in the country of nomads. And that's where the heirs of Zoltan, the first-ever diviner, intermingled with the Gypsies and produced the great, unbroken string of Gypsy diviners. These guys could find a spring at a hundred yards. It was through them that the Gypsy families of Hungary thrived. They'd go into town, dragoon a few Saxons and a few Slavs, whom the Gypsies believed were the best traders. A shiv at the throat. Separating Saxons from their purses, this was the best activity of all. The Gypsies thrived, and their leader, Andrós, decreed that no more magic was to be practiced publicly by the Gypsies of Hungary. They confined themselves to stealing loot from Jewish shopkeepers."

A small throng from the club gathers around, skeptically, but Thaddeus rises to the story, as he always does. He gives himself over entirely to charm and he smiles, and when he smiles, things happen, regardless of the existence or nonexistence of conviction.

"It was Babu, son of Andrós, a young guy who grew up straight and true, who noticed Nurit, the daughter of a jeweler, and thereby brought close these two reviled races of men. Her hair was as black as coal, and her skin was like ivory, and she was shy, with enormous brown eyes. And Babu was so bewitched by her that he was still lingering in the shop long after his fraternity of thieves had run off with a brace of necklaces. So it's Babu, the Gypsy at hand, who is set upon by a gang of Jewish shopkeepers. They tie him up and carry him back to the neighborhood where they live. And they threaten to cut off his fingers one by one unless he is willing to tell them where they can find the other thieves.

"You know what happens next, right? It's what always happens next in Europe. A gang of men with staves and torches appears to drive the Jews out of the town and into the countryside. No time to dispense with Babu's fingers, and his protestations that he's a Gypsy, not a Jew, don't impress the Magyars, who are the ones driving out the Jews. If there's a Gypsy in the bunch, from their point of view, no matter. And just as Babu's fingers aren't detached from him, neither is Nurit, the hottie, the love interest, detached from him, and during the march out of the city and into arid fields, the two of them manage to have a few wanton kisses, and Babu caresses her bosom. That's about the best he can do at the moment, and it seems amazing, the softness of her bosom, at least until they are in the scrub brush that is no man's property at the end of that country. The elders among the Jewish men — dry-eyed and fatalistic — hold council and decide that it was Babu who led the Magyars to them. They decide that they have no choice but to kill him. There's no other way to deal with it, even when Nurit pleads: 'You can see from his eyes that his heart is true! He stole nothing from the shop!' Her father tells her she's an ignorant girl, ignorant in the ways of the world. The Jews have nothing but enemies and they are driven from one place to another, always dispossessed, and she says, 'No! Babu loves me.' And that's when Babu tries his own way out of his bad spot. He boasts that he can find water for the families of this diaspora. He says, 'Do not your families need water? Do not they need to drink? My people have supplied water from time immemorial. A little gold is nothing. The true coin of the realm is water. I'm a diviner and I can give you what you need.'"

A cop cruiser slows to a stop in front of CBGB's. Some of the kids scatter or head back into the club, where a hard-core band is doing the same old thing. Of those remaining, one boy says, "But he doesn't know how to find the water!" As though he's the audience plant.

"Exactly right!" Thaddeus cries. Smiles at Annabel, who holds fast to his arm now. "Exactly right. He has no idea because his father, Andrós, has decreed that no magic shall be practiced among Gypsies. Babu has heard stories of it. He's heard the stories. And in his head, he's trying hard to know what he needs to know. Forked stick. Some kind of prayer or incantation. Is there an enchanted phrase or something? He has no idea.

"One of the elders whispers to another, 'We let him find the water, *then* we kill him.' They nod sadly. Babu makes a big production out of finding the stick. He goes searching through the low forest. Among hornbeam, alder, sycamore, yew, Serbian spruce. In the distance, the sound of wolves because, you know, it's Central Europe. There are lots of wolves. A howling over the Danube. It's just part of the whole thing. He wanders in the scrub and finally he finds a forked stick, birch, and he's walking back toward the fire circle. There are babies crying, and the women are worried. And while he's on his way back, he trips on something or something trips him, and he falls on his face, you know, in a thicket of briars. It's like he's been struck by whatever overpowering force controls the dowsing in the world, and when he gets up he can feel the forked stick trembling like the limbs of a woman in childbirth! The stick is leading him somewhere! And he follows the stick, and he knows. In an instant, he knows. 'Dig here! Dig here! Here there is water for your people! Here!' And some of the Jewish grave diggers, accomplished in their craft, dig in that spot, and down they go, six feet, and find a spring bubbling enthusiastically. Nurit kisses Babu, and there's a cheer from all the dispossessed families there, and they take him into their family, as long as he promises to convert, and they only cut off

two of his fingers, one for stealing the necklaces and one for se-
ducing a Jewish woman."

Scattered applause, very scattered, and then the limousine
again pulls near to the curb, and its door opens for Thaddeus and
Annabel as if they were born to it. And the driver says to him,
"Sir, a call for you."

Shit. His wife, Sabrina. Like she's some kind of diviner herself.
Like she can sense trouble across the planes of time and space.
Whenever he's somewhere he shouldn't be, the call comes. She
doesn't need to say anything. The call is an antique envelope,
perfumed, with a wax seal. Annabel climbs into the car with him,
but once in, she gets fidgety, staring out the window at the Bobst
Library, suicide jumper's site of choice. Nearby, boys head into
the park with their acoustic guitars. A pair of cops on horses.

The wife is saying that the commercial is going really well.
She's saying that they want her here for a couple more days. Sabrina is saying the weather in Southern California is just perfection.
It's all completely inoffensive. The goal of a marriage is deep and
abiding intimacy, that's something people say, but Thaddeus
feels like marriage is deeper when it has deception in it. When his
wife says, "The weather in Southern California is perfection," that
could mean a hundred things. There are many more layers to deception than there are to truth. Truth is a log cabin with a dirt
floor. Deception is a house with hidden stairwells, dropped ceilings, and furtive butlers. When she says the weather is perfection,
she means, "I enjoy the weather best when you are not in it."
Sabrina means, "You make the weather appalling." She means
that her life, outside of marriage, blows where it lists, like a
sirocco. She means that the weather includes the half-clothed or
entirely unclothed body of some studio executive guy with a
shaved chest. She's probably waxing his shoulders right now.
When she says all these things, she means, "I know you are doing these things, too, because you are a failed movie actor who

makes movies for teens in Kansas City. I don't expect much. But I expect you not to make me look like an asshole." He met his wife in Southern California. Later, his wife had a miscarriage in Southern California. And since then they've been too busy for pregnancy. This layer is never to be spoken of and never forgotten. She's in Southern California, where his business is, and he's in a limousine with a twenty-eight-year-old office assistant, spinning out drunken lies about Gypsies. They get stuck in traffic at the junction of West Fourth and Sixth Avenue.

"It needs more," she says.

"You do some." He pockets his cell phone.

"I'm doing it in my head. Where it's quieter," she says. "You need the Gobi Desert. It's big, and it's deserted, and it has Chinese mythology. What about a martial-arts sequence?"

He has the flask open again. "You can't just skip right to the desert. You have to work your way up. Next should be Morocco, where Babu and Nurit have Sephardic babies, who are darkly hued, and from there, in exile, they cross the Mediterranean —"

"You've got your geography screwed up."

"You think anyone cares about geography? Anyway, the Mediterranean gives you the opportunity for a lot of stuff about the Greeks. Poseidon, all of that. And then you get to the desert, and the desert is the Sahara. And it's during the Crusades, see. Their grandson is Jewish, born during the Crusades, in the Holy Land, and he's driven into the desert, where he becomes part of an Ethiopian sect. And after that, there's a kid, next generation or the one after that or the one after that, who gets abducted, in West Africa."

"You don't want it to get too much like —"

"You want narrative sweep. It's a multigenerational saga. You have to have the desert; you have to have slave traders. Did I ever tell you about Peter O'Toole and my stepmother? We were going to see *Lawrence of Arabia* at some repertory theater, back when they still had them. And my stepmother goes out of her way to say that probably Peter O'Toole was one of *them*, you know. Probably he was one of *them*, and you could tell by his —"

"I didn't know you had a stepmother."

The limousine is going up the West Side Highway. The ventilation chimney for the Holland Tunnel is before them. Jersey City like a malignancy on the opposite side of the Hudson.

"Then you have the slaves of the American South. You have the descendants of Zoltan and Babu and Kwame of what is now Senegal, and these descendants are now in the American South, and some of them are on the Underground Railroad, in the middle of the Civil War, digging for water in the frozen Cumberland Mountains while the noble troops of the Confederacy march to their deaths. It was a lost cause! But the men fought on!"

It's almost eleven when they pull up on Riverside Drive. They've eaten only salty snack items. Thaddeus Griffin is drunk. The driver comes around the side, opens the door. Annabel climbs out first, and she takes Griffin's hand, helps him out of the car. He is the American celebrity, drunken, immoral, and with an enlarged notion of his importance. He has a beautiful office assistant with him who he drunkenly believes will do almost anything. The driver, standing at attention, shuts the door of the limousine. The doorman stands at attention as the contagion of celebrity is loosed upon the world again.

"You figure out the ending," he says, in front of his apartment door.

"No. Tell me."

His voice, on the landing: "The story stops briefly at the Irish famine and then it goes, uh, from Ireland to Iceland. And from there we're in the — it's the Russian Revolution. Always the diviners are on the side of the oppressed and the downtrodden. Poland during the Second World War. The Holocaust. The Armenian genocide. The founding of Las Vegas. Very important. The whole last episode concerns the founding of Las Vegas. The descendant of Zoltan is the beautiful daughter of a mobster who's concealing the fact that he's partly black. Well, I mean, technically, he's, uh, he's Mongol, Gypsy, Jew, Tamil, mestizo, Khmer, Maori, whatever. She slips off with a tenor sax player for a romantic weekend, gets knocked up, dies of an overdose. Her daughter is raised to be a Las Vegas dancer, spurned by her, uh, illustrious mob family. And the daughter of this dancer is given up for adoption during the Nixon administration."

Annabel, who according to her New England upbringing never betrays a strong feeling, leans against the wall by the door, her body stooped slightly, like a question mark. She begins to say how hard this is for her and abandons the thought. She begins to say what an awful day it's been. And she begins to say what it's like being with him. He can't stop, however, and into the silence he drives himself; always the two things are together, the worst of him and the best of him. How beautiful she is, incandescent and full of promise. He has depleted her, he has depleted promise, he has fed on promise that is no longer his, he's kept Annabel's promise away from all other suitors, kept it away from people who might recognize it, has kept her promise in the vaults of hotel rooms, empty corridors, and stairwells, kept it in his arms, and so he tells her the ending one more time, because knowledge is aphrodisiac for the has-been or the once-was. So it seems in an empty hallway, in front of his door.

Because *she's* the baby born in Las Vegas. In 1972.

6

The bike messenger was once the centaur of the empire. During the junk bond. The bike messenger was Mercury himself, traversing the city in Lycra shorts, sunglasses, tank top. You could make a living at it; you could make fifty thousand dollars a year if you had the heart of a warrior. These nomads flanked the traffic on the avenues from midtown to the financial district and back again. Whistling at one another, shouting curses. A noble calling. As if the bicycle had been fused to the messenger somehow. As if he were affixed to the frame. Only the need for motion. And maybe some amphetamines or cannabis. He was the centaur. No message was undeliverable. Words like wind in the trees. Words at the speed of sound. The messenger made this possible. He made possible the leveraged buyout, the hostile takeover, and its dependent life-forms: lawyers, accountants, consultants.

This according to the unofficial history being compiled, on the slow days, by the owner of Omni Delivery, New York, NY: Ivan Polanski.

In due course, the junk bondsmen were in minimum-security penitentiaries practicing their squash or making license plates and pleading for leniency. After which a new age dawned, which was the age of so-called electronic mail. The age of the computerized electronic mail message, the age of endless trivia communicated as ones and zeros. Polanski was slow in appreciating the dark significance of the electronic mail message. To his regret. He had no computer at home in Glen Cove, and his kids didn't care, and his wife didn't care, and no one was trying to e-mail him messages about penile enlargement and barely legal teens. But he could see the difference on his bottom line. He had dealt with the facsimile machine. It had jeopardized his business, but he'd prevailed. He could overcome this. He faxed nothing, personally, wouldn't even allow one into the office. Screw the clients. He used the telephone and he used his team of highly trained and professional messengers. He had dealt with the facsimile machine and he would deal with this electronic mail nonsense. They waited by the water cooler, his team, they read magazines, they smoked. He didn't care what they did, as long as they got downtown faster than his rivals. Polanski believed in competition. Competition made Polanski's business lean. It had made him successful in this country, the first generation of Polanskis to be comfortable. His father spoke no English. Polanski knew what it meant to be successful here; his family had fled Communists. And yet now Ivan Polanski, with roiling innards, selected from a dwindling pool of potential employees. Retirees became part of the workforce. They took the subway trains or surface transit. They whistled while they worked. They were not fleet; they were anything but warriors. They were nice old guys.

And then there was the guilty secret of the industry. The mentally ill. Yes, in truth, schizophrenics made good messengers. They lacked compassion; they were obsessive to a fault. As long as they took their medication, they were great. When they were moving, their symptoms remitted. There were occasional difficulties. Polanski had personally intervened when one of his messengers believed he was being chased by genetically enhanced Mormons. This employee made it from Central Park West to

New York Plaza, on the southern tip of the island, in under ten minutes. No car could do it; no train could do it. Only this terrified messenger.

Polanski did what he had to do. He made a note. It said: Hire mentally ill persons. They need work. They have families who want them to be self-reliant. You don't have to socialize with them. No one else in the business will take the risk. Come hither, hallucinators. Come hither, conspiracy theorists. All of you with early stages of tardive dyskinesia and lithium-related bloating, Ivan Polanski, from the Polanskis of Krakow, welcomes you to the adventure of message delivery. Winning is about risk.

Two years ago, during this personnel initiative, he hired the messenger known as Tyrone. This wasn't the guy's name. He had a rich person's name: William Russell Wellington Duffy. That was the name on the payroll checks. But William Russell Wellington Duffy insisted on being called Tyrone. When he talked, Tyrone sounded like a William Russell Wellington Duffy. He was educated. Had a little bit of the old Bostonian in him. Tyrone was mum on all this, however. During preliminary testing, as with all Omni employees, Tyrone had successfully identified the date and time, three landmarks in downtown Manhattan, and had totaled a list of two-digit numbers. Polanski, as a matter of course, now knew some of the signs of mental illness. Facial masking. Restless legs syndrome. Low affect. Religiosity. High anxiety. Tyrone Duffy had them all.

He hadn't expected Tyrone to last. Who did last? Sooner or later a messenger was picking imaginary crabs out of his arm and then he was gone. No one lasted. Polanski might not last himself. Tyrone had not been expected to last. His bike was in awful shape, and he disappeared now and then and came back with imaginary tales of dinners with movie stars. Crazy stuff. Hard to tell what he was talking about because there were always a lot of pretentious asides mixed into the monologues. This on the rare occasions when Tyrone talked at all. He once mentioned that his dreadlocks had butterflies living in them and he observed that American cheese contained dangerous radioactive ingredients. Mostly, Polanski had to admonish Tyrone in the area of loafing. Get out there, move some damn packages, after which Tyrone would put a little effort into it, for a few days. Until he got lost again, inside the public library, where Tyrone claimed to be compiling a paper on alpha particles and gold foil. One time, a note from the library arrived in which Omni Delivery was asked to serve as a character reference for one William Russell Wellington Duffy, who wished to be permitted access to a seventeenth-century manuscript on the medicinal properties of English flowers.

Tyrone had a beard in the style of Malcolm X and big thick glasses. He was so thin that he *had* to be suffering from malnutrition. But whenever Polanski assumed that Tyrone would go the way of the other messengers, into the shelter system, into the Manhattan Bridge homeless encampment, there'd be a revelation. For example, a certain client really preferred Tyrone for all his message delivery needs. For some reason, Tyrone did have good relations with the movie business. They were always asking for him.

And so the Tyrone years lingered at Omni Delivery.

What really went through Tyrone's mind? What was Tyrone thinking about in his preoccupied way? Polanski wondered. The other messengers, like Edwin (Sanchez) from Delancey Street, kidded Tyrone. They'd give him a loving smack on the side of the head. Tyrone would scarcely indicate that he noticed. "Earth to shuttle, yo." In all places, at all times, Tyrone replied with the equanimity of the civilly disobedient. Edwin (Sanchez) from Delancey Street, Polanski's employee of longest standing, indicated that Tyrone preferred the name Tyrone because it was "more black," and he said that Tyrone had on occasion professed agreement with black separatist political platforms, especially as indicated in the lyrics of a certain hip-hop collective. Edwin said that Tyrone did not appreciate the vernacular in the work of this hip-hop collective, did not favor dialect based on ungrammaticalities, but he understood the aims of hip-hop recording artists and other local separatist movements, supported their work as educators and community organizers. Edwin (Sanchez) from Delancey Street indicated that Tyrone had studied the "great philosophies" at some university out in the middle of the country somewhere but had failed to secure his doctorate, and that Tyrone also made fine-art paintings of some description.

Ivan Polanski has seen no indication of any of these things. Tyrone's story, in any event, is simply part of Polanski's broader survey of the history of the centaurs of the empire. He knows all of the great characters, their pedigrees, he knows about their bikes, the chromoly tig-welded tubing, alu frames, clincher rims, he knows that he presides over the twilight of a way of life. And this is what he's thinking about when he gets the first call on Thursday morning. Couldn't be easier, superficially speaking. Worldwide Plaza, Eighth Avenue, coming back to Rock Plaza, Fifth Avenue entrance. International Talent and Media. Movie stuff. Look, as a manager, he needs to ascertain that Tyrone is doing the work. He needs to know how fast the job can be done. He needs to know that the centaur still triumphs.

"Tyrone," he barks, "ITM Worldwide Plaza. Going back to Rock Plaza. Here's the paperwork."

Tyrone is wearing black nylon bicycle shorts and a hooded sweatshirt. Tyrone is wearing a bandanna around his brow. Later these facts will be important. Tyrone is carrying a book, which he hides away quickly. Tyrone whispers an indication that he has heard the assignment.

"And from there downtown to twenty-one Wall. Understand?"

Tyrone nods, and then, as if wrestling with ghosts, his eyes bloodshot and narrow, he evacuates the premises, which are located above an Irish bar on Forty-seventh. All of this is not enough for Polanski. It is not enough to give Tyrone work; it is not enough to wonder about the inner world of Tyrone. It is not enough to be witness to the thinning of the ranks of the centaurs.

Polanski has to challenge his employees. So what he does is: He gets Spicer on the horn. Mr. Spicer is the one with early Parkinson's, who likes to sit in front of the McGraw-Hill building to watch the pretty girls. Polanski dials Spicer's phone. There's the usual fumbling.

"Polanski calling. Pickup. International Talent and Media, Worldwide Plaza, twenty-eighth floor, coming back to Rock Center, fourth floor, south building."

Spicer repeats it all back.

"Let me make sure I've got it, please."

"Don't do this to me."

"Read it back to me one more time," Mr. Spicer says. "I'm seventy-four years old, forgoshsakes."

A crosstown run. Ten or eleven blocks total, if you count the avenue blocks as two. As if any crosstown run were simple now. First, there are the jaywalking regulations. These have been promulgated from above, in this zero-tolerance time. Zero tolerance for broken windows, zero tolerance for panhandling, zero tolerance for the device known as the squeegee, zero tolerance for live music, zero tolerance for toplessness, zero tolerance for jaywalking, zero tolerance for dissent. On the avenues, you can still see them, looking twice, the jaywalkers, before making a dash for the other side. And yet there's the fence that has just gone up in front of Radio City. The trucks, bearing advertisements for soon-to-fail Internet start-ups, are backed up on the side streets at two or three miles an hour. People are cursing. Jewelers are swarming onto the street. There is heavy cloud cover. It is to this midtown that the contestants now go to undertake their competition.

Polanski says to Edwin (Sanchez) from Delancey Street, "Twenty bucks on Spicer."

Edwin replies, "The brother lives in the clouds. But he's fast. Spicer has corns. He will stop at the Rite Aid in the McGraw-Hill building and complain. He will make conversation with a Haitian cashier."

"Are you saying?"

"The bets are placed."

Polanski also asks Daryl Standler, dope smoker, if he wishes to wager. Standler appears to mull it over for a long while. He, too, backs Tyrone. All this gambling takes place without considering the effect of the accident: the windows and the displays of Diamond Universe, 1200 Sixth Avenue, at the corner of Forty-seventh, still shattered, inside the ribbons of police tape. The sawhorses there, snarling the pedestrian traffic at the subway entrance. All the merchandise removed from the felt-lined display cases. The street in front is swarming with rented enforcement and with Hasidic guys protecting their family business. The car is still there, in fact. And Ramon Martinez, who drove up Sixth and then made the turn at high speed, against westerly traffic, going forty-nine miles an hour, Ramon Martinez, who uttered anti-Semitic oaths, where is he, exactly? After arraignment, he will certainly be moved from his cushy spot in the Tombs to maximum security at Rikers Island, where guys will shout encouragement and vilification at him from adjoining cells. His comely appearance will be the subject of intense scrutiny. Has he had his first shower yet? Three people are deceased, two of them Hasidic. Their families are weeping, and tabloid photographers are camped out in front of the relevant homes in Williamsburg, hoping for the perfect photograph. Again, on the televised news, Ramon Martinez makes the turn. Again, in diagrams. Again, he swings his LeSabre, with a hundred and sixty-three thousand miles on it, just wide of the subway stairwell and the lamppost that has the giant facsimile diamond on it; again, he wipes out a garbage can; again, three pedestrians to the immediate south of the driver's side leap clear. One, a former high school basketball star, sustains a back injury, and two dive to the curb and are nearly run over by a taxi crossing west on Forty-seventh. Nearby: a guy holding a falafel sandwich, bantering with another guy checking his watch, and, by coincidence, an Arabic teenager. All are driven upward into the windows.

Again, we watch the Schappell footage, which confirms this interpretation. It was taken by an astute passerby from St. Louis, Norm Schappell, he of the digital camera and unsteady hand. Now the car jumps the curb, and it seems in the little windows of low-resolution imagery as though Martinez is shaking a fist, as though at this moment, when he is furthest from God, he imagines he is God's agent of vengeance. Into the reinforced storefront he goes, which should forbid such things. Again, the alarm goes off, and the taxi behind swings wide, hits a parked car on Sixth Avenue. Now the screams. On the news, the footage scrolls, the Schappell footage, and the mayor says at the press conference that this is a hate crime until proven otherwise. "There is no room in our city for hatred and ignorance, for division and prejudice. The world lives in New York City." Martinez does his duckwalk that evening in leg irons, his arm in a sling. As the reporter on the UBC affiliate notes, giving away a closely held trade secret, the police sometimes put the leg irons in the freezer, back at the precinct. Because frozen leg irons hurt like hell.

This is what the rental enforcement guys tell Mr. Spicer. He stands at the corner, taking in the expanse of the tragic incident. It's just too much of an enticement. At the three-minute mark in the competition, Spicer is just getting going. Saying to whoever might listen, "What did this city ever do to this young man? We did nothing to him! Did someone deny him a job? I didn't deny him a job! I just want to deliver messages in peace. Did I ever do anything to hurt him?"

Meanwhile, Tyrone is on the glide. Tyrone has a theory. This is his theory, which has to do with inertial bodies, bodies moving at constant speed in a horizontal direction, unless additional forces are impressed upon them. His theory of the glide is first a theory of orbit. Tyrone feels the orbit on his bike, which is to say that his bike is the *Mysterium Cosmographicum,* and his responsibility is not the delivery of messages, which is an interruption of his true calling. His responsibility is the glide, and his responsibility is the relation between large bodies, a refutation of the origins of astronomy. He flings a lanky leg over the saddle. He's off. On a Surly Steamroller, fixed gear, in baked-bean brown, no brakes, as befits a bike with this illustrious name, *Mysterium Cosmographicum.* Since the glory period of the messenger, there are no longer any brakes, and indeed, this, in the physical meditations of Tyrone Duffy, philosopher of elementary systems, painter of Newtonian phenomena, is a feature of necessity, because brakes impede the glide. Tyrone needs to glide, and the glide needs no brakes.

The pendulum's arc is the same no matter how large or how small. Newton was a man of irremediable rage. Tycho Brahe had no nose. Lost it in a duel. The facsimile was cast in a durable metal. Tycho did successfully marry, however. Tyrone, of necessity, requires that a braking force be impressed on his inertial body in order to slow the progress of himself and the *Mysterium Cosmographicum,* and that force is the gravitational pull of pedestrians. This is the value of pedestrians in the course of the glide. They are a soft landing surface. Tyrone will refuse food because a modest bodily proportion increases the glide, and the food that he refuses goes into the pool of all available foods, such that the pedestrians can be made more obese and thus softer for soft landings.

He doesn't ride on the sidewalk much. But now he must. Because of the police presence around the site of the Martinez incident, Forty-seventh is all but impassable. Riding on the sidewalk is air resistance in the glide. Obesity is air resistance, and the change in motion is proportional to the motive force impressed. Tyrone gets off the bike and he begins to walk the bike around the Martinez site. The car, which is about to be lifted free by a small crane, looks like a Christmas decoration. Promotional material. The diamonds glimmer as an afterimage, and part of this glimmering is the relation between forces, the force exerted on the carbon, which is graphite, which becomes the diamond, which becomes a legend, around which orbits the force of the

African slave labor used to produce the diamond in the mines and the use of diamonds to finance and facilitate rebel activities designed to redistribute continental resources to disenfranchised nation-states and also to dictatorial regimes. Tyrone sees Spicer at the accident site, nods politely. Spicer says, "Can you imagine? Can you imagine?" Unclear if he recognizes Duffy or not. Which means at the three-and-a-half-minute mark the contestants are briefly in a dead heat, after which Tyrone glides silently across the intersection at Sixth Avenue as though the intersection were a vacuum and he's a falling body in a landscape of falling bodies.

Spicer is so impassioned on the subject of the Martinez incident that the cops take a shine to him, as they always do, and an exchange ensues in which Spicer tells the cops that his wife died three years before, cancer, and that he liked the Mets in the series, never will quite recover from it, the series, and that that one pitcher on the Yankees is a criminal and should be locked away, and the cops applaud this, because all cops like the Mets, and they ask where he's going, and he says he's going west, but he's an old man and has Parkinson's, the early stages, and the cops violate all precepts of policing in the zero-tolerance time and they put him in the squad car and take him as far as the multinational purveyor of overpriced coffee beverages on Seventh and Forty-ninth, where Spicer repeats the whole thing to a cashier, about the wife, the Mets, never will recover from it, and what was wrong with Martinez that he felt he had to do this thing, this violent thing, while Spicer is mixing three sugars into his French roast.

For the *Mysterium Cosmographicum,* there is the problem of the door. One enters through a door, to be sure, there is such a splendid noun, but you also *door,* using the verb; that is, you are riding the *Mysterium Cosmographicum* when you strike a door or, usually, first, some soft landing surface, which is in this case someone trying to remove something from the backseat, ass first, so that you are suddenly an object in motion, separated from your launch vehicle; you are an object that has been impeded in the glide and you are now flying through the air, launched from your launch vehicle. Or there is no soft landing surface to stop you, and you are *doored*, participially. Where is the soft, fluffy white butt? It is temporarily unavailable, and there is only the door, and it happens so precipitously, the *Mysterium Cosmographicum*'s striking the door, which serves thereby as a braking device, and you behave according to the rules, wherein it is supposed that projectiles follow a curved path, your parabolic trajectory being up and over the door, including some kind of half gainer and pike position, separated from the bike, inertial energy combined with gravitational energy, in this instance at the corner of Seventh Avenue, the open door of the van from Skyline Duplication. You rise up, you come down.

This is Tyrone picking himself up just as Spicer is emerging from the multinational purveyor of coffee beverages. At four minutes fifteen seconds, still a dead heat. They nod politely again. Spicer hobbles around the corner, the folly of neon everywhere above him now, canyons opening in the downtown direction, yes, it is Times Square, and Tyrone, who is checking the tire pressure on his bike, looks up for a moment at the behavior of all those neon gases, lighting up in so many preposterous ways, advertising so many things — women's undergarments, home electronics — then mounts his steed again, *Mysterium Cosmographicum,* passes Spicer, old crank, takes a right on Broadway.

The orbits of the planets are in fact ellipses because the planets perturb one another. Ivan Polanski, Tyrone's employer, has never put together the steps in this proof, which even some elementary geometry would accomplish, equal angles here and here, nor has Polanski put together the relationship between the heavenly body called Tyrone Duffy and the heavenly body employed at Means of Production, frequent Omni Delivery client, Annabel Duffy, in Rock Center; he never got that they are brother and sister, that they are confederates, and that the Omni Delivery service is hired by Means of Production precisely because Tyrone

Duffy is sibling thereto; they are each, Tyrone and Annabel, heavenly bodies rotating around a certain Reverend Russell Hunt Duffy, of Newton, Massachusetts, minister of the First Congregational Church, and there are other heavenly bodies rotating around the same White Dwarf of high temperature and low brightness. There is a body known as the naturally produced brother of Tyrone and Annabel, the unadopted brother, Maximillian Rivers Duffy, white son of the White Dwarf, and there is the wife of the White Dwarf, otherwise known as Mom, whose idea it was, during a time of social upheaval, to adopt first one and then another disadvantaged child, meaning children of different shades, meaning African American children, and to raise them as though they were white dwarves not black holes in the Newton, Massachusetts, public school system. Tyrone and Annabel, who from their earliest ages were confederates. They were a team. Uniform deviations in velocity were always toward the White Dwarf, who was always perturbing.

Tyrone passes the Brill Building. There are many messages in the Brill Building these days; the Brill Building is a message epicenter. There are many CDRs to be taken to different addresses. And the Tin Pan Alley dudes, those remaining, are always sending the messengers around to the freight elevator. Tyrone could hum a dozen bubblegum songs written in the Brill Building, he could hum them backward with half-step key changes in them, but because he is in the uniform of the bike messenger, and because he has butterflies living in his dreads, wherever he goes he is stopped and he is invited around to the freight elevator. He knows about the Brill Building, he knows about the Armory Show, he knows about the Factory, he knows about the AbExes, he knows about the East Village gallery scene, he knows about postmodernism, he knows about the new historicism, he knows about Young British Artists, he knows, he hears, he discards the language of current events festering in him, he knows about the interruptions of the glide. *Enormous potential,* even his sister says it. The White Dwarf has always said it, as he has also said that Tyrone, whom he will not call by that name, must seek treatment. And Tyrone will not seek treatment because he thinks his problem is that he was too long stuck orbiting around the White Dwarf.

Six minutes, eighteen seconds now, and Spicer is back at the Forty-ninth Street entrance to the R train, asking directions. He inquires of a young woman the kind of bagel she's eating. He prefers the salt bagel, himself. Will only eat the salt bagel; well, also the onion bagel, and sometimes the bagel with everything, but all varieties of bagel must have lox upon them. Fresh lox. Spicer does not have a prayer of victory, does not have a chance.

Tyrone Duffy is singing "Up on the Roof" as though it were an allegory about elliptical orbits when he is again knocked from his bike, by a large pedestrian, apparently on purpose. That is, a force is impressed against the inert body of Tyrone Duffy, at point P, along velocity tangent F prime. This is Tyrone, about to make a turn on Forty-eighth, along which axis Worldwide Plaza moves into view, whereupon he is brought to a standstill by a certain pedestrian of malevolent intent. A large man, apparently of Mediterranean origin, and it seems this man has a problem with the institution of bicycle messengers, if messengers, as a marginalized populace, can be said to be institutional. A message is announced at the moment that force is impressed upon Tyrone: Something something, motherfuckers, something something. That Tyrone is heading the wrong way up Broadway is apparently inadvisable and contrary to etiquette and worthy of violent confrontation in the view of this pedestrian of Mediterranean origin.

"Broadway goes downtown, you ignorant piece of shit."

Tyrone brushes himself off with Buster Keaton understatement. The man begins to assume the stance of a combatant. The preliminary stance of fisticuffs. The planets are complex. They are not of uniform cast.

"Whoa." Tyrone mutters a reply, reaching for his glasses and his bandanna, which are scattered upon the curbside. A circle begins to form around the two men.

Another pedestrian says, "You were riding the wrong way!"

Soon a third and a fourth.

"Before the month is up, it will rain," Tyrone says, well aware of his inexplicability. His bike is upended, the Mediterranean man is coming at him, and he can see the ring on the fifth finger of the hand of the Mediterranean man, a high school graduation bauble, and he can tell that this ring is about to make a deep impression on his cheek, and he can see that the circle of onlookers is like the plasma of the early universe, gathering energy. All he can think of is "inner force," the notion that a body does what it is doing because of its inner force, and this force carries Tyrone on the glide, and the glide takes him from east to west and it takes him from north to south, and if the glide is good, then the day is good. This is his inner force. And if the glide is bad, then the day is bad, and all is darkness. The fist of the Mediterranean man is now, in roundhouse style, swung in his direction, and this blow falls across his face, and again his glasses go flying, and the bystanders, all of them white, hold Tyrone by the arms because they have all had infelicitous interactions with the centaurs of the empire. They have all had the centaurs drive them into other pedestrians, the centaurs riding the wrong way on one-way streets, the centaurs shouting at them, whistling on their centaur whistles, and now Tyrone is going to pay. One guy says, "Don't you have anything to say?" and Tyrone thinks long and hard, and he says, "$\Delta v \sim (1/R^2) \times R^2 = 1$," and he says this with such clarity that it belies everything he has done or thought in weeks. He grins. The oppositional force of the Mediterranean man, with his outer-Brooklyn accent, makes Tyrone feel alive as he has not felt in weeks. It is true that if you had but fifteen minutes left to live, it would be most satisfying to have your hands around the neck of a white man, particularly a fat, detestable, middle-aged white man, and another blow comes now, and he attempts to kick the

Mediterranean man centrally, but then a squad car pulls up close, and out come the cops, and Tyrone is let free as though never restrained. At once bystanders are consumed by the lobby ingresses of nearby buildings. "What seems to be the problem?" et cetera.

The collection of passersby that remains, significantly reduced, offers the unanimous perception that Tyrone was riding in the wrong direction on Broadway. All of these persons are unaware that Tyrone was solving elementary propositions of astrophysics. The cops slap a moving violation on Tyrone. The Mediterranean man gets clean away.

"That guy punched me in the face," he says in his throaty whisper. "For no reason. And he knocked me off the bike and may have damaged my rims from throwing my bike around. You're going to do nothing about that?"

The officers look at him as though he has just said $\Delta v \sim (1/R^2)$ x $R^2 = 1$. They hand him the lightweight *Mysterium Cosmographicum,* and he limps the last block across, until he's chaining the steed in front of Worldwide Plaza, from whence is now emerging Jack Spicer, retiree, parkinsonian patient, carrying a manila envelope. They nod.

Soon Tyrone Duffy calls into the message center at International Talent and Media and is told, of course, that he is redundant, as the package has already been picked up by an old guy. Salt is applied to the wound. On the sidewalk, he then telephones his sister. He tells her his new litany of sorrows. It's almost impossible, he says, to get out of bed. Bed has some incredible electromagnetic convection, and he can't get out of the bed, and he hasn't eaten anything but Special K for three weeks because he'd rather read Spinoza or socialist-worker propaganda than boil an egg, and it's always like that, the bad news piles up and rolls off his back, oh yeah, and he just bought a Harley-Davidson, and he's going to disassemble it and mount it on the wall of his studio apartment.

"Hey, uh, I was supposed to bring some package by there, but I guess I didn't get there in time. There was an incident."

Annabel says the word *honey* like it is the first time the word has ever been used, like honey has just been discovered by a woodland animal. And then she whispers. To explain her own conundrum. To tell him about *The Diviners,* the treatment she typed last night, late into the night, and how a friend at a film agency agreed to send it over to Means of Production as though it were a genuine submission.

"Wait a second," Tyrone mumbles. "You —"

"Made it up. With that guy. Thaddeus."

Nothing to say about this. It's clear that Thaddeus is a traditional Lothario with multiple sexually transmitted diseases and a death wish and a battalion of gossip columnists drunk on expense accounts tracking his every move.

"We're gonna see if she goes for it."

He asks the name of the author of the source material. Because there has to be an origin, even if it's a fictive origin, or perhaps because it's fictitious there has to be an origin. And she agrees that it's a really good question. The name of the author. They picked a bunch of names of dead romance novelists. The stupider the novel, the better the film, Annabel says. A novel where the prose is so horrible it's like the prose equivalent of mac and cheese in a box, that's the ticket. Add in a deformity of some kind. Romance novelists, the people who write these things, have three names. Late in the evening, she and Thaddeus Griffin worked on the three names more than on the treatment itself. They chose one from each of three different dead romance writers.

"Shelley Ralston Havemeyer."

"I may have spackled her living room," Tyrone mumbles. "It was summer when I was in, uh, school. Till I stopped showing up."

He has to be off to Wall Street. She asks if he took his medication.

Back at Omni Delivery, Spicer turns up, huffing and puffing, after taking the elevator, and Ivan Polanski whoops with joy at the forty dollars he's about to collect. Spicer has no idea. Tyrone has no idea. Polanski has picked the right horse, an old windbag who trembles and who has a job because he needs something to do. Polanski tells him to take an extralong lunch. Their business will be extinct within a year, and they should all relax. Invest wisely. Buy on the dips. And then Polanski looks at the copy of the messenger form.

"Wait a second, Mr. Spicer. How come it says Michael Cohen on here?"

"I thought you said Michael Cohen. You always send me to Michael Cohen."

"I didn't say Michael Cohen. I said deliver to Means of Production."

"What the heck is Means of Production?"

"What do you mean, what is Means of Production? It's the address I gave you. I repeated it twice."

"You didn't repeat it twice. I *asked* you to repeat it twice. But you didn't."

Polanski throws up his hands. And Edwin (Sanchez) from Delancey Street makes ready to accept the US legal tender bills.

7

Vic Freese is at reception when the old guy comes in. Typical messenger. Why are the old messengers so challenged when it comes to shaving? Looks as though this one tried to shave with a rasp. Reddish scrapes where some follicles have been ripped out, and then some big neglected areas, mostly on his neck, where there is two or three days' growth. In the nostrils, too, like stalactites protruding, like there's wheat growing out of his brain. The guy is wearing double-knit slacks and he has belted these way up around the navel, the better to display the bold tartan of his socks. The old guy stinks. No amount of aftershave will conceal it, though he has liberally applied his aftershave nonetheless.

Vic admires and pities these messengers in equal amounts because he was once a mail room kid, like the majority of agents here at the Michael Cohen Agency. Good to stay busy. Good to know the city well enough, in advancing years, to be a messenger. Good to have people to talk to, places to go. But the old guy, because Vic is standing near to the console at reception, makes a beeline for him, and Vic's pity ends immediately when the old guy draws close, because Sandra Konig is sitting right there at the desk, and the phone console hasn't even started lighting up yet. It's early. Vic points at Sandra, says nothing, and the old guy, and with him his noxious stink, moves laterally.

"Not the first time, you know," the old guy says. "There was the one other election when the popular vote didn't have a thing to do with it."

Vic indicates, with the merest gestural signification, that he has no aptitude for politics. The Michael Cohen Agency is about entertainment. Everybody loves entertainment. Besides, Vic, with arms crossed, and wearing the conservative but stylish suit from a conservative but stylish British designer, is waiting for his new client. Due at ten, and now fifteen minutes late, the new client is his *everything*, the new client is the air he breathes, the food he eats, the water that slakes his thirst. Vic has his assistant poised at the phone to page him as soon as the call comes from the lobby downstairs, as soon as the limousine has pulled up. Vic has festooned his office with swags and balloons in order to welcome the new client to the Michael Cohen team. The new client was not ensnared by Vic, it is true, he did not sign the new client, and yet the new client has become his responsibility through the largesse of the music department in the Los Angeles office. This means scraps in terms of points because the signing percentage is the only percentage that matters at the end of the Michael Cohen year when the bonuses are handed out, and Vic did not sign the new client. The guy in the music department who did will take his piece of Vic's action, and Vic will get the booking percentage instead of the signing percentage, which amounts to a percentage of a percentage. Still, just last week he was out there in Century City to shake hands with the manager of the new client. He still has the jet lag to prove that he will do what it takes.

And here is the bio. The new client records for that label in Belgium that packages singers with one name. The new client therefore has a single name, but Vic has a blockage about pronouncing the single name, since he knows, through due diligence, that the new client is actually called Tammy Gleick and that she was raised in Springfield, Illinois, until, in her teens, she moved to LA in pursuit of her big break. Her mother is the owner of a chain of hairdressing salons. The new client with one name has wanted to be a big star since she was a little girl. The new client is now twenty-two, and the new client drinks a lot, and the new client may also have a bit of a cocaine problem. This is well-known. Even Vic's kids know this much about the new client.

Vic needs the new client. Thus, the streamers in his office. Thus, a brand-new leather handbag from Hermès. A gift item. The reason Vic Freese needs the new client is that Vic Freese is not really very good at his job and never has been. Vic Freese is the agent least likely to succeed. He doesn't know why. He never tried to get other junior agents to quit when he was at the Mercury Agency, so that he could have their spots on the talent desk. He never had sex with the secretaries or the heads of departments. He never bought drugs for a client. Vic Freese has a wife and kids at home in Larchmont, and he doesn't go out. Vic eats hamburgers and watches televised golf. These days, Vic tries to get home on the New Haven line as quickly as he can after whatever dinner or drink he's supposed to have each day. He tries to see his son and daughter before they go to bed and he tries to read to them from rhyming books.

Senior agents in California have made clear that Vic Freese is operating on borrowed time. Vic has had his review with Mitch Adelstein, the head of television, who is a yeller, and Vic has been found wanting in every conceivable way, and now he has a brief few months left before he will have to move on to what would be his third agency in six years. He is the agent that other agents take great pride in leaving in the dust. Now the music department has thrown this booby-trapped new client in his lap, this handful who is unlikely to excel in television. She is five foot four inches of terror. Terror with a pierced navel. Terror in bottomless chaps. No one else wanted the new client and her delinquent past, and this was before she started snorting blow off the bars downtown. Luckily, the new client has a manager and a publicist and an agent in the music department in LA. Luckily, the new client has the label in Belgium to deal with her accidental overdoses and her diva scenes on airplanes. It is these other members of the team who must comment for the record on the inconstancy of the new client in the matter of her boyfriends.

The new client has shown no aptitude for acting whatsoever. She has never taken a lesson. When the new client did a cola endorsement two years ago, they required thirty-six takes to get her to say her one line. Then they hired a voice-over actress. It is not clear whether the new client can, in truth, read. A prominent celebrity magazine has already given coverage to her "Struggle with Learning Disabilities." And, according to the celebrity magazine, her recent single "Please Don't Send Me That Letter," in which she asks a boyfriend not to send her a breakup note, is widely understood to be a compassionate plea on behalf of dyslexics everywhere. Her scripts are always sent to her handlers, and, in all likelihood, they read and respond to the scripts for her.

The new client is why Vic cannot get into a long conversation with the old guy about the election. The new client was meant to be here twenty minutes ago, with entourage. And yet the old guy is still holding the manila envelope and looking at Vic with his hail-fellow optimism. If he has to be removed by security, he will be.

"Baseball follower?"

Vic says nothing.

"Let me tell you, when I was a younger man, I used to go down to the spring training games. I can't stand the part of the year when there's no baseball. Winter is just a bunch of weeks where I could slip and break something. That's a real danger. So why don't I go down to Florida then?"

"I'm sure that Sandra would be happy to —"

Sandra has the headset on and seems to be making bulk dental appointments for preventive scaling.

"You followed the series. Am I right?"

Vic tries to move away a few steps, toward the opaque glass doors through which any visitor must pass upon emerging from the shiny maw of the elevator. Vic mumbles some inoffensive words about golf.

"I like the team in Queens because I believe in an underdog."

Vic Freese, of diminutive size and aspect like all the agents of Michael Cohen, not one of whom is over five foot nine, was not a presence on any athletic team in the entirety of his youth but does admit to certain agonizing years in the system known as Little League.

"Wasn't very good," he remarks.

This only buoys the messenger to say, "Let me see your swing. Just let an old fellow tell you a little bit about your swing."

"Give your script to the receptionist," Vic says.

People are excited to be in a major talent agency with a hundred-year tradition of serving the stars. W. C. Fields and Don Ameche and William Shatner have walked through these doors. At any moment talent might enter. A pint-size diva with a nosebleed and a stuffed bear the size of a sumo wrestler. She will demand to be given a chocolate milk and a contract for a sitcom, for which she expects a half million dollars per episode.

"I'm just delivering. Not to say a guy like me doesn't have stories to tell. Don't we all. We all have stories. Spicer is the name. Would you like to hear about how I met my wife?"

"I —"

"My wife died a few years ago of ovarian cancer. She played the harpsichord. Honest. The harpsichord. You get a lot of stories about the harpsichord come through here? No one plays the harpsichord. Do you know what a harpsichord is? A piano but without the loud part. I was a young man in the city, and my parents were from Europe. So was my wife's family. She came here, she could barely speak English, but she could play the harpsichord. How she settled on it, I'll never know. Anyhow, one time when I went to one of the big department stores in town, I think it was Gimbels, I heard in the lobby they had a recital on the harpsichord, and this musician was playing the music of J. S. Bach or somebody like that. It was a promotion. Arrow shirts. I sauntered in a leisurely way down to where the musician was playing. It was the beginning of that, oh, what is that piece called, you know, the —"

"Goldberg Variations?"

"Just the one!"

"Look, Mr. Spicer, I'm really waiting for an —"

The elevator sighs, as if weary at having to deposit yet another payload, and the heart of Vic Freese lodges up in his sinuses. And, as the hinges moan on the glass door that gives entrance to the Michael Cohen Agency, the sullen assistant of one of the other agents appears before him eating a muffin. Crumbs on her face like a skin condition. Joelle, the assistant in question, known to keep to herself, nods at Sandra and trudges up the spiral staircase to where the offices of the agents are laid out like a strand of defective chromosomes.

"Ever after, whenever I heard the music of the harpsichord, which was a lovely kind of music, I saw the auburn hair of this musician in my mind's eye, and I saw her crimson fingernails, polished up beautifully, and I thought this was the most magical thing I'd ever heard, and I thought all harpsichord music was like that, as magical as that, so afterward I went to any harpsichord performance in the tristate area. No matter who was playing, I went. I knew all the music for that instrument because that was the music of love. And I knew one day I would see my wife again, just by following the music. This was during the war. Did I say that? Did I say that I was about to be drafted? I was. You know what that means, that means the destruction of entire cities, like Dresden, which was where some of my cousins came from before they emigrated. I was stationed in Germany, the country that my family had fled. I was there at the end of the war, the mopping-up part. All I could think of over there in Germany was the music of the harpsichord. The music I had heard before I got drafted. I was sentimental about the music, is the truth. When I got back to the city, again I chased around the music of the harpsichord, all around; any time there was a concert, I was there, with this idea that one day I would find my girl. It was months and months, though, and I never did see her, and I just about gave up. I went to work in the garment district."

Freese hates to admit it to himself, but he does sort of want to know the end of the story, even though he will have to be in the company of Spicer's smell for at least another two minutes. A prospect made even more alarming because, with each passing second, it is more likely that the new client will walk through the door and she will see him talking to a foul-smelling septuagenarian with argyle socks. And this will be her first impression of the New York office. He turns to remark to Sandra that she had best take the package from Spicer, the messenger, because Mr. Spicer undoubtedly has further deliveries to make, but Sandra is now abandoning her post for her smoke break. He knows, because he has seen her out front, that she is part of the guilty crew on smoke break. And where is her temporary replacement?

"I was going to the ballpark at the same time, which you'd think was not a place where much music got played. Not a lot of classical music at the ballpark, except when an internationally known tenor came to town. But I was at the ballpark, watching the Brooklyn Dodgers. They were my boys. Eddie 'the Brat' Stanky, Pee Wee Reese, Cookie Lavagetto, and so on. What a team. They were heroes, even if they didn't make the play-offs that year. That was the year of Jackie Robinson, if I remember correctly. So one day I was watching my Brooklyn Dodgers, the greatest team ever in the history of New York City. And it happened to be the day of a promotion. They were actually giving out nylon stockings. Nylons were brand-new at the time. The loudspeaker announced the national anthem. And everyone was standing proud. By the way, did I mention that I have eleven grandchildren?"

He asks if Vic is a man with children. Vic is horrified at the possibility of giving away personal information to a guy who may potentially memorize statistical abstracts about baseball. But yes, he admits he has two children. They are little animated characters gamboling in Vic's mind's eye. Even in the midst of important meetings there is in Vic Freese the sound of his children demanding again to dance to mopey British pop songs from the eighties. Where is the voice in him that indicates that he must put first the needs of the new client? Why didn't he cultivate that voice? If there were a scale before him now, the new client would top out at an ounce and a half. And his children would weigh thirty-eight and forty-nine pounds, respectively. If his son were here, he'd still be saying the words *campfire song*, over and over, as he has been saying for three days now because Vic made a joke about campfire songs he had to sing as a kid, like "Charlie on the MTA," et cetera, and if his daughter were here, she, too, would be repeating it, *campfire song*, because she repeats whatever his son says, *campfire song, campfire song*, until the words become, through transmutation, precious. This idea of the sound of children's voices, so adorable and so memorable, is an evolutionary triumph.

"Who do you think was playing the national anthem on the harpsichord at the baseball stadium? Can you guess who it was? Like I said, the stadium was promoting attendance by the ladies, so they had a beautiful lady onto Ebbets Field to play the national anthem. She was a tiny little speck down there on the field. She told me later that they had to truck the harpsichord out first thing in the morning and then tune it, parked at home plate. They were using a brand-new public-address system at the park, and the national anthem was never so glorious. Maybe it was beautiful because there'd been the brawl the day before where

Stanky started throwing punches at Len Merullo. Or because the war was over. I only know it was wondrous, and it was played by the woman I was going to marry. And I had a hunch that she'd stay for the game. Because it was a great game. There was another brawl, but then Pete Reiser stole home, even though he was injured. He stole home seven times that season. And the boys pulled it out, two to one. I missed most of that, however, because I was waiting out in the parking lot. I was betting that my future wife would be wherever the harpsichord was, and, sure enough, she was standing by the truck in the parking lot. They had the game on the radio."

Sandra is back, and she distracts Vic from a portion of Spicer's heartfelt monologue, the monologue that Spicer has probably delivered nine times this morning. Vic's assistant is on the line. Sandra punches the buttons and holds up the handset. Vic abandons Spicer in the middle of telling him about selling the harpsichord after his wife died, the cost of tuning and upkeep for a harpsichord. Half attending to Spicer, half listening to the emergency. At first he thinks it's his wife, because when you are a father this is always your worry. One of your kids is banged up. But it's not his wife, it's the personal manager of the new client.

It takes him a moment to put it all together. A moment until the personal manager is in the middle of saying, ". . . going to be really unfortunate from a legal angle, not to mention from a, you know, publicity angle. So, anyway, she's going to go to Europe for a few weeks, to relax, maybe to record some new things, out of the spotlight. In fact, she's already at the airport. Sorry I didn't call earlier."

Vic says, "I can't believe what I'm hearing." By which he means that he wasn't listening to what he was hearing. The handset, still warm, smells like Binaca. The manager keeps saying "Ramon Martinez."

"Ramon Martinez? Who the hell is Ramon Martinez?"

Spicer, the messenger, is listening to the whole thing, and he chimes in. Soon everyone is saying "Ramon Martinez," as though it's the adult-world equivalent of the precious incantation *campfire song,* and Vic has it pieced together that the new client, now on her way to Paris, used to be the girlfriend of someone called Ramon Martinez, and this Ramon Martinez has done something truly awful, and Spicer is saying, "Diamond District, in the Diamond District," and so is Sandra, so Vic sees the tabloid headlines assembling in the developing tray of his consciousness, that sensational newspaper photo. He starts to see Ramon Martinez driving his car into the jewelry store on Sixth Avenue, cursing the Jews. A senseless crime for a senseless time perpetrated by a senseless guy. The new client was his girlfriend, the girlfriend of Ramon Martinez. Or, at least, the new client was photographed with him, the new client had him in her private company for a span of seven consecutive nights, *canoodling,* as the tabloids will have it. Therefore, the new client, it is revealed, was consort to this known perpetrator of a hate crime. Vic Freese should see this as a dark day for the agency, he should see this as an insurmountable difficulty for his stewardship of the fledgling television career of the new client; instead, in a way, all he can feel is relief. Now the streamers in the office are for his own celebration, the celebration of his ability to go home at 5:30 and do the thousand dances with his kids to New Order instead of beseeching producers and casting agents to think Lacey, Lacey, Lacey, Lacey. Lacey with her pierced navel, Lacey with her hiphuggers, Lacey with her thongs, with her constant traveling homunculus, also known as Neil the hairdresser. Lacey, friend of manslaughterers. He cradles the handset in its postderegulation console.

Spicer says, "Now let's see that swing."

Vic says, with a new optimism, "There was always some trouble driving off my back leg. I had fallen arches as a teen."

"That can be an asset, you know. Upper-body strength. Give me a look."

And Vic Freese, soon-to-be-former television agent, stands in reception with a messenger who smells like he's bathed in formaldehyde and drives off the right leg. Spicer puts the manila envelope on the coffee table in reception, where *Variety* and *Premiere* are stacked in perfect diagonal lines. Some nice photos hanging in this room, too. Fictional film stills by the woman who is in all her own photos. Black-and-whites. Also: tiger lilies in a vase. Right before Vic swings at the second imaginary pitch, an off-speed thing that tails in over the inside corner, he looks down at the envelope and he sees the name on it. Which is not his own name. Nor is it the name of any current employee of the Michael Cohen Agency. Actually, the name on the envelope is the name of a producer of his acquaintance, at a production company called Means of Production.

Spicer has a lot of corrections for Vic. Vic is turning his wrists too soon, he's letting his shoulder drop out. Spicer argues for lifting the front leg a little higher, planting it firmly. Spicer lets it be known that he could have been a scout if he'd wanted to, plenty of guys he's met at the minor leagues have told him so. He has the eye. Knows about the importance of offense. And Vic lets him draw a diagram, including right triangles, to which Spicer adds a little analysis about why pulling the ball is a failed strategy. And Spicer actually draws this diagram on the manila envelope that is now officially delivered to the wrong address, and Vic does not stop him.

Because he has an idea. Not that he has a lot of professional ideas, but he has this little idea. Like a middle-aged mathematician, these days he has to hoard any idea that comes his way. This idea is formulated as a question: What if there's something good in the manila envelope? What if there's something to know? Some tidbit of knowledge, some insider information in the manila envelope? Isn't it now an insider information world? The envelope, in fact, is coming from the competition, from International Talent and Media. Says so right there on the messenger form. Is this not access to the world of agents who take their jobs seriously, who perform? Is this not access to the seven habits of highly effective agents: evasiveness, impatience, deceit, hyperbole, manipulation, cruelty, and love of fellow man? This idea comes from his distant past, from the days of being a trainee, when steaming open the occasional letter and reading it was considered pragmatic. Once he was startled, in the men's room, while steaming open a letter, only to discover that some other junior agent, also clutching an envelope, was about to attempt to do the same thing. And though he believed he had left behind the steaming open of envelopes, here he is. Because Vanessa Meandro has failed on three occasions to return his call. And she sweats too much. Here he is receiving a package from ITM meant for Vanessa Meandro, some project he doesn't know about, and he thinks he'll just have a look. A quick peek. To see what is to be seen.

Vic thanks Spicer for the lesson, cutting off a tiresome digression on the big band tunes of the postwar era, and invites the old guy through the smoky opacity of the door.

"Come back again soon!" He waves. "And when you develop the harpsichord story into a script, think of us."

"You bet I will!"

Once Vic Freese has decided upon that habit of highly effective talent agents known as deceit, of which expedience is one substrategy, he realizes that everything is quieter than he expected. There's a recess of autovilifications in his skull, the voice that says *too short,* the voice that says *too wimpy,* the voice that says *too passive,* the voice that says *too soft.* All of these voices sound remarkably like various heads of departments at the Michael Cohen Agency, but they have all gone on smoke break with the global conspiracy of cigarette smokers, and here he is sitting on the couch, opening the envelope, in an HVAC silence where there is only the faintest stirring of oxygen pumped into the stillness of reception. Sandra call-forwards in a murmur.

He likes the title, *The Diviners,* and he likes the fact that the treatment calls for not one but three separate films. Three films, to be filmed at once, in locations all across the globe, and thus with sequels built in. A franchise. A branding opportunity. He likes it. He likes the ambition of the franchise. He likes that there are dozens of protagonists. He likes that every single race, religion, and ethnicity he can think of is in the project. He likes that the story has Hungary in it, actually, because he is partly Hungarian (his grandmother's mother). He likes the Gobi Desert. He likes exotic settings. There's a little scene about the conflict in the Falklands. He likes it.

In fact, *The Diviners* seems made to order for Vic Freese because his taste is old-fashioned. He recently attempted to watch that television show where young people are thrown together in a house in Boston or is it Austin, where they talk in direct address to the camera about the one guy who doesn't want do the dishes, and this guy's a bleeping bleeping bleep, et cetera. He has no patience for this kind of thing. He tried watching the game show about people who want to be millionaires. He has no aptitude for this. He believes Regis Philbin is a cloning experiment gone horribly wrong and that the introduction of Regis Philbin and his hair into the larger genetic pool will result in global calamity. Vic has tried to go to the movies at the little art houses, after work, but he hates independent films. He thinks independent film people smoke too much pot. And anyway there is no such thing as independent cinema anymore, it's a farm team for the big leagues, which is why he dislikes Vanessa Meandro, besides the fact that she sweats too much. She thinks she's better than him.

Vic's formative moviegoing experiences were epics. CinemaScope types of things. Deserts, world wars, voyages in outer space, biblical stories, dragons, armies of spear-throwers, stopmotion. These are the kinds of stories Vic Freese likes, the kind where it takes a year to film and there are calamities of fire and ice. The kind of films where extras lose limbs and entire villages have to be burned to the ground. Like *The Diviners*.

Based on a novel by Margaret Howe Hinckley Firestone. Must be a real name because it's so awful. It's like she killed off half a dozen husbands with poison-laced tureens of soup and kept all the names. Hey, wait. Didn't she write the fourth sequel to *Gone with the Wind*?

It's really good. It's really, really, really, really good. It's fresh. It's fantastic. It's the best treatment he's read in a year. It's big, it's subtle. It'll make you laugh. It'll make you cry. It'll make you leave the theater and throw up your arms in joy and kiss your best friend's wife. It'll make you want to sit and think for an hour. It'll make you want to call a friend and tell her all about it. It's a film for women because it has love in it. It's a film for men because it has war. It has the man-versus-nature theme that's so important according to a teacher he had in the ninth grade. It's a movie of such potential that it can't help but give Vic Freese another idea, and he's on a real streak this morning with the ideas. This additional idea is even better than the idea about reading the contents of the manila envelope: The new client would make a really good Nurit. Nurit is a character in *The Diviners*, the Jewish daughter of the shopkeepers in Budapest who falls in love with a Gypsy boy, Babu. A star-crossed-love kind of thing. What could be better? He can see her, with a dark wig on, wearing some kind of torn shirt, the curve of her silicone-enhanced C cup just visible beneath. Her pierced navel will come in sort of handy, too. She and her lover and her family will flee across the Caspian Sea on a raft. Her belly is perfect. Nurit, the devoted and pure daughter of the shopkeepers. Nurit will wash away the bloody public relations stain of Ramon Martinez.

Vic Freese gets up from the couch in the sweet calm of reprieve. He goes upstairs to visit the kids in photocopy.

8

That afternoon, Jeanine gets the order she's been dreading all day: Go deal with the Indian guy. He's in the empty office. No one wants to go in there.

Vanessa definitely won't go because Vanessa signs the checks. Madison won't go because she had to do these errands for two years. Once you're relieved of that responsibility, you work hard not to go back. Annabel won't go because there's this general hesitation about asking her to do any menial task. Thaddeus won't go because he's a movie star. His idea of gallant is trying to persuade you that you should go to his nephew's school play in his place. Ms. DiNunzio won't go because she's the accountant. Her desk is spotless.

That leaves Jeanine. The Indian guy has had the door closed all day. You can hear him chanting. Shiva must be a melancholy deity, if the chant is any evidence. Thaddeus makes jokes about it because he seems to want Jeanine to sleep with him again. But she's not doing it. After she sleeps with him she just goes back to the apartment that she shares with her girlfriend from college and she does her laundry. The transition from love to bleach is too violent. Thaddeus never returns her calls, and then he kisses the air by her cheek and explains about Shiva the destroyer, and that's supposed to be enough.

Movie executives are aroused by people without power. Read any manual. Everyone is turned on by the girl with nothing. Tenderness offered to the assistant ennobles he who offers. Doesn't matter if you abuse the girl for weeks at a time, doesn't matter if you make her use the plumber's helper to unplug the ladies' room down the hall. If you are nice to her for three minutes on her birthday, you are golden.

Vanessa comes out of her lair and steals a doughnut from a new bag. Vanessa waves in the direction of down the corridor. "Get your butt down there and see if Ranjeet is comfortable and has everything he needs."

It's because she's younger. It's because she's from the Southwest. It's because of the disfigurement. They feel pity for her because of the disfigurement, and then they treat her even worse. That's their kind of pity.

A cheap composite-wood door with a hollow core. This is what separates the chanting from the rest of Means of Production. She knocks tentatively. *Siva yeah, Siva yeah, Siva, Siva, Siva yeah.* Or that's how it sounds. She knocks again. She can hear him shifting in the space. At last, Ranjeet opens the door. Just wide enough for his face to appear in it.

"I'm supposed to come in here and help," Jeanine says. "Do you need help with anything?"

"What is it that you need help with?"

"I don't need help," Jeanine says. "I'm supposed to help you."

"I do not have time to help."

"No, I'm supposed to help *you,*" Jeanine says. She looks down the hall to where Annabel is typing. Annabel won't meet her eyes. Annabel is pretending that the exchange is not being overheard because Annabel only really cares about her screenplay and about getting a production credit somehow. Every indie guy that comes into Means of Production, even if he hasn't showered

in five days and has needle tracks, Annabel is all over him, covering this guy with friendly caresses, giving lots of tips about submitting his work, asking him if she can get him a cup of coffee.
Call any time, please.

Ranjeet laughs like a maniac. "Just making sport with you. Of
course. Please do come in." There is only the desk and chair. And
it's dark. On the north side, were Ranjeet to look out the window,
he could see the skaters on their way around the rink. He could
see the statue of Prometheus, firebringer. In a couple of weeks,
the Christmas tree. There's a guy whose job it is to go around the
country, in a subcompact, looking for just the right tree. He stops
at diners along the country roads. He gets a feel for the region.
There must be some intuitive, magical understanding to the
task. Hello, ma'am, would it be possible to take down the tree in
your yard? You will be handsomely paid.

Coverage all over the floor. Pages and pages of the stuff. Spilled
everywhere, like a gale has swept through. She picks up a crumpled
leaf. It says MM on it, which means it's Madison's. Adaptation of a
novel by Marie Callahan concerning Napoleon's exile to St. Helena
and a relationship he had with a stunning island lass. The lass is
obsessed with prisms and lenses. She convinces Napoleon that
prisms have a military application. Madison's final comment:

> Not really clear what prisms have to do with Napoleon,
> but they're a filmic device that, in the right hands, could be
> beautiful to look at. The second act, in which Elsa betrays
> Napoleon by signaling (with mirrors) to a British frigate
> about his plans for a return to France, is heartbreaking
> and surprising, especially since she's pregnant with his
> child. Too bad the story falls apart after that.

Ranjeet is reading it over her shoulder.

"I don't know what I am meant to do with these," he says.

"Sometimes you can find some good ones."

She sweeps up a half dozen pages from the floor. Genre: sci-fi/exploitation. Budget: one hundred million. Setting: Alpha Centauri. Reader: TG.

"Sometimes finished scripts get submitted, especially to Thaddeus. We like to read his coverage."

> The disembodied robot heads go to war against one another because each group suspects that another is guilty of passing secrets to the human slave population. Technology has given the robots the faults of small-town folks. Like envy and small-mindedness. Unfortunately, the dialogue resembles an interview with an East German shot-put expert. I'd rather develop a romantic comedy about dog walkers.

"Dog walkers?"

"You know, the people who are hired to walk other people's dogs?"

The Indian guy is staring deeply into her eyes, as though he read about this strategy in a manual about the business. She's tired. She has a lot of work to do. There's something more that she should be doing, and that's why she still has this job. There's always more to do, and there's always something she has done wrong. Vanessa is pissed, for example, because Jeanine wouldn't eat any of the doughnuts. And she messed up the thing with Kinesthesia Productions, where she was supposed to deliver a script at exactly five o'clock because if the script got there before five o'clock, then one of the embittered assistants at Kinesthesia would pass on it. They pass on everything. But if it got there *right at five o'clock,* then it would go to Biedermeier's country house in Rhinebeck with him. The embittered twenty-four-year-olds wouldn't have a chance to pass on it. Vanessa has threatened to fire her three times this week. And the Indian guy is looking at her in this way like he feels compassion about all of this and yet still wants to touch her ass.

He says, "Would you like to sit on the desk, please?"

"On the desk?"

"I am going to explain something about television. Which is why I am here. I am a person who understands this medium. I learned this in my country. I'm the teacher of the meaning of television in the West. Or, to put it another way: I am the guru of television. I intend now to begin explaining."

Afternoon light dances on the wall. Outside in the world all these people are in a frenzy about *chads*. Hanging. Perforated. The Indian guy doesn't know what a chad is and doesn't care. The Indian guy can't vote. Jeanine didn't vote because she didn't have time. She was scouring the soap scum out of the corners of her shower at home yesterday because it made her feel better about things. It's her parents' apartment, for occasions when they visit NYC, and it needs to be spotless. Her roommate keeps inviting her out for things. She won't meet anyone if she's always at the office or ridding the bathroom of soap scum. But she doesn't need to meet anyone when there is an action film star who tells her that she has great tits and begs her to let him please forgo the use of a condom.

Ranjeet has her by the hand. He holds her wrist as if it were spun glass. He leads her to the desk. Helps her up onto the edge of the desk. He says, in his accent, which has the honeyed syllables of a superior subcontinental education, that first of all there were cave paintings. The cave paintings were petroglyphs left behind for men to indicate that other men had once trod on this spot. And here were the things that these men saw. They saw that there were animals, they saw that there were tigers and mammoths and hyenas, and these were the petroglyphs that were left behind preserving the glories of the hunt. History so loves the petroglyph that it never vanishes from human image-making: how to capture a hyena, how to chase down a mammoth, large game slain on the veldt. Then there are the hieroglyphs, these come next, and of the hieroglyphs we know that there are pictures of men fighting against other men, that the northern tribes fought against the southern tribes, and then each of these in turn fought with the eastern and western tribes. We know how these tribes danced and how they loved, we know all these things from these pictures, these hieroglyphs. And now there is the knowledge of the petroglyphs, Ranjeet says, and the knowledge of the hieroglyphs. Every baby that is born is born with the knowledge preserved in these pictures. At the same time, however, there was a mistake which was the mistake of the alphabet — not a picture at all, but rather an emblem for certain kinds of grunts and moans that are made by men. All is made wrong by the historical turn toward the alphabet. All is disturbed by the alphabet. With the calligraphies of the Qur'an and its Arabic tongues, there are letters and sounds of beauty; they are almost like pictures for men to look at. These are of the surpassing beauty that we associate with the pictograms of the Asian tongues. Pictograms were beautiful, and the writers wrote of cranes and bears in the forest and the archers hunting down the bears. The beauty of these pictograms created in the minds of men in China and Japan and Korea ten thousand inventions. They left behind their pictorial account of the noodle, and this learning was transmitted to the men and women who came after and who carried with them the pictures from before, the petroglyphs, the hieroglyphs, the erotic pictures painted on Greek urns, all these were contained in the pictures of the painters, the painters who introduced perspective into the world of flat drawings, the painters of cathedral ceilings, with their lenses and prisms. Then, when the time was right, these painters spawned the photograph; the photograph sprang from the obsessions of cathedral painters, you see, and the photograph was good. These photographs used the very same techniques favored by the painters of petroglyphs. Photographs of untouchables lining the streets of the city, photographs taken by imperialists, these indicate that everything is possible now, and any one man or woman may be an artist of vision, and everyone can remember the history of his city, his culture, his nation, and it is the same with the magic of cinema, where now pictures and music and stories and paintings are all made one, in this special Platonic cave; the greater the audience, the larger the audience, the more memorable the stories, better even than photographs, better even than cathedral paintings. Meanwhile, somewhere else, somewhere far distant but adjacent, there is a different story being told: the tale of written words, words on the page in alphabets. This tale is a sickness. A beautiful sickness, a way of specialized meanings that must be interpreted by monks in little cells with bars on the windows, arguing about this and that, what does this word mean, this word means that you must not eat chickens on Sunday, and this word means that if no one hears, a tree has not fallen. This is a beautiful sickness, a beautiful splitting in half of hairs, and many millions of people in cold northern regions fall ill with it, as with the illness known as plague. This is not the true way because these tales of the alphabet have no light in them. These tales are produced in dank chambers where a large ugly machine goes around and around, smudging grease on pulped boards that are preserved by monks with failing eyesight. No, as you can now see, the true way must be the way of bringing light to all the people, and there is but the one way to do that. There is the one way that cinema becomes the gift to all people of all learning and all teaching, and all beauty, and all truth, the preserved history of all mankind. There is but one way. And, furthermore, that way is the way of the little box that comes into your home or your airport waiting room or your hospital room. That way is the way of television, which is the one light, the light in the house, the light in the darkness, the light of the satellite dish, the light of the dishwallahs of India, the light of the rural places coming out of the darkness, the light of television that brings together all men and women in red bathing suits on a shore, the light of a talking horse, the light of a red-haired woman and her bandleader husband when they argue and she crosses her eyes, the light of an army hospital and its surgeons during the war, the light of a special team of policewomen who are like the three seductive fates, the light of unshaven policemen from a city in Florida, the light of a family of oil barons, the light of four women who sleep with many men and talk about it in cafés, the light of all persons who wish to be millionaires. This is the true story of men and women of today. This is where the myths and stories for the future must be sown. This is where all that needs to be told is told about the heroism of great wrestlers and beautiful women. This is where the stories are told about the houses of rich people and about the plastic surgery transformations of these people into gods. The stories are not told in the consumptive sickness of literature, of words on a page. That is for people who are dying and are sick and nauseated and are vomiting up all their hatred. You can see them dying, inch by inch, because they are homosexuals and are having sex with devices, which is pleasurable, which passes the time, but it is not the way that is delighted in by the gods. This film that you are going to make now, it must be the way of light and the aesthetic vision, it must be television, with its scantily clad sirens, and not in the movie theater that sells cappuccino instead of candies and popcorn. That is what I have been brought here to tell you, Ranjeet intones.

"And now," he says, "I must tell you about *Roots.*"

"Wait," Jeanine says, seeing at last a chance to get a word in somehow and hoping, thereby, to get out of the office. "Just how do you know all this?"

"I thought it up while I was driving for the car service."

"Your —"

"My car is outside. Parked in an illegal spot."

"What you're saying is very powerful. But actually I —"

She can hear some commotion outside now and she uses it as an opportunity to open the door. In the hall, Vanessa is standing over Annabel's desk ridiculing her, while the others, as usual, pretend to be knee-deep in work. "And the treatment lands, by accident, somehow *by accident,* on the desk of Vic Freese. And he calls me, telling me he has some treatment, says it's called *The Diviners,* and what a tremendous piece of work it is, this treatment, have I seen this treatment? And everyone is talking about this treatment. And I don't even have this particular piece of paper. Which has now been promised to me for what, three days? What do I pay you for? To sit here and talk on the phone with your friends about how horribly you are treated at the office, where your boss actually wants you to get the material before somebody else, some agent, because that's how you make the deal? You make the deal *before* the other companies, not after them. If you make the deal *after* the other companies, you don't make any money or there is no deal at all. Yeah, you are treated so badly, because you have to sit around and talk to the eleven managers and agents of some actor who wants you to come out with him to some bar tonight where supermodels are going. Horrible. Your boss actually wants you to do your *job,* how astonishing, because that's the only way your boss can meet the payroll so that you can actually pay your rent and pay your taxes and I can continue to run a business —"

It wouldn't be a day at Means of Production if one of the women there was not weeping. And Vanessa, waving a stale doughnut, looks over at Jeanine, who darkens the doorway of the empty office that is now the office of the theory and practice of television at Means of Production, and she evidently sees the half-light and the disheveled participants in the discussion of the theory and practice of television, the history of the medium, and she does a double take. But now Ranjeet simply reaches around Jeanine and closes the door. There is the sound of a siren going down Fifth Avenue. A convoy of rush hour buses.

"Think about the birth of the man called Kunta Kinte, in the program entitled *Roots.* When before in this medium which is called television has the birth of a black man such as this been as reverently treated as it is in the program entitled *Roots?* The father holds an infant up to the stars, and it is like the exaggerated dance sequences of Gene Kelly or Fred Astaire. It is the false-hood that tells a truth about the history of your nation which has never been told, which is the truth about a child born in Africa, not even born in this country, a child who didn't even choose to come to this country but who came here forcibly. It could be the most important birth in the history of the country, the birth of little Kunta Kinte, even though he is a fictionalized personage! Certainly the most important birth on television! The woman crying out in pain, pushing, pushing, and then the little child be-ing held up by the father, Kunta Kinte being held up to the stars. And then there is the youth of Kunta Kinte, and into this is cut very falsified footage of wild animals, a cheetah running in a field which is clearly not the field in which Kunta Kinte is later seen running. Or there is a monkey standing on a tree limb at the mo-ment that the young Kunta Kinte is about to be captured by a slave trader. All these many lapses, these mistakes in the editing of the material, and the misplaced comic moments of the program called *Roots*. However, above all this is the slave trade, above all this is the instant of the sale into slavery of Kunta Kinte, because no matter the aesthetics of the moment, all American stories as-pire to this condition, which is the condition of the saga. All sto-ries aspire in this direction, and all corporations aspire toward the sale and reproduction of this saga. Nothing could be more Amer-ican than this, and nothing could be more international than what is American, nothing could be more human; there are no nation-alities, there are only ethnicities and corporations, there is only the military and its collateral damage, and the land of profitabil-ity and cowboys and slave trading."

Ranjeet is so excited by the details as he spins them out that he paces the room, stepping on the coverage on the floor in his shiny sneakers, which are knockoffs from a large retailer. It's hard to tell under the beard how old he is. Jeanine thinks thirty-four, but he carries himself like he's thirty years older. There *is* something sexy about him. Again, he takes her wrist as he speaks of LeVar

Burton. LeVar Burton, who plays Kunta Kinte. And when he does, he can feel her disfigurement. She knows that he knows. She has her sleeves pulled down, of course. As she always does. Even in the summer.

Vanessa comes in. She had to eventually. Vanessa bustles in and suddenly the lights are on, and Ranjeet is picking up the coverage from everywhere on the floor.

"Give me the update, you guys."

Circles under her eyes. It's one of those days when you have to feel pity for her, which is the compassion on which the abuser depends. Circles under her eyes, disarranged hair, a shirt that's badly tucked in, a missing earring.

"He's giving me a lecture on the miniseries," Jeanine says.

"Hey, wait a second. I want *everyone* to hear this."

Everyone winces at the advent of team strategy meetings. They overcome Vanessa with a migrainous instantaneity. Though it can be said that Vanessa's attention deficit problems do prevent lengthy attempts at these or any other corporate time wasters. She leads Ranjeet, babbling, out into the hall and into the conference room with the arty glass table that Jeanine herself ordered from a catalogue. The others gather in the hall.

"Madison. Jeanine. Over here."

"Like we don't have more important things to do."

"Shut up, Madison."

Annabel, wiping away leftover tears, bringing up the rear. Thaddeus Griffin waves from his phone, points at the mouthpiece. Vanessa beckons him in, but it's nothing doing. Thaddeus won't appear in groups of women, Jeanine thinks. Too much potential for cross-referencing. When the women and the guy in the turban are all assembled in the conference room, looking at a glass bowl with individually wrapped Tootsie Rolls in it, Vanessa starts in.

"We've been educated in the American academy. We're the best and brightest. But that stops now. As of this moment, we're going to be the stealth intelligence unit, learning about this medium that we don't know anything about. Nod if you understand. We're going to learn about the medium of shamelessness. That's what Ranjeet is here to help us do. We're going to infiltrate. We're going to bite the hand that feeds us. I want to know who programs *Entertainment Tonight* and I want to know who the reporters are for *Inside Edition.* I want to know the ratings results for every appearance of Elizabeth Taylor in the past five years. The *Gilligan's Island* reunion special. Or anything having to do with Michael Jackson. The ratings for all his appearances. The Larry Hagman character. Who thought that up? Shooting him? If there's the opportunity to show women with enhanced boobs in swimsuits, let's do it. If there's the opportunity to show married women climbing into the beds of men just for money, perfect. Take lots of notes on whatever Ranjeet says. As long as he says it. Think about syndication. Just this morning I've been discussing syndication and its revenue streams with my lawyers. What I mean is, it's time to take the company to the next level. The level where the money is. I've put in all this work and you guys have put in all this work, we've plotted and dreamed, and what do we have to show for it? We've got the undivided attention of the kids with blue hair, that's our audience, dabblers, kids who use lunch boxes for their purses. We've got the bald poets with their art historian wives and PBS tote bags; we've got the film school students. And that's nice. I never thought we could even get this far, but the company needs to grow, needs to rocket toward the light . . ."

Jeanine can feel her abdomen beginning to twitch as if inside there's one of those monster larvae about to bust out of her entrails and rocket toward the light. Looking around the table at Madison, who's gazing critically at her fingernails, at Annabel, staring vacantly out a window, Jeanine can tell that Vanessa has finally driven the locomotive off the rails.

"I have to go to the hospital in Brooklyn right now. I mean, you guys know that my mother is back in the hospital, right? I'm

trying to keep the company going without any interns. Can anyone explain to me why we keep losing the interns? And why are
we in this totally awful office space? Why can't we get an office
downtown? Anyway, I'm trying to keep the company going and
now I have this, this situation with my mother. So that's what I
have to show for all the hard work. I have to look to the future;
I have to look to the possibility of a more dependable revenue
model. Which is why I have gone to great lengths to hire Ranjeet,
who comes highly recommended from the University of Delhi.
He's an important international thinker on the cinema and television from one of the largest, most successful film markets on the
globe. He's personally acquainted with Umberto Eco and Edward Said. So here he is, Ranjeet Singh, in case you haven't met
him yet, to help plot our revolution in the medium of television."

Even though everyone is desperate to get back to their desk,
desperate to pretend that Vanessa is not putting a third piece of
bubble gum in her mouth, Jeanine has to ask a question. She
even knows it's awful, but she asks anyway.

"What about reality television? Reality programming? Like
that show about . . . the one where everyone's going to an island,
and they just, they get rid of people? Because people, they just
can't make it on the island, like —"

"Ranjeet?"

All eyes turn to the expert.

"Reality programming," Ranjeet starts, hands in prayer position, "is a type of programming which comes from Europe. It is
the revenge of Europeans on the American dramatic series. People perform crazy actions. They might perhaps eat a rat. Persons
collaborate on the eating of rats, preparations for rats, which
herbs to use. You might have a program about persons doing
these things. You might perhaps find persons in a house together
with a lot of money, and you could see who tries to find the
money first, and the house has many rats in it. Or you could put
people in a house together, and one of these persons is having sex-

ual relations with another. What these programs lack is a mythology. You simply have people and money and sexual relations, and you have no mythology. Consider in the program called *Roots* the moment when the captain of the slave ship, who is incidentally played by Mary Tyler Moore's boss, and this captain of the slave ship is not comfortable with the duties of the slave ship. He finds that he cannot believe in the mission of the slave ship, but nonetheless he is contracted to bring the ship into port. The evil first mate brings first a *wench,* which is his word for the young African woman with exposed breasts, and he says, 'Captain, perhaps you'll be wanting a belly warmer,' or something to this effect, and the captain must decide whether he is equipped to have this unclothed African woman overnight in his cabin. So the captain is morally conflicted by the endeavor of slavery, and yet when there is the beautiful woman with the exposed breasts in his cabin, when he is lord of the high seas, he cannot refuse. This is mythology. This is the story that is equal to a hundred other stories. The myth of national origins is rich in a way that the reality television camera cannot be."

"People get stupid in front of the camera," Vanessa says. "People begin to grovel. People begin to lie. People begin to pander. That's the big festering paradox of reality programming."

Madison rallies briefly. "Reality programming. I mean, I think it's just the programming of sluts. If you met any of these girls who are on those shows, they're all sluts. And I'm betting the guys in the creative departments at the networks, they're just trying to find ways to meet girls who are sluts. We don't really have any sluts here, right? So I figure we don't really have anyone who understands the programming for sluts. So can we please not work on those shows? Because I don't want to look at myself in the mirror and think I could have worked on getting distribution for that new Iranian film, but instead I worked on a show about the world record holder for hooking up with guys."

"Thanks for waking up, Madison."

Then, when everyone is filing out, looking as if they won't be able to work another day at Means of Production, Ranjeet stops Jeanine in front of his empty office. His face glows with the look of a man who has a complicated future. "I have a son, and he is the most extraordinary boy, and I would like very much for you to meet my son. Perhaps you would come to dinner with my family?"

9

Preliminary reports, according to detectives, indicate that the victim is an employee of an art gallery in the Chelsea section of Manhattan. Specifically, the victim works at the gallery called 905 on West Twenty-fourth, a gallery known primarily for mixed-media work. The detectives have called the gallery and they have spoken to the owner. This owner remarked that the victim left work early on Thursday for a doctor's appointment and was not seen in the office after 4:00 PM. The victim, according to the employer and others, is Asian and is described as of slight build, attractive, with brown hair and chestnut highlights. The victim is described as wearing, at the time of the attack, clothes dark in color: black tights, black skirt, midthigh, black leather jacket. Age: twenty-six. The victim was educated at a private college in Pennsylvania. The victim's employer also indicated that the victim has been embarked for some months on gathering material for an exhibition of contemporary African American mixed-media work. The victim, according to interviews, has a considerable critical reputation. She is admired both in the office and in the field generally.

The parents of the victim were notified as soon as was feasible,

after contact information was located among the personal effects
of the victim. These calls were placed by detectives after notification by personnel at the hospital. The parents are currently staying in a hotel in midtown and are visiting their daughter during
visiting hours. They have given detectives permission to read the
address book and other effects of the victim found in a shoulder
bag at the crime scene. This address book contains seven numbers for local doctors. The parents have indicated that their
daughter was recently under the care of a clinical social worker.
Calls to the social worker were inconclusive. However, a call to
the victim's orthopedist has apparently confirmed a visit earlier
in the day. The office of the orthopedist is located in the Murray
Hill district of Manhattan, on Thirty-third Street between Second and Third Avenues. The victim suffers from a repetitive
stress complaint and was fitted for a wrist brace.

Detectives believe that the victim was making her way to the
library. Records show that she has been a frequent user of the resources of the Mid-Manhattan branch library in recent months.
The victim may have been doing research relevant to the curato-
rial project described above. According to detectives, the point of
origin for this trip was the Murray Hill office of the orthopedist.
The victim was admitted to Bellevue Hospital at 6:13 PM on
Thursday evening, so the time of attack would fall between 5:00
and 5:30, when midtown swells with pedestrian and vehicular
traffic. Thus, the volume of eyewitness accounts.

The construction site where the incident took place is on the
corner of Third Avenue and Fortieth Street. Under normal circumstances, a construction site is secure. Permits for construction at this address were up to date. However, there were reports
that early in the construction process, the Third Avenue site was
in dereliction of union agreements, such that a large rubber
rodent was deposited at the site, indicating an ongoing union
action. In recent weeks, disputes with unions were apparently resolved amicably. It follows that the site could not be easily bur-

gled for the purposes of obtaining a weapon, and yet, according to eyewitnesses, this is exactly what happened.

Eyewitnesses describe the perpetrator as male, African American, riding a bicycle. Most witnesses believe that the suspect is a bicycle messenger because he was apparently wearing bicycle racing apparel, that is, nylon shorts. This clothing, according to witnesses, was dark in color, except for a red bandanna worn around the neck. The bicycle itself had few distinguishing marks. It may have been stolen. The bicycle messenger was riding quickly, perhaps thirty-five miles an hour, when he came upon the victim and used his weapon, a brick or cinder block, on the back of the head of the victim as he passed her, knocking her to the ground. The brick or cinder block was carried away from the scene. The assault is therefore described as blunt force trauma, probably with a conventionally sized brick. Witnesses report the suspect then going east on Forty-first Street, against traffic, leaving the scene. The victim rolled to one side, with her brace parallel to the curb, as shown in the drawing. She was bleeding heavily. In no account was there verbal exchange between suspect and victim. The victim, who fell into unconsciousness almost instantly, did not have time to register surprise.

Pedestrians notified 911, which dispatched the ambulance. The paramedics arrived within three minutes, from Bellevue. They do not report any recollection of passing a bicycle messenger on their way to the scene. Nor are there reports of a man on a bicycle, in that area or otherwise, carrying a brick. In all likelihood, the perpetrator fled the immediate environs of the attack, perhaps into East River Park or even onto the subway.

The victim was unconscious when paramedics arrived. As of Friday morning, the victim is stabilized. The prognosis for recovery, according to physicians at the hospital, is guarded but positive. Full recovery of memory and brain function is possible but not certain at this time. At present, the victim, when conscious, which is only occasionally, is suffering from long-term and short-term memory lapses.

There is no evidence of rape or sexual trauma at the time of the attack. Indeed, if the accounts of witnesses are credible, there could not have been time for sexual battery. Parents report that the victim was known to date young men but is not at present involved with any male romantic or sexual partner on an ongoing basis. Her last significant romantic attachment occurred with a male, aged thirty-nine, but he and the victim separated about six months prior to the attack. This particular romantic partner is described as a painter of Caucasian ethnicity, living in Greenpoint, Brooklyn. Detectives are investigating the painter to rule out conspiracy and have made contact. This romantic partner works in galleries in Manhattan (including the 905 Gallery) as a transporter and hanger of artworks prior to openings and exhibitions in local galleries, so it is unlikely that he was in the neighborhood in question at the time of the attack. He works afternoons and evenings. Parents of the victim describe her as basically a "normal young woman" in matters of romance. She had boyfriends in college and was serially attached to men in her early twenties. In some of these cases, according to the parents, she was hoping the relationships would "go on longer" than they did. Other inquiries into the personal life of the victim are pending. The possibility of an attack by a disgruntled lover is not ruled out but at the present moment seems unlikely.

Police officers and detectives thereafter inquired of the parents whether the victim was a known frequenter of drug locations or a user of illegal drugs. The mother of the victim, to the marked discontent of her husband, indicated that the victim had occasionally smoked marijuana in college and that on at least one occasion the victim had marijuana-related anxiety, including feelings of depersonalization and alienation. Her experiments in this direction were short-lived. No other illegal drugs were known to be used by the victim. Acquaintances from the victim's workplace also professed no knowledge whatever of any drug problems. Nor were any prescription medications — OxyContin, Vicodin — obtained illegally by the victim. It's therefore possible to rule out an attack related to a drug deal or an assault otherwise perpetrated by a drug dealer of any kind. In fact, the general demeanor and biography of the victim do not suggest fraternizing with dealers or crime syndicates or known criminal elements.

It's worth noting, however, that among the doctors listed in the address book of the victim is a psychopharmacologist. The detectives assigned to the case do indicate that the victim was being prescribed a "cocktail" of medications, including an antidepressant, a sleep aid, and an antianxiety medication, BuSpar. Some of these substances were found in the shoulder bag of the victim. All the prescriptions were legally obtained. Preliminary observation indicates that the victim is now and always has been "very thin," her weight being just over a hundred pounds. Whether this information bears upon the attack is doubtful.

According to the above information, any public attack by the most likely constituencies — lovers or dealers of controlled substances or employees of organized crime syndicates, et cetera — is unlikely. The most credible theory, therefore, would suggest random attack. The perpetrator, according to this theory, was unknown to the victim at the time of the attack. Random attacks, exclusive of sexual assaults, where they have occurred in the past (as in the Eighty-eighth Street attacks or the recent Fort Greene assaults), are usually tied to the homeless population or to other persons disenfranchised from the workforce.

Detectives have also spent some time studying an important piece of evidence among the effects of the victim, namely the victim's diary of the last few months, which is described as a book of unlined paper with a black leather binding, such as would be available in any number of high-end stationery stores downtown. Obviously, obtaining this information from a person who is likely to recover either partially or entirely is a sensitive matter. At the prompting of the father, however, who is described as extremely emotional about his desire to bring to justice the perpetrator of the crime, the diary was made available in this developing case.

The victim's handwriting is small and precise, cursive, bending slightly to the right. Some letters are tall and willowy, as if blown across the page by a gust from the margin.

Some of the victim's remarks concern the weather and the pleasantness of temperatures still in the sixties in the first week of November. Some remarks concern films currently in release, including what is described as a tirade on the subject of the film known as *Pay It Forward*. The film, it should be noted, is not without favor among detectives. The victim, however, is apparently disappointed with the career choices of the lead actor in the film. To continue, the victim can't believe that she agreed to go to this movie entitled *Pay It Forward*. The people who made the film "should be towed out to sea on a barge," according to the diary. The victim writes favorably about other film releases.

One section of the diary, it should be said, was for the detectives kind of a page-turner. This portion of the diary particularly concerns the untimely death of an acquaintance of the victim. This acquaintance, notwithstanding the efforts of many in the peer group of the victim, drifted off into the "demimonde" of addiction, traveling in fast and more dangerous crowds in Manhattan, later adventuring in the crack houses of the outer boroughs, where a young gay man is likely to get into a lot of trouble. The victim describes the addicted young man in affectionate terminology, despite her exasperation at his relapses and his inability to show up for work at a competing gallery. He was, according to the diarist, "the most beautiful boy I've ever seen," and he was given to thrift store clothes that impeccably mimicked the current designers. Still, he "drifted away like a helium balloon drifts away," prompting some of the best writing in the diary. Who can understand why the scourge of relapse happens? asks the diarist.

Who can understand self-destruction? For a time, an addict will seem as if he or she might make a go of life and then, inexplicably, just when things seem to be going better, just when "his boyfriend starts to like him again, then *wham,*" the addict relapses. Which is something that the detectives have encountered many times themselves. It is a routine part of their job, and they are all but inured to it, this treachery and self-destruction. This inexplicable nature of relapse occurs to the diarist when the body of her friend is found in the Bronx, and his parents come from Durham, North Carolina, to his funeral, his parents, of whom the diarist observes that they "would never accept him for who he is." Oddly, this body, too, was subjected to blunt force trauma, according to pathologists, and perhaps sexually violated. All of this is not "something to be learned," reports the diarist. This is something to "accept the way you accept that winter will come."

It's interesting to the detectives, combing the diary for clues about the victim's own assault, that the death of the friend in the Bronx was not recent. In fact, the death in the Bronx dates back almost eight months.

Other entries in the diary amount to notes about art that the victim was considering for her group show of work by contemporary African American artists. It is likely that some of these notes were in fact taken on the day of the attack, when the victim was visiting the library. The victim feels great solidarity with persons of color, perhaps owing to the fact that the victim's parents are second-generation Chinese American. The victim observes that her interest in this art by African American artists is not "ghetto exotica," as in the cases of graffiti artists invited into the art establishment through tokenism. Of African American artists attempting work inside the traditions of art history, the diarist writes that "pretty much no one gives a shit about them or their work, unless they are putting slave imagery into their paintings or something obvious that will reassure an elite white audience." For the show planned by the diarist, she has assembled work by painters and sculptors and mixed-media artists who simply "happen to be African American" — artists who don't shy from "symbology about African American experience" but who are also about "paint handling, texture, and luminosity." She would include these painters, the diarist remarks, "because they're good, because they're moving, because they're important, because they're vital, energized, beautiful, lasting."

A list of such painters and photographers and multimedia artists follows, none of whose names mean anything to the detectives on the case, who, at any rate, are reading through the diary in one sitting and are eating doughnuts at the same time, while also talking about the trade that sent Patrick Ewing to Seattle.

One of these artists, however, did come in for more attention than others. The name of the artist in question is Tyrone Duffy. Duffy, according to highlights from a curriculum vitae included in the journals, is known, to the extent he is known at all, for shows and artwork from the early 1980s. Shows at galleries associated with what the victim describes as the East Village gallery movement. After some brief success in this East Village environment, a success that the artist didn't parlay into wider recognition, Tyrone Duffy, according to the diarist, decided to attempt to get an advanced degree in philosophy from the University of Minnesota, a degree he never completed, dropping out of the program in 1987, after which he moved to Hoboken. According to the diarist, Tyrone Duffy "falls off the edge of the world" in 1993.

What the victim likes about the early work of Duffy, which she first saw at the apartments of some friends, is that it manifests the "d.i.y. energy" of the work of the early 1980s, the violence, smarts, and sincerity of that time. What she likes is the desperation of the work, the sloppiness. What she likes, it seems, is the idea of Tyrone Duffy, an artist of some modest success who completely disappears, an artist who knew the art world legends of a certain period but who then vanished entirely. The idea only improves when the victim finds someone, a mutual friend, still in contact with Duffy. This friend reports that Duffy was diagnosed with bipolar disorder or some similar complaint. He was institutionalized on one occasion. He was not close with his family, who apparently lived in New England.

In late September, the diarist began to attempt to contact Duffy, having learned that he was now working in midtown as a bicycle messenger. The detectives take note of this sudden appearance in the diary of the apparent or alleged profession of the victim's attacker, but they decide to continue to read into the diary before presuming that the two bicycle messengers are one and the same.

What they learn about next is so-called outsider art, very popular in some circles. And what outsider art is *not*, according to the diarist, "is art." It is not like Michelangelos and Titians with their assistants and their papal commissions. Because art is a "discretionary choice" where "mimetic skill and distortions of mimetic skill" serve a higher purpose, that is, artistic vision. And outsider art, made largely by people in institutions and by shut-ins with paraphiliac inclinations, does not manifest "discretionary choice," in part because the artists do not have "mimetic skill" in the first place and also because they can often be disabled in the perception of reality.

Much of this material seems to come from a book on imagery in the artwork of disturbed adolescents by Deborah Weller, PhD, for which the victim submitted call forms at local libraries on several occasions.

"Painting by bipolar patients in an inpatient environment," according to Weller, as quoted by the victim:

> is noteworthy for wildness of color, for flamboyance. But it
> is also restless and reflective of disordered thinking, more
> so than in the work of other adolescents, and as such it has
> a compensatory aspect, a reifying and ordering disorder,
> enough so that it's hard, in all cases, to look at this work
> simply as art, as a commodity for aesthetic consumers. It

is, therefore, devoid of aesthetic choice. The aesthetic strategies indicated in this work are, on the contrary, *reflexive*. Can art that is made reflexively still reside in the same category with art made according to discretionary choice?

Weller then speaks to the art of elephants in captivity, and gorillas. What do we know about the intentionality of these artists? Is intentionality a condition of front-brain function, Weller asks, unhindered by disorder of any kind? If so, art is rather limited in terms of its effects and strategies. Art by bipolar artists is noteworthy for connections being made between disparate agencies or entities, connections suggestive of conspiracy. Members of families, for example, are considered agents of foreign powers. Teachers or clergypersons are considered secret members of fraternities and possessed of Masonic insights into the workings of the world. For bipolar adolescents, according to Weller, the discovery of these conspiracies can even be joyful, as in the case of one adolescent painter who produced in a matter of weeks a number of diagrams, painted on very large canvases, detailing connections between multinational corporations and the regimes of twentieth-century despots like Pol Pot and Idi Amin. This painter was ecstatic about his output and slept little, if at all, during the period of its creation. As Weller states:

> Perception of *entanglement*, my word for a particular set of symptoms that appears frequently in paintings by adolescent bipolar sufferers, precedes formulation of aesthetic strategy, and since *entanglement* is merely a symbolically exaggerated representation of the fact that the patient is connected to other people and feels, in this connection, exaggerated sets of human emotions, is it correct to interpret canvases featuring *entanglement* as types of discretionary choice, or rather as diagrams that offer possibilities for self-understanding or even recovery? Perhaps in this way,

as in the automatic activity of the surrealist movement, so-called genuine artwork, art in the category of the high, begins to become more meaningful as it recoils from aesthetic strategy and moves closer to the compensatory and therapeutic artwork of disturbed adolescents.

The victim, in her diary, uses these and other passages from volumes by Weller in order to talk about a particular series of artworks by Tyrone Duffy, apparently made toward the end of his productive life as an artist. These paintings, according to the victim, are known in some circles as the Thirst Paintings, at least among collectors of the work, though this title was not of the artist's own design. Thirst here coheres with a theme noticed by the victim in Weller's book:

Thirst is a frequent symptom of some of the medication used in treatment of these adolescents, both in outpatient clinics and in the hospital. Antidepressant medications, as well as lithium, used in the treatment of bipolar disorder, have dry mouth as a side effect. Inpatient psychiatric treatment centers frequently make sure that their clients have plenty of water to drink.

But, Weller goes on, as quoted by the diarist:

Doesn't this thirst stand for something else, too? Doesn't it stand for a quality that all adolescents have? A desire for religiosity and spiritual experience? A desire to be a part of adult life? A desire to have the self-determination of adults? Especially when confined in hospital, when self-determination is at a minimum, the adolescent thirsts, and so it's no surprise that this parched quality is often a part of their dialogue and even of their artwork.

Duffy's Thirst Paintings, according to the victim, here also compiling stories told by others, involve defaced works by contemporary novelists, wherein certain words are highlighted, as if to indicate patterns concealed in the work, patterns known only to Duffy himself, and although there is no indication that Duffy intended thirst to be the only theme of the work, he did, on every occasion, highlight the word *thirst*. The paintings themselves consist of paint applied with a "random energy" to leaves from books shellacked, varnished, or otherwise affixed to canvases. The paint then simultaneously conceals and reveals the secret texts, according the style known as palimpsest, so that, again, "*entanglement* is the secret being revealed, a secret web of stuff, people, themes, places, lives," according to the diarist.

In middle October, the victim apparently made contact with Tyrone Duffy himself. The meeting took place in a Polish coffee shop in the East Village known for serving twenty-four hours a day. Her first impression, she says, is that Duffy is "completely sexy." And she goes on to ask, with intuition about her own motivation, whether it's desperation that looks desirable or some inherently attractive quality.

His eyes are really far away, though I'm not even sure what I mean by that. He has trouble making eye contact. He never seems like he's looking at me at all. There's never any of that seesawing of glances you get when men are doing their seductive thing. I never look away and then catch him looking at me. But especially if I say anything about the work, about having seen some of the work, he doesn't seem to want to hear about it. His voice is a whisper, pretty much, and he mostly refuses to talk about things. He says, "Well, that was all a long time ago, and I haven't done anything like that lately." He says he just reads now. Says he started reading the books in those paintings, instead of painting on them, and that he regrets defacing some of those books. Says he figured he'd go to graduate school, where he could read more, and then he stopped going to classes. I asked him what he was reading, because it would keep the conversation alive, and he said Frantz Fanon and Michel Foucault and Edward Said. I'm not really sure he has stopped painting. I think he hasn't and just says it.

The conversation between the victim and Duffy does not last that long because Duffy claims to need to return to work. When asked his profession at present, he looks at the victim skeptically, as if she should be able to tell. The victim indicates that a certain inexplicable horror overcomes her when she first learns that Duffy is now working as a bicycle messenger because it seems so hard. It seems to the victim that the economics of fame, however brief, however long ago, should have inoculated him against a marginal working-class job. And so she is simply hoping it is not true. However, it is true. At this point the victim asks Tyrone Duffy the one question she has been intending to ask him all along, which is simply: "Do you have any of the old work left?" To which Duffy, according to the diary, responds, "I got a whole mini–storage box of that stuff. Not that I've been in there in a while." After which he makes an exit, "like a cavalier on his mount." The victim reports that her feelings afterward were like "love feelings, all confused, like he was going to start affecting my appetite. I think it's just the work, or the proximity to the work. Maybe to talk to Tyrone is to take my own job seriously, whether he can take his work seriously or not."

At this point, the detectives would like to observe that it is a salutary development for the case that the victim is such a prodigious diarist. If the perpetrator were aware that a diary existed, the perpetrator would certainly have taken steps to prevent its being obtained by law enforcement. But the perpetrator didn't remove the diary from the person of the victim, nor did the perpetrator take any money, nor did the perpetrator exert any sexual control over the victim. The perpetrator, who may have been on a bicycle, simply carried a brick in his hand until, for whatever reason, he saw the back of the head of the victim as she walked on a sidewalk, on Third Avenue, and the perpetrator then cocked his arm and battered the head of the victim. She stumbled forward and collapsed.

Once the facts are released by electronic mail message to the force about the possibility of Tyrone Duffy as suspect, by virtue of his being a bicycle messenger, the report comes back from a guy on traffic duty: He broke up a fight on Thursday morning between a bicycle messenger and some guys in midtown. *That* bicycle messenger sounds like *this* bicycle messenger. And that bicycle messenger's name is Tyrone Duffy. Soon thereafter, the story has leaked to the press. Eyewitnesses are coming forth. Amid the hysteria of the city in recent days, the car crash in the Diamond District, et cetera, the detectives admit that reading the diary has been a pleasant way to spend a few hours. Even if the diary is sad, and even if the diary is the intimate record of a woman who now appears to have very little, if any, short-term memory. Most days, the detectives find themselves with chalk circles indicating the final resting place of deceased persons, and it is nice to read about the life and loves of a young woman, a woman who may well recover, and they find that in this way, they love the victim. The victim seems to have pluck and enthusiasm for the world, and the victim seems to stand for things that a young woman of New York should stand for, like hard work and frequent use of the public library system, and they think that maybe if they were younger and not married, they could fall for her, or at least each of them feels this way in his own private reserve, and it is at this point that they decide to go to the hospital to see if Samantha Lee is alert and receiving visitors.

IO

Madison turns from the vast cabinet of beauty products in her mother's bathroom at 860 Park. She turns from honey-maple astringent chiselers, verbena pore extruders, plasma essence nucleic epidermal triage treatments. To immerse herself in the shower, Madison stands with her face under the massaging showerhead trying to ignore the afterimage of the curtain's floral print. During the next ten minutes, when she's basically asleep again — until she finds herself warming up the espresso maker, dumping a demitasse into some steamed milk — she absently spoons into herself half a grapefruit for its negative calories while her mother complains about how recycling is actually creating *more* garbage. After which, Madison needs to get out of her pajamas, and this is actually one of the most stressful moments of the day because she has all these choices. She has gone to Agnès B., she has gone to Betsey Johnson, she has gone to Prada, she has gone to Dolce, she has even gone to Bergdorf's, and she has bought these outfits, Michael Kors, Marc Jacobs. She has to wear one of them. If you buy the outfit, you have to wear the outfit. That's the rule. It's irritating and stressful. All these outfits, like strangers of whom you should ask questions at a cocktail party, at least according to her mom, who was trained to ask questions at parties by her own parents, her mom who used to be a fund-raiser at the City Opera and who now just hangs around the house complaining. Madison goes into the walk-in closet and she tries on the knee-length black skirt, then the pink corduroys, then the giant eyelet skirt, and the micromini, then superslim hip-huggers, settles on a leather skirt in claret, checks the drape of the trifle. She attempts to divine the tastes and inclinations of the male of the species by spinning around a couple of times in the mirror. Next, she goes in search of the right top, maybe something less sheer underneath something more sheer, or maybe just something black. After which there is emergency moisturizer, amber concealer, ebony eye pencil, extrahold disulfide support spray. Not that the male of the species gives Madison McDowell its undivided attention. When they do she finds reasons to resist. This one checks the length of his fingernails too often. This one is preoccupied with squash. This one uses the word *portfolio* too many times, and this one drives with one hand.

Which is why at twenty-eight she's still living here. There's no reason to live elsewhere yet. And she can't afford her own place. In summer, she has the guesthouse all to herself out in the Hamptons, where she can float listlessly in the pool. While she's at Means of Production she can save some money, and she can buy pieces (fur pants from Sean John) that are essential to the public image of Means of Production. Madison McDowell *is* the public image. That's something that Vanessa Meandro recognizes, something that Vanessa needs, Madison McDowell with high heels and an address book and an expense account. Madison McDowell in the society pages. She can call her friends on the cell phone and she can commiserate about whatever it is that requires commiseration. She can scheme out loud about world domination, about her ultimate position as a female studio head, about her imaginary husband who is thirty-eight years older than she and bound to die leaving her a half-billion dollars in stock options.

She gets into the elevator, yelling back irritably at her mother, reminding this matriarch to go to Fendi for the sale, and upon depressing the L button, she fishes out the cell phone and conference calls the girls at Vanderbilt Publicity, and the girls start in immediately about what they saw last night, for example, you can't *believe* who they saw last night, they were with that hip-hop guy, Mercurio. Almost every week they say this, they saw Mercurio, Mercurio, Mercurio, and they took him to the opening of an installation piece at a gallery in Chelsea where you could administer electric shocks to a male model, you wouldn't *believe* it, and everyone was there, here is a list of people who were there, here is a list, because even if the girls themselves weren't at an event, none of the people on the list would ever deny being at an event, that's what the girls always say, you can always just report that these people were at an event any time you throw a party, even if they weren't. The more times you say it, the more likely they are to come: Lou Reed and Laurie Anderson, Rod Stewart, John Leguizamo, Donald Trump, Matt Dillon, Isaac Mizrahi, Al Roker, Lacey, Jay McInerney, someone from the tabloids, just make up any name of someone from the tabs, because they love us, they love everything we do, and they will come to everything. How about plus-size models, there are always some plus-size models around, you can just say a plus-size model came to the party, like what's her name, any of the guys from that hip-hop label on Staten Island, and you can say that anyone from the Young Republicans was at your party. Young Republicans, they will do anything you ask. Libertarians like to be tied up. Leave your Libertarian at home watching QVC, tied to your bed. The heiresses from that cosmetics fortune, they were undoubtedly at the party, the daughter of the guy who pulled the insurance scam where the Methodist Church got taken for millions, the dashing son of an indicted arms trader, twenty cousins of the Saudi royal family, two former New York City police chiefs. You can always get the staff of the pink weekly newspaper to come to your parties, and they almost always throw up at some point late in the night, especially that guy who does the movie reviews. Or how about the heroin-addicted singer for that band, the Corinthians, or Derek Jeter will come to your party, or Fred Durst, he will come to your party, the entire staff of *Jet Set*. All these people will come.

The girls go on, yoked together in the ether of telecommunications as Madison thanks the doorman, gets into her cab. They talk about the menu at that restaurant Slab, how it is totally not that fattening, and how first they went to the benefit party for the museum, and they got so drunk, you wouldn't *believe,* and they saw a real estate developer guy, and they saw a guy from that investment bank, and they saw the guy who had the Internet start-up that only just started to tank. But that's after the stock was up a hundred and twenty percent in the first day of trading. A sweet guy and cuter than any man on earth, he's a fox, they say. His hair is the color of wheat and just a little bit messy, and he says he wants to get involved in producing independent films! That's what he said. They are serving this man up to Madison as though he were a big fish flopping on the deck, and all of this even though Madison has dark hair, which is not at all like the Vanderbilt girls themselves. They are totally being about blond, about the philosophy of the blonde. Even if you're a fake blonde, it's fine. But you have to be a blonde. They have decided to do this experiment with Madison; they are going to see if a natural brunette can make any headway in the world. But as part of the experiment, she will have to do as they say. Exactly as they say. And then, at a certain point, she will take a meeting with Mercurio. Mercurio really wants to do some film work and Mercurio is incredibly smart, you know, and he understands how it works. He really doesn't want to do an action film where he's the sidekick of some white guy, like a Thaddeus Griffin movie, because that's demeaning, although he would consider doing an action film where he has a white sidekick, like Thaddeus Griffin, say, and maybe Thaddeus gets blown to pieces about half an hour from the end of the movie, but, seriously, what Mercurio would like to do is have a small part in a film where it's not actually the worst film of the year.

Madison says, "Even Thaddeus doesn't want to do a Thaddeus Griffin movie."

Mercurio, the girls observe, is just pretending that he carries a loaded handgun and has guys working for him who are ruthless killers, because you have to have credibility with the fan base, and that fan base, the girls say, is white male private school students from large cities. Mercurio can't afford to alienate white male private school students from large cities, and so he needs a handgun, the girls say, so that the private school kids believe in him. The Vanderbilt publicists do not have the same credibility problem and they don't need handguns. They could borrow handguns if needed. They understand that credibility is imperative to all the people they represent, however, and they will do what they can at the corporate level to ensure that Mercurio's credibility survives incessant advertising, television promotions, bad marriage choices, a house in the suburbs, homosexual dalliances, insider trading scandals, diva behavior, gavel-to-gavel trial coverage, all of that. Mercurio is so sweet and he has had such a rough life, what with losing his cousin in a plane crash. So you have to find something for Mercurio. He wants an independent film where he can work outside of his established persona, you know?

"Maybe a digitally animated version of the Tibetan Book of the Dead?"

"Does it have like a hundred kinky positions in it?"

The girls miss Madison's withering sarcasm, not because they are uninformed, but because they are talking too fast. Madison is so smart! Brunettes are smart! Sometimes she has both of them on hold, the Vanderbilt girls on two separate lines, Barclay and Sophie, and she just goes back and forth between them, and sometimes they have each other on hold at the same time, and sometimes she has them conference calling her. To summarize, Mercurio would like to take a meeting with Madison and then he would like to take a meeting with Vanessa, and Madison should definitely call up the guy from the Internet start-up, hair the color of wheat, and she should take him out to lunch. The girls tell her that the Internet developer guy is really serious, he really wants to learn about the movies, he's totally cute, you wouldn't *believe*.

And of course the cab is stuck in traffic, and the driver has one of those pine-scented tree car fresheners hanging from the mirror, and it's going to pollute Madison, and she might have to puke. They pass St. Bart's at a crawl. Madison is skeptical, as she is always skeptical, about the Internet start-up guy, but she takes out her personal digital assistant and she scans through the projects that she's responsible for. Which of them might be worth bringing to the Internet start-up guy and which should she bring to Mercurio, and should she talk to Vanessa about Mercurio? And then she tells the girls that she has found a really excellent waxer, heard about her from a friend working at *Jet Set,* and the girls say, who? Like maybe they are a little irritated that they don't already know about this waxer. But Madison doesn't say who because sometimes you have to withhold information just a little bit, that's how you end up being the monthly selection for the Vanderbilt girls, so she says that she is getting the Brazilian wax, and it is really excellent, and this happens not to be true at all, hurts like hell, and then the girls say, oh, by the way, did we tell you that the Internet start-up guy is a Mormon?

"A Mormon?"

"Yeah, a Mormon."

"Really?"

From Utah and everything, and they do not know if this means that he has several wives all under the age of eighteen, but it does seem to mean that he doesn't drink very much, if at all, and he comes from a parched western landscape, and maybe his great-grandparents, his people, came over the lip of the bluff in a wagon, having endured persecution and disrespect and murder all across these United States. Okay, Madison knows what Mormon is. A Mormon is someone with strange undergarments who has an obligation to go abroad to Africa when he's fifteen to attempt to convert the Africans to his religion and who has, in the process, sexual experiences he never talks about. He has strange sheets. She says she'll have to put them on hold, and she calls the Internet start-up guy, whose stock is plummeting, and she gets his assistant, and she says that she is Madison McDowell from Means of Production and she'd like to make a lunch date for that very day, which is Friday. Turns out the Internet start-up guy does have a name, and his name is Zimri. It's the most incredible name, Zimri, sounds like a name for a Sufi dancer. Madison can understand how a half dozen sixteen-year-old Mormon girls would marry a guy called Zimri. And for a while she's on hold at the office of the Internet start-up guy, and it's playing music that is definitely not hip-hop Mercurio, and she's wondering if maybe this is the music of the famous choir, or would that be a little obvious, you know, if you were a Mormon, to have the Mormon Tabernacle Choir playing on your voice mail service. Maybe she should option the life story of his great-grandparents, coming overland in their wagon trains, enduring persecution, fighting off mountain lions, singing about saints in the choir.

She's responsible for the project about Otis Redding. Zimri might be interested in that. It's a fictionalized narrative about Otis Redding, called *Try a Little Tenderness,* and it creates a thriller subtext around the life of Otis Redding, saying that Otis Redding did not have mob connections, you know, even though some people say he did. They really were not mob connections, according to the script, what they were was connections with the Nation of Islam. Which is ironic, because he was one of the first soul singers with a fully integrated band. Well, see, it's an early point in his career, and he's still back in Georgia and he's just busting out of Little Richard's band, where he got his start in the late fifties, and he falls under the sway of the Nation of Islam because he just wants to believe that some message of hope could transform the African American struggle. What Otis Redding does, in the script, is he comes to reject both the Nation of Islam and the gradualist politics of the white man. All of this while on his last tour, you know, before the plane goes down, just like with Mercurio's cousin. Otis goes through an intellectual dark night of the soul on the last tour. He goes from the heights of ecstasy to the lowest lows; he sees into the troubled soul of this great land, and this is what enables him to write "(Sittin' on the) Dock of the Bay" while visiting friends in Marin County. There's some stuff about Herbert Hoover, but this part hasn't been worked out entirely yet, and there's some stuff about the great soul players in his band, and there's a little bit about his white girlfriends, including a woman who was married to a prominent senator from the state of Virginia, but they have to be really careful about that because Otis remained married his entire life, and the family has given permission to have the movie made, and if they don't like the white girlfriends, then there won't be permission to call the film *Try a Little Tenderness* or to use any of the original music. The third act will answer the question of who had Otis Redding eliminated. And the answer is that they haven't quite figured out who eliminated him yet, because Vanessa wants it to be terrorists, for some reason, while Madison and the writer are leaning toward Cubans, in revenge for the Bay of Pigs.

Because she's been left on hold too long, Madison puts Zimri the Internet start-up guy on hold in return and she goes back over to Barclay, half of the Vanderbilt partnership, and says, "Maybe Mercurio could play Otis Redding."

Suddenly both girls are on the line, indicating that they will consider this. They will have a quick phone meeting while she's on hold with Zimri, the Internet start-up guy, and they will also consider the Brazilian waxer and then maybe they will try to reach Mercurio. And Madison goes back to the music that sounds like the Mormon Tabernacle Choir, but there's no one there. Soon she gets another incoming call, but actually it's just Barclay, who has called back on a new line because it was faster. They are talking on two different lines now.

"By the way, who *is* Otis Redding?"

"You don't know who Otis Redding is?"

"Don't make me feel stupid, you bitch."

Barclay cackles. Madison claims to be just kidding about not knowing. But she's not kidding, and she's not letting on that she's not kidding. Meanwhile, in her innermost core, which is surprisingly sweet, Madison McDowell will do almost anything not to let anyone know that she is a virtuoso on the violin, that she was in the All-City Orchestra, first violin, and had the chance to play with the Philharmonic when she was sixteen. She has never mentioned this thing about the violin to the Vanderbilt girls, for example, nor to Vanessa Meandro, and she has put the violin under her bed, and she has not tuned it lately, because if she tunes it and her mother is in the house, her mother will get all weepy about how great Madison was on the violin. Her mother will observe that any man would love a girl who bows the violin the way Madison McDowell bows. Sometimes she waits until her mother is out of the house and her father is traveling on business, and then she takes the violin out of the case and fits it under her chin, and she tightens the bow, and she plucks the strings a few times. Then she sets the bow on the strings, and there is the long low trembling of the G and D strings, and the vibrato as she moves up through first position. And then there is the first melody she plays, when she is rusty and alone and willing to be the violin player that nobody knows. Just to have practiced something, some scales, and a little J. S. Bach. She is unthinkable without the violin because she is sublime only on the violin, and her posture is perfect, and her ear is perfect, and she hears the locking counterpoint of string quartets in her future, never to be, and that's why the other passion project she is developing is the story about the violin maker Stradivarius, who, although he made the greatest violins in history, was actually a libertine and a reprobate, at least in his early life, and, in this story, Stradivarius goes from bedding French prostitutes and playing bawdy songs on his sublime instruments to helping a Prussian general scheme against foreign intrigues. But then he experiences the ennobling of courtly love, you know, in the person of the daughter of a viscount, whom he cannot have. Something like that. And, of course, he makes the greatest violins in history in order to capture the sound of the voice of his beloved, because the value of love is commensurate with difficulty of attainment. The writer of the Stradivarius script, a guy she met at Fashion Week, a guy who tried to get her number, is still working on the third act. Vanessa has no idea why Madison likes all the historical stories, why she likes Napoleon and Stradivarius, but she thinks maybe she just identifies with the romance of women from costume dramas, and besides, girls love those kinds of movies and flock to them, like if you could get Lacey, the teenybopper, to play the chaste Elsa in the Stradivarius movie, then you'd have something that would really bring the girls into the theater in big flocks.

Barclay, on the other hand, doesn't know about Otis Redding, and she doesn't know anything about violins, and she got thrown out of a number of private high schools here in the city. Unless it's a Swedish imported car or some tacky kind of champagne that costs five hundred dollars a bottle, Barclay doesn't have a clue, but Sophie, the other Vanderbilt Publicity girl, knows about this kind of thing, a little bit, just because her father has an entire performing arts wing at NYU named after him. That's how the Vanderbilt partnership works out. Barclay Weltz worries about the billing and doesn't bother to get her eyebrows dyed. She goes to these parties wearing designer jeans and with her bra showing under her shirt, and she plants gossip items in the papers about people she doesn't like in order to have them ruined. And Sophie Fiegelman closes the deals and plays the good-cop part. It's

Sophie who told Madison that she was their choice this month and that it bespoke a *fabulousness* that Madison should be very proud of. All the more reason why it's scary when Sophie's voice rings out, breaking through the interstellar white noise of the on-hold signal of Barclay, likewise breaking through the on-hold signal of Zimri, Internet start-up guy, just as Madison is climbing out of the cab at the side entrance to the Rockefeller Plaza.

Sophie's voice is agitated. "Oh, my God, you guys, I just got the worst news! You won't believe it!"

Barclay says, "What? What?"

It's almost midday, and the skaters are already doing their thing, and the colors are bright because it's autumn. No time is as perfect as autumn, even if you're a development girl on the phone with hack publicists and you are late. Madison listens absently and walks down to the edge of the rail overlooking the rink. The holidays feel like some fever up ahead, and that's what she'll remember thinking when Sophie breaks the news that this girl she knows, Samantha Lee, from one of the galleries — beautiful girl, knows a ton of people — she was walking in midtown yesterday and this guy, some guy, he just came up behind her and he just smashed her head with a brick, just took this brick and swung it at her head and just totally knocked her out, like, knocked her down on the street; and then she was on the street with her skull all smashed in and bleeding and everything.

"Oh, my God," Barclay says. "That is so awful. That is so horrible. That is so sad. Is she dead?"

"She's in the hospital. It's all over the papers."

Madison says, "Did she go to Lenox Hill? She should definitely go to Lenox Hill."

● "What party did she come to?" Barclay asks.

"She came to a lot of parties," Sophie says. "You know who she is. She was going out with that guy, what was his name, the painter guy."

And that's what Madison takes with her, along with her impatience and her irritation, on the way into the office. She is carrying the name of a woman who got her head smashed in by some guy on the street, and it's all kind of too much, the prospect of Vanessa is too much, so she pretty much turns right around and leaves, to meet Zimri, the Internet start-up guy, for lunch at the new Indian place on Forty-eighth Street, because why not? Madison likes a guy who doesn't have to look through a hundred calendar pages before he can make a lunch date, or who at least has an efficient secretary, and she also really likes a guy who is standing when she comes in. Slow this instant down for a second, how about? Because the most important part of the day is the part you spend at lunch, and she does the important phone calls in the cab and then she just goes straight to lunch, because lunch is a legitimate expression of business.

Zimri Enderby is pleased to meet her, and Zimri is cute, and Zimri has an oblique smile that is endearing and impossible to pin down at the same time, like no matter what you say to him, you will not be able to figure out what he thinks. He holds her seat for her, and touches her on the biceps, just faintly, a brushing past of the fingertips, like he's the archaeologist and she's the intact vase in the peat bog, and then he sits. There's something stern about Zimri Enderby. That's what Madison thinks, even though he also has a button-down collar on his shirt, it's so frigging preppie, are Mormons preppies? And he orders everything as if he's familiar with it. Well, so he's a Mormon who knows how to order Indian food. And pleasantries get exchanged, according to some etiquette manual of pleasantries. Zimri hints about how he thinks the election will turn out, and Madison is tempted to say something, but the Vanderbilt girls, when they decided that Madison was the selection for this month, they insisted that she not say anything about politics for the entire month, no matter what, because no one pays any attention to politics anyhow and no one ever got a business started by caring about politics. The only thing you need to know about politics is that a check of a certain size will buy you access to politicians of any party at any time. Ten thousand bucks gets you all the access you need. Zimri is the kind of guy who could write a check of a certain size.

An Indian waiter takes away the ceremonial plates.

"I'm familiar with some of the movies your production company has done," Zimri says, "and I have to say, they're provocative and interesting. Why don't you tell me what you're doing now." Provocative and interesting? Aren't these adjectives from somebody's porch furniture catalogue? Madison pauses dramatically. She takes in her surroundings. The Indian restaurants in midtown are always decorated in crimson, like you're in somebody's mouth. Here's the soft palate and here's the uvula. She looks around at the tassels and the fringe on the draperies.

"Well, we have a couple of projects we're working on that are certain to get distribution, and, uh, we're thinking they're going to get a lot of attention at the awards, all of that. Stars are attached." She tries to think about what kinds of films a Mormon might like. Maybe he should bankroll some animated films about Native American princesses with hourglass figures or something. Means of Production is always shaking things up. This is what she tells him, using language that is straight out of that brochure that Annabel had printed and which she forgot to bring. She says that Means of Production is about "shaking things up," about "avoiding the pieties of mainstream cinema," about the "freshness and energy" of independent cinema, which means directors and actors who are "hungry for expression." She watches his face while she repeats stuff like this, like she's a waitress announcing daily specials, recommending sauces that she has never heard of before and mispronouncing the names of exotic mushrooms, and she waits to see the flicker of prejudice or disdain that she figures is hidden in the faces of the fervently religious. Madison associates any kind of religious anything with mental retardation.

But when she doesn't see the prejudice there, she gets bold and she starts to talk about her passion project, her film about Stradivarius, and anyway, it doesn't have any gratuitous bondage sequences or any transvestites in it, and it has no references to Michel Foucault in it, nor does it heroize the labor movement. She kind of warms to the whole subject, though she doesn't want to give away that she actually plays the violin. She says, "Have you ever held a violin? The Stradivarius, it's really beautiful. People cry sometimes, just holding a Stradivarius, and we want to make a movie that feels like that." And then she tells him about Otis Redding and she tells him about the remake of *Citizen Kane* from the point of view of the Marion Davies character. He has his arms folded pensively, but then he remembers that he has food, and he pokes at the chicken tikka masala, when he's not watching her as though he's waiting for her secret.

"I don't really know what I'm thinking about with the movie business yet. I'm just learning about it. And what I do when I learn about something is I just take it all in. I'm taking in the film business and I'm thinking about what I might be able to do that no one else has done."

Madison asks what the Internet start-up business is all about. Because, as her mother has pointed out, it is important to ask questions.

"I'm proceeding on two fronts, really." The one front, he says, is a company called Rural Electrification, Inc., and the goal of Rural Electrification, Inc., is to put wireless broadband service in the hands of people in rural communities. Most of these people, he says, have to go to libraries to have any access to the Internet at all, but wireless broadband is just around the corner and it would enable farmers to access information while out on their land. For example, if they have a question about soil pH balance, or a question about the water table or the possible effects of dam projects in the West. Wireless broadband would enable the rural culture of the West to feel that it was not lagging behind coastal centers in terms of information management. It would give the rural West a level playing field. That's one of the projects he tells her about, and the other project concerns privacy and privacy issues. It involves a Web site that could be used as a portal for accessing other Web sites in order to protect consumer privacy, and it would also offer software and information about privacy in an era when more and more of what happens on the Internet is being stored, saved, and sold by large Web merchandisers. "Imagine we were having this conversation on some instant messaging service, you know? That's not terribly difficult to monitor these days. Say I mentioned that I knew radicals out West, water rights activists, and I happened to know that the government had a computer that monitored users any time the words *water rights activist* turned up anywhere on the Internet. We're looking to create services and situations that will protect consumers from these malicious invasions of privacy. And the conjunction of these two projects, Rural Electrification, Inc., and the Privacy Project, will really benefit the lives of people from the part of the country where I was born and raised, a part of the country that cherishes liberty. But, you know, start-ups are sort of a side project for me, really. My father is a rancher. That's the family business. I'm just here on my passion projects, looking for financing."

"Backers, that's what I'm after all the time," Madison says. "Always hustling for backers."

"The sad part of it," Zimri says, emboldened, "is that an era is kind of fading away. An era when the markets were parched for innovation. Four or five years ago, there was this feeling that if you had an idea and you knew how to talk to it, then you were going to monetize that idea. I imagine the same thing is true in the movie business, that it's really no different from agriculture. You need the seed money and you need to tend to the crops to make sure they flourish. Most people only respect marketing, because the genius of real ideas is threatening to them. The people who come up with ideas are always the ones with the wild eyes."

She likes watching his mouth. Nothing is sexier than agricultural metaphors, really. They're so earthy. But it's sort of irritating to Madison that she can't instantly figure out what's wrong with Zimri Enderby, because there must be something wrong besides the button-down collars and that piece of chana saag on his incisor — should she tell him? — and she wishes she could ask about his strange Mormon sheets and his years as a teenage missionary. Because somewhere in there is the concealed gay affair, or the episode of sexual abuse, or the binges at Indian casinos. The secret is in there somewhere and only God knows what it is. Does he have to wear a different ring for each of the seven underage wives?

"Venture capitalists used to think like poets. They were dreamers, they were renegades. And now it's starting to look like those doors are going to be closed for a long while. And that's why I'd like to make a leap into content, you know, because content is forever. The world always needs the artists and dreamers. I appreciate the energy on the content end of the Internet story. You know, out West, back when everyone was a rancher or working the fields, there were the stars to navigate from. Men would be out in the fields with the livestock, looking up at the stars. And that was their entertainment. Stars and a campfire crackling in the desert. There are no stars here in the city, except the poets and dreamers and actors and filmmakers, the content providers, so that's where I want to concentrate my attention."

Soon after, they swap cards, and she heads for the office, checking in, on the way, with the women of Vanderbilt Publicity to offer an affidavit that, yes, the hair is wheat colored and, no, there doesn't seem to be any ring on his ring finger and, yes, he is in possession of her number and, yes, he is too perfect to be true, and has he maybe RSVP'd for anything they're doing, in the way of parties, you know, the next few nights? She would like to know so she can clear her schedule, but she says all these things because the cynic is a lapsed something or other, everybody knows that.

How quickly does the lapsed something or other begin to hope? Hope is in robin's-egg blue, tucked into the leaves of a book, like a Victorian flower. Hope is a perfumed envelope, and she can feel a little bit of a spring in her step. She hates it. She hates the hoper in herself. She notices that she accidentally flipped her hair when saying good-bye to him, and all those girls who flip their hair, blondes, always flipping their hair, what is it with them, is it a neurological thing? It should be in the catalogue of neurological disorders next to Tourette's, and so it's best to disconnect the cell phone and go back to the office and submit to Vanessa, who wants to know all about the Mormon guy, is he a Jack Mormon, which apparently means a Mormon who's not a Mormon, and she asks, of course, "Were you attracted to him? Tell me you didn't agree to go out on a date or anything, because you just can't fuck up the business relationships with these guys by going out on dates with them, okay? And what projects did you talk to him about?"

Madison, in front of a bowl of Swedish fish, admits to Otis Redding. She admits to Stradivarius.

"You didn't tell him about *The Diviners*?"

"What's *The Diviners*?"

"The miniseries."

"What miniseries? Since when is it a miniseries?"

"Since this morning, which you would know if you bothered to come into the office in the morning. Now I want you to get the writer on the phone and tell him to put something about water rights in western states into the treatment. And maybe Native American turquoise. Western guys love turquoise."

"Who's the writer?"

"It's based on a novel by Marjorie Howell Finkelstein; I think she's a big features writer for women's magazines. I think she wrote the treatment herself, but we have to get a different writer on the project. There's no way we can work with her. I called Vic Freese this morning, he claims to be repping it, but I told him we had already optioned the story and that we were going to bring all of our resources to bear on the project. We were going to make it *our* project."

Vanessa gets up, absently rubbing her neck as though it's a magic lantern that will yield ever greater reservoirs of falsehood.

"Did you actually option it?"

"We have to find Marjorie Howell Finkelstein and we have to option it before you go home tonight. Find out who her agent is, track her down. Get on it. Get western water rights into the treatment, and turquoise, and Indians, and have a copy of it on the Mormon guy's desk tomorrow, with a budget sketched out. And here, have a Swedish fish."

Then Vanessa does a thing she never does. She gets ready to leave early. She says she is going out for drinks, even though it's only three in the afternoon. The dingy black raincoat flies around Vanessa as though she's a vampire, and she's out the door. Madison remains behind, leaning against the flimsy divider of Annabel's cubicle.

"Any idea where the hell I'm supposed to find Marjorie Howell Finkelstein?"

"I think it's Melanie Horace Fahnstock," Annabel says. "That's the writer's name."

"Any idea how to contact her?"

"I might be able to find out."

"Never mind. I'll do it."

Thaddeus comes out of his lair with a crumpled-up piece of paper and, in front of the assembled (Jeanine off in the distance, looking like an orthopedist's brochure on bad posture), he attempts to do some kind of double-pump layup thing into the trash barrel.

"Do you know anything about this Finkelstein woman?" Madison asks, though she tries to avoid talking to him. "The one who wrote this *Diviners* thing. Are we really supposed to be taking it seriously?"

"You're definitely supposed to be taking it seriously, and I think the writer's name is Fedderman, actually. Melanie Fedderman. There's some middle name, too, because, you know, genre writers, they always have a middle name or two in there. The story has enormous promise, by the way."

"Nobody gives a shit about any miniseries now. We should do a show where attractive girls, like, show their cervixes to advertisers. That would make a splash."

Annabel says, "I'll write up a proposal."

Thaddeus says, "My agent knows her agent. Want me to make the call?"

"I'm supposed to make some kind of offer."

Mrs. DiNunzio rustles past, carrying a couple of files. The office poltergeist.

II

It's near upon feeding hour, and everyone, in gowns and slippers, is working his or her way out of the sunless crevices of the ward and heading for the nurses' console. Rosa Elisabetta, a leafless sapling in terry cloth robe and slippers, is ahead of the curve, ahead of the men climbing out of their beds. Men, festering, uremic, unshaven. She hasn't made their acquaintance, doesn't intend to. They tremble like candle flames at the end of their wicks. A strong breeze would blow them out. Still, near to the feeding hour, they bring forth untapped reservoirs of life, morbid jokes, gallows humor, toothless smiles.

"Go listen to the lecture," the nurse says to her, waving in the direction of the common area, with its ample but depressing population of houseplants. "Don't be hanging around here."

"I already know all that they're going to say."

"If you knew, you wouldn't be here."

The nurse's tone is patently offensive, as are her press-on fingernails. But Rosa is insubstantial, like the others, and when she reaches out for things, when she puts the flat part of her palm on the nurse's console, the result is complicated. The palm is stretched as though testing plane geometry, swooping down over the console. Her palm is a bird. Moments seem to pass, and then she feels the smoothness of it, the console. She locks eyes with the nurse, whose name she has forgotten. Rosa doesn't even know for certain if she has seen this unnamed nurse before. The nurse's eyes are big and brown and bloodshot, as if she has wept on duty. The nurse is shooing her, waving her away, as though Rosa is an insect, and what Rosa watches in particular are the nurse's hands.

"Repetition of key concepts," this unnamed nurse continues.

Bodies toddle down the corridor at the leisurely pace of detox-ification. Jocular exchanges between the penitential. It takes Rosa an interminable length to turn and look at what the un-named nurse is pointing at, namely, the death march of the ad-dict population. "Take suggestions. Go to the lecture."

Rosa Elisabetta nods, in keeping with a diminished vocabulary of dignity that is native here. And then she moves away from the console and she does her best, reaching for intermediate clinging stations, which are located around her. There is a doorknob, which is certainly a clinging station, on the way to the common room where the lecture is taking place. Also a water fountain. And here is a leaning station, by the fire stairs. Almost there. She is at the threshold of the lecture, and what she can see is that the lecturer is covered with tattoos. She can see that he's African American and he's smiling. She believes she is hearing a repeti-tion of key concepts, and the words are drifting. Surrender to win, sick and tired of being sick and tired, one day at a time, let go, let God. The lecturer makes use of strategic drifting. He har-nesses drifting terminologies, and they are almost percussive. Or else there is an echolalia, which is a pathological repetition of key concepts, as when the medication level goes down. She dreads the medication level going down because then there is the possi-bility of seizure. Again.

There are these things she hears. Earlier in the day, she heard things, she heard importunings, beseechments, and last night she heard things, all of it in a language of desire, as if want were never expressed in American English before, as if it were only expressed in these affected parts, where desire and rage are in a state of riot. Maybe these voices in her affected parts are annealed by this strategic repetition, and maybe she is redeemed by medication, because she knows, or thinks she knows, that the man who is asleep in the chair in front of the lecturer, one of four people attending, has not moved from that chair for several hours, not even to face in the direction of the television monitor, which for most of the afternoon has been tuned to talk shows. These shows are a clinging station. A clinging station is a station that must be visited prior to release. It must be wiped clean afterward.

The lecturer says something about how pleased he is to see her there, but she doesn't respond. There is a windowsill and there is the temporary pleasantness of going to a windowsill and of seeing something out the window. She has a sense of the window as an opening, onto a street, and a street opening onto a city, and a city opening onto a nation, and she considers these openings, but she forgets the particular relationship between these things, window, outside, grid system, nation, heavenly body. Her hand flutters up to the window, to touch it and to feel that it's cold. And it's a surprise, as if a dove has suddenly alighted on the scene.

The lecturer offers some further repetition of key concepts to the seats in front of him, where those four bodies are strewn as though air-dropped. And he looks over at Rosa Elisabetta, touching the window. And then he returns to his praises of God and sobriety. Getting from the window to an unoccupied seat takes a sequence of muscle contractions. A shoulder of an unconscious man is a clinging station. It's as though she is part of some peristaltic massage, having swallowed herself in an attempt to purge all things from her body. The taking in and the excreting outward. Rigors of motion seem as if they are happening on the inside, even though they are probably happening on the outside.

Eventually, she is in one of the seats in front of the lecturer, and it has taken her so long to get there that it appears that the lecturer is done with his presentation. Now he is giving his telephone number to a man in the front row, one of the few alert enough to understand. Then he comes to stand in front of her.

"How many days? If I may ask?"

Rosa Elisabetta raises her hand, provisionally, holds up the fingers.

"Three days, three days. No complaining about three days. Three days is better than no days." Here he takes her hand for a moment. Many perils to be considered in the interior of the ward, like being incarcerated with liars and drug addicts and petty criminals and fornicators, and these are so preoccupying, these perils, that she has not got around to avoiding germs. Under other circumstances, Rosa Elisabetta would recoil from allowing an African American man covered with tattoos to take her hand, but there's no time for that now because she forgot to think about it, and this is an instant in a vast conspiracy, and she doesn't know how to stop it exactly, the recognition of simultaneities, and so her hand is now in the massive palm of the lecturer, and because there is no time to stop the events spinning around her, there's no time to resist being held lovingly by an African American lecturer.

If time were expressed as a sequence of hands, then time has all but stopped, since it is eons, epochs, since either of the hands belonging to Rosa Elisabetta was entrapped in the hand of another. Her daughter is not exactly a hand-holder type, a sentimentalist. This thought dawns on her with reasonable clarity. There is this thought, and there is the hand of the lecturer, which is the leather recliner of hand-holding hands. It is pale at the palm, elsewhere dark, and it is thick, meaty, where others would be bony. In his hand, hers is shriveled, with laces of vein and artery. She is in a state of considering geologic time where a single breath in the passed-out heroin addict in the chair nearby is reduced to an infinite series of partial decisions and undertakings. That's how long her hand is in the lecturer's hand, that's how long she is experiencing gratitude, before he says, "I'll say a little prayer for you." Then back to the light speed of things overtaking, repetition of key concepts, nurses urging them down the hall to the dining room. Carts bearing the trays go by, rubber wheels moaning on the linoleum. Addicts totter after, because they will follow any smells, even if they are the same smells as last night, namely, fruit juice container, three spears of broccoli boiled until nearly liquefied, freeze-dried carcass of chicken, and a half-dozen french-fried potatoes still icy in their centers.

Somehow she finds a leaning opportunity in the dining room, bearing up her tray, and she is attempting to blow a long gray tangle of hair out of her face, away from affected parts, as she sits. With grim determination, she opens the juice and takes the plastic utensils from their plastic sleeve. Women are rare here, but still there is a young woman, no older than her daughter, sitting opposite. And the young woman rips into her unsubstantiated chicken as if this were the first hospital dinner ever consumed. Rosa Elisabetta is impressed with the display. Around the room, the sleepers attempt to eat faster than seawater turns boulders to sand, sometimes successfully.

The girl says, "Hey, can you answer a question?"

Rosa raises an eyebrow.

"Do you think I should tell them that I'm bleeding? I've been bleeding for ten days. I never bled like this before. I was living in a squat, so I just didn't get that much to eat. Know what I mean? Now I'm bleeding. Man, you can't believe. Like there's a mouse in me doing flips. Know what I mean?"

"I can't —" Rosa says. And then, as if the question were a marvel, "Your name?"

Her name is Dee. Rosa whispers the name after hearing it spoken. So simple it might be possible to commit it to memory at some point. Rosa nods, as if by nodding she can get across a spectrum of advice. Run, don't walk, where the bleeding is concerned. The girl seems to say something. Not like there are a lot of women to talk to. The girl gestures around the room, as if to prove her hypothesis. True, there is Rosa and her roommate, an obese woman who has not yet risen from her bed. This obese woman had something injected and then she slept, and she's sleeping still. And then there's the girl, Dee, and apparently Dee doesn't have a roommate, although she probably will, maybe tonight. People are coming and going. Remarks, which are observations, get condensed down to elemental gestures in her affected parts. Rosa looks at thinking from an angle and then she looks at it from another angle. She seems not to get around to saying much.

"Want to play cards later?"

Unclear. How many transactions in this marketplace of detoxified ideas would be involved in the playing of cards? The idea of *later* is almost impossibly complex, and Rosa cannot commit. In fact, while she's turning it over in her mind, dinner has come to an end.

"Rosa, try just eating the broccoli."

The nurses treat her as though she's never heard of food, as though food has never traversed the boundaries of inside and outside, as though digestion has never before degraded her, as though she has never had a seven-course meal with a pasta course and a meat course. With the resistance to these commands she feels a little more like herself; nevertheless, she does eat the broccoli, which tastes like air. And then, using the chair as a clinging station, she rises up, last to leave, and carries her tray to the cart.

The television has been fired up again, and those who are able are on their way into the common area, where Rosa imagines she can hear the sound of the theme song of one of those programs that does nothing but show police in the midst of making arrests. There is a brownie in Rosa's hand. How did she come to acquire a brownie? Rosa shoves the entire brownie into her mouth. From nowhere, her daughter appears, having brought her some clothes from home. Her daughter is a hazard coming down the corridor, and her daughter represents the flood of language. This is a corridor of perils. Her daughter comes to rest, as though made inert by her, Rosa Elisabetta Meandro, somewhere not far from the door to her bedroom, the room she shares with the slumbering obese woman who will one day awake.

"How are you feeling?" Vanessa asks.

She has made a provisional decision not to deploy the moisture arguments from her moisture ducts, but she is not in a position to make these tactical decisions, so the best Rosa can do when faced with the ambulatory memories represented by a black raincoat and its contents is to avoid comment on the moisture arguments in the hopes that they will soon abate. Or perhaps she can blame the moisture arguments on environmental insults. Too many days indoors with not enough stimulation and no exercise, and moisture arguments are involuntarily activated in the presence of the possibility of human kindness. She attempts rictus, that simple arrangement of muscle groups, but she is not sure if this offering is transmitted properly. Vanessa looks harried, as if she can't believe what she's seeing, and Rosa Elisabetta is perhaps, in some register, prepared for the fact that her daughter might not be able to believe in this place.

"Food any good?" Vanessa asks, and reaches out to touch a spot on Rosa's face, which is a residual brownie mottling site, and Vanessa harvests the residual brownie accumulation. Vanessa laughs. Rosa believes that the laughing is meant to indicate that it is widely understood that the food in hospitals is not good. This is known as a rhetorical question.

"Can we sit in there?" And without waiting to hear if that is an acceptable place for maximal cushioning, Vanessa takes her mother's arm, and they are heading back toward the dining room, even though there are residual smells. Time has shellacked the walls of the dining room with the debased categories of hospital food. Even during those hours when you are not eating, there is the smell of what you have eaten, as though it is part of the history of the place, a history of smells. The conversation is under way once Rosa is conscious of its being under way, which is after it has already begun. Vanessa is talking quickly and introducing many practical issues and much repetition of key concepts, but Rosa doesn't follow ideas easily, and by the time she comprehends one, Vanessa is already well onto the next, like she hears something about the idea of *aftercare* and something about *long-term rehabilitation,* and these things make her want to spill out of her pouch, and her pouch is still churning when Vanessa is telling Rosa what the doctor told her, a sequence of words connoting lengths of incarceration that she cannot fathom at the moment, and this is when she misses the part about the physical, Vanessa saying that the physical, something something, something, like a song Rosa can't remember, and colitis as an expression of alcohol abuse, and Rosa just winces at all of it, she just begins to fold into a wincing interval.

"You've got a few more days, that's what they think, and then we have to find somewhere else to put you. Because I can't keep bringing you here. They don't want you here anymore unless you're going to agree to go somewhere else. Do you understand what I'm saying? So we're going to have to find some rehabilitation place."

With a lecturer, there is some kind of critical layering of key concepts, so that they began to mulch and fertilize, but with her daughter, there's no layering, which means that the critical concepts are unjustified, or perhaps imported from a safe zone, which brings about further involuntary moisture arguments, and these are accompanied by a resignation in the mucous musculature, and this prompts Vanessa to take the name of the Lord in vain and to go rooting through her combination bag and sack.

"What do you expect? You're sick. What do you expect me to do? Because I leave you at home, and then you start barricading the door and you're not eating. And you practically kill the cat. And I have a job, and it's really hard for me to do my job and to make enough money to make sure that the mortgage is paid on the building, and then I have to come back home and worry about whether you're dead. And I know that you don't exactly feel like you understand me, Ma, but I love you just the same. Haven't I stayed to keep an eye on you? I have. I stayed. And I'm willing to look after you and make sure you have somewhere decent to live because I love you. But you have to make it easier on me. You aren't making it easy on me at all. I don't know whether you start drinking at nine in the morning or you drink at night, and no one else knows, either. And then you go out, and you're drunk, and people from up the block, they come and tell me you're totally drunk, walking around in the neighborhood. People leave me notes, 'Vanessa, please call,' and then I call, and people say that you've said the most awful stuff to them, Ma, and I want to let you go your own way, because you always went your own way, and that's what makes you lovable, but not if you're killing yourself, right? Do you really want to do that? I talked to the doctor. Ma, are you listening to what I'm saying? Here, use this. And what the doctor said is that your liver is really enlarged and it's probably not going to last. You could get cirrhosis. Or you could get liver failure. And that's when dementia starts to set in, you know. That might be what's causing the disorientation. And you keep drinking with pancreatitis, that's what all the bleeding is. That's the course of the illness, Ma. You're sick and you have an illness. And I have people calling saying you're disoriented and confused wandering around the neighborhood, and the doctor says you have liver damage, but no one is going to replace your liver while you are drinking. So what am I supposed to do? Do you see me going out every night to clubs? I'm not going to clubs. Do you see me going on any dates? I'm not going out on any dates. If anyone even asked me out on a date, I'd turn them down, unless it's a business thing. I'm not doing any of that. What

I'm doing is coming back to the house to make sure you're still alive. That's what I think about at the office. I wonder if Ma will still be alive when I get home. It's not even, oh, I wonder what horrible thing she's got to say to me today. That's what it's like. So now you have a few days to cool it in here, and we'll see what we can do about finding a rehab, and when you're done here, I want you to tell me that you're willing to go to the rehab, okay? I don't want to hear anything out of your mouth, I just want to hear that you understand what's going on and that you're going to a rehab. Got it?"

The cranium of Rosa Elisabetta has found that the table is the best resting area. A long silence does not diminish the need for resting, nor moisture.

"Listen, do you want to hear what else is going on? You won't believe the story that came into the office. You won't believe it. Do you want to hear this? This treatment came through."

Even in her diminished capacity, even with the medication coursing in her, Rosa can manage some guess as to the nature of the story, because all of the stories from the films that her daughter makes, they're all about drugs, prostitution, *travesti*, families torn apart, people from history who try to kill other people from history, and young people who don't respect their parents. So it must be one of those, probably the story about young people not respecting their parents. She can't possibly get all of this out, especially with her head resting on the table, but she's not diminished enough to forget what she thinks about her daughter's films, which is that she won't go to another movie opening unless her daughter stands up and thanks her personally in front of the audience. But just as she's thinking this relatively straightforward and unfaithful thought, something numinous happens to her. She is suddenly a creek feeding into some larger stream, and in this continuum of the aquatic, she is aware of the very answer to this question, as if she has been submerged into it, and she knows the answer, so she whispers, "Diviners."

Vanessa is stunned. Vanessa, who is ripple-shuffling a pack of playing cards sitting on the table in the dining room, stops everything to gaze at her mother. Deeply skeptical.

"Did Annabel tell you? Did you talk to Annabel?"

"Diviners."

"How did you know?"

That's when Rosa Elisabetta makes her first attempt to tell what happened after the seizure. She doesn't know if she should tell, because it may be that telling anyone will create dosage-escalation criteria. During visiting hours there are always people around listening. You never know. There are two men on the far side of the room now and they are playing dominoes, although it's unclear if they are actually playing the game or if they are just using the domino tiles for a construction operation that keeps their hands from fist formation. One of these men is saying, Yeah, thirteen times there and they just got tired of seeing him, couldn't get no bed, *nowhere nohow.* These men could easily be listening.

"I heard certain things."

"You what?"

"I heard certain things."

"Sit up."

"I was hearing certain conversations."

"What do you mean?"

They took the phone privileges away from her, that was the first thing they did, because after they gave her the exam and remanded her to this ward, she got right on the phone, and she would not let anyone else use the phone, and she was belittling them, because this seemed pragmatic, but then she started to feel as if there were vermin around, a bad sign. She got up out of bed to demand that something be done about this vermin. If this was a respectable hospital in a respectable neighborhood in Brooklyn, at least they could ensure that there wouldn't be hundreds of cockroaches in her room. And this was certainly criterion for dosage escalation, after which there is a gap in the story, and she is waking up on the floor of her room and they are telling her that she has had a seizure, and she feels as though a factory of aeronautics has opened in her vocabulary, and ideas appear like mobiles, but the best she can do is watch them circle. They prescribe some other thing, some other medication, an anticonvulsive, and when they give her the anticonvulsive it becomes clear that they have taken care of the vermin infestation. There are still moments she is unclear on. When exactly did the obese woman arrive in the room? No one will talk to her about the obese woman.

And in the middle of the night she began overhearing conversations, and it turns out that she recognizes some of the voices of the conversations, and these are people in her daughter's office. First she recognizes the voice of the black girl, which is a voice she always liked, and maybe she just hears a voice because she admires a voice, and a voice is a thing of comfort. As when you are falling into sleep, fretting. Not the particular words of the voice but the sound of it, like it's a melody of a song. And she always liked Annabel, called the office just to talk to Annabel sometimes, because Annabel reminded her of the children from the neighborhood. But she hears a particular conversation and then she hears Annabel talking to another person, who was a man. And the conversation is *fishy*, to be sure, not a good conversation, there are things going on there, with the man, who is, Rosa believes, the man in the office, the man from the mindless action films, and there is something going on between them. Even though he is a married man. She has an idea, in her bed, in the slipstream of detoxification, that there is something going on between Annabel and this married man, but out of this comes this idea, and that idea is —

"I heard about diviners."

"But where did you hear about it?"

"I just heard about it."

"Ma, you're on drugs."

Rosa cannot dispute certain hypotheses because it's too tiring to dispute them. The orderly comes by and tells her to sit up.

"The story, it's incredible, it's like this gigantic story spanning thousands of years," and then Vanessa, ignoring what Rosa has said, goes off on her plot summary, and Rosa is unable to follow the story, just as she was not really able to understand the voices after the seizure. She told the doctor that she had heard the voices, and the doctor asked what kind of voices, and she said she believed that they were the voices of persons acquainted with her, but they were not just any kind of voices, and the doctor asked what kind of voices, then, and she said that she was hearing voices from telephones. And he asked how did she know that they were voices on telephones, and Rosa said that she knew because there was static on the line. So, he said, you are receiving cellular telephone traffic? It had not occurred to her that it was cellular telephone traffic, because Rosa has never used a cellular telephone, and she only really knows about them because once she went to a matinée with a friend and she heard a cellular telephone go off; well, and then Vanessa, her daughter, has one, and her daughter let her try her cellular phone once, but who would she call? There was no one to call except her daughter. Nonetheless, it was a working theory that telephone calls took up residence in the affected parts, and when the affected parts were operating in such a way that one piece of information followed another, she formulated the thought that she had begun receiving the cellular telephone traffic of the city of New York *in her head.* She was now in condition of receiving and she could single out certain calls, and they were in fact the calls that had anguish in them, she could overhear only the calls that had anguish in them, for instance a call where some man was realizing that some stock that he had was going down. And she could hear that Annabel was suffering, not that Annabel gave away her anguish, because Annabel was a good girl and she would not let a little thing like a married man provoke a scene, but Rosa could hear the loneliness, all these calls were about loneliness; for example, later there was a call from Annabel to her parents, there was a call to her parents —

"So it's going to make a really great television show, that's what I think. I think we're going to try to pitch it to one of the cable stations, and maybe there'll be a way to make part of it in Italy, you know? Like, if they take it, I could just make sure that part of it's in Italy, and maybe we could go back over there."

And the other girl, is she an intern, the other girl, the one with the burns? It was late at night, and she was thinking about the burns. The obese woman in the next bed was like an oppression. Soon the obese woman would awake. And Rosa was afraid, and the part of her that was afraid was also overhearing the conversation from the girl with the burns. And now Rosa is hearing it all again, in the dining room with her daughter. She's hearing, in her head, about the burns.

"Did you hear this thing in the papers? About Annabel's brother? Ma, are you listening?"

It is almost the time of medication, which is why the voices, the telephone calls, are back, because it is the time of medication, which is the time when detoxification of addicts appears as what it is, a medical problem, and the moisture arguments do perhaps include a recognition of a retreating backward away from Vanessa, and from the neighborhood, and into the logic of the telephone calls.

"It's in the papers. It'll be the front page tomorrow. You watch and see if someone brings the paper in. A woman got hit in the head with a brick walking home yesterday, in midtown. She was just walking along, and someone hit her in the head with a brick. Just because she was there. I mean, who's surprised about that? The thing is that the woman was hit in the head by a bicycle messenger. And they released information about a suspect this afternoon, and the suspect they are looking for is Annabel's brother.

Apparently he got into some kind of scuffle yesterday. So if you talk to Annabel, be nice to her. Her brother is missing. He just took off somewhere. Didn't show up for work."

The orderly announces that visiting hours are over. Vanessa helps Rosa up onto her feet, and Vanessa tells her that she loves her, in a nonchalant way, and then they walk down the corridor together, and the only clinging opportunity, for the moment, is onto the arm of her daughter. Rosa Elisabetta is worried about what night brings, about the fresh information of the night, which is worse than the television squawking in the dayroom. The only good thing about her illness of overheard voices is that it is not an illness of overheard television programming. Now she is back by the nurse's console, and her daughter is talking to someone, and no doubt her daughter is describing their exchange, describing affected parts, describing the unusual occurrences that are now taking place in affected parts, and this is not good because it augurs a dosage escalation and a further reduction of things in their infrastructural simplicities, but there is no time for that because now the addicts are lining up.

12

His mom! His mom! Coming into the room! His mom is beautiful! He forgets his mom is coming into the room and then she comes into the room, and it's a surprise and then here she is and he loves her. He forgets how beautiful she is, and then suddenly she is coming into the room to take him home, and he remembers that she is so beautiful, because she has hair this dark, and she has dark eyes, and she is beautiful and round. And she's his mom. And she has the spot right between her eyes which is a beautiful spot, and nobody else's mom here has that spot, which means it is beautiful. And when his mom smiles, it's a beautiful smile, and when she doesn't smile, that means it's a time before smiling, and this is a beautiful time because a smile will come along soon. And his mom talks in a beautiful way that is different from the way that everybody else's mom talks. She says things in a beautiful way, a way that sounds different, because she comes from another place, but he can't remember what this place is called. He knows that he lives in Queens, and he is in Queens now, at least he thinks he is, and his mother is in the room and she is talking to the nice lady, and the nice lady and his mom are smiling and they are pointing. He is good and maybe he is the best of all the children. And the nice lady is going around the room and she is showing his mother all the things that everybody has made today, like Eddie made an airplane and then Eddie spent a long time standing in one corner with the airplane, making the noise of an airplane. He was there almost all day, and the nice lady had to tell him he needed to do something besides just make the airplane noise, and he didn't pay any attention, and later another boy went over and pushed him down and told him to shut up, took away the plane, stamped on it, and everyone started crying. The nice lady tried to explain about how they didn't need to cry and that this was a problem to solve, but Jaspreet didn't understand what she was saying and neither did Eddie or the other boy, the stamper, and anyway, Jaspreet just wanted to use the glue stick and to be left alone. He's excited about lining up the glue with the edges of things that he has cut out. He's excited because he will not use too much glue on these pictures that he has cut out. If you put too much glue on, then the picture won't stick. But if you put down just the right amount of glue, then the picture stays, and this makes him happy, like his mother coming in makes him happy. Also, there is a girl called Denise, and Denise makes him happy, he isn't sure why. When she gets mad, she throws everything on the floor and cries, and one day she wouldn't stop biting other people and she punctured the skin on Jaspreet's arm. But even when she is crying, he always wants to put his hand on the top of her head. Sometimes he just gets up in the middle of the class, and then he goes over and puts his hand on the top of her head. No matter what she is trying to do, he will put his hand on the top of her head. Usually there are pigtails or there is a braid, but sometimes the hair is all pulled up on the very top, and there is a thing that makes it stay on the top of her head, and if he puts his hand on the top of her head when this thing is making the hair stay up, then she will squeal or cry, and the nice lady will say, "Jaspreet, stop touching the top of Denise's head." Or the nice lady will tell him to stop touching her ear. Because he also likes to touch Denise's ear, the little part at the bottom of her ear, it has a gold ring in it, and he just likes to go and touch this spot. If she's in a good mood and has not thrown things on the floor or bitten anybody, then she smiles when he puts his hand on the top of her head, and they stay there like that.

His mom goes and looks at all the things that everyone made out of paper, and she tells Eddie that his plane is good, and she tells Denise that her picture of a horse is good, and then she tells Maurice that his boat is good, even though it's crusted with glue, and she tells Mohammed that his racing car is very good, and then she comes and looks at the picture that Jaspreet has made, which is a picture of the sun. The sun is smiling down on the land. And his mother comes and asks him what the land is that the sun is smiling down on, but he doesn't answer because he doesn't like to answer. But he smiles up at his mother because his mother is beautiful and so is the nice lady. Then the nice lady asks, "Jaspreet, can you just this once tell your mother what it is a picture of?" And she points at the sun, which is smiling. "What is this that's smiling here? We know you know the name of it. Just tell your mother how you know the name. Can you do that for me?" Jaspreet smiles at his mother and smiles at the nice lady, but he has a feeling like he does not want to say the name of the sun. If he had drawn a tree, then maybe he would say that its name was *tree*, though maybe he wouldn't say that, either, just because. If he felt like it, maybe. But today he doesn't want to say that the sun has a name, because he just doesn't want to, and what he wants is what he wants, even though his mother is beautiful. It's important to go home now because it's the end of the day, or at least he thinks so, and when his mother picks him up, then he doesn't have to go out into the hall with the other kids, because when he is with the other kids out in the hall something horrible happens. One time he threw up.

"Come on, Jaspreet, just one word, and it will make our day

complete. We will feel like we have had an especially good day if you will just say one word."

He says nothing. He can see that his mother is not smiling now, and actually she is making a face that is not such a nice face, and she is taking him by the wrist, telling him that it is time to go, but he has not put away the glue stick and the picture, and he begins to cry out about the glue stick, but not exactly about the glue stick, because he would rather not have to use any words, but it's just a fake cry, a fake sound coming out of his mouth, a mouth-wide-open cry, and Maurice starts to cry out, too, and some of the others, too, and soon everybody is pounding on the table, and the nice lady looks afraid because it's scary when everybody gets mad, and they could start spilling paint. Jaspreet just wants to put away the glue stick, put the lid on the glue stick and take it over to where the supplies go, where the glue sticks and the pens and the crayons go, but his mother has him by the wrist and she is telling him not to argue with her now, just come on along, please, because there are things to get for dinner and she does not have time. There's some more about the glue stick, and he wants to tell her about the glue stick, how wonderful the glue stick is, and that's when he finally gets out the words "Glue stick," and everyone hears the words, the nice lady hears the words, and everyone applauds because they know it's a good day when Jaspreet finally says something.

Later he's in the supermarket cart, standing. Even though he is way too big to be standing in it. He can see that no other kids his size are standing in the supermarket cart, just kids that are half as tall, and he has ripped open the box of cereal with his teeth and he is putting cereal in his mouth, piece after piece. And his mother is pushing him down the aisle in the cart, and he is making a trail of cereal behind him. His mother used to try to get him not to eat the cereal on the way down the aisle, but now she just lets him. She could get him to stop with the trail, but so far she hasn't noticed. One day a man frightened him by telling him not to eat the cereal. Another time he saw the same man, and the man didn't say anything. Cereal is Jaspreet's favorite meal. Sometimes in the morning there are television shows that have a lot of commercials with cereal. He just waits patiently until the television is turned on. He watches whatever is on. If there is cereal in the show it's even better.

What is the best kind of cereal? The best kind is whatever kind he is eating. Sometimes he eats cereal for breakfast, lunch, and dinner. In the aisle, his mother says there will be dried lentils, and there will be chapattis and there will be aloo gobi and there will be cashews and naan bread, which is a bread that he likes. There will be achars. He likes cereal better. Soon they are clumped in a line behind all the people clumped, and his mother hands him a newspaper with a lot of ladies in it. He is distracted by the ladies until his mother is going past the man with the machine where you rub the boxes. This man asks if Jaspreet would like to rub one of the boxes, and Jaspreet looks at his mother, and his mother sighs. What he really wants is to ride on the belt that goes past the man, but he will not do that today, since there are a lot of people behind them. Instead he will put the box on the machine. He runs around the end and stands where the man with the apron is standing, and he takes the box of cereal that he has already eaten most of, and he rubs the box and rubs the box again, and the machine beeps. He wants to do it again.

The man says, "Just once, otherwise you'll have to pay for it twice." To Jaspreet's mother: "He's a natural."

He can tell that the man is saying something that's a joke, except that Jaspreet can't understand what's so funny. And his mother, who should understand the joke, doesn't seem to think it's funny. She looks cross. Maybe there were other funny things that happened today, but he can't exactly remember. After the exchange-of-money part, they are out on the sidewalk, and he is carrying the bags because that is one thing he can do that no one else can do. Except that he gets bored. Maybe his mother will be singing something in her feathery voice while they carry the bags back to the house.

Sometimes when they get home his father is waiting in his car out in front of the building, and sometimes he isn't waiting because he is working late into the night. On those evenings, Jaspreet needs to go to bed without his father telling him a story. *Being strong* is always the moral of the story. Be strong, you have to be strong, but if his father doesn't tell him a story, then he is not strong, he's weak, because there's a moment at the end of the day when he always knows that something is going on, some joke is being told, except that he doesn't understand what's so funny and he wants to be included, except that he's not included, he's standing off to one side, no matter when it is, and if it's during the day, then there are some other kids standing with him, all of them looking like they forgot something important, and then there are those other kids in the hall, whispering. At night, in bed, he can remember all of this, in bed, and it doesn't matter if his mother is beautiful and his father is strong and drives a fancy car, it only matters that he doesn't understand the jokes. The feeling is like wanting to break something over his head.

His father is not waiting when they get home, and his mother is short-tempered, and she is unlocking the front door in a way that is not good, and Jaspreet knows not to speak. Instead, he goes into the room where the television is, and he looks at the lone fish in the goldfish bowl and he watches the fish turn and turn again. Soon someone will have to feed this fish. What the fish does is rush to the top of the water, which is good.

His mother calls, and he goes into the kitchen. His mother! She asks him to use the rolling pin, which is a special task. He likes to help roll out the dough for pastries, and he eats some of the dough, and suddenly he is hungry and doesn't know if he can wait until dinner because he is hungry, and his mother slaps his hand and tells him not to eat all of it yet. But there is a dish of dried lentils, and so he eats some. The chapattis will be better than the raw dough.

Then there is a knock on the door.

Someone is at the door! Jaspreet goes to hide in the television room, beside the couch. He doesn't know why he goes running to hide. He always does. Sometimes there is a cat living in the apartment, which is the cat belonging to the neighbors, because sometimes the neighbors go away, and Jaspreet's father brings in the cat. And when the cat comes to stay, Jaspreet tries to pull the tail of the cat, and the cat goes running and hides under the couch.

It's just his father, who is knocking at the door, and now he is putting his key in the door, and now he is opening the door, and now he is coming inside. His father is strong! His father has special gloves. His father has a beautiful turban, and sometimes his father takes off the turban and Jaspreet sees his father's hair. One day he, too, will wear the turban. Jaspreet likes to pull on his father's hair, and he likes to pull on the tail of the cat, and he likes to smell his father's hair, and his father lets him pull on his hair as long as he doesn't do it hard. He comes running, out from behind the sofa to where his father is, and he trips over a yellow bulldozer that is right in the middle of the floor, a bulldozer that his mother told him to pick up, and he did pick it up, and then he put it back where it was, and now he has tripped over it. When he dusts himself off, he sees that his father is not alone.

The pale lady has yellow hair, hair that is the color of the sun in his drawing of the sun. And the lady is thin like a coatrack. She is wearing a long red coat. A raincoat. His father gives him a hug and he musses his hair, but Jaspreet doesn't know why. Jaspreet stares at the pale lady for a long time, until his father tells him he doesn't need to be staring, and then his father says her name. And he tells Jaspreet's name to the pale lady, and she extends her hand, and Jaspreet looks at her thin hand. Then his mother comes out of the kitchen, and she is wiping off her hands on a towel, and she sees the pale lady, and then Jaspreet and his mother are staring at the pale lady, and the pale lady is staring back at them. The pale lady tries to get his mother interested in her hand, but she continues wiping off her own hands and then after a while she extends her hand. Jaspreet makes a noise in his throat that is not a word. The noise is like there's a lot of water in the back of his throat, and he keeps making it, and then he goes over and touches the raincoat of the pale lady and puts his hand in her pocket.

"He likes to see what's in a person's pockets," his father explains.

She nods and she pulls out a piece of fabric. It's many colors, the piece of fabric, and she gives it to him, and he wraps it around his head.

"Jeanine has come here to meet Jaspreet." His father is saying something else, but Jaspreet has the colorful fabric and he goes back into the television room, and the pale lady comes with him into the television room. And he's carrying the fabric, and he is holding it around his head like it's a turban. He points at the goldfish, and the pale lady, in a surprised way, says the word *goldfish*, and when he taps on the glass, the fish startles, and he points at it again.

"Do you feed the fish?" She keeps saying everything slowly like he can't understand, when he can understand fine. Jaspreet goes into the kitchen to fetch the can that has the fish food and when he's in the kitchen, he can see his mother with her hands on her hips, and he can see his father, who is tugging on his beard. His mother is whispering.

"Did you get paid for this fancy new job? Did you get paid for it? And is it part of your job that now you are bringing home the sexy Americans on a Friday night? From the job that doesn't actually pay any money to you? The one where you quit your job that paid? Like you think you are working in a movie? Maybe the white lady in the living room will start singing a ballad to you, which you can put in your American movie? You think they actually want you to work at this company? You are not a student anymore and you have a family to take care of. That is your responsibility, and you are fooling around like a child, and your employer from the taxi service is calling the house, wanting to know why you have not come in. Did you even tell him that you are not working there any longer? I didn't come all this way to raise my son in this country with a lazy husband."

There's more, but Jaspreet can't understand. He can't understand because the shouting is in the other way of talking that his parents talk to each other, and also sometimes his cousins talk in this other way, and he can understand some things and other things he can't understand. His father watches his mother, and then when they see that Jaspreet is standing there, they start doing other things, and his father goes to the cabinet where there are special bottles, and he starts pouring from these special bottles. And Jaspreet is underfoot, trying to get to the drawer that houses the can that has the food in it for the fish, and his mother bats him out of the way, but he comes back. She tells him to get out of the way and then when she looks up, the pale lady is standing in the doorway. Everyone remembers that she is there, and so his mother lets him get the fish food, and he holds it up like it's a trophy.

"Would you care to have a drink?" his father asks. And the lady says she would, and his father goes back to the mixing of special things. Jaspreet leads the pale lady back to the goldfish bowl, and there is the magic feeding, and the little mouth of the goldfish troubles the surface of the water. And they watch the fish until it is time for dinner.

The table is laid for four, and soon the four people are sitting at the table. Jaspreet does not like to sit at the table, and so he takes his chair into the kitchen and he comes back and he stands at his place at the table. His mother gets up and turns on the television because now is the time of a show that has to do with a million dollars. Jaspreet doesn't like the show that has to do with a million dollars because the man who is on the show looks like he is catching on fire. Jaspreet tries not to look at the television and the man, but he keeps looking over anyway. Whenever the television is on he has to look over at it whether he wants to or not, and he keeps seeing the man, and the man is repeating the same things over and over again. And Jaspreet's father asks if they must have the television on right now, and the pale lady is looking around the room like she forgot something.

"We have a guest," his father says.

His mother frowns.

The room smells of spices, just as the kitchen smells of spices, and Jaspreet loves the smell of spices, even if he likes cereal better. The pale lady tries to eat. She is not saying anything. His father asks Jaspreet how his school was today, and Jaspreet doesn't say anything, he just smiles. Was it good? his father asks, and Jaspreet smiles. Did you make anything? his father asks, and Jaspreet smiles. And how were the other children? Jaspreet smiles.

"Can you at least turn the program down, please?" his father says to his mother. Jaspreet's mother is pretending that she cannot hear his father, and the man on the show is asking the questions. Are you sure? the man is saying.

Next, his mother is saying something very hard to follow. This is about how she met Father when she was just a child, and how her parents knew his father's parents, and that is how they came to meet, she and his father, because this is how things were done, and for this reason, his mother is saying to the pale lady, she is meant to pay attention to Jaspreet's father's remarks, even when his remarks are not worth listening to. And she is meant to put up with him, even if he decides to quit his job for no good reason at all and begins claiming that he is a leading expert on television shows. Jaspreet understands some of this, but every time he tries to understand something his eyes stray back to the television set to watch the man who is on fire.

The pale lady says, "Maybe it would be better if I left."

Jaspreet lets out an involuntary squeal. He doesn't know why.

"No, no!" says his father.

His mother is quiet and looks at the plate of food in front of her. The pale lady is looking at the plate of food in front of her. Jaspreet pushes his chapatti through the sauce like a boat. Everybody is looking at their plates, which makes Jaspreet want to reach out and touch food. That's what he thinks he should do. He could throw aloo gobi on the floor or he could just go in the kitchen and eat cereal, he could take it into the basement, because everyone is quiet. The pale lady seems to get ready to say something, and then she is saying it.

"Well, it's true, if you don't mind my saying, that in our business, the way you make money, most of the time, is through the studios. You need to have a project in place, and then you charge fees to the studios, production expenses. Sort of like with a law firm. And that's why you have to keep costs down, you know, during the period when you don't have that many projects in production. And the thing is, your husband has an idea that we like, a great idea, and we're hoping that we can find a way to develop the project, and then when we do, he'll be able to make some money at it. The possibility of making money is an incentive for him and it's an incentive for us, too. See what I'm saying? Until that time, the time when we start charging fees to the studios, it might be a little tight as far as salary goes, that's true. But I think you should know that Ranjeet's idea is very good and that everyone in the office thinks it's a really good idea. Vanessa, who started our company, she thinks it's a very good idea. So we're moving forward with it. And that's really why I came tonight, to tell you that Ranjeet has become a part of the Means of Production family. He's well liked in the office, he's a real innovator, and we're grateful that he brought his talent and expertise to us. Of course, I also wanted to meet Jaspreet."

The lady turns to look at Jaspreet and smiles, but he can see that she is not happy about the smiling or about the talking. And her smile is not a happy smile. And that's when he decides that he will throw the aloo gobi on the floor after all. It's not a decision, really. He feels something coming to the surface of him and he either lets it happen or he gets distracted, but he doesn't think whether he should do it or not because he has a habit of forgetting. He forgets what came before, and so he doesn't know what to do, so the action either takes place or it does not take place, and if it takes place it is already decided, but it is decided in his bones and his muscles. And sometimes when these moments of activity overcome him it is like a storm, and he is doing many things, most of them bad things. That is what his parents tell him, that he is doing bad things, and if he continues doing bad things, they don't know what they are going to do with him. He may be poking someone's dog with a stick, or he may be painting the windows with nail polish, or he may be throwing things out the window, and now the thing he is doing is he is screaming, not some particular word, he is just screaming, and he is throwing the aloo gobi on the floor, and then he is sweeping objects off the table, like he is sweeping off the dish with the cashews in it, and the plate that has the naan bread on it, this is now on the floor, and soon many things are on the floor, and the shouting rises up like a balloon in the sky, and the objects must be on the floor, and things should be broken, certain plates must be broken, and he is shouting and he is making fists and he is pounding on furniture, and this all happens very quickly, so that his father and his mother don't have time to stop him before he has made a very big mess. Now his mother is crying and saying, "Oh, my Lord, what is happening to him?" And his father must get up from the other side of the table and he must start trying to hold back Jaspreet, but Jaspreet shakes himself loose and he runs into the television room, and he takes the goldfish bowl and throws it on the floor, which he has actually done many times, and he spits at the man on the television set who is on fire. He doesn't know why he does anything, but he knows that the pale lady is part of his tantrum.

"We must put him upstairs," his mother says.

"This is your fault," his father says. They are not even thinking about the pale lady now, who has risen from the table and is walking toward the closet where the coats are hanging.

"What do you mean? Is it my fault that we do not have the income that we had because you have this mistaken belief that you are now an artist? That is not my fault. And I did not bring home a strange woman for dinner. I went to the store as I always do, and I brought home my son, as I always do."

"You know nothing."

The goldfish is wriggling on the floor like a comma trying to slip between two clauses. His father makes an angry gesture in the direction of his mother and then he goes to pick up the goldfish bowl. Jaspreet takes the goldfish into his hand and it is undulating, before he in turn is bundled up by his father. He goes under one arm of his father's, and his father says, "Give me the fish."

Jaspreet shakes his head.

"Give me the fish."

Jaspreet shakes his head.

"The fish will die. Do you understand? Give me the fish or the fish will die. Do you want the fish to die?" Jaspreet is kicking, he is swinging wildly, but he will not open his fist with the fish in it. The women, his mother and the pale lady, are swarming around his father and they are telling him that he mustn't hurt Jaspreet, and then his mother has caught him by the hand and she is prying open his hand with a fork because she can't get his hand open, and the goldfish tumbles out of his hand and onto the floor, and he screams at letting go of the goldfish, and his mother shouts, "He killed the fish, you see? He killed the fish because of you. You made him kill the fish, and now we will have to buy another fish."

"The fish cost ninety-nine cents! That's how much you know about it!"

She takes Jaspreet's legs, which are still kicking, and they carry him upstairs by his arms and legs, and his father says that they are going to have to put him in the room, as if Jaspreet doesn't know which room that is, the room that they are talking about, but he does know, so he kicks and screams harder, because it is the room that doesn't have anything in it, not a thing, it is just a room with nothing in it. The room scares him horribly, not because it has no lights. Well, it does have a light, which he cannot reach, but it has no television, and it has no fish, and it has no parents in it, it is just scary and quiet, and there is nothing to do, and he doesn't like to be in there. Sometimes he is in there for a long time because he will not be quiet, and that is where they are taking him, of course. His father is complaining about how they are having to do this more often now that Jaspreet is getting older, and why is it that he is doing it more, is it because he is in America? Would he keep doing this if they were in India? Jaspreet's mother will not answer him, and soon they have put Jaspreet in the room, which is just a closet, really. Jaspreet's father is saying, "Jaspreet, you cannot ruin dinner. It is not fair to your mother, who worked very hard preparing the dinner, and it is not fair to me, because I brought home a guest, and you ruined dinner for the guest, and she came a long way from the city to meet you, and you made her never want to come to dinner at our house again. And every time that you do these things, you make us worry. We do not want to have to worry about you. You have to try to help us, rather than hinder us. Do you understand what we are saying?"

He is in the corner, and he is feeling bad at the way his father is talking, and he does not want to reply, nor does he want to say anything.

"Are you doing these things because your mother and I are arguing? Because we do not mean to upset you by arguing. We argue sometimes because we have known each other for many years, and that is what people do when they have known each other for many years. It's nothing personal and I love your mother, and she is my most perfect friend and my ally. Do you understand?"

Here the parents of Jaspreet try to hug each other in a way that will prove what they are saying. But he is looking at the floorboards in the room that has nothing in it, which is really just a closet, and he is tracing the shape of his hand, palm down, on the floorboards in the room that has nothing in it.

"Many good things are about to happen. I believe this. And we will purchase a new fish. This is my solemn vow. Many good things will happen, and we will purchase a new fish, and when the weather is warmer we will go to the tops of tall buildings and look at the view from these buildings, and we will ride roller coasters, and we will watch the horses run at the racetrack, and I will take you to the Gurdwara, and you will learn to be a devoted son and a devoted Sikh. And we are going to shut this door now, but we are not going to lock this door. Do you understand? We are shutting the door and we are not locking it, and then on the other side of this door, I am going to be making up with your mother. Do you understand what I am saying to you?"

And then the door is closed, and the silence is big and scary. Jaspreet tries to keep the silence on the far side of the room, but it's like a slow leak. The silence leaks into the room, coming in under the door first, pooling on the floor just inside the doorway, creeping across the floor to the corner where he sits, where he has rolled up his trousers so that the leak of silence will not get on the hems of his trousers. It is like the leak in the basement when the rain is heavy, and soon it will be all the way across the floor. And it will begin to get deeper. He likes the basement, and this is something he can tell himself in the silence, that he likes the basement, he likes the basement, he likes the basement, there are many things in the basement that are his friends. He likes the sound of the thing in the basement, which is a boiler. He likes that sound that the boiler makes, and he likes it when there are clothes strung up on a line in the basement. And he likes the bin full of old sheets and he likes the stacks of old magazines where he can look at pictures. He feels sure that these clothes strung up are like the other place that his parents talk about, their home, which he believes is a place with many colors strung up on lines, and in that place the houses are all full of cereal. That is what he thinks, because he is trying to think. He tries saying things, even though he does not like saying things, because it is too quiet in the room, and so he says *glue stick* a few times. He is just trying it out, he is trying out saying *glue stick* over and over, as if it is a question. Somebody must be listening at the door. Otherwise there would just be too much silence. He puts his ear to the floor because he wants to hear what is being said downstairs, but he is not sure that anything is being said. He will say things, he will try to say things, he will not be silent, and he will not make more silence in the world. He will say things. No one likes silence. He will do better, because his father loves him and his mother loves him and he will do better.

Finally, he pushes open the door, which is guarded by no one. And it is night! Night is beautiful! And everything in his house is where it is supposed to be! There is his parents' room, and he walks on the carpet because he likes the feeling of the carpet in his parents' room on the bottom of his feet. And then he goes across the hall and he goes into his room, in which there is a bed and a few banners of baseball teams because his friends at school have banners of baseball teams. He wants to be like his friends, doing the things that they do. He can hear a clock somewhere. He can hear the faucet downstairs. He can hear the distant sound of the television, which is the sound of his family, the sound of a television drifting is the sound of his household, and when there isn't the sound of the television, then something is wrong. His mother is somewhere cleaning something. He goes to look out the window because what he sees when he looks out the window is other people looking out of their windows, and then he is part of the group of people who are looking. That is good, because the street is beautiful, and the sky at night is dark pink, until the sun comes up, and people are all looking at other people who are looking, except that he can see out the window that there is his father, and his father is walking up the street with the pale lady, and they are near the stairwell that leads to the elevated trains. On the first step of the stairs, his father leans down and he embraces the pale lady and then he puts his lips on her lips, and there is the sound of the television overheard from downstairs, and then there is his father, up the block, kissing a pale lady.

13

Dialectical examination of the subject known hereafter as the 'ugly girl' (UG) was performed on a certain day in May in an American suburb by trained dialectical experts from like socioeconomic demographics, according to participant-observer methodology. Speakers in this northeastern suburb, according to the trained dialectical experts, are undergoing a vowel shift, known as the 'anomie-related vowel shift' (ARVS), best reflected in the [a/ä] transformation of *nah*, as formulated in reply to requests, e.g., Honey, will you please go and pick up some packages of chicken at the corner store? *Nah*. (See, for example, Stinson, et al., 1985.) The UG, according to the trained dialectical experts from the adjacent milieu, was unaffected by the ARVS, despite being identical in age, despite having attained, at the time of the study, the educational level of the eighth grade, along with the trained dialectical experts. A lack of participation in ARVS and in the linguistic engulfers noted by the dialectical experts, such as *fuck/ fucked/fucker/fucking*, in which the engulfer begins to muscle out other parts of speech (moreover, the *like* continuative marker, wherein a certain word is appended, without grammatical consideration, to a sentence wherever a pause is indicated), this lack of participation is evidence of marginalization and isolation within a linguistic community, by which reason the committee of trained dialectical experts determined that a meeting with the UG for purposes of study and exchange of sociolinguistic ideas was urgently needed. The UG, according to the committee, was described as diminutive and given to dress in the traditional garb of this community; viz., blue or black denim pants cut in such a way as to obscure the specific features of the lower half of her body, large hooded sweatshirt, in gray, into the marsupial pocket of which she continually thrust her hands. Face, open, gentle, but characterized by a certain sadness, according to at least one committee member (a characterization that, it should be admitted, is disputed by others, who themselves consider the UG simply 'ugly'), with an unkempt hairstyle generally restricted in the community of the dialectical experts and referred to by them as 'frizzy, corkscrewy,' etc. Lips often downturned, which according to the dialectical experts could be a biological point of origin for the back vowels that have, in the case of the UG, skidded slightly forward until they are rather nearer to colliding with her grand mean, a shift that may be ordinary in topologies of distant southern locales and on audio recordings by gangster rappers but is not known locally and is therefore not considered appropriate by the experts in this study. The recording of the UG by the committee of experts (COE) took place on Fort Point Ave., a quiet thoroughfare, after disgorgement from a standard-issue American school bus, which was, despite its quaint exterior, a veritable stew of linguistic trends and fashions. Upon dismounting from the standard-issue American school bus, the COE approached the UG and, gauging her with a preliminary analysis of her fronting advancement, asked about her boots, the heavy black boots she was wearing. Her reply of 'Get out of my way' was not considered to have resolved the question of the boot, and its relation to Fashion Vowel Supremacy, or FVS. According to FVS and ARVS, certain vowels, especially ü, œ, and ÿ, are considered imperative markers of Linear Community Formation, and that the UG would neither respond using the word 'boot' nor would she comment on the 'boots' themselves, which subsequent researches have indicated were common military jump boots, was the first indication that considerable further study would be required. Proceeding down Fort Point Ave. toward Hillcrest Place, the UG was described as withdrawn and resistant, especially in view of tests being implemented by the COE, such as the test in which the UG is invited to sit and talk on the stone wall in front of the property owned by Dan G. and Audrey L. Harrison of Newton Centre, Massachusetts. The sentence adduced by the COE, of course, by way of invitation, was an attempt to draw out the *sit/ set* reversal, but there was no success in producing this reversal, nor in any other markers of AAVE (African American Vernacular English), such as the *pin/pen* merger, etc. Did this lack of markers indicate a convergence of the COE and the philosophical and emotional and linguistic core of the UG? If so, why did the UG continue, throughout interaction with the COE, to present such an impervious exterior? When the COE asked the UG, 'Don't you like us?' they were of course attempting a sneak attack with the *like* continuative marker, and it should be pointed out in this summary that the dearth of directly quoted dialogue does not rule out the fact of the *duh* continuative marker, as well as the related *d'oh,* or contemporary shame indicator. 'No, I don't like you all,' the UG replied, avoiding the contraction *y'all* of Southern Vernacular English, which the COE claimed to have heard her employ on one or more occasions. In this instance, the reply 'No, I don't like you all' was viewed by the COE as an example of noncompliance with the study. However, noncompliance toward figures of authority, especially in the ARVS and in the case of Narcissistic Adolescent Monosyllabism (NAM), as noted by Davidoff in the *eh* engulfer, indicates a kind of mobility retardation, most notably in the double positive *yeah yeah.* And yet often these kinds of noncompliance, according to the COE, are vital, engaged political strategies. Why then the surrounding and the beginning of excessive threat with respect to the UG, as though surrounding and threat on the part of the COE were legitimate types of academic inquiry? 'Where is your neighborhood at?' the COE demanded, mocking. 'And who is your mammy?' Thereafter giving evidence of knowledge of the wealth of terminologies in the racial-slur family, without asking, it should be pointed out, if these particular lexical units were either a) offensive, or b) simply disparaging. The slurs were, however, often deployed in the history of linguistic exchange between past panels of COE and past UGs. History is littered with misunderstandings. Persons may require terms like 'brother' and 'sister' in order to create kinds of solidarity that diminish the stress levels engendered by adversaries in adversarial conflicts. Of course, a change of venue for the inquiry was considered desirable by the COE, the new venue being, ideally, one understaffed by assistants or graduate students or nosy observers, a venue such as a forest or a vacant lot behind a chain store, which in this afternoon light would not have been well traveled, the better to get a clear picture of the resistance-elongated vowel, or REV, with the hope that isolation would result in the UG's employing the antagonistic usage of adversarial slurs against whiteness, including neologisms and coinages used to describe any individual member of the COE, such as *boneys, nits, gruelies.* For this was the secret worry of the COE, namely that the UG, despite her melancholy and detached exterior, was from the true research and development wing of American language, knowing things that the COE did not and could never know. Was the UG from some special exotic other, some linguistic elsewhere? Whereas the COE itself was from the land of moribund linguists. If the UG would just be willing to collaborate on close personal rapport with the COE, then perhaps the differences between the two parties could somehow be smoothed over. This was the academic plan in terms of primary research, the plan favored by the COE. But let it be said here that the creation of a monolithic first-person plural on the part of the COE was an academic fiction. Because when one of these academics of national repute suggested the change of venue described above, then certain members of the COE, stressing academic differences, began to plead lateness of the hour. These sociolinguists began to have prior commitments to other quarterly publications, such as *Lawn-Mowing Today* and *Review of Contemporary Newspaper Delivery*. In any event, the COE dwindled, having completed the important harassment section of its study on this street, Hillcrest Place, and they therefore decamped to do their guitar practicing, leaving behind just the one member of the COE, the one with the worst skin, the one with the most unwashed hair, the one with the most harrowing situation at home, a situation much commented on by women of the neighborhood, with wringing of hands. The lone member of the COE ran wild in the streets, unencumbered by oversight. What to do with him? He was overweight and had hard-palate deformities, which of course affected his sociolinguistic picture. Here was the sole remaining member of the COE, bent on the disrobement portion of the study. Were it not for the sudden appearance of a second study subject, namely the older brother of the UG, no longer called the UG but now, instead, referred to by her pseudonym for the purposes of study, which was the pseudonym of 'Annabel,' the disrobement might have proceeded. But according to some secret code involving linguistic deviation and dereliction, 'Annabel' summoned this second subject, known simply as 'brother.' A tall, lanky figure, designed for the rescue of children, the so-called 'brother' happened upon the colloquy between the lone member of the COE and 'Annabel,' on Hillcrest Place. He was apparently in the process of returning from what was described as a 'long walk.' At first, the 'brother' thought nothing of it, thought nothing of the appearance before him of 'Annabel,' face composed in that perpetual frown of public school interactions, thought nothing of the overweight and unwashed

COE, who indeed looked like an advertisement for rapists-in-training. The 'brother,' whose name was William, though he preferred the pseudonym 'Tyrone,' was aloof from all daily events on Hillcrest Place. He was, by all accounts, walking around on some astral plane, where his studies concerned the size of black holes and whether or not these emitted radiation, etc., home on vacation from graduate school, etc., and it is no doubt likely that he spoke a tone language, or a clicking language of the African plains, etc., or a Niger-Congo dialect, or Creolist dialect, or Gullah, and the COE member would not be able to understand him, nohow, and so now the COE member, who had previously managed to exercise such admirable academic restraint, was sorely afraid, for he recognized in himself the anxiety engendered by AAVE, especially as practiced by adult male speakers. It was a thing that excluded and belittled the COE member. He would henceforth go unrecognized because of AAVE, his immensity would go unrecognized. He would receive no funding from governmental agencies, which meant, it now became clear, that the COE member should get his 'ass' the 'fuck' off of their street, which meant that the COE would go skulking back up Hillcrest, to the chaos of his own home, after which the study was aborted, and the subject called 'Annabel' fell into a hug with 'Tyrone,' and thus came to a close another sampling of normative suburban behavior.

————

The 'brother' dreams. On Amtrak. Heading northeast. Outside: marshlands of Connecticut. A state noted both for its marshes, for the fractal subdivision of rivers as they empty into the Sound. Time: late afternoon. Day: Friday. Lighting effects are consistent with the light of late afternoon in Connecticut, which is the flickering light of things passing away, the light of things coming to an end. Eschatology. Amtrak riders know that

the water side of the train is the side of flickering light. Ends of
things. What else to do here but remember? Tyrone remembers,
the better to avoid thinking about current events. Tyrone, with
ski cap pulled down over his eyes. Tyrone, having shaved his head
and chin that morning in the apartment, having sacrificed his
dreadlocks. Tyrone, sporting chinos and some shirt his mother
bought for him that had never before been free of its packaging.
He looks like the "model person of color" here on the Northeast
corridor. He counts seven people reading various daily newspapers. Seven readers who might have acquainted themselves with
the headlines and who might have the kind of intelligence that
assembles photos of suspects in newspapers and applies these
pictures to passersby. Flickering light, bare trees. Light of Connecticut estuaries. Tyrone can't, won't think of the enormity of
his predicament. He is a voracious eavesdropper, and overheard
cell phone conversations contain portions of narratives, scraps of
consciousness, grocery lists, birthday wishes, at least until the
Old Saybrook stop, where the weekenders decamp. By then he's
satisfied that it's okay to stroll the car. Tyrone heads for the snack
bar, and he's on his way there, in his chinos and his Italian dress
shirt, when a stylish and elderly woman, having recently boarded
in the village of Old Saybrook, she of the "excessive pastels" and
translucent hair, asks him if he will loft up her rolling suitcase
onto the luggage rack. He thinks about telling her to "fuck off,"
but instead he puts his back into it, hoists up her seventeen-
hundred-pound rolling casket. After which she presents him with
her ticket. Of course, because he's the well-groomed black man
in the car. In truth, the only reason he doesn't "scare" the lady
with the translucent hair is because he's clean shaven and "on
the lam." She should be scared of him, according to news reports. He is randomly felonious, according to at least one tabloid.
Indeed, he's just about to tell the "pastel lady" that "bidialectal-
ism is a natural ability" while taking her ticket and shoving it in
his mouth, or perhaps just hanging on to it so that he can cash it

in somewhere, maybe the casinos. But instead he whispers, "I'm a passenger myself," at which the woman blanches in recognition of her dangerous political mistake. Her rouged cheeks flush, and she is silenced, and he knows that she will never identify him to the interstate authorities because to identify him would be to admit that she believed he was a conductor or rail employee simply because he is a black man. She won't say it in any venue. No prosecutor can make her say it. She is humbled, and he goes back to his seat. He sleeps. The train gathers its lateness into itself, as if it is the patron saint of lateness, it bisects the marshes and then it subdivides the pine barrens of the Bay State. Cell phone gabbers shout to their neighbors about the restaurant they are going to tonight. Up the Northeast corridor, on the lam, in the shuddering and occasionally silent interior of the Amtrak train.

"Hi, Mom," the "brother" whispers, on Hillcrest Place, the interstate train having given way to the commuter train, the commuter train having given way to the taxi, the taxi having given way to the lawn of the Duffy home, which badly needs to be raked. An unused rake is balanced against a birch in the yard, at dusk.

Now that the door is opened, he feels how heavy his secrets are.

"Billy? What are you doing here?"

Awkwardly, Tyrone says, "Surprise! Just wanted to, uh, see the old neighborhood. . . ."

They're in the condition of not knowing how to stand there, as if lessons in casual standing haven't yet taken place. His mother calls upstairs. "Honey? Honey?" When there's no response, she goes up, one step at a time, and Tyrone, standing with his overnight bag in the foyer, takes in the place. The living room, where the neglected furniture is, as always, barely presentable. The furniture is coffee stained, mildewed, neglected; the rugs are matted and sun bleached. The Duffy household is prepared for the leave-taking of the last child, the natural child, Max, who has just the one year left before college, probably at Yale, where the White

Dwarf went. When Max, the natural child, is gone, the Dwarf and his wife will retire to their separate studies, but perhaps in a smaller house befitting a minister in his dotage. On cue, they clump downstairs, Indian file.

"Look at what the cat has dragged in!" the Dwarf observes. "Looking really good, Billy. Neat hairstyle, what there is of it. To what do we owe the pleasure?"

"I needed a break."

They wouldn't ask. They have given up asking. His answer, whatever it is, will entail bad news and irresponsibility. They no longer want to know, nor to feel that they caused it, whatever it is, nor to find themselves wound into the knots of his strange thinking. If a question is put to him in the wrong manner, he will go back to raving, blaming them somehow, asking weighty questions that should go unasked and doing it in an ugly, vindictive way featuring much simulated "ghetto" cursing.

"How long can you stay?"

A few days, he says, and then he tries to close out the subject. Anyway, his father is probably trying to get a sermon together. That's what he's usually doing. Do not distract the White Dwarf from the job of sermonizing. Do not distract his wife, who will be wanting her heaps of rancid cottage cheese and salad while she looks over her five-hundred-page textbook on adolescent depression. She's been sifting through the topic for ten years, for a study that has, as part of its source material, her own experience with a pair of adopted black children. Who knows whether the black children were adopted for the study or whether the study was adopted for the benefit of the black children? It no longer matters.

His father, standing one carpeted step up, reaches out for a hug. Though Tyrone doesn't budge, the White Dwarf clamps his arms around his lanky son and tells him how good it is to see him, and Tyrone almost believes him.

"Come on, get out of the doorway. Make yourself at home."

In a brief attack of the dutiful variety, he follows them, his parents, as they scuttle into the kitchen. Inside, it's the same mixture of leftover pieces of china from other people's houses, glasses with the names of regional country clubs on them, church sale finds. They all sit down at the table. Clipped hydrangea blossoms dry in the centerpiece, blue and cream and gray. To forestall silences, Tyrone panics and rushes to tell them, yes, the job is going fine, really, yes, he is making some art, yes, he just talked to Annabel, yes, he is seeing someone, yes, an Asian curator, and he is feeling well, and, yes, he's okay, he just wanted a short rest, yes, so he took some time off. They seem to be satisfied, or maybe they've just given up. Who knows? He would never be open to scrutiny, he has his notion of dignity, and his notion of dignity is about living beyond their scrutiny. They know. The agreement is for partial disclosure. Soon his parents edge out of the room.

A ragged spider plant on the pantry shelf needs watering. An article clipped from the *Globe,* dangers of herbal remedies, curls on a countertop. A distant cassette plays the cello suites, Pablo Casals sawing away. He's been there a quarter hour, in the kitchen, a quarter hour of staring absently at a dish overflowing with aspartame packets. A quarter hour of turning objects over in his hands. Feeling the heft of a soup ladle left out to dry. A ceramic bowl. His mother crosses through the room several times, appearing, disappearing, carrying more papers. He mutters some more, why can't he stop, about Annabel, oh yeah, about this story she's developing, making up details as he goes along, embellishing, "Multigenerational thing, guys out in the desert with forked sticks, rattlesnakes, scorpions, dig here, the Mormons coming across the plains, the origins of Las Vegas, water wars, a story about dowsing." His mother looks at him in that way, that I-am-still-your-mother way, that way she always looks at him. Mothers, with their night vision goggles. He pretends fascination with the matter of spots of yellowing paint here on the wall by the back stairs. His mother, with her wrinkly face and her pile of unpaper-clipped monographs, all compassion, all exhaustion, looks at him, telegraphing, *Go ahead, tell me.*

Does he want food? Because there is food of some kind, leftovers. There are plastic containers, the food of northeastern intellectuals who disdain culinary flaunting, who prefer the legacy of their forebears, leftover food of minimal flavor, wine from jelly jars. There's tuna casserole in a plastic container, which is similar in consistency and mouthfeel to chicken salad, also in a plastic container, which in turns resembles pasta salad, all from the same spot on the color wheel, yessir, jammed into the refrigerator every which way. Should he decide to eat, he will be well nourished by beige foods. There are many beige choices. He closes the refrigerator immediately, goes into the pantry, but here, too, the range of choices crushes him. How many kinds of cereal can one household have? There must be thirteen brands of cereal, and they are all varieties of flakes; there are bran flakes, oat bran flakes, corn flakes, oh wait, there are rice puffs. All the same color. The flakes are beige. It's the same with the crackers. Maybe a hint of orange or ochre. He starts taking a cracker out of each box, setting them out on the counter in the pantry. From the wheat thin to the saltine to the old-fashioned digestive, it's all in the same family of color tonalities. He needs to know. He is comparing the hue of these crackers to see if there are crackers that are different from the other crackers in any way, looking to discard anything wide of the beige family; he requires the consistency and perfection of beige.

"Max is late at school. Some kind of rehearsal. He should be back any time now."

The proof is immediate. On his way upstairs, Tyrone overhears the garage door opener beneath him. It's the Great White Hope. The "genetic copy." The White Dwarf can be heard stirring in his cloister, as if the Dwarf has an uncanny sense of the movements of the "genetic copy." The White Dwarf is saying something to his wife about All Saints' Day, which appears to have been the theme of last week's sermon, and then the "genetic copy" says something, for now he is on the scene. Soon there are footfalls on the stairs.

The first thing that must be said is that Max's lower lip is pierced. It's an innovation that Tyrone has somehow missed. Max's head is also shaved. Of course, there are two, three, four earrings. Some Maori-style tattoos on the arms. Black jeans and a torn-up flannel shirt. Maximillian Rivers Duffy, public-access television host, advocate of assisted suicide and antiglobalization. Genetic copy. Radical teen.

Tyrone nods imperceptibly from his place on the bed in what is now the guest room. A potpourri dish only inches from him, on the side table, with its bed-and-breakfast olfactory redolences.

Max says, "Hey, Bro."

Tyrone stares.

"Got someone I want you to meet."

Tyrone stares.

"Have you talked to Sis?"

Tyrone says, "Diphthongization in certain regions is incrementally breaking away into triphthongization. If the trend continues, it will no longer be possible to understand certain regions, especially those that are marginalized along cultural or racial lines."

The "genetic copy" stares back.

"I really do have someone I want you to meet."

"In certain counties in North Carolina, the word *dead* has three syllables."

Apparently, there is no choice but to stride past his brother, the "genetic copy." Back in the living room, like the caged animal he always was at this address, Tyrone now feels an additional confinement anxiety, the possibility of future penal confinement. He's flipping through the LPs collected on a shelf on the wall,

looking at some jazz from the fifties, the cover of each LP summoning up a swinging time in his parents' past. Pipe smoking
was pandemic. Sideburns indicated a knowing acquaintance with
the New Criticism, and that's the moment, in this reverie of all
things of which he's contemptuous, when there is old-fashioned
tolling of an American Telephone and Telegraph handset. Their
rotary-dial phone.

He knows immediately.

He hears his mother call out his sister's name, "Hi, sweetheart!"
He's already loping, in his rangy way, past his mother's office,
into the pantry, through the kitchen, up the back stairs again, the
maid's staircase, with all the political ramifications, never the
front staircase, into the teenager's bedroom, that bedroom which
observes all the Congregationalist trappings, a homely bedroom,
without decoration, no wall-to-wall, just a little Oriental area rug
in the middle. Max is actually sweeping his homely bedroom, and
Tyrone says, having changed his mind entirely, "Okay, let's go."

"Where are we going?"

"To see your friend."

The sweeping is undeterred by the conversation. As if sweeping enables reasoning.

"The one you were mentioning before. Let's go."

"You changed your mind fast."

"Don't waste my time."

Max reaches up to the window, opens it, the screen is nowhere
in sight, a legacy of some youthful mischief, and Tyrone says,
"Let me." He means the arachnid that is fleeing ahead of the
piles of dust. Like Jonathan Edwards's pet arachnid. Tyrone
knows about the perfection of the webs; this has all been covered
in his own diaristic commentary on his childhood, which is near
upon sixteen thousand pages in length. He takes the arachnid,
reaches one loafer-clad foot out the window.

"You don't actually have to —" Max says.

Tyrone is on the roof, where he can hear his mother calling urgently to the White Dwarf, his mother who is now in possession of the major facts. The broad outline of the facts, the allegations. He can see the shades half drawn in his father's office. There is gesticulating. There is the pantomime of alarm. The semiotics of alarm, which you can know, instantly, without fear of misrepresentation, when you see it from out the window of the house. From out on the roof. Through transparent curtains that doubtless need washing. Now is the beginning of the end of a safe place. This is what Tyrone Duffy thinks of his predicament now, that wherever he goes, he is the ill wind. In every face, now, the tightening of distrust, because Tyrone Duffy is here, with his sad story.

"Come on, brother. Take me to your leader."

The "genetic copy" doesn't have to be asked twice. They are on the roof, and the roof is a sanctuary, a retreat with access to the light pollution of the night sky. And yet the night sky is opening into the infinite. In this night sky, interstellar gas, remnants of first light, four fundamental forces, trial by jury, confinement. They pause, mismatched brothers. Somewhere nearby the arachnid, released, makes for a gutter.

Tyrone watches as his pierced brother, the "genetic copy," launches himself off the roof above the living room and into the loving arms of a Norway maple that is brushing against the house. A maple that keeps its secrets. By its permanence. Down onto the lawn they go, and then they are across the lawn in an interstellar flash, under the forgiving melancholy of willows beside the creek up the street. The maple takes in these things, this legacy of mistakes.

14

Lois DiNunzio, Means of Production accountant, first met Arnie Lovitz in the one foolproof place to meet eligible men these days, the smoker's ghetto. The civic legislation on the subject of cigarette smoking was profound, was far-reaching, or that's how the city council talked about it when they passed the relevant legislation in 1995. How profound, how far-reaching wasn't clear exactly, until these little societies of smokers began to appear at street level. Cast out of their places of employment. The tide of public opinion had turned against these miscreants, as if all at once. Once, they were worldly, they were crime novelists or backroom politicians. They were salesmen out late indulging in whiskey and women and cigars. Lois's father, Louis DiNunzio, was like that, on the road thirty weeks a year, overnight in cheap motels, with sample industrial chemicals. Who knew what he got into? Now here they were, out in front of the building.

Suddenly, your coworkers were contemptuous of you. As if the legislation tapped an enmity that had long been gathering. Madison McDowell, for example, the poor little rich girl, frequently offended with insensitive comments about Lois's smoking. If Lois closed the office door, it was her own business whether her bronchi were sprouting malignancies. It was not Madison's business. When Lois emerged from her office with the budgetary printouts for Vanessa or the paychecks, when she emerged for whatever stack of envelopes was in her in-box, the women of Means of Production were always staring at her. Oh, there's the smoker again. Lois began going downstairs.

For a while, Lois stood on Fifth Avenue and smoked. In fair weather and foul. Because she liked looking at the cathedral. Sometimes she ventured into the cathedral after work, where she lit candles for the other girls in the office. It wasn't that she cared so much about the other girls. But she liked the long wooden matchsticks, the deep red cups in which the candles flickered. In the distance, clericals in vestments scurried about. Lois had been raised on Long Island and had gone to Pace, not to some fancy school. It didn't mean that she didn't have any feelings. She did her job, and she would bake a chocolate cake from a mix if it was someone's birthday. She made a cake for Annabel's birthday. That was just a couple of months ago. Devil's food cake. Lois didn't understand why no one expected a kindly gesture from her. She was full of polite and well-meaning thoughts. Annabel was a good kid, and Lois wanted to do the right thing.

One day, she's out there smoking, and this fellow is smoking alongside her, and he's smoking a foreign kind of cigarette. It's black and it has gold foil around the filter. There's a sensual manner to his smoking. Like with smokers of old. He's a big man; Lois would say he is a stout man, even. He has a mustache, thinning hair. Mirror sunglasses. And the foreign cigarettes. She doesn't mind admitting it: She was a little boy crazy back in her day. So Lois goes straight up to the stout man with the foreign cigarettes and she asks, "What kind of cigarette you have there?" She's never picked a guy up before, even though she was a little boy crazy, but maybe now she is going to do it, because there's a first time for everything. Arnie, that's his name, replies with the brand of the cigarette, some brand she can't remember. He offers her one. Remember that stretch in summer where all it did was rain? She smoked the black cigarette in the drizzle, and what it made her feel was light-headed.

Or maybe it was Arnie who made her light-headed. Those foreign cigarettes were more potent, they were nicotine delivery systems, like the politicians said, and so she was dizzy, but there was also the stout man, Arnie. A little girl was carrying past a brace of balloons, she remembers, and Lois thought, I'm going to see this man again. The balloons prove it. And she planned to take her break the next day at the exact same time, which was 11:14. Arnie wasn't there the next day, with his foreign cigarettes, but the day after that he was, and soon they were talking about many things.

Arnie grew up in Forest Hills. Lois grew up in Great Neck. They were from the same part of the world and they had common interests. Horror movies, for example. They had both seen a whole bunch of horror movies. Of course, Lois was working for this company that made movies, but she didn't think she had seen more than one or two of the movies they made at her company. Means of Production movies were nonsense, really. They were in English, but they could have been from Timbuktu for all Lois cared. Arnie liked *Nightmare on Elm Street,* those sorts of things. When he talked about teenagers getting hacked up on-screen, he cackled in a nervous way that was endearing, as though he didn't expect anyone to feel likewise, but he couldn't stop himself.

Soon there was a good crew of them out there, a shifting constituency, a society of smokers facing the promenade and the ice-skating rink. Mostly secretaries, but occasionally there would be a middle-management fellow in his bow tie, or maybe the prim and proper office manageress in midcalf skirt and square-heeled pumps. They were all out there, and they were the society of the medically uninsurable. Laughing and gossiping and complaining. They discussed going bowling on the weekends. They were all going to go bowling one day, to the lanes in the bus terminal. But you took one look at Arnie, you'd see he hadn't done any bowling in years. If he tried to go bowling or do yard work, well then he was going to have an aneurysm, because all he did was smoke and come up with plans for his business. He was a smoker and he did all his best thinking while flourishing a Gitane or a Dunhill.

Though the smokers were warm and supportive, though theirs was a caring environment, it was months before Lois realized that Arnie had once been an accountant. Isn't that amazing! She can still remember how it came up, that day when Arnie was stubbing out one of his cigarettes and plunging the butt into the stylish metallic receptacle there. "What is it that you do, Lois?" She thought he'd never ask, but now he had, and she told him, because she liked it when people asked a question of her. He said, "I'm a consultant, myself. I do some other things on the side. I'm an *innovator,* I guess that's what you'd call me."

He'd been with a consultant division at one of the Big Five firms. He got hired onto the teams that went into large-cap companies and he advised the companies on public offerings, portfolio review, acquisitions, all kinds of things, and then he explained the angles from his unique vantage point, which was the vantage point of a guy with a proven track record who worked at one of the Big Five firms. What Arnie liked to say was there was nothing he wouldn't do for the client, the client was number one, "Anything within the bounds of law and several things without." That's what he liked to say, and then he would give Lois this look.

They went to one of those new horror movies where all the jokes are about other horror movies. The homely kid knows he's going to get killed first because he's seen it all before in other horror movies. Arnie was explaining to her, before the trailers, how he'd done anything within the bounds of law and several things without, and he was telling her not to repeat any of this because if anyone found out, Arnie said, "I'd have to kill you." After the movie he asked, "Do you think that serial killers really kill pets and all that?" It was sort of unsettling, Lois thought, but a little endearing at the same time. "They're always saying this kind of thing. The serial killers, when they're kids, supposedly they kill other people's pets. They don't feel any remorse." He laughed nervously.

She said, "So you're a serial killer now?"

That's not what he meant at all! Arnie said. "But if someone wanted me to play one in a movie, I think I'd be good at it."

People thought she could get them parts in movies. They offered up their thespian moves, their high school dramatic credentials, every day of the week, but she didn't pay any attention, and especially not when Arnie said what he said. Maybe she had become light-headed because she'd started smoking his foreign cigarettes. She was neglecting things at the office or just barely getting the work done but not in any particularly satisfying way. She was smoking foreign cigarettes and going out for Kahlua and milk at Hank's Franks with Arnie from Forest Hills. He knew the accountant for the Ramones. He had a summer rental down the shore. A weekend at Atlantic City was a good thing. At Hank's Franks, Arnie remarked that a man could certainly find that he had become devoted to a woman. That's what he said. And she replied, "Don't try to flatter me, Arnie. I know who I am." Who she was was a plain middle-aged woman without a husband, who didn't expect flattery because if she did, she would have got frustrated a long time ago. "I live a quiet life and I stay home in my neighborhood and I don't wait around for anyone." She was as serious as she'd ever been because even if the society of smokers, with its daily menu of humor and gossip, was never serious, it didn't mean that Lois couldn't be.

Arnie said, "Don't make me have to explain it."

"Don't make you explain what?"

He said maybe he was falling hard. It should have been in a nicer place than Hank's Franks. Because Hank's Franks was just what it sounded like, a place where the entrées were wrapped in tinfoil, where there were always young men at the bar whose faces should not have been so crimson. Dog-faced young entrepreneurs who came from nothing, who tried drunkenly to make it across the avenue to the bus terminal and instead did the face plant in front of a hydrant. Miracle a taxi had not backed over them. When they woke, their wallets would be gone. That's the kind of place where Lois first heard sentimental things from the mouth of Arnie Lovitz. When she was a teenager, no one ever said they cared, and even when she lost her virginity to the older brother of a friend on the girls' basketball team, this older brother hadn't said he cared, and he'd seemed uncomfortable when he passed her on the street after that. She hadn't been nervous, she liked it, the thing they had done, and she didn't care if that boy, Carl, loved her, because what she wanted was life's experiences, which included taking your clothes off. Still, it would have been nicer to hear that you were loved in a museum, in front of a beautiful painting that showed a princess in a diaphanous robe, pregnant and standing with her soon-to-be prince of the realm. That would be a nice place to be told that you were loved. But this was Hank's Franks. She needed to work fast.

The scene changes to a hotel out by the airport in Queens, because that was the kind of hotel that they could afford, if they were being fiscally sensible. Lois could see that Arnie was flush temporarily with his good fortune. He was proud of his love. The smokers of the promenade, watching the skaters go around and around, would have this bit of gossip to embellish soon enough. The smokers would be like hummingbirds over nectar. They would edit the story of Arnie and Lois into a little movie for the consumption of future smokers, Arnie's tie winched over his head without being unknotted, flung onto the grimy wall-to-wall, his suit coat and his pants, pinstripes, cast onto the floor as if they were the body of a murder victim. And how about this, the two of them in the shower, two accountants, neither of them exactly thin and neither of them exactly beautiful, and here was her nipple, and she was presenting it as if it were a delectable item, and here were his lips upon it, and if they weren't the most beautiful people God had ever put on the planet, or the most beautiful people to walk up and down the promenade to the ice-skating rink, at least they were two people in a cheap motel who could believe in this moment of love as much as anyone who ever believed in any romantic encounter. Reflections in the mirror in the bathroom were a little humbling, but soon the water vapor on the mirror made them as indistinct as any movie lovers; she wanted to laugh, it all made her so giddy, as he was putting his arms around her, because he had these gigantic arms and he was crushing her, naked in the shower, and she didn't know that any man could fit his arms around her. It made her feel like a little girl. Soon the lights came up on the lovers on the couch, just like that, and she was the one saying that she would do anything he wanted her to do, all he had to do was to tell her, just say the words, and she would be whatever kind of lover he wanted her to be on this night, she swore it, and she believed she could be this lover, believed it without any reservation, in the motel near the LaGuardia Airport, and because of her belief no lover was any better. Arnie was stammering, throbbing with his nervousness, saying that he wanted that one thing that all men were always seeming as if they wanted, or at least that's what she'd heard back when. It was a long time ago, a long time since she put that part of a man in her mouth, and she didn't know if she could do it in a way that would be pleasurable for him because she wasn't very experienced, even if she was a genius at believing. She thought that gentleness was the thing. If you treated this homely part of a body as though it were a beautiful little hatchling, no matter who it belonged to, then that person and that body would be stretched out before you like a little gossamer thread of heaven. So she treated the particular part of Arnie's body, which was actually kind of small, as though reverence was invented for it. There was an awful lot of sadness in reverence, but that was what was good about reverence, that it was not easy. It was performed with a recognition of the absence of perfection in the world, closing in on midnight. Many things had already happened that day, and Arnie was starting to thrash around, and the thrashing said that this life was not as before, and she was about to taste bittersweet dignity in her mouth, a little bit of dignity that was coming out of Arnie Lovitz for the first time, and it was salty like tears, and also it tasted a little like bleach, bleach and tears. Arnie was being made into a good man, and Lois was being made into a tramp with a good heart at the same time. That's how she felt about it; she felt that she was not sure. All she knew was that in the movies, sex was supposed to be excellent and you heard God's voice, or else it was supposed to be sinful and you got an ice pick in the temple when the marauder appeared in the margin of the shot. But it was just two people on a banquette in a motel. Arnie started crying after he came.

He said, "Lois, I have to tell you something. I know we don't know each other all that well, but I feel like I have to tell you just the same."

She said, wiping off her chin, "Don't you give me any bad news now. I don't do this kind of thing very often, and it is not fair to give me any bad news right now, because I just acted like I was a porn star. So don't give me any bad news."

What he said was that he was an embezzler. It took a good thirty seconds for the information to sink in.

"You're a what?"

"I'm an embezzler," Arnie said. "Or I have been. I've been an embezzler, a thief. And God help me."

If she were going to reach a preliminary conclusion, a snap judgment, her conclusion would have been that every good thing contains its opposite. The foul thing is all mixed up with the fair thing, they're next-door neighbors, and any time you have a good afternoon, you can bet your last dollar that some nightmare is next on your schedule. You feel warm feelings for a person, and right behind those warm feelings will be a big challenge.

What Arnie did, apparently, was set up these fictitious corporations on these islands in the Caribbean. It was just one scam at first, one fictitious subsidiary for one particular corporation, except that no one knew that it was a wholly owned subsidiary and that it didn't even exist. No one knew. There was no office in the Cayman Islands with a gently rotating ceiling fan and a rack of mainframes and an excellent view of that blue green water. The wholly owned subsidiary was Arnie's creation, on paper and nowhere else, and it was so successful that soon he was setting up a second one. In this second instance, he had the parent company selling portions of itself to a subsidiary corporation and booking the sale as income and using the sale proceeds to set up another subsidiary on these islands in the Caribbean, on an island called St. Jude, appropriately enough, an island that didn't even exist. He had even started making up geography now, in addition to office buildings. And this wholly owned subsidiary was buying and trading futures, using derivatives and other fiscal transactions that Lois didn't understand because she had always worked for small arts-related organizations.

Arnie got out of the consulting business because the rats were starting to jump off the ship at this one particular company, which company was under investigation for inflating the dollar value of some of its transactions, and that meant that soon they were going to start looking at the fine print, and Arnie didn't want to be anywhere around when that happened. And yet when he set up his own company, he was using his references from before, and for some reason he was again landing the sorts of clients who would be attracted to certain kinds of transactions, a fictitious business with fictitious offices and fictitious transactions, or maybe a company that doesn't make a product but just buys and sells ideas about products. These were all businesses where the rats were jumping off the ship. This one company, Arnie said, was being run by people from Salt Lake City, all Mormons, and their company had ties with the FBI, though that didn't mean it wasn't dirty. He got out. Except that he couldn't get out entirely, because what was he going to do? Suddenly there were no clients at all, and the phone didn't ring, and if it did, he didn't answer it because he was afraid that it was the FBI, and so what he started doing, because he had time on his hands, was that he started taking some of the business money, the stake that had enabled his consulting business, and he began moving it around. Day-trading, that's what they called it.

When he had lost that money, what he had to do in order to keep his business was to write a few things onto the books of this one client, the venture capital company from Salt Lake City. He saddled them with some bad trades. He concealed it all on their books as a business expense.

Now what he wanted was that Lois should forgive him for these things, because he knew what he'd done. Women had this magical capacity, according to Arnie, to forgive a man, and maybe it wouldn't change the situation, but he'd feel a little better for a few hours. He wanted to go legit, he said, in the hotel by La-Guardia Airport, and he wanted her to see that he was a man who had no choice but to do what he did, namely, write off fifty thousand shares of a fly-by-night biotech stock onto the books of a Mormon venture capital company. Sooner or later those Mormons were going to find out. His story was confused; his despair was violent. His mood swung back and forth all over the place, on the bed in the motel.

When he'd calmed down a little, they went to sleep.

In the morning, Lois DiNunzio slipped out of the motel early, because she slept fitfully, and she paid the bill and left Arnie Lovitz there, temporarily peaceful. She drove back to Astoria and got herself into a clean outfit for work. Where another woman would have cried on that drive, on account of how passionately she had felt the night before, Lois didn't cry, because she wasn't the sort of woman who cried over things like failure. You'd end up crying too often.

Means of Production was in one of its flush periods. The market was "top ticking." That's the kind of thing Arnie said. It seemed as if there was more money around for their kinds of movies, or this is what Vanessa told her whenever she called Lois into her office. Means of Production was on the gravy train with a Dutch conglomerate, with the guy who helped pioneer some programming language for servers, and with some French producers for a film about Catholic priests molesting kids in the suburbs. *Cauldron of Belief*, it was called. Lois thought the subject of this movie was appalling. She thought the movie painted a bad picture of her church because it claimed that the higher-ups were always protecting the lower-downs, that they didn't care what these priests did.

It was the day after Arnie had said what he said. Lois didn't have the usual DiNunzio detachment, the kind that comes from losing your mother to congestive heart failure and taking care of your younger brothers, those spoiled brats. And so she made the mistake of saying to Vanessa that she didn't think Catholic priests really did stuff like that. She reminded Vanessa that the church gave a lot of money to the poor, and it was a place for people to go who didn't have anything, and anyway the church was the sum of all its parts and it didn't need to be demonized just because of a couple of rogue priests who couldn't keep their privates under their robes.

"Leave the development issues to me," Vanessa said.

"I'm just saying."

"Have you read the script?"

"I don't need to read it," Lois said. A big mistake.

"When I start developing a movie about accountants, I'll be sure to call you in."

She was eating, of course. Vanessa was always eating when she was in a mood for a tirade. Today it was jelly beans. Vanessa turned her back on Lois, looking in the direction of the window, toward the deluge.

Lois said, "Your boorish displays don't wash with me. I've

heard it all before. You can say what you like, but I don't pay attention to your rudeness. I've worked for you for two years. I've made sure you could keep the company going. I've kept the rest of the girls in line, and I make sure they are okay when you're behaving like a little child. So you watch your mouth with me."

Vanessa needed a couple of breaths to really get going, but when she got going, it was as if she were a superhero swelling up in some fabulous demonstration of strength from the sheer force of her dissatisfaction.

"You're the *accountant*. You're like the back part of the set, where all the two-by-fours are showing. You're the classic example of a person who's never had a creative thought and who never will have a creative thought, and that may play well at the big studios, where they have not had a creative thought in twenty-five years, but in here, in this office, it means that we tolerate you. We tolerate you here just because we need someone to cover the books. But don't ever get the idea that your opinion is welcome or that it matters, because we barely recognize that you're here. You were hired to do the numbers and to shut up. And, for the record, I'm a Catholic, too, in case you haven't noticed, and every day that I have failed to slump in the pews of the Catholic Church is a day that I've improved as a person. I could show you some of the spots where I was personally scarred for life by the priests and nuns I've known, but I'm not going to because you're not smart enough for that particular conversation, the one in which I get stronger and begin to overcome these things through the vitality of *disgust*. I'm the one developing *Cauldron of Belief*. I'm the one who story-edited a story where a priest in Wisconsin abuses a bunch of boys and tries to get away with it, okay? And every day that they shoot the movie, I feel a little bit better, just on principle, but also because every day that they shoot that movie, I'm getting *paid*. And so are you. And so are the women out there in the hall, right? They're getting paid now because this movie is being made, because some French people hate the church as much as I do. So let's collect the checks, and let's deposit them, and let's bill this particular conversation as a general administrative expense, all right? Now get the fuck out of my office."

What followed did not include any slamming of doors, nor any bitter tears. Lois DiNunzio simply walked out of Vanessa's office and back into her own, passing, on the way, Annabel and Jeanine. They were blushing at what they'd overheard. But Lois didn't pay any attention to this because she'd already made her decision. She wasn't at her desk fifteen minutes before she'd cut a check made out to St. Patrick's Cathedral in the amount of a thousand dollars, which, as accountant, she was empowered to sign in the absence of Vanessa Meandro, who was leaving that afternoon for the West Coast to sit in on the beginning of editing on *Cauldron of Belief*. The check was backdated by one day. It was legal tender in every one of the fifty states. She took a package of foreign cigarettes from her purse, and she rode the elevator down to the promenade, and she smoked for a few minutes, and then, with a lightness in her step, she carried the check across the street to St. Patrick's Cathedral and slipped it into one of the little boxes where people leave coins in exchange for an illuminated candle. Lois said a little prayer, the gist of which was that Vanessa Meandro should be struck with grace, as if grace were a safe falling out of the sky, and should, in that dizzy experience of being so concussed, suffer with a love for her fellow mankind and womankind that was so overwhelming that her present life would be rendered unlivable because of it. And also, dear Lord, please make her business acumen seize up and make her smitten with some fabulous unrequited longing for some grossly unpleasant and homely person. That is my prayer, amen.

That was maybe twelve weeks ago. And in those weeks, during which Vanessa got involved in a fight to the death with the director and editor of *Cauldron of Belief,* and during which the market began its unmistakable downward spiral, Lois felt like a robin picking worms from the lawn of life. She was happy, and even her neighbors in Astoria remarked on how happy she seemed. It was a good feeling at first, because she could understand Arnie now, as she was a fellow embezzler, and she would try to comfort him, and she could take him out to see the play-offs at Shea featuring his beloved Al Leiter, and in this way Arnie could try to get comfortable with the idea that men in trench coats weren't following him each and every day. Lois felt happy because she was now charging administrative expenses to various French people that were nonetheless going straight into the coffers of St. Patrick's Cathedral, twice a month, to the tune of about six thousand dollars, bottom line.

It had been a good fiscal quarter for Means of Production. Or at least for Lois. It was all good until she got the call from Arnie in late October. One of the online brokerage firms that Arnie used was calling in some short positions. Shorts were a satisfying way of seeing the world. He loved looking for companies that were fraudulent. It was the fraud in him that loved thinking about all his fellow frauds. She'd go over to his apartment in Yonkers, and he'd be calling up reporters, telling them that some company called Primadon or something was intimidating its wholesalers. He'd be smoking and laughing about the whole thing. Until this particular call came. He needed to cover this short, on Interstate Mortuary Services, a large-scale, publicly traded mortuary company that offered family burial plans at bargain rates and shipping across state lines, but which had not even checked the federal statutes on interstate shipping of caskets and dead bodies. A great company for Arnie. But apparently they were about to be bought out in a major deal.

"Lois," he said, "I don't want to put you through this."

Living with Arnie was like plugging the dike of truth. You got one set of holes plugged, but you could see the tempest-tossed sea breaking through someplace else. Still, Lois and Arnie were an item now, and Lois didn't give up easily. That's just not what the women of the extended DiNunzio clan did. They were stick-around girls. They were loyal and they were tough. She picked up a towel from the floor of his mildewy bathroom. She carried it to the hamper in the closet. She fetched spray-on bleach.

"Don't be ridiculous."

"I'm telling you the truth."

"I've heard that one before."

Arnie said, "Just look at me." And here he gestured at MSNBC on the cable television and the scrolling of stock prices as though the scrolling of prices were somehow identical with him.

For a moment she was impatient: "Arnie, act like you can do something about your predicament. Go out there and make fifty thousand dollars somehow, and show me and the world how you can do it. People have overcome a lot worse things. People who know less than you do. Be yourself and do the thing you can do. Create wealth!"

Lois felt sort of hollow even as she was saying the words. If you tipped over a rock and looked for chicanery and betrayal, you'd find these things under every rock. In every closet there was fraudulence secreted away, next to the frilly dresses. Fraudulence was there. Betrayal was there. And fraudulence was always in greatest supply where righteousness camped out. Arnie agreed with her sentiment. He agreed that he was going to *try,* as he always said, he was going to *try* to find the money in some legitimate way, like by selling cars or something, something he could do with his bounteous charm.

Which brings us up to date. Bad news brings us up to the Friday after the election, Friday, the tenth, the day that Lois DiNunzio, the Robin Hood of St. Patrick's Cathedral, has decided to loot her employer, an independent production company known as Means of Production, of sixty-three thousand dollars, in order to cover the losses of her fiancé, who is posing as a day trader under an assumed name — the name of a deceased brother — so as not to attract the attention of the Federal Bureau of Investigation, nor the Securities Exchange Commission, which may or may not now

be looking into the matter of a certain falsely constructed subsidiary of a holding company owned chiefly by several prominent
investors from Salt Lake City, whose former accountant and
consultant was one Arnie Lovitz. Lois has not told Arnie she is
doing this, looting the sixty-three thousand dollars, nor has she
told anyone else. She is constructing fraudulent payments to
some real publicists, these publicists being known as the Vanderbilt girls, who are working to get the name of a motion picture,
Cauldron of Belief, into the paper, and she is billing this sixty-
three thousand dollars as a series of publicity-related expenses
on a series of bills she is submitting to the American distributor
of the film, which isn't even finished, and after she submits the
bill and writes the check to Arnie's all-but-liquidated consulting
business, Lovitz Offshore Consulting, she will walk out of the
Means of Production offices, and she will get in a used Honda
Civic with a hundred and forty thousand miles on it, and she will
tell her fiancé that they are going to Arizona, and then they will
begin to drive, spending, she calculates, the first night in the
Toledo area, where she has already researched a really good
place for them to eat dinner, a family restaurant. After that, they
will stop at the first mall in the area that's showing one of the season's slasher flicks.

15

The happy couples with their freshly cut lilies from the flower district; the pickup soccer players who never pass the ball; the weekend barbecue enthusiasts with their George Foreman barbecue products, their squeezable ketchup bottles, their chef's hats; the park bench romancers, mashing their chapped lips together; the carp feeders in the botanical gardens, mallards clustering before them awaiting the stale white bread, Vanessa has contempt for them all. The life-loving weenie-roasting citizens of Saturdays. Likewise, all persons who would relentlessly display their knowledge of the chad. The plural of the word *chad* is actually *chad*. Must the chad be punched out in at least two corners? Two corners or three corners or four corners? Or perhaps one single corner alone? Must you be able to see light around a chad in order for that chad to indicate intention? This is Saturday, and somewhere in a county down near the Gulf of Mexico in humid weather, members of the county board of elections are toiling, as they have been toiling since Tuesday. There are three members of the board of elections in a school gymnasium, sports mascots painted on the walls, and they are observed in their efforts by a scoundrel from each of the political parties, likewise by scoundrels of the press.

The party operatives are objecting yet again. Can light be seen around the chad? Is this chad a pregnant chad? Or is this a dimpled chad? Either way, the chad is not a legitimate chad, as a pregnant or dimpled chad does not indicate a legitimate vote. This is a nonvote or this is an undervote, depending on the point of view of the party operative making the argument. This is the news on Saturday. The light of the coastal resorts is visible around the indeterminate and partially punched-out chad, pastels of Floridian light, bleached and salt scoured. Yes, the chad exhibits intention, is perhaps pregnant with intention, and so the members of the board of elections in this county near to the Gulf of Mexico, in the tail end of hurricane season, are working furiously, their eyes itchy and red. Vanessa is not going to the farmers' market to banter with the cheese ladies who hawk their excrescences, nor is she going to the dry cleaner's to speak with the beautiful Korean girl who has changed the color of her hair for the fourth time in three weeks.

Vanessa means to work.

First, the cat must be fed. The cat comes howling to the bed where Vanessa is still lying, where she is plotting. At first she ignores the cat. She's making plans, and she's listening to news reports, and she is considering options relating specifically to the miniseries entitled *The Diviners*. Who knows if this mythology of diviners is legitimate? thinks Vanessa, lying in bed while Dade County performs its convulsions. The cat howls. The women of her office, her acquaintances in the business of independent film production wouldn't believe that Vanessa Meandro is a worrier, but there are things that they don't need to know; they don't know about the telephone conversation with her mother last night, nor about her mother's fevered whisperings. "I was just sitting . . . in the lounge and thinking, and I was hearing . . . things . . . about some kind of, I don't know, sort of a musician . . . some kind of African American man, and he's trying to get a part in the . . . in that thing . . . I heard all about it. I heard all about a man having

a conversation with . . . what's her name, in the office there . . .
promising him that if he could help to arrange financing . . . well,
I didn't understand all of it . . . had to do with some money things,
with financing . . . give him some consideration for a part . . ."

Vanessa said: "Are you kidding? You mean that guy, what's his
name? Mercurio? Right? The hip-hop guy? The guy with his own
line of beauty products."

"I don't know anything about beauty products . . . might have
said something . . . men's jogging outfits."

"Well, what else did he say?"

"That he wanted . . . that he felt that he . . . could really do
right . . . needed to break into acting . . . getting in touch with
the part of him that wanted to act . . . and he could definitely
put Madison in touch with people; I don't know . . . It gave me
a headache."

"Was there anything else?" Vanessa asked about the cellular
telephone call that her mother imagined she had overheard in
the adult psychiatric ward of the hospital in Park Slope while the
other residents of the ward were watching reruns of situation
comedies.

"Doughnuts."

"What kind of doughnuts?"

"I think they were mentioning Krispy Kreme doughnuts."

"Are you sure? Are you sure this telephone call had something
to do with Krispy Kreme doughnuts? Mom, I need to know."

"Telling you what I heard . . . and it was giving me a splitting
headache . . . and if you don't want to hear it . . . that's your
prerogative to believe that . . . You're going to believe what
you're going to believe because you never had a tablespoon of respect. They were watching television in the lounge, and I was
overhearing a telephone call between those . . . between Madison from the office and some black man . . . they were talking
about financing . . . and then they were talking about doughnuts."

"Were they talking about how I brought in doughnuts to the office the other day, Mom? Was that what they were saying?"

"They were talking about money . . . they were talking about getting money from the doughnut company. Somehow the future hinged on doughnuts."

"You're kidding me, Mom."

The conversation stalled. After reminding her mother how much she was loved, Vanessa demanded that Rosa Elisabetta put her through to whichever official was attending on the ward at this hour. Was the doctor still on call? No, the doctor was gone and would not be back until Monday, because even the doctors had to have breaks from the delusions of the patients in the ward, which meant that there was no one in authority to whom Vanessa Meandro might speak. Still, Vanessa asked her mom if she could put the supervising nurse on the phone. Her mother pointed out that, unfortunately, the nurses would not speak into the pay phone on the ward. This was against ward policy. After all, how did they know if she was really the daughter of Rosa Elisabetta Meandro? She could just as easily be a drug dealer or other codependent person. Vanessa Meandro gently bade her mother farewell, after which she got the hospital information number from directory assistance.

So the first thing Vanessa does on this particular Saturday is to begin, from bed, berating various hospital operators with threats and abuses, allusions to how these people are all going to be brought up on a variety of malpractice charges, until at last she connects with the number for the ward in which her mother is warehoused. The nurse on duty answers. Vanessa has barely completed the recitation of biographical information before she moves into the argument phase.

"Do you guys realize that my mother believes that she's receiving telephone calls inside her skull?"

The shades are drawn in Vanessa's room, and the cat is batting at her with a request of some kind. Some eerie electronic music is playing because the clock radio is tuned to the Columbia University station. The sound is muffled behind the stacks of unread screenplays towering around it.

"I'm not allowed to give information relating to our patients over the phone."

"You'd better rethink that policy, because last night I had a conversation with my mother that went on almost ten minutes in which she sounded lucid to me, except for the news about the telephone calls she's receiving *in her head*. Or in her dental fillings. Or wherever they're coming from. If you're not talking to me about it, you should at least be talking to whoever the consulting physician is over there. I want it on record that my mother needs to be getting better care for her *delusions*. She wasn't floridly psychotic when she checked herself in on Wednesday."

"Sometimes patients —"

"She had a *drinking* problem. I can't argue with you about that part. But she wasn't hearing voices. And now she's hearing the voices of people from my office talking to her. You've got to have some kind of medication for this stuff, right? I mean, haven't there been big advances in these medications? Can't you treat a complaint like this? I want to know first thing Monday —"

The nurse says something noncommittal about passing on the information. When the MD shows up on Monday, the information will be passed on. The nurse has become as silky in her delivery as a game show host hustling off a losing contestant. Requests for information need to be met with a rhetoric of delay. Requests for information are not the responsibility of this single party, a nurse-practitioner with two kids left behind at her sister's house for the day. Et cetera.

Vanessa rises and pads into the kitchen in her robe, feeds the cat, and then she calls Madison because she knows that Madison will have been out until four. It is good to wake Madison to remind her of the importance of the chain of command. Madison should be attempting to stay one step ahead of Vanessa on all things. Madison should wake with a start, worrying about Vanessa. Madison should be able to leap tall buildings; Madison should be able to accept telephone calls on a Saturday, crack of dawn, despite three or four hours of sleep. So Vanessa dials the number, gets the machine, and while scooping the bonbons of cat shit out of the box, she says, "I heard you offered Mercurio a role in *The Diviners* without running it by me. Which is totally fucking unacceptable. And I understand you're in conversation with Krispy Kreme for financing. And that's not going to work yet, either. You're supposed to keep me informed of this stuff. Call me as soon as you're up."

Having harassed Madison, she begins to feel a little better. She feels as though she might be able to raise the blinds or look in the mirror at her straw hair, her bad dye job, the rings around her eyes. But having come to this conclusion, she instead returns to the bedroom to locate her personal digital assistant, which lies on the far side of her queen-size mattress, as though she were in a long-term relationship with it. She starts at A with the stylus and she heads through the alphabet, looking for people she can call on business matters. When she gets to Annabel Duffy, she takes up the phone again and leaves a message with Annabel, who never answers. "Hi, I'm wondering why we haven't solved this intern problem yet. I want to have an intern by next Friday because we're getting behind. We need some people we can get working on these little tasks. Get some names. I don't care where you get them from. Just get some people in. If we're going to be in production on this miniseries, we need more people. We're going to be flying back and forth to the coast, we're going to be on location, and I don't trust Madison to be looking after this issue, so get on it."

Maximum friction between individuals. Instability between the players. Means of Production needs to have people competing in the same tasks. Fraternal rivalries. Catfights. The players need to be looking over their shoulders suspiciously, which is

why it is so appropriate to have Thaddeus Griffin around, a black
hole sucking in the radiant energy emanating from these talented
women. They need to be able to fend him off; they need the skill,
the power. Same thing with Ranjeet, although what Ranjeet also
represents for Means of Production is an implied critique, he
says, of Occidental meaning systems. The Occidental meaning
system is looking toward equations, see, as though the equation
is the perfect semantic unit for large organizations, he says, and
this is true in the movies and it's true in the business practices of
an operation like Means of Production. On the other hand, maybe
what Ranjeet stands for is an Asian system of meaning, which is
more like non-euclidean geometry, where the parallel lines are
actually circles; this is the theory of Ranjeet, this is the way in
which Ranjeet is going to change what they're doing, so that they
are working on a variety of approaches to *The Diviners,* not just
particular Occidental context-oriented approaches, but instead a
variety of possible approaches to story and structure. As he says,
this is more likely to yield fruit.

It's her greatest moment, the moment of persuasion. It's the
thing she was born to do. She can feel it the way other people can
feel they are ready to get into bed with someone. Other people feel
desire and they go out into the dappled sunlight of the park and
they compose sestinas using difficult-to-rhyme words like *silvery,*
and they experience love, which is that feeling when you care more
about the welfare of a person than you care about the sunlight.
Maybe Vanessa has felt that or, lying in bed with the blinds drawn,
maybe she thinks she has felt that for her mother, certain times
when she carted her mother, passed out, from the floor of her living room to her bed. Maybe in that moment, she felt something
like this epic love of poetry. Caritas. For example, there was the
time that her mother was meant to show the top-floor apartment
to this couple. She remembers this vividly. April, maybe, two or
three years ago, a Saturday like this Saturday. Vanessa was trying
to make use of the new stepping machine that she'd ordered from

an infomercial, and she intended to spend half an hour on it every day. She's on the stepping machine, weeping and pretending to ski. The bell rings downstairs, and she hopes this couple isn't an interracial couple, because there was this one interracial couple, and her mother was so rude to them that she couldn't believe it. She tried to talk to her mother about it once, and her mother shouted Vanessa down. The bell rings, and then the bell rings again, and the bell rings a third time. The third ringing of the bell is not good, and so she goes downstairs, wearing her stretchy gym clothes. She's lost eight pounds, and yet she's been weeping over the improbability of losing weight, and she goes downstairs, and here's this nice interracial couple.

The girl is light skinned and maybe part Hispanic or something. Beautiful and tall and thin, and the guy is maybe Jewish. He has the charm of an advertising guy. They are standing on the stoop, and Vanessa says, "Let's go have a look." She's on her best behavior. And she takes them up to the top floor, and they are amazed at the view. They really like the brick, they like the floors, they like the old gas lamp out front. And what they probably really like is that Vanessa does not give a shit what color they are as long as they don't make too much noise and pay their rent in a timely fashion. But on the way back down the stairs, she says, "Let's just take a quick look and see if my mother is home, because she likes to be a part of this process."

She's not sure why she did it. It was not a good sign when the doorbell tolled unanswered three times. The appointment had been agreed upon. Like many people with problems, Vanessa's mother was fanatical about her few appointments. She worried about them for days in advance. It was not a good sign when the bell rang and Rosa Elisabetta did not answer it. Nevertheless, Vanessa unlocked the door on the ground floor, after explaining that they should feel free to use the garden in the backyard, and then, as the door swung in, she found her mother passed out on the floor of the living room, arms flung wide as if in preparation for some fervent embrace, one leg of her Kmart double-knit trousers scrunched up enough to reveal a pink sock. The cat was sitting on top of her mother's stomach.

"Maybe we'd better come back," Vanessa said, giggling madly.

"Is she okay?" the woman asked.

"Sure," Vanessa said. "The only problem here is the socks."

More nervous laughter. Then there was a pause in the banter between landlord and lessees in the stairwell. And then the ad-man said: "We still really like the apartment. We'd like to sign the agreement."

She gave them the lease on the spot. They had probably seen much worse, in this challenging real estate environment. The lease was on top of the stack of papers on her mother's kitchen table, along with every other legal piece of paper she had ever needed in her life, including her will, her divorce agreement, and a suit filed against the City of New York for restrictive ballot requirements for third-party candidates in local elections. The three of them stood in the kitchen, looking at the lease agreement, while her mother snored in the center of the living-room floor. The renters had the paperwork notarized and returned, with the check, before Rosa woke.

That was a kind of love. There is love, and there is persuasion, and these are two of the colors of the universe. There is the post-modern Orientalism of Vanessa's strategy, via Ranjeet, which is a strategy of multiple fronts, all operating simultaneously. The flow chart. She's going through the scrolling alphabetical entries of her personal digital assistant, through its trove of names, Katzenberg and Meyer and Case and Bronfman and Brokaw, the telephone numbers that she has pried loose over the years, as if these telephone numbers were some kind of secret code. She uses the numbers rarely; she just covets them, keeps them in reserve. But on this wasteland of a Saturday, she is feeling that perhaps the moment has finally come. She can feel it, it's an automatic function, a reflex, and what is more true than the expression of a reflex?

She dials the cell phone number of Jeffrey Maiser, senior vice president of network programming at UBC, the fledgling network built of affiliates in the hinterlands. UBC, network of the kids, the network with lots of shows for teenagers featuring werewolves and invisible children, werewolves dealing with water-weight gain and male-pattern baldness, and, more recently, a rash of enhanced-reality programs, such as the very successful *American Spy*. Jeffrey Maiser has been linked, and this is always how they put it in the relevant publications, with a certain brainless, one-named strumpet called Lacey. A singer, if you can call her that. For whom he is now acting as Svengali, according to the relevant publications. Jeffrey Maiser is working on a deal for a half-hour enhanced-reality program in which the one-named strumpet is to lie around on casual furniture such as beanbag chairs and waterbeds with her friends, listening to songs and watching videos. They will also rate various boys, hosts of video programs, members of various bands, and so forth. Jeffrey Maiser is developing this, according to the relevant publications, and he is also attempting to secure dramatic roles for Lacey, and this will be the fulcrum of the pitch that is even now beginning to form, like a boil, in Vanessa. Vanessa needs to tell the story of *The Diviners* so badly that resistance to it is making her irritable. Yet waiting will sharpen its edges. She goes into the kitchen, where there are the makings of a particularly good egg sandwich.

She likes interior decorating that looks as though it has been shipped over from Tuscany stone by stone. And thus there are real tiles in her bathroom and her kitchen, and faux-marble counters, and she has up-to-date culinary machines in industrial sizes. Seltzer is delivered to the house. The cat, having eaten, is following her around the kitchen, making a figure eight around her ankles, just in case a saucer of milk should appear beside the seltzer bottles in the pantry. The phone is still clamped between Vanessa's shoulder and ear. And before she can connect to Maiser's line she is interrupted by the Morse code of call waiting.

"Oh, hi." Particularly unhappy at the sound of Vic Freese's voice. "Go away. Not you. The cat. I'm making an egg sandwich. Fresh basil. No, Vic, I haven't done anything. Sorry you had to stumble on it in the way you did. The parties responsible have been terminated. No, Vic. No. I haven't done much in the way of casting. Hang on a second, I have to beat the eggs."

For the sake of the pause. She looks out the window. The day is sunny, she notices abruptly. There are mutable shadows on the flagstone behind the house.

"Yeah, I thought of her, too. Are you saying that she might be willing . . . ? But isn't she . . . Yeah, that's what I heard. Guy in the Diamond District? So she's willing to come back for a big part? That's of some interest. No, no, I'm happy to do the pitching myself. I don't want to turn over the story to you. I don't want to turn anything over to you, no. What about the guys . . . You what? You already, no, I'd really appreciate if we could keep this between us. We're working on writers. Yeah, yeah. A-list all the way. A-list. Of course. You think we'd be having this conversation if I hadn't? Yeah, we contacted the romance novelist lady. Okay, okay. How is your family? Well, yeah. That's great. Glad to hear it. Yep. Bye."

Vic Freese and his nervousness are like fuel. She can put it off no longer. Doesn't matter if the egg sandwich is not yet done. Doesn't matter if it's not even eight o'clock on the West Coast; nothing matters except the pressure of language, the pressure to use language to create meaning where there was none before. Here is a void of meaning and potential that will be filled in the creation of art and value. As a producer, Vanessa Meandro was born to do this. The rest of the particulars of her job, line-producer responsibilities, casting consultant, location scout, these are of no interest to her. Seeing the film through the editing and the launch. She can do these things, but without enthusiasm. She has some of the lukewarm yolk in her mouth and some of it on her chin, and she holds an imperial blue cloth napkin, and she is ready to make the pitch. What she does is cram a big bite of the sandwich into her mouth, and she dials the cellular number of Jeffrey Maiser again, and she chokes on a mass of egg sandwich, and the phone connects, and never was there a longer silence than at the advent of Jeffrey Maiser, and in the silence, as in all such silences, Vanessa briefly regrets her ill humor with her family and friends, and thinks that if this deal works, she will attempt to calm down, she will attempt to find a way to do better, and she will begin to eat vegan entrées only, and she will look in on her mom more often, and she will invite friends out to dinner, and she will keep better track of money; if this deal will go through, she'll do all those things, she swears —

"Mr. Maiser?"

A grunt of assent.

"Vanessa Meandro here. With Means of Production? We're making the Otis Redding biopic with Wonderment? That the, uh, that the studio over there is . . . ? Right, that's the one. I'm calling today, Mr. Maiser, about something else entirely. I'm calling today about *thirst*. That's right. Thirst. I know it's a broad topic, but it's an urgent topic, whether you know it or not, a topic that is at the heart of American entertainment today. I'm a collector, Mr. Maiser, that's the first thing I want to explain to you, and what I collect, Mr. Maiser, are Moroccan pitchers. That's right. We at Means of Production are very serious about our Moroccan pitchers. They're made from a certain kind of clay, an earthenware clay, which is high in iron oxide, higher than any other earthenware clay, a clay that matures best in bonfire temperatures. Interestingly, this clay is really only found in Casablanca, Mr. Maiser. They perfected the art of the pitcher in Casablanca and Tangiers in the eleventh century, at a time when Christian and Islamic and Jewish influences in the area were at their peak. All these sects, Mr. Maiser, coexisting under the reign of one Ibn Tachafine, the founder of Marrakech.

"What I'm saying is that at the center of this bygone landscape was the notion of thirst, Mr. Maiser, and therefore at the center of this meeting of these faiths I've mentioned is the idea of thirst. You see it in the eleventh-century mystical texts of Alp Aslan, who conquered Byzantium and united the sultanates of Islam, Mr. Maiser. He understood the centrality of the pitcher and of Moroccan clay to this history of the pitcher. Think about it. You have these three faiths in the desert, in the lone and level sands, Mr. Maiser, all coming out of the compact between Abraham and his god. Abraham in the desert, desperate and thirsty, attempting to be blameless in the eyes of his god. Abraham taking his son to the killing place, willing to die of thirst, willing to sacrifice his son. Each of these peoples, Mr. Maiser, Christian, Jew, and Muslim, comes from this sort of desert, the wilderness. Which reminds me, of course, of the line from the work of Bob Dylan, *Where you want this killing done?* Are you familiar with the recordings of Bob Dylan, Mr. Maiser?"

A noncommittal groan, but Vanessa will not admit it into the terms of the discussion —

"If you're familiar with the recordings of Bob Dylan, then you are familiar with the Abrahamic faith and you are familiar with Moroccan pitchers, because in the deep space of that fish-eye photograph of Bob Dylan, next to the bellows by the fireplace, I'm speaking, of course, of *Bringing It All Back Home* here, you'll see one of the very Moroccan pitchers I'm describing, painted white. It's hard to see it in the image at first, a pitcher in which were poured many days of hard rain. The pitcher is the leitmotif in the project I'm proposing, Mr. Maiser, and what I'd like to argue is that the pitcher is *the* perfect narrative representation of the thirst of the mass television audience. And when I speak of thirst and a mass television audience, Mr. Maiser, I mean a mass television audience, I mean hundreds of millions, I mean the kind of audience that doesn't know how thirsty it is until the pitcher full of meaning is presented to it. Just think how many kinds of thirst there are in America right now, Mr. Maiser. There is the thirst of the fundamentalists in the southern part of the nation. Tired of feeling like the government and the media elites of the Northeast and the West Coast are dictating to them the terms of their culture. There are voices rising up from this part of the world, the talk radio guys and their apologists, rising up thirsty for meaning. They want a sort of millennialist vision, they want a reconstituted Jesus strolling down Fifth Avenue, laying waste to readers of the *New York Times*. And the project I'm describing, Mr. Maiser, will *not* disappoint them because it deals with ancient times and the possibility for apocalypse. What about Mormon viewers, adherents of the Church of Jesus Christ of Latter-day Saints? They are out there in the Great Salt Lake, on the salt flats, they have journeyed a thousand miles and created mythologies about the American Indians, the twelve tribes of American Indians, and they are thirsty, regionally, topographically, and they desire a clearly prophetic voice, a chaste and honorable prophetic voice, and this project that I'm proposing does this exactly, Mr. Maiser, when it depicts the Mormon exodus and, later, the founding of Las Vegas. The project delivers a story that the Southern Baptist Leadership Conference can get behind, since there are no homosexuals in it and no abortion providers, and it delivers a story that the Mormon elders can get behind, and the yogis and Buddhists of California; what could be more appropriate for their thirst, Mr. Maiser, than a story of diviners?

"That's right, Mr. Maiser, what we're talking about today is a multigenerational saga, but not one that's confined to a particular disenfranchised population, like *Roots* was or like *Holocaust* was back in 1978, a story that reaches out to every population and confers honorary disenfranchised status on it, the disenfranchised status of thirst, Mr. Maiser. Every group wants to be the group *out* of power, so that it can be restored to power through the capacity of the Moroccan pitcher to slake its metaphorical thirst, but with legitimacy and through acclamation, Mr. Maiser. The Jews, a people reviled in Europe, were driven out of Morocco, I can't remember exactly when, but I know they were driven out of there at some point, because that's history, am I right? And the one thing the Sephardim took with them, in addition to their sacred texts, was the knowledge of the manufacture of these sacred pitchers. Well, in fact, Mr. Maiser, they also took with them the kabalistic knowledge of divining, Mr. Maiser. You didn't know this? Divining is a highly secretive skill still taught in some ultra-Orthodox sects, Mr. Maiser. Divining. You saw it going back to the reign of the Hun, Mr. Maiser, and the proposal I'm going to be e-mailing you directly, so that you can have it on the desks of your people in your department on Monday morning, Mr. Maiser, will deal with the first episode of a thirteen-part miniseries I'm proposing that will depict the ancient times, Mr. Maiser, when the Hun first descended from the plains and began to rout Western civilization. The Hun brought destruction to the eastern edge of the Roman Empire, the Hun brought rape, the Hun pillaged, Mr. Maiser, and the Hun also brought, as marauders do, magic, in the person of the diviner. So when the earth was scorched, and the Romans were driven out of their empire, what they received in compensation was the diviner, leading them over the hill to the place of water."

"Uh —"

"So this is a proposal that confronts thirst on a historical basis, but it's also a proposal that actually slakes thirst. What you'll notice, Mr. Maiser, is that as you begin to contemplate the proposal, you'll see greater and greater conjunctions in your own life. Things will begin to line up. For example, I know that when I began thinking about thirst, and about how I needed to place this call to you directly, Mr. Maiser, as I began to see that you and you alone needed to receive this call, to have this electrifying opportunity to finance a miniseries that could change television history, that could change the distribution system, that could give independent cinema the place it rightly deserves in the history of cinematic storytelling, at the moment it couldn't escape my notice, Mr. Maiser, that a certain young performer was really born to play Nurit, the daughter of a Jewish shopkeeper and the love interest in this story. What is thirst, Mr. Maiser, but another name for erotic need? Am I right, Mr. Maiser? When we have the itch, we need it scratched. Why else, Mr. Maiser, are we so thirsty ourselves, here in this land rich with water? Where does this thirst come from? Why else those advanced embraces? Why do they leave us so in need of a good swim and a cool drink? I know you know, Mr. Maiser, and I know that you know how a certain young performer could bring in the teenage audience that so badly needs to slake this particular kind of thirst. We want young, charismatic performers, we need them, the perfect curve of a breast, that ephemeral thing that only lasts for a few years, the rippling muscles of a young buck striding across a high-definition screen, and this is the story that can really deliver to the network a teenage audience because every generation has an attractive thirsty teenager who finds the truth with a forked stick, do you hear what I'm describing, Mr. Maiser?"

"Listen, I —"

"The hydrophobia passage in, what was that movie, with the, *To Kill a Mockingbird*, right? The dog is mad? Right, it's a hydrophobia passage, serving as a metaphor for exile, the exile that the African American characters feel from white society. The hatred of water? The recoiling from water, such that water creates a kind of madness in the person or animal until they go wild, trying to spread an illness, after which they themselves die. Did you know that it has two phases, Mr. Maiser? Hydrophobia? The dumb phase and the furious phase, exactly coincident with the two kinds of political disenfranchisement? Well, *The Diviners*, Mr. Maiser, is a story that does the opposite. It works a metaphor of inclusion, a metaphor of, well, I guess you'd call it spiritual renewal, like night swimming, Mr. Maiser, a spiritual renewal that fully recognizes the importance of carnal appetite. We'll be getting a prominent A-list writer to bring to the screen the thirteen two-hour episodes we're proposing for this miniseries, Mr. Maiser, and we know, because we have admired your accomplishments at UBC, that you are the man for the story, the man who recognizes thirst as a historically urgent theme and who knows how to bring this story, with modern music, a sound-track spin-off, maybe some divining-rod merchandising opportunities at some of the fast-food chains, like maybe we could have a McDonald's promotion that would feature divining rods with the hamburgers, Mr. Maiser, or a Krispy Kreme divining rod, a little plastic divining rod that has some knots carved into it so it looks like a bough from a birch tree or a maple or something. What do you think, Mr. Maiser? Do you realize what an opportunity this would be for your company, especially since it would bring you close to the world of independent cinema, which has the critics and pundits on its side? Don't you and your friends want to get involved with a project that will lend you indie credibility *and* a mass audience? Can't you see a poster for a project like this, Mr. Maiser? Isn't a poster for a project like this materializing in your mind right now, a poster that can be run on the crowded subway lines of New York City and on city buses across the nation? Can't you see tie-ins, movie spin-offs, novelizations? Can't you see magazine profiles, the front covers of weekly newsmagazines, Mr. Maiser, can't you see third-world feature films, can't you see spinning off *The Diviners* into a thirteen-part cinematic extravaganza to show in all the relevant countries, like Hungary, or perhaps in countries like Bulgaria that can't afford the rental fees for new Hollywood releases? What about an edited, feature-length edition of *The Diviners*? With voice-over commentary for the DVD release? What about a director's cut with nine hours of additional footage? Don't you think, Mr. Maiser, that this is an opportunity that your company can't afford to miss? Can't you imagine that if you turn down this opportunity some other network will instantly jump on it, such that your job with the president of the network will be jeopardized and your stock will plunge and you will go down in history as the man who refused to sign up *The Diviners* when he might have, Mr. Maiser? Don't you just want to say yes now, Mr. Maiser? Don't you want to say yes now to this historic television narrative?"

"Stop!" Maiser cries out. There is approximate silence, cellular phone static standing in for silence, a stunned, faintly sublime silence. "I've got stuff to do. Just send me the damned proposal, for godsakes. I'll get back to you on Monday."

After which, Vanessa again takes to her bed.

16

It's Monday midday in Santa Monica, and Melody Howell Forvath, writer of novels of international intrigue, doesn't give a
goddamn what anyone thinks. She's going ahead with the party.
Melody Howell Forvath hasn't given a good goddamn for many
years, except about the state of her pool, the newest restaurant in
her neighborhood, and the best beaches within driving distance.
And this is because she has paid her dues with novels of international intrigue. She's published twenty-seven, the first twelve she
wrote herself, up until *Double Dutch* (1973), the one about the
twin spies operating as prostitutes in an Amsterdam brothel.
They broke open a heroin case, et cetera. Then, beginning with
Envoy of Desire (1975), she hired a string of well-educated and
presentable graduates of Smith and Wellesley to write the books
according to her instructions. Here's how she works. Melody
goes to the magazine store and plucks from a well-thumbed
Travel & Leisure a few promising locales. Then she sits down with
whoever is the ghostwriter, and they hash out a thrilling story
that features adultery, champagne, a hail of bullets, and a sexually independent woman. That's her stipulation, that the novels

have sexually independent women in them. She's certainly not writing these books for men, who only care about how big the warheads are.

In truth, Melody Forvath's job is the job of advance woman for a corporation called Melody Howell Forvath. After she goes over the proofs, her only genuine responsibility is to undertake the book tour, something she rather likes. She goes to the good hotels, the Ritz in Boston, the Carlyle Hotel of Manhattan. She greets bookstore owners and employees, the names of whom she carries with her in a leather book. After each event, on the plane, she writes postcards thanking every local benefactor.

From modest beginnings in Kansas City, Melody Forvath has become a writer any publisher would love to have on her list and a hostess of renown in the Los Angeles area. She has lots of friends, and there are still others who'd like to be her friends, and that's why she's the logical person to mount the gathering being thrown today on behalf of Iveshka Maevka, MD, whose practice has been a great comfort to her now that her profile is not the promotional tool that it might once have been. As you know, it's tough for a woman of a certain age. Melody Forvath made the acquaintance of Iveshka Maevka, MD, through her daughter, Ellie, who works as a buyer for a stylish boutique in town. Iveshka Maevka is a swashbuckler who wears double-breasted suits and surgical gloves, and he is up-to-date on the latest techniques, and he is eager to live a life of opportunity here in his adopted land. Melody Forvath wants to make sure Dr. Maevka, in his new line of business, receives the social introductions he needs. To this end, she has written a few words on one of those pink sticky pads.

Dr. Maevka has followed the progress of this medication through the Food and Drug Administration. He argues forcefully that a substance that is basically a toxin can nonetheless be a boon to modern medicine, though he recognizes that this medication, or its raw material, is still going to cause the occasional health emergency, when foods are not protected properly or when canned goods are spoiled, things of that nature.

As Melody Forvath understands it, eye twitches, excessive perspiration, and spasticity were among the first applications for the medication. (And before you make fun of people with twitches, let's just point out that Melody Forvath has known a friend or two with these kinds of problems, and they are no picnic.) From there the cosmetic uses became obvious. She's eager to get this part of medical history into her next book, if possible. Maybe a detective who is also some kind of dermatologist. A glamorous dermatologist.

From the treatment of excessive perspiration, the medication soon became widely available as a treatment for some of the humbling signs of advancing years, namely the wrinkles that appear around the eyes or the forehead.

This is what Dr. Maevka has told her, during their one-on-one treatment sessions. Dr. Maevka has long been known as an expert in surgeries that tighten the face or hoist a sagging buttock, also in the removal of unwanted liver spots using laser beams. Melody Forvath has, in fact, suffered the attentions of his blade. But no longer. She doesn't want her husband to have to see her with the bandages and wearing the hooded sweatshirts. Dr. Maevka is the first to admit that the medication in question is less invasive, and already there are many actresses, some as young as their late twenties, who are worried about lines on their forehead. They are all getting the treatments. It's no big drama anymore, it's just a step that a lot of women will be taking. Women are always ahead of men on these kinds of things. Later, men will get the bug, and the men will do it in secret, so that no golfing partner ever finds out.

The hors d'oeuvres are little dainty sandwiches for people who like to eat when they're nervous, and then there will be iced tea, fruity and minty, with fresh leaves drifting lazily in pitchers from Steuben. Dr. Maevka is willing to prescribe tranquilizers for people who are hesitant, but he's hoping that there's not going to be a lot of drinking, because that just isn't medically sound. When you have a lot of drinking at a party, then people get sloppy. He'd rather sell the reputation of the medicine among the sober and alert, because with anything that causes paralysis, there's bound to be misunderstanding.

Wouldn't you like to know the names on the guest list? She's not so indiscreet as to give away information like that. People in this neighborhood depend on their anonymity. She will admit, however, that the wife of one of the major studio heads will be there, also the wives of several hot-shot entertainment lawyers and a few screenwriters.

Melody has these parties because it's a nice way to give back to the community. In fact, she says this to one of the cater-waiters, an attractive young girl who is almost certainly an actress. She says, "I really like to have parties like this occasionally because it's a good way to give back to the community." She asks the cater-waiter to hold out her hand, and she notices that the nails of the cater-waiter are lacquered maroon, a shade Melody also favors, Bordeaux or maybe California Bing. The girl places a Tiffany platter of canapés on a nearby table and she takes from Melody the item that is being offered, which is a lilac-scented eye pillow. Just like the ones that will serve as party favors this afternoon.

Melody asks, "Do you think it's too much?"

The gap-toothed cater-waiter, bless her heart, knows exactly what an eye pillow is for. She leans back and sets the eye pillow across the bridge of her pretty little nose and she takes pause. The sound of industry is so reassuring around a house, the mustering of hospitality, the caterers layering saucissons onto little sandwiches, the stirring of aromatics into the iced tea, the preparation of the smart little bags with the favors in them, including cleansing lotions admixed by Dr. Maevka himself, as well as the lilac-scented eye pillows, selected by the hostess. The cater-waiter lingers in the center of the room with the eye pillow across the bridge of her lightly freckled nose.

She says, "I can definitely feel a nap coming on."

"Then you keep that one for yourself, sweetheart. For when the party's over."

The cater-waiter smiles and curtsies, both earnest and playful. But there's no time for playacting because now there's the chiming of the front door and the party is begun! Melody Howell Forvath would continue in a discursive vein on her thoughts about botulinum toxin and the history of cosmetic surgery in California, or partygoing in general, but she barely has time to complete a sentence because each close personal friend is now immediately followed by another. Here, for example, is Darlene, with whom she plays tennis, Darlene who always makes a questionable call or two but has perfect ground strokes; and here is Lois Maiser's ex-sister-in-law, she comes on like a freight train, and before Melody even has time to ask her about her son the skateboard champion, she starts in with the doubts she's having. "Doesn't the toxin cause dystonia?" Melody pretends not to hear, sweeps out of the foyer, grabs the cater-waiter, points her in the direction of the office, "Look up something for me: *dystonia.*" In record time, the cater-waiter, who certainly does resemble the celebrated gap-toothed Wife of Bath, comes trotting out of the office, the planes of her cheeks faintly flushed. Fewer than half a dozen guests have slipped past her when the answer comes: "Involuntary contractions of the musculature." She says it to Lois's sister-in-law with the forgettable name. How horrible to forget the name of someone she knows so well. Then, abruptly, it comes back to her. "Actually, Janet, dystonia is what it's used to *treat*, but you can ask these questions of Dr. Maevka, whom you're really going to like, sweetie. He's a dish."

They're here, the women of Santa Monica, for the Forvath party. Melody greets each in turn, holding her long-stemmed rose, white with an elegant scent. She smiles sweetly, she welcomes each, one by one, into her living room. She can see the gap-toothed cater-waiter again, who with a sweep of the arm is sending forth the guests, until the Forvath sitting room is like a wild-animal display — one of those drive-thru ones — of the most powerful women in the Los Angeles area. Diana Collins, the lawyer; there's Kennedy McCord, the children's book writer; Sherry Horst, the psychoanalyst; Ellen Evans, the publicist. That interior decorator, Leni Jankovich. Dozens of others. The only person missing is Lois Maiser herself, who's all broken up about her husband's trading down for some young thing. In fact, ever since, Lois has taken to Dr. Maevka with a vengeance. She's already an initiate. And yet Melody Forvath doesn't know if it's the best thing that Lois isn't here. Lois risks finding out about the party through some other channel. Through loose talk. You know how people are. Lois's depression verges on the morbid, and Melody has heard tales of Lois not getting out of bed for days at a time and giving away personal possessions. Melody doesn't know what to do about it yet, but she will do something. She'll take Lois to a desert spa, in Scottsdale or Taos. Or to a wine tasting with that fabulous wine consultant, what's his name. In the meantime, however, Melody Howell Forvath follows a guest into the living room and slips her ornamental rose into the vase by the Plexiglas lectern. She takes out her notes, on the sticky pink things, and she holds these notes up to the girls as though some secret is held here.

"I had all these wonderful remarks I was going to make because of course I'm a writer and so I'm maybe a little too fond of the sound of my own voice! But seriously I think it's fair to say that you're not here for me but for the man of the hour. So why don't we invite him in right now, girls?"

He's Dr. Iveshka Maekva, from San Diego, by way of St. Petersburg. He's elegant and stylish, in a charcoal gray pinstripe but with some of those rakish details that younger designers bring to things, a robin's-egg tie with red tennis rackets on it. His hair, though thinning on the top, has an effect more virile than vulnerable, and it's swept straight back and oiled with something French. There are curls behind his ears. He wears tortoiseshell glasses, which somehow give him an Omar Sharif gravity. If Dr. Zhivago were a dermatologist and cosmetic surgeon, this is what he'd look like, and his accent would seduce whole blocks of Santa Monica wives.

He seizes the microphone roughly and adjusts it. The amplifier crackles to life. "You will want to be knowing about the positive benefits of this treatment. And so now I would like to enumerate these benefits. First, I can promise that you will lose many if not all of the lines around the eyes and in the area of the forehead. This is the first of my promises to you." And now Dr. Maekva has parted company with the lectern. He has moved forward to the edge of the sofa where Kennedy McCord is sitting. Immediately, as if he were the sea breaking upon the sand, he is caressing, in the most methodical way, the top of Kennedy's forehead, where even her close friends would agree there has been some grooving, owing to the grimacing and the impatience with which Kennedy daily struggles. "I can promise relief from repetitive stresses acting upon these muscles here. I can promise that for about three months after this treatment, these lines will completely disappear. I can promise that the muscle tension here will completely evaporate. Here your skin will again resemble the smooth, unlined skin of a young woman in the bloom of youth. Or perhaps even better than a woman in her

youth. Perhaps you will have the skin of a little child." He takes
Kennedy's hand briefly and then sets it back in her lap, and then
he pauses briefly to straighten a cuff link before moving toward
Sherry Horst, possibly the most impervious of the RSVPs.
Sherry Horst, who never met a salesman or a politician she
didn't dislike.

"You will be wanting to know the costs of such a magical cure.
And there are costs. Beyond the monetary investment, of course.
I can promise, in a spirit of full disclosure, that you will have
slightly diminished sensation in the particular area of the treatment. We are paralyzing the muscle groups, after all. Certain
kinds of facial expression will be difficult, if not impossible, during the effective period of the treatment, as there is paralysis. A
quizzical expression, for example, out of the question. The result
is a kind of appearance that skeptics would perhaps call masking,
but others would simply call beautiful."

Now Dr. Maevka uses his most calculating bit of persuasion,
which, the way Melody Howell Forvath sees it, is really more like
a Las Vegas spectacle. From his briefcase, Dr. Maevka removes a
rolled-up reproduction of the painting by Leonardo da Vinci
known as the Mona Lisa.

He unrolls it.

"I would ask you to look at Leonardo's definition of beauty,
which is inscrutable, which is dignified, which is not a pandering
beauty, not an immature beauty, but which is rather the beauty
of wisdom and understanding. This beauty will be yours for the
duration of the treatment.

"There are minor side effects, of course. How could it be otherwise? But these are mainly owing to the injection and to the inert materials contained in the injection, and these minor side
effects will include for some of you respiratory infection, flu, headache. Transient effects, I think you will agree, and nothing compared to the restoration of your radiance. You will be beautiful,

you will be good at poker, and you will smile like a Renaissance masterpiece."

A sigh of acclamation sweeps through the Forvath sitting room. Melody thinks she sees it even in the face of the gap-toothed Wife of Bath standing like statuary at the door. Dr. Maevka has the audience in the palm of his hand, and because of this, he now lifts from his bag the rubber gloves of his trade, and he snaps these onto his wrists as if this were part of the Hippocratic oath, after which he produces the last hurdle to be surmounted today, the needle required for the application of the toxin. "As you know, the needle used for the treatments is slightly larger than those used for injections you may have had in the past, and I think it's important that you have an opportunity to see the tool that is to be used. I disclose it now. Nothing to be afraid of, of course. If you contracted rabies, for example, you would be in a much worse position. In fact, in that case we would have to inject you in the abdomen."

Kennedy asks if there is any pain associated with the injection.

"Of course, there is the injection itself, which is a pinch of nothing, and then, because we use distilled saline to preserve the toxin, there is some minor stinging, but beyond this there is no real pain associated with the injection itself. Any other questions?"

"Is there any danger of infection from the toxin?"

"A good question. Most of you will know that the toxin is commonly found in . . . I believe in the United States that the prejudice is for mushroom soup. Because we are giving very minute injections in very localized regions, however, we are not spreading the toxin throughout the body, like mushroom soup would spread it, if ingested. It will stay where it is injected and it will perform its magic there. The answer, therefore, is that notwithstanding the seriousness of the toxin itself, these are very focused injections in particular locations, and there is no worry about toxin escaping into the body as a whole and causing trouble. No worry at all on this point. If these are all the questions, I suppose I might ask for a volunteer?"

Well, it's her party. It's Melody's party, and she has gathered her friends here, and she has put her credibility on the line, her literary celebrity, and there's really no option but that she should be the first, the first to have the injection or the series of injections. The first to be in the strong, masculine hands of Dr. Iveshka Maevka as he passes this milestone in his practice, his first Santa Monica Botox party. The occasion is momentous in so many ways. Melody raises her hand, and there's nervous laughter in the room as her friends realize how brave Melody is and how sweet for bringing them all together like this.

"It's material for the next book," she says, "so don't worry!" Everyone laughs. "And I'm even writing off the catering bill!"

Dr. Maevka gestures toward the daybed situated strategically by the enormous potted fern. From here, Melody can see the ripples on the surface of the pool through the French doors. She can hear birds twittering in the palms. Was any afternoon more deluxe? She sits up straight, since her posture is never less than good, and she looks up at Dr. Maevka as though it's a conversion experience that is promised in this moment, and before she knows it, the injection is upon her, a slight pinch. She's conscious of the fact that she feels nothing, really, in the spot of the injection. The pressure being relieved as the needle is withdrawn, nothing more. When you get right down to it, how few things there are that really deliver on the promise of eliminating sensation. How many hedonistic pleasures are about acuteness of perception, roller coasters and white-water rafting and casinos, but how precious and few are genuine moments of relief, as when one is in bed, and the light is extinguished, and the oncoming dreams are confused with the afternoon's appointments. Then there's a sharp sting of an additional injection, two more, right above her eyebrows, as if she's having her third eye drained, and the sting narrows, intensifies, and Melody swallows in the sting, the chemical aftertaste, and the light opens up, and it contains people, and stillness, and faint chlorine fumes.

Sherry Horst. That's Sherry's ring, that awesome rock with its many facets, glimmering above the heads of the other women. Her hand aloft. This is amazing in itself because Sherry is never early out of the gate on anything. She's fond of lawsuits, since that's what her husband, that poorly dressed oaf with the worst teeth in Los Angeles, does for his livelihood. Dr. Maevka has certainly sold his product well — through the inexorable cheer that makes his practice so profitable — if he has sold Sherry Horst. Melody makes a mental note to be sure she has the number of Sherry's platinum card.

"Does it hurt?" Sherry asks Melody, as the doctor with his impressive needle approaches, an attractive nurse trailing behind him submissively.

"Of course not." Although Melody does feel a little as if she's been attacked by hornets. She hopes it's nothing serious.

The doctor again performs his clinical benedictions. Four or five aging women in sequence, all of them speaking of nothing but boutique sales in town and what certain movies have grossed and who is pandering to the tabloids, as needles plunge into their faces. They are thirsty for good news, these friends of Melody's. Because what has this nation told them, here in the new millennium? This nation has told these women to get out of the way. It has told these women that if they are not wearing blue jeans with their, what's that word, with their booties hanging out of them, then they are not real women. It has told them that if they do not have a ring hanging out of their navels they are not women. It has told them that they are the leftovers of domesticity, they are the residue, they are what child rearing leaves as its waste product, they are what the nineteen-sixties and -seventies left in their wake. They are decades of ill-considered license. They are the end stage of bed-hopping and jet travel to the Caribbean and experimentation with pot and Dubonnet and low-tar cigarettes. They are what America once said it wanted. And so the least that capitalism can do is to give these women a way to feel a little dignity now while the sluts in the low-riders get themselves compromised and go through it all, the day care and the nannies and the private schools. It's no wonder, when you think this way about it, because of all the sorrow and all the paradox, that at this moment there is a commotion at the front door, an overheard sort of commotion. It's almost a beautiful sound at first, commotion on expensive tile work, or maybe it's just the side effects of the treatment, the hornets careening around the room, maybe the hornets lead to increased echo. It takes a minute for Melody to grasp that her name is being bandied about in the commotion. Sluggishly, she rises from the daybed, looks back toward the foyer.

Ohmygod. It's Lois Maiser. A crisis. It's a genuine crisis! And she knows! Lois knows she wasn't invited! She wasn't invited to the party, and all of her friends *were* invited, and now Lois is here, and all these other people are here, and they all RSVP'd! How could Melody have been such a horse's ass, how could Melody have willfully overlooked the possibility that such a moment was lying in wait for her? The sense that propriety has failed is in the room and it's as certain as billowing curtains and sunlight and peppermint tea and chlorinated-water vapor. The women look down at the expensive Italian tile beneath them, as if by studying the tile they will at least not make the situation worse. It's just like one of those movies, one of those insipid television movies where a fellow shows up who would never be there at all, in order to have the dramatic confrontation! My God. Actually, it's like *Reign of Frogs,* that novel she once wrote about a counter-espionage agent who is incarcerated in a Chinese psychiatric hospital and forcibly medicated, only to find her own husband is being held in the same ward. What a coincidence!

"Lois, I . . . Come in, sweetheart. Come on in."

In truth, Lois's face just now resembles nothing so much as an African mask. Well, it's an African mask with a perm and blond highlights, but it's still a mask, the kind of mask that you see on a shelf in an expensive psychiatrist's office, which is of course where Lois has spent a lot of time recently. Her serotonin levels are like the roller coaster on the Santa Monica pier, first up and then down, down, down. And one of her side effects must be ravenous hunger, because Lois has packed on a good twenty pounds, and without replacing her wardrobe.

"Melody," Lois starts slowly, without the hysteria to which she resorted to get in the front door, "I'm really sorry to show up this way —"

"Oh, it's nothing, honey. Come, sit."

"It's not like I'm here to break up the party. That's not why I'm here. It looks like a lovely party, and I'm hoping that I get invited next time, and that I'm not too late to get one of these lovely eye pillows . . ."

Melody Howell Forvath might laugh were it not beginning to dawn on her that Lois is not here to make a complaint about the hostess, nor about the fact that she wasn't invited. No, there's something far more terrifying going on, something far more inimical to partygoing merriment. Lois means to make a complaint against Dr. Maevka. Melody can see the recognition dawning in him now, the recognition of Lois. Lois as the accretion of bad luck. Dr. Maevka's lantern jaw is set in a hard way, as though he's a tight end who is going to have to fight his way over linebackers.

"Listen up, everyone," Lois is saying, holding one of the lavender eye pillows in a clenched fist. "I think most of you know me here, and so I think I'm not without credibility. You know it's me, someone from your own community, who's about to say what I'm going to say. And what I'm going to say is that the procedure you're undertaking today —"

Is that a blob of spittle yo-yoing from Lois's mouth, detaching, heading for the marble floor in fancy filmic slow motion? It certainly looks like a little dollop of some foamy something. Spittle, in all likelihood. Detaching. Catching some California sunlight before striking the tile with a gentle plop. Melody is sure that it is. Melody even whispers, "Is that drool?" to herself and notices Diana Collins nodding. Diana sees it, too. It's drool, proceeding in a steady trickle from Lois's mouth, the mouth set in that African mask of a face. And Melody begins to understand. It's not that Lois is depressed over her husband! It's not that Lois is hiding out because of the little tart her husband ran off with, though this would be a perfectly good reason to hide out. Instead, Lois has been concealed in her Laguna Beach mansion because of ineffective cosmetic treatments!

"Botulinum is dangerous, you guys, that's what I'm telling you, and there's a lot that can go wrong with it. I didn't want to interrupt the party, I didn't want to ruin the party, but I thought you should see what can happen before you get seduced by the story someone's telling you about the miracle."

It's unmistakable. Lois is *drooping*. She has the telltale eye droop. It's the left eye, teardrop shaped and drooping, and the edge of her mouth is drooping, almost as if she's had a stroke. An entire side of her face has somehow been, well, *smooshed*. She has had some reaction on the left side and she looks like that actor, what's his name, the one that won't stop making public appearances even though he can no longer talk. Melody would be the first to admit that Lois has no lines in her paralyzed, drooping face, that's true. Her paralyzed face is without lines, and if it weren't for the cascading saliva, she would look pretty good. Melody wonders whether available men in California would have trouble making sweet love to a sexually independent woman who drools.

"I'd be remiss if I didn't say that I got my injections from the very office that is here today making the house calls. I just thought you should know."

"Just a moment! Mrs. Maiser, I object!" Dr. Maevka shouts, and now it's really a carnival. He pulls a surgical glove from one hand, a punctuation mark, and thrusts it to the floor, where he stamps on the glove as though he were challenging Lois to a duel with Russian eighteenth-century pistols. "Mrs. Maiser! I will not stand by while you calumniate my professional practice."

Lois's voice is beginning to rise, to ascend to its more shrill register. "I have brought myself here as a cautionary tale, and people are free to make whatever conclusions they want to make!"

In the voluptuousness that is the sun and its reflection and the westward retreat of daylight over the swimming pool, the women begin to sneak out of the house of Melody Howell Forvath, without making even abbreviated good-byes. It's stealthy at first and then more like a stampede. And Melody, a little light-headed, as if the hornets have got the best of her, doesn't know what to think. Friends clutch at her hand as they sneak toward the door. Diane Collins clasps Melody's hand between her own and she says nothing, because Melody has the stuff *in her* now, as if it's her secret, her postmenopausal fetus, the botulinum toxin, slayer of American mushroom soup eaters. She doesn't know who to be angry with first, so she puts ire aside, for now, and she goes and stands with the Wife of Bath, who is stooping before a sculpture of a water nymph. The Wife of Bath is cleaning away a dollop of lobster salad that somehow landed there.

"There's a phone call for you," the Wife of Bath says. "In the kitchen."

She holds up the offending lobster salad clotting a lavender cocktail napkin. Nearby, Lois and Maevka are referring each other to their lawyers in apoplectic whispers.

Melody leaves her own party behind as though it never happened. There's no other conclusion but that it was a disaster as a party, a blot on the escutcheon of Melody Forvath. She has no intention of lingering. Maybe she, too, should sue Maevka, that quack, who claims to have a license to practice in California and who probably has no such thing. Melody leaves it all behind, for the kitchen, where the portable phone is handed to her as if it were a baton. Her office is beyond, and she hasn't visited her office in days, but now she takes a long slow stroll in its direction. Vic Freese's voice reverberates in her poisoned head. He has a weak voice, a loser's voice, as if he was never taught to breathe properly. He's the television agent, or at least she thinks he's the television agent, and television agents share most of their genetic material with cockroaches, that Ceylonese subspecies that hisses loud enough to scare dogs. Melody much prefers her American literary agent, though sometimes her British literary agent is nice, and also his Italian co-agent, who is very sexy, and then there's also the French agent with that beautiful accent. They all send her gifts at Christmas.

"Melody, didn't you once write a big fat novel called *The Diviners*?" Vic Freese asks.

"Do you remember what it's about?"

17

The two detectives, according to reports filed later, spend the first hour of the stakeout arguing about doughnuts. They introduce various facts into the discussion; for example, that Krispy Kreme sells a billion doughnuts per year and thus cannot be considered inferior to the more popular brands, that Krispy Kreme can produce, in situ, up to twelve thousand doughnuts an hour. Imagine if twelve thousand original glazed doughnuts were to become suddenly available at a particular Krispy Kreme franchise, for example, the World Trade Center location. What a boon to New York City policing. The detectives feel that the more complex doughnut varieties, such as the chocolate ice cream filled or the glazed lemon filled, are tasty, but these are not really the doughnuts that the detectives consider the essential business line of the Krispy Kreme corporation. The essential business line is the original glazed doughnut. The detectives speak of the cultural penetration of the original glazed, how it has acquired an almost fetishistic reputation among consumers. Consider, for example, tiered doughnut wedding cakes. Concentric rings of original glazed doughnuts, in a fractal design, with lightweight bride and groom ornaments at the summit. This wedding cake design is taking off now, and it proves that the only way to go, with a business line like the original glazed, is up. Original glazed no more than five hundred feet from every American household. Original glazed on every block in every major city. Original glazed available at other fast-food addresses. Original glazed in public schools. Original glazed when you register to vote.

The detectives are considering investing in the Krispy Kreme corporation, a common stock listed on the NYSE, one that has been doing quite well, a fact noted with pleasure by the detectives, who are currently getting their asses kicked on some of their other securities, for example, QualComm. Krispy Kreme has the Krispy Kreme "mythodology," which is based on the work of the critic Joseph Campbell. Krispy Kreme has strong brand recognition, a proven growth record, as well as the Doughnut Theater Concept, which is more than you can say about QualComm. The Doughnut Theater Concept is the on-site Krispy Kreme production event made visible to the consumer. Better even than the Ford production line. The Doughnut Theater Concept begins when the red light comes on, the red light indicating the presence of the core line of business, the original glazed doughnut. The Doughnut Theater Concept is the detectives watching as the original glazed doughnuts begin to come off the production line, twelve thousand strong, toppling onto cooling trays as if they were lemmings free-falling into a ravine. Yes, with the Doughnut Theater Concept, the detectives can know the business in which they are investing and they can conduct surveillance on the core line of business, which conforms to the style and habits of the metropolitan detective, who does not have time to figure out which parts of his cellular phone use QualComm technology.

The stakeout continues in this way until one of the detectives, the one *not* reading the tabloids, announces that the sister of the suspect is now on the move. He uses the code agreed upon earlier, "The worm has turned." The sister of the suspect is now leaving her East Village address, she is slamming the front door of the walk-up behind her, proceeding west, and so the detectives stir like ravens in a dead tree. That is, the detectives abandon their vehicle, and each brings a doughnut. It is Sunday, and the detectives would normally have the day off, but they are concerned that the suspect, the older brother of the young woman currently under surveillance, may have fled the metropolitan area to points unknown. The sister may be the only credible link to the suspect.

There will be observation of the movements of the sister of the suspect, in the event that the sister makes known the whereabouts of the suspect.

The sister of the suspect, according to reports, is, it should be noted, "very attractive," and is wearing "leather pants" on the day in question. It's another day of steady drizzle. Nonetheless, the detectives hasten westward, following the sister of the suspect at some remove. What they know: The sister is an employee of a boutique film production company, which boutique has made a number of films that the detectives have not seen. The boutique film production company hires out work to the very messenger company at which the suspect in the assault case previously worked. A connection has therefore been established, between suspect and sister, first in the identical surnames of these two persons. Second, this connection was verified in a quick data search of credit and medical records, confirming that the suspect has been both a failed graduate student and a client of a variety of mental health professionals. He is, in fact, "bipolar," or manic-depressive, whatever the current terminology is. According to the detectives, it is established that the suspect has a history of mental illness, and this is likely to be material to a jury trial, especially in view of the fact that the assault incident is being prosecuted as an attack without motive.

The detectives have leaked this information to the press.

They know, and the knowledge is bittersweet, that both the suspect and his sister, the woman currently under surveillance, are adoptees. They know that the children were adopted, some years apart, by white parents, though both the suspect and his sister are African American, and to the detectives this is a sorrowful part of the investigation because one of the detectives, while educated in the city college system, is himself from the projects. The projects speak through him, and the projects are with him, and there is no shaking off the projects, which are an engine of African American identity in this city. He knows: When you take a black kid out of the neighborhoods and you put this black kid in the white neighborhoods, this kid will be like a duck raised by geese. And in this instance, the adoptive parents are church folk. The father is a minister of some kind, and the mother is a psychologist. The suspect and his sister were adopted and they were raised up in New England. The detectives also happen to know the names of the natural parents of the two children, and they know that one of these children was born in Chicago and one in Las Vegas. They surmise that the two siblings are as close as natural siblings because they are two supererogatory kids. Later there was a natural sibling, a white baby, born to the formerly barren mother. This is why they think the suspect will contact his sister. He can't do otherwise. They want to be there when it happens.

The sister of the suspect proceeds up Avenue A at a brisk clip past a Mexican joint. Mexican food in NYC is almost always a disappointment. Nevertheless, the detectives duck inside this establishment briefly and throw away their tabloids, inhale cilantro and tomatillos, wait for a suitable interval, and then they exit and continue the surveillance. The detectives continue west on Eighth Street, passing examples of a genus that doesn't seem to exist in any other neighborhood, the men and women wearing black leather jackets, all of them with dyed black hair, all of them with various piercings, all come to the region around St. Mark's Place. The sister of the suspect, picking up the pace further, makes a right-hand turn at the cube sculpture, a known squatter and runaway hangout, past the still unpalatable Kmart franchise, first of its type in the city. To what destination would the "very attractive" sister of the suspect be bound? Might she be making for the cheap hairstylists of Fourteenth Street? For the extremely large music and media store nearby? Is she going to kill time in the park, reading some tome? Or perhaps she is bent upon the farmers' market? Not possible. No farmers' market on Sunday.

It is the best of all outcomes for the detectives. They have eaten little but doughnuts since the stakeout began. They could not have hoped for *this*, for how the sister of the suspect passes through the threshold of a restaurant in the Union Square neighborhood, a restaurant beloved by the detectives, a restaurant that is, yes, "model owned and operated." Indeed, the restaurant, which was once a run-down Greek American coffee shop, is painted a nauseating teal on the outside and is notorious for attracting only the most delectable of feminine examples, each of them over six feet and with legs of limitless majesty. The detectives do not seek out such places. They are made of sterner stuff. They will stake out the Fulton Fish Market if required, they will stake out mortuaries in the outer boroughs. But if their work brings them to the former coffee shop, they will allow themselves a moment of bedazzlement as the hostess takes them to their table, a table where their concealed audio recorder can pick up some of the conversation at the next booth, the booth that currently contains the sister of the suspect and a certain coworker from the film company known as Means of Production, namely Jeanine Stampfel. Born: Scottsdale, Arizona, July 15, 1976. Educated: University of Arizona, BA, in English. Moved to New York City: 1998. Lives: Upper West Side.

The detectives settle on entrées as follows: media noche and paillard of chicken. They each order a mochaccino beverage. Then they eat and listen. Christmas lights festoon the walls. Synthetic hits of the nineteen-eighties throb on the sound system.

"It's . . . I . . . just thought, you know. I, uh," Annabel Duffy replies. The detectives have missed the opening of the exchange. However, exact transcription of the remaining conversation follows: "I mean. It's stupid that we never get together at all. We're . . . I mean, working together in the same office and everything. We should be . . . And especially with all the pressure that this—"

"Television thing —"

"Yeah," Annabel Duffy replies. A waitress saunters by, and the detectives begin to speak to the idea that there are secret affiliations between these women who don't eat enough food. Look at that waitress. It's as if they recognize one another or something. They are morphological kin. They are like greyhounds. And they are exchanging secret signals about what might be eaten without danger of caloric intake.

"I don't know what to think. I hate television, know what I mean? I don't even want to work there if we're just going to be thinking up television shows."

"I don't even have one. A TV. I mean, I have one, I guess, but I don't have it on very much. No cable or anything. I watch what's that show the —"

Stampfel mentions the name of a certain show, and this show is not as audible as might be wished, and yet, using the most up-to-date digital editing tools, the detectives will later be able to surmise that Stampfel mentioned a popular television show about a pack of werewolves, *The Werewolves of Fairfield County*. By night, suburbanites are transformed into baying, lonely lycanthropes, and so forth. It's a program that the detectives have not seen, though they have heard it is very popular among the young, for nearly four seasons now. In four years, many things can befall a lycanthrope. Meteor showers, droughts, floods, spontaneous forest fires, suburban sprawl, the complete elimination of nature, mad love. Such things make for ratings, which make for syndication.

"I watched some of one of the World Series games," Jeanine says. "With a man."

"Right. With —"

"How are we going to develop television stuff if neither of us watches any television? And Madison is going out to parties all night?" To the waitress: "Another one of these? When you get a chance?"

"Minivan is acting weird."

"Totally."

"She's totally out of her mind, even on a good day."

"I go home and cry," Stampfel says. "I can't do anything. My parents are worried. They're saying I should just come back to Arizona. What's so great about the movie business? Why do you have to be so far from home? Arizona is not as glamorous, but it's . . . it's —"

"We should film *there*," Duffy says. "I mean, Arizona would be great. We could stay at some really good hotels, right? We could get massages."

"Have you read the coverage?"

"Sure."

"I thought it was really *junky*, personally. I don't even think Madison reads the stuff. She just passes it on."

"I didn't think it was so bad," Duffy says. The detectives turn, as if to signal for more hot sauce. It's part of their undercover cloak of veracity. They only briefly attempt to catch a look at the awkward conversation of Annabel Duffy and her friend. The two of them are stabbing at salads as if they're trying to put the salads out of some misery. "I like epics, big things, politics. And maybe it's sort of fun to think of stories that anyone could like."

"That's so cynical. I don't mind being, you know, the priss on the staff, so that everyone can feel all superior, and, well, yes, I guess I *do* mind it, it kind of hurts my feelings, but don't expect me to pretend everything is fine. The story sounds like it was written by some romance novelist or something. In fact, Madison was telling me that the author *is* a romance novelist."

"Come on, Jeanine. You know I —"

"Sorry . . . I'm —"

"Maybe it's just, like I said, I'm worried that if we're just doing television, then we're all going to become —"

The suspect's sister signals the waitress again, plunks down a large ring of keys on the table, keys as numerous as if she were a prison guard at a county jail.

Stampfel says, "I dated this guy from Harvard one time, and now he's writing a reality show where people try to inform on their coworkers."

"You don't really —"

"No, you're . . . you're . . ."

"Look," Annabel remarks, "Minivan wants us to hate each other; it's like, it's really easy to hate each other. That's what professional women do, you know. They're like, they're supposed to hate each other and fight over the same men, all of that," Duffy says. "I'm supposed to hate your projects, you're supposed to hate mine. We're both supposed to hate Madison's projects, and we're supposed to talk about what a bitch she is."

"She is kind of a bitch."

"And we're not supposed to talk about Thaddeus."

The detectives asphyxiate, momentarily, on extremely spicy Brazilian fare, because one bit of information available to the detectives that is perhaps not available to the two employees of Means of Production in the next booth is that a Casanova named Thaddeus Griffin has been romantically involved with *both* of these women. And that's the least of it. One of the detectives tailed Mr. Thaddeus Griffin very recently, just for fun, and went to the gentlemen's club with him and, just for fun, asked Thaddeus Griffin for an autograph in this gentlemen's club. Contrary to stakeout protocol, of course, endangering the security of the investigation, et cetera, but the detective in question considered it information of a kind. Would Griffin bolt if recognized by an action film fan in a mob-owned strip club? Or would he return to the Asian lap dancer, the one who looked much like the victim of the crime they are investigating? Griffin brushed off the overture of the detective, shoved aside his black laundry-proof marker without comment. Later the same night, Griffin was observed outside the building of Annabel Duffy.

"You aren't . . ." Stampfel stutters, can't get it out. "Are you saying what I think you're saying?"

"Big deal. So we both slept with him," Duffy observes. "He gave me chlamydia. That's a boundary for me."

"Do you think he slept with Madison? This is so embarrassing. I can think of some embarrassing things in my life, but I have never talked with someone who slept with the same guy as me. It's just, uh, you know."

What the waitress brings now is carrot cake and dessert forks, and the two women appear to have arrived at complete unanimity in the matter of dessert, the better to negotiate the awkwardness of their revelations. Further commentary on Griffin follows, some of it extremely embarrassing, as in the portion of the recording wherein Duffy asks Stampfel if Thaddeus Griffin started talking with her about "taking it to the next level." Duffy guffaws at the recollection. No, Stampfel did not have any discussion about the next level, but Stampfel naturally asks, What is the next level?

"The next level is the level of *pain.*"

Which means? According to Duffy, as summarized briefly in the report of the detectives, the level of pain is chiefly the level of clothespins. And it is not the woman who must wear the clothespins, it is the woman who must apply the clothespins. Which means, deductively, that Griffin is the wearer of the clothespins. The target area for the clothespins is apparently the nipples of Griffin. At first. Then later, when the nipples have too reliably become the target area, the scrotal region becomes the target area for the clothespins. "It's a lark," according to Duffy, applying the clothespins to the scrotal region of Griffin. Maybe the scrotal application of clothespins to a major Hollywood action film star makes Annabel Duffy want to jangle her keys — this is more than audible on the tape. And yet the detectives also wonder how Duffy, sister of the suspect in a major felonious assault, can casually eat a luncheon and discourse on scrotal application of clothespins. And yet they are enough bemused by the scrotal application, and the application of clothespins to inner thigh, likewise the words *binder clip,* which in this context must be considered extremely painful, that they fail to notice some of the rather strange twists and turns of this conversation.

"He never asked any of that sort of thing of me," Jeanine says, devouring the last bite of cake. "I guess it didn't get that far. I started to feel guilty about his wife."

"That's the thing that made me *want* to attach the clothespins. The fact that he hurt so much when they were on, it was like he was feeling as bad as he should have felt about his wife. He'd be sweating and whining and saying 'ouch' over and over. It was kind of funny. The worst part, you know, is the part where you take the clothespins off. That's the part that really hurts. You get used to them while they're on, I mean, not that I know personally, but that's what he said. But then he would take the clothespins off, and he would just be crying out when he did it. I put all this in my screenplay. You know, he promised to help me with my screenplay, that liar, so I guess maybe he finally did, because at least now I know that clothespins hurt more when you take them off."

"If my parents found out about this, they'd make me get on a plane immediately. If I said New York was like a man who can't get an erection and who wants you to attach clothespins to him."

"He couldn't —"

"He tried to make up for it in other ways."

"I mean, not like I'm a size queen or anything. It's a cute little one."

Another piece of carrot cake appears, as though agreed upon

earlier in the secret signals of the union of anorexic women. Where the conversation seemed awkward and even tense before, now a common ground has been established between the sister of the suspect and her coworker, and the detectives are beginning to feel as though they have held their table longer than they ought. They are wondering whether they might repair to Union Square Park, there to await the next move of Duffy. One of the detectives stands, stretches languorously, heads for the men's room. Here is what he glimpses as he strides past: He glimpses the moment when Annabel Duffy has taken the hand of Jeanine Stampfel in her own and is examining the "life line" of Jeanine Stampfel as if they were thirteen-year-old girls engaged in teen occult behavior. What's with young people these days? Is adolescence now decades long? Thinking of none of this, the detective takes a deluxe leak. Much needed after sitting in the car all that time. While soaping up, he wonders if his wife will have the football game on when he gets home. Will there be chips?

Back at the booth, his partner is ready to leave. The audio recorder is hidden away on his person. After paying, one detective says to the other that they have a lot of paperwork ahead. The other replies that they should cut it short. There's always tomorrow. All of this while they are walking past the two women, as if they and the women have no connection at all, as if the city is not a chaotic network of lost connections and near misses. Only after they pass the hostess does one detective look back, one last time, to see that the Duffy woman has now rolled up the sleeve of the other, the Stampfel woman, and what she has revealed on the arm of Stampfel are tremendous third-degree-burn scars.

Burn scars? Is that really what he saw? Did he really see what he thought he saw? wonders the detective. A man of inexhaustible fact, our detective, a man of inches and yards, a man who admits to nothing in the way of uncertainties. A man who is now seeing a beautiful blonde with third-degree-burn scars over the majority of her arm, perhaps both arms. And what about the high-necked blouse she's wearing? Because of burns? Where do you get that kind of burn? And what does that kind of burn feel like, and how many weeks are you in the burn ward with that kind of a burn? Sometimes he is suffocated by the darkness of his job. He thinks longingly of the purity of the original glazed doughnut.

The door swings in, and an I formation of hungover Europeans clogs in the threshold, impeding the progress of the two detectives. Bound for Bloody Marys and football games on inaudible monitors. Were they as observant as detectives, these carousers would overhear the end of the conversation, would overhear the Duffy woman ask the Stampfel woman how she got this, this molten bubbling along the length of her forearm.

"Because I noticed the, uh, you know, in the office, I think I noticed like the first or second day, how could I not notice."

Quietly. "I was in a fire." And then, inexplicably, the Stampfel woman asks: "Are they gone?"

To which the Duffy woman replies, "Yeah, I think." In the lowest of tones, while the scars lay exposed to the air, the drama of burns. "They always *look* like police, you know? Not like I had any doubt. Their sneakers are too new."

"Where is he?"

"In Massachusetts. I think. Or he was there Friday. He might be still moving around. He knows not to call me now. But that only makes me more worried."

"And he didn't do it? Whatever they're saying he did?"

"Guess how many black bike messengers there are in New York City?" Annabel says. "Okay, look, what I want you to do, I mean, if you feel like you *can* do it, is to take the key to his studio, see if you can get into his studio, get his computer and his cell phone. Because he says he was in his studio during the time when the woman was, uh, assaulted. Then if you can, just bring it all to work tomorrow. The computer and the phone. Just bring them in. There should be stuff on the computer that will prove —"

Even more urgent is the confederacy of the moment.

"His computer has everything on it, lots of his work, lists of things he ate, proposals for new works, and it'll have some kind of alibi on it, and the phone bill will have his phone records on it. I'm supposed to take the computer and the phone to a lawyer in midtown. I know it's a lot to ask, and I won't, you know, I wouldn't hold it against you if you can't do it. But if you can, it's like the sweetest thing anyone ever did."

"It was . . . it was, um, kind of nice getting to talk."

"What? Oh. We should, uh . . . Okay, I'm going out first, and I'm going to take these guys, the police, on a little shopping trip to find the most expensive lingerie in the Village. Hey, did you hear?"

Stampfel is standing, one hand on the vinyl lining of the booth.

"Shelley Ralston Havemeyer."

"Who?" Jeanine says.

"She wrote *The Diviners*. We actually found her."

"I thought her name was Marjorie something."

"Don't believe everything you hear. She has two studios fighting over her."

Annabel, having had her only meal of the day, makes for the door, her Celtic tattoo just visible above the rim of her leather pants, in that sacral zone between belt and shirt hem. Out she goes into the rain. The Bloody Mary drinkers, aligned at the bar, in an intensity of forgetting, don't see. The runway models, still irritated at waitressing or hostessing when by now they ought to have become supermodels, don't see. Even the detectives, calling in to the precinct, indicating that they are just about done for the day, have not seen. The person with a scoop on the way these events connect is the woman in the conservative and sensible outfit, the one with the burn scars and a dead-bolt key.

18

"With that," he says, and he means the masking tape, on the desk of the False Guru, in the office of the False Guru, in the Ashram of the False Guru, where he's located with a woman named . . . what's her name again? Her name is Nora. He has removed many items from this desk, just in case a surface is needed. His good fortune owes to the fact that he has agreed to be a part of the next gala benefit thrown by the False Guru for the Foundation of the True Practice, a foundation that aims to bring remnants of Eastern wisdom to the thirsty Western masses. The False Guru has the cooperation of a number of persons with perfect skin and large fortunes, and Thaddeus Griffin has now agreed to lend his name, in concert with these persons who have fortunes, and this has caused the office of the False Guru to be made available on short notice, for an important private lesson with one Nora Richards, whom he'd earlier thought to be merely another student of the False Guru. But no. She's not simply a student, she's a yoga instructor in training, and she has proven her willingness to conduct this private lesson in the office of the False Guru, a lesson commencing in seated posture on the Oriental carpet. Quite a lovely and expensive carpet, when you pause to consider that the False Guru was at one time a practitioner of the fine arts, a free-wine-in-plastic-cups-drinker at local art openings. But then the False Guru traveled to India to learn the binding poses. He practiced renunciations and the diverse skills that would enhance the business that he was launching here on the fringes of Noho.

One with the carpet, one with the tumbleweeds of dust on the carpet. Thaddeus accepts a gentle correction in the performance of the auspicious pose, bhadra-asana, bringing the soles of his feet together under the scrotum, hollowing the hands above the feet in the shape of the tortoise. He allows Nora to push roughly upon his shoulders because the problem is that his shoulders are always up around his ears, and this is inauspicious. Thaddeus makes the shape of a tortoise, indicating receptivity. There is a siren going past the Ashram of the False Guru, and somewhere there is the faint tinkling of the indoor fountain installed at considerable expense, also the chittering of beautiful yoga practitioners in their expensive outfits. This is the poetry of sounds, respiration, siren, fountain, and the liquid vowels of practitioners, and this is the magnificence of incense, and this is the raising up of prayer, and this is the knowledge of subtle things, a knowledge of things that are hidden away, which is one of the tasks of the yogin. When the yogin knows these subtle things, then shall he mash his mouth against the mouth of his yogini.

She was once employed in the helping professions. She told him so. She was once employed in the profession of exotic dancing, and so it does not seem as though she will turn away from the desperate collision of soft tissue, this mashing of faces. She has an Indian guru. She has learned to play the harmonium. She is allowing herself to be kissed by Thaddeus Griffin, movie star and practitioner of yoga, and she is kissing back a little bit, and this is the pose called the Adulterous Union, wherein two practitioners, who are elsewhere participants in love's vast covenant, conjoin their mouths on the Oriental carpet in the ashram.

"I really can't help myself, you know, I can't help what I'm going to say, so I'm just going to say it. Because why hold back, you know? You're just incredibly beautiful, do you know? Do you know how beautiful you are?" The yogin says these things as though to say them were a chant. It's no falsehood to speak in this way. Falsehoods are not noble truths. She is beautiful, even if it is also true that the yogin thinks virtually everybody is beautiful. Fully two-thirds of the yoginis he passes on the street are ravishing. They don't know this about themselves because a ravishment doesn't know what it is. For example, the way a certain woman wears glasses, tiny spectacles, pinched onto her nose like a fence that protects the male of the species from the memorable hue of her eyes. She probably works for Internal Revenue. There's a way she shifts her weight from side to side as she walks, she has the most beautiful ass he's ever seen, and this ass was created as an evolutionary novelty so that men would see the ass of this Internal Revenue employee and these men would beg to be with her, and she would preserve her rajas, or genital ejaculate, and suck up bindu, thereby ensuring fruitful multiplication, in turn creating the chromosomal reproduction of the perfect ass, and thus the continuity of a brave line of Internal Revenue employees.

However, upon seeing this woman on the way to the Ashram of the False Guru, the yogin's reverie about her ass is interrupted because passing close by her, in the opposite direction, is another yogini in a conservative suit who is wearing a high-visibility hard hat. She is so beautiful with the hard hat on that it is almost impossible not to propose to her on the spot, and the fact that she has a mole on the side of her nose is completely irrelevant to the enlightened yogin, she has to wear that hard hat, she must keep wearing that hard hat, and as a matter of course he'd still be thinking about her, except that now he passes a woman with that little calf muscle, the calf muscle from too much high-heel wearing, or perhaps it is just the advanced practice of uttankoormasana, resulting in a sculpting of calves; she smiles as she walks, the yo-gini, and the smile of a yogini is philosophically overwhelming, emanating from the third eye center; it is as if the yogini knows that the universe is situated in her body; it is as if the yogini drinks the water from the cranial bowl of the yogin; if they all smiled while walking, yogins would be as idiots stunned by the multitude of smiling yoginis, and still he is thinking about these calves, that smile, wondering if he should run after the yogini in order to get to know her in her quintessence, in her rajas, who-ever she is, this as he enters into the ashram, signs in for class, only to find, again, by the sale leotards and the CDs of thunder drums, as the fountain spills into its retaining pool, the afore-mentioned Nora Richards.

"So how much for a private lesson, anyway?"

Which brings us to this moment. Nora is attempting to ob-serve the rigors of private tutelage, pushing against his pelvis as she tries to get him to do the second warrior pose with binding, reminding him to lock in the belly, performing in this way the mula bandha. Close the anus and strongly draw upward the ex-creting energy. She reaches under, and she must know how en-lightening it is to have her reaching under him in this way. He is truly experiencing the enlightenment and the freedom from re-birth. And it is then, in a state of enlightenment where there is no room for individual consciousness, that Thaddeus suggests that she masking-tape his wrists together in order to ensure that the binding in the pose is performed according to tradition.

"What?" Nora asks.

He is balanced in sushumna, between inhalation and exhala-tion, between the masculine and the feminine. He is thinking that this is a bad idea, this private class, in that it does not observe ab-stinence from the eight kinds of erotic action, namely, to think it, to praise it, to joke about it, to look with desire, to converse in private, to decide to do it, to attempt to do it, to perform it. And yet it seems like a very, very good idea at the same time, because self-discipline splits the personality in two, as the masters say, and without self-discipline one drinks in the fluids of the moon.

"With that." He selects from among the personal effects of the False Guru. Standard-issue American masking tape, the sign of a well-equipped desk.

"Isn't it going to hurt?"

"It's going to make it so that I do the pose right, you know, and that's what I'm after. I'm all about trying to do the pose right. That's why we're here." He's in the pose and he really does feel like a warrior, because he is a warrior of the Adulterous Union, he is a warrior of expedient decision making and inadvisable se-ductions, and he's in the pose, the warrior pose, and this is the presentation of the lingam, the gesture of the lingam, in which concentration on longing is in the shape of an arrow shining like a thousand suns, and this is good, because sometimes he has to resort to the philters of Western medicine to achieve the proper presentation of the lingam, and he reaches one arm under him-self and one around his side and says, "Bind me."

"What about getting it off later? That's going to burn."

His impatience is plain to see. For this is the lingam gesture. Nora peels up the end of the tape, wraps it around his wrists twice, and then, under pressure, a third time. This is the pose of the Humiliated Pupil, and once in it, he scuttles, as if crustacean, closer to her, where he can plant his five o'clock shadow on her hams, and she giggles, and he kisses her thigh. Her thigh has the excellence of distant galaxies.

"Take off the gear." He means that the time is so short. And she does the perfect yogic removal of layers, one leg at a time, like a pink flamingo of yogic abandon. And because she has the expe-rience in the helping professions, she has eliminated coarse over-growth from her body, except for a landing strip, in the Brazilian style, and she giggles as he cranes with his neck, winching for-ward to make a landing in the folds of her, though she cannot help but say, "Flat back, shoulders down, please. Shoulders down," and then there's a little rush of the breath of the ocean, a silencing, as he has now placed his tongue where he would prefer to have his tongue, his subtle tongue of the candle flame. Exertion is involved because his hands are in the binding position and so his hands cannot be used. And it is said that meditation upon the mandala on the wall in the office of the False Guru shall alleviate conditions of suffering, the mandala on the tapestry, that representation of Shiva the destroyer, but this causes distraction from the presentation of the lingam, which causes the lingam to fail. There is no other explanation but the explanation of unnecessary concentration upon the mandala. How could this always happen? Losing himself in the shambhavi mudra when he should be engaged with the tantra and the yogini. How could it happen?

He collapses onto the floor. "Bow pose. Can we do bow pose?"

The yogini expresses hesitation at causing pain to the yogin in the pursuit of the bow pose, which is better performed by seasoned practitioners. And yet the entire alimentary canal will be toned in this practice, which is the practice of dhanurasana, likewise adrenal glands and thyroid gland.

"Tape my ankles, too, when I —" and he rolls onto his stomach, the bow pose, with one arm pinioned under him, left over from the binding, "and then you can sit on top of me and you can do a correction. On top of me."

The instructor must know the shape of the cosmic being. The shape of the cosmic being is the guise of the star of the action film, star of distant light, star of the eternal cosmos, and the yogini is a drinker of the light of the cosmic star of the action film. And she kneels over him, reaches in through his shorts, massages his buttocks, as if he were clay and she the potter, and then she shoves his ankles together and starts circumnavigating these ankles with the standard-issue American masking tape, twice around, three times around. And then she yanks his workout shorts down, without even asking, there he is, the cosmic being, in the office of the

False Guru, extremities taped, and his shorts around his ankles, and he's a cosmic being who has a most fleshy lingam, and he needs something more, something, in order to perform the gesture of the lingam. It has to be real suffering for him to be able to do it, something that increases the wattage of the prana. And this is what he says to Nora: "Can't you put some fingers up me? Could you maybe just put a few fingers up me or something?"

Which, as has been explained above, is the digital exploration of the mula bandha, root contraction, which conquers old age and death. It would be better, of course, if these things did not need to be explained. When the breath is held, the prana is still, and so the yogin holds the breath, and the prana is still, and there is the digital examination of the mula bandha, which is a part of the tantric exploration, which is the moving of the lingam without allowing the seed to fall. And so we have again the placement of the mouth of the yogin at the yoni of the yogini, which is the gesture of the beginning of the worship of the yoni, where a thousand petals crowd the mind of the yogin, and the deities dwell in the subtle centers, and what could be better, for the lingam once again desires to perform the lingam gesture, and the yogin thinks now of all the crowding images of humility that are upon him, on the carpet of the False Guru, under the tapestry with the mandala upon it, the image of humility in which he could perhaps be on the desktop of the False Guru, with his mouth against the yoni of the yogini, and then even more than this there is the expelled cleansing of the yoni, bahish-krita-dhauti, perhaps there could be an expelled cleansing of the yoni onto the yogin, for the yogin believes that his practice could improve significantly in the presence of this magnificence of the yogini, because the life force lies in knowing these things, in doing all things with the body of the yogini, the things that he has not yet done, or at least has not done recently, and what about gajakarani, or elephant technique, perhaps the yogini could teach him of this ritual cleansing, because if anything, the yogin needs cleansing, needs to be cleaned

of the wastes, mucus, gas, and acidity, there is a shortage of
cleanliness, and he presses his mouth against her, and there is the
bellows breath. The yogini is practicing the bellows breath, and
then perhaps the yogini is performing the humming bee breath,
which stretches back to the centuries before the birth of the Bud-
dha, the breath that is indicative of tantric ascension, and that is
when the yogin asks about the amorali, reminding the yogini that
we need not think of amorali as consuming something unclean,
like solid wastes, because the practice of amorali, the yogin thinks,
is about immortality, except that he uses more coarse language,
to ask about it, and he asks about it, because the drinking of the
urine will be of the midstream, for the midstream has no bile in
it but rather hormones, enzymes, and other by-products that are
a surfeit, a supplement to the harvesting that the body does, and
therefore it will be —

"What did you say?" she asks.

The yogin asks again.

"Are you asking what I'm thinking you're asking?"

"It's not going to be messy," he says. "I'll be careful."

"Are you kidding me? Who do you think —"

It's so sudden! The way the yogini performs the pose known as
smacking the face, after which she makes her exit. Drawing up
her workout clothes as though she is shuttering her own personal
lingerie shop. The class was going so well, there was so much admirable work being done by the yogin, who really is getting close
to being able to do a split, and to be here making this completely
admirable progress, and to be entirely willing to pay the yogini as
much riches as she desires, and then to have her perform the
smacking pose while he's in the middle of an extremely demanding asana, well, it's inexplicable, and it's sad, and, moreover, the
lingam is limp on the carpet of the floor of the office of the False
Guru, and his limbs are all taped up, his limbs are bound, and he
is wearing no shorts. His shorts are around his ankles. He is
wearing a loosely fitting T-shirt, and the room smells as if it was

sweated through by professional wrestlers, and he is having a little trouble getting onto his knees, and there are pens and pencils
that he swept off the desk in his enthusiasm, and they are on the
floor and he has made a real mess, as always. He needs to get to
a pair of scissors. He's sliding awkwardly to the floor and attempting to loft himself somehow onto his feet so he can reach
backward with his bound hands. He uses his head on the seat of
the desk chair to lever himself up. He hops several times, closer
to the desk. He's fervent in his wish that there are some scissors
in the desk of the False Guru that he can use to cut the tape, and
then he can be on his way.

This is what is called the after-loneliness of the Adulterous
Union. It was loneliness that launched him upon this difficult
pose and it is loneliness that will accompany him onto the street.
He is lonely, enfeebled, not like a proper yogin, not like a proper
star of the firmament. He is not like the wandering mendicants
of yogic practice, who withstood loneliness for two thousands of
years. He is not a meditator in a cave of loneliness. Why can't an
actor in matinée films with a beautiful wife withstand loneliness
for even a day, for even twelve hours?

Once freed, having torn out a surfeit of wrist and ankle hairs,
he flees past the front desk of the ashram, past the battery of attractive employees at the console, checking people in, and his
cheeks are flushed as he heads east, on foot, into the East Village,
waving off a guy on crutches, a true mendicant, who recognizes
him from *Single Bullet Theory* or some other action film from his
oeuvres complets. Thaddeus shouts a half-hearted hello to the mendicant and to Asian tourists on St. Mark's place, "Hey! Thanks
for your support!" until he is below the window of one Annabel
Duffy, and it is dusk, in November, and he is yelling at the window of Annabel Duffy, "Come on down! Hey! Let me in! Let me
in! It's me! Let me in! I haven't smoked in at least seven hours! I
won't smoke in your apartment, and I'll be nice to your cat, and
I'll buy . . . stuff! I'll go home with you for the holidays! I swear!"

But there's no answer, no way in, as if the after-loneliness we have just mentioned is a condition of the improper practice of the hatha yoga, which is only exacerbated by the presence in the world of laundromats, shuttered television repair shops, half-abandoned shopping malls, feral cats. A neighbor calls out her window that he should please shut the fuck up, "And your movies are *not* good." He can see the arm of the woman, the silhouette of her arm, as she backs away from the window and pulls the blind. The glimmer of a bracelet.

The cell phone rings as he's heading back toward Avenue B. His agent. There's a *great* opportunity here, his agent is saying, a really *fabulous* opportunity, in a picture that's getting set up at one of the large studios, called *Assassins*. Big-budget picture. Set in the Middle East. He would get to ride camels and sleep under the stars in the desert and see a politically unstable part of the world, and it will be directed by that director of action classics, Waldo Schmeltz, the guy who made the one about the Amsterdam hookers who are informants during the Nazi occupation.

"I can't talk right now," Thaddeus tells him. It's more that he doesn't want to talk.

"Hey, pal, I'm sorry about the thing in the paper."

"What thing in the paper?"

"You know . . . that *thing?*"

"Which paper are you talking about? And what *thing?* What do you mean *thing?*"

"Listen . . . there's my other line. I'll get back to you. We'll catch up. Pal, think about *Assassins*. Let me know how you feel in the next day or so. Could be huge. Could be top ten. Plus the possibility of awards."

"You said *thing* just now. What is that? And I have a question for you, too. About *The Diviners*. Have you heard —"

But the connection is severed. Too logistically difficult now to duck into a men's room in order to rinse off this conversation. Usually a powerful antibacterial soap will get rid of any oily residue associated with a film agent. Now he's in a cab. The cabbie is fleet, but why the fuck does Thaddeus live on the Upper West Side? He hates the Upper West Side, with its socialism lite and Zabar's and people wandering around with new food processors and fancy cheese assortments and laser-whitened teeth. Perambulators clogging the sidewalks, SUVs double-parked, all because they have to pick out some cheeses to serve tonight, out in the Hamptons, to their friends from the corporate-law firm. They will eat veggie chips in the SUVs stuck on the LIE on the way to the Hamptons to serve up their cheeses. Thaddeus wants to live in Tribeca, in the shadows of Wall Street, where it's all painters with drinking problems flinging pigment straight out of the tube onto the canvas before going to some screening of a Hong Kong action film. Painters with lead poisoning, short-term memory loss, tossing back shots at Fanelli's, because they're willing to die for what they do. That's how passionately they feel about their craft. Thaddeus is willing to die *in* what he does, at least if someone else does the stunts.

He lives on the Upper West Side because his wife's father gave them a duplex. At the time, they were scrambling. Her dad the corporate lawyer was on retainer for the tobacco manufacturers of the world. And Thaddeus is stuck here with his wife, who's out in San Diego filming a commercial. What is the commercial for? He can't even remember, feminine products maybe. She's filming a commercial for feminine products, and soon he'll be making a film in the desert, where he gets to ride a camel and eat hummus until it becomes impossible to eat it again, and his wife will be making a commercial for feminine products, and they never will see each other again, except in airport lounges. Thaddeus strides past the doorman with a salute and a lopsided grin that says, I know I'm supposed to feel lucky.

In his apartment, Thaddeus Griffin is nobody. In the living room, in the pantry, in the dining room, in the spare room that is never used for anything at all. Most of all in the bedroom, he's nobody, and his condition of being nobody in his apartment dwarfs the lack of privacy that is his burden in every other place. He's afraid to go outside and he can't wait to go outside. On the street, he's somebody, can't walk a block without being Thaddeus Griffin, but here in his apartment, he's another lost guy with another case of after-loneliness. In his apartment, he watches television, plays video blackjack, practices darts. He's really good at darts. In his apartment, he's among the best player of darts ever.

The lights are off.

And he's not alone.

Because, sitting in the dark, in the living room decorated by Marcus Atkins, is his betrothed. His bride. In one of the big stuffed easy chairs, bent over as if she's hinged, face in her hands, her hands hollowed like a tortoise shell, holding her face. Sobbing. How long has she been here, he wonders, when instead she was supposed to be hawking feminine products for a network commercial that would have meant residuals, et cetera? How long was she just waiting for him? In order to perform these sobs? Is this an Equity-approved showcase?

"Honey, I didn't —"

She's so startlingly beautiful that people draw up short on the street. As if she were the diagram in the physics textbook labeled "Electromagnetism." Dark hair, which right now has blond highlights in it, falling all around her face, blue eyes the color of a blue screen, easy smile, freckles that the makeup people like to cover up for some reason, especially across the bridge of her slightly pudgy but adorable nose, and she is often to be seen in bulky sweaters that cover the swell of her completely perfect breasts, and tonight, when he turns on the light, he sees that she is wearing an old pair of jeans, used to be his, and they always look really good on her somehow, because she's tall enough that she doesn't even have to cuff them or anything. Yes, his wife implies an eternal question, one that has haunted him through the seven years of their union. How can someone this beautiful have an inner life? And if she does, why is it that he has never, ever had a part in it?

"Did you happen to look at this?" she asks. A newspaper cylindered into the gap next to her in the chair. When she flings the paper into the space of the living room, the leaves drift in several directions, separating. "Did you happen to see your picture in the paper today?"

"I don't know what —"

"Don't be full of shit."

He didn't read the tabloids this morning. Because he didn't go into work. He took the morning off because there was nothing going on at the office and the scripts on his desk looked dull. He was thinking he would go to an audition or two today. He wants to play a romantic lead instead of an action hero, and if he has to audition, well, okay. But then he didn't go to any auditions, he just called his broker and played solitaire on the computer. He made an omelet with week-old Brie. When he went into the office, in the afternoon, it was quiet because it was Monday. Vanessa had already left. He didn't talk to her, nor to the girls in the office. Was there a *reason* that the girls in the office were so quiet? This afternoon? Was there a reason that Madison didn't come out of her office when he went past? Was there a reason Jeanine was pretending to be involved with some new intern? And why was Annabel all cool and businesslike? Why didn't she say anything about the script? Was there a symbolic meaning to the moment when Annabel walked past and went to the water cooler? Could he construe this as a judgment of some kind? A moral disapproval? He and Annabel were supposed to be talking about sketching out the miniseries, they were going to do it together, it was going to be their thing, and she didn't say anything about it, not a single word. She walked by him on the way to the water cooler and she filled up a plastic bottle at the water cooler, and she turned smartly on the heels of her boots, and he didn't think any more about it, not then.

His wife rises, crosses the room, finds the correct page from those disparate on the carpet. The picture of him. It is, in fact, unmistakably a picture of him leaving Annabel's apartment over the weekend. He recognizes the large Hispanic woman sitting on the stoop behind him. It's kind of a bad picture. He seems to have a number of chins in this photograph. And below the photograph there's an item about him leaving the apartment, including the time that he left the apartment, which was not long before sunrise. Waking up in a strange bed makes him feel more ashamed. Always a problem. The item goes on to note how much weight he seems to have put on.

"Don't say anything, okay? I think you should give me, you know, at least four or five minutes here where I get to be the one who talks. And the first thing I want to say is that you are just so incredibly *stupid,* Thad. Do you know who this girl in the office is? You're carrying on with some girl in the office? Do you even know who she is? She's related to some guy who . . . who committed a *crime,* you know, who just hit a woman on the street with a brick; isn't that what the paper is implying here? You don't think that the sister of the guy who hit a girl in the head is going to be of interest to the papers? Doesn't cross your mind? While you are getting your freak on with this girl? Didn't cross your mind that you might try to keep your name out of the papers, *for me,* for example?"

"Uh, actually, her brother didn't do it, the thing with the . . . whatever. He didn't do it."

"How do you know that, Thaddeus? The newspapers don't know, and for the moment they don't care. They only care about this juicy story. The issue here —" A stifled gasp and some more tears. "The issue is not whether this guy really hit the woman with the brick, Thad. The issue is whether *you* have any respect. For your marriage. For anyone at all. The issue is whether I'm supposed to do anything about it, the fact that you don't have any respect for me, or the fact that you stood up in front of our parents and friends and vowed certain things, in fancy language, and we released doves, and five years ago you even danced in an Italian fountain with me, and now you are spitting in the face of —"

"Of course I do have respect for my —"

"Then you deny —"

"I —"

He tries to figure out a position that he can take. He tries to figure out a debating position he can occupy, and he finds that there is no such position. He goes around the room turning on lights, in a madness of switching things on. He realizes that he is still carrying his knapsack with the warm-up clothes in it, all this time, and so he sets the knapsack on the floor. The warm-up clothes seem to come from an entirely different epoch, the epoch before this. Time is divided, there's a forking of events, and the time before now is commercial and jovial, like a holiday billboard advertisement for advanced shaving technologies.

"You don't deny it?"

"I thought you were out filming the commercial in California."

"I had an emergency."

"Well, I thought that you were getting with what's his name, the director. With the ponytail."

"You thought what?"

He can feel that the point is Neanderthal; he can feel that everything that comes out of his mouth is Neanderthal. He feels like a schoolyard antagonist who has beat on the fat kid and who is now quivering in the hands of the relevant authorities. And if he's been anticipating this moment, the moment when the scam unravels, he has nonetheless managed to deny its foreshadowing. This moment seems as though it has two moments in it, one in which he loves the truth and one in which he loves to lie to himself about how much he loves the truth. He loves the truth in which there is the comfort of the fiction about his wife and the commercial director. It has been the big happy fire in the fireplace of his consciousness, so refreshing that it felt better than the truth, which is desolate.

"What are you saying about Derrick?"

"I'm saying that you were getting next to Derrick. And I hate the way you say the guy's name. How can anyone really be named Derrick? He sounds like a lacrosse player or something. I bet he does a lot of stomach crunches."

The argument is vaporizing before him. It seemed so good when it was propping things up, but now it feels like one of those defense-lawyer strategies. Your Honor! My client's dental work receives radio signals!

"Derrick is happily married, believe it or not. Some people really *are* happily married, Thaddeus. Some people really love their wives and their children, really cherish them. And maybe, just maybe, these men who are happy with their wives and their children, maybe these guys just like the work of certain actresses and look forward to working with them. Has that crossed your mind? That Derrick likes to work with me just because I'm good at my job? Maybe I'm not as important as you are to the teenagers in the malls across the country. Maybe I'm not as important to you, but I'm an *actress* and I do my job, no matter what the job is, I do my best, and if it means that I have to go three thousand miles away to work, and I have to leave you alone, and I have to sleep in some pretentious hotel with fresh flowers in the bathroom and watch wannabes in the bar on my way through the lobby to go sleep by myself, knowing the whole time that the second I'm not here you're going to be out all night, so that I don't know what to think, that you're going to injure yourself somehow, that you're going to be belly up in a ditch, run over by a taxi, out-of-control drunk, falling into the Hudson, because you don't have enough sense to respect yourself, or me, if I have to live like that, well, I do it because I just want to try to have my own job. You don't even have the sense to know that I'm working for my own self-respect. And because I love you enough to leave you alone. And so this is what you do for me. You get your picture in the paper coming out of the apartment of some black girl whose brother committed an assault, and I don't even know what the next thing is, what the next problem is going to be, what to think of next: your drinking, or the women, or some gambling rampage, whatever. I don't know what to think. Except that I should be allowed to work, just like you. My work shouldn't call our marriage into question, and it shouldn't be disrespectful to you, and it shouldn't be an affront to you. Maybe I'm not the greatest actress or maybe I am a really good actress, I can't tell anymore because I'm used to feeling awful about myself *because of you*. Because I try to pretend like I don't care about what's going on with you, but I care, I care about how everything always seems to be falling apart, and I don't want to live like that. Get it?"

What is there to understand? With a pathetic grin on his face, he goes to embrace her, because he really does feel impressed with her commitment and her sense of fairness, and he admires her. The admirer can stand beside the Thaddeus that is the failure in the room, and he can admire his wife, so he tries to embrace her, though she gives no indication that this strategy is welcome. In fact, she fends him off.

"Isn't it something we can fix?" he inquires.

"Not if what you're going to do, while we repair things, is mess around some more and pretend that there's no problem and pretend that you don't know the extent of the damage."

The phone rings, and then his wife's voice, on the outgoing message, sings out in the front hall. The machine mumbles with the tones of some whispery caller.

"Do you want to tell me what you've done?" she says. "Do you want to begin by telling me what you've done? Because if you tell me some stuff, then maybe that will shine a little more light into the dark spaces. The way I see it, it's like this, Thaddeus. It's like you traded all those moviegoers for me. The people in the theaters in Sandusky and Pittsburgh, you traded what they know of you, the you who is filmed carrying firearms, for me. I've known you for eight years, and apparently I know nothing. So why don't you start by telling me what you've done. Tell me just one thing that you've done, so that I can get to know you, the you that exists in real life, instead of in front of some blue screen."

It was important that the apartment look as though it could be in some magazine. When Marcus Atkins decorated it. So that now, as they are sitting in it, it's impossible to sit in it as though it wants to be inhabited, this room, as though it means to be comfortable and inviting. Its inhospitality makes it hard for him to get his tongue wagging, makes it hard for this moment to be what it ought to be.

"I don't think you really want me to do that."

"Why?" Sabrina asks. "Because it's *awful?*"

"Pretty much," mumbles Thaddeus, action film star of the side of right and justice, the guy who prosecutes the corruption, the guy who brings down the international cartel of terrorists. Usually when he's supposed to cry on film, he needs the glycerin, and he needs strong direction.

"Maybe it's not an isolated case."

"I'm aware of that."

"What do you want me to say?"

"Well," she says, and appears to ruminate. "I guess I want apologies that last for days at a time, and I want them in the press. I want your apology to be as public as your bullshit has been."

"How?"

"You can go to the window right now and shout out of it. Or you can call the papers. You can call the papers and pretend to be an anonymous source. Or you can call your publicist or you can call your agent, and you can have them issue a statement. Or you can write a press release where you list all the movies you've made before going on to talk about what a wretched philandering fuck you are, and how you have arrived at this amazing decision about the spiritual value of telling the truth for a change, even though you're a philanderer. But whatever you decide to do, you'll have to do it by yourself, because I'm going across town to stay with my parents. I don't want to have to feel like all I do is harass you about this stuff. I don't want to be that person. So I'm going to stay with my parents, and you can begin the publicity campaign to save your marriage, and then you can go to sex-addiction rehabilitation or whatever else your team of psychiatrists advises, and we can meet each other at marriage counseling and discuss it there, and that's the way it will go for a few months. You can do it my way, I mean, unless you want my lawyer to contact yours."

Now she's standing, hands on hips.

When she's gone, it's as if she wasn't there at all, as if the conversation never took place. It's all silences again, inhuman interior decorating, after-loneliness, and he can do what he wants. He can go play a computer game, or he can do some sun salutations, or he can go looking for hotties on the Web. He can call Annabel. Or he can feel this burning sensation. The burning sensation wants him to act, even if he doesn't want to act. There are remedial steps in human behavior, and these could be first. He could change the sheets. In the master bedroom. There's a woman who comes once a week to do the cleaning, but it suddenly feels as though changing the sheets will ensure a really good night's sleep. Changing the sheets will muffle the burning sensation. It has been years since he changed his own set of sheets. So this is medicinal, going into the closet where Sabrina, his wife, has stacked up the sheets just so, and he takes a pale blue top sheet and a pale blue fitted sheet, king size, a couple of pillowcases, really high thread count, or so Sabrina has told him. He goes into the master bedroom and rips the bedclothes from the bed and makes a tangle of them on the floor of the bedroom, and then he falls into this tangle, facedown. When he gets up, he will start to do something, maybe write that miniseries. Yeah, he'll write.

19

The consultant from Poseidon Management Systems is backlit at the front of the conference room, a windowless inner sanctum. La Casa Grande, an exclusive West Coast convention center, San Diego. Wearing a polo shirt and pleated slacks, sporting an unmistakable rub-on tan, gesturing at the projection above, the consultant begins his song of bulleted points.

The company is Universal Beverages Corporation. The product is quality. The theme of the conference is Growing Quality. Across diverse product lines, Universal Beverages makes and sells quality to a considerable portion of the consumers in this country and the world. The product lines are: alcoholic beverages, snack foods, television broadcasting, film production and marketing, and, the newest line of business, interstate mortuary services.

The goal of the three-day off-site management conference, here at La Casa Grande, will be creating synergies between the divisions so that the Universal Beverages Corporation can increase market share and Grow Quality. And the company will Grow Quality because quality is like small potted cacti, which are to be given gratis to each and every conference participant to take back to his or her office, where he or she will Grow Quality, symbolized by these thriving and persistent cacti. Growing Quality is not an easy strategy. It depends on fundamentals: a healthy seedling, abundant sunlight, water, fertilizer, and excellence. The Poseidon Management Systems team will be here, during the off-site, to help the employees of Universal Beverages find analogies for sunlight, water, fertilizer, and excellence in the rough-and-tumble worlds of entertainment, comestibles, and mortality. Tactics such as team building, creative innovation, and sales maximization will be explored over three days in the spirit of Growing Quality. Quality assurance, quality control, quality innovation, quality as expressed in synergy and cross-marketing opportunities, quality in human resources. These are the watchwords of the conference.

Which indicates to Jeffrey Maiser, head of network programming at UBC, that the stock has fallen off the edge of the earth. Like he doesn't know already. Like he doesn't know about the condition of his options. Like he doesn't know about trending downward, 11 percent, since the high in March. Like he doesn't know that the guys at the top of the Universal Beverages pyramid are not happy about the studio, with its recent shutout at the Oscars, and the television subsidiary and its grim efforts during the ratings sweepstakes. Like they don't call him several times a week, threatening him. Just as he has called the news and sports divisions and demanded that they meet their targets for the quarter or else contact their headhunters.

The moderator introduces Ibn Al-Hassad for the morning session. Al-Hassad got his start during the Human Potential Movement. He's a veteran of Alan Watts's seminars and an expert in the art of archery. He's a protégé of Abraham Maslow, Fritz Perls, et cetera. Al-Hassad has demonstrated fire walking in public and is an admirer of spoon benders, past-life regressionists, mediums, diviners, and other wackos. The title of his book, featured recently on the UBC morning news program, is *The Revelation of Finance*. Al-Hassad, according to bulleted points PowerPointed above the head of the moderator, will speak first on finance and spirituality, and then he will speak on salesmanship, after which he will touch on Growing Quality. In the video feed, with its stirring and faintly military music, Maiser can see that Al-Hassad has the perfect television face. His face is a slate cleaned of all its markings except for traces of inoffensiveness and self-regard. Not a wisp of profundity remains to challenge the UBC managers.

And yet Maiser doesn't give his full attention to the mesmeric face of Ibn Al-Hassad, for the simple reason that the chief executive officer of Universal Beverages Corporation, Naz Korngold, decreed at the kickoff dinner last night that several things would happen during this management off-site: "I just want to say from right here at the podium . . . what I want to say is that tonight somebody will drink too much of our own product," at which there was mock dismay and consternation, "and tonight somebody will sleep with someone else's wife or husband, and tonight someone will reveal that he does not have the wherewithal to do what we are here to do, which is to grow quality. There will be evasions and denials of our estimable mission. That's the way off-sites go. The wheat is separated from the chaff at these off-sites, or, to use the metaphor of our newest division, you have your pine box and you have your deluxe, silk-lined, diamond-encrusted, with pillows of eiderdown. If you are part of the hard-working majority of Universal Beverages, you have no cause to worry. You're here to make our business *universal*, like it says on the logo, to make our products dominant in the competitive global environment. Each of you should strive for this goal, each of you make sure it's not you who fails to innovate, make sure it's not you who resists growing quality. Get to know the manager to your left and to your right. One of the three of you will be fired by the end of the year. Now, drink up and get to work!" Stunned silence and then anemic applause.

As evidence of all this madness, for example, the decree has come down that the heads of the divisions should fill out the Myers-Briggs personality test and the MMPI-2, and write a personal essay, as described in the packets at the registration tables. The heads of divisions should return these items to Korngold's assistant by the end of the first day, after which they should extract the same materials from their subordinates. And so on down the line.

At the Saturday dinner, Maiser sat next to the ivory-maned battle-ax of Interstate Mortuary Services, Lorna Quinson. The red snapper was timidly prepared, and the strolling mariachi band was persistent, and after playing with his flatware for a while, Maiser found himself wanting to know a little about Quinson. About the billowing blue midcalf dress she had on, about her ringless fingers, about the dreams and nightmares of her childhood. Lorna looked like a great comic actress from one of the seventies sitcoms. Battle-ax with a heart of gold. How did someone with this kind of poise come to flourish as a leading light of the mortuary business, selling what had initially been a string of floundering family-owned mortuaries to one of the largest corporations in the country? And was she put off by being here among the big names of broadcasting and entertainment? Maiser made a few tentative inquiries during the fifteen minutes or so they were chatting. And just before each swiveled in the opposite direction, according to the obligations of dinner party politics, he asked her, "Did you write your essay yet?"

Lorna Quinson, with a cocked smile, shook her head.

This conversation gave him the opportunity to gaze. In the way that television executives can gaze. Quinson's hair was gathered into an orderly bun, and he could see a bit of the back of her neck, the nape of it, and it was straight and comely. As he listened to a flunky at his right droning lengthily about his favorite network shows, Maiser was thinking instead of Quinson's neck. Everybody knows that cop shows are about social control, the flunky droned. Quinson's neck. *The Werewolves of Fairfield County,* best and most creative use of serial narrative in years. Quinson's neck.

In the course of dessert, Quinson reached not for the pumpkin cheesecake but for her BlackBerry portable messaging device, which she carried in a small patent leather clutch. She stared down into its impenetrable secrets. Then she dabbed her lips, the color known as Cherries in the Snow, refolded her napkin, and excused herself.

Maiser went to the men's room himself, where he called the office immediately, told his assistant to get Lorna Quinson's e-mail address *now*. He brushed off the men's room attendant, who, while Maiser rinsed his hands, claimed to be part of the Universal Ministries — which probably would be a division of UBC by the next fiscal quarter. Why not? The Ministries could provide boilerplate grief counseling to families at Interstate Mortuary Services, could furnish *The Werewolves of Fairfield County* with genuine apocalyptic subplots, and could offer apoplectic commentators to the new conservative talk shows that were being churned out like widgets. Maybe Maiser should leak news of the acquisition to some prominent shareholders and see what happened.

Back at the table, a case of expensive French whites, emptied, was toppled on the linens. As if some malcontent had yanked on the end of the tablecloth. Now, in the center of the ballroom, Naz Korngold, with a flourish, indicated he was turning in for the night. Upper management followed in a retinue, including Lorna Quinson. She was gone, the queen of morticians.

Maiser slipped out the back himself, trying to ditch the overeager guys from the news division, which he would have to dismantle before long. Outdoors, it was an Industrial Light and Magic night, with a myriad of shooting stars and orbiting satellites, and Maiser wondered if Naz Korngold had ordered it especially for the weekend. Maiser cursed golf and the people who had invented golf, on the way to his private casita. The MMPI and the Myers-Briggs tests hung over his head: *I think nearly anyone would tell a lie to keep out of trouble;* mark *T* for "true or mostly true" or *F* for "false or mostly false." *Horses that refuse to move should be whipped,* true or false? *There is often a lump in my throat,* true or false? *I can easily make other people afraid of me, and sometimes do for the fun of it,* true or false?

Who is Jeffrey Maiser? That was the essay question, printed right there along the top margin of a blank piece of paper. It was in his packet at registration, to be filled out in ballpoint pen and returned to Naz Korngold. Underneath, Jeff wrote, "Who's asking?" And then he whited it out so that not a trace of this initial response remained visible. *I work best when I have a definite deadline,* true or false?

And so here he is on Sunday, having erased four more false starts for the essay while ignoring the speech by Al-Hassad. "Quality is present at the instant of the big bang," Al-Hassad is intoning. "Quality is twelve billion years old, as old as the *prima causa,* like the carbon cells that make up each and every one of you. Each and every one of you *is* quality. You can be confident of that." Maiser is chugging aspartame beverages and throwing away potential essay answers. For example: his participation in the occupation of the president's office at Columbia. He was just a kid then. And it was not that he agreed politically with all the protesters. He just liked the drama of camping out. All that wood paneling and those gold-plated pen-and-pencil sets. Those kids with their heads full of Whitman and Hendrix and Eldridge Cleaver. He was a guy who always knew the potential of a good story, even then. Was this the Jeffrey Maiser of the essay question?

The true essay about Jeffrey Maiser would also have to talk about his marriage, which fell apart last year, and about his bad relationship with his daughter, who is at NYU film. It would have to speak of his inability to do well in the department of romance. Oh yeah, and there's another thing he's worried about, the thing that might show up on the MMPI-2, might skew him statistically toward category two, the category of the unstable.

What about Jeffrey Maiser the practical joker? Back in college days, he'd been tasked by a dean with serving as amanuensis and guide for a visiting professor, an important law professor from the state of Ohio. Instead of taking this Catholic and conservative law professor to the faculty club, as dictated by his schedule, Maiser took him to a brothel up on Upper Broadway someplace. He can still remember the look on the impressionable young law professor's face when he saw the array of African and Latin hookers available for his delectation! The dope smoke was like a curtain over everything! What a laugh! The guy went on to become a Supreme Court justice, too. Later in his professional life, Maiser exchanged all the cars in the reserved spaces at the studio parking lot with the pink Cadillacs of Mary Kay Cosmetics, so that when the brass came out one afternoon they all had to drive a pink car home. Then there was that time he showed a trainee a broom closet in the building and told him that this would be his office from now on. He allowed the trainee to stay in the closet for nine days. Maiser even made up a television reviewer, Don Stankey, and wrote Stankey's columns for one of the popular newsweeklies for two years in order to create strong buzz for UBC programming. Those early raves for *The Werewolves of Fairfield County,* those were Stankey's columns, after which Stankey had a regrettable car accident on the Saw Mill, leaving behind a wife and three kids, one of whom had cerebral palsy. If only UBC had had a relationship with Interstate Mortuary Services in those days, Maiser could have thrown a proper memorial service for the guy. There would have been baroque music and a dramatic reading from the stories of Jack London.

A large number of people are guilty of bad sexual conduct, mostly true or mostly false? If you tested any of the managers in the room, any of those guys around him doodling little slashing, angry lines on their legal pads right now, they'd all have their obsessions, their dark secrets. None of them is talking. Edward Jones, the studio head, had himself filmed at an orgy with a bunch of male models back in the late seventies. You can download photos of the party on the Web. And the head of the beverages division, Stew Ledbetter, is so badly alcoholic that he never turns up at a meeting before noon, and even then with a cola can full of vodka. It's widely known. Priscilla Rankin, in finance, has lost hundreds of thousands of dollars gambling on college basketball. There are ass men, men obsessed with breasts, there are men obsessed with youth, there are men who drive into the desert and weep, there are self-mutilators. All of them ambitious and successful professionals.

His own predilection dates back to a specific moment, or so he tells himself, back when he was a producer, back in the early eighties, when he was working on a film about a girl with bone cancer. She had come to wear the *halo,* this girl; you know, the contraption they attach to you that allows you to keep the head up straight in the midst of your hardships. Anyway, he hadn't even noticed this actress, Celine something or other, Celine Thorpe, when she was hired for the job. She was just another actress in leg warmers trying to impress the director, who was a no-talent commercial guy who'd made his reputation directing spots for antacids. Maiser had only intended to be on the set the first day of filming.

In the meantime, the costume department had outfitted Celine Thorpe with the halo. She looked scared at first, coming out of the trailer. Her outfit was not terribly flattering. No designer threads that she could try to make off with when the shooting was done. And then there was the halo. Maiser ought not to have seen Celine Thorpe that day, ought not to have, ought to have contented himself with the little dead spots and recriminations in a long marriage. That's what he ought to have done. But here he was, in the park, sitting in a canvas chair, and here was Celine Thorpe, coming down from the trailer. It was the magic hour, the hour when the light was just so, and the palms were just so, and the kids on the softball diamond were just so (here's the crack of the softball coming off an aluminum bat), and the sun glinted from the glimmering halo. The scene involved the character with the debilitating bone disease managing to go to the park for the last time in her short life, and during this last visit she notices the preciousness of all things in the park, the softball players, the dog walkers, the butterflies dive-bombing the blossoms of bougainvillea. The fog machines were blowing up a subtle mist. And Celine was in her brace, and the unsteady way she walked through the moist grass of the park, it was just a beautiful, understated piece of acting. Maiser felt the conjunction of youth and metal cage, and it was as if he were being reflected in the light coming off the halo, and he realized that a bit of his heart began opening right then, by reason of fetish.

It was untrue what they said about angels, that angels were quaint birdlike agents who oversaw your daily life and ensured that you got the best of all parking spaces. No, these were not angels. Angels were apparitions of dread. Their annunciations were impossible burdens, and you greeted them only with terror. The angel that appeared in all the Annunciation paintings, that was no sweet angel. That angel scared the piss out of the Virgin Mary, who undoubtedly didn't want to get knocked up by an abstraction. The same thing with Celine in her halo, she was a dark annihilator in the life of Jeffrey Maiser.

He threw himself into work, of course. He tried to distract himself from feeling. But when the disabled groups started writing in about how great the broadcast was and, boy, was that Celine Thorpe amazing, she brought such dignity and beauty to the role of the girl with the debilitating spinal disease, well, he realized something had changed. Bedding Celine Thorpe for the next few weeks in a suite at the Chateau Marmont was the least of it. She wore the prop without the least bit of hesitation, or that's the way it seemed. There was a way the prop made any blemish, or even a couple of extra pounds, look *great* on Celine. He didn't care if she was perfect. On the contrary. It was her imperfections that made her so sweet. And yet when he started seeing her out of costume, wearing a slinky gown at an awards show or being interviewed on *Oprah*, well, he felt like she was all wrong.

He volunteered to serve as the network emissary at a fund raiser in Santa Barbara for the disabled. The publicists at the studio should have attended in his stead. He had already RSVP'd for the baby shower of some news anchor. But he went to the fund raiser himself and he saw a half dozen women in back braces, halos, even the lowly neck braces of whiplash, and he could feel himself getting all sentimental. How could it be? He was a strong man, a man with a national reputation as an executive, and he was following a woman with a neck brace out of the hotel in Santa Barbara and watching the awkward way she walked, and he was feeling that he was about to beg this woman for a caress.

His daughter, the tomboy Allison, brought home her pal Firth. When was this? During the Gulf War, maybe. Firth was an Asian girl, so he was a little confused about the name. One of those adolescent things, probably. Her name was Yo Yo or something similar, but she changed it to Firth because that's what you do when you're thirteen. Anyway, Firth had scoliosis, and Maiser had become enough of an expert that he could recognize that this was front-to-back scoliosis, not left-to-right. Maiser took one look at Firth and realized that he would have to start working late at the office, whether it bothered his wife, Lois, or not, in order to avoid salivating over the thirteen-year-old Firth, who was meant to start wearing her back brace full-time during summer vacation. He would have been altogether too happy to administer deep tissue massage to the spot on her behind where the hamstring connected to the femur head.

You get into one of these groups of girls, adolescent girls, and the group is like a swarm, and suddenly there are more of these girl children, all of them broken in some way, all of them bearing one another up, each of them the crutch of another, each of them both nurse and patient. There's the wall-eyed girl, the speech-defect girl with her twisted *r*'s and *s*'s, the girl with the clubfoot, the girl with the harelip, the girl with the prosthetic arm, who often goes around without. All of these girls at his house, around his pool, at one time or another, as though his daughter was a collector of them, though there was superficially nothing wrong with her. His daughter favored the broken girls because she thought the broken girls were superior to the blondes with their boob jobs and their Lexus convertibles.

Maiser was trying to stay at work through all of it, trying to get lost in the reports from advertising on the projected price of a thirty-second spot during a show they were developing, *The Werewolves of Fairfield County,* but some days he was weak, just as anyone would have been weak, and then all the broken girls thought he was the greatest dad of all time because he'd be coming out with dishes of sorbet or a tray full of crackers and cheese, and saying, "Just thought you guys might want a little snack," his cheeks stinging as though he'd just been acupunctured. He remembered the time he helped a girl with no legs onto the raft in the pool. Another man might remember a trip abroad with his family, might think of the Caribbean Sea and some sunlit beach, the tranquil aqua cove where he had a daiquiri with his wife. Instead, Jeffrey remembers the day he helped a girl with no legs onto a raft in his pool. The smell of the water and the way the light danced around her. What perfect shape she was in, from all the wheeling around, and who could say she wasn't the most beautiful woman, the woman who would have launched Greek ships? Her smile was diffident, sure, was self-conscious, but there was something wanton about it, too. "I have secrets," she was saying in her way, "that you'll never know. I have secrets, and they are only unlocked with respect." He can remember the way he fumbled climbing the steps, out of the pool, as if he were just another pedophile brought to his knees.

Then there was the girl who turned up just before Allison went off to boarding school. This was the last spring of the broken girls. She was younger than the rest. There was nothing special about her. A nondescript girl with a herniated disk. She came with a walker. There was something so poignant about a twelve-year-old girl with a walker, just beginning to have breasts, just beginning to flower into womanhood, and here she was with a walker. What made her the one? This girl from Illinois? Allison was contemptuous of the girl with the walker, as if she knew that this time of broken girls had come to an end. As if she were already off at boarding school, back east, where there was not going to be a steady supply of the deformed. On the contrary, there would be a lot of WASPs with season passes at the local ski resorts. Allison called the girl Granny, like it was a nickname of long-standing, and the girl withstood it, inching toward a piece of patio furniture as if it were the only safe spot for miles around. As soon as she had lowered herself onto the chaise longue — Maiser remembers seeing it from the window upstairs — Allison just got up and strode off, leaving Granny with her walker beside her like a trusty friend. The light was failing, but the kitchen in the guesthouse was lit up as if on fire. Norm, the caretaker, was making ramen noodles. Jeff remembers seeing Granny patiently sitting by at first, and then less patiently, and then attempting to get up with the walker, and failing, and beginning to cry. Until he went out to help.

She said her name was Lacey.

He got her up from the chaise longue, and he helped her into his car and drove her home, and he admonished his daughter on the subject, and he sent Lacey a card when she was getting ready for her spinal fusion surgery, and then he gave in, and the giving in was delicious. He visited her in the hospital, and he fed her Jell-O in her bed, and he buzzed the nurses and demanded more Vicodin on her behalf, and he made her a thousand promises in her hospital bed. He was a middle-aged man pronouncing absurd oaths of fealty, and this was before he even planted a kiss on her forehead, not to mention before he planted a kiss on her lips, and he begged her not to give in to his demands, and then cried out with joy when she did, and then he deflowered her, telling her how he wouldn't do it unless she was sure it was what she wanted, and he paid for her singing and dancing lessons, because she said that was what she wanted. She wanted to be transformed from the girl with the bad back and incipient osteoporosis into the one-named entertainer of legend, the one who didn't have a Jewish last name. So he secured her management, and he got her her first recording contract, and he read the fine print for her, and he knew that what had made her beautiful when she wasn't beautiful was gone, so that the announcement of eternal fealty was an announcement of abridged fealty, the announcement of true love was a betrayal of true love, because with the broken girls (like Dante and Beatrice, when you think about it), love is breached at the moment of its honor. Jeff Maiser was forever fielding calls complaining about the apartment he got for her, from Tammy Gleick, a.k.a. Lacey, complaining that it wasn't like it had been, even for her it wasn't, even she knew that everything he gave her was corrupt, until there was nothing left of her in his life but articles in the tabloids. Lacey, the one-named international superstar, breast implants insured by Lloyd's of London, Lacey and her string of Hispanic bodybuilder boyfriends who trained her and her bionic body parts.

Only a television executive can know this stuff, that the image is the thing, and the image is the secret, and the secret is that the broken girls are things of myth, things you can devote yourself to, and that the devotion has to be in secret because only things in secret last, because when the broken girl leaves and takes up with a sequence of club rats, a sequence that may or may not include a guy who drives his car into a diamond merchant's display window, then you know that you still have your secret, and you treasure your secret, your humiliation, while your own body wastes away, and your career dwindles into twilight, and your wife leaves and begins her insane sequence of plastic surgeries, only a television executive can know all these things, all these sorrows.

It would show up on the MMPI. *I am worried about sex,* mostly true? *I am often looking through glossy magazines for women with back injuries,* mostly true or false? The women with the back injuries are going to show up on the test, and there is nothing to do about it. He is going to spike in the paraphilia section of the results. A whole day of presentations about Growing Quality passes with reveries such as this. Before Maiser knows it, it's dinnertime, and he goes right over to the table where Lorna Quinson is sitting, and he trades his place card with the guy sitting at her right, and he banishes this guy to a table between the head of children's programming and someone from the art department.

"What a surprise," Quinson mumbles.

"Not really," Maiser says. "I mean, I —"

"And to what do I owe the pleasure again?"

"Feelings of desperation?" Maiser says. "I can't accept any more offers of sexual slavery from young producers. It's going to tarnish my squeaky-clean image."

"I'm sure that's not what *I* heard," says Quinson, without looking him in the eye. She fingers a barrette and does not elaborate.

"Your ideas on programming," he says, with the charm tap now firmly screwed into the open position. "I'm here because I need your ideas on programming. You know, my guys are not performing like they're meant to perform, and I need to take the pulse of the entire television-watching community. Wherever I might find them. Tonight that means you. Tonight that means let's take some time, here at dinner, and you tell me what you watch and why you watch it, what the medium means to you, what makes you laugh and what makes you cry. Then I'll get to work on a few programs that reflect your insights."

At last, she could be said to be imperceptibly smiling. But before he can take pleasure in the certainty of this uncertain smile, there's a hand on his shoulder. It's Naz Korngold's obsequious secretary, Georgia, a southern gal with a peroxided mane coiffed with military severity. Korngold refers to her as Georgia the Peach.

"Jeffy," she says. "Naz wants you at his table. Last-minute sort of thing. Analysts."

No! There's no recourse for the unavoidable dinner that lies ahead but frequent deployment of the term *synergies,* always in the plural, and aggressive, salesmanlike alcohol abuse. Indeed, he pursues these strategies in a single-minded way so that the rest of the evening shuts over him like the curtain after the bloodbath of act five —

———

Abruptly, he wakes for day number three and its schedule of team building and Growing Quality in the Context of Community, and, yes, he has the kind of headache that led primitive man to assume he was possessed by evil spirits. Maiser drags himself out of the king-size bed and throws on some jogging clothes. Turns out that La Casa Grande is located outside of San Diego in a small neglected desert village, though no one at the resort would admit to it. When Maiser calls the front desk and asks how far it is to town, making clear that he intends to walk the distance before breakfast, they urge him to reconsider. Maybe some time in the sauna instead? A massage? But Jeffrey knows about the evil spirits and he knows what it takes to rid himself of their spells. The brisk constitutional. And so it is out of the climate control and onto a two-lane road with a speed limit of seventy-five. No sidewalks. The desert of Southern California has never looked more Saharan. A few last-chance palms rise up from otherwise scorched expanses of white sand. A roadside billboard advertises four hundred acres at rock-bottom prices. Up ahead, in the distance, whether from the physics of mirage or from hangover, a Dairy Queen staffed entirely by morose teenagers shimmers. Nonetheless, he quickly establishes that he should turn back, except that when he does so, another vision materializes before him, a revelation of the worst kind. It's a battalion of laborers, mostly Mexican, building a large plywood wall.

Maiser kicks aside a few busted bricks while he watches. He wipes a slick of hundred-proof perspiration from his forehead.

There's only one purpose for a wall out here in the elements. There's only one purpose for this wall on the day for which team-building exercises are called in the schedule. It's the Obstacle Course.

He hails the poor sons of bitches from Mexico who are working hard and trying not to get shipped back across the border. "Muchachos? Hola!" A guy with a Padres cap on backward and a goatee dusts off his hands and comes over slowly, as though it's a chore.

"It's okay, sir. We speak English."

"Sorry to bother you. Do you guys have any idea why you're building this wall? Any idea at all?"

"We're told to build a wall to certain specifications. We build a wall." He gestures at it as if it's a thing of beauty.

"That wall looks like it could easily hold a very large man or woman," Maiser says, expecting no reply. The implications are there for anyone to see. Without taking leave of the laborers, he trudges back along the road to his casita. In the meantime, of course, the more ambitious corporate managers are coming in from the putting green in their smart little golf carts, looking tanned, rested, and self-satisfied.

Jeffrey Maiser should be happier about being right, about the wall, about the tragic course of the management off-site, about human nature in general. But he's not happy about being right, insight and contentedness being on opposite ends of life's superstructure. Within a half hour, he will be here, unbreakfasted, slouching in front of the wall, getting instructions from some management consultant bonehead. As usual, Maiser will not be listening carefully, precisely because the facts of daily life have a shocking tendency to be easily forecasted, and he still has not written the essay required by Naz Korngold, nor has he completely filled out the MMPI; *I used to like to play hopscotch and jump rope,* false or mostly false?

There is now a rope affixed to the wall and it is swaying gently.

And Jeffrey Maiser is standing in front of the wall next to some of the most important people in the Universal Beverages Corporation family. Stew Ledbetter, the president of the beverages division, who looks and smells as if he has recently emptied the contents of his stomach; Leslie Aaronson, the thirty-one-year-old head of the UBC film studio, who will probably be out of a job in under a year, just like the last three studio heads; himself, Jeffery Maiser, one of the most driven, respected, and astute minds in television; and Len Wilkinson, the word guy.

Boy, does he fucking hate Len Wilkinson. If Ibn Al-Hassad had devoted a portion of yesterday's speech, a mere bulleted point, a fancy software-enhanced graph, to the greatest enemy of Growing Quality, Maiser missed it, but he knows nonetheless that the greatest enemy to Growing Quality is "dissension in the ranks." Naz Korngold, if he remembers correctly, mentioned it at dinner last night before Maiser's brownout. Naz pointed out how it was the natural tendency of people during "times of crisis" to begin to "take it out on one another." It was natural for there to be an upsurge of "dissension in the ranks." And yet in truth, this was a time to "pull together," according to Naz, a time to "keep our eyes on the prize." The implication being, perhaps, that Maiser is himself one of the problems, a guy who trusts nobody, who keeps his own counsel, who is merciless and solitary, like a timber wolf.

There's one good reason for trusting no one, and that reason is Len Wilkinson.

Wilkinson came up through corporate communications, straight out of some state school, University of Ohio, maybe, where he'd been a sportswriter. He had great dreams of a journalistic vocation ahead. And there he would have stayed if not for a moment of stunning creativity, the kind of breathtaking moment that can really launch a career. That moment was the composition of the expression "inspired by a true story." Yes, somebody had to be the coiner and promoter of this piece of etymological flab, and that somebody was Len Wilkinson, who'd gotten his start in the mail room at UBC films. It was not long after that the studio was having a bad spell. Nothing was doing the kind of business it ought to have done. UBC had worked the market for sequels for a good five or six years, and still the public was less excited about the sequels than the superior original products. Wilkinson was given the task of writing a press release for a little-known telefilm, developed by the studio and cross-marketed to the network, based on the wartime career of a recent president of the United States, and in the midst of this press release, he had described the film as "inspired by a true story," with all the religious nuances implied. He went on, of course, to argue in meetings that television had no mission to document but rather to "inspire." Naturally, the press release was recast in a dozen major reviews for the film, so much so that "inspired by a true story" became an industry-wide, if not global, standard.

He didn't stop there. Wilkinson later repeated his theory of television in various offices in such a way as to bring down the head of television production, whose name Maiser can't even remember, arguing that television was a medium of modest ambitions in the first place. People who watched television knew and accepted the origins of the form, vaudeville and old-time radio. They weren't interested in the news division and its veracity, they were not interested in current events. And television news was inferior to news sources available elsewhere anyhow. The key to television was to develop *mythologies* that had some of the allure of news programming without the bitter aftertaste of factuality. Jeffery Maiser would have been impressed with the naked ambition of the man if he didn't hate so much about Wilkinson, who loved televised golf, who didn't drink, who had a comb-over, and who wore cardigan sweaters in the office.

Of course, once the "inspired by a true story" formula began to lose its PR luster, which it did inevitably, Wilkinson began to argue precisely the obverse, in yet another attempt to curry favor with Naz Korngold's floor. The next Wilkinson coinage, the phrase of the new millennium, the phrase of the postmodern television ethos that had brought about such must-see events as the confirmation hearings of a certain Supreme Court justice, the murder trial of a certain football player, this week's contested election, et cetera, was "enhanced reality."

The other networks were developing the idea, too, like sows thundering toward a trough of rotting vegetable rinds. That game show about wanting to be a millionaire, the couples on the island where their commitments were tempted, the jungle Machiavellians, and so forth. It should have been called "enhanced avarice programming." But no. Wilkinson had written the first press release in which "enhanced reality" was explicated as such. It was a way for Americans to see how Americans really behaved. It was edgy! It was enhanced! And even though Maiser had signed off on the first twelve episodes of *American Spy*, the UBC enhanced-reality product in which contestants competed to be the best possible espionage agents by spying on neighbors and associates, evaluated in their performance by retired military intelligence specialist Norm "Star" Spangler, he could feel intuitively that the "enhanced reality" programming model was really about eliminating programming. The long-term goal was the elimination of the *mythologies* that Wilkinson had prized earlier, the elimination of those nasty SAG employees, those players strutting and fretting upon the little screen and cobbling together a living in the process.

Wilkinson wanted Maiser's job and, given Maiser's rather public domestic problems of late, he probably had a good shot at it. Wanted it last year, wanted it this year, wants it ever more fervently at the base of the wall out behind La Casa Grande. About the only good thing Jeffrey Maiser can say about Wilkinson is that he has a withered thumb. Maiser doesn't know the cause of this deformity, what peculiarity of genetic material brought about the thumb, which resembles the little penile nub of a newborn. There is no way that thing is opposable. Wilkinson is forever clapping you on the shoulder with the left hand, so that you get a close-up look at the nubbin, whereupon his face will fall in some expression of beleaguered self-consciousness. In these moments, it is hard not to feel compassion for Len Wilkinson.

Oh yeah, the fifth member of the four horsemen of the apocalypse, here at the wall, is none other than Lorna Quinson, who is wearing an attractively modest dress from the Lands' End catalogue. She tugs at Maiser's shirt. "I think I'm woefully overdressed, Jeffrey," she says, gesturing at the outfit, in which her socks match the deep blue of the dress.

The management consultant expert interrupts his spiel in mid-enthusiasm. "Listen up, ladies and gentlemen. You are going to have to pay closer attention if you want to actively pursue the goal of excellence here this morning. You are being timed against your subordinates. Everyone's being timed here today, and there will be tremendous prizes, not to mention bragging rights, for whichever team brings in the best time."

"It'd make a good midseason replacement program, Jeff, don't you think?" Wilkinson crows. "*Management Olympians* or something like that. Where Fortune 500 CEOs and their subordinates compete for the reins of their corporations? Tuesday night, maybe, right after the soft news."

Still, it's obvious Wilkinson is a little nervous. He's shifting from foot to foot as though he's got some kind of prostate infection and he's jiggling change in his pocket. And Stew Ledbetter is sopping his face with a brightly colored handkerchief. Leslie Aaronson is reapplying her lipstick.

"Team building," the management consultant continues, "working in concert, working together as one, finding commonalities, synergies. You'll have to decide who goes over the wall first and who helps the others up from the top, and you'll have to decide who waits at the top while the rope is being used on the far side, because the wall is eighteen feet, and there's only the one rope."

Suddenly it's as if the consultant is looking right at Wilkinson's deformity, the thumb. It's as if Naz Korngold has assembled this crew of misfits precisely to put the colossal hurt on Jeff Maiser. And Maiser, who is a three-times-a-week-at-the-gym kind of guy, sees the way it is going. He sees that he is outdoors in the ninety-degree heat with an alcoholic, a mall doll in leather pants and high heels, an embalmer, and a guy with no opposable thumb.

"Okay," the consultant guy says. "You have five minutes to prepare."

An interval of reflection settles over the participants. They're looking at one another with unalloyed contempt. Each one, the way Maiser sees it, is thinking that he or she is the one surrounded by deadwood. Each is jockeying for position. Each is closing in for the kill. Each is thinking, I have to make do with *this?* This is the best management team at the best multinational entertainment and coffin provider in the world? This is it?

"Stew," Jeff ventures. "How you feeling? Feeling like maybe you want to go up first?"

"Never better, Jeff," Stew says. "I'm feeling nothing that a nap and a couple of those migraine pills wouldn't cure. But I'm ready to go; I'm ready to contribute. In fact, I *want* to contribute."

"How were you in the chin-up department? You good for five or ten chin-ups back in your day?"

"I got the draft deferment, Jeff, if that's what you mean. I went back to business school. And I can't say that I have done a lot of chin-ups since that time. But I'm willing to try."

Leslie chimes in. "Look, I think I should just go over really fast, because I can do it expeditiously, and that will bring us that much closer to winning. My husband is a trainer."

"Leslie," Jeff says, "you might as well just take off the heels right now, and maybe the leather pants, too. Don't you think the pants are a little too constricting for this exercise? We don't need you to lap dance here, we need you to scale a wall. Personally, I'm happy to avert my eyes."

"I bet you are, Jeffrey."

"Have it your way, girl."

Lorna stays out of the infighting. Modestly, she removes her flats and her navy blue socks, modestly she sets these aside, under the partial shade of a yucca, along with her sweater and a pair of bracelets. Forty-five seconds, thirty seconds, fifteen seconds. Lorna has this humility about the demands of the wall, an almost philosophical humility. Must be the mortuary business. Must be the way she has made her money. She has some of the serene efficiency of the mortician. And then it hits Jeffrey Maiser, at once, who Lorna reminds him of. And it's not in any obvious way at all, but that doesn't make him less of a moron. It's in some throwaway gesture, an offhanded refixing of a stray hair. She reminds him of the thing that he lost, the person he lost so completely when he embarked on the madness of Lacey. He lost the grace of women his own age, the way they survive. Those were the few quiet years in his life, the years when his marriage was good. Those were the years when the yammering in his skull was quieter, and those years are gone, and there's no one to blame but himself. When the management consultant calls time, this is what Maiser is thinking, that he misses his wife.

Lorna's hand around his wrist calls him forth from the past, because Len Wilkinson has thrown Leslie Aaronson aside, in a pretty rough way, so that she has fallen to the ground beside the rope, twisting her ankle. The two of them, Lorna and Jeffrey, watch in an almost ecstatic paralysis as Wilkinson, with only the one hand, attempts to fling himself up the wall in such a way that the potential for severe back injury is unignorable.

"Jeffrey," Lorna says, "I've been thinking about what you said last night. And I know this really isn't the right time to bring it up. But I just thought I'd let you know. About the programming issue. I'm not really the most terrific sleeper, and last night, instead of writing my essay, I made a list of television programs I've liked over the years —"

Wilkinson is grunting with the exertion, and Stew Ledbetter is pushing against his ass, trying to help but in a sort of halfhearted way, as though he wishes the whole thing would end.

"You son of a bitch, Len! You think I'm going to let you work on *The Green Lantern* publicity with me this summer? No fucking way!" says Leslie, massaging her ankle. She castigates the consultant guy, too. "I hope you're taking notes or something."

"— It's the miniseries, Jeff. Gosh, I know, it's just the most old-fashioned thing imaginable right now. That sort of thing is banished to cable television or something, and no one watches them, or that's the theory. But what I like is a big multigenerational story, Jeff, with a lot of characters, and I like the big themes — love, death, war, adultery — and I like a sense that there is order in the universe, that we're not all out here clawing our way to the top for no reason. So that's what I'd say. I'd watch Richard Chamberlain in *The Thorn Birds* any day, and that little girl who later becomes his wife, just adorable. What a pretty landscape!"

Maiser says, "You know, it's really funny you'd say that, because I was in the hotel the other day and I got this call —"

There's no time. He could stand and talk to Lorna for hours, but there's no time. Somebody has to stop Wilkinson, who is hanging by one hand from the rope, about four feet up, and is calling out for help. Before Maiser knows it, he is running, and he can feel himself running, can feel the decision being made in the quads and the delts, and it's not some corporate type of decision, it's a reflexive decision, as if he is a character in a miniseries himself, and before you can say *enhanced revenue stream,* he has Wilkinson around the waist and is lowering him back to the floor of the desert, after which, with a dexterity he doesn't think he still possesses, he has his own boozy body halfway up and a hand over the top, where he scrapes off a couple of layers of skin. The shadows are all on the other side of the wall. If only they had known that the shadows are there, and that all they have to do is drop over the other end and they will be in the shade, where a cooler full of bottled water awaits.

"Leslie," he calls, upon lofting a leg over the summit so that he can sit. "Get your ass up here. And forget about retaining counsel. You can sue over your sprained ankle tomorrow. Today, you're getting your ass up here. Get on it, sweetie. Now."

And the amazing thing is that Leslie *has* taken off the leather pants. Admittedly, she's wearing a long silk shirt, but she has done what needs to be done, and he has to admit, her body is a traffic-stopping kind of a thing. Never let it be said that those young women who spend all their time in the gym are not *strong*, because they are incredibly strong, because she's halfway up in the time it would take to have a station break and she's got a spiel going the whole time: "Do you want me to stay at the top and help to lift Stew up? Or do you want me to go over the other side? Just tell me the plan!"

"Go over," he says, and by the time he says it, she's already there, flipping the rope as if it were some trick she learned as a cheerleader in high school, when she wasn't snorting coke and copying other people's essays. He gets a quick look at her backside, notes that that is definitely *not* a thong, and then she's over the edge. Leslie swings hard against the other side, halfway down, and lets go, landing like a Romanian gymnast, except that she shouts, "Motherfucker!" About the ankle.

"Stew!" Jeff calls.

Ledbetter is standing at the bottom of the rope as it pendulums in front of him. "Jeff, I don't know. Maybe I was being a little ambitious before!"

"Stew," he says, "we just don't have time, pal; we just don't have time. Want your division to get spun off?"

And that's the thing that does it, and Stew Ledbetter is up, huffing and puffing until he's near the top.

"Jeff, I'm worried I'm going to vomit. I'm just really not that good with heights."

But in fact Stew is coming up, with much grimacing, and soon he has one flabby hand grabbing at the top.

"Leslie, get ready down there, he's coming down!"

Maiser hoists up the rope. And Stew tips over the top as though he's falling into his grave. There's an ominous thud. But Jeff doesn't look because he can see that Len Wilkinson is at the bottom of the wall now, awaiting his turn. He hears Leslie call that she has Stew and that Stew is indeed throwing up, but there's no time, no time.

"Len, get the hell out of the way; we're doing Lorna next."

"But Jeff, I can help pull Lorna up."

"You could, Len, but you're not going to. Get out of the way."

Wilkinson seems to have no intention of doing that, however, until Lorna kicks him hard in the shin. With her bare foot. It's a gutsy move. Wilkinson crumples, bent over his hematoma. And now comes the difficult part, which is where Jeffrey leans down to pull, because Lorna is just not going to have lifted herself up any ropes lately. To his amazement, though, she seems to have choreographed rope stylings, as if there was some past of rope training or something, or maybe water ballet, one of those grace-filled girlhood activities.

"Lorna, are you going to need —"

"I *was* a gymnast as a kid. Until I had a fall."

"A fall? Was it a back injury of some kind?"

"If you could just give me a hand at the top, please."

She has the rope fed between her bare feet, which feature painted toenails, and she contorts herself, like an inchworm on a blade of grass, with each fresh upward convulsion, until her hand reaches for his, and their hands are connected, and he pulls her up. He can see her bra strap. And her bra strap is good. And her hair has come unfastened. And her hair is good. The fact of her past upon the balance beam is good. Flushed cheeks. Heaving bosom. The gleam, in her green eyes, of exertion. And the two of them are on the top of the wall, and on the one side, they are watching Leslie and Stew drinking bottled water in the shade. And on the other, in the glare of the desert sun, Len Wilkinson.

"I guess the Americans with Disabilities Act doesn't cover this one, Len," Jeff says. Lorna makes no move to go down the far side yet, and her dress billows under her from the other side of the wall.

"Are you going to make fun of my disability, Jeffrey? That doesn't seem like team building."

"I don't give a shit about your disability. I have better things to worry about than your little baby penis. Len, listen, I can't help but notice the view from up here. It's a sensational view. Clear day, bright sunshine. The view is just great."

"What do you mean?" Tugging on the end of the rope as if he's going to attempt to go it alone again.

"What I mean, Len, is that it seems to me that we have the opportunity to make a deal. That's the view I'm seeing from up here, Len. I'm seeing a view of corporate structure before me. Or maybe that's not really the thing, Len; maybe it's not corporate structure that I mean. Maybe what I'm seeing is an idea of corporate ethics, of the way things might work, and maybe that's what team building is all about, all pulling in the same direction in terms of ethics, Len, right? The scales have fallen from my eyes up here, Len, and suddenly I'm feeling really good about things —"

"Gentlemen," the management consultant guy suddenly intrudes in the action, "I remind you that you're being timed, and lengthy conversations are really going to eat up a lot of time."

"Fuck off, pal. Now, Len, here's the deal. I like my job and I like having the kind of responsibility that I have, because I think I'm good at it, and I like the other people in my division, the people I've worked with for the last twenty or twenty-five years in some cases, and I don't want to see anything happen to my division. I mean, I'm willing to make a few changes to swing with the fashions of the moment, but I'm not willing to see a fifty-year tradition of news broadcasting taken over by a few punks with too much gel in their hair, and what I'm looking for, in general, are some assurances that my division is going to survive the next shake-up, and this is where I think you can be of some use to me."

"Jesus, Jeff, we're —"

"We're going to be announcing some bold new programming in the next couple of weeks, Len, and these new programs are going to be anything but the enhanced-reality model. What I'm wanting from you is that you are going to come up with the ideas we need to launch these new programs. You're going to use your skills, you're going to promote the hell out of this sonofabitch, and you're going to stake your reputation on it."

"Jeff, what are we talking about?"

"I got one word, Len, one word for you. And that word is *miniseries.*"

"Jeff, let's just get this over with."

At which Jeffrey Maiser turns to his helpmeet, the embalmer, and tells her to hold his feet, he's going down.

20

Eduardo Alcott has sequestered Tyrone in the basement, where they are hunkered on a couch with vinyl protective covering. There are many power tools nearby, and serpentine coils of extension cords. And there is the smell of sawdust. The forlornness of basements is well-known. Alcott has made sure that Tyrone's brother, a.k.a. the Great White Hope, is no longer acting as his brother's keeper. The tutelage and indoctrination must be undertaken in a precinct free from interference. The process must be given space and time, as with Chinese reeducation. This, at any rate, is how Tyrone explains the situation to himself.

Today's lecture, according to Eduardo, is about the perforation of the skull. The theme of today's lecture is the communication between the contents of the interior of the skull and the environment. The theme of today's lecture is the urgent need of these two regions to communicate more freely. The theme of today's lecture is blood-to-brain-tissue ratios and the fluidity of blood. The theme of today's lecture is the mystical surgery known as trepanation, the boring, scraping, drilling, or cutting of the skull, using such tools as have been explored from Neolithic times up to present times: the cylindrical crown saw, the Woodall trephine, and the cone-shaped cylinder with center pin.

Eduardo, the Mexican ideologue, a fiery and passionate man, claims distant ancestry to the founder of a local collectivist experiment in Utopian thinking, in the following way: the initial Alcott, the Utopian Alcott, for all of his theoretical expertise, got with child a young woman of the Indies who was in his employ, and this unwanted young woman was exiled to the tropical latitudes of her girlhood, where, after prolonged and grueling labor, she whelped a boy, whom she called Alcott after his father, and this Alcott grew up scorned and hated. The lot of bastardy is hard. Nevertheless, this young Alcott, by the name of Neville, was proud and strong. He read widely in the writings of his father and his father's friends, for example, a certain Walden Pond camping expert. And Neville learned of the immensity of nature, the perfection of nature, and of the pestilence of man. He likewise learned, by virtue of his coming of age in the tropics, of the many religious and mystical practices favored by the so-called savage cultures, among these being cannibalism, incest, sacrifice, ritual amputation, dowsing, and the like. Neville Alcott retired to a cave on a lone island in the Caribbean Sea, taking only his wife, who was a dark woman, a Moorish woman, a former slave or perhaps the daughter of slaves, and together they produced a great line of Alcotts, a coffee-hued line of Alcotts, and these Alcotts rose up in the Caribbean Isles. They were as one with the freed slaves, the abandoned slaves. They were as one with workers of the sugarcane plantations, they brewed rum in the hot sun, they lived in palm-frond shacks when hurricanes blew, and when they had become as strong as an army, these Alcotts were a part of every attempt to overthrow the European oppressor in this hemisphere. The Alcotts rode into Havana in tanks with Fidel, Eduardo said. In fact, Eduardo himself rode into Managua with Daniel Ortega and the Sandinistas, and he composed position papers for the Zapatistas, and he abducted villagers with the Shining Path. In every place where the Alcotts could oppose the power of the Anglo and his lackeys, the Alcotts shone forth, until, through the magic of counternarrative and alternative historical systems, as explained by Gramsci and Fanon, this Alcott came back to the place where the original Utopian Alcott once lived himself, to Concord, Massachusetts, where the Revolution of your pestilential country began, and here he intends to begin the process of bringing down the fiendish American power, bringing it to its knees, so that America can know how it subjects the many peoples of the world to its bad television programs, its repellent and decadent movies, its fascistic foreign policy, and also its inferior mass productions of cut-rate goods, such as bad beer and coffee and cars that are the laughingstock of the globe.

Today's lecture is about the operation "for the removal of stone," whose history was first articulated by one Paul Broca, a French gentleman who was given a skull by an American prison reformer named Squier, who in turn got this skull as a gift from a Peruvian woman. The skull, sundered from its identity, made the rounds and was for a time much studied by a phrenologist with unusually large ears, called Horsly. Why was this skull so valuable? Every age has its abundance of skulls. The Khmer Rouge, e.g., paved roads with skulls. The skulls in Rwanda outnumber the bowls. The skull in question was of interest because it had a perfect parallelogram cut from its surface by pre-Columbian Peruvians, Peruvians before the pestilence of Columbus and Cortés and their rapacious hordes. This skull had a parallelogram cut out of it, after which the owner of the skull apparently survived for a time. Because, if you believe the writings of Paul Broca, there is evidence of some of the bone *growing back*.

"There are thousands of these skulls found in the area of Peru," Alcott says, droning on in his interminable way, licking his lips, running his hands through his wavy gray locks, refixing the aviator glasses to his nose. "Peru is the capital of this historical surgery, the surgery known as trepanation. Peru and surrounding areas, and this is what we wish for you to understand, comrade. From here the operation was exported around the globe. From Neolithic times, from the times which are before writing and history, you find the Peruvians boring holes in the skull. And soon thereafter you find peoples in the Pacific Islands also performing this operation, having in all likelihood learned this operation from the Peruvians, and this we know because of the revolutionary peoples of New Caledonia, where trepanations were as common as the extraction of teeth. And this is the case even in New Ireland, where women frequently carved the skulls of their own children so as to make sure their children would grow up tall. It is possible, of course, that peoples made these journeys by canoe, from the coast of Latin America to the islands, because of prevailing winds. The word *kumara,* for example, denoting a kind of sweet potato, this also made a transpacific journey, according to linguists, and just so with the operation for the removal of stone.

"Many times"— Eduardo pauses to increase the mystery — "many times, these operations were for legitimate purposes, maybe depressed skull fractures, you know, when a piece of bone is actually driven into the tissues of the brain and surgery is in order to remove the bone fragments and to drain out the pus. As you are aware, my revolutionary brother, there is also the operation that is about the humors, about allowing the bad air to be released, the bad air of humors. The trepan was used to release this bad air into the room, after which the healing would begin to take place, because when there is pressure upon the brain or when the blood in the brain begins to coagulate, according to valid and historically sound medical theory, there is illness and death.

"But many other times, the operations took place in order to release demons who were harassing the medical subjects. Or the operations took place for spiritual purposes. For example, in Eastern Europe, which is the last place this type of surgery reached because this was the most backward place on the globe, you have the Bronze Age Russians, who were really just isolated bands of tribes in the region of the Minussinsk Basin or the Dnepr River. Still, using various scraping tools, they too performed trepanations, after which these tribesmen carried harvested pieces of the skull around with them as amulets. In some cases, you know, we've even read of buried remains of tribesmen, in bogs, carrying sacks with them in which there were contained bits and pieces of numerous skulls, all of these fragments removed from living persons. It is to be supposed, my revolutionary brother, that the magic was increased if the piece of skull that was obtained was from a living person.

"Left parietal lobe, almost always the proper region for the trepanning in these Bronze Age times, in Italy, Austria, Portugal, for example. There the skulls were beveled."

The basement is damp and cold. The furnace is shuddering as if desperate, just a few feet from where Tyrone is sitting. One of Eduardo's flunkies, a high school kid named Hal, has gone off for more food, returning with hummus and tabbouleh bought in large tubs from the local health food market. Eduardo is very passionate about the health food market. Eduardo is passionate about many things, unless perhaps this is just part of the indoctrination process.

It happened this way: Tyrone and the Great White Hope had jogged up the street, under cover of night, fleeing the residence of Tyrone's adoptive parents. It seems so long ago. They fled, and there was a brief moment, in the air of autumn, when Tyrone's liberty seemed grand, like he was a dove released. Then there was some waiting, and shivering, underneath an oak, in the shadows, until an unassuming Econoline van appeared, a van featuring the sort of unsettled idle that is an augury of future muffler trouble, and before he could think twice about it, Tyrone was jumped, blanketed with some rough wool, bundled into the back of the Econoline, which unfortunately did not have the all-purpose Sears love mattress, and then Tyrone, who did not struggle, was blindfolded. Tyrone was told not to ask questions. Tyrone was told that if he cooperated there would be no need for force.

The Great White Hope had appeared to be just returning from some after-school activity, basketball practice or whatever it was he did, oboe lessons. The Great White Hope appeared, notwithstanding excessive bodily ornament, to have his middle-class white-boy routine down pretty good. But appearances deceive. Because the Great White Hope was attempting to shake off the chains of his elite birth; he was attempting to be with the people, alongside his pals, these revolutionary types, who favored the rhetoric of high-powered cranial saws. You held the saw in place with your forehead while you winched the boring mechanism into the head of the sufferer, who was bleeding like a stuck pig.

At first, Tyrone believed that the Great White Hope had given him up to the authorities. But of course he couldn't figure out why he needed to be blindfolded in order to be extradited back to the Empire State. Tyrone's revolutionary spirit was clouded at this time. He had a feeling of loneliness, and he believed that the Great White Hope needed to turn him over, perhaps to claim some reward, or to get his photo in mass-marketed periodicals, or simply to indicate his supremacy over his darker adopted brother. Tyrone's feeling was sorrow, but sorrow is for the weak. In years past, Tyrone had attempted to instruct the Great White Hope. In fact, this was an area of some nostalgia. Tyrone wanted to be certain that the Great White Hope got beyond the standard-issue education of the rich suburban kid. Maybe Tyrone's kidnapping, in a van that smelled of spoiled milk, was proof enough that the Great White Hope had now come into his own. There was the silence of the van, and then there was incense burning, sandalwood, to cover up the dope smoking and the spoiled milk. Tyrone began to relax, to feel that a condition of permanent flight was paradoxically useful to his legal situation. If he had no idea where he was going, it could hardly be bad for him.

Three or four persons hustled him into a little shack apparently somewhere in the northeastern suburbs. They led him stumbling into a cheap living room, which was done up in the cut-rate paneling that indicated the permanent vegetative state of National Football League enthusiasts. This he knew when the Great White Hope removed the blindfold.

"Sorry, bro. Hope it wasn't too uncomfortable."

Tyrone said nothing. Nothing had served him well before. The revolutionaries stared at Tyrone, blinking, as if he astonished them. He noticed that the table was cluttered with ceramic ashtrays of the sort made by fumbling elementary school students. Whoever acted as leader, and it became obvious quickly that the leader was this Mexican man with wild hair and fervent, unblinking eyes, had a school bus full of sixth graders on his payroll. Further evidence of this was to be found in the knit pot holders in the kitchen, where the revolutionaries all ate together. One of the four teenagers standing by offered Tyrone a beverage: Gatorade, the popular sports drink, complete with electrolytes. No telephone anywhere to be found, and a television with only a coat hanger for an antenna. For a time, they all said nothing. Later, the comrades played cards in silence.

After some hours, it came out that the Great White Hope needed to return to the home of his parents. They needed to come up with a story for him to provide these genetic parents. Eduardo silenced the deliberations, motioned to Tyrone to stand up, and took him down into the basement, where, in his stiff, academic English, he began the first of his study sessions on the theory and practice of the organization known as the Retrievalists. Tyrone said the syllables over and over, as if the repetition would give some clear evidence of hidden meaning. The Retrievalists. The first lesson concerned the bogus history of the Alcotts, described above, and when it was over, a wordless teenage girl stretched out a down sleeping bag for Tyrone on the basement floor. The Retrievalists would have him sleep there.

What was it they wanted? Eduardo asked rhetorically on the second day. Naturally, they had many answers to this question. What they wanted was the rescue of this continent from its oppressors. They wanted relief from the oppressors who had wrongly seized the American lands and visited upon the natives a genocide, who had all but wiped out the mighty bison, who had sown among the native peoples such foul illnesses as smallpox and alcoholism. When they had completed this mission, they would move on to other continents, in the following order: Europe, Asia, Africa, Australia, South America.

What were their origins? Their origins — and here Eduardo hoped that Tyrone, as newly installed Minister of Information, would soon come up with a better recitation of the facts — were in the environmental movement. They had originally been an autonomous cell in a decentralized organization with no leader, which had no revolutionary position and whose goal was felonious attacks on property. It should be noted that the Retrievalists still supported the cellular structure of this environmental organization, they just needed to enlarge the political debate to include other legitimate modes of instruction and resistance, such as prisoner exchange, propaganda, black-market financing, counterfeiting, cyberterrorism, et cetera.

"We are aware of certain problems of a legal nature in your own situation," Eduardo remarked on Saturday, in the middle of the indoctrination, "and we want you to know that we applaud your dramatic efforts in the city of New York."

"If you're asking about the, uh, the Asian woman," Tyrone said, "I had nothing to do with that. She's my friend."

"We understand that it is important to keep the story streamlined and in a condition where it can be repeated without mistake. We applaud the rigor of your preparations."

"I didn't have anything to do with it, sir. I got enough problems."

"For the time being, you are in the care of our organization, and we would like to present you with some intelligence on the strength and militancy of our efforts, so that you may indeed become our Minister of Information."

It was like graduate school all over again, that was the truth of it. In graduate school there was always the solemnity and the forced language. Eduardo had a trait in common with the graduate students of Tyrone's acquaintance, and that trait was facial masking. Schizophrenics used the technique, too, especially when speaking to the manifest and latent content of symbolic systems. Tyrone knew this because he'd had the occasional hallucination himself.

After each session would come the catechism. What is our name? Our name is the Retrievalists. What is our origin? Our origin is in the struggle against the pestilence of humanity. When did we begin our struggle? We began our struggle in 1994. What is the nature of our actions? The nature of our actions is random and discontinuous, but we seek the violent destruction of the property of the oppressor. Who is the oppressor? The oppressor is the large multinational corporation and its allies. When will our mission be completed? Our mission will never be completed. How long do we serve? We serve until death.

———

On Monday, after some more ranting while the kids are at school, there is a period of a couple of hours when Eduardo Alcott has other responsibilities. What could these responsibilities be? Some kind of computer-programming job that he uses to finance both his living situation and his revolutionary cadre, where he might also have access to a server that conceals the Web presence of the Retrievalists. When Eduardo goes out into the poisonous atmosphere of the world, he leaves behind sentries. For Tyrone's security. Hal, the guy with the unwashed hair, and Nina, the sullen blonde who always seems to wear her sleeves at such a length that as far as Tyrone knows she has no hands. A big lug with a heavy-metal mullet and a Korn tour jersey, named Glenn. Maybe the conversation that ensues is completely scripted. Impossible to know.

"Our parents are perfectly nice and everything, and we were never mistreated by them," Hal says.

"Yeah," Nina says. "Our parents are perfectly nice."

"We came to believe some things, know what I'm saying? We feel like you walk outside, you see certain things, you know, bad things. How can you not walk around and feel like things are getting worse, you know? Once there was some mystery to this life, now there's none. Now there's just waking up and taking the standardized test, making sure that you get into a good college, you know? So you can go work for the Bechtel Corporation or the Carlyle Group. And, like, all this pressure about college, what's that about?"

"Yeah," Nina says. "College."

"I know how to clean my room and I know how to pick the lock on the liquor cabinet. That's about it."

Glenn, across the room, adds his own perceptions of the revolutionary situation while sharpening knives. "I had to take the door actually off the hinges at my mom's. She had it all in this closet with a really strong padlock. I just took the door off the hinges."

"We're normal kids. We're not statistics. But we've got to this point where we feel like we have to act, get it? And that's why we're going to do what we have to do. Because that's how a revolutionary movement functions, you know, it acts."

Tyrone takes in the nuances of the scene. The television, with the sound off, is unwatched, as ever, though it happens to be broadcasting, at present, *The Werewolves of Fairfield County.* A repeated episode he happens to have seen. Time, in this rerun episode, is moving backward rather than forward. Only the werewolves seem to know how to deal with it.

"We've been thinking about it, you know, and we have, like,

deliberations. We debate," Nina says. "What should be the first direct action? Like, what will be the thing that gets us the right kind of attention so that we can continue to attract other soldiers, or whatever, and to promote what we believe in?"

Gradually, as though a curtain is being retracted by an offstage dwarf, the plan under discussion emerges. The plan, like many such plans, involves the element of fire, which in Tyrone's fevered and heavily sequestered imagination is the most ominous of elements. The plan has been dreamed up by a committee of teenagers, and the plan involves a firebomb, homemade, which shall be used on a local chain business, which does not belong in such an estimable place, a place of nature and wildness, namely Concord, Massachusetts.

"Like, what makes those people think they can just bring a franchise like that into a town like this?" Hal asks. "What makes them think they can do that? Don't the people who live here have any say in these kinds of things? They don't have any say because these things are all being figured out someplace else by real-estate assholes and —"

"By some idiot," Glenn says, grinding another knife.

"By some guy who probably has kids that he needs to put through school somehow, and how is he going to put his kid through school, and he can't figure out any way he's going to do it because he shouldn't have gotten his wife pregnant in the first place, they should have used some kind of birth control, or they couldn't get an abortion because of where they live, or whatever, so he has no choice but to get a job at this lousy place, and then it's up the chain or get fired by the big corporation, and so now he works his way up, like, until he's got the job that is oppressing other people every day, and that's the job of figuring out where the franchises go."

"I don't even like doughnuts," Nina says. "I mean, I maybe liked doughnuts when I was a kid, but now I think doughnuts are eaten by people who don't know any better. Like, the whole idea of the doughnut is to dumb you down. People, they eat the doughnuts and they can't think straight, and they have to take a nap, you know, and then they can't understand the forces that are working against them, like, they don't even know whether a doughnut is nutritious or anything, because how are you going to find out? The doughnut is a symbol of how people don't have any power, and so the doughnut has to go."

"We tried thinking up some revolutionary slogans for a protest," Hal says. "You know, like, WE CALL IT DOUGH*NOT!*"

The three kids laugh, and their laughter is open and inviting, as if it comes from a more innocent place. Tyrone hears fervor, and hears youth, and hears how lovely and frail youth is, how open to the bad ideas in any room, so easily sent on long, erroneous rambles, and these things can coexist, the frailty and openness of youth, the mercilessness of it, and that's how you get a pair of Cambodian twelve-year-olds who smoke opium to persuade an army of adults that God speaks through them.

"So you're going to firebomb a Krispy Kreme?" he asks.

"Reduce it to cinders," Hal says.

"Leaving a black, smoky pile of nothing," Nina says.

"And when is this meant to happen?" Tyrone asks.

"Can't tell you that," Nina says, and she goes and puts her hands on the shoulders of Hal. "Eduardo knows all of the specifics, and we only learn things bit by bit, and that's because we're not, you know, so old yet. But we're in on all the planning and deliberations and stuff."

"You're expecting that I'm going to hang around and watch you guys blow up a doughnut restaurant?"

Glenn lines up knives on the counter. "Eduardo says you are a revolutionary."

"I'm a bike messenger," Tyrone says, and then says more than he's said in a long time. "Man, I'll tell you what I am, I'm a bike messenger. But once I, too, had a lot of ideas about things." Warming to the subject as he goes, "I had all these ideas that

I could change the world, the kinds of ideas that you guys have. I thought I could run for office. I thought I could help the other people who have my color of skin, because I was lucky enough to get a good education, which most of the people with my color of skin don't have. For no good reason did I get any of this. The dice just fell my way. And I could go back and teach these people how to do better in the world, make more of the world. And the way I thought I was going to do this was first with words, and I went and worked with the words, you know, in graduate school, and when the words wouldn't bend the way I thought they were going to bend, when I woke up one morning and the sentences all looked like they were going places I never expected them to go, then I gave up trying to do that."

"That's exactly what we —"

Tyrone raises his hand, knowing that in this group, if in no other, he can command attention.

"And then I thought that maybe I could change the world by making art, you know, and I started in doing just that. I would take a book and I would mark out all the words except for the few words that represented a secret code, a code assuring that certain systems were in place, big impenetrable systems. I would open these codes for the reader, and I did this obsessively, all night long sometimes. I would do these things, I would do violence to books, and open them up, you know, so that people could see what was really written inside, and when this didn't change the world, I started, well, I guess I started to get a little desperate, I started making collages, and then videos of collages, mismatched words and books and pictures, all those seductions in the world; I would stay up for nights at a time, and I wouldn't go out, I'd believe that I had worked out important artistic statements, and when I didn't make any money at it, as I always thought I would, I got a smaller apartment, still, you know, holding on to this idea that I could change the world, even if I had to economize. And then I got another smaller apartment, always so

I could keep the studio where my work was stored, and then I didn't have enough money for the studio, so I had to get this bike messenger's job. And that was a blow. At first I said I wouldn't do it for long, you know, because I had this other important responsibility, but then a couple years went by and I wasn't young the way I was young anymore, and I was a guy who had this job where I could run free in the city, and eventually these patterns emerged, and I would ride in the city, between all these addresses, all these corporations or agencies or law firms, whatever, and that started to seem like that was the art, that was changing the world in a way. I was making patterns, just like I was trying to write something or draw something; I was going where the addresses told me to go, and I was sort of like the elements, and so I started not going to the studio as much, and the world wasn't getting changed by me at all. Gradually, it was sort of like the world was a place that had almost no traces of me in it. I was the messenger; I was the person who made it possible for meaning to happen. A word, or a tape recording, or a compact disc with some information on it, these were never meaningful on their own because they didn't go from one person to another. They were never complete until they were transmitted by me, so I was a thing that was always missing. I was the completion of the circuit, a device for meanings to get made, but in this way I'd stopped meaning anything at all, myself, I was just a guy a split second between when a letter got written and when it got read. I was the time between meanings, a time that grows shorter and shorter the longer you live, until it seems to be going backward, and all of this meant I had not changed the world, and it meant that I had done some good by not changing the world, by deciding to leave it as it was."

When he finishes his disquisition, there is stupefaction in the crumbling interior of the kitchen, a stupefaction among the revolutionaries. A werewolf bays at something on the television screen across the room.

"But your brother said —"

"Never mind what my brother said."

"But what about the woman in New York?" Hal asks.

"Why is it a good thing if I hit a woman on the sidewalk with a brick? Which I did not do. Why is that a good thing for me to have done that from your point of view? Did you ever hit anyone in the head? Do you know what head injuries are like?"

Glenn arises from his stool, from his knife sharpening, and he comes to the uncomfortable folding chair where Tyrone sits. "We're willing to do what needs to be done."

"You know what's going to happen if you get convicted of arson?"

"We're not going to get caught," Hal says.

"I'll let you in on a little secret, before I leave, which is maybe what I'm going to do here in a second, and that is that I was actually *talking* to, uh, to Samantha Lee, the woman, the victim, on the phone at the moment that she was hit, the woman, the victim. She was on the phone, and I was talking to her from the studio, at the moment she was —"

He didn't realize it, until this dusk, in this safe house, somewhere in the suburbs of Massachusetts, the momentousness of what happened. He fled the city of New York because, as a messenger, transit was his skill, because that is what he did. He fled the scene and he prepared for the worst, which is the lot of the black man, and then the worst came to pass, which is also arguably the lot of the black man, followed by further and further examples of the worst. All of this. Yet now it seems that there is a miserly portion of redemption available to him, and this redemption is in the fact that he meant to say something kind to this woman, Samantha Lee, he had called to do so in the first place, to say something kindly to this woman, who believed in what Tyrone had once done, as an artist, and this is what he meant to say, "I am in the studio tonight" because of you, because of you, because of you, but the line went dead, and now, in front of a bunch of teenagers, he feels the unmistakable import of that moment.

And that is when Eduardo returns.

Eduardo turns off the television. Flings house keys onto the kitchen table.

There is silence in the room.

"Tonight is Monday, and this is the night that I've set aside for further loyalty tests," Eduardo begins. "As you know, I've designed loyalty tests for each of you, to make sure you're up to the revolutionary actions ahead. I've just returned, in fact, from making sure that our other comrade, Max, who is presently operating as a double agent, is functioning effectively and that his cover has not been compromised in the first phase of the loyalty tests, in which he gave up his own brother to the movement. He seems fine, except for the fact that his mother says he is grounded for the rest of the semester.

"I can also tell the Minister of Information that news of his case has now reached the Massachusetts Bay Colony. His parents are aware of the situation and they have contacted the out-of-state police.

"Now, what we have scheduled tonight is the next phase of the loyalty tests. Revolutionary brothers and sisters, I have to bring the Minister of Information up to speed and so I must revisit ground covered earlier, and my apologies. We speak again of the ancient surgery of trepanation and of the use of the ancient surgery as a treatment for maladies of the mind. I think we have spoken of its use for depressed skull fractures, most of these resulting from battles where slingshots and rock throwing were common, and we have spoken of its use in situations where demon possession was the diagnosis, also with seizure and epilepsy, but have we spoken of its use with respect to migraine? Yes, the ancient surgery was used as a cure for migraine because migraines were considered a kind of demon possession. And what was the result of the ancient surgery, my revolutionary brothers and sisters? The result was increased feelings of well-being and peacefulness, greater alertness, and increased sexual feeling. This is the truth about the ancient surgery, that it has a very modern capacity, and that is for increased feelings of well-being.

"I hesitate to give you the proof, my revolutionary brothers and sisters, because I'm guessing that you just won't believe it's as simple as this, but it is, and this is where loyalty comes into it, my brothers. So now if you could just step forward here and feel this part of my skull."

There's no getting around this phrenological obsessiveness of Eduardo's, and Tyrone watches the kids step forward to where the older man is seated, by the oven, which is set at broil to help with the heating problem. Eduardo bows before the teens, in order to present the crown of his head.

"Please don't poke at it, my brothers, because the bone hasn't healed over all the way, and if the skin were to be perforated, well, you know, I could get a bruise on the tissue itself. And this would not be good for the movement."

The spot is overgrown with hair, so it's hard to say exactly where or what the evidence is. Glenn is first, massaging the top of Eduardo's head.

"I can't feel anything," Glenn says. "Is this the right spot?"

Eduardo takes his hand, and there is the strangely gentle probing of the skull, the older man, holding Glenn's right hand, stroking the mild curve at the top of his head.

"Oh," Glenn says, "I get it. There, right?"

Eduardo drops the hand suddenly, as if it has now grown foul, and he points at Hal. Hal wipes his hand on his grimy jeans and presents himself. Eduardo takes his hand and swipes the hand across his head, like a caress at first and then, as if the hand were some kind of swooping bird, sets it down on his skull, and Hal's brow, furrowed in concentration, seems to soften.

"You mean that little divot thing there?"

"What else would I mean?" Eduardo snaps.

"What did you use to do it?" Hal says.

Of course, Eduardo points out, he did not perform an auto-trepanation, and he is reasonably sure there are no examples of auto-penetration in the literature of the ancient surgery, especially because it would be impossible to both fold the skin flap over the eyes and simultaneously complete the procedure. However, Eduardo points out that the medical industry in his own land is not as tightly regulated as it is in this country, where the industry is compromised by manufacturers of drugs and by large health insurance conglomerates that control medical practice by virtue of their normative idea of what the human body is and must be. In his country, a trepanation can be procured under sterile circumstances for a modest fee. He points out that the Peruvians had a much higher success rate, in the pre-Columbian era, than the doctors of Europe because they practiced their surgery in the open air, whereas the western doctors performed theirs in operating rooms, where vulnerability to infection rendered the survival rate no higher than 10 percent or so, and that in the rare instance in which a doctor agreed to perform the surgery.

"Of course," Eduardo says, and now he seems to be making his pitch directly to Tyrone, "we have a migraine sufferer here. And for her loyalty test, she has gratefully agreed to be the recipient of our efforts today."

Is it possible? Has Nina agreed?

"Because of our situation, we are going to have to make do with the tools at hand. I have spent some time making sure that we have a drill bit that will not penetrate beyond the skull into the brain tissue. We will also need a small hand vacuum cleaner to suction up the fragments from the hole. I think under the circumstances, the boring technique is going to make the best sense. In this technique, a number of very small holes are bored into the skull, in the shape of a circle, after which we gouge out small lines connecting each hole until we pry loose the circular piece of the skull. We would like to offer Nina, the revolutionary sister, the piece of skull fragment when we are done, so that she can make an amulet out of it. And we would also like to assure the revolutionary sister that we have, in advance, procured enough prescription pain reliever to ensure that the operation will be virtually free of pain. So whenever the sister is ready, we will commence."

Nina begins to cry softly in the corner where she's sitting, and the crying is so base, such a violation of the revolutionary code, that there's a flurry of activity in which all of the Retrievalists gather around her. Tyrone has to get her out of Eduardo's shack somehow. Immediately.

"Does the revolutionary sister want the pain medication now?"

"Look, my brother," Tyrone says at last, edging closer to the front door, "I think there might be some better ways to test her loyalty than to put her life in jeopardy in order to cure her migraines."

"What does the minister propose? Unless of course he proposes to call the authorities, who would take a great interest in his own case."

"Give me the drugs," Nina says. "Give me the drugs."

"Uh, you could have her go get work at the Krispy Kreme franchise. She could bring back, I don't know, information on the time that they close up shop. Which parts of the store are vulnerable to fire. A blueprint, whatever you need."

"The minister is not taking into account the fact of the ancient surgery creating feelings of well-being and fulfillment. And also there is the matter of allegiance."

Tyrone could turn the drill on Eduardo and perforate his left shoulder or his wrist or his ankle, so that Eduardo would be in intense pain. Or he could depress the spot where Eduardo's skull surgery is healed over, bringing upon him a deep and heavy sleep. Or he could hold Eduardo down and give him a half dozen of the Percodans or Percocets that are secreted away on him somewhere. He could persuade the teenagers to turn against Eduardo, in the process giving them great lessons about the preciousness of some aspects of contemporary life, even in these dark times. For example, look at the mountaintops; there are mountaintops all over the place. There are mountaintops in the state of Massachusetts; on any day you could just decide to go walk to the summit of a mountaintop, on the trail that passes over it. Tyrone is no hero, but he could do one of these things, or he could simply do what messengers do. He could flee.

There is no one to stop him; there are no guns in this turn of events, even if Eduardo does yell, "Get the gun!" as Tyrone opens the door. There is no genuine snub-nosed, pearl-handled anything, there are no perforations with bullets, no high-speed chases, or that's what Tyrone hopes when he resolves upon telephoning the constabulary, come what may, just as soon as he figures out where he is, out in this neglected part of the suburbs, a few filling stations, auto repair shops, the front door of Eduardo's place swinging wide behind him, looking back to see the room lit up, running and yelling, "Call the police! Call the police!" running and yelling as if he has never used his voice this way, as if he hasn't spoken in years. The four of them staring, pointing. As he hightails it up the street. Never did a used auto parts shop and a bunch of customers loitering in front of a mini-storage facility seem so wondrous and full of peace.

21

Something really strange is happening in the office, Madison Mc-Dowell, the diarist, scribbles, in a hand marked by excessive balloons, balloons intent on lofting the *i*'s of her composition above the other letters. She's in bed, just before sleep, surrounded in a bunker of throw pillows and stuffed animals. *Like for example what was that outfit that Annabel was wearing, she came into the office and she was wearing this suit, you'd probably get it at Ann Taylor, gray with pinstripes, some kind of cheap silk shirt, not even a good one, pumps with ankle straps, and get this — white nylons, and that's a weird look on a black girl. So I ask around a little and Jeanine tells me that Annabel has to go see a lawyer. Something to do with her brother again. I have definitely been avoiding her since I heard about the whole thing, because I wouldn't say I knew Samantha Lee well or anything like that, but I saw her, you know, at parties. There's all kinds of girls from the art world that you see them around, but you don't want to seem like you don't care about somebody who got hurt. Maybe she's going to have really horrible scars. Of course, Annabel says her brother didn't do it, and that's what they all say. The truth is I never trusted her that much to begin with. I can work with anyone pretty much, that's one of the qualities that anyone would have to talk about if they were writing a reference letter for me or something, or if I were doing an interview, I can work with anyone.*

Which reminds me, we're trying to hire an intern again, and since Annabel had to go wear her Ann Taylor outfit out to see a lawyer, that only left me and Jeanine to do the interviewing for the interns, and they were all these boys who have to know everything, like one guy comes in and wants to talk about how horror movies from the fifties were like revolutionary texts or something, and Czech psychoanalysts, and The Crawling Eye *and* It Came from Within, *this is supposed to impress me, but it doesn't impress me at all. Thing is, the interns always want to direct, but they'd be a lot more interesting if they wanted to produce or they wanted to be marketing experts. Besides, all they're going to do is messenger videotapes and file things, whatever, write coverage on scripts that somebody's aunt sent to the office. I don't give a shit if* The Crawling Eye *is meant to be an allegory, I just really don't care.*

Vanessa's mom is rehabbing out in some hospital in Brooklyn, so Vanessa's been even weirder than usual. Honestly, I don't know where she thinks the company is going and if she even has it together enough to keep the company going. Of course, my mom is in the living room, drinking dessert wine and watching reports about politicians arguing in Florida, and that's pretty good when you compare it to your mom being in some rehab in Brooklyn with skanky crackheads.

Anyway, in the afternoon, the Vanderbilt girls called, because they had finally gotten out of bed, and they said there's going to be a righteous party on for when Mercurio launches his clothing line, which is going to be called PussyWhipped, already he has this logo that's going to be on everything, it's going to be the best logo ever, that's what they were saying, and they tried to explain to me what the logo looked like, but come on. That's just stupid. You can't describe a logo over the phone. Logos are meant to be seen, not digitized. And making the logo before you make the clothes is like making the movie poster before you make the movie, but I guess a lot of movies do get made that way. In fact, I have been making little sketches of the bus poster for The

Diviners, *because I figure this will really help us. Okay, my idea is that the beginning of the show, the first episode, has to start with this big army sweeping down over some big plain. I mean, Mongolia, right, somewhere around there, it's some country no one ever heard of, like what are the names of those countries over there? Like Uzbekistan or something. So the army is sweeping low down over some plain in Uzbekistan, I bet if there's not a desert plain there, no one will know any better, and anyway they're supposed to be Huns, so the Huns are sweeping down across the plain, pillaging and raping innocent girls, whatever it is that these armies do and the camera is sweeping above the army, like from a helicopter, above these men, just a ton of men, a whole bunch of men, and they're all sweaty and wearing jerkins, right? I don't care if the Huns didn't wear jerkins, it doesn't have to be historically accurate, it has to be sexy, and lots of the guys have bloody slices or cuts on their biceps and maybe on their faces, with just a little bit of blood, and that's what's going on down there with a lot of hacking and stuff and people are getting sliced. There are men on horses, but if you look up the hill toward the top, you see one general, I mean, did they have generals? Whoever their leaders are, one is riding down behind the marauders and one other man is turning the other way, and he's got this bright light on him, and he's raising this stick high above his head, could be a crutch from some old war injury, at first you're not sure, but then you are, it's not a crutch, it's a diviner's rod, and he's raising it above, because it indicates that there's another way to do things, and this guy, this really sexy guy with the divining rod, he's raising it above everything, and he's indicating that the diviner's rod is the way of peace, or whatever you want to call it. And that's my idea for the poster. It would look really good on buses. You know, buses have that big advertising space there.* The Diviners: A New Mini-Series brought to you by UBC. *Then some kind of marketing line:* Love, famine, war, thirst, half-naked men, ethnic cleansing, the creation of Las Vegas. Produced by Means of Production, in association with UBC. *Something like that.*

Here's the really strange thing I forgot to say. Lois never came in to-day. Never called or anything.

———

Okay, so let's just say I had the greatest idea ever for the company, just the greatest idea ever, Madison writes, the pink vinyl journal in her lap, last curlicues of smoke from a stubbed-out joint hovering over her bedside table with its pile of unread scripts. *The idea is so good that I should get my paw print in front of that theater in Hollywood, way ahead of Brad Pitt, who doesn't bathe enough. Anyway, here's the idea, which is about the intern problem. We have all these boys coming in, with their stupid ideas, like one boy comes in with the train station sequence from* The Untouchables *all storyboarded, like that's supposed to impress me, because the point is that we're a company that's mostly women except for this one womanizing jerk I wouldn't give the time of day to and an Indian TV wonk. We need a girl intern! So I'm invited to the program of student films at NYU, and I hate going to those things, because all the movies are about whether or not some French woman influenced Freud's conception of the death drive, or whatever, Jesus, get a pedicure or something. Anyway, so I noticed that the screenwriter for one of the films was a student called Allison Maiser. You'd think everyone in New York City would have the idea I was having, the idea about seeing if this Maiser was related to that Maiser, you know, head of UBC programming — I think Vanessa pitched him over the weekend. So I did a little checking, stealth phone calling, or maybe I made Jeanine do a little of the checking up, and it turns out that it's her, all right, only question is how can we get hold of her. So I call up the Vanderbilt girls, get them on the phone, they're back to talking about Pussy Whipped again, everything is Pussy Whipped this and Pussy Whipped that, I tell them to quit with Pussy Whipped, because my pussy is not whipped, I say look I have to figure out how to find this girl, this Maiser girl, and they put me on hold, seems like it's only five minutes, but I'm reading a script anyway, and that's okay because I love a story when you can just sink into it like it's the best boyfriend you ever had, which is what this script is like, seems like it's only five minutes later, and they say, we know how to get to her, we have her number, but we have something we need to tell you, it's really important. What's that? I say. They're interrupting each other. Are you sure you want to know? Of course I want to know. Well, she's like so not your type of girl. Who isn't? The Maiser girl. She might have her bottom lip pierced or something, or her tongue pierced. She's like a girl version of Dennis Rodman. I say, Forget about it! Dennis Rodman is so nineties! I say, it doesn't matter if Allison Maiser doesn't have any arms and legs! Because we'll put her to work licking stamps, even if we don't have any of those licking stamps anymore. We'll do that because as soon as she walks in the door, we can call her father and say, your daughter is the best intern! Your daughter makes all the interns seem like, I don't know, bricks of cheese! The Vanderbilts are skeptical, because they are almost certain that Allison is not a blonde either, not even a dyed blonde. She might have blue hair or something. They're giving me a warning. Who gives a shit, I don't always have to listen to them.*

So I give the Maiser girl a call later, and I put on my best office voice, and I say where I'm calling from, I say the magic words that work on any college student, I say that I'm from Means of Production, I say we're working on a Michel Foucault biopic, and we definitely need more help in the office, and we have heard good things about her short film, and it's not like she is immediately jumping for joy, which I guess figures since her dad is like the most powerful man on earth, but she agrees to come in around ten the next morning, assuming I can get to the office by then. I tell Annabel that she has to interview her first, and I don't tell Annabel who she is. I don't tell anyone who she is, because I want to savor the idea for a little while. It's worth savoring, because it's the smartest idea ever.

Oh yeah, other news. It's in all the papers! I don't know why this kind of thing should always be in the tabloids first, but you'd have

to be an idiot not to read the tabloids. This article says that there was
a rumor going around that Samantha Lee was on her cell phone at
the time she got hit in the head with the brick. I mean, maybe she
got hit because she was on the cell phone and talking really loudly
about bloating or something. I've wanted to kill a couple of people,
especially when they were talking about stuff like that during a movie.
I was watching one of those French movies, but you know it had
a crazed nymphomaniac in it, and suddenly, right at the big death
scene, someone takes a cell phone call. Takes the call and promises
to call back but she can't talk because right now she's in the theater,
and then the person says which theater it is, and how the movie is
really great, and it has a crazed nymphomaniac in it, when are they
going to get together.

The rumor in the paper says that there's a cell phone, and that the
cell phone will prove that Annabel's brother, a suspect in the case, was
actually calling Samantha at the time of the attack, and so he could
not have been the attacker, because he was calling from a land line,
and now there are all these police swarming around the spot where it
all happened, except that no one can quite find the cell phone, you
know, because it got knocked loose when half of her head was crushed
by the brick that the psychotic guy hit her with. The weird part is that
Annabel doesn't seem all that surprised by the news. Still, if she
planted the story, then I'm pretty proud of her, because that's a good
skill to have at your command, you know? I try to plant things in the
press all the time, and if I had better contacts, I'd plant even more stuff,
like that Mercurio is definitely going to be in The Diviners and that
I am destined to head one of the major studios.

I didn't go out tonight. I just came home and painted on skin care
products. Then I ran around the house terrorizing the dogs. They don't
know it's me, because my facial mask is purple.

P.S. Still no Lois.

The super went to Lois's apartment to see if she was dead, Madison writes on Wednesday, after the big party for PussyWhipped, Mercurio's sportswear line. Because she's a little drunk, she's writing in her lingerie, feeling fat, like a porpoise splayed on an expensive mattress. *So far all we know is that Lois is not answering the door, and we should probably file a missing persons report, but Vanessa doesn't want to do it yet, because someone from Lois's family should do it. As far as I'm concerned the question is whether Lois actually has a family, because I'm betting she was spawned by an adding machine or a calculator or one of those slide rule things. Right from the first second when I got into the office Vanessa was on the rampage, and first it was back to that thing about how we had to get the* fuck *out of the* fucking *office because it's a* fucking *dump and it depresses the* fuck *out of her, like I rented the suite or something. I asked where she wanted to move the office, and she says downtown of course, because everyone wants to be downtown, but personally I like the office here. Because my commute is really easy. And if I had time to skate now I would, at the rink, and I would wear a cashmere scarf and I would skate backwards under the big tree, and I would drink hot chocolate and tell some man what a hunk he was.*

I pass this kid on the way in, I don't even know whether it's a boy kid or a girl kid, it's just some kind of kid thing, and it's sitting on the folding chair by the front door, near Jeanine's desk, and this kid thing is wearing some shredded black stuff that got thrown out in the Dumpster at some heavy metal club, I mean, I guess it's clothes, but who knows, the fishnets are so full of holes that the net couldn't catch orca, and she's got so much metal sticking out of her face that you could hang tinsel on her and stick an angel on top, and the amount of eye makeup, don't even get me started, and her eyes are totally closed, so it looks like she's sleeping, in the chair, and I sort of look at Jeanine, and Jeanine looks at the girl, and since the girl is sleeping, no one wants to wake her up. It's amazing that she's sleeping, because Vanessa is on the rampage, but she's definitely asleep, and Vanessa, who doesn't pay any attention to things if she doesn't want to, she doesn't pay attention, and I just go into the office, and Annabel comes in, looking worried and still wearing the Ann Taylor outfit, although she seems to have changed her blouse, and I ask her if things are okay, because now the papers think that there's some kind of conspiracy between the guy who drove his car into the store in the Diamond District and the Samantha Lee attack and the desecrated temples on Long Island and some one-eye sheik on Atlantic Avenue, there's headlines about Waves of Hatred, *of course, it's got to be some kind of Islamic thing, like when that guy blew up the building in Oklahoma City it was supposed to be an Islamic thing, but it turned out to be rednecks. But Annabel is not feeling great because the police still want her brother. He was supposed to be at her parents' house, but then he left or something, and supposedly he's just moving around, by train or who knows what.*

The good news today is that Vanessa thinks UBC is really seriously considering The Diviners. *Who knows how they decide this kind of stuff, I guess they talk to advertisers, and they get the poster guy to come up with some kind of poster. Of course, I told her that I have a really good idea for the poster, but she just waved me off. The bad news is that there seems to be like three different people out there claiming to represent the project, and Vanessa has been calling Vic Freese at the Michael Cohen Agency, and I could hear her yelling in my office. Later she comes in and tells me that Vic is representing the writer of the original book, who is named Melody or something, and then there's another version out there with Leonard Nimoy attached as a director, that version is by Shelley Ralston Havemeyer or somebody, and then there's our version, which is totally different. Apparently, we have coverage of the Nimoy treatment, and there are no Mongolians in it. How could there be no Mongolians? The whole point was to start with the Huns! I feel like I want to have Huns in the story, and I'm especially happy with that poster that I sketched out. What if they change it and the story winds up being about a dysfunctional family in the suburbs with a misfit kid who gets voted the most likely to succeed at the prom?*

That would suck. Maybe one diviner is like another, because they're all in touch with some kind of magical power, and we should just take what we can get, and if that means executive producer credits for Vanessa and me, well, okay, move on.

I called the Vanderbilts to say that there are three different versions of our story out there, and it can't be like with Weird Science, *you know, there was some other science movie that came out at the same time, oh yeah,* Outbreak, *or whatever that one was, the plague movie glut, you know, there are just not going to be competing versions of the mini-series about diviners out there, not if we have anything to say about it, and then we go on this whole thing about Ranjeet, you know the Indian guy from the office, he was at the party for Pussy Whipped, and I guess he has taken off his turban, because he was wearing this Prada suit at the Pussy Whipped party, and somehow he got into the V.I.P. section, I don't know how he got over there, but actually he looked really hot. He's shaved his beard down to a little soul patch, and he has his hair all slicked back, and he's wearing the Prada suit, and of course I think he's just trying to get with all the girls, but he's not talking to the girls, he's talking only to the industry people, and when I go over to him, he gives me an air kiss and says that he's been talking about some British version of a Jane Austen book that I never read, and he's saying that it serves as a really good example of what* The Diviners *might mean, and I can see that he's nervous, there's a little line of sweat on his upper lip, and for a weird second I think maybe I should kiss him, that's the part that I'm really shocked by, that and the Vanderbilts saying who was that hot Indian guy, and I say he's not Indian he's a Sikh, they come from a tradition of peace and spirituality, and the Vanderbilts are like what the hell are you talking about, and even I don't know what I'm talking about. The thing is that Ranjeet was a car service driver, and now it turns out that he's smarter and more hard-working than anybody who works in our office, which is why he hasn't been around in a couple days, because Vanessa says he's seeing a lot of agents, talking about various projects, trying to find people to line up behind the mini-series.*

It has to be one o'clock when Annabel comes in the office laughing. Ohmygod, she says, I just figured out who that girl is. I say, what girl, and she says the one who's asleep out by Jeanine's desk. And I say, oh my god, that's a girl? Because I just wasn't totally sure it was a girl, I thought it might be like some kind of vole, and Annabel says that's no vole, that's a girl who wants to be an intern! Oh my god! I say, that's no girl that wants to be an intern, that's Jeffrey Maiser's daughter! Not the Jeffrey Maiser! Yes ma'am! I say, and it's your job to interview her first, and remember to be really nice to her and say yes to whatever she says she wants to do, because we just want to keep her on the hook for a while, at least until we get the whole mini-series thing hooked up, and we're still really laughing and I'm thinking why do I always forget that actually I really like Annabel, because when she's laughing it kind of makes the entire world seem good somehow, and that's when Thaddeus walks by, but it's like a ghost goes over our grave because neither of us wants to say anything in front of Thaddeus anymore. It's only a matter of time before he's not here, that's what I think, because Vanessa doesn't want to work with him, and he keeps turning up in the tabs, and he seems like he just got spanked, which he definitely should be.

I go out to the good sandwich place across the street that has the pesto, and I get a grapefruit and a Diet Coke, but not pesto, and when I get back Annabel has Allison Maiser in the conference room, and I can see them in there, and Annabel is pacing back and forth, and the girl looks like she might still be asleep. By the time I've eaten half of the grapefruit and thrown out the rest, it's my turn with Allison. Annabel sighs and holds the door open.

Okay, I say going in the door, so here we are, and you've met Annabel, who will be your boss, and you've met Jeanine, who will also be giving you some things to do when we need them done. What else do you want to know about what we do?

Allison is just digging out some hangnail. She says, I don't think any of your movies are so great. I say I don't think they're all great, either, but my job is to make it possible for Vanessa to produce the kinds

*of movies she wants to produce, and then when I have learned every-
thing there is to learn about that I'll make my own movies, and hope-
fully all of mine will be great. She says, you guys need a lot of help with
story editing. I say, actually what we need is an intern who can do the
intern stuff and who wants to learn. You'll be going to the houses of international stars, like, say, Marcia Firestone, we worked with her on
our last project, and you could go over there to her apartment, and help
her get ready for the shoot. Our last intern got to go over to her place,
make her coffee, make sure she got to the shoot on time. She's just not
choosing her roles very well anymore, Allison says. Well, listen, I say,
why don't you tell me what you think you could contribute. She
launches into this amazing speech, well, I'll tell you what kind of
woman I am, and of course I can tell that she'd have a "y" in
"womyn" somewhere, because it's just that kind of thing, she says: I'm
the kind of woman that can't read for a very long time, because I have
a really short attention span, so I don't want to sit around reading
things, and I get really nervous when there's a lot of pressure, I just
can't stand it when people yell at me, so I don't want to be yelled at,
and I don't care who's doing the yelling because if anyone yells at me
I'm just going to walk out the door. I have a really upset stomach, they
think I might have Crohn's disease or something, and I need to know
that I'll have access to a bathroom, and that no one is going to say
anything about the fact that I have to use the bathroom frequently.
And I only want to work on the experimental projects, I don't care
what other stuff you're working on, I don't want to have anything
to do with any Hollywood movies, and I don't want to talk to anyone
at the big studios, because they're all stupid. What I bring to you is
my future, and my future is going to be big, and you guys can be a part
of that, or you can not, but I know that anyone who has me working
for them is going to employ one of the most promising talents of her
generation, that's what I think, and I don't want to have to come in
until eleven, and I get as many personal days as I want.*

Okay, I say to her, the job is yours. Welcome to Means of Production.

Tonight I had another date with Zimri Enderby, Madison writes, wearing silk pajamas, for the hour is late, _but before I get to that, I should just say that today Vanessa didn't show up at the office, and I can't remember the last time that happened. I guess it's something to do with her mom. Also, there was a note from her on my desk, I guess from yesterday, at the end of the day. The note was about Lois DiNunzio, and it said that she was pretty sure Lois hadn't been murdered, because she'd been going through the books, and it's clear that there's a lot of money missing over the last few months, and she thinks that Lois probably took some of the money with her, and she thinks it might be something like fifty thousand dollars missing. Maybe even more. Who knows what we'll find once we start poking around in accounts payable and all the expense accounting? And since tomorrow is Friday and that means payday, we have to make sure there's money to pay everyone. She asks if I can keep it to myself, maybe we'll talk to Thaddeus if we have to._

It's pretty scary, because what are we going to do when the rent comes due? We need to get something going, like the Otis Redding project, or the mini-series, or else we're going to have to lay some people off. At least we don't have Lois's salary to worry about, this pay period, but we also don't have anyone looking after the books. Probably we'd lay off Jeanine first, but Jeanine's smart enough that she could do the books for a while. Until we get some project going somewhere. It was like a dungeon in the office, and we're all waiting to hear if someone will call about UBC. I even called up the Vanderbilts and told them that we had to spread some evil rumors about Vic Freese and the Michael Cohen Agency, or else they're liable to get their especially dumb version of The Diviners _sold, and we'll all be getting day jobs in retail. I could always audition for the holiday show at Radio City, they always need subs in the violin section._

Which reminds me, Vanessa called in later saying that her mother might have left the hospital, at least one nurse told her that her mother left the hospital, but her mother isn't answering the phone at the house. I know I should try to help out, but what do you do with Vanessa? You sure don't try to hug her or anything, because she's just not the type of girl that you'd go hugging. I'm not sure I could hug her, for one, and another thing, she just hates me. It wouldn't really do any good.

Anyway, it all gave me the idea to call Zimri Enderby for dinner. I could tell that the Vanderbilts were still hot for him, because I kept seeing his picture in the paper at philanthropic things. Like there was a picture of him with Mrs. Astor at the library, or somewhere else his name was in boldface. It said he was a venture capitalist specializing in Internet-related ventures, and it said that he had also been an early investor in a business called Interstate Mortuary Services, which sounds pretty creepy, but I guess dead people have to go somewhere.

Zimri met me at this sweet new restaurant in Tribeca called Slab. The chef was trained in Lyons, and it's like his third restaurant, and I had to work extra hard to get the table, like I basically had to promise that we would shoot something at the restaurant or have an entire movie catered by Slab, but I don't know if we'll do that because some people are vegetarians, you know, and Slab is not for them, at Slab you get to choose your own cut of meat, and you get to say how you want it done and with what kinds of sauces and so forth. Zimri thought it was the greatest because he comes from Utah, and apparently there is a lot of meat out there. I was looking around to see if there was anyone I knew at Slab, I'm pretty sure that I saw whatshername, that actress from movies of the seventies and eighties, Pia Zadora.

I was explaining it all to Zimri, about Harold Robbins, how when you read Harold Robbins it was all about zipping through the narrative sections to try to get to the dirty parts. Never enough dirty parts, as far as I was concerned, and I learned a lot about things from these Harold Robbins books. He always had bad euphemisms for body parts. Zimri says he wasn't allowed to read any books like that when he was a boy, because of how strict his parents were. Mostly he read westerns, where there were wholesome descriptions of the range life and battles with the Indians, but even that was sort of borderline material. I keep thinking that people basically all believe the same things, but maybe I just have no idea. Also, Zimri tells me that I look really pretty, and that he's lucky to be out with such a beautiful woman, but I still feel like I'm fifteen, because I'm living at home, and I wonder when that waiting-room feeling of being adolescent is over. But I tell him that I'm touched by what he says.

Next, I ask Zimri why if he's such a good-looking man, and if people from where he comes from get married young and start families, why isn't he married, and what's he doing in New York, which is about the last place most people from Utah would want to be. Zimri gets a serious look and says that in order to explain all this he has to explain more about the idea of mission, which is this idea that when you are of a certain age you have to go out into the world, and you have to try to evangelize for the church. (I already know this stuff but I let him tell me anyway.) Some people go far away. They go to Zimbabwe, or they go to Congo, or they go to Malaysia, or something, and they know that their faith is with them, except that sometimes the faith isn't with them. This is what I'm pretty sure Zimri was trying to say. It's the first time some people are away from home, and they've never had a drink, they've never even had caffeine, and they're out there in the world, in Zimbabwe or something. It's a big world, Zimri says, and he says it in this gentle way, like he wishes he could protect even me from it.

The thing is, Zimri came to New York on his mission, and he worked for a while in the branch of a genealogical library that they have here, up near Lincoln Center, and he filed stuff, and that's how he paid his rent, filing pieces of microfiche, although his parents also gave him money, and he went out into the streets sometimes, and he tried to talk to people who were living in the streets, and most of the time no one would have anything to do with him, he says, and he didn't think he made more than one or two converts in the time he was in New York, and he never got into much trouble either, although, and here he says he's being really honest with me, he says, he saw beautiful women

*every day, everywhere he went, he saw women of such beauty. And he
went to the opera, and he went to hear jazz, and he learned that black
music was this beautiful thing, and everywhere in New York City there
was this beauty and this despair and the two things were right next to
each other.*

*The reservation had to be for late, so Slab was clearing out a little
bit, and we'd been there a while, and Zimri had been telling me about
trying to convert some guys down near the Bowery, because there were
still a lot of homeless guys down there, they were like historical characters, the men who still remembered the old Bowery, and one of these
guys gave him the flask and said, taste this, and as if he were punctu-
ating the story, Zimri picked up my glass of wine, because he didn't
have one, and he held it up and got a good long smell of its smell, and
his eyes sort of went crossed for a moment, and he said, that's got a real
kick to it. And that's when I thought, well, I really like this man.*

*It'd be a lie if I said that I didn't think about how Zimri was good
for me and good for Means of Production, maybe even good for* The
Diviners, *and I don't want to start lying in my journal, so I'm not going to say I didn't think about those things. That's why I went out with
him in the first place. But suddenly I didn't feel like that was why I
was here, suddenly I thought that I liked this man, and that maybe I
was wanting to kiss him and maybe I was wanting to do some other
things that I don't exactly feel like writing down yet.*

*Everybody looks good in candlelight, and Zimri looked handsome
in candlelight. You wouldn't think a place called Slab would have such
a nice interior, all maroon and navy blue and everything. It's just for
cigar-chomping bond traders and their cronies. But Zimri looked handsome. Maybe it was because I wasn't supposed to kiss him that he looked
so sexy. Maybe it was that I didn't know what would happen next.
Maybe it was that you weren't supposed to think certain things about
a man who believed in God, and that's definitely the case with some of
the things that I was thinking about. The Vanderbilts were always asking why I didn't date anyone. Who was I supposed to date? Some musician with his underwear showing and he probably had some kind of*

disease? After I was with Thaddeus, I said to myself that I didn't want to go through that again, especially not with some idiot actor guy with not a single brain cell in his head and no heart where his heart should have been, and so I just made my job something I loved, and it still is the thing I love, that's the truth. But I also loved this moment when I finally asked a man if I could kiss him, just like that, and it was like a big emancipation to say that I wanted to kiss him.

He said yes.

Well, his hotel room was as big as my parents' apartment, which is big for a hotel room, and it was at the top of the hotel, and his hotel was downtown, it was the Soho Grand, and he walked me past the bar, with his arm entwined around my arm. At night that bar is all willowy girls wearing not enough clothes, and they were all dancing by the bar, they didn't even buy those outfits, they were paid in those outfits, and Zimri was saying to me, we're just going to kiss, that's all we're going to do, and suddenly I thought he was the boy on the mission again, the boy on the mission who had the wine glass of New York City held up to his nose. And soon we were through the lobby, and soon we were in the elevator, and soon we were in his hotel room, and soon we were on his bed, and not a single item of clothing was coming off, and I don't even know if I want to write about the stuff that happened after this part, because maybe some things are meant to be in your memory only, not even in your journal, because I don't want my older self looking back at these lines and saying I shouldn't have done what I did with that poor man who didn't know what he was getting into, because I heard a man calling out my name, and I loved hearing my name, I loved it, and I'm not going to say I didn't love it, and when we were done he had his face in his hands, and he said he was grateful and he held me like he was grateful and like he wanted to be grateful again soon.

He said he intended to work with us too.

22

There's a commotion taking place beneath the study of the Reverend Duffy, on the first floor. But he's not ready yet to take a hand in this commotion. He applies himself instead in the matter of homiletics, as it was passed on to him by his teachers and as he has practiced it for thirty-five years, most of it in this parish, here in Newton, Massachusetts. Less through dogged persistence has he practiced his calling than through an inability to think of what else to do. It's his portion and his cup. He has remained in this parish, and this parish is full of stories. Why, there was the time his choral director took up with one of the parishioners. The story would have barely risen to the level of gossip were it not for the fact that the choral director, Brian, and his inamorato, Archie, were both married to women at the time. Quite a story, and it required all his pastoral skills. The wives declared that their sex lives had been more than adequate.

Stories of parish life sustained him when he wasn't sure if there was anything new to the job after the fifty or seventy-five marriages and just as many funerals, who knew how many baptisms and confirmations. The church calendar often looked to

him like a child's roller coaster, with gentle, predictable acclivi-
ties and declivities, and not much else. Here he is again at the
end of the church year, coming up on Advent, that time of reflection, when the symbolism is so comforting: the all-powerful
disguised as a defenseless baby in mean estate.

Well, not quite yet. First, the end of the church year. Time of
eschatological imaginings, as in the week's reading from Hebrews: "It is a dreadful thing to fall into the hands of a living
God." Not yet the advent of the baby with the fancy halo, not yet
the time of the dove fluttering above the baby. Not yet. Instead,
we are here where the metaphors are not comforting. So perhaps
it's appropriate that his wife is downstairs shouting at his biological son, which, it should be said, is an unusual thing in the
household of the reverend. The shouting mostly came to its conclusion when the older, adopted son left. Still, some shouting
does not mean that he must be immediately involved. When
William Duffy, the eldest, was young there was much gnashing of
teeth. There was never enough of anything to salve the open sore
of William's adoption, not to mention the unforgivable fact of
William's being of a different race. If only they had known of
identity politics in the seventies what they know now at the *fin de
siècle*.

At present, William is in difficult legal circumstance, and it is
this circumstance that leads the reverend to the commencement
of next Sunday's homily, the notes on which he will embellish ex-
tempore, according to his usual style. Start on Sunday, work the
whole week in a leisurely way, avoid the oppression of deadlines.
He types the words on his old Smith-Corona, with its warm, percussive music:

```
You may be surprised to learn that it has been
nearly two decades since I felt any certainty
about the existence of the Almighty ---
```

A relief when he types the line, and how many times he has thought of typing it before, never feeling that it was right, always feeling that it would shock the parish, perhaps even more than the liaison between Brian and Archie. The instructor in homiletics always advised getting down associations first, whatever they were. So he will get down all the thoughts and, likewise, all the uncertainties he has at the end of this jubilee year. He is uncertain about many things. His uncertainties are the "dreadful thing," as advertised in the epistle to the Hebrews. Where are the saints who are supposed to be abroad in the land, in whom we might delight? The Reverend Duffy does not know where they are and he doesn't know if they will come again in such a way that there is no doubt associated with them. The saints will not come on a particular day, wearing a particular robe, and with a particular program, and this is because the time of saints is past:

```
You may be surprised to know that when I pray
I often do not know what to say and in reply I
receive only silence ---
```

He can hear his wife begging to know where his younger son, Maximillian, has been. Where has he been spending these last nights? With which of his friends did he allegedly stay, and will the parents of these friends vouch as to the facts? It is known that William, the elder, turned up briefly in the house, on Friday, speaking only of a need for a short vacation from his work, though in fact his entire life seems to have been a vacation. It is known that William is in an enormous amount of trouble, because almost immediately after his appearance the Reverend Duffy and his wife began to receive telephone calls about William's trouble, which trouble came to pass in New York City. First among this sequence of dreadful revelations was the call from his daughter, Annabel, the middle child, whom the reverend loves most, though a father is not meant to love one child above the others. His daughter explained to them about the young Asian woman, and the reverend's wife, Debby, wept there at the kitchen table, and she asked why they had all this going on *now,* alluding to other periods of trouble in their union and their family. The reverend held her briefly, though he was no good at holding people. He was better at a certain stiff resolve, and this is perhaps what made him effective at the weddings and funerals of the Congregationalists of Newton, Massachusetts, where stiffness has a long history.

His daughter called, and then his wife went upstairs to do the reconnaissance. In their younger son's room she saw the curtains blowing in like sails on the sea vessel of calamity. Her two sons had gone out the window and shimmied down the tree, as though they were teenage hoodlums, and the window was open, and now they were gone. If this was not a story as full of metaphors as the powerless baby in mean estate, well, then the Reverend Duffy did not know his biblical stories.

The Gospel reading for the last Sunday of the church calendar is from Mark, and the homily had better deal with it. The only problem, seeing as how the reverend is cataloguing his uncertainties while his wife interrogates their son downstairs (she will not be trifled with, et cetera), is that the reverend doesn't believe that Mark actually wrote the passage attributed to him here. The fiction of Mark is perhaps one of his uncertainties, as is the liberally embellished narrative of Jesus, especially in passages such as this one, wherein it feels that powerful bishops or church leaders are retroactively attempting to foreshadow kinds of martyrdom that had probably already taken place by the time of their subsequent redaction, in order that the wandering mendicant Jesus of Nazareth should come off as a fine prognosticator:

9 You must be on your guard. You will be handed over to the local councils and flogged in the synagogues. On account of me you will stand before governors and kings as

witnesses to them. 10 And the gospel must first be preached to all nations. 11 Whenever you are arrested and brought to trial, do not worry beforehand about what to say. Just say whatever is given you at the time, for it is not you speaking, but the Holy Spirit. 12 Brother will betray brother to death, and a father his child. Children will rebel against their parents and have them put to death. 13 All men will hate you because of me, but he who stands firm to the end will be saved.

This is just the kind of End Times nonsense that supports an entire industry of televangelist frauds, who learned their skills, the reverend thinks, not from theologians but from manufacturers of underarm deodorant. It nauseates the Reverend Duffy, this type of scriptural passage, it depresses him, but at the end of the church calendar, it is unavoidable. The people who incline toward this kind of bunk, or the Book of Revelation, are the ones with borderline personality disorder or a deluxe helping of delusional narcissism. They need clinical care. His son William, for example, always liked the Book of Revelation best because of all the special effects. And there are plenty of those in the reading today:

```
I don't care for the readings, and I question
their relevance. There's always evidence of an
ending, if we look for it, but where there's
an ending there's always evidence of a begin-
ning. I say look for the beginning. Look for
the opening of the blossom. For the intimation
of spring.
```

His wife and he were on separate extensions when they got the news. The Reverend Duffy asked Annabel if it would be possible to contact the family of Samantha Lee, the injured girl, and this was his rather insistent question for the first twenty-four hours. Is there a way for us to contact the family of the poor girl? So much so that his wife asked him if he did not care for his son. The reverend, stricken by the remark, looked deep, and he determined that he did believe it possible that William had perpetrated the attack. He had no trouble believing it, in fact, though he would tell no one this, not even his wife. Moreover, believing that his son had committed the assault, he nonetheless had no trouble continuing to love his flawed, reckless, impossible son, who knew more about physics and linguistics and engineering and a thousand other things than the Reverend Duffy would ever know, but who seemed unable to hold down any job more complicated than message delivery.

Downstairs, again, his wife, slamming some kitchen implement on a countertop, demands to know of Max how he expects what he has done — helping his brother avoid the authorities — will reflect on what the Reverend Duffy does, and his son replies in a measured voice, which the reverend can clearly hear through the floorboards (the parsonage is no vast mansion), that it's his father's ministry that has *allowed* him to do what he did. He says he would do it again. Well, his mother says, the window has new hardware on it now, and you owe it to your father and myself to respect our wishes, and you can go up there and look out the window for a while and imagine what you see on the far side of it because you're not going to be on the other side of that glass until the daffodils blossom.

```
The end, as we learn of it in Mark — a time and
place when certain people will be rewarded for
perfection and others consigned to the lake of
fire — is a convenience for those who are un-
able to shoulder the responsibilities of the
present ---
```

He turns off the typewriter with the sheet of paper still in it. He closes the office door behind himself. Down in the kitchen, he finds his wife, expert on adolescent psychology, with text-books spread wide around her. The boy has retired to his room. They are a couple of common laborers, the two of them, and if there are things that are never thoroughly discussed between them, then at least there is the sensation that they have worked in concert, they have labored, and it is in this feeling that gratitude sweeps through him, and he puts a hand on his wife's back and looks over her shoulder at the book, at its scientific language.

"I don't even know if he's been staying after school like he says," his wife remarks. "I don't know where the beginning and end of the truth are with him, and I hate the sensation of it. He was such a sweet little one."

The reverend grunts in assent. They will be in bed early, as they have always been, and there's no use eating some snack before bed, because it will not agree with him, even though he has a powerful hankering for a cookie. His wife will not tolerate crumbs in the bed.

"It's all going to work out," he says mechanically. "And if it doesn't, we'll be strong. We have always been strong."

Then he trudges up the back stairs.

Once, and this was fifteen or twenty years ago, he'd been at a party in town. The reverend had been at a party, which wasn't unusual, because he was often invited to parties. He was invited to play golf or tennis occasionally, and sometimes he was invited to give a speech at the high school or to officiate at a classroom debate on some ethical issue. He was a minister of the Congregational Church, and Massachusetts had Congregationalists before anything else, except the Pequods. He preached at a plain church building in the center of town, on a green, the First Congregational Church, and he lived in a small house two blocks away, because he needed room for his children. He was a pillar of the community.

And he came to be at the party, and there was a girl there, just fourteen or fifteen, and he realized that he had seen this girl a

hundred times over the years, with her friends and on the holidays. It was another of those instances when he realized that he
had been at the church long enough to have watched children
grow from their baptisms to their very adulthood. He had baptized this child, in fact, had made the watery cross upon her
forehead, her parents beaming proudly. He knew them well
enough, John and Barbara.

He'd come across her in her ballet class years, in her tree-
climbing years; he'd watched her in her homely years with the
braces and the skinny legs, and then he'd watched her in her
cheerleader years, and now he was seeing her in the flourishing
of her adulthood, at this party. He was watching her because she
was employed this night by her father, John, to serve drinks to his
friends, the other pillars of the community. She had certainly developed in a way that the Reverend Duffy had never expected.
He had never expected a girl that he'd baptized to be one of the
great beauties of her age. You never knew to expect such a thing,
but this was just what she looked like now: at the bar, with a
dozen bottles in front of her and a pitcher of water with which to
water down the whiskeys, just as if this, too, were baptismal water.

So much time should not have passed. Not with him doing what
little he had done, which was to pace through time as though it
were stepping-stoned with church calendars, without learning,
without growth. The girl was a symbol of this, of how miserly was
time in his life. Time had made him good at one thing and horrible at everything else, so that the blessings of the world were always elsewhere, never his. All the conversations he had that
night, he approached these conversations in the same graceful
way he always approached them. The people of Newton told him
what they had to tell him, with a certain cant of the head, a certain nervous gesture, how they were proud and terrified, and he
listened well, that's how he remembers it now, that he listened
well, and he spent the night stealing glances at the girl at the bar,
and she was a goddess of wine, so resolute, so statuesque.

The party proceeded into the kind of cheerful disorder that marked these events. The people who stayed were the ones you wished would leave. His own wife had left because Max was still in diapers then. And William was going through a rough patch in high school or maybe college. He can't remember which. The reverend himself became one of those guests you wished would leave, standing out on the patio. The more recognizable constellations were just visible through the light pollution and the cloud cover. Bare trees waved in the breeze. He saw the daughter, and the daughter was picking up drinks and coasters, and she was drinking from the drinks, surreptitiously. She was drinking and carrying the glasses off to the kitchen, and he followed her into the house, observing the methodical performance of her responsibilities, and then he watched as she went upstairs, already tipsy, no doubt. His body carried him along with her, as if he was drunk, too, upon her shadow. Then he surprised her in her bedroom.

In bed, on Sunday night, in his sleeplessness, he thinks of it again, as he has often thought of it. Here he is again, wishing that he could remember the language of the moment, because if he could remember it, then maybe he could undo it. How he surprised her, how she was slipping a sweatshirt over the polo shirt she'd been wearing. She remarked that he'd surprised her; he said he wished he hadn't. A simple exchange, at first, and innocent enough, for the moment.

Next, he invited himself to sit on the edge of her bed. She was standing before him because she was hoping he would leave, and he could see himself through her eyes. He wasn't so stupid as to think that she would want him, because he was the one who'd baptized her, after all, and he was bald, with the worst kind of baldness, not even a widow's peak, just patchy, and the hair sprouted everywhere else on his body, in his ears, in his nostrils, on his shoulders and back, and his brows grew together, and he had an ugly beard that grew all the way to his eyes, and he was puffy and soft, and he never ran, nor exercised enough to stem the tide of pudginess, and his appetite was enormous, insatiable, and the problem was constantly getting worse, and here were his squinting eyes, and his thick, embarrassing eyeglasses, and his bowlegs; he could go on with the litany of all the things that she could see in him, the first and last items being that he was old, old enough to have sired her. Where he'd once been young and revolutionary, now he was old. He'd gotten old in the church. And the church, it struck him, was exactly like this girl before him, a thing out of reach, a glimmering in the distance to which he could never quite get, because no matter how far he journeyed, it always seemed that he was still in the spot where he began. When would the heavenly annunciation be his annunciation? When would there be just a little whisper from the great voice in the ethereal skies? A pat on the back?

He could see himself in her eyes, and this should have stopped him.

What did he imagine he wanted? To offer some praise for her beauty that she would not have understood or that she would have thought *cheesy,* to use the language of the young? She was sixteen, or maybe seventeen, and even if she looked older, with her womanly breasts and her weary, off-kilter smile and her auburn hair and her green eyes, she was still a child. She would launch ships, maybe, or she would launch magazines and clothing lines, and there was no place in this for the likes of him. He can remember what she said next because she said it with a kind of generosity, and she didn't need to. She could have screamed, called for her father. She could have screamed, but she didn't. She said, "Reverend Duffy, have you maybe had a little too much to drink?"

Who hadn't? Everyone had had too much to drink. His own wife hadn't had too much to drink, because his wife was impossibly good, with reservoirs of goodness that debased him. She always had more energy for another homemade dessert that the kids would ignore. His wife had not drunk too much, but many others had, all the people who stayed too late at the party. If only drinking too much would explain it away, if only the gin bottle had an advisory about reckless behavior. Unfortunately, he'd drunk just enough to remember and to know better. Though his exact wording was lost, fifteen years later, the matter of his request was not. What he asked was if this sixteen-year-old girl would hold him.

When he reimagines it now, he reimagines it as if he were the fluttering dove himself, the holy spook, up near the corner of the ceiling, near some recessed source of interior illumination. Here he can watch as the Reverend Duffy asks a teenage girl to hold him. He can watch when, without waiting for assent or dissent, the reverend launches himself into her arms. What a foul tableau it is, for there is much music and merriment coming from elsewhere in the house. The music is the old rock music from the sixties, something like the Association or the Lovin' Spoonful or perhaps the sound track to *Hair*. There are whoops of laughter from out on the patio, and the Reverend Duffy has launched himself into the arms of the goddess of wine. The girl doesn't know she is beautiful yet, but she knows enough to recognize that she should not have a middle-aged man wrapped around her. She also knows that this middle-aged man should not be aroused.

Drink is said to increase the need and to decrease the ability, but it did nothing to dampen the arousal brought about by the teenage daughter. He could feel himself sweaty and desirous, in a way he had not been with his wife in a long time, though they had their loving and generous middle-of-the-night encounters. This was different; this was the lust that intended to conquer, that wanted to possess and overcome, that wanted to bend philosophy and history to its will and that broke the will of its subjects if it had to. This lust would admit of no opposition. What could the teenage daughter do to fend off the first part of the debasement? She crumpled backward onto her bed, with him piling onto her as though he were a rugby enthusiast. He was in her arms, or some portion of her arms, as little as she could get away with, and he tried to wrap his hands around her. In recollection, this is a fine moment in which to examine the particulars of her room, its immaculateness, the football team banner, the guitar case in the corner, the stuffed animals piled on the hope chest, the lacy curtains, the baby blue bedspread, the sliding closet door, which was open just enough to glimpse some of her girlish outfits.

She began to wriggle free. She spoke of his post, emphatically, "Reverend, Reverend," the very thing that he was and is not, worthy of reverence, as if saying this would loosen him up somehow, and he was pouring out his all but drunken heart, the reservations that he had then and still has now, that any person of substance would have, that his profession was founded on the kinds of horseshit that you tell sensitive children to get them to sleep; he told her that we all lived here in emptiness and desolation, recognizing ourselves nonetheless as isolates in the infinitude of space, little asteroids of frozen rock in the endlessly expanding nothingness of creation; he tried to get out a couple of lines of poetry in some language that the girl could understand and then, and this is the worst part, he attempted to caress her breast. He remembers this part particularly well. He remembers that he attempted to touch her breast. He remembers that he put his hand down upon her breast, as if he might feel its fullness, as if he might feel where the nipple slumbered, where she would be as the Madonna once was, a feeder of human potential, and perhaps he even wished to suckle at the nipple of the girl, but the girl, who in this time had not ceased from saying "Reverend, please, Reverend, please," pleading, came up with some surfeit of strength, and she heaved him sideways off of her, and with tremendous haste, she skittered into the bathroom next door, where he could hear the little *ping* of the push-button lock sealing her in.

His clothes were disarranged. His shirt needed to be tucked in. He went to the bathroom door. Probably she could hear him. She could hear him brushing softly against the bathroom door like a house cat against a shin. Most likely, she could hear him listening to her as she listened, and then she could hear him giving up, could hear the dawning of woeful recognition on his part as he headed down the staircase, straightening his tie. Maybe she could hear him talking to her father, telling John and Barbara what a fabulous party it had been and how he hoped to see them again soon, and then maybe she could hear him, just down the street, starting up his ten-year-old Volvo. If she could hear it, she did so without any pity, because no pity was owed.

That's what he thinks about in the middle of the night. Waiting still, after all these years, for the repercussions.

———

On Monday, having slept fitfully, he is back at work on the sermon, for a few hours, before walking over to the church to see if there are any calls. There he will banter with the elderly widows who work for him selling picture postcards of the beautiful old church on the green and helping to plan potluck dinners and Bible study classes.

His wife, the forgiver and forgetter, yells to him that he should come down and have some breakfast, and she is right, of course, so he comes down. He's been up since dawn, in his office. He asks, shouting as he descends the stairs, if there is any news on the answering machine. His wife says not. He asks if Annabel called again. She says not. He says he slept badly, and she slept badly, too, and yet there was no moment when they reached out for each other across the old lumpy king-size mattress. She asks what he will do today, though she knows what he will do today. And he knows what she will do, which is work on her textbook and then go to the office, where she has a couple of hours of private practice, and during these hours he agrees to be back at the house, to answer the phone and to keep an eye on Max.

"What's the sermon about?" she asks.

"'It is a dreadful thing to fall into the hands of the living God,'" he says. "Oh, and another section: 'You sympathized with those in prison and joyfully accepted the confiscation of your property, because you knew that you yourselves had better and lasting possessions.'"

He pries a piece of burnt toast from the toaster, butters it without conviction. "Good news, if true."

"Maybe if we told Max that his property would be joyfully confiscated?"

"He'll come around," the reverend says.

He doesn't even sit at the kitchen table. He stands. The toast is a disappointment.

"I have no point of view," he offers. "My angle is that I write this sermon at a dark moment in human history, and I am a mediocre man, and these are mediocre times. None of the gauzy apocalyptic promises will cover over all of this, the daily horror of people at their worst and most selfish. I don't quite know what to say after that."

His wife has a gentle expression of disapproval, which involves some mix of eyebrows and one corner of the mouth appearing to smile while the other frowns. This is her commentary on the sermon he proposes. He chokes down the toast in silence before banishing the crusts to the trash barrel. Then he rinses his plate and houses it in the drying rack.

"I wish you lots of inspiration," she says, and excuses herself. Her office was formerly Annabel's bedroom. It still has a few movie posters in it, as well as a radically sloping ceiling that would make it uncomfortable for the men in the household. His wife's voice disappears into the living room, reminding him of various responsibilities, and there's more, distantly, from upstairs. The telephone rings as soon as he has alighted at his own desk, and it's the police from New York City. Wanting to know again if William has made contact with the Duffys. The reverend has the typewriter turned on. He has just written these lines:

```
If you believe the reports, Martin Luther King
Jr. was not, when writing his dissertation,
good at citing his sources. If you believe the
reports, President Kennedy kept files on his
opponents and had chemically enhanced romps in
the White House.
```

When it is his turn, he tells the police what he knows, that his son appeared on Friday night and disappeared almost immediately, and they have not heard from him since. He says that his son did not perform the crime of which he is accused, and he says this as a matter of course. And he whites out some of his homiletic text by hand while he talks to the police. There is some back and forth with the detective on the other end of the line about the exact time that William appeared in the house on Friday, the time he left, and so forth. What was he wearing? "He was well turned out," the reverend says, and the police ask if he would please call if William attempts to contact them, and the reverend says, "Of course." Soon after, Annabel calls and offers to come and stay with them until it is ironed out, and she asks how the reverend can get any work done, and the reverend tells Annabel not to come. She has her job, her scripts, and she should have time for these things. His wife, who has by now picked up the other extension, agrees.

"Where's Max?" Annabel says.

"In his room," his wife says. "Where, for the moment, he belongs."

"Did your mother —" the reverend says.

"She told me," Annabel says. "I have a feeling he's going to —"

"Good-bye, sweetheart, work hard," the reverend says, and leaves the women to it.

Has he mentioned in the sermon yet that everyone needs to

get their pledge cards in? Yes, it's the time of year when every sermon features a hundred different appeals for cash money. 'Tis
the season to remind the affluent that the First Congregational
Church of Newton is a symbol of civic pride and that its upkeep
is not inexpensive, since the building was constructed in 1721, after an earlier church was outgrown. It has been in continuous
service ever since. It has had only twenty parsons in all those
years, in part because of a pair of long-suffering types in the
nineteenth century. It is worth reminding the congregation of
this eminent history, and that the Reverend Duffy is now in
fourth place on the all-time list in terms of duration of service.
He scrawls on a notepad: *Remember to ask for pledges.*

In the middle of the afternoon, the reverend does what he
never does, what he abominates as a pastor and an ethicist. He
goes to watch television in the family room. Max is down there,
wearing a pair of torn jeans and a T-shirt and an old mohair
cardigan. Father sits next to son, on the couch, and neither says
anything for a while, especially as the space of conversation is
currently occupied by some kind of talk show featuring women
of the plus sizes. The question is whether plus-size women are as
sexy as women of regular sizes. What the reverend does believe,
in the chatter of the indignant plus-size women, is that Max
knows where his brother is.

"Do you know where he is? Because I think you know where
he is. And I think your sister knows, too, and I wish you would
tell me, so that we can make sure he is all right and isn't making
things worse for himself. This is not a matter for individuals. It is
a matter for families."

Max pretends to be watching the plus-size women.

"He didn't tell me where he was going."

"Your story is full of holes. It's all going to come out eventually, and I don't want you feeling worse for what you have done
later. I'm offering you the chance to tell me what you know so
that you won't feel ashamed. Telling me will lighten your heart."

Max gets up unceremoniously, goes upstairs. Slams his door. The Reverend Duffy is now alone with the plus-size women and he sits through several commercial breaks, always coming back to the talk show, and then he falls into a stuporous slumber that comes on like fever. There is a sick member of the congregation, Mrs. Milliken, but he forgets about her. There is the bereaved family, the Ericksons, whose son just died of lymphoma. The stupor wipes away the Ericksons. The great forgetting of afternoon television is upon him, and he is asleep, and the commercials are singing their jingles into his slumbering ears, and they are telling him about excellent medications that he should ask his doctor about, Lipitor and Nexium and Elysium, they are telling him about feminine products, and they are telling him various things that will help him with the family wash, and they are telling him about other programs that he might enjoy, and all of these things are much louder than the responsibility of the last Sunday of the church calendar and the manifold signs of the end of the age, and he hears of Lipitor and Nexium and also of the stars falling from the sky and the heavenly bodies trembling. Never have the End Times been more apparent than in the combination of ranting of plus-size women and the traumatic napping of an insomniac Reverend Duffy, and when he wakes a half hour later, with the television unaccountably turned off, he feels acutely the disgust of a violent waking. He's nauseated and disgusted and hates the world, and hates himself for having watched the plus-size women when he should have been calling on the Ericksons, but instead of calling on the Ericksons, he goes directly upstairs to the office and to the typewriter, which still trembles and hums in the way that typewriters do:

1 As he was leaving the temple, one of his disciples said to him, "Look, Teacher! What massive stones! What magnificent buildings!"

2 "Do you see all these great buildings?" replied Jesus. "Not one stone here will be left on another; every one will be thrown down."

So it follows that edifices will fall, just as we all are fallen men and women, just as I am myself, who has given to this parish things he does not have, namely charity and love. Your faith gives me faith today, when my own family most needs it.

Dusk already! The days are getting so intolerably short, and the end of the year is coming, with all the dread of winter. His wife comes back into the house, and he doesn't even call out to her. She has gone and she has returned, and he has taken no notice of it. The tension would seem to call for something, but what is the something that it calls for? He has not had a stiff drink in many a year, but maybe tonight is the night for a stiff drink. He doesn't know how to sit still, nor what to do with himself. He hasn't done a legitimately ministerial thing all day, nor has he spoken to anyone but the police and his wife and son.

When he goes into the kitchen, his wife has some pasta boiling, which he might as well have made himself, as he is an expert boiler of pasta. They are here when the knock at the door comes. The two of them go to the door, he with the dishrag in his hands because he just tasted the pasta and pronounced it not quite ready, and when they open the door it is the door opened on the lesson of prodigality, on the lesson of the son who wastes his advantages and resources only to return home to be loved, to be loved because the prodigal son is now in the light on the front step, here he is, and the prodigal son is loved! He looks as if he has never been looked at, he looks as if he has set a new world record for dishevelment, and he has on no shoes at all, and his shirt is untucked, and his hands are waving madly, as if his hands have now liberated themselves, and he is crying this low, savage cry, the cry of relapsed madness; or the son seems to come in from the wilderness, even though there is no wilderness in Newton; there is no topographical wilderness here, the reverend knows, and yet tears are streaming down the face of the adopted son, and his parents are on the step, and they have their son in their arms, because the son has come home, and he is in their arms, and the three of them are there, in the light of the step, and the neighbors must be watching, but what does it matter if the neighbors are watching, damn the neighbors, what is God to the reverend and his son but an inadvertent thing, unless of course there is the action of grace in the moment of the return of the son, the son on the front step, wearing no shoes, cuts upon his feet and hands, who may or may not have done whatever it is he is accused of having done but who is now here, is now home, and his parents are with him, for he has no other place to go, and his father is the agent of forgiveness, and the agent of forgiveness is bringing the son into the house, all the things that divide us should not divide us, because those things are nothing, those things are just hesitations, and the wife of the reverend, the mother of the son, is saying, "Mercy, mercy," and she is picking up the phone, but the phone will not help, because the son's wickedness is now commuted, whatever it is, whatever it was, because the reverend is holding his son, his gigantic son; his son is in danger, and his father has not yet done everything he could do, nor has he believed as strongly as he could believe, but now he will, and now the father loves the son again, because the scriptures are correct:

It is a dreadful thing to fall into the hands of the living God.

23

You would think that the ward throve at night, that the inpatients of detoxification were at their best overnight, in half shadows, stirring up from their apnea. You would think that the wraiths would be up and wandering, mumbling as they passed. But you'd be wrong. Rosa alone is up, gazing out the window at the neon of the chain bookstore on the next block over. Maybe if she listens carefully enough to the sounds of the nightscape, cars toiling up Seventh Avenue, sirens, jets overhead, then she'll hear what's genuinely taking place, rather than what is not. It doesn't matter, though, how loud she gets them to turn up the television in the dayroom.

There are events that are almost certainly taking place, and then there are dubious events. Those conversations she heard today, those girls, the ones who work in publicity or whatever it is that they do. They were gabbing with the development expert at her daughter's company, gabbing about some intern she'd hired. "You wouldn't even believe how lazy this girl is; she sets a new record for laziness. She's so lazy that she can't be bothered to *refuse* to do anything, because it would take too much energy to refuse. She's so lazy that it's amazing she even comes in; she just sits there like a bump on a log, and it's not like she's doing her nails or anything because she doesn't have any nails. She chews at her nails, all the black nail polish is chipping off, and she bites them anyway." "Doesn't that make you sick? Plus, aren't you supposed to avoid eating your nail polish?" "Totally. You shouldn't eat it. I guess someone should design edible nail polish; maybe we should tell Mercurio." "Reminds me of those . . . those *edible panties* that that girl, who was that, used to talk about, remember?" "Wait, why does it remind you of . . . never mind, ick." Then, after Rosa overhears this conversation in her detoxifying head, she can't stop saying the words *edible panties,* as if these words are somehow the key, as if they are deeply relevant to the present, *edible panties,* and over dinner she can't stop herself from saying it. When she's at the dining table with the girl, the one with bleeding problems, she keeps saying "edible panties," and the girl keeps asking why. But Rosa, who finds the whole notion of these underdrawers shocking and improper, can't figure out why she keeps saying it, she just does.

That's a conversation composed of people she likes. If she has to be overhearing cellular phone traffic in her head, at least she'd prefer to overhear the conversations of people she favors. She could offer advice to the voices. "Is it true that you're having a problem with . . ." Whatever it might be. Unfortunately, her difficulty is not just with conversations of people she knows. Now if she stands too close to the window, she hears these telephone whispers from the entire expanse beneath her. They are out there in the universe, conversations drifting over her like a layer of digital smog. "Honey, no one is hotter than you; you are just the hottest thing I've ever seen in my life. Are you alone?" "Sure." "And what are you wearing, baby?" "You're not going to start in with this again, because last time you didn't talk to me for like three weeks afterwards, and it made me feel dirty." She doesn't know for certain what these people are talking about, but she has an idea. No one should have to overhear these conversations, which are a layer of pollution.

She heads for the pay phone, the one in the corridor that they all share. At the nurse's console, there's a night nurse, asleep in her chair, chin planted in the middle of her chest, mouth open. A fusillade of snores issues from that mouth. Rosa pays the nurse no mind and slips past her to the wall phone. She presses the zero in the keypad and waits. A sequence of beeps. An actor's voice comes on, the voice of Darth Vader. Before she can evaluate the particulars of the Vader voice, there's a hiss and another voice comes on. This voice asks her what she needs. "Well, you see, I'm in a . . . I'm in the . . . I'm indisposed . . . and I'm finding myself in this unusual situation. . . ." She waits for supportive words from the operator; none are forthcoming. "The situation is . . . well, uh, the situation is that there are certain telephone calls that are . . . that are —" Rosa tries to whisper the complaint, so that the night nurse won't be disturbed. The operator replies, "Do you need a number? Because that's what we're supposed to —" "Not at all," Rosa says, shuffling in her paper slippers, back and forth. "I don't need any numbers, I have all the . . . " "You're complaining about people who talk too loudly on their cell phones? I'm sorry, but you can't blame the telephone company for people who talk too loudly into their phones; you should take that up with the —" "That's not . . . ," Rosa says, "I'm saying that I . . . I'm saying . . . that I can *hear* the conversations —" "But where can you hear the conversations?" "*Everywhere,* everywhere I go, I can hear them in my head. . . . I can hear the people and they're having the . . . and I can hear what they're saying, even if . . . people I don't know very well. I keep expecting . . . I'm going to hear my ex-husband . . . with his floozies, I haven't . . . he hasn't . . . probably twenty years, but my daughter . . . she might want to . . . since he's her father, and if I could hear that conversation, maybe, but instead . . . or I

hear some businessman who's making some deal in a . . .
acquaintances . . . or I —" "Excuse me, ma'am, we can't —"
"She ought to be able to talk to that . . . her father. . . . I don't
give a goddamn whether I ever speak to him, but that's just not
right, and I want you to talk to whoever it is there that . . ."
"Ma'am?" "Your manager . . . I am a person who has connections. . . . I was . . . I used to know people who could get things
done, and maybe now I'm . . . maybe my circumstances . . . no
reason why your company needs to pick on an old woman," and
she tries to remind herself to pipe down, to keep it to a whisper,
but she can't help herself, because it's an outrage, you know,
these corporations, just not answerable. "You can't go filling my
brain up with these calls . . . no reason why a woman like me
should have to hear . . . and I guarantee you . . . you don't want
to have that kind of trouble on your hands —"

A dial tone by the time the night nurse comes over and takes
the handset from her, replaces it in its cradle.

"You can't be up doing this sort of thing."

"I was . . ."

"I don't care if your ass falls off, you can't be out here on the
phone at this hour. Now, get to your room." The night nurse puts
an arm around Rosa and walks her down the corridor. For a second, it's as if there's no time but this time of the corridor. As if
she needs just one thing to bring about the cessation of voices and
that thing is another person's arm around her. If human kindness
were reliable, then Rosa might leave behind these fortressed walls
and return to Eleventh Street, where she left off, to store up a new
supply of backdated magazines and newspapers while forgetting
to eat. But the fact is that human kindness must come to an end,
and it comes to an end right before the door to the room that she
shares with the slumbering obese woman. Inside, a darkness
more perfect and terrifying than any she has known. The nurse
says nothing, points into the space, and then Rosa follows the

end of her arm, the crooked pointing finger, and continues, tentatively, into the room as the night nurse firmly closes the door behind her. Immediately, Rosa can hear the voice of some politician, the mayor of the city, and the mayor is calling somebody, city councilman, or maybe it's the chief of police. Must be. The mayor is talking to this personage about his new program to prevent the spread of some menace that she can't, at first, identify. "Look, we've got to have something in place that deals with it; we have to indicate that we have *zero tolerance* for it because you know any time of day someone could be just walking down the street," and then gradually the nature of the call emerges, "and could allow *waste* to spread on the block, someone else comes along, you know, they could . . . there could just be a spreading of waste; we just can't have that." "But," remarks the other, "are you sure that you want to allocate resources on this? After all, even with the . . . and do we really think this is a pressing issue when we —" "Listen, your job is to implement, and what I think would do the trick is a small mobile force deployed at all the frequent locations, like around the parks, and we could issue summonses for people who don't discharge their obligations, and the reason we need to do this is that if someone sees one . . . one mound of waste, then he is going to feel that it's really not a critical situation and actually it's rather cold here in the middle of November and maybe it would be all right for Rover here to . . ."

Rosa gives a moan at the content of the exchange, and she whispers the words "dog waste initiative" to herself in bed, hoping that she can put aside these phrases, that the night might swallow her into its river of forgetfulness. But just as she's imagining the possibility of sleep, notwithstanding voices, the obese woman, whose somnolent form has uttered no word since first it was installed in bed, speaks out: "You can tell me."

"Tell you *what?*" Rosa asks.

"What's bothering you."

"I don't need to . . . This certainly isn't . . . My being stuck in here with no freedom . . . of movement . . . and the medication is making . . . it's making my foot twitch."

"Tell them."

"Who?"

The obese woman rolls over so that her massive form is facing Rosa's bed, and Rosa is almost certain that she can make out the glimmering beacons of her tiny eyes.

"You've been here for a week. They can't hold you unless you're a danger to yourself. So you tell them that you aren't suffering with whatever you're suffering with. Then they have to release you, because you are not a danger to yourself."

"What about —"

"There's an insurance angle, too. Insurance doesn't want to cover rehabilitation. Halfway houses, everybody knows. Even the doctors don't believe in them. Really, they just want to send you home."

"I'm as fit as —"

"They'll hold you if you mention hearing things or seeing bugs."

"I don't see any —"

Rosa glances at the clock on the table between them. After three, and she's no closer to sleeping than two hours ago. She doesn't know why she tells the obese woman about the telephone calls, which she feels she should conceal, but she does.

"What kind of telephone calls?"

"I can listen in."

"People are saying things about you?"

"Nobody says anything about me. . . . I'm an old woman. But I can listen."

"You can hear these conversations and not even one of them is about you?"

"Wait," Rosa says —

"The darndest thing I ever heard," the obese woman says. The obese woman has been in bed a week, having been lifted into bed and then occasionally turned by a team of four men; the obese woman is addicted to some incredibly powerful opiate, because of her aching knees and her stress-fractured feet; she'd been camped in front of the television for another week, looking forward to another episode of *American Spy* or whatever her program was, swallowing down the pills, in the chiaroscuro of narcosis, trying to decide whether or not the Clapper would really be a good thing to have in the living room.

"Wait," Rosa says. The static overcomes her. The crackle of the cellular telephone, as though the calls are not transmitting properly, as though the service is given to interruptions. Every third syllable is impossible to make out, the voices beginning to tell her the things she's not meant to hear. This one is coming from Washington, and she doesn't know if she can stand it if she has to listen to a lot of people talking about things having to do with Washington. "Got to get our people down there, get them down there in force; we need people, we need placards, and we're going to have to start paying people to do what we need them to do, *now*, which is that we need them on the ground there, because we need to make disbursements, get some of the young people working on the campaign, and we have to start paying these people to get on the planes right now. Hell, we have to start booking the seats, and we have to get them down there and we have to have them observing, we have to have them on the ground, wherever people are counting votes. Because we can't have them redoing what has already been done, so we need to start spending the money." Like the voice is not even having a conversation with another person but just rehearsing a conversation that will take place at some future moment. The words are so close in her head that they are louder than any other sound. Sometimes it's as if they are louder than even the things she sees, and she wants to swat away the voices. She's not even sure if she can see anything because the calls are so loud. Should be some kind of volume control.

"What's happening?" the obese woman is saying.

"Somebody's talking about the election."

"Everybody is talking about that."

"What do you mean?"

How could she have overlooked the possibility before? Suddenly, it's possible that the obese woman herself has something to do with the telephone calls. Maybe she is some kind of dispatcher or a router, some kind of personnel manager of the people talking. "Do you have something to do with it?"

"I haven't voted in twenty-five years."

"Then why did you say that?"

"What?"

"About the election?"

"I'm just making conversation."

Everything that's happening is happening below the threshold of the visible. The same outside. The people who voted, they don't count, because it's happening below the surface. Everything she sees, the city out the window, the cars, the parks, the skyscrapers. Somewhere even farther down, underneath the lowest part of the subway system, there's another layer, where the decisions are made. It's like two hundred people, and their sons and daughters go to parties together, and they meet on Friday nights down in the bunker and they play cards and they decide who gets what country. This one gets to put a nuclear power plant in the middle of Kazakhstan. That's what the Friday-night card players say, and they divide up their winnings, and they divide up their businesses, and they give one another a pat on the back. Some people get to see these things, some people are special and they can see below the layers, and these people are gifted.

"I think you need to be medicated," the obese woman says.

"I am medicated."

The obese woman will not discuss it further. As precipitously as she began talking, she has stopped. Conversation is a brief eruption in the expanse of silence. And in the midst of considering ideas about silence and conversation, Rosa hears someone pounding on the door, announcing that breakfast is going to be over if she doesn't get up. Rosa treads quietly past the massive bulk of the obese woman, dons her robe and her paper slippers, and shuffles out, squinting, into daylight.

More bodies wobbling ahead of her. Down toward the dining hall. The light is a disinfectant of particulate material that has been sprayed liberally to cover the stench of poisonous darkness. Breakfast is the same dispiriting meal she's had every morning here, and she can eat none of it. The tray comes and goes. After which, the consulting physician ambles in and asks if he can have a word with her. Rosa nods.

"Right, good. Well, uh, I'll . . . We're wondering if you happened to notice anything unusual last night, with your, uh, with your roommate."

"Unusual?" She begins to hear a buzzing in her ears, and her eyes dart across the field of the room, as if stray sounds might be coming from anywhere, and she tries to fix on a possible origin, as if by alighting on a cause, she could relax a little into the singularity of her condition.

Rosa tries to shout, "I didn't hear anything!"

"Anything at all? Because we have, uh . . . Well, the problem is that she has . . ."

He doesn't know how to put it, what will soon become the problem of the entire ward. But she can tell. The obese woman has expired; she has gone over. It's true. There's a troika of orderlies, and they have managed to heft the obese woman onto a gurney, and they are wheeling her out of the ward just the way she came in, and a cluster of the detoxifying is there to watch, gathered by the nurse's station. The large shape goes out with the sheet drawn up over its head. The obese woman never even got to have a name. No one visited her, and no one called for her, and now she is going off for disposal.

"We're going to have a meeting to discuss it in a few minutes, so that anyone who has any feelings on the subject will have an opportunity to share his or her feelings. It's important in times like this for the community to gather. There will be grief counseling. If you need it."

"I'll tell you what I need," Rosa Meandro says to the doctor. "To get out of . . . I don't want to go out of here like she did. . . . I have served my seven days; it's time for me to go. I am not a danger to anybody."

"We can discuss that later."

"I'd like to discuss it now."

The issue, technically, is that she has to be released *to* someone, the doctor says grudgingly, and this person will have to meet with the social worker, go through an outtake process, and so forth. But Rosa doesn't want to be released to her daughter. Vanessa will not agree to the release, and Rosa doesn't want to be confined in her apartment, telephone conversations or not, because confinement makes her problems worse. She doesn't have to put up with it anymore, she feels stronger, and if they won't let her go, she'll bribe her way out, she'll go out for a candy bar and then she'll pay the elevator operator, and then she'll be on the ground floor before anyone knows what has happened. She'll be gone. But just as she thinks this, just as she should be explaining to the doctor about how important it is for her to be released, she begins to listen in on a stray telephone conversation. "You don't understand, the thing is he was on the phone with her at the time that she was hit, he was actually talking to her from his studio, it's the most beautiful —" Giving way immediately to some strategic planning conversation about gross volumes of doughnuts, interrupted by Vanessa calling from somewhere to check up on the miniseries, bothering some man and then another, also about the miniseries, "We're going to do it, we're going to get it *done,* and we're going to get it *done* because no one else is doing anything like this, and I want you to consider this a green light, and I want you to pick whichever version of the story you think is the best one, and I want you to get the budgets together, and I want you to bring them in here where I can see them by first thing tomorrow morning, and that's the last I want to hear about it," then the prospects for a long winter with much precipitation, and a conversation about the fastest route from Albany to Providence, "Just shoot on over on I-Eighty-four," and in the midst of this the doctor asking her something, but she can't really understand, except that suddenly she *is* curious. Why don't any of the conversations mention her? The obese woman should never have brought it up! Even her daughter's conversations never mention her! The conversations are about market share, or they are about venture capital, or they are about how the campaign needs to protect its investment by sending operatives down to Florida, it needs to get the public relations initiatives on its side; none of these conversations mentions Rosa, as if she's not even here anymore.

Rosa says, "Call my daughter; you can release me to my daughter. Have the . . . someone can call my . . . you can release me to my daughter." But the doctor is retreating to the dayroom. By the time Rosa fathoms what has been said to her, he is underneath the television set, rubbing his hands together nervously, and now Rosa is shuffling toward the dayroom. She is listening to the radiator and wondering if the radiator is actually making the noise that it seems to be making, the sound of someone strangling. The ward is talking excitedly about how wonderful the obese woman was, even though nobody actually interacted with the obese woman because she never came out of the room even once.

In the afternoon, her daughter is meant to come and collect her. Rosa is wearing the clothes she was wearing when she was admitted, and she is frail, and yet she is filled with a grandiose hope. She has come to have a purpose. She has survived this reversal and she is repaired, more or less, and the sunset over the western expanse of Brooklyn, out the hospital windows, is magnificent, and the beauty of the sunset on Thursday is a metaphor for her indomitability, no matter if she's going to have to return on an outpatient basis so that they can monitor the blood levels of the medication that makes her mouth so dry she can barely peel her lips apart to complain. She is special, in her way, because she has been chosen to hear conversations, and if she is to hear the conversations on the outside, then she will be special there, too, because she knows things that no one else knows, and this makes her worthy and important. The inner workings of politics and culture and conspiracy are revealed to her and her alone.

At 4:30, Rosa asks the nurse, since she's standing in her street clothes (overnight bag at her feet) by the door marked Exit, if she can just go down the hall to get herself a nice candy bar, a little snack. The nurse has two calls on hold, as well as, in front of her, a snaggle-toothed man in his underwear demanding special treatment in Cantonese, and she can't be bothered to think twice about Rosa and the candy bar. Maybe if she were thinking, this nurse would think about why Rosa needs to take her overnight bag to go to the candy machine down the hall, but it doesn't cross her mind, and by the time it does, Rosa is already on the elevator. By the time they check the elevator, Rosa is already on the street. By the time they check out the front of the hospital, she's past the chain bookstore, heading for the liquor store.

It's important to choose a liquor store that is different from the last you visited. This is known as freedom of choice. When was the last time you went to the liquor store? Which liquor store were you going to? How is that liquor store laid out? Were you just a couple days away from being incarcerated in the detoxification ward? Then you must certainly go to a different liquor store because your patronage at various establishments ensures that there will be competition among package store businesses in your area, as it also ensures that you do not get personally close to any of the owners of these businesses. No choice but to go farther over, onto Sixth Avenue, where Rosa hopes she can find a store where she has not been lately. This she does, in a state of apprehension.

It's rush hour, and the weather seems sharply colder than when she was incarcerated, and she might feel bad about her daughter, who will be at the hospital any minute now and who will be wondering why her mother is not in the hospital, and the hospital employees will be sheepishly searching the premises, but Rosa cannot worry about this now because she has a mission, and the first part of the mission is the liquor store, and when she reaches it — there are the usual warped linoleum floors and the reek of fresh industrial detergent — she is overwhelmed with hopefulness. The liquor store is owned and operated by Spanish speakers. She selects a pint of cheap rye whiskey and she asks the owner-operator if he will dust off the bottle, and this he does, when at last he understands, making use of a handy feather duster he keeps behind the register.

Rosa takes the bottle onto the street, where everyone is hurrying home, and she opens the bottle, nestled in its paper bag. When the blended whiskey hits the back of her throat, she can feel her throat close up, out of stunned delight, and she can feel the spiny points of anxiety begin to diminish, and she can feel the telephone conversations receding into some distant chamber of intelligence, from which only the occasional word or phrase will rise out of the murk, "marinade," "pomegranate," "mons pubis," and this is exactly where she wants to be in the battle against hallucination and mental illness, because it enables her to pursue the next stage of her mission.

It's months since she rode the subway, many months more since she rode the subway during rush hour, but perhaps the spectacle of her, a woman who has quarreled with the basic chemistries of human identity and who, in the process, has been given access to the entire global network of cellular telephone calls from which to pick and choose in her analysis of contemporary mores, is enough to induce people to move out of her way. She makes for the rearmost car of the train, and here she secures one of the seats that are meant to be left for invalids, and she sits in the invalid's seat, and she drinks and passes an agreeable trip into Manhattan, to Forty-second Street, where she disembarks. Now Rosa Elisabetta walks through the long stinking tunnel that takes her to her destination, the bus terminal of fever dreams, where she hastens to the ticket booth, pink neon framing the disconsolate face of a woebegone bus company salesperson. She removes from her wallet some of the last of her rumpled cash, and she pushes it through the slot to the morose ticket agent and tells him that, yes, she's going to Florida, where she's going to put a stop to all this election madness.

24

The Krispy Kreme franchise in flames.

An impossible thing to fathom, that someone would come here to Concord, a sleepy suburb, home to lawyers and venture capitalists, drive past Emerson's grave, and firebomb the local Krispy Kreme, the first in the state. Where did these fiends obtain the incendiary devices? Where did they get the will and the means to firebomb the Krispy Kreme? And was it true, as rumor indicated, that Concord was now home to a small mobile revolutionary cell? The Krispy Kreme was located on Main Street, of course, and now every citizen could walk by its remains. They would smell scorched yeast, burnt plastic, and electrical panels. The picture windows of the storefront had been shattered by the all-volunteer fire department in an attempt to contain the blaze, and this mission was successful. The only related damage was to the floor above the doughnut restaurant. Well, there was some smoke damage in the adjacent florist's shop. No one was hurt.

The conflagration had erupted at eleven or just after, according to the newspaper accounts. A man "purchasing a six-pack" at the convenience store up the block saw figures rounding the corner. He wondered why these figures were running. A light sleeper whose apartment backed up to Main Street heard everything. She could verify the time. Occupants of a car passing at the appointed hour saw a pair of suspicious persons in tan overcoats in front of the Krispy Kreme.

No doubt, it was a terrorist group of some kind, as editorials opined. Some kind of domestic terrorist cadre had come here to Concord, or to the Boston area, and had brought with it the suspicion and fear attendant upon such things. There were terrorist groups in other places, in Israel and Palestine, in Chechnya, in Indonesia, but not in Concord. Until now. Even if this was some kind of radical environmentalist group with "humane" ideas about the destruction of property, it was still a terrorist group. The aim of terrorist groups was to produce anxiety about the future, and this was in fact what this terrorist group had produced "in spades," according to an editorial on the subject. This is exactly what Max Duffy's mother is saying on Friday afternoon, thinking out loud, as she slows in the bottleneck at the former site of the Krispy Kreme franchise, believing, according to her theories about the psychology of teenagers, that if Maximillian Duffy is to understand the error of his ways, he needs to see what revolutionary principles have wrought in one New England town.

"The bus driver lived up there," she remarks, pointing at the blackened window casements above the Krispy Kreme restaurant. She's made sure that her son has seen the articles in the local press. She's made sure that he understands that the FBI promises to be involved in the investigation. The ancient Volvo belonging to the Reverend and Mrs. Duffy halts, like the cars ahead of it, and mother and son rubberneck past the black shell of the doughnut purveyor. Shattered glass, forlorn interior, police barriers, orange cones, scorched industrial equipment dragged out onto the sidewalk. At a Dumpster, scowling municipal workers heave up bits of wreckage.

Of course, they'd already taken Eduardo Alcott into custody. That's the part that Max can't figure out. Apparently they came for him after Tyrone called the police. And if the other Retrievalists were now remanded into the care of their parents or guardians, awaiting the possibility of charges in Eduardo's case, then who actually performed the firebombing? Since the Krispy Kreme arson project had never been written down, as nothing was ever written down at Eduardo's, there was no evidence of their plans. Who brought about this bold threat to unchecked multinational franchising? Was it really a terrorist group? Or was it a bunch of teenagers who had smoked too much pot and who just got into the pyrotechnics of the thing? Were they freedom fighters? Were they ordinary criminals? Were they rogue employees who couldn't make ends meet at minimum wage and who were making a statement about pay scale? Was it somebody who wanted fresh original glazed doughnuts and was unhappy that none were for sale?

The town fathers had their theories. The town fathers had each been photographed in front of the rubble, decrying the national mood of permissiveness and complacency that led to such unthinkable tragedy. None of them knows any more than Max knows himself, probably quite a bit less, because they have never heard from the kids who hang out in the Krispy Kreme parking lot, smoking. The doughnut restaurant was practically new, was part of a rollout of Krispy Kreme franchises here in the Northeast, and now it is gone, and with it almost a dozen good jobs and a place for kids to go on weekends.

He asks his mother if she'll at least let him go for a walk, to think things over. She's kept him inside these last few days. Since Tyrone came home, Max hasn't even gone to school, and he's going as crazy as his brother. Anything to get out of the car, anything to get out of her sight, anything to have a moment in the company of nature.

"You could just take me over to —"

"Oh, to the —"

If it's *those* woods she can hardly refuse him, because *those* woods have literary pedigree, and whenever Max seems to be living inside the parental dream of a fine education, no problem. So she takes the county road, congested during the evening commute, and soon she is alongside the celebrated pond. Deborah pulls the car over, and Max gets out of the car and says he'll be back in ten.

He had school lectures in these woods, he had plant identification classes. He knows the varieties of ferns, Christmas fern and ebony spleenwort, and a good portion of the birches and firs and maples. He can identify the nuthatches and the wrens and the warblers, chickadees, and red-winged blackbirds; according to his indoctrination, he recognizes part of the Utopian vision of Eduardo Alcott, whose goal is the rescue of Gaia, or Mother Earth, from the one true pest species, *Homo sapiens sapiens*.

Naturally, there is more to the Alcott narrative than Max has told his mother. There is more to the story than the rights of the forest, the rights of Mother Earth to be free from the meddling of the human animal. For example, with each of the Retrievalists, Eduardo attempted to inculcate a particular environmental skill. With Nina, Eduardo taught her to fire rifles and shotguns, so that she might use these to prune the population of hunters and sportsmen; and with Glenn, Eduardo taught him to lay traps. (In fact, Glenn came out of his training well-versed in survivalist techniques, which is probably going to come in handy during his summer job at the local nursery, where he will be heaving bags of pine bark nuggets into the backs of sport utility vehicles.)

What Eduardo taught Max was the skill of divining. This may have been an indication of some special esteem for Maximillian because divining, as Eduardo put it, was the most recondite of these Retrievalist disciplines. There had to be complete trust for the lessons to take place, there had to be an absence of worldly distractions, there had to be attention and humility. Eduardo took Max out into the dwindling forests of the region. Sometimes they went driving for an hour or more to find a suitable place. They went to the old New England, the vanishing New

England, the New England of gothic tales and Indian clashes. Then, when the forest was thick enough, Eduardo would pass on the arcana of dowsing.

The first thing to learn was that there was no explanation for what was about to take place. There was no empirical explanation as to why it worked, any more than it was possible to explain why Catholicism worked. If you believed, it did. Perhaps dowsing had something to do with geology, and with the geological history that was imprinted in each and every human body; or perhaps it had something to do with magnetism, with the tiny particles that conveyed the universal force known as electromagnetism; or perhaps it had something to do with Druidic wisdom, the white magic of the Druids that the Romans failed to suppress; or perhaps it had to do with auras and chi energy and the orphic wisdom of New Age bookshops, like the bookshop two doors down from the Krispy Kreme restaurant of Concord. Whatever the cause, dowsing worked. This was the first lesson: Utilize, don't analyze.

They were up near Monadnock, the most hiked mountain in the United States. "Science is the stooge of capitalism," Eduardo was saying. "Science serves the pig. It has no creative abilities, it has only this tendency to do what is expected of it, which is to accept the logic of *product* and the merchandising that is its lifeblood. The vassals of capitalism do as they are told. And the vassals of capitalism are research and development lackeys. So don't believe that this skill I'm teaching has anything to do with science."

These were the lessons of the survivalist cadres, of Maoist guerrillas in the Amazon. And to prove the lie of science, Eduardo now grasped his Y rod, the traditional forked stick of divining — a polished piece of the witch hazel — and he held the ends of the stick between the third and fourth fingers of his upturned hands, thumbs on the ends, as he explained to Max, with the point of the stick upward. Then he spun in a clockwise direction, eyes closed, so that the strain and anxiety of Eduardo's veined face yielded a little bit. He went on spinning until an incredible thing happened, a thing that even Max was able to witness, notwithstanding disbelief. The stick seemed to tremble violently at first and then, despite all the energy that Eduardo used against it, the stick began to fight its way in a downward direction, until it was drooping past the median point of Eduardo's belt line. It was now definitely pointing toward the earth. Eduardo came to a stop, opened his eyes, and, grinning, he pronounced the results of his experiment: "I am now facing magnetic north."

He explained that the forked stick, in terms of design, was mainly of interest as an antique. Nobody used the forked stick anymore, really. What they used were metal rods, L-shaped rods, like this:

⌐L

and these metal rods were contained in plastic sleeves, usually the grips from bicycle handles. You could make the L rods from conventional wire coat hangers, the kind you might get at your neighborhood dry cleaner. You placed them in the bicycle handles, Eduardo said. And then you went out into the natural world and you waited to see what the metal rods would tell you. If the rods fanned out in a V shape, that was a "yes," and if the rods crossed their tips that was also a "yes," in reply to whatever question you were asking, such as whether there was water in a place or whether there was a vein of silver ore. Only if the rods failed to react was the answer in the negative.

"For today," Eduardo said, "we will content ourselves with finding potable water, since that's a bit of magic that you can easily make use of. Let's empty our canteens first, so that we can experience the sensation of thirst like our revolutionary brothers in the Mexican desert. And then we will see what we can see."

He took the L rods from the small kit bag he'd brought, an old messenger's bag with the name of a local newspaper fading from its side. And he presented the L rods and the grips to Max in his brusque way.

"You try."

While Max was getting used to the feel of the grips, Eduardo was giving him the second lesson. The second lesson was as follows: It is not in the material of the divining rod that the divination resides but in the dowser himself. Didn't matter what you used, Eduardo said, and the excessive attention that some people paid to the Y rod and its perfect varnish was fetishistic and against the spirit of dowsing. Some people used fishing weights on fishing line and they held aloft this little pendulum item and they waited for it to arc back and forth. Some people, Eduardo said, used their hands alone. They went into the woods with their hands aloft, in a receptive state, and they waited until they felt their palms get moist or they waited for the hairs to stand up on their arms, at which point they knew they were in the presence of silver or gold or other eternal mysteries.

"Go ahead," he said. "Ask it."

"Ask it what?"

"What do you want to know?"

"Is there water?"

"Be more specific."

So Max asked, on that chilly day in April, if there was a spring nearby where they could refill their canteens. And immediately the L rods opened in what Eduardo described as the "yes" position, the V position, and Max wondered, even as it was happening, if he was causing this to happen, the way impatient teens gathered around a Ouija board will always immediately summon the dead kid from up the block. Was Max tilting the rods down because he wanted to pass this examination so that Eduardo would quit looking at him that way? Still, the L rods had given the answer he was looking for. There *was* a spring. Eduardo laid a gloved hand on his shoulder.

"Now ask in which direction."

He asked the L rods in which direction the water lay, which felt really stupid because it was like talking to his hiking boots or something. Immediately, the L rods crossed, and he found that the direction was not straight ahead, and not to his left, but exactly in the direction of magnetic north that Eduardo had indicated before. Max walked carefully forward, with Eduardo following behind, and the forest closed around them as if the divining rods were in collusion with the wisdom of the primeval forest. When the rods gave an ambiguous message about how to proceed, he waited, turned slightly, until he felt that tug, as if he had caught a fish on the end of them, and he hurried forward anew. Before long they heard voices, and then they saw other hikers in their brightly colored jackets, filling their water bottles from a pipe that protruded from igneous rock. They drank.

Eduardo congratulated him, and the two of them began to walk back, Indian file, the way they had come, toward the van. It was as they walked that Eduardo told him that the halos of the saints were not halos but auras, this was well-known, and that the divining rods could measure the auras of all persons, and that before they went back to Newton, Eduardo was bound, by his belief in the sanctity of the revolution, to ensure that Max's intentions were honorable, through the measurement and calibration of his aura. So, Eduardo asked, would Max please stop where he was at the moment? Would he please stand completely still?

It crossed Max's mind that he was about to be executed, that he was standing in the traditional posture of executions, like in WWII movies where victims turned their backs and laced their hands behind their heads. Hard to tell with Eduardo whether he trusted you or was about to put a bullet in you. Still, maybe the one thing Max did believe in was belief, and maybe it wasn't the kind of belief that his father, the Reverend Duffy, believed in. He felt as though he wanted to believe in something, some great system, and that the opportunities for this kind of belief were few, because the only thing that you could believe in these days was an acne cream that contained enough fast-acting agents to clear up your blemish before the big dance. Or maybe you believed that if you went ahead and busted your ass on some standardized test and didn't just fill in little circles in the shape of a bunny, you would get a chance to go to some school that would make sure you learned about business administration, so that, later on, working on behalf of a very large corporation, you could, with a straight face, say the words, "The public was never in danger at any time."

Max believed that Eduardo believed in something, and he therefore hoped he would not be shot. So, in the stillness of the forest, when Eduardo said, "Tell me, does this man have the true heart of a revolutionary?" he thought that it would probably be okay, and that he would not fail the test. When he was invited to turn and face the Y rod and its assessment of his character, he was happy to find that the device was pointed down. It was in the "yes" position — because he did have the heart of the believer.

Was that at Monadnock? Or was that the first time they'd come here, to the pond? And was it with the Y rod, as he remembers, or did Eduardo do the test with his hands? As if he were in the process of bestowing some Andean blessing? Max wasn't sure, because it was the spring, the time of gorging himself on the orthodoxy of the Retrievalists, a dizzy time with a flood of ideologies, and as he tramps through the woods now, around the pond, with the commuters whizzing past on their way home to cocktails, he thinks about how the price of enlightenment was that he needed to hide a lot of things from his parents.

Eduardo's third lesson concerned ley lines, or lines of power, which "came from above," Eduardo said, though he never elaborated on the nature of this above. Maybe it was a cosmic thing, you know, or maybe it was a religious thing. Whichever it was, you could dowse these lines of power with your dowsing rod. Just as you could dowse the water supply. And what you would find was that spiritual places, houses of worship or other alternative systems of knowledge and understanding, inevitably cropped up along these lines of power. Like you might find that there was a shaman living here, or you might find that an old church was on one of the lines of power, which made Max want to dowse the First Congregational Church to see if the church where his father practiced was a true place of spirit. At the same time, he sort of didn't want to find out that his dad was a huckster.

The third lesson definitely took place here by the pond, because Eduardo had gone running like a madman into these woods, looking for the approximate site at which a certain environmentalist and revolutionary, always referred to as the "civil disobedient," had once resided. Here beside the pond. Eduardo claimed that the "civil disobedient" had lived along a ley line and Eduardo claimed that it was possible to prove this. If you took a map of the countryside and you dangled a pendulum above this map, you might draw a line, Eduardo said, that ran right from the spot where the "civil disobedient" had once lived. The "civil disobedient," H. D. Thoreau, Eduardo observed, knew that American civilization was about corruption. He knew that the laws of American civilization were corrupt; and he came to this place because this was where the energy originated. Eduardo, with the Y rod dipping in front of him, dashed madly into the undergrowth, to where the "civil disobedient" was granted his vision, a diviner's vision, Eduardo said. The "civil disobedient" came here with nothing, with pittances of cash and meager possessions, and he came to make his union with the energy of this place. The union was good, because the "civil disobedient" never again wrote anything as flawless as what he wrote here. He never wrote anything flawless about the Maine woods and he seemed to have paddled the whole length of the Merrimack without crossing a single line of power.

The pond doesn't seem so magnificent now, as Max bushwhacks through the skunk cabbage. Night is falling, and it's starting to drizzle. And his mother is calling to him, "Honey! Where are you? Don't go too far, okay?" But there's always a good reason to go farther into the woods. They're going to chop down the woods and put in a bunch of condominiums, lakefront properties, it's already decided, with a boat landing for the Jet Ski guys. And something weird happens to Max just as he has this thought about the Jet Ski guys. He remembers something Eduardo said. Maybe it was the fourth lesson, and maybe the fourth lesson was mumbled one day when they were here by the pond, offhandedly, and the fourth lesson was that, Eduardo said, "If they ever come for me, look here, and I'll leave a message."

Max didn't give it much credence back then. He never paid much attention to Eduardo's more apocalyptic observations. Still, he's doing what he never thought he'd do; he's pulling down a live branch from a maple sapling, and he's pulling off stray bits of bark, exposing, in the process, some of the green pulp underneath, and why? Because he thinks he'll give it one more try. He'll make a satisfying wishbone of a twig. He doesn't want his mom to see what he's up to, and he doesn't know why. The pursuit of magic is like masturbation or sentimentality; it's best done alone. When he has a hurriedly constructed Y rod, he does what he was taught. He puts the bifurcated section between the third and fourth fingers of his upturned hands, with the point facing upward, and he asks the Y rod the question he has for it today, and that question is: "Did Eduardo leave a message here for me?"

The important thing is to empty your mind. The distractions are the encroachments of the commuters, the possibility of Jet Ski guys in their pastel-striped wet suits, the distractions of home. His mother, and his father, and his brother. Tune out his brother's legal situation, his sister is coming up from New York. Oh yeah, and where is he going to go to college? "Adherence to truth is the cornerstone of dowsing," Eduardo told him, and the truth is what he is after. He waits for the Y rod of antiquity to dip. He waits for it to struggle with him. He waits for it to confer on him the honor of a reply. He waits to be made more than he is, more than the kid who is grounded and who has to take the trash out and do all the laundry for everyone in the house, not failing to remove the delicates before putting the bundle in the dryer. He waits. The Y rod does not disappoint.

The Y rod says "yes." The Y rod thrusts its prow toward the fecund earth. With uncanny self-sufficiency. He asks if the message lies ahead of him, and the Y rod continues to say "yes." He follows the "yes" farther into the woods, "yes" past the little forest of silver birches, "yes" past a guy who is letting his springer spaniel run free, "yes" past the remains of a party from last weekend, a campfire circle and a couple of empty six-packs, "yes" farther into the forest, "yes" unto the moment the tip of the Y rod unaccountably rises up again.

"Is this the place where Eduardo left a message for me?"

The Y rod indicates "yes." As if it's trying to wrest control of itself away from him.

He flings the stick to the ground, and he gets down on his hands and his knees, in the drizzle, until his knees are covered with mud, pushing aside leaves and pushing against downed limbs and rocks, looking for he doesn't know what. Until he finds it at last, when he's covered with the topdressing of the forest floor, when his vintage windbreaker is dotted with decomposing leaves, when his jeans are soaked all the way through. Only then has he found the tree stump, on the ley line of the "civil disobedient," where Eduardo has left the note for him. Folded into halves, these sheets of legal paper, shoved into a crevice in the stump. He sits beside the Y rod on the forest floor, so that now his ass is wet, too. In the dwindling light, he attempts to interpret the ink-smeared lines on the pages.

Dear Maximillian,

If you're reading this it means that I'm probably in custody or have left town. If so, I apologize for leaving you all in the way that I have done. And that's not the only thing I have to apologize for, but I'll start there. And I'm sorry for bringing you all this way, out into the woods, just to tell you what you probably already know, that I'm gone.

I guess I should tell you that my name isn't Eduardo Alcott, although maybe you've guessed this part already. Actually, my name is Sy Molina. Though I was raised in Rhode Island, my mother is from Guatemala, so I am Central American along the maternal line. I was educated at the University of Rhode Island in social work, and most of my life I have been a child welfare caseworker for social services in Massachusetts.

For a few years, I thought my job was honorable, if difficult. It was what I'd been trained to do. But after a while I started to feel like my place of employment was the one place not to be if you really cared about kids. Because I was seeing all these kids who were breaking my heart. I was seeing all these kids who were left out in the cold by the system, getting shunted around from house to house, mostly to places where the adults were being paid to shelter them, and these adults didn't care at all.

I had hundreds of kids in my caseload, and I couldn't remember the names or the details of most of their stories. I began feeling like I couldn't do anything, couldn't make a difference. In fact, when there was a problem, sometimes it seemed like it was just a hassle to correct it. I felt this burden, like I knew I was going to have to deal with all this paperwork and bring action against some of the foster parents, and the kids had already been beaten or their parents had left them or the parents were addicts, whatever it was. I just couldn't live with the fact that I brought these kids more trouble instead of less. I had tried to help them out, and often I placed them in these homes where they were even worse off.

This was my job for twenty years. I'd read the case reports at night. I couldn't tell which kid was Evan or Juanita or Lance. Had I gotten this kid out of South Boston or Dorchester or Worcester? I didn't know, but I'd put him with some couple that already had four foster kids, and they had more spaces now because the last one had gone into the juvenile-detention system after assaulting his science teacher.

Everyone burns out eventually. One day, I chewed out my manager, told her that she was responsible for the trouble that all my kids were going to get into. We were making it worse for them, I told her, and I said this to her in front of a bunch of other caseworkers. I told my manager that the work we were doing was worthless, and after I left there that night, I didn't get out of bed for almost six months. At the end of that period, I was living in the house and in the circumstances in which you came to know me.

I met this heavy metal kid in the mall by the interstate, and I was talking to him in the food court about what kinds of bands interested him, that kind of thing. I remember I was reading a book about the Black Panthers that I'd bought in a used-book store. Glenn seemed like he was impressed with anything having to do with the Black Panthers, and I have to admit his approval made me feel good. That was the very moment when Eduardo was born, out of thin air. It was a big relief for Sy Molina. Because Sy Molina had lived for his work, but he had also failed at his work, and his relationships hadn't turned out too well, and he was making do in a dump of a rental in the commercial part of town, and he was reduced to talking to kids at the mall. No one else would talk to him.

Glenn wasn't like other teens. Glenn felt like Eduardo was someone he could look up to. And this was the first time, in all the years that it had been my job to look after young people, that I felt like I was really interacting with kids, really having an impact. Back when I worked with child welfare, I would look in on a kid and I'd tell him, You aren't using drugs, are you? Because you really shouldn't use drugs. And then I'd go back to my house and smoke reefers, like I'd been doing since the seventies, and meanwhile the kid was probably sniffing glue and he wasn't paying any attention to anything I was saying. Why should he? Glenn didn't feel like I was an asshole, and when I was Eduardo, with Glenn, I had this sudden need to teach him things, to learn the kinds of things myself that I could pass on to Glenn, in the process proving to him what a special kid he was, how brilliant, how full of energy. It didn't make any difference if he was using drugs. Eduardo's attitude was that if Glenn was using drugs then maybe he was learning something about himself and something about his identity.

When Glenn brought Nina around, that was a big bonus, because it was like my caseload had expanded. I was starting to merit the kind of responsibility that I'd had when I was working for the state. Nina was sensitive. I could really learn some things, some crazy things, alternative philosophies, and I could tell Nina about these things, and she would really listen and her eyes would get wide. All the things that seem so impossible in the world, like genuine change, you could tell Nina about these things, and she would just eat them up. Maybe I did fall a little bit in love with Nina, I'm not sure. I know I never laid a glove on her, never even hugged her, but I know I wanted to impress her.

What do a bunch of teenagers get from listening to teachers at school, where the curriculum is about the same old shit in the same old way, making sure that you fit into the mold that society wants you to fit into? That wasn't going to work for you guys, because you were special, and I just wanted for you what nobody else wanted for you. I loved all the crazy things about you, your ideals, and I guess I created ideals for you to love even more. The fact that you guys wanted to come over to my place and hang out with me, that made me feel like I could do better, and go further, for each of you. Like I was the parent who really loved who you were, instead of wanting you to be a certain kind of person so that you were easy to love.

I designed everyone's training along these lines. I designed stuff so that people could improve at being who they were. I designed stuff that would build on your confidence, make you feel better when you left my house. So you could go to school and you could mess with some football player if you had to. You could walk around with head held high. Each of you had secrets, and they were good secrets. Bits of wisdom.

But the more I lived out the lies of Eduardo, the worse things got. I began feeling paranoid everywhere. I would walk out on the street,

*and I would think that people were going to find out. I would think
that people were going to call me Sy. I worried I'd run into some guy
from social services when I was out with one of you. I started wearing
glasses and I grew a beard and everything, just so that people wouldn't
recognize me, and maybe this way I'd bury Sy Molina for good.*

*You've probably figured out that I don't know anything about
dowsing. I think dowsing is very interesting but I don't know anything about it. That time up in the woods, well, I knew where magnetic north was before I dowsed, because I had a compass with me.
And as for your finding the spring, I had my hand on your shoulder. I
was trying to steer you in the right direction.*

*Things changed when you showed up, Max. First of all, you're a
brilliant guy, and I expect you'll go to Harvard to learn about liber-
ation theology, or whatever it is they teach there now, and you're going to make a difference in this world, and if your parents have been
too busy lately to remind you how brilliant you are, then accept this
letter for the message it contains. You have a brilliant life ahead of
you. I knew it from the second that Nina brought you through the
door to my house. I knew that you were a kid who wasn't going to be
deceived for long. I'll never forget your brother getting into the van. I
was scared shitless about the trouble he was in back in New York, and
I was scared that he was going to bring the police down on us. At the
same time, I was trying to be credible, so that your brother wouldn't
tell all of you kids that I wasn't who I said I was. I could see in your
brother's eyes that he was a troubled guy but also that he wasn't going to be taken in. I could see all of that.*

*I never would have hurt Nina. You know that. I mean, I don't know
if you can understand that now, but I never would have hurt Nina. I
was starting to panic and I had some idea that maybe I could get
your brother to move on, go back out wherever it was that he was supposed to go, to the county jail, or whatever. That was a little selfish,
considering that I always had a real affection and respect for you.*

*All of this was about loving kids, see, and that's what I'll leave you
with here, that I loved you kids, because I never had any kids of my*

*own, and it looks like I never will. I got into my job because I wanted
to make the world better, and I never felt like I did until I met all of
you, and then I felt like I had accomplished something, for a while,
anyway. People like me want to give something away to the world,
and then when we get the chance, it comes out wrong. That's not how
I wanted it to go, because I loved you kids, and I never wanted to do
wrong by you. I wanted to prove to you that the world is good, that
you can make a difference. See, you can go out there with no more
than a forked stick and find all the good in the world.*

Viva la revolution,

Eduardo

Max hears the rustle of his approaching mother and he crumples the pages and shoves them into the pocket of his jacket. His mother, out of breath, leans against a sturdy oak.

"So what are you doing out here?"

He holds up his divining rod. His scanty twig. As if it will explain.

"Looking for water."

25

Midmorning on Friday, Vanessa takes a pad from her desk drawer full of skittering pens and paper clips, and begins writing down the list of horrible circumstances: her mother going into detox, dealing with all of that; her mother having fled detox for points unknown; Annabel's brother, and whether or not he hit some woman on the head with a brick; Lois DiNunzio, missing at first, presumed dead; the fifty thousand dollars that Lois embezzled; how to pay the rent next month because of Lois; the miniseries, the six different versions of the miniseries out there, and the eight different women who supposedly wrote the novel, or play, or whatever, on which the miniseries is supposedly based; all the producers and agents insisting that they came up with the idea or packaged the idea, an idea that now seems to have some kind of *buzz* attached to it; and that's just a beginning on the list of horrible circumstances, at least until Annabel knocks on her door, and she waves her in.

"Got a second?"

"Have you and Madison made any headway working on a writer for the . . ."

"Not a problem."

"Does that mean you have someone? We have to have a writer, that's the thing. And it can't be some movie guy. Has to be someone completely uninterested in art. It could be a woman. It could be a woman with no conscience. Someone who lives and eats and breathes the small screen, the social Darwinism of the small screen, the sentimentality of the small screen. Someone really calculating, really heartless, bloodthirsty."

"We don't have a *particular* someone yet, but we have names and we're working on them. We're ahead of you, and we're expecting to, um, have results really soon."

"Let me know as soon as you —"

"Well, that's actually why I —"

"What? Are you going to *resign?*"

"Well, actually —"

A sharp, puncturing wound, here it comes, to go with the others. An awl driven into Vanessa. As if she's a faux-leather belt being manufactured by some sweatshop preteen in Malaysia. She sets the pen on the pad, gets ready to write down *Annabel quits* before it even happens.

"A leave of absence, that's what I want to talk about."

And then Annabel launches into this explanation about her brother. Something has happened with her brother, a breakdown of some kind. Her brother was abducted, she says. She's using all this language that you'd hear from cop shows: abduction, deprogramming, secret terrorist cells. Vanessa doesn't quite get the details. Supposedly Tyrone hit some woman with a brick, as mentioned above, and then maybe he hadn't hit some woman with a brick, and then he had taken flight, and then, Annabel claims, he was involved with some kind of ecoterrorist organization. Isn't that just kids from Ithaca or Santa Cruz smoking weed and going without showers? Sort of like that. Not like the Red Brigades or Baader-Meinhof. Has he built himself a tree house and refused to come down? Has he started protesting in favor of hemp? No, this was some dangerous nationwide organization in which discrete cells operated without mutual contact and without any central organizing authority. The organization may have performed some kind of brainwashing on Tyrone. And on her younger brother, too. What is certain is that Annabel needs to go back to Massachusetts and be with her family while they begin the process of healing. This healing process might involve a couple of weeks. Annabel wears this resolve on her pretty face as though she has rarely been as sure of anything. She is already immersed in her journey of healing, and her resolve makes it impossible for Vanessa to complain about the timing and about how the office is shorthanded as it is because of Lois DiNunzio. How is Vanessa going to hire someone to fill Annabel's spot? The arrangement is that you always have to hire your replacement, but Vanessa can't say anything about it because of the journey of healing, and she just begins to sweat with anxiety about the whole thing, which is when she remembers another thing that she forgot to put on the list. Her period. She hates getting her period.

"I know you have a lot going on right now," Annabel continues, "and I know you're really concerned about your . . . Well, my situation is important, too, otherwise I wouldn't ask, and I just need to be up in Newton, where I can be closer to what's going on."

Vanessa wants to point out that she, Vanessa, is at work, and her mother has escaped from detox, and she is here at her desk while her mother is hiding out with Emilia Commito, matriarch of the Park Slope ravioli empire. Her mother is attempting to punish Vanessa for carting her off to detox in the first place, and so Vanessa's mother has gone to Emilia's, where she's lying on the couch watching talk shows and complaining about Mark Green's mayoral campaign, and Vanessa feels distraught and awful and has been having Jeanine call the police and the hospitals every few hours.

"What are you going to do up there? Isn't it going to be kind of *boring?*"

Annabel gives her a doe-eyed look, as if Vanessa has said something really awful, and that's when it strikes Vanessa. Vanessa always forgets that the entire office is and has long been synchronized in this area, the menses. But Annabel doesn't cry; she shimmies up some metaphorical flagpole of resolve, to rest there pridefully. Where the healing is.

"It doesn't have that much to do with what *I* need," Annabel says. "It has to do with just thinking, like, what's the best thing for Tyrone? The best thing is if I go up there and help out."

"I don't really think it's that great a thing for your career. I mean, I think if you are expecting to have a long career in independent film, you need to put this organization ahead of everything else. Like Adam Weinstein, who gave up his apartment so he could sleep on the editing-room floor. That's letting no one come between you and the project. That's creative control. Or Hope Oliver, maxing out her credit card, persuading her mother and stepfather to take out a second mortgage, you know. Then selling the broadcasting rights for millions. People do what has to be done. That's the way to do business."

"We don't always agree," Annabel says. She's standing by the door. She must not be feeling as bad as Vanessa usually feels when the cramps really start roiling in her. Maybe healing and closure are even more powerful than ambition and sentimentality and cramps, and who is Vanessa to criticize closure, although she just hates the fact that anything could be more important than Means of Production. Annabel tells her to take care, and then she's gone, and Vanessa thinks she'll probably never be back again.

She puts Annabel's name down on the list.

The intern comes in. The intern has a bag of doughnuts. The wordless intern, who looks as if she's about to play the role of victim in a women's self-defense class, in her torn fishnets, miniskirt, and black long-sleeved rock-and-roll tour T-shirt. The intern has brought the original glazed doughnuts of the Krispy Kreme empire. The intern sets these on Vanessa's desk and then she stands there digging at a hangnail while Vanessa plunges a hand into the bag of doughnuts and selects one. Nothing could be better at the present stressful moment.

The intern has been associated with Means of Production for a number of days now, despite which Vanessa has not yet thought to ask the intern if she has a name, or any interests, or what she is working on. Yet suddenly she wants to ask the intern this information because the intern has brought doughnuts (the cane, that is, loosens the tongue), and also because it is definitely the case that the intern has not been here long enough to have her period synchronize with everyone else's. She is therefore the one person who is free of abdominal suffering.

"Hey, so what's your name?"

The intern gives her first name.

"Do you have a surname, Allison?"

"Maiser."

Vanessa chews the doughnut in silence, doesn't let on that she has heard anything out of the ordinary. But she *has;* she has heard syllables that could change her entire future, that could change everything for Means of Production in this trying organizational moment. Visions of a new office in a hip downtown location again dance in Vanessa's head, likewise awards speeches, a country house, a personal trainer, cheese of the month.

"Do you want a doughnut, Allison Maiser?"

"I already had two."

"Where are you from, anyway?"

"Santa Monica."

"They have Krispy Kreme out there?"

The intern contorts herself into some kind of scorn that Vanessa believes is meant to convey that Allison cannot be bothered to think about doughnuts. However, Vanessa doesn't want anyone, any staff member, even any intern, demeaning the integrity of the doughnut. Not in a bad-luck environment. Not now. There is bad luck everywhere, there are bad circumstances, and the least the intern could do would be to honor the integrity of the doughnut. However, because Allison Maiser is who she is, Vanessa says nothing. The intern is back to chewing at her hangnail when Thaddeus Griffin sticks his head in the doorway.

"Got a second?"

Griffin has not been around much in a few days, and when he has been around, he has been more than remote. Just another example of the kind of intrigues taking place out in the corridor beyond Vanessa's control.

"Got something I want to tell you."

He looks at the intern and then at the decorative palm in the corner, as if the two are equal in his sight.

"Don't mind her. Have you guys met?"

Allison Maiser will not budge unless ordered. Vanessa points at the vacant chair. Thaddeus, running his hands nervously through his colorist-enhanced movie star hair, slinks across the office, clearing his throat several times. He sits in the empty chair next to the intern. He reaches for a doughnut.

"I'm not supposed to eat these."

"No one in Hollywood is too smart for doughnuts."

"But some in Hollywood are too thin."

"If Atkins said eat doughnuts, people'd eat them by the dozen."

He looks at the intern again, hoping she will remember some other assigned task. "The thing is, I got an offer for a big film, *The Tempest of Sahara*."

"You got what?"

"An offer. *The Tempest of Sahara*, a big costume picture."

"That can't be the title."

"It used to be called *Assassins*, but then they changed the title to *The Tempest of Sahara*."

"That's funny because —"

"Filming is in Morocco. Starts in January. Morocco. How often do you get to see Morocco? Yeah, and the wife wants to come. So we'll be shipping off to Paris in December, for rehearsals, and from there to Morocco. Where we'll smoke a lot of hashish. Probably be gone for four or five months."

"I thought I . . ." Is the sinking feeling just a sinking feeling or could it be something worse? There are definitely going to be bad cramps today. Sometimes the cramps are so bad she wants to curl up and die. Is there ibuprofen in the desk drawer, skittering around with the paper clips and half-empty jars of antidepressants?

"It's a great script. I think there are only three lines in the last half hour, and those are monosyllables. A lot of scantily clad women in their twenties. The ammunition budget exceeds the GDP of some of the African nations where the second unit will be shooting."

"Are you —"

"I don't feel like I have that much choice right now. It's not like much else has been coming from my agent."

"What about the miniseries?" Vanessa says.

What is it with actors? When a genuine emotion passes through them, a rare enough occurrence, it's as if it's a dental emergency. That's how Thaddeus seems, like the dentist is going to send him out to specialists. He's going to need implants, and his face is going to swell. But at the mention of the miniseries, he rallies, and the sullenness that perfumes him vanishes. He gathers himself up in the chair and starts riffing on the possibilities.

The networks can't *help* but snap it up, he says. One of the cable affiliates, maybe. Lately, the cable networks are taking on a lot of this kind of thing. And Thaddeus says he has some ideas for writers, really great writers. And there are some subplots that she should really be thinking about. He gets so excited that he smacks the intern on the shoulder and then fishes a second doughnut out of the bag.

"The Mormon exodus. Think about it. I mean, they walked across the desert to Salt Lake City, pursued by murderous bands. There was a lot of division in the church at that time. The polygamy thing could play really big on the screen. You could have a strong leading man playing Brigham Young. De Niro. He'd look really good with a beard, a big beard, and he'd have all these wives, and it would sort of be like Charlton Heston not making it into the promised land, right? Brigham Young with his wives, and they're pursued by murderers, going over the Rocky Mountains. They ring the wagons and they take out their guns. How many of the heads of Mormon households will get murdered? And not just a little bit murdered, but cut up and fed to the wolves out there? How many wives are cut down because the Christian oppressors won't accept that the polygamous Mormons are God's chosen people? And there's never any water, and there's a day where Brigham Young, he's just had enough, and maybe he really thinks that Joseph Smith made up the entire business about Moroni, and he just doesn't know; his faith is weak. He calls up a diviner from his midst! Brigham Young, he's just always taken these women around him for granted, he's got all these wives, cousins of his other wives, and he's just always taken them for granted, and he's never known that they had special skills, and he retires to his tent to pray to God to ask if this is the right thing to do. And the dowser turns out to be Brigham's wife Honora, who is played by Susan Sarandon or one of those other beautiful older women! Will the Indians, who are supposed to be the special allies of the Mormons, allow them free passage through the plains? It's a great story, see, and that would be the way to ensure that Madison's new boyfriend —"

"Her what?"

"Yeah, you know. He wants to —"

"Oh, yeah. The Interstate Mortuary Services guy."

"I heard it out in the hall."

Vanessa asks Thaddeus about his last day, and he says he'll come in next week to pick up stuff and after that he's on his way. He stands behind the chair now, drums on its seat back. Thaddeus Griffin, of *Single Bullet Theory*. A guy who's no good at saying good-bye, who's no good at anything except holding steady a firearm full of blanks. Vanessa writes on her pad, *Thaddeus goes to Morocco*. He comes around the desk to give her a hug.

"I still work here," he says. "You need help with anything, you know what to do."

He gives the intern a wary glance and makes for the door.

It's the sentimentality part that she can't stand. With the menses. The mother bird feeding the little birds on the nature program. It was a while back, she was flipping around the dial, as if all she ever did was flip around the dial, and whether by chance or design, she landed on this channel, and there was the mother bird feeding the little birds the regurgitated worm or grub or whatever it was, and the little birds were really hungry, edging out one another to be the first chick to devour the regurgitations. What could be more tender on this earth than the little birds and the awful New Age music? The whole phenomenon was so irritating that she took the remote and hid it in the closet with the hardware and the cat litter, and she couldn't find it for a week.

Maybe Thaddeus would do it, knock her up on a noninterventionist basis if she asked in the right way. She'd have to learn some basic romancing skills. She'd have to ask if he were having a good day and how was his wife, and she'd have to ask if she could help him with the crossword. Whatever that stuff was that people did. He's fucked everybody else in the office. Nobody has to tell her; she's not an idiot. Is she that much worse than everyone else? She's a fashionable dresser, and even if she has not exhibited much interest in men, it's not that she doesn't *like* them —

"Do you want lunch?" the intern breaks in.

"Huh?"

"I thought I'd ask if you wanted lunch, because I'm going to go out and get some lunch."

"What are you getting?"

"Tofu scramble. A shot of wheatgrass."

"You just ate three doughnuts."

"Well, if they're in front of me —"

"Get me some fried dumplings at the Chinese place."

The intern stands up and puts out her hand. For the cash.

"No one's given you the lesson yet?"

Vanessa makes up the lesson on the spot. The lesson is how to extract a free lunch from the good Chinese place by claiming to be part of a movie filming on location in the area. You go into the Chinese place, you say that you are making a movie with the biggest star imaginable. You say you are making a movie with Julia Roberts or you say you are making a movie with Tom Cruise or a movie with Brad Pitt or a movie with Nicole Kidman, whoever. You use the name of the most famous movie star imaginable and you say that you really have to have this order as quickly as possible. The difficulty is that the guys in the Chinese place speak very little English, and they have grown up in some unheated cinder-block project in a city like Shanghai, and they have been beset by graft-addicted informers their whole lives long, and they probably owe some toothless slave trader twenty thousand dollars for getting them out of China, and they don't give a shit about Ms. Kidman or Ms. Roberts or Mr. Cruise. And therefore you are going to have to start to cry, you will need to produce tears at the Chinese place, and you will have to say that your job is on the line. If you don't bring these dumplings over to the trailer right now, your job is on the line. You will have to say that you are having a really bad day, and you will have to say that you are getting your period and that you are about to get fired and that you forgot to bring the petty cash from the office, and can't they just give it to you this one time, you'll bring the cash tomorrow, and you'll also bring them the autograph of one of the big stars tomorrow. And you might mention that the movie is being underwritten by some multinational entertainment conglomerate, like, try Universal Beverages, and see if that gets the attention of the heartbroken maître d', try saying "Steve Case" over and over again and see if that gets their attention, because they understand Steve Case and they understand Bill Gates and Naz Korngold. Tell them that Naz Korngold is underwriting the movie or that Bill Gates will give you the money tomorrow and that you will get the signature of Bill Gates or Naz Korngold, who is definitely making a movie with Thaddeus Griffin, and see if that works. And so your objective is to bring back lunch without taking any money and to do it *fast*.

At the conclusion of these remarks, Vanessa feels better, and there is a poignant light moving through the confines of her office, illuminating bits of dust. The light is moving across the piles of paper, the light is passing. And then the phone rings.

Vic Freese has been promoted this week, that's the word. He is codirector of the television division and he is brimming with confidence, which is almost impossible to take. Vanessa has felt, in the week of conversations with him, that he is getting closer and closer to edging her out of *The Diviners*.

He says, "Lacey has definitely signed on to play Nurit in the Hungarian section, and we have been discussing the idea of her playing a second part later in the film, too. You know, maybe an old woman in the . . . uh, Mormon episode."

"What Mormon episode? I just had Thaddeus in here, and he was making up all this shit about the Mormons; I thought he was just —"

"Van," he says, "you have to stay up to date. The Mormon section was a condition of sharing expenses with Interstate Mortuary Services."

"Interstate Mortuary Services?"

"A subsidiary of UBC."

"I know who they are."

"They want to get involved in content. Content is the future. For Interstate Mortuary Services and their shareholders. Every consumer that they can get acquainted with the Interstate Mortuary brand is more likely to call on them later, when they are confronting a fatality situation."

"A fatality situation? Listen, I just want to make sure that we're . . . that Means of Production is the development arm of the series right now, because we have all our people working on it. We have it out with two writers, and I'm going to see who comes up with the best treatment for the first episode, and then we're going to move the ball forward."

"You don't even have a writer yet? Jesus. We're talking principal photography no later than September."

"We have *names.*"

"Look, I don't know how long I can hold the place for you. There are other parties interested. Big names, names I'm not at liberty to reveal. There are people who think there's theme park potential here. Everybody loves a water ride. There's cross-marketing potential with the divining rods. The toy companies have been contacted. And did I tell you about the really great product placement underwriting agreement we have right now?"

"Uh, don't tell me . . . doughnuts."

"Exactly!"

"My people *secured* that Krispy Kreme financing."

"Vanessa, don't bullshit me. My assistant here is in close touch with the chairman at Krispy Kreme. . . . Hang on. Gretchen? Gretchen? How many calls have we made to the guys at Krispy Kreme on the thing? The *thing!* Hang on. Vanessa, did you hear that? Did you hear what she just said? She says we've made at least twenty calls this week to the Krispy Kreme guys alone. In the last two weeks. Their involvement was a prerequisite for all the talks with UBC."

"You didn't talk to UBC, Vic. I talked to UBC. I talked to Maiser right after I talked to you . . . what day was that? Saturday? I talked with him right after that. He didn't mention talking to you. It was all me. I did the pitch, and I'm in touch with the guy. Don't mess with my contacts."

"How long can I hold the spot for you? Can I hold it forever for you? Vanessa, I can't. I would like to, but I can't. That's all. Get your story together. Tell me who's attached, and as long as they're clients of this agency, we're in business. I think I can get you the line producer job on the actual filming if you want it."

"Line producer, my ass. How many days do I have?"

"You have a few days."

"Because you have no idea —"

"I don't care what's been going on."

"Okay, okay. Judy Davis for Brigham Young's wife . . ."

"Are you crazy? Can you say the word? The word is *Australian.*"

"She's *not* Australian."

"She's Australian as puddles of beer vomit."

"I don't believe it."

"Gotta go!"

The intern appears with the dumplings. She pulls her chair up right next to Vanessa's desk and she spreads wide the plastic trays. She arranges the little pools of dunking sauces. She makes her preparations with a minimum of conversation. She holds up chopsticks in one hand and in the other she holds a plastic fork. Vanessa wants the plastic fork but takes the chopsticks.

The intern says, "I told them we were in discussions about a reality show called *Take-Out.* Who can deliver the items the fastest, that kind of thing. They knew all about reality television. They kept repeating Regis Philbin's name in the form of a question."

The intern has one expression and the expression is boredom. And the question is, in this time of unprecedented prosperity and budget surplus, why all the boredom? The intern eats a dumpling. And then, in a ruminative spirit, she offers the following: "My father is ready to give you the green light, but you have to tell him that I'm here. And you have to tell him that I'm going to do the location scouting. That's what I want to do first. My career trajectory is up the production side. In this case, I want to be able to drive around the Southwest for a few weeks, looking for the right locations."

Never once does a flicker of interest pass across her vampirically pale features.

"How do you know that he's ready to give us the green light?"

"He's embarrassed by my mom. By the divorce settlement. By his stupid girlfriend. He's looking for a place where he can make a stand. And he's embarrassed about the news division. He's going to have staff reductions in the news division, and he's going to have to do more tabloid television type of stuff, and he doesn't want to, because the news guys are the only guys he likes. He'd rather do anything than have more reality programs, but he has to do it. And when he has to do stuff like that he's always looking for something else. What's the thing he can do that's completely different from whatever everyone else is doing? A miniseries. Why would he want to do that? It's stupid. A miniseries is just a bad idea. Who actually watches these things? Nobody watches them."

"What do you mean?"

"Some Civil War thing with Robert Duvall in a hairpiece? Nobody watches that except your grandparents and the Civil War reenacters. Get drunk and eat a lot of fried chicken out of buckets and then pretend to fire your musket at your neighbor the muffler repairman. Then you pretend to have your leg cut off by the Walt Whitman character. That's who watches the miniseries. Nobody wants to do them, and that's exactly why my father will want to. He's going to want to look like he's a man of principle."

"You think I should call him?" Vanessa nervously wipes off her lips with a take-out napkin for the fifth time.

"He's going to call you. But you have to be completely ready. If you don't have a writer, lie about having a writer. If you don't have directors lined up, lie about having directors. And when he says to fly out there, don't take any meetings with anyone from the network where he's not present. By the way, my scouting ticket has to be business class."

Then they go back to the dumplings. After that, a couple more doughnuts. The intern gives Vanessa a disquisition on her interests. The intern likes Antonioni, the intern likes Tarkovsky, the intern likes Fassbinder, the intern likes Sirk, the intern likes Kurosawa, the intern likes Ozu, the intern likes Wenders, the intern likes Herzog, especially the Kinski films. She wrote her senior thesis on Kinski. And Vanessa makes up a list of movies that the intern should watch that she hasn't yet seen, and she does it with zest, even if her stomach suddenly feels as if something is inside her, intent on gnawing its way out. When the intern finally goes back out to her desk to chew on her hangnail some more, Ranjeet and Jeanine peer into the office as if they've been waiting.

"Got a second?" Jeanine says.

Vanessa looks for her pen and her list of problems.

Jeanine wears an expression of forced joviality. Ranjeet is dressed in an expensive suit, and he wears a matching tie and pocket square, and he has removed his turban and shaved his beard. Ranjeet is beaming. He has been living in the office, Vanessa knows, because the kitchenette has become a chaotic scene. It smells like vindaloo in there. Vanessa should feel concerned. She's sure he once mentioned a family. Maybe he's not in close contact with his family this week. What she likes is that she has an employee who stays long after she has left for the night and who is there before she gets into the office in the morning. If he has to shave in the kitchenette, fine. He's out there trying to meet with the big agents, and he's talking to casting directors about the miniseries, and he's going over the treatment, sentence by sentence. He's a postcolonial onslaught.

"I am here," he says, "to make a presentation. My assistant, Jeanine, has helped me in the matter of this presentation."

What he does is stretch wide his arms, as though he's doing some kind of special Sikh dance or something, and he says that the prologue to the miniseries must begin with the four fundamental elements, these elements being earth, air, fire, and water. Remember, he says, that when the Hun sweeps down from the plains, what the Hun brings is fire. Remember that the dawn of civilization is a moment of much fire. The hunters and gatherers, Ranjeet says, shiver in the dark on the plains until they remember that the fire can be *fed*. The fire can be fed with sticks and branches and it will continue to warm them. Turn toward the fire! This is how it is with the Hun, sweeping down from the plains, bringing conflagration to the decadent civilization of the Romans and the Saxons and the Gauls. So the miniseries itself, Ranjeet says, begins with fire, and the first image is of fire, and the camera sweeps through the forest at the moment when three separate fires are about to converge on a fourth, a moment of pure immolation, the kind that firefighters dread more than all else. And, yes, this fire could be anywhere, this fire could be in forests of the United States or it could be in Siberia; the audience doesn't know at first, Ranjeet says. We know only that it is fire. And what feeds the fire? What feeds the fire is wind. And so in the midst of these fires, we feel the gusts blowing, we feel the flaming trees swaying in the gales, and then there is a shot from a helicopter, sweeping along the treetops as they burst into spectacular combustion, as if the conflagration is gobbling up trees by the hectare. And now we come to the edge of the wood, and the camera is actually dollying backward, down a hillside, a hillside already scorched, left with nothing but blackened stumps, as a cavalry of

Huns flees out of the forest before the massing of the three fires, north, east, and west, before the windswept conflagration, Ranjeet says. They sweep down the hillside, and now the camera pivots as the cavalry of Huns goes past, and it gallops with them farther down, where, ahead, we can see a village of farmers and traders, and we can see now that the Huns are intent on descending into the village, and once the marauders have rushed past the camera, we see a last straggling pair of Huns, one with a crutch, and his companion, a Moor. Clots of dirt are flung up by the hooves of horses, Ranjeet says, fouling the surface of the lens, and into this hillside of ash and dirt plunges the man on crutches, falling to his knees and then onto his side. When he rises up slowly, he looks at the dirt in his hands. The fire is behind him and around him. The wind has changed direction, violently, and now the fire is flanking the little town of farmers and traders of the Silk Road, and the man knows, the man on crutches knows this, and he looks at his companion, the Moor. No words are exchanged between these devoted friends, but the sentiment is clear.

Only the pure of heart, only the humble of intent, the look seems to say, only the faithful, only the believers, can rise to a moment so fraught with peril. And then the man, Ranjeet says, lifts up his crutch, and what the camera sees, Ranjeet says, is the crutch against the flaming sky, here are the flames, and here are the black clouds and flames so hot that you would throw yourself on poison-tipped pikes to escape them, the flames on all sides, and I promise you this part could all be done with models and with found footage of American fires, but against all this is the crutch, and suddenly we find our hero, because that's who he is, a hero, seizing the crutch in the forked V where he has placed his arm all these many years that he has been lame, and it's like he has been healed in this moment of peril, healed by his need to do the thing that must be done, and he is holding the crutch aloft and he is saying these words, with all the anguish and grandiosity of a man who is saving an entire civilization from itself: "The innocents of this town shall not perish for want of rain!"

The Moor raises up his cloak over his head against another gust of the wind that is controlling the events of this storied day, and above him we see the great black clouds that have been gathering, the clouds that we have not been able to make out because of the smoke from the forests, but now we can see, because the camera is level with the clouds scudding over the scenery; yes, there are great black clouds that are heavy with rain, that are pregnant with the possibility of rain. And this is the moment, the moment of the pronouncement of our hero, when the rains begin. In a tempest. Again, Ranjeet observes, this could all be done with models and digital enhancements. There will be no need to actually film these storms.

"I tell you these things," Ranjeet says, "because I want to say to you that I am the man who must direct the miniseries. At the very least I must direct the first episode, and also the episode which concerns the founding of Las Vegas. I am the man because I have the vision. I must direct."

26

Behold, a portrait of the family, in the year 2000, as preserved on the digital video camera of aspiring filmmaker Annabel Duffy. The family assembled in the living room. Duffy residence, Newton, Massachusetts. First, the Reverend Russell Hunt Duffy, in casual clothes, a pair of easy-fit jeans ordered from the L.L. Bean catalogue, a turtleneck in brown, cardigan sweater with cables. He's wearing slippers, too, but they're not in the shot. The camera captures the Reverend Duffy's discomfort. The vacant smile, as if pasted into his salt-and-pepper beard, is the indicator that the Reverend Duffy doesn't know what to think. He squints. He gives nothing away. The Reverend Duffy, depicted as a man of strident routines. A man who has made sure that the used books in the bookshelf behind him are rigorously alphabetized, though many of the books are unread now for decades.

Beside him on the couch is his wife, Deborah Weller, PhD, who has her arm around the reverend, not vice versa. She's the one who's laughing about the whole thing, laughing about the slow pan, about the idea that Annabel should film the five of them while they are all there, because it's what she can do, because it's her gift. Annabel promises not to do anything with the film, not if they are unhappy with the results. It's what she can give them, a portrait, when they are doing the one thing they can do, which, she says, is loving one another. Her mother is the one with the surfeit of love. Her mother on the couch, her mother laughing as if nothing in years has been as good as having the five of them here for this unscheduled time, even if it is a gathering that has an unfortunate premise, Tyrone. But that's forgotten during the duration of this slow pan from right to left. Her mother is wearing navy blue corduroys and a paint-stained chamois-cloth shirt, cream colored, and her long brown-and-gray hair is shaggy around her shoulders, and her expression is both exhausted and joyous. If she had to lift a Volkswagen off any of them, she could do it. And yet is her mother anything else *besides* a force for selflessness and love? Where is that other woman, libertine, the hidden lover of sensuality, the drinker of too much wine, and why is she never in the shot? Why always laughing, selfless, and full of joy?

Next, her older brother. Her brother, the last few days, has remained in bed until the early afternoon. At midday he skulks down into the kitchen to look at the newspapers, with his glasses on, in whatever outgrown formal clothes remain here in the house, a pair of khaki pants that he had to wear for his confirmation however many years ago, and a button-down oxford that isn't tucked in. He still looks like the smartest guy Annabel has ever met. If only there weren't his difficulties, the weeks where he doesn't sleep and calls her at all hours with ideas about the interconnectedness of banking, drug cartels, and descendants of the *Mayflower* families. Followed by the months of muteness and retreat. If only. Here on the couch, you can see him trying on three different ways not to stare, and then staring just the same. Staring into the camera as if this is to be the mug shot they might have taken of him at central booking.

Even as she looks at his face in the monitor of the camera, she can see something else happening, slowly at first, the hand of her older brother, reaching toward the free hand of his mother, the black fingers of her brother's hand walking across the couch toward his mother's white hand, and the filmmaker is observing a rigorous cinematic detachment while this little thing happens, the black fingers of the son interlacing themselves with the white fingers of the mother. Nothing is said; it's just a moment worth studying. Her brother's face never changes, and her mother's face never changes, and the camera pauses, and then it continues its journey.

The younger brother is wearing whatever it is that he thinks he has to be wearing these days, because he's still in this moment when he has to be wearing something that indicates dissent. Some protest is always being implied. He has on the baggy jeans, and he has on his so-called wife-beater, and he has donned the jewelry, the jewelry that will have the maximum impact in the right-to-left movement of the camera across the text of the Duffys. Her younger brother. He has so quickly assumed the mantle of the Duffy who has to call the revolutionary police down on the rest of them, her younger brother with his pierced face and his multiple tattoos. Her brother who won't even talk about the sinister group of teenagers he was associating with, and who won't say anything about whether they were involved with the arson at that franchise restaurant in Concord. Nevertheless, here he is flush against his older brother, though there's another three feet remaining on the couch, crushed up against his older brother as if it's his older brother who's going to solve the problems of the world. The younger brother looks as if he's about to lean his head on his brother's shoulder, and now the camera retreats to a wider angle, until they are all in the frame, and then the filmmaker herself jogs past the coffee table and past the stack of art books, past the decorative fern on the side table. There's the sound, from off screen, of the dishwasher in the kitchen changing cycles.

The filmmaker almost pounces on the shot as she dives in next to her younger brother and reaches her hand all the way down the line until she manages to get her arm around three of them, around her younger brother, her older brother, and her mother. Behold the family. What does the camera know? The camera knows that the American family consists of at least one adulterer, that the American family consists of a mother with depressive symptoms undiscussed with the other protagonists in frame; and the American family consists of at least two races; and the American family consists of at least one young man with a serious mental illness; and the American family consists of at least one young woman who has had sex with her own gender on a number of occasions and who thought it was kind of hot; and the American family consists of at least one screenplay writer and one master of divinity; and the American family consists of one teenager who is a total outcast at his school. Behold the family, sought after by the police of large metropolises, compulsive about sexuality and psychiatric medication, uncertain as to its political beliefs, argumentative, dismissive, except when loving, brilliant, broken, sad, and about to do one thing all together, as one. And that one thing is *not* to sit and discuss their many problems in a sober and loving way. No, the American family, as soon as the digital camera is shut off, is going to perform its one regular activity. It's going to watch television.

And what are they going to watch?

The Werewolves of Fairfield County! Because it's a Sunday at 8:00 PM. And this is the Thanksgiving episode, as broadcast on the UBC network, the network of the American family. UBC has been heavily promoting the Thanksgiving episode of *The Werewolves of Fairfield County*. Because the network knows a hit when it sees a hit. Everybody, for some reason, is now watching *The Werewolves of Fairfield County*. The cast was on the cover of a major newsweekly a fortnight ago. The Halloween episode is normally the big episode in the fall season, but the creator, Christine Katz, has spoken in recent interviews of the need, in this the fourth season, to come up with new creative challenges for herself and her staff of writers. This year it is the much-ballyhooed Thanksgiving episode.

A synopsis of the general themes of *The Werewolves of Fairfield County* is in order, for those who have somehow missed the previous three seasons. Of course, it's important to note that the lycanthropes of the program are not afflicted with an illness, some disease, some contagion, caused by the bite of another werewolf. No, this is not the lycanthropy of your Lon Chaney Jr. films, from the high period of horror films. Nor is it dependent on *I Was a Teenage Werewolf*, the nineteen-fifties articulation of this condition. No, the lycanthropy of *The Werewolves of Fairfield County*, which is the lycanthropy of the new millennium, is genetic, part of a spontaneous evolutionary mutation. In Fairfield County, stronghold of the affluent and powerful here in the northeastern megalopolis, the human species has spontaneously come to express a genetic crisis. In Fairfield County, the human species has mutated, such that the tennis stars and swashbuckling fiscal experts of the county number among them those who grow hair on their knuckles and howl for blood at every full moon.

The werewolves have formed themselves into a pack. Season two, in particular, was organized around this principle. The pack protects the individuals from being pruned by the police or by the unscrupulous hunters of the area. The pack keeps its members from needlessly taking human life. And so, in season two, the werewolves began to exhibit a certain crude moral rectitude. For example, during the second episode, the werewolves happened upon the mayor of Waterbury, who had embezzled funds from his education budget, and they tore him limb from limb in a sequence that was considered too violent for the hour at which it was broadcast.

The older wolves look after the younger wolves. The Caucasian wolves of Fairfield County, who outnumber the others, protect the Asian and African American wolves, though there is no discerning the racial origins of the werewolves when they are under the sway of the full moon. The rich wolves, of whom there are many, protect the poor wolves. The strong protect the weak. It's true, the social conditions of the pack would seem an improvement on the relationships that are formed by "human civilization." This was driven home, e.g., in the third season, whose theme was the mixed blessing of wealth. Ezra Montgomery Scott, one of the alpha dogs, was being tried by an overzealous state prosecutor for insider trading, while at the same time he was caring for a teenager at his home, a new member of the pack. The young man, of course, was frightened by and unprepared for the manifestation of his mutation. He was a caddy at the Round Hill Club and he was an orphan, and Ezra Scott, while playing a late round of golf with his lawyers, thought he recognized something in the boy. He took him home to give him a talking-to.

The moon was nearly full. Scott locked himself and the boy in the basement, as was his habit for the entirety of the three days, and when the two of them weren't baying lonesomely, in a way that drove Scott's pair of greyhounds wild, he tried to persuade the boy that though his new identity was a cross to bear, there were things that were salubrious about being a werewolf. For example, there was a sense that you belonged. There was the certainty that there were always others who had compassion for you, even when things were at their hardest. This Ezra Scott explained to the young inductee, though in doing so Scott missed meetings and hearings relevant to his court case. When the boy manifested suicidal ideation, Scott cared for him, and when the boy tried to attack Scott at night, Scott managed to keep him from getting injured. All while Scott was meant to be rehearsing talking points with his defense team. For the price of his kindness, Ezra Scott was convicted of stock fraud and sent to the penitentiary, from which he escaped at the next full moon.

Even among fans, the first season was noteworthy for clichés of the horror genre. The first season was mainly about teenagers. If the program had considerable insight into middle-class teenagers and their fashionable obsessions with copyright infringement and low-riding jeans, it was right in step with most fare on the UBC network. But when the second season introduced the grizzled railroad employee from Stamford, Mike Woodwell, it was clear that something new was happening on network television. Ratings began to creep up. A lineman on the swing shift for Metro-North, Woodwell lost his wife early in the second season to lupus. Never did the howl of a werewolf on a windswept city street sound more heartrending or more appropriate. Woodwell's subsequent courtship of a black barmaid from Port Chester, Felicia Adams, and his affection for her two sons, one of whom is disabled, was one of the most graceful introductions of an inter-racial romance in television history. As the critics remarked, there was chemistry between the two. It was about this time that Deborah Weller, PhD, Annabel Duffy's mom, began to fall for the charm of the show. She got her daughter hooked the next spring when the DVDs of the first season, with extra commentary, became available.

The Thanksgiving episode of the fourth season, according to teasers, also concerns Felicia Adams. Adams has long since broken up with Woodwell, who nonetheless pines from afar. (He seems destined to be one of those television characters who can never work out how to live.) Felicia is now in love with a strong, charismatic African American character, Edwin Watson, who works at the Life Savers plant in Port Chester but who is currently in danger of having his murky past as a low-level drug dealer revealed by a woman who wants to have an affair with him. In fact, at the end of episode nine, Edwin quits the job at Life Savers, without telling Felicia, though he continues to bring back a roll of candy for the two Adams boys each day.

Felicia is not a perfect mother, nor a perfect barmaid, since she tends to go missing several days a month. Occasionally she's had jobs that were offered her by other members of the pack, but even so she's between positions at present, except for fill-in shifts at an Irish bar at Thanksgiving. Where is the holiday turkey going to come from? And the stuffing and the cranberry sauce and the pies? Who's going to bake the pies? The predicament is made even worse because her elder son, Bennett, a scholarship student at the elite Fairfield Academy, intends to go to a big party tonight at the home of the Burns family. You know, the Burns family. The twin brothers of astonishing good looks, and the sister who's already tearing up the Seventh Avenue fashion shows as a model. Of course, Bennett is aware of the ironies of eating Hamburger Helper and then going to a party with the high-fashion-model daughter of the Burns family, who he's pretty sure has a crush on him, just as he does on her.

Naturally, each episode has its narrative crisis that can only be faced by the pack as a whole. In the Thanksgiving episode, this crisis has to do with the fact that the ubiquitous deer of Fairfield County are beginning to suffer with a strange, inexplicable wasting disease, and the governor of the state, an independent in the tradition of Lowell Weicker, has declared open season, with high limits, for the deer hunters of the Nutmeg State. No one is meant to *eat* any of the venison until state regulators are certain that the danger is passed. But it's okay to shoot at deer. The wolf pack, which will be gathering this weekend for the full moon, is in grave danger not only of being pruned in the indiscriminate blasting away at bucks and does but also liable to be famished, too desperate to go without deer, notwithstanding the wasting disease.

This is where the episode begins. In a state park near Bedford, where, at dusk, a pair of bow hunters is sharing a flask and trying not to make a lot of noise. Suddenly, a commotion in the woods.

A buck sweeps by, followed close behind by a pack of wild dogs. What a moment of great beauty. Must be an eight-point buck, his rack a beautiful thing to encounter. The crossbow hunters raise their medieval weapons — which have carbon arrow shafting and vibration dampers and pendulum sighting systems and cat whisker string silencers — with intent to take out this white-tailed specimen. They have fantasies of venison steaks in their freezers all winter long. But suddenly there are these dogs and they are, uh, they are extremely large dogs, dogs such as these hunters have never seen before. The pack of wild dogs seems to swell and grow in ways that begin to frighten the men. There must be thirty or more of them! The men shrink back under the canopy of a pine, which gives comfort for a moment, until the pack takes note of them. A group of fifteen or so of the younger pups, eager to kill and flush with their own mad energy, turns and heads for the bow hunters.

Now the credit sequence with the moonrise over Darien and New Canaan. Moonrise over the soccer practice at Wilton High. Then the short takes of the cast changing into wolves while there is mournful slide guitar and harmonica wailing in the background. *The Werewolves of Fairfield County,* brought to you by the United Broadcasting Company. In Newton, Massachusetts, Annabel Duffy notices during the commercial break that instead of watching the program, her brother Tyrone has a book in his lap. And in his hand there is a black felt-tip marker. It can mean only one thing! Her brother is making art! Defaced books! Her mother brings in popcorn from the kitchen and sets it on the table, and the Reverend Duffy takes the popcorn, forgetting to thank his wife, and fills his mouth with it.

———

In Santa Monica, Jeffrey Maiser is by himself, in an enormous family room that has no family in it. On three walls there are books, the vast majority unread. He faces a massive entertainment complex with all the latest bells and whistles, accented with a few tennis trophies from his wild youth. The television itself has a plasma screen, and there are so many speakers in the family room that he can't even remember where they all are. He has a scotch on the rocks, and he is sitting in the black leather recliner, and he has turned off every phone in his gigantic and empty house, and he has put his cell phone under a pillow on the sofa, and he has prepared himself for the one unalloyed bit of good news in his programming week. He can't remember exactly what happened in the last episode, and he can't remember what's supposed to happen for the rest of the season, but he can remember what the advertising rates are for the program. The programming executives should be really pleased, even if they will have to pay millions per episode to renew beyond the 2001 season. But that's what's so great about a television program where any character could be killed at any time. You can always hire a new cast.

So where were we? A pack of wolf pups is trained on two bow hunters, all of whose machismo, all of whose high-visibility gear and Ted Nugent rhetoric, cannot save them now. Hesitating only momentarily, like hunting dogs pointing at prey, the pups now stutter-step toward the two huddling figures. One man has let his weapon drop out of his hands in perfect terror, while the other manages to fire off a single camouflage-colored arrow from its high-tension firing mechanism. Because a network television show doesn't have the budget to do one of those camera-mounted-on-the-arrow-as-it-rips-through-the-forest-and-into-the-flesh-of-the-enemy shots, we just hear the arrow sizzle in the dusk until there is the searing howl of one of the werewolves. Someone is hit! This of course doesn't stop the pups. In fact, it emboldens them, and in seconds the two hunters are a pile of bloody laundry. The rest of the pack, almost casually, brings down two magnificent bucks.

When dawn comes, the wolves rise up out of their satiety in a circle around the vivisected bucks. The wolves, human again, with their human clothes in tatters. There's Devon Porter, the daughter of one of the founders of the Central Intelligence Agency and one of the best interior decorators in Greenwich, her mouth ringed with gore. Beside her is Laney Carrington, also an heiress, who seems to have torn a rather expensive gown during last night's feast. Beside them is Laney's housekeeper, an Irish lass called Siobhan McCallister, and Siobhan is making a joke about how venison is not meant to be eaten as sushi is eaten. The three women have a good laugh. A contractor from Norwalk, Bob Gallace, wearing an expression like he is full of worries, is dusting off Clay Goldberg, the internist from Scarsdale. Bob tells Clay he really ought to wipe around his mouth and offers him a handkerchief. Clay says, "If only venison was Thanksgiving fare. I'd take a side of it home to the wife."

"Good point," Bob says, and then shouts generally, "Hey, does anyone want a steak or two for Thanksgiving? I can bring out the pickup and a hacksaw." There are a couple of laughs. "Or maybe one of the heads for the wall of your library?" They'd meant to kill some of the wild turkeys. That's the irony of it all. This town is crawling with wild turkeys.

However, there are those in the pack who are not worrying about turkeys. They are shocked by what the camera reveals now. There was trouble last night. The adults gather by the bodies of the two fallen hunters, where the young pups are shocked by what they have done. They all agree that someone is going to have to dig graves for the two men. And yet a woman moaning nearby alerts them to another tale, just as dark. Liz Carter, the very young, newly accredited English teacher from Fairfield Academy, took the arrow that one of the hunters managed to fire off before his demise. She's pinned against a maple, impaled at the shoulder, still bleeding.

It's Bob who calls out, "Oh my god, Liz!"

Vanessa says to the intern, over at her place to watch, while they eat Cajun pizza, "It's great that they're willing to let the women fight just as violently as the men. There should be, I don't know, bruises on their cheeks, and they should have to shake off the hurt and get back into the fray and stuff. I mean, look at her. She's a mess." That is, look at Liz Carter, pale, fatigued from loss of blood, but very much alive. She's going to have to go to her English class and explain why she has a very deep puncture wound in her left shoulder. And that's after she goes to the hospital and has a large composite arrow, only inches from her heart, removed by the region's best surgeons. When Clay and Bob and Mike Woodwell attempt to carry her out to the road, she lapses quickly into unconsciousness.

The action cuts away to Felicia Adams, who arrives back at home, in tattered jeans and sweater, to find her lover, Edwin, waiting for her at the door. He takes one look and shakes his head with a knowing weariness.

"I'm *still* supposed to believe this line that you have some kind of overnight job three nights a month, and that this is what happens to your clothes every time you go to this job? This is what I'm supposed to believe?"

Felicia says, "You can believe what you want. Remember when I told you that I was a woman who had some issues? Well, one of my issues is work. One of my jobs isn't terribly pleasant."

"If you're carrying on with another man, Felicia, you know it's going to come between us."

"I'm not *carrying on,* as you put it, Edwin, I've told you already. And if I was, this wouldn't be the outfit that I'd be wearing to see him! I don't have time to carry on, I don't have time to love anyone but you and the kids. That's all I want to do, and I can barely keep up with it. C'mon, Eddie, it's Thanksgiving, and we don't have any of the stuff we need for Thanksgiving dinner! We don't have any turkey and we don't have any cranberry sauce. We don't have anything for the kids!"

Felicia's disabled son, Vern (played by an actor who actually has cerebral palsy), walks, in his rickety way, into the shot. As always, he understands more than he's saying. He says almost nothing. With his crutches, he drags along his withered legs. Felicia and Edwin lay off the fighting at the appearance of the boy with the preternatural calm.

On Eleventh Street, in Brooklyn, Allison Maiser argues that the moment is, she says, just like in Ibsen, just like *A Doll's House*. That is, the moment is rich with dramatic irony. Edwin thinks Felicia Adams is a gentle homebody who works hard at the bar, but actually she's trying to cover up that she's just been out in the woods eating deer from the bone with a pack of wolves. Every character, Allison says, knows something that no one else knows. This is the law of the pack, which is therefore the secret of the show, that you cannot give away the secret knowledge of the group. Those who have given away the pack have mysteriously vanished or met a grisly fate. Felicia can't tell Edwin about it and she can't tell him about what has really been worrying her for months —

"The kids," Vanessa says.

The intern says, "Shhhhh."

It's what they all worry about, the adults of the werewolf pack. That their precious kids, the towheaded snowboarding or waterskiing teens of Fairfield County, growing up with all the comforts and advantages of affluence, might turn out to be bloodthirsty animals. They might be playing Pop Warner football one afternoon at dusk, they might be at driving school one afternoon, and, to their horror, they will begin to sprout an ungainly growth of facial hair. They will dispatch three raccoons and somebody's favorite house cat, and they will howl. The pack lives in dread of this familiar turn of events. Though the pack looks after its own, the pack wants only that the gene for its mutation should be recessive. The pack would have its ranks remain thin. In the meantime, the members worry.

Felicia is no exception. The younger boy, Vern, is just twelve, and should he become a werewolf, he will be a werewolf eaten by the others the first night out. And then there's the older boy, Bennett. She's so happy that Bennett is fifteen already, because fifteen is quite late to discover the lupine truth about yourself.

Back to the main action! Edwin, the boyfriend, is furious with Felicia's meager excuses, or so it seems, and he announces he's going *out*, to where we do not know. We see Edwin at a pay phone in town, where, with a furtive expression, he dials what is clearly a bad-news telephone number.

"Yo, brother. Yeah, it's your man, E. Watson. No doubt, no doubt. Had to take care of a few things. Some obligations. Letting the heat die down. But now E. Watson is back, real deal. Look, yeah, I'm going to pay what I owe, my brother, know what I'm saying? Most certainly. Thing is, can you be fronting me? Today is Thanksgiving Day, bro; I need to bring home something for my girl or else I just cannot show my face no more. Have pity on a brother. You will get the first part of the profit, for sure, the second part will be going toward a turkey, then I will work for you for free until all is forgiven."

Edwin has gone back to dealing? On this day of all days! He's such an ineffective drug dealer! And there's no doubt something horrible will transpire the minute he arrives at the house of the evil drug dealer, Alfonse Tilden, who lives in the projects over by the railroad station. (Mike Woodwell, the lineman, tangled with Alfonse last season in one of the two episodes in which no one at all changed into a werewolf.)

Now there is a commercial break.

Vanessa and the intern cannot stand the narrative tension, can't stand the waiting, can't stand *not* knowing what's going to happen, can't stand the time between episodes, can't stand the time between seasons, can't stand the time during the commercials. Though they are tacticians of story, they are taken in by the sweep of narrative, and they want to know what happens more than anything. And this narrative tension somehow brings them together onto the same couch. Until moments ago, Vanessa was on the couch, eating her lukewarm wedge of pizza, and the intern was on the floor, plucking the black olives off a slice and eating only these scarabs, and now the intern is on the sofa, too, as if the sad truth that Edwin is going to suffer retribution, gangland style, on this, Thanksgiving Day, is too much for them. The distance between their bodies begins incrementally to diminish, as though they were glaciers drifting ominously toward each other in a great arctic sea. *To Be Continued . . .*

27

Ranjeet exclaims, "This is the most important moment of the entire season, this moment when these characters must sit down for the Thanksgiving meal! It is the region of New England, and they have nothing for the Thanksgiving dinner, they have only the cold cut variety of turkey, such as you might find at any delicatessen! You could get it anywhere, and it is always inferior! It's a loaf of turkey, nothing more! This is all they have! This is meant to be the feast that proves that America is most bountiful and can survive the entirety of the winter with its bounteous harvest, and yet all these persons possess is the cold cut turkey, and they are attempting to make instant potatoes from a box of potatoes, and they have the Jell-O and it has small bits of fruit floating in it, and this is the great bounty of America! It is not even real food. It is chemicals. And this is what they have because they are disenfranchised by reason of their color and by reason of a disadvantageous political system."

Jeanine tells him: Put a lid on it, because the moment is poignant, and he is actually talking through the program, and she wants to see what the kids are going to say. Because the kids are gathered around the character named Felicia Adams in the kitchen, which is tiny, with just a couple of cupboards that will not close because they have been painted over too many times, and inside these cupboards is her great collection of mismatched plates bought mostly from tag sales. And yet despite the grimness of the Thanksgiving, the Adams boys are gathered around their mother. They know, even if she doesn't say so, that she's trying hard. That counts for a lot on Thanksgiving. Even Bennett, the older boy, is attempting to be kind of generous. Still, young Vern asks, "Mom, this all we're going to have?"

"It's what we've got for now," his mother observes. "You think the Pilgrims had Jell-O? They didn't have any Jell-O. They didn't have one piece of fruit or anything. Orange slices in that Jell-O? Oranges come from Florida, probably. Florida was a swamp back then. The Pilgrims all had scurvy. Their teeth were falling out, and they never flossed."

Bennett says, "It's because we're poor."

"We're *not* poor," Felicia says. "We're busy. And sometimes we're too busy to manage. Folks are penalized for being busy these days, at least in our tax bracket. There are a whole lot of people who are a lot poorer than we are."

The doorbell rings.

In the Means of Production office, in the conference room, with the tiny little office television on the brand-new conference table, Jeanine shifts in the arms of her Sikh lover, thinking not about the poignancy of Felicia's attempts to fix dinner for her family, and not about how family is always capable of rising above grim circumstances. No, Jeanine is thinking about her lover's wife and son, and the Thanksgiving they are going to have this coming week. This ushers in a sinking feeling. It's a sinking feeling that she imagines is not unlike the feelings of the television character Felicia Adams, who is in a race against time to fix Thanksgiving dinner by 2:30 so that she can get the dishes cleaned, including the pots, before moonrise. Because as soon as the moon rises, Felicia will not be in the mood for housework.

Jeanine imagines that her situation is like Felicia's situation, in that their lives harbor secrets. And this is the way that *The Werewolves of Fairfield County* does its job, not through the richness of its screenwriting, nor through able performances, but by virtue of the simple human tendency to see one's vulnerabilities in others, to be, in these instances, full of pity for the frailty of both human beings and werewolves.

At the sound of the bell, Felicia goes to the door, and there, framed in it, is Edwin. Down the corridor, she can see neighbors peeking out of their own units. They all gander at Edwin because Edwin is carrying the most enormous turkey, the most enormous turkey Felicia has ever seen, housed in a beautiful new turkey pan. It's as if he stepped out of a Dickens tale.

Felicia says, "Where did you get that turkey?"

As smiling Felicia attempts to take the pan from him, hefts it out of his arms, Edwin slumps to the floor. Bleeding. Yes, Edwin is bleeding from a gunshot wound in his left shoulder. Edwin has been shot.

Felicia Adams cries out. Because it's one more thing. Because she just doesn't have time. Because the meal is not ready, and if the meal is not ready, we can easily surmise, the meal will not be done on time, and if the meal is not done on time, Felicia will turn into a werewolf before it is done. And so there is no time for more catastrophe. And yet here it is. Now Bennett and Felicia (the latter having set down the turkey pan in the front hall) drape Edwin's arms around their shoulders and they drag him into the apartment. He's groaning in pain, and it's a sort of feral moan. Mother and son drag the injured man through the corridor and into the bedroom, where they lift him as best they can onto the bed. Felicia hurries into the kitchen to make a compress. She seems to suspect immediately what's going on.

"You want me to call the doctor?" she says with a frosty reserve.

"No doctors," Edwin says, according to his part.

Then, in a moment that is so artful it doesn't seem to belong on television, the audience realizes that the enormous turkey, in its enormous Williams-Sonoma turkey pan, is still out in the hall. The camera has paused upon this culinary item. A beautiful amber light shines upon the turkey. The camera is panegyrical. We hear Felicia and Edwin in the bedroom, and Felicia is whispering, "What did you get into? Did you get into what I think you got into? What were you doing down there? Do you have something you want to tell me?"

"I'm so sorry, I'm so sorry. All I wanted was to provide, I swear to you. I wanted to provide something. For you and the boys. For the dinner. All I wanted to be was the man who provided."

The camera has never once strayed from the turkey in the hall, and gradually we are aware that there's some kind of scraping taking place in the hall, right behind the camera, and only incrementally do we realize that it's the sound of crutches, crutches edging into the shot. And then Vern is everywhere in one margin of the frame, like a seal pup on dry land, flopping in the hall. It's just Vern, trying to get himself down to the level of the turkey, which involves dropping the crutches. Now he tries to lift up the pan. He tries in different ways, to no avail. Soon he tumbles weakly onto his side, on the floor, beside the turkey.

Felicia says to Edwin, "What am I supposed to do with you?"

"It went clean through," Edwin says. "Just leave me for a few days. It'll be fine."

"I can't look after you all day, Edwin."

"Don't worry about it. Don't worry about the money or the rent or anything for right now."

"I don't want you coming back here telling me not to worry about money and bleeding from a gunshot wound in your shoulder!"

Vern, who has given up trying to lift the pan, gets a grip on one of the turkey legs and rips it off. He pauses at the sight of his good fortune at first, as if there's some built-in hesitator in him. And this is when we hear Bennett's voice for the first time, back in the other room, and Bennett is saying, "Is he going to die, Mommy?" At the word, the camera slowly tracks back from Vern, back toward the kitchen. With a Hitchcockian uncanniness, it enters the bedroom, where, in afternoon light, the tableau is as in the Northern Renaissance. The potential is for another missing father, like all the fathers missing from the life of young Bennett Adams, who once had a real father, and who found a replacement father in Mike Woodwell, only to suffer when his mother could no longer live with Mike, because of Mike's paralyzing sadness, and now here is Edwin, lying wounded on the bed, and Bennett is unable to lose another father. Felicia says, "No, he's not going to die; he's going to live so that I can yell at him some more," at which point she looks out into the hall and calls, "Vern, you put that back in the pan right now! Darn it! We're *not* going to eat that turkey. We're going to take that turkey down to the church and we're giving it to people who really need something to eat."

"Oh, come on now," Edwin says.

"I'm not eating the turkey if it's an ill-gotten turkey," she says. And then, looking out into the hall, "Vern!"

And Edwin says, "Look in the coat, at least look in the coat. A neighbor gave me those, I swear. Look in my coat."

The camera closes in on Bennett, who is nearest to the blood-stained bomber jacket flung on a chair. And he reaches into the pockets and pulls out . . . three turnips.

Edwin says, "No Thanksgiving holiday is complete without turnips."

What to make of these root vegetables, in the eyes of Jeanine Stampfel? She knows these are not stories well told, if judged against a Chekhov or an O'Neill, but she has cried at commercials for antidepressants and at medical programs with deformed children on them, even though she knows better. Should she be judged for crying at this moment because of turnips, and because of Vern, who can't get up without his crutches and who is laid out sideways next to the turkey, dutifully refraining from any pilfering? You would think Ranjeet would be crying, too, but he's not crying, he's saying, "Root vegetables! Root vegetables! Of course! The root vegetable is the symbol of the thing that is being forged in this family, which is a provisional family, but which is nonetheless better than many biological families! They must eat the roots to feel the roots! The thing which is born of the earth! A tuber!"

————

A motel just off the interstate in the great swing state of Ohio, the interstate that goes all the way from coast to populous coast, this is the place that two miscreants, Lois DiNunzio and Arnie Lovitz, have holed up for the past five days, imagining that if they lay low and pay for everything in cash they will not be traced to this motel. They imagine that every day spent in this way is an improvement on the day on which they ran off with the funds. It is a part of their every transaction with the world, the money, not as a guarantor of ease, but of ultimate condemnation. They have this money, but sooner or later they are going to be found out. Is it possible for them to love each other with the stolen monies hanging over them? Is it possible for them to love each other in a sequence of motels with names like Defiance Motor Court? The answer to these questions is yes, they don't seem to have a problem loving each other, at least so far. They put the dread about the money in one compartment and they put their love in a different and more roomy compartment. They try to keep the two separated as much as possible. And so they love each other and they worry, and tonight they are loving and worrying in front of *The Werewolves of Fairfield County*, except that so far Arnie has been expressing some disappointment with the episode because, he says, when there's not enough werewolf stuff in the program he just doesn't like it as well. He's got control of the remote. He clicks it relentlessly. While dragging on a Gitane cigarette, his third in a row.

"Lay off. I want to watch the end," Lois says.

"Checking the scores." He exhales deeply. "Anyways, how can you have a show that's supposedly about werewolves and you don't have any werewolves in it?"

"If you'd be patient, you'd probably get what you want."

When the show comes back from the break, it's one of those transitional sequences that is mainly a teaser for the ongoing serial narrative, namely, a sequence of Bob Gallace and Clay Goldberg talking on the phone as the light dwindles. Bob is calling Clay because he's worried. He's in his little house in Norwalk, and his kids are out in the yard, throwing a football, and he's got the game on, and he's whispering.

"Clay," he says, "I'm feeling really fatigued today. I just feel like . . . well, I don't know what I feel like. I feel like I can barely stand up without . . . without fainting or something. You feel okay?"

"I feel okay, partner, I sure do. I can give you the once-over before the moon crests, if that'll help. Running a fever?"

"I am, Clay. Nothing serious yet, but it's a little bit of a fever. And I'm just incredibly thirsty, you know. I just can't stop drinking. You don't think I have that wasting disease or anything, do you? I mean, it's not like —"

"Creutzfeldt-Jakob? I think that's a big stretch, Bob. I think our . . . our particular genetic differences might protect us from stuff like that, and anyway, the incubation period on human spongiform encephalopathy is ten years. Talk to me about it when you're on Social Security, okay? In the meantime, be sure to hydrate."

Bob cradles the hands-free receiver. He's pacing in the living room nervously, and while he is pacing it comes over him, the convulsion. The kids are visible through the window, throwing the football, and the football spirals in slow motion in the shot while a shank of mammalian fur trembles in one corner of it, and a long, desperate howl freezes everything.

"Excellent!" says Arnie.

———

Thaddeus Griffin, screen actor, turns on the show in the middle, just in time to see Bob Gallace suddenly overcome by supernatural transformation, and the cannabis he just smoked is so powerful, so much stronger than it was when, long ago, he was a teenage doper wannabe, that he's not sure if he can watch this show without freaking out a little bit. It's a bad idea to watch these shows without anyone else around. Like if you are smoking a lot of pot, for example. Like if you are a guy whose wife has just moved back in with her parents, or say you are a guy who has pretty much walked out on his producer's job and who is just waiting around to go make some piece-of-shit movie in Morocco, it's a bad idea for you to be buying dope on the street, where you could be photographed doing so by some tabloid. Bad idea. There's something about that image of the wolf's fur coat that's so *freaky,* and Thaddeus starts to feel like, what does he feel like, he just feels really high, and he quickly changes the channel; he has to remember not to watch this fucking show, it's too fucking scary, definitely he should not be watching it when he's . . . so he changes to some reality thing; there are these people, and they are, where are they, they're on some island, and they all look like they need to . . . they look so skanky, like they really need to bathe, and the guys all have these beards and everything, it's like, uh, actually the guys kind of look like werewolves, if you really want to know the truth, and suddenly Thaddeus is kind of worried that maybe one of them *is* a werewolf, maybe that one guy, maybe he's . . . He flips the channel back to the *Werewolves,* but he can't even stand a minute of the thing, can't stand it, but if he doesn't watch it, then he's just thinking about it, which is even worse than watching it, in a way, and now there's some, uh, some black kid going to . . . he's going to a keg party or something, nothing so bad, it's just a party, see? It's just a party, it's nothing to get so freaked out about. But soon Thaddeus starts feeling like something really horrible is going to happen to the black kid, and soon there's going to be that kind of music, you know, dissonant chords and stuff, and you know, and he can't take it, he thinks the whole thing is just really freaky, and he shuts off the television because his breathing has become erratic, it's all about his hyperventilations, if he can just get his breathing to settle down, then he won't go on with this thinking that he's, um, he just doesn't even want to think it, but he's looking at his arms, and his arms are incredibly hairy, his arms are all covered with this fur, he never really noticed it before, and if it weren't for the perfect blond locks that the colorist gives him, wait a second, it looks like it must have got darker, he thinks it's getting darker, the hair on his arms, and he tries to calm himself down, and he thinks he should call someone, maybe he could call his wife and tell her, and his stomach is bothering him, and maybe that's the first sign, maybe stomach pain is the first sign, and he could call Annabel, he should call someone, come on, don't be ridiculous, he's just being ridiculous, but no, it's not ridiculous, it's incredibly serious. Nothing has ever been more serious. He starts peeling off layers, feels better if he takes off some clothes, his skin just needs to breathe a little bit, that's it, his skin needs to breathe, it's like everything is constricting, so he takes off his sweatshirt, it's like a three-hundred-dollar sweatshirt, but he takes it off, drops it on the floor, and he takes off his T-shirt, that's a lot better, things are better when he is not wearing a shirt, and then he takes off his jeans, and this is okay, at least for a moment it's okay, until the *panic*, and he's looking at himself, in the recessed entertainment den of his over- or underdecorated apartment, and there is no other conclusion, there is no other way to think about it. Yes, he is even more hairy than he was just a few minutes ago, he's almost sure of it, and there's the stomach pain, and he feels like he's almost doubled over with the stomach pain, and he takes off his socks, because a man should never appear anywhere, not even in the privacy of his own home, in Y-front briefs and dark socks. The question must now be asked, there is no avoiding the question: *Is mine the body of a werewolf?* Has Thaddeus gone from being an actor in action films, highly regarded action films, to being a werewolf? Is this the fitting and karmic end of an actor in action films who has been prone to infidelity, like that singer who was unfaithful, and his wife waited until he was soaking in the tub one day and then she brought in scalding water and dumped it on him? At once, Thaddeus strips off his Y-front briefs, and now he's nature in all its glory, he's the animal in the human animal. Five hundred stations of cable and a hundred more radio stations, and even cable Internet hookup, joystick, and gaming options, and he cannot be distracted from thinking that there is definitely some kind of wolf taking over in him, because he is hairy everywhere, he is lupine, hair all over his back, all over his nipples, and the fur on him is thicker than it ever was, and he is going to need what a wolf needs, he's going to need sides of raw beef, and he's going to need woman flesh, and he's going to have to go out tomorrow and have the whole wolf hide waxed off of his body, because, you know, he can't show up on a movie set in Morocco looking like a wolf or he never will be able to work in the business again. Maybe if he showers he can calm down somehow. He's not a wolf. Just go take a shower and put on some Yanni or something, one of the cable radio stations will have Yanni, all Yanni all the time, maybe there's that video of Yanni playing, that always calms him down, when no one is around, he can put on Yanni and wait for the cannabis to wear off, Yanni will have the proper effect. The swelling repetitions of pan flute will move through him, and the lycanthropy will fade. When the sun comes up tomorrow it will all have been some horrible mistake.

Felicia has forbidden her strong-headed son Bennett Adams from going to the party at the Burns residence. Because of the trouble with Edwin. But that's not the kind of forbidding that's going to keep any teenager from doing exactly what he means to do. Felicia has to go out "to work," or that's what she tells Edwin and the kids, and there's a van waiting at the curb, driven by Rose Liggett, also a werewolf, and it takes Felicia into the woods, where she will meet the thirty-five other members of the pack. The boys are left behind to finish the washing up, and Edwin is slumbering in Felicia's bed, moaning in pain. Vern, who might have a little touch of obsessive-compulsive disorder, is lining up the flatware on the countertop in the kitchen, the knives with the knives, the spoons with the spoons. He doesn't even see when his brother goes right out the front door.

Bennett telephones for a cab on the corner, and he gets in the taxi, spending money from his part-time job at the sporting-goods store at the mall in New Rochelle. He ditches the taxi on the road a block over from the Burnses' house. He's going to walk in the front door as if he's come from the wilderness or as if he's the hero from a Maupassant story, which he sort of is. He comes from New York, not from Connecticut, he comes from the disadvantaged part of Westchester County, but he can put on a good masquerade, and he's putting one on now, having dressed up in the wardrobe of the kids of Fairfield Academy, featuring the threads of J. Crew and Banana Republic. He passes between the antebellum columns of the Burns residence, and then he crosses the imperial threshold. Inside, the kids are hanging off of every piece of furniture, and the music is blasting, the kind of music that occurs only at the parties of television shows.

Meanwhile, back among the audience, in the Park Avenue apartment of Madison McDowell's parents, who, like the Burnses, are away for the night, Madison tells Zimri Enderby that she doesn't know why they can get so much right on television, things that the movies can never get right anymore, like discomfort and awkwardness between people, and the long, slow development of characters, the ups and downs of long-term relationships, but they can never get the music right. Zimri doesn't know much about it, since he was never allowed to go to parties as a kid, except parties where they served ginger ale and there was bingo and sing-alongs. He doesn't know what the music should sound like. Zimri is sitting on the floor, so he can get closer to the television, and Madison is touched by the fact that he is on the floor and still wearing his impeccably polished loafers. Her cell phone rings, and she looks at the number, and she realizes that it's the Vanderbilts calling. They always call during *The Werewolves of Fairfield County*. The Vanderbilts are just really pissed that this stuff is happening, that there are these shows, you know, that are just, like, really popular, and they have nothing to do with this popularity, mainly because the producer is, like, such a bitch. The Vanderbilts could really give her some *phat* ideas about guest stars, like models and recording artists who should definitely be on the show, but Madison doesn't answer the cell phone, she just flings the phone across the room and then she tumbles back into the middle of the story.

Bennett Adams sees Merry Burns coming down the stairs! A blessing is promised in the moment, because Merry sees him, and he sees her, and the contagion of desiring passes back and forth like in a closed-circuit diagram. Everyone sees them seeing each other, and we see them seeing each other. Everybody knows better than to get in the way of that binding of gazes. There's a hurtling movement to the episode, to the way that two beautiful teenagers draw near to each other. And there's some witty repartee, as when Bennett says that he's especially thankful this year that her parents have gone out to some cocktail party, and Merry says she's thankful that they thoughtlessly "left the liquor cabinet open, wow, how did that happen?" She also tells him that the

teacher from school, Ms. Carter, who was supposed to chaper-
one, called and said that she'd had a medical emergency and
wouldn't be able to fulfill her obligations. When this banter is
over, the two of them are dancing to some slow ballad, and their
heads are on each other's shoulders, and it's adorable, and Madison McDowell and Zimri Enderby, like so many other watchers
of the program, are almost convinced that the episode is going to
have a happy ending. It's almost like Bennett Adams is not going
to have to agonize for the rest of this ominous school holiday.
Maybe he can forget about the drug cartel that left Edwin for
dead on a street corner, and the legacy of his own absent father,
and the money problems faced by his mother, and other forces
too dark for him to understand yet. Merry Burns takes him by
the hand, and they head up the stairs.

Madison slides down onto the floor, in her silk pants, and she
rows herself across the floor to where Zimri sits, and she tells him
that he's sexy for a guy from Utah, and then they fall into their own
forbidden embraces, during another commercial break. Before the
break is over, he has lifted her up off the floor, so that she won't get
her pants any dustier, to carry her down the hall to the bedroom.

If Annabel's mother, the psychologist, has a view on sexuality
as depicted on television, it's that the excessive saccharine of this
sexuality is bound to create expectations, and not just among
young people, who are almost honor bound to expect that when
they finally get naked with their friends the earth will tremble or
there will be the sounds of rockets going off in their ears or they
will feel an overwhelming and intoxicating love, more addictive
than heroin, and this love feeling, called forth by the commin-
gling of bodily fluids, will never take leave of them, until death
comes for them. The male characters on television, of course, are
noteworthy for abandoning the girl characters. This is one of the

guarantees on television these days. The male is often a cad. Whereas no feminine protagonist can possibly be wanton, nor can any girl toy with the male affections, according to the psychologist, and that's according to some sort of misguided affirmative action, and perhaps it's not the worst thing. Even the adults, according to the psychologist, are at risk in viewing these sexual encounters. It's possible that they may feel a faint trace of jealousy about the long decades of adult sexuality, which are generally of muted and gentler tones. What television needs, according to Deborah the psychologist, is *more* sex, not less. Lots and lots and lots of sex, but sexuality that is resplendent in its many hues, not just this young man chasing the young woman up the stairs, and then getting into bed and pulling the covers up, and then banging away in missionary position. What television needs is bad sex, it needs premature ejaculations, and women forgiving men for premature ejaculations, and it needs impotence, lots and lots of impotence, it needs dry vaginas, it needs lubricants, it needs Viagra, it needs pornography as a marital aid, and it needs other performance enhancers, vibrators, perhaps dildos. Entire episodes devoted to these things. How often does a dildo get mentioned on television? Surely the Southern Baptist Leadership Conference wouldn't begrudge the FCC a dildo or two? Nobody is hurt by a dildo, unless it's boys using them on themselves without adequate preparation, or groups of girls using those two-headed jobs without knowing how.

"Shut up, Mom," Maximillian says to his mother.

The camera picks up a pair of house cats in the Burns household. The cats just happen to be in the room with the two young lovers, and the cats are fighting, as house cats will do, one batting the other around the head. The cats freeze, dash just out of the shot and then back into it. We hear the breathy importunities of Merry Burns on the bed, and then we hear something else. We hear something very different; we hear something *almost animal*. . . .

"I *knew* it," Annabel says. "It's because he's black. Everyone else gets to have sex on this show, but he doesn't get to have sex just because he's black. There's never a shot of just black characters in a store or anything or discussing politics. They're always the mutants."

"Annabel!" Max says, who, though he is a strident critic of television culture and its seductions, is the one paying the closest attention. The Reverend Duffy, who has been known to use *The Werewolves of Fairfield County* in his sermons, is soundly sleeping. And Tyrone, who has said not a word about what's going on, has been concentrating on the book in his hands. "Anyway, Edwin is black and he's not a werewolf."

Not yet, anyway.

The transformation, one of the things that initially set apart *The Werewolves of Fairfield County* from other programs, is by now so predictable that it's difficult to bring anything new to it. The transformation of man into wolf, here in the fourth season, is just digital nonsense. The same makeup morphing through the same predictable stages. And yet each season, Christine Katz, the producer of *The Werewolves of Fairfield County,* has tried to hold in reserve a little improvement in the matter of the transformation. The hard-core fans of the program know to wait for the razzle-dazzle of this moment of improved metamorphosis. Sunday, during the Thanksgiving episode, it turns out, is the day of something new. So: Bennett Adams, just like his mother, Felicia, *is* a werewolf, and it is the moment of orgasm that has brought it out in him. The uninformed viewer will perhaps not be certain it's an orgasm, but still. The scene is powerful, it's almost garish, the way he arches up off the reclining, sweetly moaning body of Merry Burns and stretches up his arms, because it's his virginity that he's casting off, too, his innocence, and of course the irony of the moment of any deflowering is that the body always knows what it's doing, it knows and loves the moment of its new awareness, as if it has always known; the body loves its animal exhibitions, and this is especially true of poor Bennett Adams, who is not only knowing and loving the animal aspect of his splattering seed, but just as he comes, the bristles of fur seem to burst out on his face *instantly,* not gradually, as in all the traditional werewolf programming of the fifties and sixties, but immediately. And that's the great new effect in this episode. His cry is his own voice and the voice of the wolf simultaneously. The one is an aspect of the other, and then, again immediately, his shirt, his preppy polo shirt, which he's still wearing at the commencement of the love scene, the polo shirt that his mother actually ironed for him, shreds like confetti, and you can see the threads hanging off of him, others flying out into the room. His old body is a piñata giving way to the new. He knows that something awful has happened, that he is not just a boy who has known the inside of a girl, and he knows, all at once, that he's a *thing,* not a boy but a *thing,* and as a thing he should flee, and that the proper place for all animals is in the state of nature's wildness, which is not in some mansion somewhere just up the street from where Martha Moxley used to live. He doesn't even have his pants on, of course, he has nothing on, but he's a wolf, and nakedness is not a shameful thing to a werewolf, and he goes bounding off the bed and down the stairs and into the thick of the party, which at this somewhat late hour has given way to intoxicated lassitude. It's not the giddy carnival that we usually see depicted on television but is, rather, a lazy, fumbling, inert affair where boys who are too drunk to perform make passes at girls who are too drunk to refuse, and the werewolf bounds past all of them, and the few who are awake or alert enough to understand that they have just seen something supernatural rub their eyes, looking, nonetheless, unsurprised.

———

Vic Freese's wife, Lise, says, during the commercial break, "You know, I can't stand it that you're suddenly taking notes during the entire show. Couldn't we just sit here and watch the show? You used to watch the show because it was fun to watch, and now you just sit here and you take notes, like television is nothing but an opportunity to work for you. If we can't sit together and have a quiet night together, like we used to do, then what's the point? Now it's all just the agency, agency, agency, agency, and how everybody is jealous of your success and how everybody wants to steal that teenage slut client away from you. But what about your kids, and what about me? I liked it better when you were a failure, if you want to know the truth. I liked it better when you used to say that work was neurotic and all the people at the agency were neurotic and never had any fun in their lives and they were all going to die young. Are you going to die young, too? Now that you're mister codirector of the television division? Or are you just going to sit there taking notes and not even listen to me when I'm talking to you? You're going to pretend I'm not even talking to you? I don't really care if I wake the kids up. I want the guy I dated and the guy I married. He was sweet and gentle and would play miniature golf, and I think the kids want that guy, too, not some guy who never comes home or who comes home after they're already asleep, and then when he does come home, all he does is turn on the television and start taking notes and blustering into his dictating machine. Is that what you want? Is that what you really want, to be like that? Forget it, I don't even care what happens, I don't care if the werewolf gets the girl, and I don't care what happens to your miniseries. I'm going to bed."

———

The director of the Duffy family documentary pans again over the assembled, as the final four minutes of the show begin. She's part of her own melodrama now. Though it is so far unspoken. She has her own multigenerational secret, one that she has not

464 | Rick Moody

announced to the American family, which lounges around her

464 | Rick Moody

announced to the American family, which lounges around her in its American-family tableau. It's a melancholy secret, to be sure, an unwanted secret, and yet perhaps a hopeful secret, too, this secret of conception. Even in such a fraught moment, when her brother's future is uncertain and the election is uncertain and her employment situation is a little uncertain, the chromosome-hauling spermatozoan will, given the right conditions, and notwithstanding the frequent impotence of the father, nonetheless occasionally perform its endurance-swimming trick and crash through the wall of the ovum, even if the birth control pill is said to be 99 percent effective. It's melancholy that Thaddeus isn't answering his cell phone, that he has apparently decamped for California, or that's the rumor, before going off to Morocco to shoot his swashbuckling epic, and she doesn't even know how to tell him about the spermatozoan and its accomplished mission. But because she hasn't told him, hasn't told anyone yet about her idea that she just might keep the little fetus with the action film–star daddy, it seems like nothing but good news, as if somehow it's going to turn out all right for all the generations of the family; somehow they need one another, even if they can't stand one another, and the little fetus needs everyone to give him or her a break, give him or her a while to turn into an actual person rather than just the potential of personhood. Love is best expressed as the likelihood of a little mixed-race baby for now, she thinks, over the forms of half-conscious family members in the living room, while ministering with her camera.

It's going to be an amazing documentary, probably much better than her script about the wife of the Marquis de Sade, and one thing about it that will revolutionize filmmaking is the pacing. Instead of a lot of stuff happening all the time, the newly pregnant filmmaker has decided on a static approach, as in avant-garde film. There are going to be large patches of film where nothing much happens at all. The film will have mimetic aspirations. It will attempt to re-create the pacing of real family life, the long periods between revelation in which the manipulative and semifascist plot structure of Hollywood and contemporary television serial narratives will have no place. That fascist kind of work creates attention deficit disorder in audiences, and it probably creates that spike in the rates of autism that everybody talks about, too. And that's why the newly pregnant filmmaker lingers on the sleeping form of the Reverend Russell Duffy, who can be expected to sleep through almost any after-dinner television programming. He always expresses strong opinions about what they watch: *no* on comedies, *no* on teen films, *yes* on Provence or Tuscany and anything with a classical music theme. But having expressed an interest in content, the reverend cannot stay awake longer than fifteen minutes, and often the volume has to be turned up so that everyone can hear over his snoring.

The others talk freely, despite the slumbering man of God, but before the newly pregnant filmmaker can capture the tenor of their conversation, the television program is back, and the flickering of the monitor plays across their faces.

What they are seeing is Felicia Adams in the morning. The morning after Thanksgiving, in the kitchen, at dawn, trying to straighten up things in the house before the others wake. Suddenly she hears the front door open. There she finds her eldest son, holding some scraps of a towel around his middle so as to conceal his Edenic nakedness from her. The close-up on Felicia's face captures the slow play of meanings in her. He must have gotten into some kind of devilment with his friends. He must have gotten into some trouble with a girl. Or he must be . . . The surprise is in how long it takes, considering that the notion can't have ever been far from her thinking. It's always darkest right under the lamp. Apparently she has tried to believe anything but the notion that her son has the lupine gene, as any mother would.

"Mommy," Bennett says, "something awful happened to me last night. I don't even know . . . I don't even know how to say it. I'm so scared, and I don't know what to do."

Now there's one of those Madonna-and-child moments in the front hall of the apartment, where lately Vern reclined while romancing the carcass of a turkey. The two of them slide to the floor, the boy weeping as though he's still just a kid trapped in the expanding body of an adolescent. There's blood all over his hands and arms, a volume of blood that no person should have to see, especially no one as young as Bennett. His mother lets him cry for a while as he tries to describe what cannot be described. "There was something happening to my body. I was over at Merry's house, and suddenly something happened to my body, and I was . . . I was covered in *fur*, and then I can remember that I ran out of the party on . . . on *all fours.*" And then a fresh helping of tears.

When she has said nothing for so long that it is maternal callousness, Bennett Adams finally looks up at his mother, and suspicion begins to pass across his own features. Her gaze is level, determined, unsentimental.

"We've got to get all this blood off you before your brother wakes," she says. "Come with me into the kitchen."

And the two of them, confederates, tread softly into the kitchen, where she turns on the tap in the big sink basin and immerses his hands in the water. With a generous bar of soap, she soaps his hands in her own, and the water cascades across his bloodied knuckles, and this water foreshadows developments in next week's episode, the hydrophobia episode, about which there has already been voluminous conjecture on the chat boards.

"Mom?" he says, and the nakedness of the interrogative tells much about the suffering of werewolves, from their origin in Middle Europe to their postmodern anguish in the evolving genetic picture of the new millennium.

"Yes," Felicia says.

"You, too?" he says.

"Yes," she says. She knows. She has felt these things. She, too, has suffered. "But don't say anything more about it now. Don't say anything more." And she gives his hands another round of soap and water and then dries them with a dish towel. Now Felicia leads the boy into the back bedroom, where his bed occupies most of the available floor, and she lays him down on the mattress and pulls the covers over him.

"It seems like it's a curse," she says to him. "It seems like you are doomed every month when the moon is full. But there comes a time when it seems like a blessing, like you're better somehow. You know the taste of warm blood still pulsing, and that's something that most people will never know. You're special now, because you have ripped the limb from a living animal and watched it bleed to death, and because you no longer have to pay attention to property lines or the laws of the politicians or the morals of the churches, or any of that. You *are* the laws of nature. And yet after a while, even that becomes a curse, and then you learn the one bit of grace in all of this, and that's the law of the pack. The pack is the one place you're understood now. The pack is the place where your mistakes and your failures are your assets. The pack is where you can get out of any jam that you can get into. If you can't find a job, go to the men and women of the pack. And if you don't have a friend anywhere, go to the men and women of the pack. If you can't believe in anything good on the face of this earth, go to the men and the women of the pack. They're everywhere around you, though you've never seen them. Your mailman might be a member of the pack, and your teacher might be one, and your doctor might be, and even your own mother might be, though you've never known until now." She smiles at him. "Okay, better get some sleep, because you're bound to get into trouble again tonight."

He's already asleep. Or nearly so.

Felicia rises up from his bedside and she closes the door to his bedroom behind her, and on the far side, she slumps against the door, stifling sobs and wondering how she can take this, too, this on top of everything else. How much stronger can a woman be?

Closing credits. And theme music. The announcer tells all to stay tuned.

At which point the assembled constituencies, in all the millions of living rooms, the living rooms of some huge portion of the industrial West, exhale and begin to abandon the television set. There's nothing worth watching after, and in one living room in Newton, Mass., the newly pregnant filmmaker of a powerful new documentary about family life looks down at the book that her older brother has been marking up throughout the episode of *The Werewolves of Fairfield County,* and it looks like this:

such

thirst

28

There are days when the only question in the waiting room of the hospital is about the quality of her consciousness. And yet the victim has no consciousness of her habits and opinions, only the consciousness of the brick. The brick has no consciousness itself, or so it is often believed. And yet here is the brick considering its manifestations. Or perhaps the consciousness of the brick and the consciousness of the victim have become twinned in their perceptions. For the victim, the consciousness of impact is lost. Not so for the brick. The consciousness of the moment of the impact, when the victim is talking on her cell phone, walking briskly to or from the library, depending on the account, is alive for the brick, when it becomes an instrument of death, collides with her, crushes a portion of the side of her skull; when she is facedown on the sidewalk, and the cell phone has gone skittering, and the blood flows liberally from her skull; when the brick is cast aside, to return to its formerly inert state. Lost to history, lost to the victim, except that she hears the brick calling to her.

Of course, the victim does not know that she has collided with a brick. She knows only that she is in a serene blackness of indefinite duration and proportion. In this space there are murmurings, and these murmurings are disconnected and without meaning, and they appear amid portions of blackness that have nothing at all associated with them, no variation, no density, no volume. If there are words overheard, murmurings, they are heard at such a distance that they sound more like a massing of insects.

The brick comes from an oven somewhere, a kiln, from some locale plentiful in the labor necessary to produce a brick, an area that offers costs of labor far cheaper than what is available here in the metropolitan region. The brick is from Romania, or the brick is from the Yucatán, or the brick is from a factory in West Virginia, where the brick-producing factories are soon to shutter once and for all. Men and women there have manufactured bricks for forty-five years, but they soon will be looking for work in the service sector. This brick is made of clay, and the brick was fired at high temperatures, and there was a medium that bound the clay and gave it pigment in a giant convectionary bowl of some kind, where the mixture was assembled, and thereafter the brick was shaped and fired. The brick is nothing but earth. It has no history except in recollection, as an agent of death. In this instant of the victim's life after the collision with the brick, the first instant that the victim recognizes as such, what she is conscious of is the brick.

The eruption of color is terrifying. The eruption is painful, and the pain is associated with this perception of the brick and its history. And there is a word written on the side of the brick, it must be that a word is written there, this occurs to her, a word that will identify the factory where the brick was made; she is aware of wanting to read the word, though words and letters are impenetrable to her, and she is not sure what an alphabet is or if she could ever read from one. Still, this name on the brick will have some kind of lesson for her.

The victim has no name, and in the intervals of hearing nothing and feeling nothing and seeing nothing, this namelessness is of no consequence. In fact, it's a blessing. Without a name, there is no sense that the not-hearing and not-seeing and not-feeling of the victim are anything but aspects of a system that never loses any energy, never winds down. There's no need in a system like this for a name, so the victim does not know that she has no name, nor does she experience herself as a victim, except as a victim of eruptions of light and color. Light, associating itself with some agony in her skull, implies she *has* a skull, that she is not simply a brick that has some name written on it, for example, the word *Utica*. What a shapely and beautiful word *Utica* is because it must be the name of a something. The name must be other than the brick; it must be a recognition of some other system of things, a system that includes light and sound, and that includes an overheard pageant of insects chirruping words like *Utica*, which is or must be a place where bricks are made and which may or may not be the place that *this* brick was made.

She has only a brief time to notice and evaluate the history of the brick, which is a history of the land in a place called Utica, however, because there is blackness and the blackness is without period or characteristic, and when she is enveloped in it she *is* it, except that she isn't, because more and more the chirruping seems to resemble certain things, words, though she isn't sure from which past she remembers these things, because if she is a brick, how would it be possible that she could remember things, unless, for example, she remembers the earth. Still, she remembers these words or thinks she overhears these words, and these words are indicators of something having to do with a brick and having to do with a woman.

One day, from a mothballed place, she performs a trick that she can't remember ever having performed before. Suddenly, for a moment, she *sees*, and this is a monumental event for the victim because when she is a seeing apparatus, she believes that she may not be a brick, but rather a woman, or at least attached to the body of a woman. And there are other things she knows, in this brief moment before the system is shut down again. She believes, for example, that she knows about blankets.

There is such a thing as a blanket, and a blanket is blue, because this is its color. The place where she is, this thinking and seeing apparatus (which may or may not be a brick or a woman), is *in bed*, and she is looking at a blanket, and this is what a blanket is: a blanket is a thing that is draped across a body to prevent it from growing cold, and whoever it is who puts the blanket on the body, if in fact a person puts the blanket on the body, this is an entity of *kindness*. There are sheets here, too, this is another word she remembers, and there's a feeling to sheets, depending on what kind of sheets they are and whether these sheets are thin or heavy. Sheets feel a certain way when they are crisp, starchy, or draped across your body. Still, the woman has had enough of thinking, and so she sleeps again, and this sleep may last for a day or more, and the sleep may include a portion of consciousness that may be partly awake and partly asleep, and these portions of consciousness may include scraps of things that are said to the victim, or these portions of consciousness may not, or that is what a doctor says within earshot of the victim, that it is okay to speak to her and to touch her, as these things may help her.

Which implies that there must be others in the room. There are people in the room. The brain injury that the brick caused makes it hard to recognize these others or to tell anything about them, and so she sleeps through the notion of other people, perhaps she forgets them for an entire day, so that it is Monday, or even Tuesday, and she has entirely forgotten that there are people in the room. But it becomes unavoidable, the conclusion that she is a mind exercising itself, and in these days when she is asleep or unconscious, she begins to have certain tasks that she performs; one of these is the cataloguing of colors, since she is often seeing colors: mustard, orange, rust, russet, mud, black.

What is a brick for? A brick is for building things. And what is it that is built with the brick? Certain kinds of buildings. And where are these buildings being built? In a town or city, mostly. These things are elementary, and even a brain that has been badly distressed, and on which there have been performed various surgeries, has stored enough information, somewhere, to know these things. Bricks are for buildings in the cities and towns. And who builds the buildings? The buildings are built mostly by men. There are men with wheelbarrows, and they are moving many bricks from one spot to another. Or there are men driving forklift vehicles with many bricks being transported from one place to another, so that buildings may be made of these bricks.

These bricks are from Utica, and Utica is a place in Asia. She assumes that Utica is in Asia, and therefore it follows that many Asian men have cooperated in the making of these bricks, and these bricks have come from Asia because they are cheaper in Asia, or the creation of these bricks is inexpensive there, that is why bricks would come a long way, because she believes that New York City, where she imagines herself to be, is a long way from Asia. She believes that she is a woman who is in New York, and the bricks are in New York, too, having come from Asia, by boat.

What does the idea of the woman have to do with the brick? When she is seeing things again, she is in a place that is white and pale green, and there is a television mounted on the wall, and there are these people, and the people are looking at her, and she can see and hear. People are blinking at her, and there is something unusual about the people that she can't understand at first. They look unusual, not like the people that she would have expected to be in the room. They blink and stare. Is blinking a method of communicating? She stretches her arms above her, and they cannot, apparently, believe what they are seeing. They begin saying something, and the thing that they begin saying is probably her name. At least she later believes that it might be her name, because they keep saying it. Samantha, Samantha, Samantha. She doesn't know anything about this word, which would imply that it must be a name, because a name is a word that has no other useful associations. A name is a word that doesn't do anything. "Samantha, can you hear us? Samantha?" Could it be possible that these are her parents? These little disheveled people? What's wrong with their eyes? They have strange eyes. It occurs to her, after a while, that this must be the way people look when they are from Asia, but maybe she is only thinking this because of the brick. The brick comes from Asia, after all, so now everything comes from Asia. The nurse probably comes from Asia. Everybody is from Asia.

She says, "Can I have a glass of water?"

Pandemonium. The man who may or may not be from Asia goes rushing out into the corridor, calling for a nurse, and the woman who is still in the room runs back and forth thanking God. Many things are getting clearer to the victim now. For example, there is some reason why she keeps thinking about Utica and about the factory there that makes bricks. But a lot of other things are not clear, like whether she is truly Samantha, and who these people are. The nurse comes, and the nurse is followed by a doctor, and the doctor is followed by a policeman, why a policeman she does not know, and they are all in the room, and they are laughing, and the people who were waiting, the Asian people, are hugging her, and this goes on for a moment, until composure sets in generally, and then the doctor asks if he can make a brief examination. Not being able to think of much else to say, she agrees.

He produces a small flashlight of some kind, it is clipped onto his shirt, and he says that he is going to shine this flashlight in her eyes, and he does so, and the light is so bright that it seems to be shining all the way into the dark places of her body. She closes her eyes. He asks her to open her eyes, and she opens them, and he shines the light, and then she closes her eyes. He says okay let's move on. He asks her to stretch out her arms. She stretches out her arms. He asks her to keep her eyes closed and to please touch her nose. She doesn't know what this means, really, and yet she attempts to touch her nose, but unfortunately her hands go wide, her hands seem to have no force guiding them, no volition. After she attempts to do as she is told, there is some silence in the room, and she recognizes that she has not passed this particular test. The doctor asks if she can turn sideways in the bed, so that he can see her feet, and he asks her to close her eyes again. He asks if she can feel this and this, and she wonders what he is doing, because she can feel something, but she is not certain what it is, nor where it is meant to be occurring on the surface of her body.

The doctor introduces himself and tells her his name, and she says, "Pleased to meet you."

"Can you tell me how you came to be here?"

"Where am I?"

"You're in the hospital."

"Why am I in the hospital?"

"You've had an accident," he says. "And I'm interested for the moment in whether you remember anything before your accident. Am I right in assuming that you don't remember much about that time?"

The questions seem difficult. They must be trick questions. She thinks there are right answers and wrong answers, and also answers that are both right and wrong, and answers that will have something to do with Utica, with Asia, with bricks, and with women, but she is frightened at the possibility of giving the wrong answer or of people knowing the degree of uncertainty that she has about the questions, and so she begins to cry. The tears are involuntary, and she does nothing to conceal them, and because of the tears the doctor says that probably it is best if she rests. And the rest is not like a gentle interval in the day, a sweet and relaxing nap, it's like a sickness, which apparently it is, because before she knows it she is back in a place that is no place and that is indefinite and characterized by blackness; in this place there are emotions now, and the emotions rotate through her chaotically: frustration, boredom, sadness, apprehensiveness. It is worth noting that never does she feel a pleasant emotion.

Why shouldn't she just feel happy about the fact that she has consciousness and that her consciousness is separate, she now realizes, from the consciousness of a brick? Why can't she feel good about not being a brick? Wednesday would perhaps be the day to feel good about it, but Wednesday is the day when they begin to assume that she is going to be awake on a regular basis, and because she is awake, they now believe that she should be doing some things besides simply sleeping and eating and listening to the horrible television on the wall. She doesn't know what she thought before, if there even was a before, but she knows that she hates that device because everything on the television is like the explosion of lights in her head, and that explosion was so violent that she hopes she never has to experience anything like it again; better to be asleep. Yet every day, every minute, the television is like an explosion of light, and at the end of every one of these explosions it seems as if someone is getting punched or shot or stabbed or arrested by the authorities.

Meanwhile, the torture that is designed for today is the torture referred to as physical therapy. They mean to take her to the floor where exercises are done and see how much she can do. And this is because she has begun attempting to make it unassisted to the bathroom of her semiprivate room. Thus, there is a pair of nurses, and they lift her up, and she puts an arm around each of them, and they lift her away from the bed and they put a robe on her, and now her feet are touching the ground, or, if she looks down, it looks as though her feet are touching the ground, and one of the nurses says that they are going to walk toward the door, and they just need her to put one foot in front of the other foot, that's the job for now. This sounds so easy when it is said in this particular way.

One nurse says, "You're our little miracle, right?"

The victim says, "What?"

"We're just so glad you're up and around, Samantha. You're our miracle of the eighth floor."

"Thanks," she says. "I guess." And she thinks that she should get used to the fact that she's named Samantha. No one seems to be calling her anything else.

Walking is harder than anyone explained. The phenomenon of balance seems as if it must be magic. Is it something that people have to learn or can they just balance themselves? Because whenever the nurses loosen their grip on her, in the thirteen steps to the door, where there seems to be a wheelchair waiting for her, she slumps sideways, collapses, and feels horribly dizzy. The dizziness is overwhelming, and her legs do not do what they are supposed to do, and she begins to tremble at the difficulty of the whole project. Where are those people, the people who must certainly be her parents? They are always here, but today they are not. Why aren't they seeing this?

Nonetheless, there are things out in the hall. And there are people to see. For example, there is a policeman who seems to guard her room and only her room, though she doesn't know why, and, though he probably has other things on his mind, he always seems to smile at her. He smiles when she makes it out of the room and into the hall, and he says, "Looking good." And there's something about the officer that she forgets at first but then recalls. The officer is an African American police officer. Some of the nurses are also African American. How could she have forgotten about these things?

Everyone seems very happy to see her in the wheelchair. She is the sort of person whom people are very happy to see out in the hall. People actually stare at her, which reminds her that she should know what she looks like. She must look either beautiful or repulsive if everyone is pointing at her. But she doesn't really have time to think about this too much. Before she can think about it, she's asleep. Right there, in the wheelchair.

In the night, in the incomplete darkness, there is time to think, and she knows that there was something about being African American that was important. She has to make a note to look at herself when she gets the chance, because she keeps forgetting.

When she is next aware of the day it is a weekend, and the breakfast tray is in front of her. How is it possible that she has been awake for hours before noticing? She has eaten half of her breakfast, and maybe she has even carried on conversations, before being aware of any of these things. How can she eat this appalling food? Everything in her body hurts, and something terrible has happened to her, because she was not always this way. There was a time before this time, and there was a self before this self, and there was a Samantha who wasn't this Samantha, and therefore this is the moment when she asks of the woman who is often by her bed, "Tell me what happened to me. I want to know what happened."

The woman looks at her husband, and this is how the victim knows that this woman must be her mother, because, she thinks, a mother is a person who does not want to give bad news to a person, and apparently the victim is a person who is loved by this woman, and so this woman must be her mother, because the mother looks so stricken at the idea that she has to tell the victim what has happened that she passes along the responsibility to the father, who sets aside his newspaper, because he is a man who spends a lot of time reading the newspaper, and so it is given to the man to be the husband of the mother. A father is the person who brings the worst news.

"You were walking down the street and you were attacked by someone," he says. "You were struck in the head."

"How was I struck in the head?"

"You were struck with a brick or perhaps a cinder block," the father says. He looks pained to be saying it.

"Where was I going?"

"You were going to the library."

"Why was I going to the library?" she asks, because now she has a great number of questions. Every question sends her scurrying off in a number of directions, and each of these questions generates further questions.

"You were going to read," he says, "or you were going to do research. We don't exactly know why you were going to the library.

We think you were going to do some research for a project that you were preparing."

"You were always going to the library," her mother adds. The two Asian people have risen from their chairs now, as if rising from their chairs were some kind of synchronous ballet that they have prepared for this moment. The mother takes the victim's hand.

"And then what happened?" the victim asks, because this is what she wants to know. How does a thing cause another thing to happen? How does one event become another, as when a brick becomes a sort of vengeance? Or is this just a condition of her brain, to believe that one thing always leads to another? Some days she goes from her room out into the hall, and from the hall to the elevator, and from the elevator to another floor, where she is meant to attempt to walk and to move her limbs in a coordinated way, and in the complexity of this there is nothing for her but to marvel. Because there are so many persons rushing around the hospital, and for these persons and for the persons recuperating in the hospital, there are all these causes and effects. Things causing other things.

"After the brick," she says.

"Then you were very badly injured, and of course people called for an ambulance."

"I want to see it," she says.

"What do you want to see?" her mother asks.

"I want to see what my head looks like," she says, because she knows now that they have concealed this from her. They have waited for a time when she will be sturdy enough to see. They have been in possession of the story for a long time, the story of the brick, and they have doled out portions of the story, and they have discussed the story when they believed that she was not conscious or was sleeping. There was a time when she was not able to be in possession of her story, when the two people who are her parents were its stewards, and they concealed things because there were many things that she might have known, but she was not ready to know them. Now she is ready.

"I don't want you keeping it from me. I want to know what it looks like."

The mother gives the father another one of those wounded expressions, and then the mother begins to go rummaging through a handbag beside her chair. The word occurs to Samantha now before the mother even produces the object, and the word is *mirror.*

The victim says, "I know about the brick. I learned about it. The brick is from Utica, which is in Asia."

The mother and father look at each other, and the father begins to move toward the door, but the victim shakes her head no because she does not want the doctor and she does not want any restriction on the liberal flow of this catechism. She wants the free exchange of information because she will be asleep again soon, and while she is awake, during this brief day, let her experience its dramas. The father stands at the foot of the bed while the mother takes from her handbag the object known as a mirror, and now she is beside Samantha, and Samantha seizes the mirror, and she moves it around, and she tries to arrange it so that she can see her face, but the mirror keeps pointing in the wrong directions. She sees the wall behind her or she sees the curtain that separates her from her roommate, who is about to have brain surgery. She can't hold the mirror steady, the mirror is capricious, and she feels some sensation in her, the feeling is known as rage, and she demands that her mother should steady the looking glass. She needs for it to be held where she can see it, because her hands don't work, not the way they ought to, and nothing in her body works. It is a useless piece of equipment, this body, it is a *mess,* she tells her mother. "Now, just hold the mirror up where I can see and don't say anything," and the mother has to reach around her, to the far side of her head, because it is on the right side of her head, because the brick was used on the right side of her head, because whoever used the brick was behind her, and then alongside her, and so they hit the right side of her, and she was thrown to the ground, and her brains were dashed out of her head on this right side; of course, her cell phone went flying, and now she and the brick and the rage are one, and she can see, she can see how they have shaved all of the hair from her, and she can see that there is a scar and stitches, and the scar runs the length of her skull from her forehead back and down, to her ear, and the shape of her head is irregular where the scar is, there are some bulges here and there, it is not a round head or a smooth head, her head is not shaped like a head, it is shaped like a mess. Her head looks like something in a butcher's shop.

She also notices that her eyes are strange. That she is Asian.

"What kind of nationality am I?"

"You're Chinese American. Your grandparents came from China."

"Who did this to me?"

It's the question that they aren't prepared to answer, these people. The question of who did it to her. Also the question about why she is not dead. She knows now that these are the questions that they don't want to answer and don't want to talk about. Maybe it is a Chinese characteristic, not wishing to discuss things that are painful to discuss. Maybe before, she was the kind of person who accepted this reticence. She doesn't remember. She will not tolerate it now. She knows which questions to ask because she feels sick when she asks them. She feels as if the room itself wants to scream.

Again, it is given to the father to answer. "We do not know who did this to you. They believed they knew who did it to you, but now they are not so sure."

This is all on a Monday, or so she thinks. She will wake tomorrow and she will ask more questions, and they will not want to or will not be able to answer.

Will she have to have more surgery? They do not know. What

is wrong with her brain? She has had several strokes. When will she be able to walk? They do not know, but she has to keep trying. What's wrong with her arm? She has carpal tunnel, from typing. What did she do before? She worked in an art gallery. Can you explain art to me? Well, art is the category of human endeavor that has no purpose. Art is what people do to describe general human aspirations. Why was I interested in art? Your mother and I do not know why you were interested in art, because we do not understand art very well. Your grandfather worked in a laundry, and I worked as an accountant so that you could go to the university. When you went to university you became interested in art. You taught us a lot about art, her father goes on, but until you grew up we knew nothing about it. It was something you put over the sofa, if you were lucky enough to have a sofa. You took us to see paintings, her father says, and you took us to see photographs, and they were so complicated and so powerful that we didn't know to what to compare these things. What kind of art did I like? We don't know how to describe the kind of art you liked. You liked very modern things. Whereas we liked very old things, things that reminded us of China. The people you worked with, they can explain to you about art. How will you put me in touch with them? You could telephone them. Who were my friends? Your friends were people you knew from the gallery and from when you went to college. We didn't know many of your friends. Why not? Because you didn't choose to bring them home to us. Was I in love? We don't think you were in love. Are you sure? We don't think you were in love. You had a boyfriend for a while, but then this romance ended, as things often do when people are young. Why do you say that? Because young people do not understand love.

Her mother says, "Don't say these things to her. She is ill."

And her father says, "Why shouldn't I say these things? I'm not going to sugarcoat things while she is learning what she has to learn, because then she'll get the wrong ideas."

Samantha has more questions. Was she a happy person? She was a mostly happy person. And was she happy growing up, wherever it was she grew up? She grew up in the suburbs west of Philadelphia and yes, she was happy as a child, if a little shy. Who was her last boyfriend, because she can almost remember, she can remember things about him, or at least she can remember things about being next to his body, a body next to hers, and she can remember something about the joy of being next to another body, and there is no such feeling here in the hospital, which, though it is full of people and family, is a lonely place. Her last boyfriend, she is told, was a packager and transporter of art. Or, as her father seems to want to say, despite her mother's diplomacy, he drove a moving truck. When did her parents meet? Her parents met a long time ago. How come she doesn't have any siblings? Because they were not able to conceive any more babies. And do her parents still love each other? Of course. And why is everyone staring at her, wherever she goes in the hospital? Because she was in the newspapers a lot. Why was she in the newspapers? Because of the nature of the crime. And is she still in the newspapers? Sometimes. And who was the person the police believed committed the crime? This person was named Duffy. That was his last name? Yes, his name was William Duffy, but he preferred to be called Tyrone. The police believe that she was acquainted with this person, perhaps for some time.

At the sound of the name, something happens in her. It is as if a whole second window of consciousness opens up. It is the window onto ornament, onto all the things that are inessential on their surface, and yet, when this window is reopened, she wonders how she lived without it, because in here are consigned the memories with no names attached to them, such as riding down the FDR in a taxi at night with the windows open in spring. How beautiful this memory is, and how beautiful are the lights, and how excellent is the FDR Drive. Likewise, the memory of the leaves changing color in the suburbs in autumn, and the memory of ballet class as a girl, and what it felt like to lace up her toe shoes, and also the memory of the taste of ice cream, especially mint-chocolate-chip ice cream, which in her girlhood tasted like cough syrup, only better, and the smell of people's lunch bags in elementary school, and what it felt like to have to climb the ropes in gym, which she always hated, and how she always liked to look at the cards at the back of library books as a girl, and the satisfying sound that a videocassette made the first time she ever fed one into a machine. These images come tumbling out at the sound of the name Tyrone, and she can't attach a significance to any of them, except that she knows that they all belong to her, all these memories belong to her, and she doesn't know why she forgot them, nor why they are returning now, except that they are followed by colors and light, and the only possible idea she has of all these things, as she thinks of them, is that they are paintings, and there are a thousand images of cracked bits of pottery and illuminated manuscripts, and then there are the flattened devotional images of medieval painting, and then there are the Madonnas, all the Madonnas and all the little babies with them, and then all the deposition altarpieces, and then there are the court paintings of the Enlightenment, and then there are the scenes of country life, and then there are the early photographs, and then there are the paintings of the Impressionist period, she sees them all, and then there are the Cubist paintings, and the Fauvist paintings, and then the provocations of Dada and Surrealism. It all comes back to her, that she was once an art historian, that this was what made her go to work at the gallery, that she loves all these paintings, including contemporary art, she loves the anarchy of the contemporary, paintings that are nothing more than colors hovering in front of her, like windows into the original quality of colors, drips and scratches and lines and nothing more, just color, and paintings based on soup cans, and paintings based on comic strips; somewhere in here she recognizes that the paintings she's seeing are by Tyrone, as if the entire history of art that she's remembering while her parents sit and watch her leads to the paintings by Tyrone Duffy, and his mangled books, as that's what a lot of his work is, mangled text, words torn out of their context and made new again. She feels a sudden excitement at having unlocked the door to where all the things were stored, this door has been kept closed for so long, and maybe she didn't even know these things before, maybe these are only things you can know when you come back from some really empty space, or that's what it feels like today, that she's had some kind of insight, because of her brain injury, for no other reason. She can't read, she barely remembers anything from the past, she barely knows who her parents are, and she only knows her name because they keep repeating it to her, but she knows for certain that Tyrone didn't use the brick on her; there was no way that Tyrone used the brick. She tells her parents, "It wasn't Tyrone; that's ridiculous. I had a big crush on Tyrone . . . and . . . and . . . I think I was actually talking to him on the phone when I was hit, I think I was . . . I think I was trying to get him to go out with me."

29

He is Randall Tork, the greatest wine writer in history. He is the writer of innumerable wine articles and wine books, and the author of an eponymously named franchise of annual wine-collecting guides, the *Randall Tork Guide for Discerning Collectors*. He is popularizer of such terms as *barnyard* and *gymnasium* when used in the description of fine wines. He is the man who made the Battenkill vineyard what it is. He created its reputation; no one else did it, though many stake their claim. He's the one who destroyed a popular sommelier at one of the French restaurants by spreading the rumor that this so-called professional had no sense of smell. He did it with glee. He cares nothing about his subjects, the vintners, not about their feelings, not about their multimillion-dollar investments. They are the enemies of true invention.

What he despises: the delusions of wine connoisseurs, how they actually believe that they can taste all those faint traces, tobacco and chocolate and toasted almond, how they defer to whatever costs the most and is most prized by the heirs and heiresses who haven't spent a sober afternoon in forty-five years. The look in the eyes of wine collectors at the word *Bordeaux* makes Randall Tork want to drive forks into these eyes, and when he encounters these people at wine tastings, he invariably selects the "best" wine at random and then argues for the perfection of the vintage, saying that the rest of the region tastes as though it has formaldehyde in it, and he then adheres to the result unswervingly.

He wrote the column that is whispered about by every informed collector, the remarks in which he compared the entire run of 1997 California chardonnays to the actress Elke Murnaugh. Who could forget?

These wines are flabby in the way the cellulite bulges from the too-tight pouches of her nulliparous behind, they are fruity like the desserts that are favored by the disadvantaged children that Murnaugh and her never-to-be-mentioned partner take into their house so that she can be photographed leering, like a wine taster, surrounded by her brood, on the covers of celebrity weeklies. These chardonnays have the mouthfeel of neglected vaginas begging to be brought beseechingly out of retirement, musty, undeodorized, and sentimental. They have the aftertaste of excessive reuse of Lysol spray in the bovine bathrooms of salacious celebrities who are otherwise lax about germs, and they are garish like appalling Broadway productions, the casts of which are full of malnourished thespians who would do anything for a plug from her flatulent fabulousness. Have I neglected to mention the overused dance belts of Broadway dancers, ossified with eons of sweat and antifungals? These wines have hints of these exquisite tastes. And the so-called wine drinkers who favor these chardonnays are, like Murnaugh herself, pustular pretenders to the great tradition of wine producing who would never save a bottle of anything, who would drink a capful of cheap perfume and call it French wine, if only they have been told by some online sewing circle of hacks that they should do so. Let these Murnaugh urine specimens be drunk by the aforementioned imbeciles and then praised to the stars. Persons who use words like *zippy, zingy,* and *fun* should be lined up and shot, and perhaps their moldering remains will bring a more satisfying fermentation process to the creation of a wine than we find in this repellent grape.

The fact that he once had to sit behind Elke at a certain performance of a certain Broadway spectacular did not enter into the review, of course, and how dare the suggestion be made. Randall Tork is the greatest writer in wine history, and his contempt for the edifice of wine consumption is owing to the fact that he cares about the truth. Indeed, at forty-nine years of age, and completely repulsive in the matter of his physical demeanor, being rather short, rather fat, and rather covered with acne scars, and having large muttonchop sideburns, and eyes too close together, and given to wearing a beret because of hair that is thinning on the top, there is nothing else for him to care about but wines.

His parents, who separated in his earliest childhood, found him unlovable and his feminine primping and mincing worthy of contempt, and they abused him mercilessly, and may they rot in hell. He had no friends as a child, and in the instances where people were moved to pity by his circumstances, he spit on these people, reviled them, and felt good about it after the fact.

Today's august task is to work the term "festering boil" into a review of a Moselle, and to compare the owners of a restaurant in Marin County that once failed to honor his reservation to Vichy collaborators, after which he will return again to one of his favorite leitmotifs, the "gentle crushing of the fruit." The foot crushing the grape in the bathtub is where wine began, in an intimacy, in a humanness. What enology has lost, and there is always something lost, is this very humanness, the slave in the bathtub crushing the grape at the behest of his cruel master. There should be slaves, of course, and there should be masters, and there should be a calm, serene attitude about the fermentation process: Keep the room cool, require absolute cleanliness, make certain that the man who is monitoring temperatures is a man who knows to check every hour. Don't forget about *elevage,* the interval between fermentation and bottling; it is an art that has been handed down through the oral tradition. Randall can talk about these things. He can talk about *triage* and malic acidity and cap management, and the role in this era of the great French families, the way *père et fils* have conspired generation after generation to do this one perfect thing, and how this has not happened in the appalling United States of Baptist wine swillers because what have we here? In this country? We have the kind of tradition in which a fawning twenty-three-year-old wine writer comes to call at your vineyard, though he is unable to recognize appropriate tannins and wouldn't care if the wineglass was filled with antifreeze.

Thus, Randall begins to compose:

> Is that what you want for your vineyard? Do you want to have an expensive meal with a twenty-three-year-old with genital herpes, so that when you attempt to bed him in order to ensure the fine review of your pestilential product he infects you with his suppurating sores? Is that what you want? Maybe if you calved off his finger warts and mixed them in it would improve your beverage.

The language is closing in on what he needs. Truth is a condition of language, and when the outrage is pure, then the review is accurate.

What about the piece he fashioned entirely of similes? Reviewing the wines of Paraguay? Magnificent, really.

> What are these wines like? They are like the teenage sacrifices of the Aztec peoples at the moment that these sacrifices

wet themselves; like the smoked banana peels of banana republics; like the scorched smell of freebasing at the coca-producing factories of the Colombian cartels; like the acidified pages of the tomes of the Magic Realists; like the revolutionistas, unwashed and unfed; like the Disappeared after a good six months in their unmarked graves; like the punctured rectums of the fervent Catholic altar boys on their way to another round in the confessional with the good Father; like the smoking sky over the scorched rain forest; like the rainwater running down the gutter of an Indian village with no plumbing; like the throbbing bosoms of the sun-ripened, thong-wearing transvestites of the humid slums; like the discarded thatch of a continent's worth of Brazilian bikini waxes; like the cannibalism of the interior tribes; like the moldy grooves of another box full of warped tropicalia LPs; like the nectar of slug-infested mangos; like the ear-splitting cry of the toucan and like its gaudy, excessively colorful exterior and its thinly constructed beak; like the bomb shelters of the hidden Latin American Nazis; like the still throbbing organs of their victims; and like the soiled loincloths of the victims of cannibalism at the moment of their demise.

Yes, he is the greatest, and no one can take the mantle from him, and yet there is the one thing missing, namely a personal life of any kind. There were some married men, in his later teens, the sort of men who liked much younger boys, no matter the appearance of these boys. He has been with some of these men, and he loved these men, and he learned a lot from them, including something about wine. But many years have since elapsed with nothing to show for them but the occasional tawdry sally with a vigneron or a sommelier. These never did satisfy, especially when he tried to get them to tie him up properly.

In the wake of this realization, there was no choice, really, but to take the search for love out into the world. And that was how he, Randall Tork, the greatest wine writer in history, came to conduct wine tastings at the hospices and in the chronic-care wards of the Bay Area. To be Randall Tork, stripped of his reputation and his franchise, in a hospital ward, with a couple of bottles of swill and a box of digestives, filling plastic cups for men and women who had cast off all but the last few pounds of their body weight, this was actually a rather moving experience for him. He got the okay from *les médicines:* a glass or two would not unduly affect the tripartite cocktail of chemicals routinely prescribed for his *étudiants.* He began spinning out his tales of wine excellence, how the grace to make a good wine did not take just root stock and ample sunshine, it took five hundred years of perfection and the beneficence of the gods, and he spoke of the kinds of political stability (monarchy being especially good) that made this perfection possible and of the secret languages that needed to be handed down, and in telling these stories, he found that he suddenly had a greater purpose. He found that he could feel great affection for the HIV afflicted, even when they made uninformed evaluations of the wines. He looked forward to getting out of the house.

It was in this context that Randall met a certain handsome gentleman. Raoul was not exactly who Randall Tork was imagining when he went to speak in the wards of the damned. Many of the men in the hospices at least dimly recognized the importance of wine, perhaps as part of their dining lives. Some of them even had strong opinions on the subject. They would occasionally take issue with him, and there was vigorous back-and-forth. Raoul was not one of these men, and Randall was of the opinion that Raoul had never even tasted wine before he had his first plastic cupful on the ward. He knew so little of wine that he had no idea that the stuff in the chalice at church on Sundays was reputed to be the same beverage that Randall Tork was now handing out. Raoul, it seemed, was mostly interested in professional baseball, the argot of which he pronounced in a charming Hispanic way.

Whippet thin, with short curly black hair, Raoul also sported one brown eye and one that was sort of greenish, a combination so lovely that Randall Tork felt a need to compose lines on the subject. It turned out, of course, that the vehicle for these lines was a review of a New Zealand white that everyone said was so vivacious, *full-bodied, like an Oakland hooker, with the fruit of her cheap douche and the overtones of a Sumatran boar barbecued on a spit. Yet still this wine reminds me of the multicolored eyes of a beautiful man who once offered to take me to see the legends of local baseball frolic on their fields.* Always Barry Bonds this, Barry Bonds that, Barry Bonds is a Greek god, he will live into eternity. This was Raoul's sweet song, along with the fact that his surname, he said, proved that he was related to someone called A-Rod. Raoul was full of strong opinions about baseball, as befitted a young man, and seemed to come to the wine tastings with the cross-purpose of perseverating on America's pastime.

Raoul said he was straight, which is what they all say, especially those men of the Catholic countries to our south, notwithstanding that they have all been around the block, pledging their eternal love to their boyhood friends before going and knocking up some she-vixen because they are too prideful to use a condom. Raoul said to Randall at the first tasting, "I am not a fruity wine like these others here," and then he giggled as if he had never said anything so amusing in his life, which was perhaps true. Maybe he was straight, because who knew about these things? The libido is as mysterious as soil and sunlight and precipitation and the vine.

One fact was incontrovertible, however, and that was that Raoul had been an intravenous drug user during many years. He had lived on the streets for some of these years. It was likely that Raoul had been a male prostitute, perhaps in the Tenderloin. And this dark history of Raoul was, for Randall Tork, especially thrilling.

Accordingly, Randall visited this particular ward more often. Other locations of the needy began to get fewer lectures, less exacting attention. And then abruptly Randall Tork was visiting Raoul on a nonprofessional basis because Raoul was very sick and very thin, with a lingering pneumonia, and some days he could get out of bed, and some days not. Raoul was never less than enchanting, in his consumptive ghostliness, and he was always gallant when Randall Tork came around. The question was why. Why would a former male prostitute and IV drug user who claimed to be straight, whose main interest was Barry Bonds, get excited about the attentions of a stumpy, middle-aged wine writer with muttonchops and a beret, who sat around all day trying to decide whether to repaint his living room while checking the prices of his stock portfolio?

There was no reason on earth why Raoul should care for the attentions of Randall Tork, and thus the reasons must have been abstract and perfect, and Randall Tork, the greatest wine writer in history, did, of course, attempt to divine the nature of these abstractions while considering the force and meaning of the Castello di Ostuni, 1999 Chianti Classico (fifty-five dollars a bottle):

Why should this be the top Chianti from Ostuni, a region not widely noted for its fine wines? Why should this estate, which has been in the family since 1580, suddenly produce a wine that I love, after a run of the worst, most undrinkable table swill of my considerable experience? To answer these questions, reader, there is no choice but to speak of sweet love generally. When in love do you not see depth where once depth was unapparent, and when in love do you not see elegance where once elegance feared to tread, and when in love do you not see complexity where hitherto all was simplistic, and is not a condition of willingness and openness to novelty the most succulent of trances? Does not love eventually work its magic on even the unworthy? Yes, complexity is love's highest aim, and in the case of a wine, its symbol is in the full-bodied nature of the vintage, and by full-bodied I mean the kaleidoscope of liminalities in one sweet goblet. Hold it up to the light, hold up the beloved wine to the light and see how when your love is decanted his blood is deep and red like history. Now drink of its bouquet, the bouquet of this sweet Chianti, its bouquet of musk and lilies and warm semen, and now you are ready to see the precarious balance in the taste of your love, citrus, honeydew, and birch, and now and only now are you ready to sip, oh yes; here are the fierce tannins, which ask for your courage and which call after you, reminding you of the responsibility of this sweet instant; now let the echo of that taste linger, bringing with it a sweet waiting. It is yours to delight in love and to remember that love and wine call you to the same reverence, to take and delight and remember and describe and teach and succumb to the sweet wrestling, the longing for what will soon be gone, for a bottle of wine must end, like the greatest love story told.

He threw caution to the wind and read the column aloud to Raoul. And though Randall wasn't sure that Raoul would really understand all of it, the critic nonetheless performed his love poem, acting out his Keatsian excesses with stylized sibilances and exclamations. If Randall Tork could not answer why Raoul should favor him with attentions, perhaps it didn't matter any longer, because the column proved that Raoul brought out the best in him. He even took Raoul out to a Mexican restaurant in the Mission, and he actually drank *beer* with Raoul, which he previously would never have been caught doing with anyone, and he laughed uproariously at Raoul's tales of the street, of the camaraderies of the street. He didn't care if the louts and toughs of the authentic Mexican restaurant used that horrible Spanish slang word to describe the two of them. Then he took Raoul back to the hospice, giving the taxi driver very exacting directions, which if not followed to the letter elicited torrents of abuse, because he now cared about the vintage known as Raoul and, notwithstanding the haste of the decision, he wanted to know if Raoul would come and live with him in Marin County, in his little house on stilts.

Of course, it occurred to Randall Tork that Raoul might be lying about various things. It occurred to Randall Tork that he was taking in a felon with a past full of shadows, but he was willing to do what needed to be done, which was to administer the tripartite cocktail when it needed to be administered, and to cook healthful soups from scratch, and to laugh when laughing was possible, and to give constant updates on baseball scores, and even to watch televised baseball if that was what was needed, to help the patient dress, to bestow kisses on the patient, and when Raoul began improving a little bit, when he seemed to rally such that he was even talking about getting a job, perhaps at a discount-beverage center, then Randall Tork knew that in addition to being the greatest wine writer in history, he was also a person whose love was curative. How to tell Raoul this, that he had never ever before been such a person, that his principal motivator had always been the urge to despoil? Now he wanted only to despoil the vineyard owners of Sonoma and Napa Valley, no one else. Passersby seemed more benevolent than ever.

There was the wrinkle: that Raoul would never make love with him. Would not, at any rate, have an orgasm with him. Raoul said that his spunk, which was the word he used, was toxic, and that it was not fair to subject Randall Tork to it, when the truth was that the very poison of Raoul's little frogmen was what made them more ambrosial and heavenly. Randall would have delighted to eat them, as a testament to his sacrifices, since there was no apparent link between this practice and viral transmission. But no, when it came to these moments, Randall had to beg of his

Hispanic lover, and this was proof that there were always further depths of humility for Randall to know, if he would know love.

The amounts of money that began to go missing were mainly inconsequential, because Randall Tork did not leave a lot of cash around the premises. He hated cash, in fact, and dealt almost exclusively in debit and credit cards. He was an inveterate saver, and most of his fortune, which was not much, considering the reach of his annual paperback and his Web site ratings, was tied up in mutual funds that had nosedived, along with everyone else's, earlier in the year. Yet he was frugal and thrifty. When two hundred dollars disappeared from his wallet just after these monies were extracted from a cash machine, he didn't fail to notice. Nor did he, however, immediately confront Raoul. He waited to see what would happen. Would the two hundred dollars be converted immediately into a speedball or whatever the term was? Six weeks later, there was another precipitous disappearance of cash. Randall asked himself what the saints would do. Would the saints thank the heavens that Raoul was feeling frisky enough to go in search of drugs? Would the saints forgive and forget?

One afternoon about dusk, in early October, which is after all a perfect time for a shocking revelation, Raoul, weeping, put his hand on the knee of his patron and said that he was again putting the needle in his arm. It was not what he wanted to do, he said, lapsing into the Spanglish patois that was so divine, "The thing calls to me, and I cannot refuse."

Randall listened to the circles of Raoul's reasoning, and his disgust was with himself, more so than with the rampant lies that peppered the confession. Because he had not yet sacrificed enough, as anyone could see. Holding the emaciated head of his lover in his lap, he said, "How can I help?"

"I must stop. I don't want to hurt nobody."

Randall said, "I could just give you whatever amount of money you need to ensure that if you are going to use drugs you buy from the most reputable dealers in these drugs, that you get the safest drugs, and that you always use the cleanest needles, and in that way, you take the fewest risks. Because if money is going to enable you to feel comfortable, then I need to help, because I am the man who loves you."

After consideration, Randall added, "We can go through this together."

Raoul wept for a while and when he again met Randall Tork's eyes, it was with a kind of gratitude that Tork was not used to seeing, even from the wine publicists who had dodged the exploding ordnance of his malice. Randall could tell that Raoul was high even at the moment of confession, because he knew the look. The look of the simulation of self-knowledge by one who is able in deceit. He knew Raoul was high and he suspected it would get worse, that there was no ending ahead but a bad ending. This bad ending might contain the assault of his own person, the robbery thereof. Still, he had come this far, and for the moment there was no course but to trust further and to attempt to lead Raoul to the light of nobility, especially as this light was indicated in the tradition of the production of wine. He urged Raoul to come to tastings with him, and Raoul attempted to comply on a few occasions. But for each boondoggle that featured Raoul's guest appearance, there were days when he was gone, and, for all Randall knew, he was out on the street, playing the *putain* for an extra twenty or thirty clams. Randall Tork tried to make sure that the boy never left without cash, and he always snuck a half-dozen condoms into his pocket when Raoul's blue jeans came out of the wash.

As Halloween rolled around, Randall Tork began to get an even more desperate notion. That he would like to *marry* Raoul. Marry him? He could not marry Raoul, for so many reasons, chief among them that Raoul Rodriguez was Catholic, and in the Roman Catholic Church there was no such thing as the love between men. The blood of Christ congealed at the very notion. And there was also the law of the land, the nauseating Defense of Marriage Act, which prohibited two men from meeting in the nuptial bower to celebrate their love. Formidable problems, indeed, and yet Randall Tork, the greatest living wine writer, did not accept that anyone could tell him what he might do. He would marry Raoul, and they would promenade down the steps of some church, sparklers sparkling everywhere around them. He would utter his vows to the boy and he would know the joy the vows brought down on their utterers.

Was it delusional? He'd known Raoul three months. Three delicious months during which he had never once shrunk from holding the boy's head when he upchucked, nor from cleaning up after his bouts of diarrhea. He cherished every joke and every moment of kindness; he loved every landscape that had Raoul in it. He was occasionally struck by the notion that Raoul would not live out the whole of his term. For example, Randall Tork should have been finishing a big article for a big glossy magazine about the Afghani vineyards that were springing up in place of the once plentiful fields of opium poppies. But he could not finish the article because he was too busy thinking about getting married. Where might they conduct the ceremony? Should they travel to some faraway country that recognized their type of union? Would Raoul be able to fly without having to give himself an injection? Which designer should they select for the creation of their wedding suits? And, most important, what would be the wine? In the past few weeks, Randall Tork had been vacillating between two different choices: the 1945 Mouton Rothschild, with its light amber edges, and the 1959 Lafite Rothschild, memorable for, dare he say it, the black truffle overtones. He found himself curiously irresolute, as if the idea that he might now be married had begun to affect somehow his professional credentials in the matter of this selection. Scandal!

Into these interesting times, as if dropped from the air, a movie star projected himself. Randall had met the movie star at a wine tasting at a Sonoma vineyard, Lonely Lake, owned by a certain film producer. Randall Tork felt that the wines of Lonely Lake were beneath contempt, as were all but a few American wines, but he had made an exception and graced this tasting with his presence for the simple reason that Lonely Lake had the best wine *label* he had ever seen. It hadn't escaped Randall's notice that some of the California vineyards had brought to the design of their labels the expertise and sublimity that their wine making lacked. The pen-and-ink elegance and the almost Victorian calligraphy of the Lonely Lake label appealed to Randall, as did the invocation in its title of that most romantic of emotions. What did Randall know better than wine? Just the one thing. Loneliness. The idea that a purveyor of popular pabulum like the producer who owned this vineyard would willingly invoke that most perfect word, *loneliness,* in the pursuit of a drinkable simulation of a Malbec, it was enough to roust him from Raoul and his house.

Randall Tork recalls that he was talking to a thoroughly moronic author of mystery novels, whose visage looked as though it had been face-lifted by a drunken home renovator, and she was boasting about how her next novel was going to be about a wine writer, when all at once there was a commotion in the room, and the movie star and his wife made their entrance. Of course, Randall Tork is not the sort to be surprised by stardom. He has seen stardom come and go. He has seen great chefs laid low by pedophilia and vainglory, and he has seen vineyards that were red-hot in one vintage produce nothing but detergent for a decade. He has seen it all. Still, Randall Tork admired a fine entrance. When the movie star and his wife entered the party, the general astonishment of the wine tasters was a fine thing to behold. The wine tasters laid aside their gossip about the movie producer and his wines long enough to take note of the white minidress that the wife was wearing and the ensemble that the movie star himself sported, a pair of torn blue jeans, a silk T-shirt, a blazer from Armani, and cowboy boots.

Randall Tork was introduced to the movie star as the world's greatest living wine writer, and neither he nor the movie star disputed this characterization. There were two giants in the room now, and this was one of those moments when those destined to greatness must sniff around each other's behinds to settle the question of whether or not to attack.

What impressed Randall about the movie star immediately was that the movie star ignored everyone for the rest of the afternoon and devoted himself exclusively to Tork. This indicated, on the part of the movie star, a developed palate. He believed that the movie star showed promise. And the movie star, unlike many straight men of reputation, was not at all uncomfortable around a man of Randall Tork's persuasions. On the contrary, the movie star seemed to enjoy talking to a wine writer no matter *qu'il fait la drague*. It was only when they had been talking for some fifteen or twenty minutes that the movie star admitted that he actually did collect a little bit, under the tutelage of his father-in-law, who really knew about these things, and it happened that in this context, the wine-collecting context, the movie star had indeed read some of Randall Tork's reviews.

"You're a madman, and I can't get enough of it. I don't care about the wines. I only care about the way the language tumbles out."

"Of course you do."

"You're like Proust."

"Proust is like *me*. I'd never change the boys' names to girls' names."

"He — ?"

"I was not pampered as a child. I made myself up in a fever dream. It was not a taxing project. Now Randall Tork rules the world."

Of course, the movie star had many demands upon his attention. Eventually, the vineyard owner, that briny lump of tissue, pried the movie star loose from his colloquy with Randall, and Randall recognized that this was inevitable, if boring. But before the movie star moved on to dally with the vacuous, diaper-clad elderly of Sonoma County, he leaned in to Randall and said, "Give me your card. We'll get together."

And Randall's card is rather special. It's from Smythson of Bond Street, the London office, special ordered, and it is on heavy stock with gilt edges, printed in Edwardian script from a hand-engraved copperplate: *RANDALL TORK. IN THE CON-SIDERATION OF FINE VINTAGES.* E-mail address below. During the events described, Randall delivered the card with the ennui that appropriately suggested that the movie star could never have been luckier than just now. Indeed, the movie star smiled, before disappearing into the throngs.

This personage, Randall later admitted to his consort, Raoul, was called Thaddeus Griffin.

"Single Bullet Theory?"

"The very one."

"Was he a handsome man?"

"Exceedingly handsome, his handsomeness chiefly located in his tonsorial effects. He is a man with perfect hair, hair whose disarrangement is among the most calculated statements of beauty I have seen in many years."

"You going to make room in your bed?" said Raoul mischievously.

"Fool," Randall said. "I'm promised to you. You are my appointment and my disappointment. Moreover, this is a man who loves his wife. I can sense these things."

Evidently the movie star managed such feats as producing from thin air the unlisted and fervently guarded telephone number of Randall Tork, because suddenly, out of the blue, in the middle of the crisis of Raoul's addictive relapses, the movie star called not too long after the tiresome general election. He said he had something he wanted to discuss with Randall Tork and could he come out to Sonoma, just after the Thanksgiving holiday, to meet with him. There was no description of what was to be discussed. And yet Randall Tork, the greatest living wine writer, was not above a little adolescent excitement. An excitement that he elected not to display, lest his passions bring about one of the inexplicable torrents of Latin rage in Raoul.

Today is the day. Having completed six column inches of negligible interest and having fretted briefly over whether his powers are on the wane, Randall Tork has washed behind his ears, and he has brushed his teeth again, and he has set out a lovely Château Lafite from a year before he was born on a silver platter, alongside which are two glasses from Tiffany's, and he has gone out into the living room, where Raoul is sobbing over a talk show about a woman who cannot accept her daughter's navel ring, and he has hugged this dear boy, and he has asked if Raoul would make sure not to ask the movie star anything about his movies or his upcoming projects, because these people, he tells Raoul, do not like to have to talk about how they live. It would be better if he would just continue watching the program until Randall gives him the secret signal, and then he can go ahead and talk.

"You trying to hide me away from your famous boyfriend!"

"Raoul! Absolutely not!"

"You saying that I'm not good enough?" It's just what he was afraid of. The outrage gathers momentum, like a chain reaction, beginning as a peevish jocularity and moving through bitter resentment into full-scale meltdown.

"I am saying no such thing! I'm saying that we do not yet know what the movie star *wants,* and in the absence of information, we should wait and see what it is that he wants, and that requires the stealthy strategy of a feline —"

"You calling me —"

"I'm not calling you anything except my dear sweet boy who has made my life tolerable. I'm just explaining —"

"I can go out on the street and wait for you there, if that's what you want. I come into your house like this, you ought to treat me with *respect*. Because I have things I can do. I can go away!"

"Raoul! Please don't do this! Not now. I am your cheering section and your federal agency. I love you no matter what. Please just understand —"

In fact, Raoul has taken a bad turn in recent days. Raoul has stopped looking rosy in the way he was, even though Randall is making sure that he takes what he's supposed to take, and he has stopped expressing the joy he was previously expressing. Raoul has mostly lain around on the couch, complaining about a program called *American Spy*, which bothers him because he thinks the participants are unpleasant. Perhaps it will be this way until spring training, when his pastime can again lighten his heart. Whatever the cause, Randall Tork does not have liberty to ponder it, because the doorbell is ringing — because it is twelve noon sharp on the Monday after Thanksgiving, the appointed day and time — and now the movie star has come to call, here at the little house on stilts.

The movie star is graceful and full of humility as he stoops and crosses the threshold. The movie star hands over his scarf and his leather jacket, and he smiles at Randall and compliments him on the house, on its elimination of inessential furnishings, the concealment of all books, the warm light that suffuses the premises with genteel hospitality. All things, it should go without saying, that Randall Tork has premeditated in the presentation of his modest bunker. If the movie star notices the lump on the couch, he doesn't say anything about it, and neither does Randall. At the kitchen table, after the wine is poured from the decanter and after the movie star performs a neophyte's swirling and sniffing, the conversation at last begins.

"Let me know what you think," Randall says. "Grape juice. Just a trifle. I have a couple of other things I want you to try."

"Excellent."

The movie star gives the wine pause, a pause that the movie star apparently thinks he must observe, before getting onto the subject he has genuinely come here to address.

"Listen, Randall — it's okay if I call you Randall, right? I didn't really come here to discuss wine, which I'm sure is kind of an unusual thing to say under the circumstances. Since that's what you're known for. I really admire what you do as a writer, and that's why I'm here. It's like I said the last time we saw each other. I think I said then that I didn't think you were *just* a wine writer, any more than Hemingway was just a writer about bullfights. I think you're one of the great contemporary writers, I really do, and believe it or not, I do read. Once you get locked into doing what I do, you're sort of stuck there. There are lots of compensations, sure, but there are lots of costs, too. For example, no one believes I got a good education at a good college. No one believes that I love to read and that I admire the great storytellers, you know? It's true. I even write.

"I wouldn't exactly call what I do writing; it's more like blocking out big chunks of story. You know. I try to develop scripts and stuff. That's what I've tried to do for the last few years, in New York. And recently I've had a little good news. That's really why I'm here. I've finally got something set up, or just about set up, something that has the potential to be a really big project, you know, the kind of thing that has major-studio involvement, major money on the table. A blockbuster."

"Is this a —"

"Not a motion picture, actually. It's a . . . well, it's sort of a television thing, really. It's a . . . miniseries."

"A what?"

"Just listen for a second. It's not every day that I have a conversation like this, Randall. Let me tell you a little bit about what's really going on. Let me tell you a little bit what it's like. My name has been in the papers lately, and not in good circumstances. The kind of coverage that you don't exactly want to get. And that sort of coverage has not exactly endeared me to my family, if you see what I mean. I'm about to go film a movie in the desert, Randall, a movie called *The Tempest of Sahara,* which has to be one of the dumbest scripts I've ever read. And when I'm through filming there, in three months, and I come back to the wreckage of my married life, I don't exactly know what I'll find. The production company that I helped found is at death's door, money problems, embezzlement; I have every bit of bad luck you could think of.

"Still, I had this idea about a month ago, for a miniseries. About diviners. Diviners, Randall, you know, the guys with the, with the —"

"Forked sticks."

"And this prompted me to read a little bit about the arid places of the world, Randall. It started out as a joke. The whole story started out as a joke. I guess I can come clean, Randall, because you seem like a guy who could, who has been . . . I feel like you'll understand, and the thing is, the story started as a joke to impress someone, Randall. It was spun out on a cocktail napkin in a bar. But then I started reading about the deserts, about the American West, and about the struggle for water, which, you know, is a struggle as old as man. There's always been this class of magicians, Randall, and they're, like, they're the priest class in the desert, they get to wear the best outfits, these ones who know where the water is; I started to see that there was always something magical happening in the desert, there was this awesome deprivation and savagery going on, and then on the other hand, there were these little moments of grace, from generation to generation, whenever the diviners were on the scene, and that's when I got the idea for this series. Once I started writing I couldn't stop. The words were just pouring out, Randall, I never had an experience like this before, I'm not . . . I'm probably not really an artist. I'm not a guy who lies awake at night with bits of inspiration floating through my head. But once I got the idea to start writing this story, Randall, I couldn't think of anything else. It was like I was the desert, like I was the parched landscape, and the rainfall, the storm was breaking over me, for no reason other than I was in a bad patch and I was being given this chance to make something out of it."

The movie star's earnestness is commanding enough that Randall Tork can hardly look away. He refills the wineglasses. The movie star drinks his down as though it really were grape juice. Randall, who normally tastes the stuff and spits it out, feels somehow compelled to keep up, as the movie star begins to spin out his deluxe plot summary. Can anything on earth truly be duller than a movie or book digested by some brainless hunk of protoplasm who didn't read carefully in the first place? Randall would rather die than listen to plot summary. But that was before he got pitched by a movie star. Now, as the movie star tells him that the story begins at the dawn of time and moves up through the Dark Ages, into the Crusades, he's thoroughly charmed. The movie star could give the plot summary of the new post-deregulation phone book, and Randall would think it rather adorable. This is how the colloquy goes, until something really special happens.

What is the thing that happens? The thing that happens is that the movie star begins to tell Randall Tork about the discovery of Las Vegas. What was Las Vegas? Las Vegas was nothing; it didn't exist. Nothing existed, for the Spanish, on the road to Los Angeles, except a dozen days or more in the open sun with just the brackish water that the wayfarers managed to carry with them along the way. Many were lost, as the movie star tells it, many were lost, and that's without bothering to mention the assaults of the natives, who came from out of limitless nothingness where no one should have lived, to surround each and every band of Spaniards, stealing their women and scalping their men. Sometime in the

early nineteenth century a young Spanish adventurer, Rafael
Rivera, on a journey across this very desert, decided that the natives had to be coming from somewhere, from some verdancy
out there in the wasteland. There had to be water; there had to be
waving fields. There was no other explanation. And Rafael Rivera
set out across the desert with courageous confederates. No one
expected anything of him, only that they would later find his
shiny skeleton, picked clean. But what did Rafael find? He found
an oasis, and he named it for its waving fields, Las Vegas. It cut
the trip to Los Angeles in half because it was no longer necessary
to go *around*.

A beautiful little story, of course, and as part of the larger narrative, it would necessarily include a dowser as one of the courageous confederates. But what piques the interest of Randall Tork,
of course, is the role of Rafael. In general, the rest of the story is
a little silly. Who cares if there were other, older explorers along
for the ride? Who is going to play Rafael Rivera in this miniseries?
It seems completely natural to him that Raoul, his intended, his
plighted troth, would be perfect for the part, since he is already
Hispanic, and he is beautiful to behold, and the gravity of his illness would look entirely appropriate out in the merciless desert.
So overwhelming is the idea of trying to cast Raoul in the role of
Rafael that he doesn't at first pay attention to what comes next.

"The thing is, Randall, you know and I know that the world
hates a guy with two ambitions. The world wants me to do the
one thing, and that's fire off blanks from an automatic weapon.
Especially with all the trouble I've gotten myself into recently.
Everywhere I go lately, there's a guy with a beer gut and a tele-
photo lens waiting for me to pick my nose. I had to change cars
twice and duck into a men's room just to get here without anyone following me. And so it's just not for me to try to be the
writer on this script, even though I'm really proud of what I've
come up with. I don't want to go through the whole process of
coming up with a pseudonym or any of that nonsense. I want

someone to flesh out the story for me, Randall; I want someone to be the writer for me. I want someone who really has something, who really has the gift, who really has the inspiration that maybe I have had this week but that I'll probably never have again. I want someone who has the real vision to do this for me, to be the name on the poster for *The Diviners*. You could work on the script with me if you want, Randall, it's really up to you. You'd get a cut on the whole project and a credit that you can use to your advantage later on if you want. You've got a name and a reputation, a great reputation among the people who could really help to finance a project like this, and you're a natural, so why wouldn't you write a script?"

Why wouldn't he, indeed? Is he not Randall Tork, the greatest wine writer in history? And has he not always, in the back of his mind, known that one day he would turn his abilities toward something that served as a more likely platform for world domination? His editor has often told him he has a novel in him, for example, and if not a novel, why not a thirteen-episode miniseries, with a three-hour pilot, that goes from the dawn of man up to Las Vegas? He is a natural, really, as long as one point can be negotiated. And that point is Raoul.

"Well," Randall says. "This is all so sudden. All so very sudden. But I must say, Thaddeus — if it's okay that I call you Thaddeus — I'm touched and honored. I really am. Because there must have been any number of writers, experts in other fields, whom you must have considered — although I'm obviously more qualified than all of them. Still, I'm honored. Touched and honored. Obviously, I'll need to think about it for a few days, and would it be possible to take a gander at some pages from your script? I think that might be the way to proceed, just so that I can see to what I might be signing my name? It's really a very provocative proposal you bring, and I will give it my utmost consideration."

Then Randall says, "Oh, and by the way, there's someone I want you to meet."

If his husband-to-be, Raoul, is going to secure the role of Rafael, it would be best if the movie star could meet him first. He certainly hopes that Raoul can hold his tongue and not say any of those incredibly impulsive things he says sometimes, because here it is, the movie star's proposal, delivered in a passionate and intensive forty-five-minute tête-à-tête over a Château Lafite, and could anything be so wonderful and so sudden as this proposal? Nothing could. He just wants Raoul to share in the outrageous wonderfulness of it, and after the shoot they will perhaps wed, in a large ceremony in Sedona, because it wouldn't be all that far from Las Vegas, and so perhaps they could get married in that spectacular Frank Lloyd Wright chapel up in the rocks, and perhaps the movie star would agree to be the best man for the both of them. Randall rinses the crystal out and then he points at the living room. Thaddeus tarries in the doorway. Beyond, the television screen murmurs hopelessly.

"Raoul, honey?" Randall says. Though he never employs cheap endearments. "Raoul, honey? Are you awake?"

30

The desperate venture to the city of Las Vegas on Interstate Fifteen. They don't fly in. Airports are for frauds. Hip-hop impresario Mercurio? He's in town, convening a high-stakes game of poker at the Venetian. Mercurio flies into town on the record company jet. Lacey? She is said to be in town, having returned from Europe. Europe, she says, is boring. Lacey has been drinking in the bars at the Bellagio. There are governors and congressmen here, there are judges and CEOs, there are sheiks and organized-crime figures. They all use the airport. But the desperate, those who pay for the bricks of the empire, they do not fly into Las Vegas. They come through the desert.

Therefore, Ranjeet and Jeanine want to see the city rising up from the depleted water table, they want to see the shimmering mirages of Las Vegas, or at least this is what Ranjeet says. Jeanine is no longer sure. She's beginning to think that having staked her future on a foreign national who only a few weeks ago was driving for a car service in Brooklyn may have been a bit hasty, especially because Ranjeet persists in believing that he's going to direct both the big three-hour first episode of *The Diviners* and the spectacular Las Vegas episode, a.k.a. episode thirteen.

Ranjeet has gone native. He doesn't run his plans by Vanessa or Madison or anyone else. He doesn't care about Means of Production or its legacy. He orders Jeanine around, implying that she doesn't know about her own culture. He says that if the Liberace Museum is not, as she sees it, an absolute necessity for their trip, then she should not have accompanied him. He especially wants to see the capes. And so Jeanine has become the woman behind the megalomaniac. She can arrange many things according to instructions. She can book flights, like the flight into Salt Lake, where they went briefly to see the temple of the Church of Jesus Christ of Latter-day Saints. She can insist on a larger car, which is a dusty Mustang convertible, by which conveyance they are approaching Las Vegas. She can secure hotel rooms. And she can listen to the *strophes,* as he calls them, when they overcome him, his songs about the plenitude of jerky in truck stops off the interstate, about the poisonous American coffee of these wastelands. Is the foulness of the coffee in Elko a test for the immigrants who have come to this New World? And what about the women painted on the mud flaps of the rigs that they pass? Ranjeet sings of all these things.

He has somehow swindled the rental car through someone at UBC. She doesn't even want to know. He is on his cell phone all the time now, and she overhears more of his conversations than she has conversations with him. Maybe he is dictating the strophes into some answering machine someplace. He seems to believe that the appearance of cell phone use is a necessary part of his job. "There is no actual city here, no actual place, no content of any kind, that was why this was the perfect locale for Benjamin Siegel, also known as Bugsy. Because if a place has nothing in it but mirages, then any kind of fantasy may be built upon this place, and the economy of such a city is composed of the ephemeral nature of fantasies and the massaging of fantasies into the possibility of gratification. It is a very fine word, *gaming,* because it implies that there is a complete elimination of serious endeavor."

They streak past another billboard: Topless girls! One hundred miles!

"There's something I need to tell you," she shouts, as he barks into the cell phone.

"I would like to hear what you have to say when I am done with this particular call."

They are looking for the Spanish Trail. They're looking for where the caravan of Mexican trader Antonio Armijo might have traveled in 1829. This would be a very good place to film any desert sequences. To film in the actual place of this caravan will bring a much-needed legitimacy to the project, especially as Antonio Armijo is himself a character in episode thirteen. They can hire the specialists they need, the gaffers and grips, the assistant directors, the second unit, in the Las Vegas area, which now boasts professional crews and a city department of film projects, just as with any thriving metropolitan center. There will be a reverse caravan of professionals to this desolate spot along the Spanish Trail, which could also be ideal for any featurette about the making of *The Diviners*.

They have passed through towns called Death and Devil's Paintbrush, and they have seen expanses of craggy mountains and empty valleys, and it all looks the same; it all looks like a canvas on which the developers have not yet daubed their computer-aided pastels, and yet, at a certain moment on the interstate, which could as well be anywhere, Ranjeet cries, "We must stop!" He pulls the car off the highway, muttering about the geological survey of the Bureau of Land Management. It is right, he says, that he should be able to drive his rented vehicle wherever he should choose to drive it, through Russian thistle and mesquite. That is the great democratic principle. The convertible, which, rented at a luxury rate, is not designed for this kind of punishment, kicks up storms of dust as they streak into the midst of Ranjeet's folly. They move out of the range of the cellular telephone, away from its roadside comforts, and Jeanine feels herself cradled in the emptiness of this place. Ranjeet presses on, thundering over the tracks of an all-terrain vehicle, until they can no longer see the interstate, and its hum sounds like a signal from interstellar space. Finally, Ranjeet says, "Here." He's out of the car before she has even registered that they are parked. Ranjeet scampers into the desert and falls to his knees.

"They came this way," Ranjeet says. "They came here, believing that they were going to be a part of the historic rush for the nuggets of gold." He picks up a hunk of rose quartz and studies it as if no other piece of rose quartz has ever been found. "I believe I am seeing flecks of gold here. Come quickly and look."

"The gold rush was later."

"Fool's gold is perfectly serviceable. It matters only that I have re-created the anguished journey of Antonio Armijo and his band of sixty, men bent on the promise of the Pacific Ocean, about which they have heard so many things. They have heard of palm trees and coconuts, salacious women, they have heard of the vast western ocean, but here in the desert, they can see none of it. They can find only these glimmering minerals. They can read in the patterns of the rocks their own fates."

"Aren't you worried about snakes?"

"The water," Ranjeet says, "is beneath the floor of the desert. And that is where Rafael Rivera emerges into the story. He is the diviner of rivers and he is an all-important member of the posse of Antonio Armijo. He comes from the ancient family of diviners, which stretches backward through time. Rafael is the finest scout in the history of the Spanish territories, but even so, no one believes he can find water in this parched region. No one knows exactly how he does it, as he has never allowed anyone to see him in the practice of his craft."

It goes on like this, only more elaborately. Jeanine admires Ranjeet's hard work and the way he remains kneeling in the sand. Here she is standing by the car, like the women of cinema, who are always to be found with their behinds against the passenger door, perfect hair blowing in the desert winds, each of these women wondering if she's getting paid enough to offset the inevitable disappointment of life. In any road movie, you can be certain the actress would rather be back in the car than standing outdoors. Everyone would rather be back in the car, moving past the motels and the towns that are no more than a gas station and a general store and a few rusted pickup trucks.

"You *could* kiss me," she says, advancing one tiny step away from the car, away from the eight cylinders and the mediocre gas mileage. "That was one of the reasons I came."

Ranjeet looks up from his hunk of quartz. "I am a Sikh. According to my faith, I regard another man's daughter as my own daughter and regard another man's wife as my mother. I have coition with my wife alone. However, we will have a hotel room, to which we are entitled as contractors working for a large television network. In a flush of entitlement, we will embrace, even though I am a married man."

"Do you have to keep bringing that part up?"

When she kissed Ranjeet by the subway after that uncomfortable dinner, because she was weeping over his son's beauty and innocence, wasn't it already apparent that she'd made a big mistake? Hadn't she made a big mistake when she asked him to take off the turban? Hadn't she made a mistake when she told her roommate that she'd found a man of honor who probably could do his own laundry and cook fabulous Indian cuisine? Hadn't she made a mistake by forgetting the good advice about mixing the professional and the personal? Of course the real mistake is to spend five minutes in the condition of longing, because the minute you desire a thing, you and it are lost.

Ranjeet, dusting off his hands, rises, comes to her side, and holds open the car door for her.

The desert ends almost as if there's a dotted border where the despoilation begins. There's the desert, and then there are the cookie-cutter ranch houses of the greater metropolitan area and the billboards advertising the local spectacles: a pair of magicians with white tigers, topless dancers, the lowest interest rate of any pawnshop in the city. Jeanine can see the pox of the city in the distance. She can see the cartoon exaggerations of the casinos from here. The sun has dipped its fingertips in the wading pool beyond the horizon, and the chill of desert evening in early winter begins to overcome her. She can feel Ranjeet getting swept up into the gigantic con of the place. The strophes begin anew.

"What Benjamin Siegel recognized," Ranjeet says, "was the great energy potential. What Benjamin Siegel knew was that every single citizen was either part of the spectacle or part of the audience. There are the two categories of persons, the entertainers and the entertained. According to Benjamin Siegel, his organized-crime syndicate needed to control the entertainment. Indeed, the spectacle must extend outward from a theatrical space until it engulfs the city surrounding! There must be a Strip! Benjamin Siegel came into this place after the right to gamble was secured, which is of course enshrined in your law, and he saw that there had to be spectacle. He did whatever he had to do to find the capital resources necessary to realize his dream, though to do so he lost himself, lost his fantasy to women and beverages which overflowed the very containers in which they were housed." Then some more about mobsters and about Del Webb, former owner of the New York Yankees, who learned everything he needed to know from the hustle and vigor of the game of baseball.

They're staying at the Luxor because the Luxor, with its pyramid and its sphinx, is designed to resemble the legal-tender dollar bill of the United States of America. The hotel is large enough to hold an army, and it is full, and people are ambling everywhere in the stunned thrall of casino visitors. It is impossible to feel that one belongs in a place like this, a place that is a giant toilet for flushing away the discernment of consumers. No matter where you go in this city, you pass the pit, and then you must hear the sound of the slot machines, that hypnotic tolling, promising the undeliverable, flushing you away.

The receptionist has a face like a gambler's dream. Jeanine looks down the long console of the check-in desk, and there are ten or twelve of these women, all of them ripe with erotic promise or fiscal promise, at least until they graduate to the next echelon of global entertainment and power.

"We are here as guests of the Universal Beverages Corporation and, specifically, we are guests of Jeffrey Maiser, the head of network programming for the UBC network. I believe that the Universal Beverages Corporation owns a portion of this hotel, and therefore it is necessary that the luxury suite is to be complimentary for us, and that there will be complimentary chips for gaming purposes, and we are very grateful to accept this honor."

The model/actress scarcely blinks because she has heard it all before, every plea, every story. She has welcomed people of extreme penury, as well as arms traders and Saharan warlords. She excuses herself and goes down the line to speak to a manager, who stands by in a rakish suit. The two of them hover over a console, and then the model or actress returns. She brings the bad news. "We're *very* sorry for the confusion, but we have no notification from Mr. Maiser or from anyone at Universal Beverages Corporation that your expenses are being taken care of. However, by way of apology, we're willing to give you a room now, and some complimentary chips, to tide you over while we attempt to straighten out the situation. In the meantime, we'll just need a credit card to secure the room. We'll credit your account, of course, once we get the direct-billing issues resolved."

Ranjeet writhes with discomfort.

"But we were told by one of Mr. Maiser's staff people that we would be able to —"

"That may be true, of course, but we'll need a major credit card, at least for the time being."

Ranjeet looks at Jeanine, as if to plead, *Don't ruin my illusion.* And yet Jeanine pretends not to understand this request, just so that she's not a pushover. Then from her handbag she pulls the Means of Production corporate credit card. Ranjeet seizes the card, presents it to the hotel employee. The hurdle is hurdled, and they are off to the elevators.

"It was very nice of them to present us with these complimentary chips," Ranjeet says in the elevator. "Have I mentioned to you that I am a very good gambler?"

"You haven't."

"Your embraces will create in me the desire to gamble. I'll order champagne and food for the room, and then you'll bathe, and I'll watch you bathe, and there will be a gentle and spiritual embracing, and these things will make me want to gamble."

"What kind of gambling do you do?"

"Please guess. If you should guess correctly, you will receive a deluge of embraces."

"I guess blackjack."

"Exactly correct."

The elevator launches them onto their floor, and they make their way down an endless corridor in search of the correct numerical digits. This is the storage bin of the desperate, and, should they open the door to their room, it's as if an agreement has been reached. Their last chance to resist the spectacle will have evaporated.

The room is sweet and quiet, and in it there's no hint of the madness that lies below, except perhaps in the oxygen-rich air. Jeanine is feeling a little better, though every minute alone in a room with Ranjeet reinforces the fact that he is avoiding making love with her. While she doesn't exactly think that a married man *should* be making love with her, he did embrace her by the subway station, and she did stay late in the office with him watching television that one night, and she could feel that he was aroused then, that she caused a stirring in him and does still, so why should there be this unanswered question? He seems to want to make love sometimes, and then other times he seems not to want to, and this is how it goes again, when he starts the water for her and pours the capful of bubble bath under the open tap. He says that he is going to telephone for champagne and he closes her into the bathroom.

After she has taken off most of her clothes, she makes the decision to entice Ranjeet, in her lingerie, and this is perhaps more evidence of the oxygen-rich delirium of the place. She's a woman covered with burn scars, and she is in her lingerie, and she's hypnotized into believing that this is the moment when she will be known in her complexity as a woman who is loyal and a woman who is covered with scars, a woman who is a little turned on, a woman who wants to make love at least once in a while in the arms of someone enthusiastic and caring, in the arms of someone who wants her in return, and who, in wanting her, creates the same in herself, the condition of wanting, which is who she thought Ranjeet was when he first appeared in the office, when he first began unreeling his strophes as though they were written on scrolls. This is the moment, and Ranjeet can make what he wants out of it, and what he makes out of it will be an indicator of the state of play, and the water is thundering in the tub, and the water turns her on a little bit, actually, she has occasionally used it in the project of self-satisfaction, and she looks at herself in the mirror, which is beginning to steam up, and she determines that she is not fat, that she is genuinely attractive, if not perfectly beautiful, and any guy would be lucky to have her, and she determines that yes, she is going to go out and seduce him, because that's the kind of place this is.

The door to the bathroom eases shut behind her, and the rush of the bathwater recedes. She finds that her Indian lover is sitting on the edge of the bed in nothing but his socks, and he is attempting to touch himself in impure ways, and this might be good, this might be part of the contagious sin of Las Vegas, except there's a problem. If he were aroused, he might be touching himself with abandon and delighting in it, and she might think it was okay, even with the socks, because he was maybe planning on sneaking into the bathroom or something, leaning her over the sink, but here he is, trouble twice over, because he's not sneaking into the bathroom, and he can't seem to get himself aroused at all, and also he is crying; Ranjeet is trying to masturbate, and he's wearing only black socks, which is the biggest fashion faux pas ever, and he's saying something about praying to God and that the true Sikh shall make "an honest living by lawful work," and he is saying that "all food and water are, in principle, clean, for these life-sustaining substances are provided by Him," and he's saying that love is the state of a "single soul in two bodies" and that the woman should "ever harbor for her husband a deferential solici-tude and regard him as the lord and master of her love." And af-ter saying all these devotional things, he adds, "Please tell me what it is we are doing here."

Jeanine kneels by the side of the bed, against his leg, looking up at him. And what happens is that he sees the scars, the scars that he, like everyone else, seems to forget about, because of the long sleeves, and he grabs her arm roughly and he looks at the scars. "You are a woman who has been injured. I have another woman at home who is injured, and that woman is devoted to me, for her I performed matrimonial circumambulations, and I have not honored the marriage that I said I was going to honor. Now what is to become of me?" But instead of pushing her away or telling her that she must dress, he begins to kiss the scars and he says, "I must kiss these scars, because if I kiss the scars then I will have paid back what I have plundered." And he begins to kiss the scars, and she lets him kiss the scars for a while, and it's okay, although sometimes when people kiss the scars it reminds her of the burn ward.

In the long run, nothing is going to happen just from the kiss-ing of the scars. He has to kiss her somewhere besides the scars.

She pushes Ranjeet back on the bed, and she removes the socks from his feet, and she now gazes upon what turn out to be his incredibly beautiful feet. Most guys have bits of sock fuzz nestled between the toes, and most guys don't clip their toenails enough, or their toenails are mottled with fungus. But Ranjeet's feet look as though he's spent his life walking on pillows. How could he have worn socks over feet so beautiful?

"I'm going to . . . let me . . ."

Ranjeet says no, no, no, but he's still lying on his back, covering his eyes, and she takes the little shriveled thing into her mouth, as if it's string cheese, and she tries to make something happen, and the minutes pass, and she gives it all the determination she can give it, but maybe she's just not so good at this kind of thing or maybe he's thinking of his wife. She has heard that adultery is meant to be electrifying, but it turns out to be tawdry and dull, like life in a casino, and so she just kisses him once softly on the thigh and then gets up and retreats to the bathroom.

By now, the bubbles are halfway up the wall. It's a big tub and it still hasn't filled. All of this romantic failure is revenge for her foolishness. Her foolishness for coming out here, for driving eight hours across the desert, like all the other people who came across this desert, believing there was anything genuine here. The people who came to enrich Meyer Lansky and Lucky Luciano or their heirs. The people who came because a flamingo is good luck or who came because Frank Sinatra performed here and bullied a dealer who dealt from a shoe. She's more foolish, because she knows better.

She leans back in the tub and steadies herself with one hand, and she walks her feet up the wall a little bit, trying not to eat any soap bubbles, until the tap is trickling down upon her, and she's in some grotto of moisture and disillusionment, where she belongs, for all her foolishness, and if she comes, she'll just feel worse about it, but that seems like what she deserves. When the door opens, she doesn't turn to look, she just lets the tap do what the tap will do, and she lets her fingers knead her, and so there are two of them there, with their dashed hopes, in some casino out in the middle of nowhere, trying to come up with a story that they can sell to the television executives in Los Angeles, and the two of them can't even get an arm around each other where it means anything, she thinks, feeling her legs trembling, but she shouldn't think about it at all, she should concentrate on thinking about nothing, she should concentrate on the sound of water, if she thinks about him, she'll just get distracted, so she just keeps at it, and she thinks that there's nothing to look forward to at all and that the whole story is built on lies and misrepresentations, the miniseries, and the office in New York, and her friendships there. She hasn't made a good decision in three months. She thought she was being prudent, and it turns out she wasn't prudent even once. She was always getting ready to do what she is doing right now, which is to blow everything in such a spectacular way, and this is when she hears Ranjeet at the sink, saying her name, blessing her a thousand times and promising all kinds of crazy things, saying that she is the One Timeless Being, promising that he will give her a half dozen children and that he will jump into a fire for her, and what he's saying sets off some kind of chain reaction in her head, and when that part is over, she flings herself backward into the bubble bath, so that her feet are periscopes and the rest of her is immersed.

After dinner, Ranjeet and Jeanine head for the gaming pit.

There's a whole method to selecting a proper table at which to play blackjack, according to Ranjeet, and this method involves divination. The first requirement is that there can be no other player at the table. As they are in Las Vegas on a Wednesday night, and as they have arrived at the pit with little left to say to each other, they go in search of the table that has no players, where the cards are fanned out in front of the dealer like plumage. However, Ranjeet can't find a dealer whom he likes. He doesn't want to reckon with a *white* dealer because, he observes, in a strophe of remarkable bile, the white dealers have contempt for immigrants. "There are a billion of us from India in the world," he says, "and there are more than a billion of the Chinese persons. Do these salaried employees not think that we are going to come here and overrun this land? We *are* coming to overrun it, and we are going to remake it in our image, with our beliefs, our ethics. Why do you think there are so many Japanese here in the casino? And so many Chinese? Here in the casino? Because we are coming for your country. We will dispossess you because it pleases us to do so." And he's right; the rest of America, those who are not in a private suite with Mercurio or Lacey, looks like the rest of the globe. Ranjeet walks nervously around the tables reserved for blackjack until he finds the one African American dealer, the dealer avoided by the rest of the players, the dealer with the gleaming skull made perfect with some waxy stuff, and then Ranjeet sits in the fifth seat and he lays down the complimentary chips, failing to offer even a single chip to Jeanine. They wait for the dealer to finish his ritual of shuffling.

Jeanine says, "It's time for me to tell you the thing I meant to tell you."

A fantail swept out in front of the Sikh.

"This happened when I was a teenager in Arizona. Believe it or not, I was a really rebellious girl, and there was nothing that my parents could do to keep me in the house. I wasn't like I am now. I was running around with my friends, in their parents' cars. We'd go driving in the desert. We drove east. Less civilization. North and east there was nothing but the reservations. We thought we had more in common with the Indians than we did with our parents. Used to spend nights out there. We'd lock the car doors, push the seats back. It made my parents mad, of course, and I'd get grounded for a month. Then I'd go right out there and do it again. I liked the reservations, especially the Navajo reservation. From the road, it was empty as far as you could see."

The dealer asks Ranjeet to cut the deck. They are ready for gaming. Ranjeet bets the minimum, which is fifteen dollars.

The dealer draws twenty-one on the first hand.

"You don't want to be out there in late summer, because if you're out there for very long you're just going to cook, you know. There are stories about people who leave their baby in the car in the summer. They go into the convenience store. They come out, and the baby is like a piece of dried fruit. Or dogs. They forgot to leave the window open a crack for their dogs, and now their dogs are sun-dried tomatoes. Everyone is trying to avoid fire. You can hear it on the radio. 'Today the alert is code red.'"

Ranjeet draws fifteen, takes a jack from the dealer, goes over. At this rate, he will last seven or eight more hands. He looks at Jeanine, pleading, as if by pleading he can get her not to tell the story. She waits and then she continues.

"I was going out with a boy named Philip. Philip was not a good boyfriend. My parents didn't want me to go out with him and they didn't like how I dressed with him or how I did in school when I was with him, and they didn't like anything else about him. Philip had planned this party for Saturday night, and we were going to drive north, to Skull Valley. Up near the Bradshaws. Just grasslands as far as you can see. Not as dry as the lower elevations, but the fires are just as dangerous. Up in the mountains you have the piñon and the ponderosa, and those make for good fuel. It didn't stop us. You go through there into horse country, and then you go beyond all the horses, and then you're in Skull Valley. We found a place off the road, where Philip and his pal Ryan and Ryan's girlfriend, Skye, got out and set up a couple of tents."

Of the next three hands, Ranjeet wins two. Then he doubles down with two sevens, wins one. Suddenly he's feeling kind of good about things. He bets forty-five dollars on the next hand, loses, and just as quickly he's exhausted half of the stake.

"Who wants to cook? We had some trail mix and we had a lot of beer and dope and some hummus that Skye brought. She worked at a health food store in town that nobody really patronized except us. She was always in there reading books about crystal magic. So Skye brought the only food we had, which means that we probably didn't have as much as we should have. The first thing we did was start drinking the beer and smoking a lot of dope. Philip and Ryan started saying a lot of stuff about how they wished that Skye and I would start kissing, because they wanted to watch. Actually, I never really talked to her much, because Skye didn't really talk. I told them that they should just lay off of Skye, but they didn't lay off. They'd probably set the whole thing up beforehand; that's what I think now. Let's get the girls drunk. They had some adolescent idea that they were going to set up an orgy on this big camping trip, but obviously they didn't know us too well."

"Could you please," Ranjeet says.

"I want to finish."

He bets forty-five again, draws thirteen, the number that gives every amateur blackjack player chest pains. He takes one card, and then another, and manages to work himself up to twenty, after which Jeanine watches as the dispassionate and professional African American dealer draws a six at fifteen, for twenty-one.

Ranjeet says, "I need more funds."

"You're welcome to use any funds that you have at your disposal," Jeanine says.

"I don't have any funds at my disposal."

"Call your contacts at UBC."

Ranjeet says, "Let me have the credit card."

"Why should I give you the credit card? You're playing like my grandmother."

"I am very sorry. Please finish your story."

He bets the rest of his chips. A whippet-thin guy with gin blossoms and a martini approaches the table, and Ranjeet waves him away.

"I figured I should find a way to escape with Skye. So we told the boys we were going to go out into the brush to get comfortable with each other and they should come along in a few minutes, like maybe they should come along in fifteen minutes, and we would be more comfortable, we would be native girls in the brush. And then we ran off. It was dark, you know, and we could smell the campfire even while we were running away through the fields, running as far as we could, out into the prairie, and I remember thinking that I was a little worried about the campfire because of the warnings that summer. Even if the fire alerts never stopped us before. We were drunk and high, and I remember that I saw Skye smiling and laughing for the first time. We thought we would circle back to the road, laughing the whole way. We thought we knew the direction of the road, but as far as we went we didn't see any road, and we didn't see any cars or even any lights. We'd thought we'd hitch a ride, because no one was going to leave two girls by the side of the road at night. But we couldn't find the road."

Ranjeet holds out his hand for the credit card.

"The story is finished, correct?"

"Incorrect. Go negotiate a second mortgage on your house. That'll give you liquidity."

Ranjeet walks away from the table, mumbling to the dealer that he will return in a quarter hour. Jeanine takes a drink from the first scantily clad waitress who comes by and she tips this waitress generously, feeling bad about the outfit and the hours. When Ranjeet comes back, he is furious and he is clutching a number of hundred-dollar bills. He says, "Are you happy now? I did not want to use these hundreds of dollars, because a Sikh does not form dubious associations or engage in gambling, and because these are the last dollars in my bank account, and I was saving them for the expenses relating to my son. Even if I am here and I have degraded my marriage with you, it does not mean I do not love my son, who I think will be an honorable man."

He places the hundred-dollar bills on the green felt, and the dealer calls over his supervisor to oversee the exchange of bills for chips. Immediately, Ranjeet bets a hundred.

"We're out in the middle of some prairie that should belong to someone. But we don't see anyone or any ranch house. There were wild burros out there, according to the signs, and I was starting to think about wild burros, and I was starting to think about other animals of the mountains, you know, bobcats or javelina. I didn't know; I was kind of worried. It was getting late. And we started calling for the boys, but we weren't hearing anything. We weren't hearing anyone calling back to us. I think Skye was really scared. She told me how she didn't have any family in Arizona, how she had come out west to go to school and then she dropped out of college right away and started working in the health food store and living behind a gas station. We called out some more, and no one answered our calls."

He wins the first hand, and then he wins the second.

"We figured we were going to have to stay put for the night, so that in the morning we'd be able to see where the road was and then we'd find our way back to town. We thought we needed a fire to keep the animals away from us. There could easily have been snakes out there, you know. Skye had a lighter because she smoked. If we had a fire, someone might find us, too. If people saw fires burning in the night, the fire department would get notified, and they'd come out and dowse them. So we tried to make a little campfire circle and we went looking for twigs and sticks, and all the time we were calling out to each other so we wouldn't lose each other on top of everything else."

Up a thousand dollars! A miraculous thing! A God-given thing! A thing that prepares the way for tomorrow's work, which will involve taking photographs of the locations they are going to use for the Las Vegas episode!

"I'm not done," Jeanine says. "I was telling you about how we made the little campfire circle, and then when we had the little campfire, we lay down beside it and we told each other stories, like I'm telling you a story right now, and we thought we would keep each other awake, telling stories, so that we could be sure to keep an eye on the fire, or in case the boys saw the fire, or if someone else did and called the fire department."

Ranjeet puts down five hundred dollars with a flourish. At which point the dealer deals himself an ace and a face. With a studied calm, the dealer remarks, "Bad luck, sir."

This is followed by two more top-dollar bets, desperation wagers. With the remaining five hundred, Ranjeet moves down to one-hundred-dollar increments. Of these, he loses three, wins one, and loses two more.

"You know the ending? You already know the end, so I'll just tell you the end, which is that I woke up to hear Skye screaming. The wind had blown up, which is the special requirement of a wildfire, and Skye was screaming. I was wearing a nylon windbreaker over a halter top, and I don't really remember what Skye was wearing, because at the moment when I woke up, Skye was already in a lot of trouble, with the campfire having blown out of the campfire ring. Skye's clothes were on fire, and I ran over to help her. I remember thinking that we didn't have anything at all that would be good for putting out a fire. We didn't even have any water. We were just a pair of stupid girls who didn't have anything and who hoped our boyfriends would turn out to be better guys than they seemed. We didn't have any water and we didn't have any shovels, and I could see that Skye was trying to pat the fire out on her arms and back, and I jumped on her, and I was trying to put out the fire on Skye and I could feel that I was not really getting the fire, that something was making the fire burn brighter, and maybe that was my nylon jacket burning, but I didn't have time to pay attention to it because I looked up and I saw that there were flames all in the night to one side of us, like the night itself was burning up. Before I could even deal with Skye, I said, 'We've gotta run, we've gotta run,' and we were both running, and I was patting down my arms, and I remember that I was trying to put out the jacket and I was trying to figure out if I could pull it off, but I couldn't pull off the jacket because it had already melted. The only good thing about all of this was that we could hear the sirens in the distance. We could hear where the road was, because that was the direction that the sirens were coming from, and we were running toward the sirens, and Skye was wailing, and I was running as fast as I could, and finally we got to the road, and that's where I passed out or went into shock. And I just want to tell you, in case you ever wondered about trauma, that I didn't forget how I got to the hospital, or the first skin grafts, and I never did forget the fire. I wake up a couple of nights a month feeling like I'm running from fire. That fire burned four days. My name was in the papers, and everybody knew what Skye and I had done and what the boys had done, which is that somehow we started the Skull Valley Fire, and after that I never went outside to a party ever again. As soon as I finished school, I came east to New York to get away from the Skull Valley Fire, from the horses in their paddocks who died because of me, because of my stupid teens. If I came east, maybe no one would know how I felt about what I had done."

When Ranjeet has lost the last of his money, they get up from the table, taking leave of the new dealer, an Asian man with none of the complicated style of his predecessor, who is now gone on his break. It's only when they're passing through the maze of slots that Jeanine takes a quarter from her clutch, throws it into a one-armed bandit, pulls the lever, and waits as the alarm goes off crazily on its summit, indicating a major payout. The coins tumble into the tray below, more coins and more coins and more coins, until the tray can't begin to contain the scale of the payout. Thousands! More than thousands! Ranjeet looks around, stunned, waiting for the uniformed employee. Jeanine says she can't believe it, but somehow she can. Sometimes this is how it goes. Can he wait here for a second? She really has to go to the bathroom, just wait, just wait. And while he's waiting for the money, she heads for the elevator, for the room, for the car key. It's only four or five hours to Phoenix.

31

Sagebrush, creosote, ocotillo, waving fields of parched grasses uninterrupted to the horizon. The occasional juniper like a blemish on the emptiness. Even the tumbleweed doesn't seem stagy, doesn't seem added for effect; that's how Vanessa knows she's where she's supposed to be, in a place where the wind on the rails really does howl, where the freights do rumble through the crossings for the rest of the day, where the best bar in town can't afford a neon beer sign, where the one dilapidated market has an entire aisle of tortillas. A swirl of dust blows up around you, as if the range has a quarrel with you for cluttering its absences. You startle an antelope or a deer when you go out walking, but you shouldn't go out walking, because no one does.

Alpine, Texas. She's come here to find that it's among the last places in the country unexploited by the film business, an exploitation she now means to bring about with a vengeance. She means to line up a bunch of trailers, longer than the longest freight train, and she means to assemble a bunch of union guys who will descend on the local bars by the dozens, and she means to send extras in Mongolian outfits into this rangeland, and these Mongolians will be stabbing at one another, with the fight choreographer yelling from just offscreen. There will be helicopters hovering over all of the action, equipped with cameras and massive lenses.

Her itinerary: first, the Gila National Monument. From there, she moved south and east. Vanessa liked it better in Truth or Consequences, New Mexico, and she liked it there for one reason. The Low Rider. Well, there was also the possibility of Alamogordo. Yes, Vanessa favored the idea that a Geiger counter might pick up echoes of long-ago blasts. But what Alamogordo looked like was like everything else. On the second day, they turned south toward Carlsbad. Why is it, at these caverns, that there's always a tour guide who has to point his flashlight at a stalagmite and compare it to an elephant? No way. Cutting short Carlsbad, they decided to head east toward the Big Bend. It was a long drive, and they let themselves stop at whatever picturesque roadside beguiled.

Then, while driving east into the dawn, in a Pontiac Grand Am in teal, Vanessa managed to stumble on this place, scarcely of note on any map, except for its state university. Alpine, TX. She had no reason to know that she'd long been yearning for such a place, a place so slow and backward and lost. Maybe the whole month of November had been bringing her near to Alpine. With each bit of bad news in the prior weeks, she had drawn closer. Fuck Dallas and its oil culture; fuck Houston and its art museums. Out here was a plateau the size of Rhode Island with only seven thousand legal inhabitants, a few starveling longhorn steer, some horses, and antelope. Heartbroken towns full of tumbleweed and excessively large pickups with tinted windows.

Her room at the Javalina Motor Court smells like a swimming pool, and the hot water isn't hot, and Vanessa's stomach is knotted from the taco she ate in town, and there are a half dozen distressing messages on her voice mail, not one of them from her mother, who she still expects will call. There are the frequent messages from the department of Missing Persons. Madison, meanwhile, claims to have found a good office rental in or near to the World Trade Center. Means of Production will be closer to Robert De Niro and the other classy addresses of Tribeca. But still. There's no cell phone contact out here in Alpine, so there's no point in trying to return the calls now at the inflated motel rate. If you drive up into the mountains, she was told by Jack from Brewster County Properties, you might be able to make contact with a satellite.

And speaking of space junk, Alpine is a known location for unidentified flying objects. So it is that Vanessa attempts to roust Allison Maiser, intern and location scout. They are going to drive into the hills to watch for UFOs. Jack knows the guy who knows where to go. It's big business hereabouts. Vanessa saw a store-front that boasted trips for prime viewing. This sounds like something that could be worked into the script. Maybe dowsing, the skill passed down through the generations in *The Diviners,* was first learned from interstellar wayfarers. Maybe there should be UFOs or space aliens at the end of the story.

Allison's door is beige and is peeling, and the room number has come loose, is dangling upside down, revealing an aqua paint coat underneath, from a cost-conscious period of motel admin-istration when bright colors prevailed.

"Get up!" Vanessa pounds on the door. "I have an idea."

Allison sticks her nose and homely eyeglasses into a narrow space between the door and its frame. In her hand, a dog-eared paperback that she picked up in Albuquerque, Louis L'Amour.

"Unidentified flying objects! When else do you think you're going to get the chance!"

"I was reading —"

"Divining is some kind of genetic mutation, and maybe there are UFOs at the beginning and end of the story, and the dowsers are touched by the lights given off by the UFOs, and that's how they develop the skill, and the mutation is passed down. Should

I call Ranjeet? At the end of the story, the last dowser is conscripted into NASA."

Vanessa explains how she saw the storefront advertising expeditions, and about the tip from Jack the Realtor. Allison Maiser could refuse, of course, because she's Allison Maiser, but she ultimately gets a coat on, though she's still wearing her pajama bottoms. It's back into the Grand Am. Soon they have met up with their guide, Bo Fontaine, a one-time military man who has seemingly spent the last twenty years drinking too much and who has failed in this period of time to perfect the art of shaving without a mirror. For fifty dollars, Bo says, they get to go for a drive and hear his spiel, which is about a woman called Brenda Mae Millerton, who, in these very parts, just north of the town of Alpine, was taken up into a shining disk, probed, and released, during which adventure she learned, above all, that the aliens have been visiting the southwestern United States simply for the reason that the landing surfaces here are amenable to their craft. These aliens also visit the Nunavut Territory, and that's why the Inuit drew those unusual drawings.

The aliens understand and are attracted to love, Bo continues, in his four-by-four, and therefore, "It's pretty likely that they have a conception of Jesus. In the beginning was creation, and that means *all* of creation; it doesn't just mean creation here, it means creation far and wide, creation scattered about in the night skies, creation amongst the galaxies that you see from that telescope . . . what's that . . . the Hubble telescope. Creation means the creation of galaxies; it means those are real pictures coming from real galaxies, black holes, and such, which means He was there when the aliens were created, as He was always there. He'll be there when we travel to the stars. Put it another way: The aliens are aspects of creation. The aliens are in His own image, just like we are.

"No need to fear the unidentified flying object because even if the pilots of that craft have three heads or eyes in the palms of their hands or whatnot, they know love, see what I'm saying?" Bo goes on without self-consciousness. His chatter is transitional: from the lights of Alpine to the blackness of the farm road that leads due east. Again and again, in the days of driving, Vanessa has found herself at night in a landscape that has more *nothing* in it than anywhere she's ever been. Here it is again, producing a feeling both soothing and unsettling. The arresting nothingness of the back roads, jackrabbits hopping off the tarmac before their headlights. It could be mountains out in that darkness ahead and behind; it could be a stately sequence of ridges. It could be nothing.

They don't know anything about Bo. They don't know, really, that he's not a rapist in training or a world-class serial killer. There must be more serial killers in the great state of Texas, because they execute so many of them. Vanessa knows how to kick a guy in the balls hard and she knows how to punch at the Adam's apple of a man with a sharp jab so as to choke and incapacitate. She'd do either of these things before she'd let a sweaty redneck dishonor her or the intern.

In fact, if she needs to, she resolves that she will maneuver herself into a position where she can inflict bodily harm on Bo, after which she will tell Allison that she has been wanting to kiss her. Because ever since the night when they watched *The Werewolves of Fairfield County* together, the night when Vanessa found herself in bed with Allison the intern, who was definitely a top, there has been no consort between them. It should be, when women love women, that the male tendency toward callousness, toward the recoiling from intimate talk, sharing feelings, never rears its head. Women shouldn't fuck and run. But once Allison had wrapped her arms around her, and inserted some things in her, and used her tongue on her, and told her that she was now Allison's possession, until Vanessa was laughing because it was all so funny and so new, laughing until the moment when she started crying, once Allison had done all these things, it was as if she embarked on a campaign of neglecting Vanessa in the office. If not for serving as location scout, which Vanessa offered Allison in hopes that they would then share a hotel room, she would probably be as far away from Vanessa as she could get. It has been a little tense. Nevertheless, Vanessa will tell Allison that something has come over her, some feeling has come over Vanessa out here in the desert, in the limitless night. She will tell Allison that she thinks that this life is made for more than work and pizza and television. She wants Allison to understand that they could address these philosophical issues together. This conversation would involve a fair amount of kissing. And more.

"Is there a reason why we have to be so far out of town?" Allison asks Bo, from the backseat.

"We have to be this far out of town," Bo shouts, and he seems to like to shout, "because right near here is where Brenda Mae Millerton was when she was abducted by the disk-shaped object I was telling you about. Right along this road is where the *visitors*, because that's what we like to call them, *visitors*, made themselves known to Brenda Mae."

"How did they make themselves known to her?" Vanessa inquires.

"That's what I'm getting to," Bo says. "Brenda was on her way into town from her family's ranch, she was fixing on going to a restaurant, and she was on this road when she looked up and saw something gleaming in the night sky. What she saw was a disk-shaped object performing a rapid-fire Z-shaped maneuver —"

"What's a —"

"This is military country. We know what kinds of maneuvers could be performed by the modern aircraft from our arsenal. We know it wasn't any fighter jet or what have you. No stealth bomber could perform the kind of maneuver I'm speaking about. Brenda Mae saw the rapid-fire Z-shaped maneuver of the flying disk, and she felt cocky about it, prideful, because she knew that we live in a region where unidentified flying objects are part of life. I'm guessing you ladies might not feel the same way about it. I'm guessing that you think this is a big laugh, how this is the region where the *visitors* come. You think you've paid your fifty dollars and that's a big laugh. And you get to hear a local citizen tell you tall tales of the night. Am I right?"

Vanessa says, "We're here on a very important mission."

How long have they been driving? Forty minutes, and there has been nothing. Less than nothing. No city in the distance. No light pollution from a town twenty miles away. Nothing to separate or divide the immensity of the night from itself. Anything could happen here. Things without explanation, things that make mockery of the United Broadcasting Company and its parent corporation, all the employees thereof.

"Brenda thought she was safely out of the way of the craft that was performing the Z-shaped rapid-fire maneuver, and she thought, Well, it's probably some kind of border patrol, and she kept driving, singing along with Tejano music on our local station until, at a certain moment, and for no reason other than a little bit of restlessness in her heart, she looked into the rearview. What she saw was that there was a light hovering right behind her, hovering above the road right behind her automobile."

Of course, Allison looks behind, because she's sitting in the backseat, and Vanessa looks back at Allison, longingly, and there is nothing out the back window at all.

"How big was it?" Allison asks.

"How big was it? Many have asked, of course," Bo says. "And the answer is that questions of size are earthbound questions, because, according to Brenda Mae, the scale of the lights of the visitors varies depending on where you are in the story. At this point, when the lights are flying right behind her vehicle, the lights are about what you'd expect on a standard-issue farm tractor. But before you get the idea that these lights are just the headlights of the car following her, you need to know that they were hovering *above ground* and they were, as she watched, rising up above the stern of her car, up above the trunk, and, as she looked back, the lights were now above her car, and she was afraid."

"What kind of sound did the thing make?"

"A very good question, and it's not a question that most people would think to ask. Most people just want to know about the shape of the unidentified aircraft and the size and stature of the visitors. Most people get right to those kinds of questions, and those questions would indicate that they haven't thought much about issues of propulsion, fuel, aerodynamics, plasma, things of that nature. The question of what kind of sound the unidentified aircraft made is an interesting question, of course, especially for the reason that the aircraft made no sound at all."

"Oh, come on," Vanessa says. "How would she know if it made no sound at all?"

Bo applies the brake as though he's test-driving the four-by-four for its manufacturer, as though he's in one of those commercials invariably filmed in landscapes just like this and he wants to highlight his antilock braking system. The four-by-four, recently driven well above the legal limit, lurches to the dirt shoulder with a minor skid. Bo shuts off the engine.

"The answer to the question, ma'am, is that she knew the unidentified aircraft made no sound because she pulled the car over, just like I've done, and she shut the car off, and, you know, this was in early September, and so it was the time of year when you might have your windows open because you like a breeze. So Brenda Mae had her windows open, and she pulled her car over because she was afraid, and she turned off her car, and she heard nothing. In the wide open plains of the great state of Texas, here, she heard nothing, not even crickets, like everything had come to a stop, like the night had come to a stop, and she could feel the light shining on her from above because the light had warmth, heat, even, and she knew that there was something up there, all right, but all she could hear was her own breathing, her shortness of breath, and that was when the light, because the aircraft was experienced by her as a kind of light, got in the car with her, into the backseat of the car with her, just like if the light was your friend back there. What's your name again? What I'm saying to you is that the size of the vehicle, the unidentified flying object, seemed to expand or contract based on a lot of individual factors, and for now it was small enough to waver like a mobile of lights in the backseat of Brenda Mae's car."

For dramatic effect, Bo throws open the door on the driver's side of his four-by-four and climbs out onto the pavement. There are some pinging tones — the engine cooling from its gallop — but otherwise, around them, there's only the night. Vanessa and Allison get out, too, and they are brought up short in the perception of the night sky. It's a night sky that they would never see back east, where industrial residue enhances the sunset but forbids the glow of unmediated stars. Here they can see the planets low on the horizon before them and, above, the ceaseless churning of the Milky Way and its constituents.

"The period of her blackout started right at this point —"

"Her —"

"Memory loss," Bo says. "Could have been traumatic, of course. Because she was seeing things no one has ever seen before, things that you don't expect to see in this life. Maybe she bumped her head somehow and suffered a concussive injury in her brainpan. The fact is that Brenda Mae was in her car, and she remembers having pulled over the car, and she remembers seeing the blinding light in the back of the car, and she remembers looking out the window and seeing it, seeing something out there, and asking herself *What is that thing?* And then she remembers nothing. She doesn't remember walking away from her car, even though she certainly did walk away from her car, since she was found wandering, in an unclothed state, forty miles from here; and did I say that those forty miles were in the middle of the range? Forty miles as the crow flies in the middle of the range. By roads, it would take hours to get there, and you'd still have to hike in. Maybe, you're thinking, she used some kind of ATV, the kind that leaves no tracks. Maybe she parachuted in. I'm in no position to judge, but that range, that meadow where she was found, is this very field, that's what I'm saying, this very field right beyond the road here. If you look out in that direction, that's the field where Brenda Mae was found thirty-six hours later, wandering in an unclothed state, disoriented and measuring extra high on a Geiger counter. With a story about being shoved out of the craft, the unidentified flying object, and no memory of what the visitors looked like."

Good thing they paid up front, because one question Vanessa asks herself is whether the story is worth fifty dollars. The whole way back to town, while Bo chatters on about other sightings, she's thinking about Brenda Mae, who he says works at a hotel in the next town, as a waitress. Is the story worth fifty dollars? Did Brenda Mae Millerton go to the psychiatrist after her experience? Did she go to the church of her choice? Did the evangelical church help her with the feeling that she'd been abducted and probed by the visitors? Would the Seventh-Day Adventists or the Jehovah's Witnesses welcome such a parishioner?

Bo says, "All of these persons I'm telling you about were administered lie-detector tests by the sheriff of Alpine, who considers himself an expert on alien encounters. Brenda Mae passed the lie-detecting test with flying colors, indicating that she believes without reservation that the events took place as I'm describing them. She was also hypnotized, by a fortune-teller from Midland, and the fortune-teller believes the story, too. In fact, this oracle actually hinted at some of the experiments that might have been performed on Brenda Mae, tests that probed the cellular dimension of human tissue, things of that nature. The last thing I'll say, before I conclude for tonight, is that Brenda Mae reports that in the weeks after her abduction she was suffused with warm feelings for humanity, feelings of love. She believes that the lesson being imparted by the visitors was the lesson of love. She believes that she was being probed so that the visitors could try to understand why there was so much hatred here on Earth. Brenda Mae wishes she could travel back up into the craft now because of that sweet feeling of union."

Back at the hotel room, Vanessa's mother's voice beckons to her from the complexity of silences, her mother's unearthly voice, reached by remote, on Vanessa's machine back in Brooklyn: "Don't want you to worry . . . in *Florida,* honey . . . don't want you to . . . now, I want you to promise that . . . everything . . . got an important . . . taking marching orders from an important . . . nothing to . . . people making the decisions . . . in close contact . . . calling me and . . . front of the courthouse . . . because there's just . . . hang on, just a, I've got to . . . who would have thought . . . old mother . . . weather is . . . only just a couple of weeks . . . young men in suits . . . people have to stand up . . . proud . . . moments like this . . . in case you have forgotten . . . just as soon that I . . . not thinking too clearly . . . really ought to give it some more thought . . . got a swimming pool . . . a long bus ride . . . very nice man came today . . . the justices are . . . the ruling is . . . that woman is . . . my stomach is . . . don't worry about a . . . back before you . . . on the next bus and . . ."

The part that gives Vanessa the creeps is not the slurred speech on the message, the marginal clarity, but the fact that the call seems as if it's all part of the same evening's entertainment. The call should be reassuring, because at least her mother is still her mother, doing the things that her mother seems to do, but of course there is no number where she might return the call, and she can't shake the feeling that her mother is one of the *visitors.*

Vanessa wants to go to Allison's room. She wants to knock on Allison's door, and she wants to be admitted to Allison's room, and she wants to wrap herself in Allison's arms, and she wants to tell Allison what's going on. She wants to have one of those heart-to-heart conversations that other people seem to get to have, especially after they have slept together.

———

But next morning Vanessa's all business. If life is love and work, and the love machinery has blown an important fuse, well, at least you still have work. So in the morning, all Vanessa can talk about is the border, how they need to get closer to it. The Chisos Mountains, for example, she has the map to indicate the mountains, the Rio Grande, the thousand species of cacti, the geological layers. Allison has barely finished her coffee and huevos rancheros before they're driving south, into a landscape so flat that it's easy to see why Bo Fontaine's visitors would have landed. Mountains hover in the distance, bisected by clouds and heat mirages. Vanessa gets the rental car up near a hundred miles an hour, since there are no other cars, until the Grand Am rattles as if it's going to break apart from the g-forces of her fanaticism.

Past the entrance to the national park, of course, because it will be full of college students on Thanksgiving break. Nothing ruins the feeling of adventure like kids sporting hemp products. She turns right just beyond the park entrance. And the next town on the road that shadows the river is:

"Terlingua Ghost Town," Allison says, reading aloud. "Blah blah blah, mining company once employed thousands of workers, vanished as quickly as it was established. *Countercultural types* in residence, blah blah."

"What could be better?"

"On the other side of town is the new state park. Four-wheel drive only."

They stop for gas in Terlingua, and the first local they observe is in his fifties with a ponytail tickling his lumbar region, riding a bicycle with a Chihuahua in the front basket. The guy looks as if he might be carrying gas back to a jalopy that ran dry somewhere on the roads out of town. Or maybe he needs to restart his tractor, so that he might harvest some righteous bud, completely organic. They disappear into the low mesas, where the road threads through the abandoned mines, the quicksilver mines of Terlingua's former glory.

Beyond, the road is rutted and pitted to such a degree that the Grand Am must slow to a proverbial crawl. To the right of them, the state park rises unvisited. To the left is the river and, therefore, the border. Between the two, the dirt road on which they travel. A bird twitters somewhere and falls silent. A breeze whispers.

They get out of the car.

The two women pry apart the barbs of the fence and they trespass onto the state land, because Vanessa wants to be on the top of the hill about a mile distant, because she wants to see all the way into the interior across the muddy river. Vanessa won't hear a word about snakes. She threads her way around the prickly pear and agave and starts toward the hill. This is what John Ford saw, this is what Edna Ferber saw, when they looked over to the other side. The border across which all is uncertainty, radical factions, kidnapping, persecution of the natives, executions by the police, disappearances, diviners, sorcerers, visionaries, penitents, this is what they saw when looking out from here.

It's Allison who breaks the silence.

"So who came up with the idea, anyway?"

Vanessa's already sweating horribly. She keeps dabbing at her forehead with the sleeve of her sweatshirt. "We should have brought water."

"I mean, who really came up with the miniseries? If everybody has a different version of the story —"

"It was just some piece of coverage that Annabel had. I don't know. Some novel."

"I kept trying to, you know, find the original manuscript, but every manuscript that I found that was supposedly *the* manu-

script, it turned out it wasn't anything like the coverage, the stories were completely different."

"Melody Forvath? Or whatever her name was?"

"I don't think Melody Forvath wrote anything about dowsers.
She's friends with my mom, you know."

"Your mom is friends with her? We could have saved money!
You could have said it was a film school project or something!"

The river and its flagstone bottom begins to come into view,
winding away like a lasso. Beyond, the neighbor to the south.

"I don't think there is a book," Allison declares.

"If there's no book," Vanessa says, "then what is there?"

"I don't know. But there's no actual book," Allison replies. She
stops. "I'm getting blisters."

Not much farther. Always a little farther. Always a little more.
The farther up you go, the farther you want to go. Once you get
to the top of this hill, you just want to crest the next. You want to
see the Solitario, the crater from the dormant volcano, and then
you want to see the butte beyond.

"That doesn't make any sense —"

"Unless Annabel —"

"Did it herself."

"But why would she —"

"Well, she has this awful script about the wife of the Marquis
de Sade. Handcuffs and ivory dildos and all that. I always put off
dealing with her script."

"I thought it was good."

"You read it?"

The ridge of the hill, just another fifty paces. Only when they
have trudged the fifty paces, thinking about a story idea that has
apparently sprung into being without an author, only after they
have gazed solemnly on the land to the south, across the border,
only then do they see what is on the north side of the hill, cow-
ering in the shadow of a rock formation. A family of Mexicans.
Not exactly a family of Mexicans, or not certainly. The group of

Mexicans has no patriarch. The family of Mexicans is composed of women and children, namely a woman who looks as if she's maybe in her early thirties, a little heavy, careworn, wearing a nylon tracksuit; and a girl in her teens, in denim and halter top; a boy about fifteen, with a first faint growth of mustache; and two little boys, maybe six and eight.

What Vanessa notices right away is that all of them are *wet*, the legs of their trousers are wet. They have been immersed, maybe in a place where it is possible to ford the great muddy creek.

"Ohmygod, they scared the shit out of me," Allison blurts out.

It's the teenager, the boy, who looks as if he might do the two women harm. The others are frightened. And dusty. And wet.

Vanessa says, "Uh, hello. We're really sorry we bothered you. We were just going for a . . . for a hike."

The absurdity of her worldly concerns, talking about some miniseries, who wrote the miniseries, who came up with the idea of the dowsers, when nearby this is taking place, the drama of woman and children in pursuit of things that this place offers, this country.

"You guys speak any English? *Ingles?*"

The woman shakes her head. The teenage boy nods, then changes his mind.

"Allison, you speak any Spanish?"

"I can order dinner in Italian."

"Where are you going? Can you answer that question?" Vanessa tries, with the family. "Can you say where you are going? What town? Terlingua?"

The woman in the tracksuit, whom Vanessa thinks of as the mother, shakes her head violently. But even if the family could answer where they were going, they wouldn't, because where they are going is El Paso or Las Cruces or Albuquerque, where they have cousins or other relatives or neighbors who are going to help them slip quietly into the American economy.

"Do you have *agua?*" Vanessa asks, and she gestures as if to drink from a flask or canteen. The Mexicans stare at her, as if the question is an impropriety, and then, as if there is some preliminary agreement among themselves to scatter in the face of Anglos, especially these filmmaker *yanquis* wearing too much black and standing in the middle of the desert without water or sunblock, the Mexicans start down the hill, heading north toward an expanse that will take them the whole morning to get across.

"Wait," Vanessa says. "Wait."

Allison says, "What are you doing?"

"They can't," Vanessa says. "There are bears out there and stuff. They can't sleep out there."

She addresses herself to the teenage boy, trying to act it out. "Don't go, don't go."

But the mother begins to head off again, and the boys follow her soon after, and it's only when they begin walking that Vanessa sees that the teenage boy has a good reason for looking fierce, for looking menacing, namely that he's limping badly. It's only after they've watched the Mexicans attempt to descend into the valley that Vanessa feels the beginning of responsibility in herself. For certain, this is a tonal color that she has read about but never quite known. She's skeptical about the Mexican boy. She's skeptical about what she should do about it. She's skeptical about the part of American movies where the sentimentalists rush in. She's skeptical about epiphany, about the Greek origin of the word, the making manifest. Simplicity nauseates her.

But in the moment of being undecided, intellectually, her physiognomy leaps into decisiveness without hesitation. There's the border patrol somewhere in the distance, and the border patrol will be coming this way. And there is the danger of exposure, and there's the danger of hypothermia or death by thirst, which is apparently a horrible way to die. She doesn't know what she feels; she feels something in the crimson range, something in ultraviolet, but she knows she's going to do something about the Mexican family and she doesn't care what gets lost in the process.

"You have to help me," she says to Allison, and she begins running down the hill after the *pollos,* and Allison the intern follows after, and in the illusionistic space of the desert, the *pollos* are a hundred yards away, though they seem much closer, and she seems to run after them without ever getting closer, calling all the while to the teenage boy. In the distance, she can see the mother, carrying one of the younger children now, as though the younger boy were a papoose. The little one nuzzles at her, the cuffs of his jeans pushed up so that Vanessa can see that his socks are lime green.

"Wait," Vanessa says, "*wait.*"

And as if he understands, the teenager turns and stops, his face sweaty with discomfort.

"Do you need money? *Dinero?* We can give you *dinero.*" She goes into her wallet, and she pulls out twenties, and she starts putting them into the hand of the teenager. "Take these. Just take them." And then she points at her ankle. "Don't you want to let me see your ankle?" And Vanessa pulls off her own hiking boot, hopping up and down, and then her rag sock, and she shows her ankle to the boy. She's never realized that she has a perfect ankle before. But that's what it looks like now. The perfect ankle of privilege. She has made her ankle available to him just so that she can point at him. "Let me see. Let me see if you're injured."

The mother has doubled back now, and she and her teenage daughter, if that's who the younger woman is, are repeating the word *no* to the boy, over and over, and there are some other bits of advice in Spanish: *No es tiempo de haraganear, de todos modos seria demasiado peligroso quedarnos por acá, y aquellas son unas locas, a lo mejor estan drogadas, así que deben alejarse de ellas,* but the boy has taken the twenties and he is going to display his ankle now, with a kind of bravado, and he sits on the dusty hillside, and he pulls off his damp sneaker and his muddy sock, and he smiles gallantly, and Vanessa can see how his ankle is already swelling up.

"When did you do this? Did you injure yourself in the river? Trying to cross? You know it's going to get worse, right? It gets worse for forty-eight hours. That's what happens with a sprain. It's a sprain, right? You didn't get bit by a scorpion or anything, right?"

When she touches him, she touches him as if she knows, as if the skills of the nurse-practitioner are suddenly hers, though she's just a hypochondriac with a home medical encyclopedia, nothing more. "You should let us drive you, wherever you need to go."

Allison chimes in. "We have a car, back there. We have a car. Pontiac? We have a car and we can drive you wherever you need to go. Because of the border patrol. And we can get you water. *Agua.*"

The mother says *no* absolutely and firmly, and then the group of them is standing there in the middle of the desert, the Mexican border jumpers and the two Anglo filmmakers, without having ten words of a common tongue between them. It's only performance that is going to make the point clear, Vanessa thinks, and it's not even a performance, when it comes to her. Who's even thinking about the movies now; the movies are for kids in private colleges, so that they won't feel lonely on weekends. Movies are so that she'll have something to tell her grandchildren one day, about the people she met. Movies are because it's the thing you can do here in this place; you can make a movie with your millions of dollars. Movies are nothing compared with the boy with the sprained ankle and the faces of his little brothers, sun burnished, etched with concern, desperate.

"We can't let you go walking into the middle of the state park, where you are going to get picked up by the authorities, so that you'll be delivered to Immigration and get deported immediately. We can't let you do that to yourselves. If you came with us, you could come back to our hotel, and then we'll find a way to get you into the interior of the state somehow, away from the border and the border patrol, and then we'll leave you with whomever you want, in whatever city that you want, and then you can try to get some work somewhere. I'm not saying that I have any comparable experience, but I feel like you *can* understand some of what I'm saying here, and I'm being genuine about what I'm saying, that we just can't let you do that. There are coyotes out there, there might be mountain lions out there, and it's dangerous. We have a car, and we have unlimited Avis mileage, and we think you should get into the car with us, and we'll bring you to the new life, if that's what you're after. We'll bring you to the life on this side of the border, even though we sort of think this new life isn't all that great. We don't want to judge what it looks like to you, we just want you to have what you want, because we have enough to share. We can give you the chances you want, at least for now. We can give you the promise of this side of the border, if that's what you think you need. Please just don't go walking toward that volcano crater in the middle of the park when you can't even walk, because you just don't know what's going to happen out there."

Can't the Mexican family, with their ruddy features, understand the human truth of the moment? The truth in the earnestness of Vanessa's "please"? They must understand. They can understand that the teenage boy cannot walk into the desert with his ankle as it is, and they can understand the shoulder that Allison offers him now as they begin to head south, toward the car.

At the top of a hill, Allison tries her cell phone, on a hunch.

To the teenage boy, she says, "Ever tried one of these?"

"Sí," he says.

"Hey," Allison says after a moment. "There's a message from my dad!"

Epilogue and Scenes from
Upcoming Episodes

The distinguished jurist, at work, in the temple of jurisprudence, District of Columbia, tenth day of December. The distinguished jurist, in the consideration of his part in history. The distinguished jurist, in a state of aesthetic arrest before the busts of the many noble judicial minds who have worked, labored, cursed, and cheered in these august halls over the course of the two hundred years of our national experiment, viz., the Constitution of the United States of America. Black, Burger, Hughes, Story, Holmes, et alia. The distinguished jurist, in a heartfelt and philosophical moment, knows well that, as the son of an immigrant, and having made his way through myriad barriers via the practice of such elementary virtues as thrift, loyalty, hard work, rugged individualism, et cetera, there is little in his early life to suggest, ab initio, that he should be present at such an important judicial moment. Which of these other justices, depicted in these busts, these marble opulences, was called upon the way this jurist and this court have been called upon to render judgment unto history, to fashion, as it were, an epilogue to democracy?

Every age has its landmark legal conflicts. The distinguished jurist was not birthed into the age of *Gompers v. Buck's Stove and*

Range Co., where he would have affirmed forcefully with the majority on the matter of property rights. Nor was he raised up so as to add his voice to *Feiner v. New York,* where it was precisely correct that a no-account hoodlum was carted off to a penitentiary. And, of course, he would like to have ruled during *Stone v. Graham,* since its outcome makes him miserable, serving as a precedent for his contention that his adversaries on the bench do not know how to read, cannot defend their votes, and cannot see the truth when it is right there before them. Alas, the distinguished jurist had not been called to judge these cases.

And yet the distinguished jurist has been brought here to this place now, and so he means to seize the moment. Well, he's always here on Sunday. In that sense, it's a day like any other. He partakes of the Holy Eucharist, et uxor and with those of their nine progeny who might happen to be visiting, and then he comes in. He is always working on Sunday, on petitions for certiorari, likewise the useless in forma pauperis petitions, writs of habeus corpus, which, by virtue of *Barefoot v. Estelle,* take less time than they did formerly. He works on his concurrences and dissents, which of necessity must include corrections of the imprecise grammar of his colleagues, whose lackluster rhetorical constructions are as delusional as their arguments from history.

This Sunday is not like those other Sundays. On this Sunday, there has been a summons from the chief justice, the man with the specially tailored robe, to discuss the case before them. The justices have assembled, the justices have stayed late, including those of their number who are of advancing years, and they have spoken to one another by memo and by phone, and finally they have met briefly in conference, where there were a number of heated exchanges concerning the preliminary opinion, per curiam, that the clerks are at present drafting. The tone in the building, not that the distinguished jurist worries about tone, is almost as bad as during *Furman v. Georgia,* wherein every one of the justices wrote, each with a different and in most cases equally specious opinion, on the matter of the penalty of death. Of course, it is not the place of lily-livered citizens of weak temperament to make the law of the land other than what it is and shall ever be, because the law of the land is that a man shall be hanged, or shot, or electrocuted, or injected, no matter whether he or she is old enough to vote. He shall be hanged on earth, and afterward he shall be commended for eternity to a lake of fire.

Here's the interesting part. Notwithstanding the course of extraordinary events, the distinguished jurist has a long-standing dinner engagement scheduled for this evening and, while pacing the corridors, he is pondering whether or not it would be unseemly to break his dinner engagement. The distinguished jurist is looking at the busts of the justices and is wondering if the justices of the past would have kept a dinner date on a night like this. And it's not just any guest who comes tonight. It's his law school chum. How fondly the distinguished jurist feels about his chums from law school. They collected palindromes, they bet informally on outcomes of capital rulings, they rooted for the New York Yankees or the Boston Red Sox, never both. They stayed up long nights, slept badly, pressed their own shirts, never went without neckties. The distinguished jurist had no firm idea, notwithstanding his magna cum laude, that he would ever come to have the opportunity to serve here in a place so august, and as a result he was, in those days, relatively speaking, fancy free. He could spend an afternoon trying to come up with a palindrome like "Star comedy by Democrats." He could spend an afternoon debating the issues raised in the *Republic* of Plato, wherein he concurred with the idea that poets should be banished from the city limits. They were close, the chums of law school, and this particular chum was his bosom buddy and his especial pal, because this particular chum would sing. What they did when they needed to blow off some steam was find a piano wherever they could on the campus, and there they would sing from the musicals of the period or they would sing light operatic songs, Gilbert and Sullivan, et cetera, and they would find that the singing of these songs choked them with emotion. They were young men who dreamed grandly, and though there was no certainty that they would come this far, they knew they were destined to do great things, and the songs they sang were a recognition of the scale of their dreams, from which dreams they never once deviated.

His friend's road led into the world of business, where the special chum served first at Debevoise and Plimpton. Specifically, the chum worked on several pro bono cases that the distinguished jurist considered unworthy of such a legal mind, e.g., *Massiah v. United States*. This early work made the special chum aware of what he really wanted to do, which was entertainment law, and it was in this cause that the special chum relocated to the dangerous land across the mountains, California, after which the distinguished jurist saw far less of him.

For his part, the distinguished jurist was for some years involved in the education of meandering and unfocused law students. While the special chum was trying to establish the D.C. office for Debevoise, making the acquaintance of such memorable persons as could exist in the heavily perfumed air of the Kennedy and Johnson years, the distinguished jurist was languishing instead in Cleveland, and this, as anyone will tell you, is not a place where one makes a long-standing contribution to national jurisprudence. At one point, he attempted to relocate to a more suitable environment, Georgetown, perhaps, or Columbia, but when he visited the campus of Columbia, he found it peopled entirely by communists of dubious hygiene, including one remarkably unpleasant and outrageous young man who had the audacity to take the distinguished jurist to a house of ill repute! He was meant to be going to a faculty soiree of some kind, and instead this appalling young man took him into a building on Upper Broadway populated with scantily clad women of a different color from himself. It was only when he made clear that he was an adherent to the pre–Vatican II tenets of the Roman Church that his kidnapper relented.

And so the distinguished jurist remained for some years in Cleveland. He thundered in the classroom about tort reform, about the necessity of constitutional limits on claimants. He would thunder in the classroom about the so-called right to privacy, which is not a right but a weakness of character, since it exists nowhere in the Constitution of the United States of America, neither in the Bill of Rights, nor elsewhere, and he thundered thus because he did not really wish to be in the classroom. His wish was to be in government, and at last he was given a chance, when again justice was being meted out appropriately by the men and women of a benevolent administration. In this capacity he served until a delusional peanut farmer from Georgia appeared on the horizon. In the following years, first at the University of Chicago and then at the American Enterprise Institute, he was given the chance to evaluate his positions and to refine them such that he came to see that by *not* opposing the usurpation of power by judicial activists, the distinguished jurist was giving material aid and comfort to the forces of evil.

Relief appeared once and for all in the person of a godly man, a man who had come in from the wilderness, a man who had once called himself a unionist but who was now a man of belief, and this God-fearing man plucked the distinguished jurist from a think tank, raising him from nowhere to the Court of Appeals and later to this very temple of jurisprudence, according to a senatorial vote of 99-0, so that the jurist might write his blistering concurrence in, e.g., *Webster v. Reproductive Health Services.*

It is fateful, after all, that the distinguished jurist was redeemed by a veteran of the entertainment world, a former movie star, because, as noted, this is precisely the direction traveled by his chum from law school. His special chum, who had once been a vigorous outdoorsman and sportsman, and a swashbuckling swordsman with the ladies, packed up and settled in the city of Los Angeles. This vexed the mind of the distinguished jurist, who felt that the place was peopled by drunkards and child molesters, notwithstanding the beauty of some of its flora. Moreover, in the case of the special chum, there were, concurrent with the relocation west, a number of modifications of comportment and habits that did not seem in keeping with the wearing of neckties.

In fact, there was a period during which the distinguished jurist and the special chum didn't speak at all, and this had in part to do with a rumor that began circulating among classmates about the special chum, namely, that perhaps the special chum had a certain weakness proscribed in the Old Testament and in other enduring scriptures that do not change because of evolving standards of decency. Language is fixed and perfect, and the company of heaven sings when in the presence of perfectly deployed sentences. Even more disappointing were some of his hires, including a person alluded to above, whose name the distinguished jurist cannot bear to mention, who went on to become the heir apparent at the conglomerate of the special chum. How was this possible?

Christmas cards still arrived, and birthday cards still arrived, and this was no small feat on the part of the special chum, as the distinguished jurist has a goodly number of children, after all, and yet the special chum remembered the birthdays of all these children and even a couple of grandchildren. There were telephone calls now and then, and the distinguished jurist did his best to discount the rumors and he paid no attention to the diminishment in the excellence of the written grammar of the special chum, which he believed was owing to the influence of the film world. The special chum had advanced swiftly and decisively in the world of entertainment, until, at first, he was the head of a film studio, and from this aerie the special chum advanced through the ranks of the parent company that owned the film studio, which parent company was in the business of spirits and intoxicants, a business that, in the view of the distinguished jurist, was only marginally more harmful than the film studio itself. And in due course the special chum became the chief executive officer of the company in question, a major Fortune 500 corporation with holdings in beverages and entertainment. The company boasted operations national and multinational, and a myriad of contentious and opinionated stockholders.

The apotheosis of the special chum took place during or contemporaneous with the decision in the case that came to be entitled *Maryland v. Craig,* which case, as many will remember, had to do with the alleged molestation of a certain child. The child testified during trial proceedings via one-way closed-circuit television in a separate room. The Court of Appeals overturned, complaining as to the use of this novel form of cross-examination, et cetera. The distinguished jurist, naturally, finds the idea of child abuse abhorrent, perhaps worthy of the ultimate penalty, and he believes, naturally, that people who have the problem that the special chum is rumored to have, the love that dare not speak its name, are more likely to behave as child molesters behave, and the distinguished jurist, naturally, would no more hold on behalf of a child molester than he would favor a Soviet, and yet, in thinking about the special chum, and in thinking about the Constitution of the United States, the distinguished jurist, during the conference on *Maryland v. Craig,* came to feel that perhaps there are aspects of what he might call *the human* in people who are afflicted with this dread sin, and perhaps *the human* merited, in this particular instance, an opinion that was not entirely alien to the cause of the molester, whose case went down in flames nonetheless, as the distinguished jurist knew that it would.

His perambulations now bring the distinguished jurist into the empty, reverberant cavern of the spiral staircase of the Supreme Court of the United States, a design element that is so splendid that the distinguished jurist often pauses to gaze upon it, and it's here that he arrives at a decision, Solomonic in its evenhandedness, viz., that he will tell the special chum, Naz Korngold, that if the special chum would like to meet him in chambers, then perhaps the two of them could dine briefly as planned while the jurist's clerks work on his concurrence. Perhaps in due course he might be able to give the chum a little tour of the premises, including the hall on level one where his own portrait will hang. Perhaps he can bring him here to the spiral staircase. When he returns to his chambers, this offer entire is dictated to the distinguished jurist's secretary, Mrs. Edith Wilbur, who then places the call while the distinguished jurist watches, standing by the edge of her desk, mouthing the words to make sure that she makes the offer just as he has dictated it. Mrs. Edith Wilbur is schooled in making these telephone calls in such a way as to produce maximum impact with the announcement of the caller, indicating that she is calling from the Supreme Court of the United States. And therefore Mrs. Edith Wilbur gets through immediately to the assistant of the special chum, the executive assistant being known as Georgia the Peach, and Georgia the Peach patches the secretary through to the mobile phone of the special chum, and the secretary makes the offer and she then nods thoughtfully, without making eye contact with the distinguished jurist, whose hovering is not ideal but effective nonetheless. Then Mrs. Edith Wilbur announces, having terminated the connection, that the special chum would indeed be glad to appear at the Graeco-Roman temple of jurisprudence, especially since he has a matter of personal import to discuss.

It's only after the terms of the meal are settled, and after fending off his one especially sycophantic clerk, that the distinguished jurist remembers the last time he saw the special chum. This was perhaps eight or nine years ago, on the occasion of a shooting expedition in the state of Maryland. On, or about, or during *Feist Publications, Inc. v. Rural Telephone Service Co.*, and this he remembers because he recalls explaining to the special chum about the implications for copyright raised by *Feist*, wherein originality triumphed over "industrious collection," to the detriment of phone book compilers henceforward. He recalls the special chum laughing grimly and asking if the vogue, in his own business, for film "sequels" might be affected, since those films seemed less the products of "authorship" than works that were simply compiled by the "sweat of the brow" from preexisting narratives. The distinguished jurist remembers these things, and he remembers that it was early spring, and that the weather was overcast, with light winds, and that the smell of sulfur and ejected cartridges was wonderful, as ever, and he remembers, naturally, that the special chum was not doing very well in the matter of obliterating the little clay pigeons. The special chum was made increasingly uncomfortable by his abject failure.

Of course, the distinguished jurist was not born into the condition of firearms enthusiast. It's more that his position on the Second Amendment has made it natural. In the march of life, strange bedfellows do we become. In truth, the distinguished jurist, as a young man, rarely found himself in the company of those who had been reared up with firearms and the sport thereof, and yet as he rose through the ranks of national adjudication, he found himself learning about firearms and connoisseurs of firearms. He found himself appreciating the ritual of cleaning, preparing, shooting, caring for the gun, nailing up the kill, plucking the kill, and here the distinguished jurist will admit that he does take care of the plucking himself, disbelieving that his wife should be burdened with such things. And though the distinguished jurist was not born to carry a gun, like many men of leisure, he is rather good at the sport, and so he was handily trouncing the special chum on the day in question, at least in numbers of clay pigeons dispatched. Even the young man who was accompanying them in the marshes of Maryland, the young man from the local rod and gun club, found himself saying nothing in the tense silence as the special chum shouted "Pull" again, and again the clay pigeon traversed the sky unperturbed.

Because the location of the shooting expedition was outdoors in a rather rustic part of the state of Maryland, there were about them some examples of what remained there of wildlife, the few species that had not yet properly come under man's dominion. There were a few buffleheads, and there were a few cormorants and other such waterbirds, and there were a few geese. Canada geese, in particular. On a number of occasions, the special chum was heard to exclaim that these birds were pestilential, and he used a number of obscene epithets for the geese, and he noted that when he was a child, these geese were given to leave droppings on the lawn of his summer home, on the windward side of Cape Cod. Goose droppings, the special chum remarked; horrible. You'd go out there in the morning, you'd better be sure to wear Wellingtons if you didn't want to step in the mounds. The birds were unfriendly, too, the special chum observed, always trying to run the children off the estate. The distinguished jurist took pause here, since he could not help but notice that the special chum's dream of a Cape Cod childhood was at variance with some of what he knew of the special chum's curriculum vitae. The special chum during his time in Hollywood had apparently gerrymandered the locale of the story, because the special chum was, by virtue of his religion, occasionally picked on as a lad, and this was something that on the most drunken nights in law school the special chum would share with the distinguished jurist, calling him by his diminutive name, saying that they understood each other because they were here at the law school at a time when the scions of Protestant legacy would not have any truck with them. They had each overcome the prejudices of the nation, the special chum indicated back in law school, and yet, out in the marshlands, with his gun loaded, the special chum, as if he had something to prove about the rumors that the distinguished jurist had heard about him, had felt a need to seem other than what he was, that is, a person whose summers had taken place in Mamaroneck, by the Long Island Sound.

Accordingly, what happened next was perhaps natural. It was perhaps part of the natural order that the special chum should call "Pull," that the clay pigeon should rise up into the sky like a tiny emblem for Apollo making his journey across the day. And yet, just when the special chum might have fired on the clay pigeon, he instead turned the barrel of the gun in another direction. Both the distinguished jurist and the young man operating the slingshot for the clay pigeons ducked, flattened themselves, and there was a pause and a pathetic squawk as the shot perforated the hide of one of the Canada geese settled nearby beside some brush. The other geese reared up, astonished, and the whole of the gaggle took flight, except for one, who remained behind momentarily, looking, no doubt, at its now mortally aerated mate. Then this bird, too, lifted off. There was a silence as the special chum took all this in, the fact that he had finally hit something. Then he ejected his cartridge.

"Fifty years of irritation rectified," said the special chum.

Their rod and gun club guide mumbled something about how they were definitely pests and needed to be shown a thing or two, or that's how the distinguished jurist remembers it. The rest of the day, no more than three quarters of an hour, passed in uncomfortable silence.

Though there was an aggrieved apology, next day, when the distinguished jurist reached his chambers, a little handwritten note about the nature of sportsmanship and how the special chum, by his own reckoning, had failed the test of sportsmanship (and would the distinguished jurist please accept this gift in his name to Ducks Unlimited in the amount of et cetera, et cetera), the distinguished jurist found the event, the dispatching of the goose, unsettling, distasteful, and so further years passed without much consort between the two friends.

However, one finds that old friends are gilded by the lateness of the hour, the headlong rush to the beyond. We are thrown into this life to fend for ourselves, and everywhere there are disappointments and conspiracies that can drive us from our charted course. We are only given a few bosom mates. No lapse in judgment should separate us — for whose slate is without its chalk marks? — and though the distinguished jurist has spoken out to any number of groups against the love that dare not speak its name and how its pleas for special rights must be repelled — notwithstanding these things, the distinguished jurist always did like the special chum. Though the special chum is thicker around the waist now, and though his blue eyes have dimmed, and though he is craggy and not the rake he once was, the distinguished jurist feels that he will not give up on the amity of long lives lived together. Such is loyalty.

In fact, this is what he is thinking as he waits at security in the rear of the building, when the special chum arrives and passes through the metal detector.

"Good buddy!" says Naz Korngold.

"Special friend!" says the distinguished jurist.

The two hug. The distinguished jurist takes in the outfit, the pleated pants, the silk shirt, the sport coat.

"You are looking especially natty," he says to his old friend.

"You're hale as ever," says the special chum. "I was expecting you'd look like you'd got no sleep in the last couple of weeks. But you look ready for combat!" Here the special chum smacks the distinguished jurist on the shoulder, as he might have done forty years ago. It feels only a little forced.

Then the special chum takes pause and gazes down the length of the corridor where they stand, which, because it is a Sunday, and because the special chum has entered from the back, looks like a public office building anywhere in the District of Columbia.

"They spend the redecorating budget upstairs," the distinguished jurist offers, meaning the courtroom itself, with its opulent swags of drapery and its allegorical murals.

"But this is where it all happens," says Naz Korngold.

The distinguished jurist prides himself on a spotless office.

The piles of briefs and memos are tidied up and put in their particular areas, and at the end of each day the distinguished jurist insists that Mrs. Edith Wilbur should clear off his desk in its entirety, because he cannot think properly with his desk covered in papers. This is the condition of his desk when he enters with the special chum. Mrs. Edith Wilbur enters behind them, to make sure they have everything they need. The distinguished jurist sends her away. Next, the particularly sycophantic clerk also tries to stop in for an introduction, no doubt recognizing the special chum from photographs, but the distinguished jurist also sends the sycophantic clerk packing, telling him that there are some capital cases that must be dispatched. At last, the distinguished jurist points to the empty chair by the desk and then he indicates the table across the room, where there await two steaks, two salads, some French bread, and a bottle of *vin ordinaire,* procured especially for them.

"Pull up your chair," the distinguished jurist says. "Lend me your troubles."

The special chum says, "I'm grateful to you for taking the time when you have so much before you. And, of course, I don't expect you to compromise the extraordinary sensitivity of your office."

The distinguished jurist uncorks the bottle of wine with a flourish.

"The situation is this." The special chum drinks from the proffered glass. "As you probably know, our stock is plummeting badly. Getting hammered, in fact. Since the beginning of the year. There's dissent at the board level. Certain persons are attempting to infiltrate the board. People who are not loyal. I've tried doing what I can, cost-cutting, downsizing, diversifying. You may have heard about our new —"

"The Interstate —"

"First-rate product. My acquisitions are in the name of making the core business sturdy, as you know. So that we can weather the downturn in the near term. Perhaps we'll be situated for a surprise in the second quarter of next year and going forward from there."

The distinguished jurist asked for rare. This simply cannot be considered rare at all. This would have to be considered *medium*. By no properly considered assessment could this steak be rare. He is on the verge of calling in Mrs. Edith Wilbur.

"Never have I felt as irresolute as I feel now," says the special chum. "I know what I want out of the business. I know what I want as a manager. But I feel irresolute, like I don't know which way the weather is going to turn. Like I'm just killing time, without any sense at all. On the other hand, I do have an even more radical scheme that involves rolling a number of heads of departments."

"How many heads, exactly?"

"One head in particular."

"Whose name is —"

"I'm sure you don't . . . Look, you are performing a meaningful labor here, friend, whereas I'm out there in the trenches producing booze and movies with numbers after the titles. I'm embalming corpses, transporting them across state lines. Our experiences are really so different —"

Then the distinguished jurist says, as though he is some sort of fortune-teller, as though he does not already have an opinion on the subject, "Jeffrey Maiser."

"Impressive. You're reading the papers."

"The clerks brief me on what I need. And the wife reads the occasional magazine."

"A troublemaker, a man who has defaulted on . . . a man who had the audacity to . . . I don't even know how to describe it to you. He actually proposed giving over massive expenditures to . . . I don't even want to talk about it. I have this fabulous movie in production, pal, a film that's going to really require all our resources, a fabulous picture called *Tempest in Sahara*. Desert battles in WWII, the Bedouin, and so forth. This guy, knowing that this project is going to require a great deal of our promotional energy, or synergistic marketing, has the audacity to propose a miniseries on virtually the same subject and it's —"

"A miniseries?"

"A miniseries. Do you have any idea what a stupid idea that is?"

"And," the distinguished jurist says, "unless I am wrongly informed, has he not been frolicking with a certain —"

"Your facility with the contemporary moment is, uh, impressive."

"When indisposed, I look at the periodicals."

"I'm going to start over entirely in network programming. I mean to cancel everything that boob has in production, I mean to cancel every contract, and foreclose on his ridiculous miniseries, and I mean to make the network *the* venue for a twenty-first-century vision of programming. I can see the future, tantalizingly, before me, things like interactivity, synergies between television and the Internet, downloadable programming, video on demand, and especially enhanced-reality programming, cameras running twenty-four hours a day in the homes of Americans, where they'll be able to watch cheats and thieves in the moment of their apprehension by the authorities, Americans catching terrorists, domestic and foreign, Americans rooting out sex offenders in their neighborhoods. Of course, I recognize that I have a fiduciary duty to the shareholders, as I also have a duty to the medium in which we work. So it follows that I need a head of programming who sees these things the way I see them. I mean to make sure that the next head of programming can't even *relieve* himself without my seeing him shake off, and in this way we will be leading rather than following. If that suggests a new model of programming that requires fewer employees and lower costs, so be it. I say *yes* to inexpensive programming that makes you, the viewer, the hero of the series, I say *yes* to the common man, and

I say *yes* to the narrative of everyday life. I mean to drive up the stock price and I mean to make those analysts in New York take notice. So, buddy, there's just the one thing I need to know. . . ."

The distinguished jurist, maintaining a veneer of thoughtfulness and impartiality throughout the impassioned monologue of his special chum, has had the chance to work his way through the steak. The steak wasn't as bad as he expected.

"What is it that you need to know?"

"I need to know the future, buddy."

"Which future is it that you need to know?"

"Well, ideally, I need to know if the markets will stabilize going forward. With this decision you're about to make, can you assure me that the markets are going to be stable, tomorrow and the day after. That's all. It's just a tiny little question."

"Are you asking —" says the distinguished jurist.

"No, no, no, I wouldn't ask that —"

"Then what are you asking?"

"Look, I'm about to embark on the biggest downsizing campaign in the history of one of the nation's largest media conglomerates. I'm about to meet with lawyers. I'm about to lay off an extremely well-known —"

The distinguished jurist rises up from his desk, holding, in his hand, the cloudy glass of *vin ordinaire*. He rises up, an imposing presence, a man whom others fear, a man who creates the truth, uncovers it, wherever he goes and who brooks no dissent, a *flagellum Dei,* and he begins, "Special friend. Now is the moment that we brook no irresolution. Now is the moment when we tolerate no weakness. Now is the moment when we withstand no hesitation. You come asking for certainty, and I say, special friend, that you should look into your own innermost heart, the sanctum sanctorum of your most fervid wishes. You should look into your heart, special friend, for any vestige of weakness that you find there, and you should take in hand this weakness and squeeze the very life out of it. As if weakness were a rodent that wandered into your bedroom. Weakness has no business in the future that begins today, friend. Weakness is a relic of a past. What remains for the weak are the courts of Europe. What remains for the weak are the commissions and the tribunals of a continent without belief and stamina. Human rights are for slaves. A man should die before he allows himself to be a slave, and if he is not dead yet, he ought to rise up to kill his master, today. Weakness and irresolution are for women and little children. And the people who can be crushed should be crushed, because that is the order of things, that is nature, and nature is what God made, and what God made is power. Yes, special friend, that's what we put in the place of weakness. Power comes only from divine law, and what divine law says is that power is just. You may recall the King James Bible," and here the distinguished jurist quotes from memory, "'*Wilt thou then not be afraid of the power? do that which is good.*' And so I remind you, tomorrow, not to hesitate. For what is the good, special chum, but the decision on which power settles itself? The states know this, the states know that they can draft the law in their borders and that all will be well within the borders of these states, and they will not be subject to reversal from a disenfranchised elite from a corrupt law school somewhere. This is not what power is. Power is the people in the moment of attempting to divine God's justice, wrestling with God's justice, knowing that the state is God's scourge here on earth, and if the state says that a man should die for what he has done, then a man must die. If the state says a woman's fetus must live, then the woman's fetus must live, and so what is the lesson of obedience? The lesson is that God controls all things, and you have no recourse, and so you obey, that you may have everlasting life, special friend. The lesson of obedience is that there is no other path to travel, for every other path of life ends in madness or death. Every other way but the way of obedience is death, *E quali agevolezze o quali avanzi ne la fronte de li altri si mostraro per che dovessi lor passeggiare anzi?* What are seductions of the world that they are more alluring than what obedience can do for you, special friend? Power is the sign that a supernatural authority has visited a place. If power is given to you, then power is yours to exercise, and, more than an option or a choice, it is your *duty* to exercise this power. Life is the unremitting exercise of power, and if power is the ability to fire a dullard who is no longer performing his appointed job, then you must fire that dullard and you must have him escorted from the premises under armed guard, and you must seize his personal computer, and you must copy all of his files before he erases them. And if power is the ability to have a camera in the office of his successor, so that you can make sure that the successor does what you want him to do all the day long, then you must exercise this power and you must shrink from irresolution; you must delight in power, in the exercise thereof. Power is given to some men to prove that God's reign is just, and those who seek to preserve the tradition of the law will not whimper in the face of responsibility. So if you come to me, special friend, asking what's going to happen tomorrow, I can't tell you what's going to happen tomorrow, but I can tell you how to live, and that is to live the way we lived when we were young, special friend. How did we live? We proceeded as if the world were ours. We loved our parents and neighbors, but we couldn't help them. Special friend, we have come to places like this temple of jurisprudence, and are we now going to be faint of heart? No, special friend, we are not. We are the linebackers on the front line of the divine, and we spike the quarterback of the opposition, and we do not worry about breaking his neck. Compassion is faintness of heart; compassion is a lie told by people who are afraid to rule. What will the meek inherit? Social Security benefits that will not last another twenty years."

The distinguished jurist, having drained his goblet, looks to the special chum, who holds aloft the bottle. In the middle of the room they meet, and each glass is refilled. The special chum looks as if he has just witnessed a faith healing, or perhaps this is how the distinguished jurist perceives it, that the jurist has healed. No matter if the people do not understand, because they will understand one day.

"Squash Maiser like a bug," the distinguished jurist says. And then: "Let me walk you out."

In the corridors of power, two old friends. The report of their heels the only sound of their progress, a progress that with each pace brings closer the end of a long day's labors. When they have come near to the back entrance to the Supreme Court of the United States, the distinguished jurist asks what has been on his mind for most of an hour: "Naz, you know, I have half a mind to try a screenplay myself. Something with patriotic themes. Perhaps one day. What do you think?"

"I think it's a brilliant idea."

"How do you end a story about God and country, though? That's potentially a problem."

"That's easy. A story about God and country ends the way all good stories end."

Availing himself of a theatrical pause, the special chum goes through the doors to where the limousine waits for him in the distance. Then the special chum's voice sings out as he disappears into the night: "All good stories end with a fireball in the sky."

About the Author

Rick Moody is the author of the novels *Garden State,* which won the Pushcart Press Editors' Book Award, *The Ice Storm,* and *Purple America;* two collections of stories, *The Ring of Brightest Angels Around Heaven* and *Demonology;* and a memoir, *The Black Veil,* winner of the PEN / Martha Albrand Award. He has also received the Addison Metcalf Award, the *Paris Review*'s Aga Khan Prize, and a Guggenheim Fellowship. He lives in Brooklyn, New York.